TAYLOR QUINN

goes straight for the heart with

The Birth Mother
Nikki is Bryan Chambers's niece.
And Jennifer Teal's daughter.
He knows it. *She* doesn't.

Another Man's Child
Marcus Cartwright is giving his wife, Lisa,
her freedom...to have another man's child.

Shotgun Baby
Con Randolph's fathered a baby.
Now he needs to find a wife!

Dear Reader,

I'm excited to be bringing you these three very special stories. Inspired by the world around me, all three of these stories were books from my heart.

The first, *The Birth Mother*, was inspired by a billboard featuring a young teen, about six months pregnant. The text promised that there were always alternatives, choices. The image was of a young, frightened, lonely girl. She could have been any one of my daughter's friends. I had to give her a happy ending.

The second book, *Another Man's Child*, came to me while I was sitting at my desk one day. I'd been thinking about how modern technology was changing the world. From computers, I somehow ended up with artificial insemination. Guess that's the romance writer in me!

And the third story, *Shotgun Baby*, was born when I heard that representatives from the state of Arizona could legally knock on a man's door for his signature to give away his baby, when nothing requires anyone to let the man know he'd even fathered a child. I tried to imagine how that man might feel, how he might have found himself in the predicament to begin with.

In all three of these books there are no easy answers, but hopefully you'll find some enjoyable hours with people who have what it takes to go the distance.

I'd love to hear what you think of these stories! You can reach me at P.O. Box 15065; Scottsdale, AZ 85267; or ttquinn@home.com.

Tara Taylor Quinn

TARA TAYLOR QUINN

Mother's Day

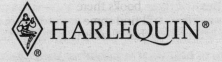

HARLEQUIN®

TORONTO • NEW YORK • LONDON
AMSTERDAM • PARIS • SYDNEY • HAMBURG
STOCKHOLM • ATHENS • TOKYO • MILAN • MADRID
PRAGUE • WARSAW • BUDAPEST • AUCKLAND

HARLEQUIN BOOKS

by Request—MOTHER'S DAY

Copyright © 2001 by Harlequin Books S.A.

ISBN 0-373-20187-7

The publisher acknowledges the copyright holder
of the individual works as follows:
THE BIRTH MOTHER
Copyright © 1996 by Tara Lee Reames
ANOTHER MAN'S CHILD
Copyright © 1997 by Tara Lee Reames
SHOTGUN BABY
Copyright © 1997 by Tara Lee Reames
This edition published by arrangement with Harlequin Books S.A.

Visit us at www.eHarlequin.com

Printed in U.S.A.

CONTENTS

The Birth Mother

PROLOGUE

SHE WAS ALONE when she went into labor. But six-teen-year-old Jennifer Teal expected nothing else. In the ways that mattered she'd been alone since the day she was born, which was why she'd been so ripe for Tommy Mason's pickings. All he'd had to do was say he loved her...

The pain came again, gripping her lower body so tightly it squeezed the breath out of her. She pushed back into the couch, fighting the panic that wasn't far from the surface.

Her stomach muscles relaxed, and she tried to con-centrate on the book she'd been reading. The pains were still almost ten minutes apart. She didn't want to call her parents home from work until it was time to go to the hospital.

The hospital. Tears sprang to Jennifer's eyes as she thought about the cold sterile place. Oh, please, little darling, please don't come yet. She rubbed at the huge mound of her belly, comforting the baby girl who'd stolen her heart the second she'd seen the barely dis-cernible outline on the ultrasound film. She couldn't bear to think about what was going to happen.

The next pain froze Jennifer's tears as she concentrated completely on riding it out. She let the pain come, let it rip into her lower body. She wished desperately for someplace she could go to escape what had to happen, someplace where she didn't have to be afraid. She knew better than to wish she didn't have to face it all alone.

The pain faded and she thought again about calling the dealership to tell her parents it was almost time. But she didn't reach for the receiver. No. She was going to savor these last hours she had with the baby she loved more than she'd ever loved anything in her life. She was the only person in the world who wanted this baby—other than the couple who were out there somewhere, waiting, with a nursery set up, a whole wardrobe of tiny newborn clothes ready. Jennifer had never met them, didn't even know their names.

Worried that her water might break and soil her parents' couch, Jennifer took advantage of her reprieve from pain and hoisted her heavy body up. She didn't want to mess up the carpet, either, so grabbing her book and a pillow from her bed, she went into the bathroom. Using the wall as a brace, she slid down to the floor. If her water broke she could have it cleaned up before her mother got home. Not that Eloise Teal would be angry about the mess, but Jennifer didn't like to be any more of a hassle to her elderly parents than necessary.

The next twenty-one hours became something of a blur to Jennifer, remembered only in pieces of mind-robbing pain intermingled with snatches of blessed peace. The peace she took from her baby. For sometime during her pain-induced delirium she'd realized she wasn't the only one sharing the incredible experience. Her baby was with her one hundred percent of the way, through the phone call she finally made to her parents, the agonizing trip to the hospital sitting in the back seat of her father's used Coronado while her parents sat silently in front, the disappointment when, in the emergency room, her mother opted to stay with her father out in the waiting room.

Through the long hours of pain, the brief moments of relief, the times when medical personnel prepared her body for childbirth, and even during the minutes she attempted, unsuccessfully, to push the baby from her body, Jennifer's daughter was with her all the way. She wasn't alone, after all.

And then they injected her with something to knock her out. It was nighttime when Jennifer finally came to, when she learned the baby had been delivered by cesarean section, when she realized she'd been denied the few seconds after the birth to meet the tiny being she'd brought to life. She was no longer the mother. Another woman, a grown woman, was waiting for that right.

Jennifer wasn't even sure how much time had passed, what day it was. She wasn't sure it mattered. She didn't try to stem the tears that ran silently down her cheeks. There was no one there to see them. She hadn't known it was possible to feel so empty and still be alive.

She turned her head away as the door to her private room opened. She didn't want to see anybody.

"You having troubles sleeping, honey?" The soft words fell into the darkness.

Jennifer looked toward the nurse's shadowy figure walking toward her. She remembered her from the labor room. She was young for a nurse, and pretty, too. She'd been nice to Jennifer through those long agonizing hours.

"I can give you something to help you sleep or help with the pain if you need it, sweetie. You just say the word." The nurse lifted Jennifer's wrist, feeling for her pulse.

"Is my baby gone yet?" Jennifer asked. She was afraid to fall back to sleep. Afraid they were going to take her baby away while she was unconscious. Not that her being awake would make any difference; she just couldn't bear to think of sleeping through it.

The nurse's eyes filled with pity as she smoothed Jennifer's hair away from her forehead. She hesitated, as if she wasn't going to answer Jennifer, and then she shook her head.

"She's still here."

"Is she pretty?"

The nurse smiled, her knuckles rubbing Jennifer's shoulder. "She's beautiful, honey. And healthy as a horse. You did a great job. Now—" she stepped back and tucked the covers around Jennifer "—why don't you try to get some sleep, huh? The doctor said you get to go home tomorrow."

The thought panicked Jennifer. Not that she liked the hospital, but when she left, she'd never be near her baby again. She watched desperately as the nurse walked to the door of her room.

"Can I see her?"

The nurse stopped just inside the door. "You know it's against regulations, honey."

She didn't say no. "I haven't signed any papers yet. Doesn't that mean that technically she's still mine?"

The nurse moved quickly back to the bed, frowning. "You aren't thinking of changing your mind, are you? You're so young, honey, barely sixteen. What are you, a senior this year?"

"I'll be a junior when school starts, and no, I'm not going to change my mind. I just need to see her."

"It's not a good idea, honey, believe me. It'll be so much harder to give her up if you see her."

"Have you ever given a baby away?"

The nurse looked shocked. "No."

"Then how can you know it'll be harder? I'll tell you what's hard—lying here knowing my baby is only a few feet away and I can't tell her how much I love her. Doesn't she deserve that, at least? To know that even though her own mother is giving her away, she still loves her?"

"I'll tell her you love her."

Jennifer sat up, mature beyond her years, not only because of the past nine months but from a lifetime of trying to make life easier for her elderly parents. She'd never really been a kid. And especially not now.

"I need to tell her myself. I promise I won't change

my mind. I just need to tell her goodbye. Is that too much to ask?'' Jennifer's words dissolved into tears.

The young nurse hesitated, tears in her own eyes as she looked at Jennifer, and then she turned away. ''I'll see what I can do, but you change your mind and it'll cost me my job.''

She left the room, not giving Jennifer a chance to reply.

Jennifer tensed when her door opened fifteen minutes later and the young nurse crossed the shadowy room carrying a blanket-wrapped bundle. Jennifer's heart swelled till she thought it would burst.

Giving no thought to tomorrow, to an hour from then, she reached up to take her daughter in her arms. She was beautiful! And so soft and warm and sweet-smelling. Jennifer's arms trembled as she held her baby against her breast, where she belonged.

She was barely aware of the nurse hovering at the end of the bed as she studied the precious little face, soaking up a lifetime's worth of loving in those few brief moments. She wanted to unwrap the baby, see her tiny fingers and toes, actually touch the little feet that had been kicking her for so many months. But she was afraid to, afraid she'd make the baby cry.

So she just continued to hold her, smiling as she watched the sleeping infant. Suddenly, the baby stiffened, stretching her tiny legs and arms, and opened her eyes, those big blue eyes, to stare up at Jennifer. And then, just when she thought the baby was going to fall back to sleep, she stiffened again, and one tiny hand popped out of the baby blanket, flailing in the air until it caught Jennifer under the chin.

Jennifer reached for the little fist instinctively, raising it to her lips, kissing the soft, sweet skin. Then her daughter's mouth opened, and she turned her head toward Jennifer's breast.

The nurse came forward. "I need to take her back now, honey. It's time for her to eat."

Jennifer nodded, her eyes never leaving the child in her arms. "I love you, baby girl, I love you so much," she said, her whisper thick with tears. She lifted the infant, burying her face against the baby's warm neck—and kissed her daughter for the last time.

Please, God, just give her a happy, loving home, and I promise I'll never bother her again or go looking for her or anything. And I'll never have another baby to replace her or ever make love with a boy again, either. Not if you'll keep her happy for me. Please, God.

She sobbed as the nurse took her baby away from her, sobbed and hated herself for not being strong enough to fight them all and insist on keeping her child. Logically she knew she'd made the right decision, the only decision, by giving her baby to a loving couple who could provide a much better life for her than Jennifer could ever hope to.

But as she cried long into the night, Jennifer couldn't silence the part of her that said there were places she could go, places that would help, places designed to make it possible for unwed mothers to provide for their babies. If only she was strong enough.

A part of Jennifer died that night. The tender, vulnerable, young mother in her was slowly suffocated until all she had left to tell of its existence was the hospital birth picture the young nurse slipped to her just before she went off duty.

CHAPTER ONE

BRYAN CHAMBERS hadn't had sex in eight months. His chair, which he'd had tilted back on two legs, came down to the floor with a bang. Damn. Maybe that's what was bothering him. He stared at the little calendar lying on the side of his drafting table as if it would prove he was mistaken, as if he actually made a notation when he took a woman to bed.

He didn't collect notches on his bedpost, never had. Hell, until eight months ago, he'd never even owned a bedpost. But he'd always had his share of women.

Bryan pushed himself away from the sketches he'd been working on all morning, a campaign for one of his newest clients, a national soup company. He was too restless to be creative. He started to run his fingers through the hair at the back of his head, but stopped. It had gotten so long he was wearing it in a ponytail.

"Jacci!" he hollered, ignoring the intercom on his desk.

His secretary poked her head inside his door. "Yeah?"

"I'm outta here. If Wonderly calls, put him through on my mobile."

"Did you get the sketches done for tomorrow's meeting?"

He tidied the morning's clutter, shoving the Wonderly client folder into his sketchbook. "Nope."

"You want me to see if Calvin can give them a shot? The meeting's tomorrow at nine."

"I'll get them done." Bryan didn't need his partner pinch-hitting for him. And if Jacci wasn't such a damn good secretary, he'd fire her. She had a tendency to forget who was boss here. But he had to hand it to her. She'd lasted longer than any other secretary he'd ever had. What was it now? Six months? Seven?

"How long you been here, Jacci?" he asked, crossing to his supply cupboard to put away his charcoals.

"Since eight," she said, frowning as she watched him.

He frowned back at her. "Not today. How long you been with the company?"

"Going on two years. Why? Is it time for my raise?"

She had a point there. She probably deserved a raise after putting up with his moods these past months. She kept the office running like clockwork, too.

"Maybe. How much of a raise we talking about?"

She shrugged, naming an outrageous sum.

Bryan pulled his aviator sunglasses out of his shirt pocket and put them on. He shoved his calendar into the back pocket of his jeans. "If you'll settle for half that, you got it," he said, heading for the door with his sketchbook under his arm.

"What happens if I don't settle?" Jacci asked, following him out to her office.

"Then you're fired."

She sat down behind her desk and started typing on her computer keyboard as if she'd never been interrupted. "You really should carry a briefcase, you know," was all she said.

"Forget it," Bryan mumbled, heading outside into the bright Atlanta sunshine. Jacci's nagging irritated him almost as much as the thought of carrying a briefcase. He hated the trappings of conventionality, hated being tied down, even to a briefcase.

Which was why it was so strange that he was eager to get home. He'd never bought himself a real home, either, until eight months ago, always preferring to live in generic, though elegantly furnished, condominiums rather than tie himself down to a bunch of belongings that would make mobility difficult. But all that changed in the split second it took for a tornado to touch down in Shallowbrook. All that changed the minute he got Nicki.

"HEY, BOBBY, how's it going?"

"Just fine, Ms. Teal." The young mechanic smiled at her from beneath the Tempo hoisted up in his bay.

"And how about your boy? Is he completely recovered?"

"Yes, ma'am, he's back in school this week and bragging about the accident like he's a hero or something. My wife and I sure appreciate you being so understanding with me missing so much work this past month.''

''I'm glad we could make things a little easier for you, Bobby. Now, how's Mr. Corales's car coming along?''

''Almost done. He won't find another thing wrong with this car, ma'am. Not unless he breaks it himself.''

''Good. He's been more than patient with us. I want him happy.''

''I can guarantee it, Ms. Teal,'' Bobby said, grinning at her as he stepped back beneath the car.

Jennifer continued on through the mechanic's bays behind Teal Ford, one of a half-dozen big sparkling dealerships in the Teal Automotive chain, taking in every last pristine detail as she exchanged pleasantries with her employees. She ran a good ship, an unusual ship, an honest ship. She was proud of that.

Reaching the last of the sixteen bays, she stopped. ''Okay, Sam, what's wrong with her?'' Jennifer's gaze was focused on the Caspian Blue Mustang convertible up on the mechanic's rack.

''I think it's the rear axle, Jen.'' The gray-haired man had his head buried underneath the car.

As soon as she'd noticed the clunking sound when she'd switched gears that morning, Jennifer had suspected that the internal gears in the rear axle were stripped, but she'd hoped she was wrong. ''What about the U-joint?'' She had to ask the question, though it was a waste of time. If Sam thought it was the rear axle, it was the rear axle. In the twenty-odd years she'd watched Sam Whitfield work, he'd never been wrong about a car. Which was why he was the only one she trusted near her Mustang.

Shrugging out of the jacket of her suit, she stepped beneath the car, as familiar with its underside as she was with the driver's seat.

"See this?" Sam grunted, tapping a length of U-shaped piping with his wrench.

Jennifer slid her fingers around the casing that connected the rear axle to the transmission, finding it as solid as it should be. "We're going to have to drain the transmission fluid, aren't we?" she asked. It was Friday, and she'd hoped to have her car over the weekend. She didn't like being without it.

"Yep. Be a sin to drive it like this."

Jennifer nodded, taking another cursory look before stepping back from under the car. She pulled a towel out of the dispenser on the wall of the bay and wiped the grease off her hands. She had an important lunch in less than an hour, and it wouldn't do to have dirt under her fingernails when she shook hands with the mayor. She needed the rezoning if she was going to get that lot next to Teal Chevrolet for her trucks.

Slipping into her jacket, she said to Sam, "Would you mind doing it tonight? I'll bring dinner just like—"

"I'll be here, Jen. Ain't I always?" he interrupted.

"Six o'clock okay?"

"Yep. And don't bring none of that Chinese crap, you here? A man's gotta have something more substantial than that if he's gonna keep going."

"How about a T-bone steak?" Jennifer asked, grinning at the old man encased in greasy overalls. No Teal Automotive uniform for Sam. He was still wearing the striped denim overalls he'd worn when he'd been the only mechanic here, back when her parents had started Teal Motors with only one small lot of used cars.

Sam cursed as his wrench slipped. "Burgers'd do."

"See ya at six," Jennifer said, making a mental note to call her secretary and ask her to arrange for a steak dinner with all the trimmings to be here at six o'clock sharp. Rachel knew just how Sam liked his steaks.

Jennifer was already looking forward to getting into the jeans and sweatshirt she had stashed in the trunk of the Lincoln she was driving today and joining Sam beneath her baby—the 1964½ Ford Mustang convertible she'd rescued eleven years ago. She couldn't think of a better way to spend a Friday night.

But first she had to convince the mayor that the deserted plot of land next to Teal Chevrolet would be much better suited to a truck lot than to the garbage- and graffiti-strewn crumbling foundation that resided there now.

"HEY, KID, YOU WANNA go up with me for a while? See the sunset? Go to Florida for some ice cream?" Bryan leaned against the doorjamb of Nicki's bedroom, trying not to worry that his niece was right where he'd left her that morning, lying on top of her bed. He knew she'd been to school. Not only because they were under strict orders to call him if she didn't show up, but because her book bag had been moved from the kitchen table where he'd left it after packing her lunch that morning. But she needed to be up out of bed for more than six hours a day.

"You don't have to take me. I'm big enough to stay home alone," she said, scooting up to a sitting position. Bryan watched her, frustration eating away at him. He knew she'd only made the effort to sit up for his sake. The minute he left the room, she'd lie right back down. Dammit, would she ever again have traces of the impetuous imp who'd stolen his heart more than eleven years ago? Did that child even exist in Nicki anymore? Or had she died right along with the rest of his family?

He wandered into her room, noticing how neat everything was. At least *that* was Nicky. "I don't want to go alone, sprite. What fun is ice cream if you don't get to share flavors?"

"But it's Friday night, Uncle Bryan, and you always said a Friday night without a date was like pizza without the cheese."

"I don't want a date, Nick. I want you. Won't you come?"

She sent him a look that said she was certain he was humoring her and she didn't need to be humored. But she slid off the bed.

"Okay. But if you really want to invite a date, instead, I won't care."

She wouldn't. And that was what worried Bryan the most. Nicky didn't care about much of anything

these days. Not since the tornado had hit Shallowbrook eight months ago, wiping out half the town and
an entire family, as well. Nicky's family. Nicky's and
Bryan's. His parents, Nicki's grandparents, his sister
and brother-in-law—Nicki's parents—and a mass of
cousins and aunts and uncles. They'd all been having
a cookout, celebrating Nicki's eleventh birthday. God
knows why Nicki had chosen that moment to run inside to use the bathroom, the one room in the house
without a window. Bryan only knew that when he'd
rolled into the mass of rubble that had been his hometown, two hours late for the party, he'd found his
niece, speechless and trembling, in the arms of the
preacher's wife. That good woman had been the one
to tell Bryan that Nicki was the only family he had
left.

"YOU WANT TO TAKE HER for a while?" Bryan said
into his headset an hour later, glancing at the child in
the copilot's seat.

Nicki shrugged. "Nah." Her voice, coming to him
through his earphones, was as lifeless as her eyes.
There wasn't a hint of the glow he used to see when
he took her up with him.

Bryan despaired as he looked out from the cockpit
of his four-seater Cessna. Even flying didn't excite
Nicki anymore. He was running out of ideas. Keeping
a close watch on the myriad gages in front of him,
he set a course for his favorite airport just inside the
Florida border, remembering the first time he'd seen
Nicki, the only child of his only sibling.

Though he'd been well liked in Shallowbrook, the son of the town doctor, he'd never found the small community to be the nirvana everyone claimed it was. To him, during the long years of his growing up, it had seemed like a prison. He'd always yearned for whatever was in the next meadow or over the next hill. Within Shallowbrook's slow-paced, if loving confines, he'd never been able to find the peace, the serenity that his parents and older sister had thrived on. He hadn't been content just to live his life; he'd wanted to shape it, to make it happen. By the time he'd graduated from high school, he'd felt like an explosion waiting to happen, and had hightailed it out of town as fast as his old Jeep could carry him.

But he'd never forgotten the family he'd left behind, never abandoned them. No matter how claustrophobic he got, he made a point to visit them several times a year. And always, after a few days in town, he was more than ready to return to his condo in Atlanta, to a city full of opportunities, instead of one so predictable it made him want to run naked in the streets just to see something different happen.

But he'd been in Shallowbrook the day Lori had brought Nicki home. He wouldn't have missed that day for anything. Half the town had turned out at his mother's house to welcome home the much-awaited newest addition to the Chambers-Hubbard clan. Just as they'd all grieved with Lori when she'd learned she couldn't conceive, they'd rejoiced with her as she'd walked up the front steps with her newly adopted daughter in her arms and happy tears streaming down her face.

And for once, as he'd taken his turn to peer down into the curious blue eyes of his infant niece, Bryan had felt magic, right there in Shallowbrook.

Recognizing the terrain below him, Bryan banked the plane, waiting for landing clearance from the control tower.

"What flavor you gonna have?" he asked the silent girl beside him.

Nicki continued to stare sightlessly out at the lush green Florida landscape, her earphones seeming to swallow up most of her head. "I'm not very hungry."

"Chocolate, huh? I thought so."

That brought her eyes to him, if not a smile. "I really don't need any, Uncle Bryan."

"No one *needs* ice cream, Nick. It's a treat. So, you want two scoops or three?"

He received clearance from the tower and headed in.

"One," Nicki said wearily, closing her eyes on his spectacular landing. Bryan felt completely helpless as he glimpsed the tear that slid slowly down her pale young cheek.

"IT'S RISKY, Jennifer."

"Yeah."

"So why mess with a good thing? We're not in high school anymore. You don't have anything more to prove."

"You think that's what this is? Me proving something? To whom?"

"I don't know, Jen. Your parents maybe."

"They're dead, Dennis."

"Okay, maybe to yourself. But you don't have to do this. You're an incredible success. The business could run itself you have it so well established. Why would you want to screw that up?"

"I don't happen to think One Price Selling will screw that up, but if it does, that's a risk I'll have to take. As soon as I find the right agency to help me, I'm launching One Price Selling."

Dennis Bradford looked hurt as he fell back into the padded leather chair behind his desk. "What am I, vice president in name only? My opinion doesn't count?"

Leaning her hands on the front of his desk, Jennifer looked him straight in the eye, imploring him to understand, just as he always had. "Your opinion matters more to me than anyone's. I wouldn't be here, or probably anywhere else for that matter, if not for you. I need your support on this, Dennis."

He watched her silently for several long moments. "I need to know why, Jen."

"Because it's right." She sat down in the rich blue armchair in front of his desk. "We run an honest business here, which has a lot to do with our success. But One Price Selling is the step beyond that could make Teal Automotive more than just a successful business. It could make us great."

"It'll give your competitors a golden opportunity to eat you alive."

"Which is why we need the best ad agency this city has to head them off."

"It won't matter, Jen. Either way, we stand to lose. You may sell the idea to the public—hell, I'm sure you will—but as soon as some of the shysters in this business start doing the same, or *say* they're doing the same, it'll tarnish the whole thing. You'll begin to look like all the others, just peddling some new gimmick."

"But that's just it! It's not a gimmick. We'll have price tags on every car showing the factory list price and the lower Teal Automotive price right next to it. No haggling, no hard selling, just a fair honest price, take it or leave it. It's just what the automotive industry needs."

"In theory, I agree with you one hundred percent. But what happens when everyone else starts saying they're doing the same thing, but instead of following through in good faith, they jack down a trade, or make the 'fair' price a different price for each customer who walks in the door? We're right back to the same old way of doing business, and we've cheapened ourselves by gimmick-selling."

"The difference will be that every customer who walks onto a Teal lot will get the same fair price for his trade and for his purchase. No exceptions. Period. If I've built the reputation you say I have, people will give me a chance to show them *I* mean what I say."

"You're not going to budge on this, are you?"

"I can't, Dennis."

"Still paying for past mistakes?"

Jennifer smiled. "Nothing so melodramatic as that, my friend. I just want to do things right."

"This doesn't have anything to do with a certain birthday coming up, does it? You always push a little harder this time of year."

"I resent that, Dennis. I'm not going to make a business decision as important as this one on the basis of past pain."

Dennis studied her silently for a moment, then nodded. "Okay, Jen, but we better hope there's a damn good advertising man willing to take this on."

"We'll find one. But I need you behind me, too. Not only for the support, but for a lot of the decision-making, as well. We're going to have to retrain our entire management and sales team, come up with a pay-plan alternative to the straight-commission policy we now run under, choose new incentive programs..." She grinned at him.

Dennis came around his desk and pulled Jennifer up out of her chair. "You know I'm behind you, Jennifer. I always have been. If this ship goes down, we'll be swimming for shore together."

Jennifer squeezed his hands, telling him with a look all the things she couldn't say, before heading toward the door of his office.

"Oh, Jen, I almost forgot. Tanya wanted me to ask you to come for dinner tomorrow night before the city-council meeting. She needs your opinion on her newest creation."

Jennifer turned with her hand on the door and smiled at him. "Her paintings are selling for thousands and she needs *my* opinion? Your wife has a screw loose, Den."

"So you'll come? She's already phoned twice today, nagging me to ask you."

Jennifer thought of the pixie-faced four-foot-nine-inch woman she'd brought home from college one summer several years ago with the express purpose of fixing her up with Dennis. "Yeah, I'll be there."

She was still smiling as she walked down the hall of executive suites to the door marked President. She was lucky to have such good friends.

CHAPTER TWO

"CAN I TALK TO YOU, Uncle Bryan?"

Bryan's heart hammered as he spun away from the layout he'd been mulling over for most of the evening. Nicki was instigating a conversation?

"Sure, sprite, whatcha need?" *Anything. I'll give you anything. Just tell me what.* In the week since their impromptu trip to Florida, he'd barely been able to coerce her out of her room for dinner.

"My mother."

He stared at his niece. Had she gone over the edge? Had she forgotten Lori was dead? Blocked the whole tragedy from her mind? The doctor had mentioned the remote possibility of such an extreme reaction, but Bryan had thought they'd passed that point months ago. *Come on, Nick, hang in there,* he silently implored her. *We'll get through this together if only you'll let me help.*

"We can head to Shallowbrook first thing in the morning, hon. But we just visited the cemetery two weeks ago. You sure you wouldn't like to go shopping or something, instead?"

Nicki slid into an armchair, her skinny body barely filling half the seat. "I mean my *real* mother."

"Lori *was* your real mother." Bryan's words came out more sharply than he'd intended. He felt as if he was soaring over the Rockies in a plane whose engine had just died.

Nicki didn't budge. Her long auburn hair lay around her bony shoulders like a cloak as she stared at her fingers, fidgeting with them in her lap. "I want to find the woman who had me," she whispered.

He froze, on his way to a crash and burn. He wasn't prepared.

"I don't think you can do that, Nick. They have laws against stuff like that." *Why, Nicki? You're Lori's baby. And now mine.*

She looked up at him, her hazel eyes pleading. "I think you can do it now sometimes. They have places you can go to find out."

Her look tore at Bryan, making him wish he were Superman. There was nothing he wouldn't do for this child. But find her biological mother? The woman whose blood ties made Nicki more hers than his? The woman who'd given her away? He kneeled down beside her, sandwiching her thin cold hands between his own.

"I don't think it's that easy, honey. Adoption records are sealed. What you're talking about is when someone *wants* to be found, there's a place where they can register their names and give pertinent information."

Nicki's eyes were almost determined as she looked at him. "We have to go to that register, Uncle Bryan.

Maybe she's there. Maybe she's been looking for me and we don't even know it.''

''And maybe she isn't, Nick. Why set yourself up for disappointment? I know how much you miss your mother. Hell, I miss her, too. But she's still your mother in here—'' he tapped her rib cage ''—and she always will be. That's the way the woman who gave birth to you wanted it, honey.''

Nicki looked down at their clasped hands. ''She coulda changed her mind.''

''That's not the way adoption works, honey. It's for keeps. She would've known that when she gave you up.''

''But what if she *did* change her mind? What if she wants me?''

''*I* want you, Nick. We're doing okay together, don't you think?''

Nicki looked at him again, her eyes swimming with tears as she nodded. ''I just gotta know who I am,'' she whispered, her young body tense as if begging him to give her this, to move mountains if need be to find her missing link.

It was just another of life's ironies that the one thing in which Nicki expressed interest in the eight months since she'd come to Atlanta was the one thing he didn't want to give her. But, looking into her eyes, Bryan knew he had no choice.

''I'll see what I can do.''

Nicki smiled at him through her tears. The first real smile he'd seen in eight long months. He hoped to God he was doing the right thing.

JENNIFER SMILED her goodbyes to Ralph Goodwin, the general manager of Teal Pontiac, and his wife at the door of the Teal Automotive suite in Hawk's Stadium. She felt good. The Hawks had won in overtime. It had been a great game. And she'd just gained Ralph's support for One Price. He hadn't been nearly as hard to convince as Dennis two weeks before. He hadn't even asked why. But then, he didn't know her as well as Dennis did.

She was still smiling when she pulled her Mustang into the parking garage below her luxury apartment building an hour later. It felt good to be home. She'd been out every night that week, and as much as she loved the socializing that went with her job, she was looking forward to a long soak in the Jacuzzi she'd had installed in her master bathroom. Taking a moment to exchange a few words with the doorman about the Hawks' victory, she entered the elevator, inserted her key and pushed the button for the penthouse apartment.

Yeah, Ralph had been a much easier sell than Dennis. And tomorrow night she'd tackle Frank Dorian, the GM of Teal Ford. She was going with him and his wife to the Peachtree Celebrity Cook-off where they were going to prepare pots and pots of Celia Dorian's chili in an attempt to raise money for the city's homeless. Celia was a quiet woman, kind of reminding Jennifer of herself in an earlier day, back before she'd figured out that more people liked her if she reached out to them. She'd discovered a whole new side to herself, a happier side, when she'd learned to be a little more outgoing. She'd also found out that a talkative gregarious teenager had much less chance of hearing the voice in her head than a quiet introspective one.

But that time in her life was long behind her. There was only so much grieving a body could do, only so much self-loathing. The past was sealed as tightly as the records that gave proof to it.

Soft lights were glowing in the foyer as she let herself in, and Jennifer took a moment to soak in the calm cool atmosphere of her spotlessly clean, professionally decorated home. She'd surrounded herself with the same blue-and-white color scheme that was found in all the Teal Automotive offices and showrooms.

Leaving the lights on, she headed across the plush white carpet to the master suite. She'd check messages in the morning. Right now she just wanted that soak.

And some music. The house was too quiet. Backtracking, she slipped her original recording of Rogers' and Hammerstein's *Sound of Music* into her compactdisc player. And then ejected it. Not that one. Too many children. She glanced down the rack. *Oklahoma* was too much of a love story, *Carousel* too noisy, and *The King and I* too surreal. Irritated by her indecision, she grabbed the double CD set of *Phantom of the Opera*, dropped the discs into the player and jabbed the play button. *Phantom* suited her mood. The phantom was in control. He lived alone. He didn't fall in love and live happily ever after. And he was fiction.

Taking one more detour, Jennifer poured herself a glass of chilled white wine before finally heading for the bedroom. She hadn't been so restless in ages. She assured herself that it meant nothing, that with the deliberate fullness of her calendar over the next few weeks, the feeling would pass.

She'd make sure of it. She didn't have time to be sidetracked. Not even for a second. Because the by-roads she traveled were all the same—they led to the same deserted place. She'd spent years learning how to stay on course; she was not going to let The Day, which was looming, send her hurtling back, not like it had last year.

But she took her wallet with her when she went into the bathroom. She laid it on the marble vanity as she brushed her teeth and removed her makeup. Routine. Control. They served her well. Detours did not.

She meant to undress, to take her wine and step into the tub. But Christine's hauntingly beautiful voice floated to her from her built-in sound system. Christine. The Phantom's one true love. *Think of me... Remember me...*

Jennifer froze, her eyes glued on her wallet. Slowly, as if of its own accord, her hand reached for the wallet, unfastened it, her fingers searching unerringly beneath her health-insurance card. She slid the battered hospital photo out of hiding and gazed at it. *Remember me...* It never got easier. It never got better. Never.

THE WOMAN hadn't signed up with any register. At least none in the state of Georgia. Bryan didn't know whether to be glad about that or not. He only knew he had a knot in his stomach that wouldn't go away.

He couldn't leave it like that. He couldn't just tell Nicki that her biological mother hadn't even thought of her enough to register in the slim chance Nicki might be looking. But he also knew, considering the fact that the woman was making no effort to be found in these times of open adoption, that chances were good she wasn't going to be receptive to having her eleven-year-old castoff suddenly show up in her life—if and when he did find her. Nicki wasn't strong enough to handle that. And maybe the woman had a right to her privacy. Not sure what he was going to say, he walked slowly toward his niece's room.

She was sitting on her bed, brushing her hair. Just brushing it. Over and over. The new fashion magazine he'd brought home for her lay unopened beside her. At least she'd carried it that far. He was pretty sure the last one had never made it off her desk.

"Hey, Nick, can we talk?"

She looked up, her hazel eyes filled with alarm. "What?"

For the life of him Bryan couldn't understand that look. He'd been seeing it more and more often lately. He understood Nicki's grief, but what in hell did she have to be afraid of? He stayed in her doorway.

"I did what I promised. I looked for your biological mother in the registries."

"Did you find her?" Nicki's face lit up; the knot in his stomach grew tighter.

"She wasn't listed, Nick."

She looked away and went back to brushing her hair. "Oh."

Bryan entered her room and sat down beside her. It was tearing him up to see her hurting. "Maybe it's best this way, honey."

She shrugged—and then sniffled. *Hell.*

"She loved you enough to give you a good life, Nicki, but in doing so, she had to say goodbye to you. That had to have been a really hard thing, going on with her life without you. But if she hadn't, you wouldn't have had your mom and dad, or your grandma or grandpa, or me. We need to be really thankful to her for giving you to us. And maybe the best way to thank her is to leave her alone. If she's gone on with her life, made her peace with the past, said her goodbyes, then she has the right to continue as she is. That's the right *she* got when we got you."

Nicki started turning the pages of the fashion magazine.

Lori, help me out here. What in the hell do I do now?

"You said you needed to know who you are, but you don't need to find some stranger to know that, sweetheart. You're Nicki Hubbard, the little imp who stole my heart the first time I ever laid eyes on you."

Her lips twitched, almost smiling, but she still wasn't looking at him.

"We're a team, Nick, you and I. You're all the

family I have left in the world. You just stick with me and we'll come through this. I promise."

She glanced up at him, but didn't look convinced.

"Have I ever let you down before?"

She shook her head.

"Remember the time you wanted to go on that roller coaster that went upside down and your mother wouldn't hear of it?"

She nodded.

"Who came through for you? Who explained the physics that convinced her to let you go? And then held your hair back when you threw up afterward?"

Nicki did grin then. "You did."

"That's right. And who helped you out that year you wanted to surprise your mom and dad with a new puppy for Christmas?"

"You did."

"And what about that birthday party when Miss Debra What's-her-name was inviting all your friends to her party at the same time you were having yours— and was promising them a magician if they'd come. Didn't I come through for you then? Taking all those little girls up in my plane so they'd come to your party?"

She nodded, but her eyes were getting cloudy again. *Damn. I'm losing her.*

He took her brush and turned her back to him, pulling the bristles through the thick chestnut locks. "Have I ever lied to you, Nick?"

"Uh-uh." Her voice was so soft he could barely hear it.

"So trust me, honey. I said we'll make it just fine, you and me, and we will. I know I can't take Lori's place, or your dad's, either, but I love you with everything I've got." And they *would* make it, no matter how penned in he might someday feel, because he'd die before he let Nicki down.

She sniffled again. "I love you, too, Uncle Bryan…"

He continued brushing. "But?"

Her thin shoulders lifted in a shrug. "But who gave me my hazel eyes? Mom's were brown like yours, and so were Dad's. And what about my hair? No one in the family has red hair."

"Neither do you. It's auburn." *Great answer, Chambers. Way to come through.*

"And what about how tall I am? Mom and Grandma were both short."

"And what about your ability to see the good in people? Even when old Debra What's-her-name tried to steal your party, you still invited her. You said she'd only done it because she was lonely and wanted friends. Remember? You used to do stuff like that all the time, Nick, and you know why? 'Cause that's how your grandma was. It used to drive me and Lori crazy when we were growing up 'cause anytime we complained about anything she'd find something good about it. You know how hard it is to get riled up when everything's so rosy?"

Nicki turned around, nodding, a sad little smile flitting across her lips.

Bryan tapped the brush against the fashion magazine in her lap. "You've always been interested in dressing well, and that came straight from your mother. As long as I can remember Lori claimed that just because she lived in a small town didn't mean she couldn't look as good as the girls on TV. And your love of science? That came from your grandfather. I can remember when you were about a year old, barely walking, and he had you up on the kitchen counter, showing you how he could mix things together and make them fizz. You used to make him do it over and over, until Lori finally complained about him wasting all her cooking ingredients."

"Did he stop?"

"Of course not."

"Did Mom get mad?"

"What do you think?"

"Uh-uh."

"You're right, she just stood there and watched right along with you. And look at this room, Nick. You've always kept things neat. Just like your dad. He made a game out of picking up your toys with you when you were still a baby. When he played with you he'd race you to see who could put away one toy first before getting out another. By the time you were three, you were driving your mother crazy insisting she put the lid back on the shampoo *before* you'd let her wash your hair."

Bryan thought of his sister, how happy she'd been every day of her life after she got Nicki, what a great mother she'd been. He felt that familiar pang, the crushing weight he got every time he thought of his family. God, he missed them.

"But...but what about other things?" Nicki's tentative question interrupted his thoughts. She was crying again. "You know, like medical stuff you can get? Diseases and things. And maybe..."

"Maybe what?" He was brushing for all he was worth.

"Maybe other stuff, too. What if my mother was crazy or something and that's why they gave me away? What if I take after her?"

Bryan was beginning to get the picture and he didn't like it one bit.

"You're not crazy, Nick. And I'll find her if I have to, just to prove it to you."

IT TOOK SIX WEEKS and a professional search consultant, but Bryan finally had Nicki's answer. Or at least he thought he did. He sat in his office after hours on Thursday, Nicki's packet in front of him, and knew he could no longer put off opening it. It was stupid to feel threatened by a few pieces of paper. Knowing the name of Nicki's biological mother wasn't going to change anything. Nicki was his legally, and every other way that counted. He wasn't going to lose her. He couldn't. She was his family.

He opened the packet, read for a few minutes, then stared. He couldn't believe it. According to these reports, Nicki's mother was Jennifer Teal. *The* Jennifer Teal. Of Teal Automotive.

Everyone in Atlanta who watched television or listened to radio had heard of Jennifer Teal. Her ads were memorable if for no other reason than Ms. Teal claimed to be an honest car dealer. And judging by her success, Bryan figured she might just be.

Or else she had one hell of a sales staff.

Balancing on the back two legs of his chair, Bryan shuffled through the forms until he found Nicki's original birth certificate, listing Jennifer Marie Teal as the mother. No name was listed for the father. Nicki had been born at one in the afternoon. Her mother's birthdate was…Bryan read the date, then looked again, doing some quick calculations. Good God, she'd been barely sixteen when she'd had Nicki, which would have made her barely fifteen when she'd conceived. That was just four years older than Nicki was now.

His chair came down with a crash and he reached for the phone.

"Sandra, Bryan Chambers here. Sorry to bother you at home, but I was just going over these papers."

"Yes, Mr. Chambers." The search consultant's tone was as sympathetic as it had been for the entire six weeks she'd been working for him.

"How sure are you that these records are referring to *my* Nicki?"

"Quite sure, Mr. Chambers. As you can see, the original birth certificate matches Nicole's modified one exactly, with your sister and her husband's names inserted for Ms. Teal's as the parents. And the other documents support the same findings. Ms. Teal signed the adoption papers that were on file with the state, giving custody of Nicole to Lori and Tom Hubbard.''

Bryan nodded. ''Thank you, Sandra. You did a great job.''

''I'm glad I could help. Have you thought of how you're going to approach Ms. Teal? Assuming that you are, of course. I'd suggest a letter of introduction to begin with. That usually works best, giving everyone a little time to get used to the idea before actually meeting face-to-face.''

''Thanks for the advice. I'll think about it.'' Bryan rang off.

He didn't want to write to Ms. Teal. He didn't even want to accept her existence. But Nicki did. His niece was showing no signs of picking up her life. Bryan had called the counselor he and Nicki had seen right after the tornado, and she'd been concerned enough to speak with Nicki again. Nicki had gone because he'd asked her to, but the session had done no good. It was up to Nicki now. Nicki and him. And hadn't he promised her, promised himself, as he'd seen his family's caskets laid in their graves, that he'd do whatever it took to take care of Nicki?

But he couldn't just introduce Nicki to her birth mother. Not yet. Not until he'd met the woman, assured himself he wasn't setting Nicki up for another blow. Until he was certain Ms. Teal wasn't going to reject Nicki, he was going to keep the fact that he'd found the woman to himself.

And until he was ready to let Nicki know about Ms. Teal, he couldn't tell Ms. Teal about Nicki, either. Not until he was certain he could trust her with the information. Which meant he was going to have to orchestrate a meeting between himself and Ms. Jennifer Teal. He reached for the phone again. He needed all the information on Jennifer Teal he could get.

DENNIS POPPED his head around the door of Jennifer's office late one Tuesday afternoon. "Tanya wants to know who you're bringing to her opening a week from Friday, because if you don't have a date yet, she knows someone who would love to take you. And before you even suggest it, she says she absolutely won't allow you to come alone because then you'll leave early, and she hates it when you do that."

Jennifer looked up from the customer letter she was reading and smiled at him. "So who does she have picked out for me this time? Let's see, we've done a stockbroker, two doctors, an accountant, three attorneys, and wasn't there a professor of something in there once? What's left?"

Dennis shrugged. "Who knows? But you can bet he's cover-model material and ready to settle down. You know as well as I do Tanya's not going to rest until someone is sharing that 'big lonely penthouse you go home to every night,'" he said, mimicking Tanya.

"Yeah, well, tell your wife to quit her matchmaking or I'll bring Sam, and the closest thing he has to a suit is a semiclean pair of overalls."

Dennis raised both hands in the air. "Hey, she was

your friend before she was my wife. You deal with her," he said.

"She never listens to me," Jennifer replied, hoping that one of the men she dated occasionally would be free to escort her to the opening. Because the men Tanya chose for her all had one major flaw. They were ready to get married. And she wasn't—not yet.

JENNIFER CONGRATULATED herself on her choice of dates. He was charming, intelligent—and no readier to settle down than she was. The fact that he'd left early to attend to a problem at his plastics plant, a problem that could probably have waited until morning, was his only drawback. Having promised Tanya she wouldn't leave early, Jennifer was left without an escort for the rest of the evening.

"Interesting painting."

Jennifer glanced over her shoulder at the man standing just behind her and nodded politely before turning back to the painting she'd been considering.

"Tanya said you were an expert on her work. She thought you might be willing to show me around."

Damn. Apparently she'd underestimated Tanya's determination. Because if Tanya had sent this man over to her, it could only mean one thing—he was her newest marriage candidate. Trust Tanya to have him around tonight just in case.

Jennifer wondered where she'd found this one.

He was gorgeous, with his deep brown eyes and strong chin that jutted just enough to give him character without being obnoxious. And the clothes he was wearing definitely fit his body to perfection. While they weren't as formal, even with the tie, as the occasion demanded, they were courtesy of one of Atlanta's more expensive tailors, according to the label on his pocket. And he had a ponytail. She looked back at the painting she'd been studying, ignoring him. She was going to get Tanya for this.

"Kind of thought-provoking isn't it?"

His voice did things to her he should be ashamed of. "It's supposed to be."

He stepped forward, just as Dennis's senile old aunt came wandering around the corner.

"Oomph!" Aunt Abigail exclaimed as she careered into Jennifer's handsome companion, dumping the contents of her purse all over the floor in the process.

The man was on his haunches before Jennifer was even sure what was happening, helping the flustered old woman gather her belongings. Jennifer bent down, as well, retrieving a lipstick that had rolled to the wall.

"Where you headed, Auntie?" Jennifer asked, concerned that the woman was on her own. The members of the Bradford family took turns keeping Aunt Abigail in their homes and included her in everything they did. They also never let her out of their sight.

"Oh, Jennifer, it's you," the old woman said, patting her breast as she smiled at Jennifer, obviously relieved. "Dear me, where did all this stuff come from?" She was kneeling down beside the man, holding her purse open while he deposited the various notes and hankies that Aunt Abigail always carried back inside.

"I think that's it," he said, the tenderness in his voice doing strange things to Jennifer.

"I dropped my purse, you know," the old woman said, as if he hadn't been there to see the whole thing. "I came around the corner looking at one of dear Tara's pictures. Such a sweet girl Dennis married. Dennis is my nephew. The son of my only sister's daughter, Abigail the second. She was named after me, you know. He's quite a fine lad, don't you think?" she asked, turning to Jennifer.

"He's the best friend I've ever had," Jennifer said, as if it was the first time she'd told the old woman that. Truth was they had this same conversation every time they saw each other. Aunt Abigail's memory was almost nonexistent, but she always remembered that Jennifer was somehow associated with the family through Dennis.

Tanya's marriage prospect glanced at Jennifer over Aunt Abigail's head, his dark eyes full of understanding. Jennifer looked back at the old woman, willing her heart to settle back to its normal pace.

"I think that's everything, Auntie," she said, rising. The man helped the old woman to her feet, holding her gently by the shoulders until she steadied herself.

"Thank you, young man. You're a true gentleman. I must say." Aunt Abigail held up her wallet, opening it with slightly unsteady hands. "I'll bet you've never seen this before, have you."

"I don't believe I have," the man replied.

Jennifer watched him, impressed with his patience. Aunt Abigail went through phases where she had her wallet out every few minutes, looking through it and trying to show its contents to whichever family member was closest.

She pulled out a plastic card. "See this? It says Abigail Swenson. That's me."

The man nodded. "That's your health-insurance card. A good thing to have."

The old woman preened under his praise, pulling out a driver's license that was no longer valid.

"That's me, too," she said, pointing to the name printed there. "Abigail Swenson, it says. But what's this?" she asked, frowning at the little plastic card.

"It's your driver's license, Auntie," Jennifer said.

"Oh, yes, yes it is. My driver's license. Issued by the state of Georgia, see? Did you know they won't let me drive anymore?" she asked, looking at the man.

"I didn't know that," he said, "but I can see where it has its advantages. You don't ever have to be designated driver that way."

Aunt Abigail giggled. "I never thought of that. I like you. You're a smart young man—"

"Oh, there you are, Auntie. I've been searching all over for you!" Dennis appeared around the corner, looking relieved.

"You worry too much, dear boy. I was just making the acquaintance of Jennifer's young man."

"Sorry, Jen," Dennis said, nodding briefly at the

man standing beside Jennifer as he led his aunt away. If Jennifer had needed any confirmation that the stranger was one of Tanya's handpicked marriage contenders, she'd just had it. Dennis hadn't been able to escape fast enough.

"I guess I'll go look around. Care to join me?" the man asked. *Damn.* That ponytail interested her more than it had any right doing.

"No, but thanks. I was just leaving," she said. Okay, so she was a coward, but getting involved with a gorgeous man who wanted to settle down was pointless when Teal Automotive was consuming so much of her life. And men with marriage in mind were the only type Tanya ever sent her way. *Damn.*

BRYAN STOOD in the gallery watching Jennifer Teal walk away. He'd never liked society functions, but this one had him more on edge than most. He was a little too warm, his heart beating just a little too fast. And his tie was suffocating him. He desperately wanted to rip it off and get some fresh air, and not just because of the melodious voice still ringing in his ears. He'd just met Nicki's mother. That was all that mattered to him.

Impatient with the time it was taking the private detective he'd hired to find him an in, he'd decided to attend tonight's opening as soon as he'd read about Jennifer Teal's expected presence at the gallery in the morning paper. He'd thought he'd missed her until he'd accidentally bumped into the diminutive artist, Tanya Bradford. That good lady, while involving him in a recitation about one of her paintings, had pointed Ms. Teal out to him, simply because Ms. Teal had been standing in front of the piece in question.

She'd surprised him. He'd expected her poise, her wit, even her intelligence. He just hadn't expected to find her so attractive. He hadn't expected to like her.

Bryan caught a glimpse of the old woman who'd bumped into him earlier across the room. Auntie, Jennifer Teal had called her. And suddenly, seeing Ms. Teal not only as Nicki's birth mother but as a woman with a family, made him feel guilty as hell about what he was doing. Barging into a beautiful woman's life with an agenda of his own, fully knowing he might hurt her. It wasn't his style, but then neither was a home, possessions, the tie he was wearing. But for Nicki...

Jennifer Teal might not look like anybody's mother, but he knew better. Loosening his tie, he turned to go. Nicki was depending on him.

CHAPTER THREE

JENNIFER STILL HADN'T found her man. She and Dennis had interviewed people from more than fifteen advertising agencies in the two weeks since Tanya's opening, both local and out of state, and though several had seemed promising, not one had fully understood what she was trying to do.

Most of the ideas she'd seen would sell One Price to the public. But she didn't only want to sell One Price. She wanted to sell integrity. She needed someone with enough sensitivity to see the difference.

She pushed away from her desk and the file she was supposed to be perusing in preparation for another interview with another representative from another fast-paced, nineties-type ad agency. She didn't need to see the file. She could probably recite its contents by rote, having read fifteen other identical folders over the past two weeks.

She walked around her office, looking at the paintings Tanya had done for her. She wished she had more of her friend's perception, envying Tanya the inner peace that allowed her to see the world around her so clearly.

Her secretary's voice piped into the room. "Your appointment's here, Ms. Teal."

Jennifer punched the intercom button. "Thanks, Rachel. Please send him in."

Dennis wasn't going to be joining her that morning. He'd had to go someplace with Tanya. She'd heard his secretary mention a doctor's appointment. And based on the fact that he and Tanya both had to be there, and the knowledge that neither of them had been sick, Jennifer had a suspicion what it might be about. She wondered who'd be more thrilled, Dennis or Tanya. And she wondered why she wasn't more excited for her two best friends. Maybe she was just feeling a little left out because they hadn't let her in on their secret.

Her office door opened. "Mr. Chambers to see you, Ms. Teal," Rachel said, her tone as professional as always.

Jennifer offered her hand automatically, her mind still in the doctor's office with her friends, until she saw who'd just walked into her office. The man from Tanya's opening. The one she'd been thinking about ever since seeing him that night two weeks ago.

"Oh. Hello," she said, hoping she didn't sound as uncomfortable as she felt. She was barely aware of her secretary slipping silently from her office, but she knew when Rachel shut the door behind her. The huge room was suddenly confining, and a little too warm.

"So we finally meet. Officially, that is." His deep voice was just as she'd remembered.

He was still holding her hand as he smiled the sexiest smile she'd ever seen. She pulled away from him and moved behind her desk. "I guess we do."

She didn't know why he was here, but she wished he hadn't come. He was a little harder to resist than the rest of Tanya's husband prospects. He hadn't told her his name that night at the opening, or she would've known when Rachel announced him that he wasn't the appointment she'd been waiting for.

"You don't sound too pleased. Have I done something to offend you?"

She may have remembered his voice, but her memory had done an injustice to the rest of him. His jeans, so faded they were almost white, were tight enough to leave very little to the imagination. And his shirt was equally sexy. It was faded, too, and cotton, and the sleeves were rolled up to his elbows, leaving his tanned muscular forearms right out in plain view. And his hair...

"I was expecting an ad man," she said, wondering why she was so fascinated by his ponytail.

"And you got one." He settled into the chair in front of her desk.

Damn. She had to admire Tanya's ingenuity. Tanya had known Jennifer was looking for an ad man, but Jennifer had no idea how Tanya had managed to find one who was also ready to get married. Jennifer sat down, feeling foolish standing over him, and overdressed, too, in her stylish business suit. "Okay, you can tell Tanya you tried, but you're wasting your time," she said.

He stood, but instead of leaving as she'd expected,

he moved to the couch, taking his sketchbook with him. "I happen to believe I'm using my time very wisely. Coming over?" He indicated the spot beside him on the couch.

His jeans were even more illuminating when he was sitting down. It was hard not to stare. Grabbing a yellow legal pad and pen, she crossed to the couch and sat down beside him. If he'd actually prepared something to show her, the least she could do was listen. But she wasn't going to hire him.

"I'd like to center our campaign around you," he began, "because you *are* Teal Automotive. The entire basis of One Price Selling is integrity, gaining the trust of your customers. They need to trust *you*."

Jennifer got goose bumps.

"One Price Selling is not a gimmick," he went on, "so the usual gimmick advertising will sell it short. Which is why we need to approach this up front, from the top—which again means you. You have a sterling reputation, Ms. Teal. You've built your success on honest business practices, on fairness and customer service, and now it's up to us to make sure that everyone in Atlanta knows that."

The man was good. He was dressed like a construction worker, carried a sketchbook for a briefcase and wore a ponytail, but he knew his stuff. And more important he'd seen what she was trying to do. She suddenly had a vision of him reading Aunt Abigail's health-insurance card.

"What did you say your name was?" she asked.

"Bryan Chambers, of Innovative Advertising," he

said, looking perplexed. "Didn't you get the file I sent over?"

The File. She should have read the damn file. "Tanya didn't send you?"

"Your secretary called mine to set up the appointment."

Jennifer could feel herself turning red, a reaction left over from the days when she'd been so aware of being a burden that self-consciousness had become a way of life. "And you weren't at the art gallery that night because Tanya wanted you to meet me?"

"Tanya Bradford, the artist? I'd never met her before that night."

"Oh." Suddenly, as much of a fool as she'd made of herself, Jennifer felt wonderful. She looked at the unusual and oh-so-sexy man beside her and smiled. He wasn't there because he wanted to get married. He was just an ad man. A *gorgeous* ad man.

He smiled back at her. "I'm missing something, aren't I?" he asked. His sensual brown eyes lingered on hers just a little longer than was necessary.

"I'm afraid so, Mr. Chambers. But I'm impressed with your ideas. How soon can you make it back to meet my vice president?"

"Call me Bryan. And is tomorrow soon enough?"

CALL ME, Uncle Bryan. Please call me. Nicki lay on her bed staring at the clock, watching the second hand tick past the two, and then the three, constantly ticking, until five more minutes passed with a still-silent phone. He'd said he'd call.

Her stomach was filled with butterflies. She wasn't going to cry. It made her more scared to cry. But what if he didn't come home? What if...

Her future stretched out before her, a gray scary blob. She blinked, making the picture go away. She wasn't going to be scared. Nothing was going to happen to Uncle Bryan. He'd probably just forgotten he'd said he'd call if he was ever going to be later than five o'clock. 'Cause he'd never had to check in with anybody before.

It was just that he'd always been home by four-thirty—every single day since she'd come to Atlanta. She knew. She watched the clock every day. She always felt tons better the minute he walked in the door. She loved him so much. She didn't know what she'd do if she lost him, too.

Maybe he was tired of having her around. Other than him dying, that was what scared her most. Sometimes she lay awake in the middle of the night and got crazy just thinking about him not wanting her anymore. She'd heard her mom and grandma joke about Uncle Bryan's wanderlust often enough. But Grandma used to worry about it sometimes, too. Nicki had heard her telling Grandpa once that she was afraid Uncle Bryan's roots were going to shrivel up and die if he didn't plant them somewhere soon. Nicki didn't know about all that, but she knew she just couldn't picture Uncle Bryan ever settling down to a normal boring life.

Oh, God, please help me. Please let Uncle Bryan

*come home. I promise I won't get in his way. Just let
him come home.*

Five-thirty. The clock kept ticking. Nicki's eyes
were so dry they hurt, but she kept watching the
steady rhythm of the second hand going round and
round. Her legs were getting stiff, but she wasn't going to move. Not until Uncle Bryan got home. She
just had to wait long enough. He'd be home.

He might've gotten in an accident. He could get
hurt bad if somebody ran into his Jeep. Especially if
he took off the roof and let it all be open. Maybe he
was at the hospital. Maybe they were working on him
right now! Her stomach started to ache like she might
throw up.

Even if he was at the hospital, it didn't mean he
was going to die. Maybe he just had some broken
bones or needed stitches. He might not be able to take
care of them while he was healing, but Nicki didn't
care. She could take care of both of them. She'd stay
home from school and fetch and cook and clean all
day if she had to, and she didn't even care if he was
a really grouchy patient like Grandpa when he'd had
that heart surgery. Uncle Bryan could yell at her all
day if he wanted to, just as long as he came home to
her.

Nicki started to shiver. She got cold a lot lately.
She thought about pulling her bedspread around her,
but she didn't want to move. Her fingers were cold,
too, but they were still sweaty against her cheek
where she lay on them. Her future stretched out before her, a gray scary blob—

The phone rang.

Nicki's heart started to pound so hard she could feel it in her chest as she stared at the Snoopy phone Uncle Bryan had bought her. What if it was the hospital? Or the police? But they came to the front door, didn't they? Especially since she was just a kid. She started to relax. It must be Uncle Bryan.

Jumping up, Nicki ran to the phone, counting the rings. She knew Uncle Bryan's machine picked up on the fifth ring, so she'd get it on the fourth. She didn't want him to think she'd been waiting by the phone like some ninny. She didn't want him to feel like he had to report to her or anything.

The third ring pealed into the silent house. Nicki took a deep breath. "Hello?" she said, making sure she didn't sound too eager.

"Nick? I'm so sorry, honey. I've been with that new client I told you about for most of the afternoon, taping a series of radio spots, and after I dropped her off there was a huge wreck on Peachtree. And the damn battery on my mobile went dead so I couldn't call, but I'm back at the office now, and just as soon as I drop these things off I'll be heading home. You okay?"

"I'm fine," she said. He didn't sound like Uncle Bryan the way he was rambling on. He sounded upset. Probably because he'd had to worry about checking in. If it wasn't for her, it wouldn't have mattered that his phone battery was dead.

"I'm sorry if I worried you, honey. I'll buy an

extra battery for my phone so next time I'll have a backup.''

She was causing more trouble and she didn't even mean to. ''It's okay, Uncle Bryan. You don't have to do that. I wasn't worried.''

''Oh.'' A pause. ''So whatcha been doing?''

She looked over at the clock, at the name written in little black letters where the second hand connected to the minute hand. ''Reading.''

''How about if I come get you and we head to the Lightning Bolt? We can get some hot dogs or something from the concession while we play.''

Nicki didn't mind about the hot dogs, but she hated the arcade Uncle Bryan seemed to love so much. She wasn't much good at the games he wanted her to learn so badly, and she probably made him bored she was so easy to beat, not that he'd show her he was bored. But even worse than the games, all those people made her nervous. There were more people in the Lightning Bolt at one time than had lived in the whole town of Shallowbrook. And lots of them were boys almost as big as Uncle Bryan, and they wore dirty blue jeans. ''Okay,'' she said. She'd already been enough of a pain for one day.

When they said their goodbyes she hung up the phone slowly, glad that Uncle Bryan was all right. And a night at the Lightning Bolt wouldn't be that bad. Not if she was with Uncle Bryan. She was just going to have to get used to all the people in Atlanta, to going out a lot. She wanted to live with Uncle Bryan forever, and she knew that before she came he'd never stayed home. She couldn't make him change any more than he already had or he was going to get tired of her way before she was all grown-up.

She brushed her hair and changed her clothes, putting on jeans and the Atlanta Hawks T-shirt Uncle Bryan had bought her. She was going to need a bra soon. Most of the girls in her class already had one, and sometimes Nicki wondered if there was something the matter with her that her breasts were only just now starting to grow. She wondered if her mother—her *real* mother—had been a late grower, too. One thing for sure, there was no way she could ask Uncle Bryan what he thought. He'd probably never come home again.

And as she sat on her bed counting the minutes until she heard Uncle Bryan's Jeep pull into the driveway, she wondered for the hundredth time what would happen when she turned eighteen and Uncle Bryan didn't have to keep her anymore. She wondered if he'd be so tired of her, so mad she'd ruined his life for all those years, that he'd leave and she'd never see him again.

Her future stretched out before her, a gray scary blob…

BRYAN CHECKED his mobile as he pulled onto the lot of Teal Hyundai. He was spending the afternoon with Jennifer Teal again, today taping a couple of television commercials, and he wanted to be certain that Nicki could reach him if she needed to. Not that she'd ever called him. But it had scared the hell out of him the week before when he'd realized his mobile had been dead all afternoon. He'd had visions of Nicki needing him and not being able to reach him, of her being all alone and unable to cope. He'd been tempted to abandon his Jeep in the traffic jam on Peachtree and walk to the nearest phone just to assure himself that she was all right. Only the thought that he'd probably get there faster by waiting out the traffic had kept him in his seat.

Teal Hyundai was a far cry from Teal Cadillac, the dealership he'd visited the day before when trying to determine where to shoot the commercials. Gone were the glitzy mirrored windows and high-tech design he'd first thought would make a good backdrop for the TV spots, and in their place were brick walls and plain glass windows. The only decoration was the Teal Hyundai painted on the windows alongside the blue-and-white Teal logo.

This is where he wanted Jennifer's viewers to see her. Teal Hyundai would appeal to the lower-income car buyers, and her appearance there would make her seem accessible to them. Or so he hoped. He wasn't at all sure how well the classy lady would look in such humble surroundings. Maybe he should have gone with the Cadillac dealership, after all.

And maybe he should never have taken the job in the first place. But when the detective he'd hired had called him with the news that Jennifer Teal was looking for a new advertising firm for a special project she was working on, he'd decided the chance was too good to pass up. He wasn't so sure anymore. He was spending too much time thinking about his newest client.

Jake Landers and Bob McKinney, his film crew, were already set up on the lot just as he'd instructed them. They waved as he parked his Jeep. All they needed now was Jennifer. He got out of the Jeep and crossed the lot toward the tile-floored showroom. She was probably waiting inside.

A sleek blue vintage Mustang pulled onto the lot in front of him, and Bryan stopped, admiring the car. He'd always had a thing for Ford's famous sports car, the older the better. He'd bet this one was at least a '66. Maybe even a '65. Now that he had a garage, he should look into getting one himself. Could be that was just what he needed—a new toy.

Bryan was so busy admiring the car that it took him a minute to realize who'd just climbed out of it.

But only a minute. She looked more beautiful every time he saw her, every bit as sleek and elegant as her car. She was wearing a black short-skirted suit, a perfect contrast to the wavy auburn curls pinned up in that twist thing on the back of her head. He wouldn't mind her for a toy, either, only this one he'd keep in his new bedroom.

Except that she was Nicki's mother.

"Nice car," he said, meeting her in the middle of the lot.

She smiled at him, a friendly glad-to-see-you smile. "Thanks. Sorry I'm late, I got stuck on the phone. I've never been good at cutting people off."

"No problem. I just got here myself." He smiled,

too, putting his hand in the small of her back as he guided her toward the camera.

His fears about her looking "right" at this dealership were quickly put to rest. She fit into Teal Hyundai as naturally as she had Teal Lincoln Mercury the week before. After two hours of following her and Bob and Jake around the dealership, Bryan was as perplexed as ever about her. She had a hell of a talent for names. No matter who they passed, from janitor to sales manager, she was outgoing, friendly and called every one of them by name. But what was even more impressive was their obvious ease with her. They treated her with respect, which was probably a given considering that she signed their paychecks, but they seemed to genuinely like her, too.

She turned to speak to an elderly female customer waiting in the service area, and for a second there, he saw Nicki in the tilt of her chin. After listening to the woman's complaints, Jennifer led her into the dealership's waiting lounge and to the comfort of a couch. Then she brought the woman a cup of coffee and promised her she'd get someone on her car as soon as possible.

She did, too. She walked back out to the service area and conferred with the service manager about how to get the woman's car fixed immediately without inconveniencing any other customers. And then, outside in the lot, she apologized to Jake and Bob for the interruption, the Atlanta sunshine catching the gold glints in her chestnut hair. Nicki's hair.

He was puzzled. How was it a woman so outgoing,

so giving to others, could keep herself hidden from her own child? He could certainly understand why, at sixteen, she gave up the child, but it seemed odd that a woman like her wouldn't have, at some point, wanted to meet the child she'd given birth to. See if she was well cared for, happy, especially in these days of open adoption.

She obviously hadn't, though, because the birth had not been registered with any of the search-and-find services.

Didn't Jennifer care that her daughter might be out there somewhere, wanting to know her, needing her?

Or was Teal Automotive the only child she cared about? Bryan was aware that public knowledge of her having had a child out of wedlock and giving it up for adoption could damage Jennifer's reputation somewhat and possibly hurt the One Price campaign. So was her business the reason she hadn't registered?

She caught his eye as Jake stopped to load another tape. He gave her a thumbs-up and she smiled, not looking away until Jake called her back to the cue cards Bob was holding. So she felt it, too, this attraction between them. Damn.

He wondered if she was seeing anyone. He knew she lived alone, that she wasn't seen publicly with the same man with any regularity. But that didn't mean she didn't have a private liaison going on. He wondered about Nicki's biological father. Was she still in contact with him?

Nicki's birth certificate had said "father unknown." But Jennifer had only been fifteen when she'd conceived Nicki. Surely there hadn't been a lot of candidates for the daddy. Or, God forbid, had she been raped? Surprised at the rage that filled him at that thought, Bryan determined he had to have some time alone with her, get her to talk to him. As soon as possible. For both their sakes. True, Jennifer was trusting him to do this campaign for her. But Nicky was relying on him, too. And if push came to shove, Nicky's interests were number one.

"As soon as possible" turned out to be two hours later as he and Jennifer sat in her office, viewing the videotape Jake had shot that afternoon.

"I'd like Dennis to take a look at this before we make any final decisions," she said, "but I like the service area for a background better than the lot. What do you think?"

Bryan sat beside her on the couch, smelling her perfume as they leaned forward studying the console television screen. He'd never seen such a naturally beautiful woman in his life. As hard as he looked, and he'd looked damn hard, he couldn't find anything artificial about her.

"I think very few people are going to notice the background," he said.

She looked startled by the compliment, but pleased, too.

"Thank you."

"You're welcome."

He knew he should look away, that their eyes were saying things to each other that should never be said, yet he couldn't seem to break the silent communication.

"How come you've never married?" he asked, the videotape rolling on without them.

She shrugged and turned her gaze away. "Never found the right guy, I guess."

"Maybe you've just been looking in the wrong places."

"Maybe." She glanced back at him. "What about you? I don't see a wedding ring on *your* finger, either."

"I'm a bad candidate for marriage. My soul's too restless."

She laughed. "What's that supposed to mean?"

"Just that I've never been able to stick at *anything* long enough to make me think I could stay with one woman for eternity."

"You're too hard on yourself. I finally read that file you sent over, you know. It said you've had Innovative Advertising for almost ten years. That sounds like sticking at it to me." She grinned at him.

"I also have a partner. I can take my restless soul off when I need to."

"Why do you need to?" Her grin faded, her eyes now serious.

"You ever have the feeling that something great is happening on the other side of the hill and you're missing the whole thing?"

He thought he saw a flash of pain in her eyes. "Sometimes."

"Me, too," he said. "A lot of times. So I guess,

until I know why it is I keep feeling that way, I'll keep heading over that hill.''

''Be careful you don't get lost.''

''Yeah.''

He wanted to kiss her. He was pretty sure she wanted him to kiss her, too.

''I'll bet you loved the Ferris wheel when you were a kid,'' she said, smiling again.

''You think I like going around in circles?''

''No!'' She touched his arm, her fingers cool and featherlight. ''Don't you remember how high it used to go? Almost to the sky. Certainly high enough to see over that hill.''

He couldn't look away from her lips, couldn't stop wondering what they would taste like, how they would feel beneath his. He'd been wondering for weeks.

She was looking at his lips, too, and running her tongue across her own.

Bryan wasn't aware of leaning toward her, but he wasn't surprised when she met him halfway. Her lips were hesitant as he covered them with his own, not really kissing him back so much as allowing his caress. He pulled her into his arms and deepened the kiss, opening his mouth to her, coaxing her to invite him inside.

He lit like a flame to gasoline when she did. No woman had ever excited him as quickly, as completely, as this one did.

Holy hell.

He pulled away from Jennifer, stunned. ''I'm

sorry," he said, rubbing his hand across his face. "I was out of line there. I don't know what's the matter with me. I've never attacked a client before." His attempt at a joke failed miserably.

"It's okay. It was only a kiss," she said lightly, but she wasn't breathing any easier than he was.

He'd just kissed Nicki's mother. *Where in hell's my brain?*

"So what's the real reason you're not married?" he asked, needing to get his answers and get out.

He reached for the TV control and turned off the videotape, while she scooted farther away from him on the couch.

"I got burned once."

"What happened?"

She got up and went over to her desk, leaning back against it. "Nothing very unusual, I'm afraid. You know the old story...I loved him, he didn't love me back kind of thing."

Bryan found that hard to believe. The guy must have been crazy. But was he also Nicki's father?

"And you never met anyone else?"

"Believe it or not, I just haven't had the time."

Bryan stood up. He was getting nowhere. "You haven't had time to date?"

She smiled. "I've dated some great guys. I'm just not ready to invest the time a good relationship takes."

Did that mean she wouldn't have time for a daughter, either? "What about a family?"

"Tanya and Dennis are all the family I need."

Bryan would have stopped right then and there. He would have gone home and told Nicki that he couldn't find her mother, that she was dead, anything to keep his niece from coming face-to-face with a mother who didn't have time for her. He would have—if he hadn't seen the wistfulness in Jennifer's eyes. He didn't know if the look had anything to do with Nicki. He had no idea if Jennifer had any motherly tendencies at all. He just knew he couldn't leave it like that.

"I've got tickets for the symphony Thursday night," he said, hoping Calvin hadn't already given the tickets away. "A couple of days isn't much notice, but can you come?"

"Yes. I'd like that." Her smile had him wanting her all over again.

CHAPTER FOUR

JENNIFER FELT like a girl preparing for her first date. She'd never met a man who attracted her so much, who seemed so perfect for her. He was intelligent, successful, gorgeous as sin—and no more ready to get married than she was.

She wore her navy silk jumpsuit with matching pumps, liking the way the outfit pinched in at her waist and covered enough of her chest to be circumspect, but still left an enticing amount of skin bare. She even pinned a navy silk bow into the twist on the back of her head, which made her feel particularly feminine. Jewelry was something she always allowed herself, and tonight she felt almost sensuous as the cool gold pendant settled between her breasts and gold glinted from her ears and wrists. As she took a last glance in the floor-length mirror in her bathroom, she felt like laughing. She was actually having fun.

She did laugh when she answered the door to Bryan half an hour later.

"What? You don't like my tie?"

It was blue and patterned with little yellow airplanes. "Your tie is fine. It's the suspenders I'm not so sure about."

He hooked his thumbs into the matching blue-and-yellow suspenders. "Too much, huh?" he asked.

Jennifer looked him over one more time. The suspenders held his shirt tightly against his chest, giving testimony to the fact that the man was all muscle. "No, I like them," she said. And she did. A lot. Almost as much as she liked his ponytail.

"Nice place you've got here," he said, looking over her shoulder into the penthouse.

"Thanks," Jennifer said, self-conscious all of a sudden. She had a feeling he hated her home. To a man like him, it probably looked incredibly boring.

She locked the door and followed him out to his Jeep.

BRYAN HATED the symphony. Even more than he hated briefcases. He hated the stuffiness of it, the yuppiness. He didn't want to keep up with the Joneses; he'd left them behind years ago. He certainly didn't need to see or be seen. And he preferred his music with lyrics—and a little more volume.

But he couldn't remember when he'd enjoyed an evening out more. He refused to call it a date; he'd set down the law for himself on that account. But whatever it was, it was the best one he'd had in years. Jennifer was different. She didn't play games or flirt, didn't make him wonder if she had a hidden agenda. She wasn't shy, or coy, or easily embarrassed. And she didn't seem to care about the Joneses, either.

But neither did she say a lot about herself. Teal Automotive, sure. Her activities, the last charity din-

ner she'd attended, the Hawks' chances to make it to
the NBA playoffs, all were open for discussion. But
Jennifer Teal, the woman inside the successful entre-
preneur, remained a mystery.

The second half of the symphony was well under
way, and Bryan was still wide-awake. Amazing. He
stole a glance at Jennifer. Her lips were lifted in just
a hint of a smile as she watched the stage, engrossed
in the music.

His mind wandered from the concert hall to his
bedroom, with Jennifer in it, her long wavy hair loose
from its pins and spread across his sheet. There were
no pillows on the bed. They'd been shoved to the
floor hours before, and the covers were gone, too.
Jennifer didn't need to cover up. She lay sprawled
before him, looking up at him with sleepy eyes and—

Somebody's beeper went off. Bryan was catapulted
back to the present, irritated with whoever was being
paged. One hell of a great fantasy had been interrupted.

The beeper sounded again. Jennifer nudged his
shoulder. "Shouldn't you check that?" she whispered.

His beeper. Damn. It was the first time in all the
months he'd been carrying it that the thing had gone
off.

He jumped up out of his seat with complete dis-
regard for the people behind him. "I'll be back," he
said to Jennifer, already climbing over feet to get to
the aisle. He didn't need to check to see who was
calling. He knew. There was only one person in the

world who had his number. Only one person to whom he'd given twenty-four-a-day access to his time.

His chest felt like it was being squeezed in a vise as he asked the first usher he found for directions to the closest phone. *Dear God, let her be all right.*

Dropping a quarter into the slot, Bryan punched in his number, his finger frustratingly slow on the numerous buttons, and finally heard the line to his home phone ringing.

"Nick? You okay, sweetheart? I can be there in twenty minutes," he said as soon as his niece picked up the phone.

"I'm fine, Uncle Bryan. I'm really sorry to bug you. I wouldn't have, but Calvin called and he's someplace where he can't be reached, so he's calling back in half an hour. He told me I had to page you, or I wouldn't have, honest."

Bryan sagged against the wall in relief. "Bother me already, okay, Nick? It's what I bought the pager for, remember?"

"Yeah."

"So what's Calvin want? He's not coming home, is he?" Bryan's workaholic partner had just left for a vacation with his family, the first he'd taken since he and Bryan had opened their business ten years before. Bryan had a feeling it had been either that or be served with divorce papers.

"He didn't say he was. He wanted to know if you heard from a Mr. Wonderly about some kind of tapes."

"Tell him everything's fine and to quit worrying

and enjoy his vacation. Better yet, tell him I'm not taking any more calls from him until next week."

"You want *me* to tell him that?"

"Yep. And if he starts to give you a hard time, you have my permission to hang up on him."

"I can't do that!"

Bryan smiled as he listened to the horror in Nicki's voice. At least he'd managed to get a rise out of her.

"Sure you can. It's easy. You just put the phone back in its cradle without saying goodbye."

"Okay...if you want me to." She sounded like he'd asked her to burn the house down.

"I do. So whatcha up to?" Bryan was reluctant to hang up. Not just because he'd rather talk to Nicki than listen to the symphony, but because she'd finally called him. He wished she'd do it more.

"Watching TV."

"You got all your homework done?"

"Uh-huh."

"And you got Mrs. Baker's number right by the phone?" he asked. Their next-door neighbor was a widow, and a godsend, checking on Nicki for him whenever he couldn't be home.

"Uh-huh."

"Did you feed the fish?"

"Uncle Bryan, we don't have any fish." She sounded like she was smiling.

"Right. I knew that. So, anything sound good for a snack? I can stop by the store on my way home."

"No. That's okay."

And just like that he'd slammed into that brick wall

again. It wasn't okay. Not to Bryan. It wasn't okay at all. Because Nicki needed a hell of a lot more than she was telling him. And suddenly he remembered Jennifer, the woman waiting just beyond the doors for him to return. Not his date. Not someone he could fantasize about taking to bed with him. *Nicki's mother.*

"I'll stop for some of those cupcakes you like. If you don't want any tonight, you can take them to school with you tomorrow."

"You don't have to, Uncle Bryan. Honest."

Bryan slouched against the wall, suddenly more tired than he'd ever been in his life. Month after month went by, and they were making no progress. "I know I don't have to, Nick. I *want* to." He paused. "I'll be home soon."

"I can stay home late by myself."

"You do great alone, Nick, but I still don't like to leave you there by yourself. The symphony's almost over, I'll drop my client off, grab the cupcakes and be home. We can watch *Taxi* together. How's that sound?"

"If you want to. But you can stay out later if you want. It doesn't matter."

It doesn't matter. Those were the words that worried Bryan most of all. Nothing seemed to matter to Nicki anymore. He'd been warned to expect apathy from her, as well as himself, as they went through the grieving process, adjusting to losing their entire family in the blink of an eye. But it had been almost a year, and while he sometimes still woke up with that sick feeling in his gut, he was able to look forward to things again. But Nicki wasn't. He was getting more and more concerned that her apathy was passing the boundaries of normal. Nothing mattered.

Nothing, that is, except finding her biological mother. She'd just asked Bryan about it again the day before. And Bryan had lied to her. He'd told her he hadn't found her birth mother yet—because he was still no closer to knowing whether or not Jennifer had a place for Nicki in her life. If he had to guess, he'd guess not. And there was no way Nicki was strong enough to hear that. So, with no other choice, he'd lied to her. Just as he was, by omission, lying to Jennifer. Nevertheless he wasn't going to tell either one of them about the other until he could be surer of the outcome.

He hung up the phone and went back into the auditorium, determined to do whatever it took to get Jennifer to open up to him and get the whole thing over and done with. No more fantasies. Reality was just too important.

JENNIFER LOOKED forward to his good-night kiss all the way home. She'd been thinking about it all evening, every time she'd felt his arm brush against hers or he'd leaned over to whisper something to her. She'd been anticipating his kiss like a silly schoolgirl, and yet she couldn't seem to stop. Had it just been a fluke the other day in her office, the way he'd made her feel?

Her blood was barreling through her veins as Bryan

pulled up in the visitor parking at her building. Tonight they weren't at the office. Tonight they weren't
working. Tonight the kiss would be more than an accident.

"I love this time of year," he said as they walked
together toward the ornate front doors of her apartment building. The Georgia air was warm, balmy. A
gorgeous spring evening.

"Because of the basketball play-offs, right?" It
was all Dennis talked about when they weren't talking
about work or Tanya.

"Nope. The flying." He held open the door for her
before the doorman could get it.

She looked at his tie. "Flying."

"Mmm. It stays light longer now, but it's not summer vacation yet, so the skies aren't too crowded."

"You're a pilot?"

"Yeah. Since I was a teenager. I was barely eighteen when I bought my first plane."

She pushed the button for the elevator. "Do you
still have your own plane?"

He nodded. "A Cessna four-seater. There's nothing
like being up there in a world all your own. You're
never going to get freer than that. Do you like to fly?"

"I don't know. I've never flown in anything
smaller than a 737, and I'm usually working the
whole time we're in the air."

"I'll take you up some time, if you like. We can
go to dinner at a great place I know in Huntsville."

"Alabama?"

"Yeah, and they've got the best red snapper I've ever had."

The man was incredible. And maybe just what she needed. "If you're serious, I may just take you up on that."

The Day, Jennifer thought, was coming up fast. Another couple of weeks and it would be twelve years. Twelve long years, and facing that day never got any easier. No matter how she tried to convince herself otherwise, the what-ifs, the recriminations, the guilt were always there. And the wondering. But maybe this year she wouldn't have to be alone with her guilt. Maybe, if she spent the day with Bryan, she wouldn't hurt so bad.

"I'll give you a call next time I'm going up," he said.

The elevator came and Jennifer stepped inside with him, glad to find they had it all to themselves. She put in the key for the penthouse and pushed the button that would take them up to the top floor. And when she turned, he was looking at her.

"So what did you think of the cello concerto?" she asked, nervous again.

He grinned at her. "The truth?"

She nodded.

"I think the Wonderly-soup account is going to benefit from it greatly."

"The Wonderly-soup account?"

"Mmm. I think it was during that concerto thing that it finally hit me what was missing from the campaign."

She grinned. "You didn't enjoy the symphony, did you?"

"There were some good parts," he said, holding her gaze with his own. Jennifer felt as if she was going to melt right there beneath his sexy brown eyes.

The elevator doors opened, and she stepped out, sliding her key into the lock that would let them into her penthouse.

She didn't really know what to do next. She'd never brought a man here with anything intimate in mind.

The penthouse door opened and she turned. *Invite him in, idiot.* "I really enjoyed myself tonight."

He brushed his fingers along her cheek. "I did, too."

"In spite of Mozart?"

"He wasn't that bad. I think half my problem is the setting. I'd probably like him a whole lot more if they'd put on an outdoor concert, up on Stone Mountain, say, with everybody wearing shorts and lying around on blankets in the grass."

It sounded wonderful to her. Especially if he took her along. "I'll let you know if I ever hear of one," she said.

"You do that."

He was looking at her the way he had in her office right before he'd kissed her. And this time she was ready for him. She wanted him to kiss her. She wanted to feel his arms around her again more than she'd wanted anything in a long time.

"Well, good night," he said, and stepped back into the elevator.

Jennifer hadn't even noticed that he'd been holding it open. Before she had a chance to respond he was gone.

"How's Tanya?" Jennifer asked Dennis the next day over a midmorning cup of coffee in his office. She hadn't slept much the night before and it was her fourth cup of coffee so far.

"Great! Just great. Her show was a huge success. Requests have been pouring in for more paintings. She even had a call from someone in New York. He wants to set up a one-woman exhibition for her."

"A New York show? All by herself? How long will it take her to get ready?"

"It'll have to be after—" Dennis stopped.

"After?" *After another five or six months?*

"After she, uh, gets enough new paintings done to carry another show," he said, stirring more sugar into his coffee.

Damn. How long were they going to wait before they told her they were expecting a baby? She knew lots of people who'd had babies.

Just none that were close to her.

She pictured herself listening to the intimate details of the growth of Tanya's baby and having to celebrate every development with them. She thought about walking into an infants'-wear department, of looking at the overwhelming array of garments, holding them up and hearing Tanya marvel at how tiny they were.

"How long will that take?" She should just tell Dennis that she knew about Tanya's pregnancy. That she'd probably known before Tanya did. That even if Dennis's secretary hadn't slipped the news, Jennifer had recognized the symptoms, anyway.

"She told the guy it would have to be next summer."

"And he's willing to wait that long?"

"Yeah. He's already booked the date. The second week in July."

"So you're going to New York," Jennifer said, forcing a smile. She was happy for her friends. They deserved it—and more.

Dennis fidgeted with the picture of his wife he kept on his desk. "Tanya's counting on you coming with us, Jennifer. She says she can't do it without you there."

Jennifer thought of the baby Tanya was carrying. It would be seven or eight months old by then, and the focus of every moment of their lives. She started to sweat. "I don't know if we should both be gone at once," she said, hating herself for her sudden weakness. She didn't understand what was the matter with her.

"We'll see what happens when—" His phone rang and Dennis broke off.

Jennifer couldn't help noticing he hadn't tried very hard to persuade her. Was Dennis really that unsure about her ability to handle being around their baby? Even for a few days? He knew her better than anyone else on earth. And yes, she generally avoided being around babies because they made her remember, but it wasn't like she couldn't handle those memories if she had to.

"Yes, I did see them…I agree…Great, we'll look forward to seeing the finished product." She listened to Dennis's conversation, telling herself she was over-reacting. Dennis was probably just waiting for Tanya to tell her their news. And she'd be excited about their new baby long before it arrived; she just needed a little more time to get used to the idea.

"Sure, she's right here," Dennis said, holding out the phone. "It's Bryan Chambers."

Jennifer stood up. "I'll take it in my office."

"He's on line two," Dennis said, his brows lifting in surprise.

But Jennifer wasn't thinking about Dennis's reaction as she left his office. She needed to know what she'd done wrong the night before. And she certainly wasn't going to ask within earshot of her vice president.

"Hi," Jennifer said, picking up the phone as soon as her office door was closed behind her. She sank into the blue upholstered high-backed chair behind her desk.

"Jennifer? Good." Without waiting for her to speak, he went on, "I'm working on the next series of television ads for One Price, and I've got an idea I'd like to run by you." He sounded so formal. So impersonal.

"Shoot," she said, picking up a pen to sign a couple of letters Rachel had left for her.

"So far we've appealed to your wealthier customers, to businessmen and to the working class. This time I want to go for the housewife, the family man and Grandma."

"All at once?" She put the signed letters in her out tray.

"If we can."

What had happened to the man who'd come to her door wearing bright blue-and-yellow suspenders the night before? "How?"

"By including children in the scripts. We show you in a series of short spots, giving a Teal Automotive coloring book to a couple of kids while their parents shop for a car, explaining One Price to a little boy who's in with his parents buying a car, and fastening a baby into the built-in child seat in a Windstar."

Jennifer set her pen down slowly, deliberately. "I'd rather you think of something else." She pushed up the sleeve of her pale pink suit, looking at her Rolex.

"Of course, if you insist, I will, but I think you ought to at least give the idea some thought. Talk it over with Dennis, if you'd like. A series of spots like this would not only be cost effective, but time effective, as well, reaching several markets at once."

She didn't hesitate. "I don't need to talk to Dennis. I'd rather not do it."

There was a pause on the line, and Jennifer knew she was handling the situation badly. Still, she felt like she was being bombarded with babies all of a sudden. It should have helped her to realize that her reactions were largely because of the impending anniversary, that she was always a little sensitive this time of year, that she'd be fine once The Day had passed again, but she still didn't feel any more inclined to hold someone else's baby.

"Mind my asking why not?" Bryan's voice, softer now, made her feel like a heel.

"I'm not very good with kids."

"What's to be good about? They say their lines, you say yours, you smile at them, and it's done."

Except for the baby. If it cried in her arms, they could have to redo the take. Heaven only knew how long she'd have to be holding it. "I'd just feel better if you could come up with something else," she said, looking over her schedule for the rest of the morning.

"Well, whatever you say..."

She'd disappointed him. "Bryan?" She pushed her calendar aside.

"Yeah?"

"Did I do something wrong last night? Something to send you away?" She was beyond caring if she made a fool of herself. She needed to know.

"No. Why do you ask?"

"One minute we were having a good time, and the next you were gone."

"The symphony was over."

"But that didn't mean the date had to be. It wasn't even ten o'clock."

"Is that what it was? A date?"

"I thought so," she said.

"So is that how you treat all your dates? With vague answers any time they get too close?"

"Is that what I was doing?"

"You're doing it again. You answer my question with a question."

"I don't have many dates that mean anything. I really don't know how I treat them."

"Are you saying ours meant something?"

"Maybe. You're different, Bryan. And you don't apologize for it or flaunt it. And you don't seem to care that I'm the owner of Teal Automotive. It's refreshing. It also helps that you're no more interested in marriage right now than I am."

"It may not matter overly much to me that you *are* Teal Automotive, or that you're one of the richest single women in the city, but I do like to know the people inside the women I date. Getting to know you is like trying to break into a cement cell."

Jennifer's hand started to shake. "It's...it's hard when you're in my position. You never know what people want from you, or if they even want you at all, rather than what you can do for them. You tend to get cautious after a while."

"Poor little rich girl, huh?"

"Maybe. Except that I have a couple of close friends I'd trust with my life, so I don't consider myself all that poor."

"So what does it take for someone to become your friend?"

"Are you saying you want to?"

"Maybe."

She smiled. If his "maybe" meant anywhere near as much as hers had, things were going to be all right.

"Then I guess you ask me out again and see what happens."

"I'm getting kinda hungry for some red snapper."

"If that's an invitation, the answer's yes."

"Monday for lunch?"

"Okay."

"Good. And, Jennifer?"

"Yeah?"

"You're right to be cautious—about what people might want from you, I mean. See you Monday."

Jennifer held the phone long after the dial tone was humming in her ear. He understood. And she was in trouble. For the first time in her adult life she'd met a man she could fall in love with.

But just how attracted would he be if he learned the truth about her? How much would he admire a woman who'd apparently once had the morals of an alley cat? Who'd been stupid enough to get pregnant?

CHAPTER FIVE

SOMETHING WAS WRONG with her—in the head. Nicki didn't know what. She'd never been around a crazy person before to know what one was like. But she knew something was wrong. Nothing was fun anymore.

She tossed aside the book she was reading and stared into space. The book was stupid. The kids in it had stupid problems. They spent all their time worrying about who their best friends were inviting to parties, and whether or not their moms were going to let them go to the movies with boys. Like any of that stuff really mattered. Nicki couldn't believe she'd ever found books like that any good.

She heard Uncle Bryan turn off the shower. As soon as he got ready, he was driving her to the mall to shop for summer clothes. He was making a really big deal out of it, taking the whole day, since it was Saturday, and even taking her out to a fancy lunch like her mother used to do when they came to the city to Christmas-shop. Nicki used to look forward to those trips for weeks, counting the days and making lists so she'd be sure not to forget anything. She used to love shopping.

But not anymore. Shopping was stupid. Who cared about all the fancy stuff in the store windows? Clothes were clothes. They didn't really matter. They didn't stop things from happening. And what did she care if she looked good? There was nobody around to dress up for. Uncle Bryan mostly just wore jeans and T-shirts, and it didn't matter to him if that was all she wore, too. Besides, dressing up was dumb. A waste of time. It wasn't going to bring back her parents.

"Ready to go, Nick?"

Uncle Bryan came into the living room, still pulling on his shirt. His hair was wet, but already the long part was in its ponytail. Grandma would've had a fit if she could see it, but Nicki thought it was neat.

"Yeah. I've got my list, just like you told me," Nicki said, getting to her feet. She was going to try really hard to make herself have fun today. Uncle Bryan wanted her to, he was trying really hard to make the day good, and she so badly wanted to make him happy with her.

He didn't get it about what colors didn't look good with her hair or which stores carried the nerdy clothes, but he was friendly with all the clerks, and Nicki didn't mind shopping with him at all. He made her try on every outfit they picked, and then come out so he could see her in it. Which made her feel sort of special, even if he *was* only doing it because of her mother.

She pulled on a baby T with a big daisy on the front and a pair of matching daisy shorts, and looked at herself in the dressing-room mirror. The outfit seemed okay, and she'd seen lots of girls at school wearing daisies lately. And it didn't have any red or orange that would look bad with her hair. But still, she wasn't sure if she looked geeky or not.

She peeked out the door of the dressing room to make certain nobody but Uncle Bryan was out there, and then slipped out.

"Is it comfortable?" He'd asked that same question with every outfit.

"I guess."

"Well, I gotta tell you, Nick. You look wonderful in it. That top shows how slim you are, and the shorts make your legs look miles long."

Nicki blushed, but she felt like smiling.

"But I don't know," Uncle Bryan continued, and her stomach tightened up again. "It might be a little old for you. Maybe you should wait a year or two before wearing those short shirts."

"Okay," Nicki said, trying really hard to hide her disappointment.

"You're only eleven, Nick. We don't want boys noticing how cute you are for a while yet."

Nicki nodded and went in to change. He didn't have to worry. Boys didn't notice her. But she didn't feel so bad about not having the outfit if it was because Uncle Bryan thought she was cute.

Uncle Bryan paid for her clothes, including a longer daisy T-shirt to go with the daisy shorts. She added the bag to her other packages and followed him out into the mall, wondering again what was wrong with her. She was glad to have all her new things.

She just wasn't excited about them. In the old days, when she'd come to the city to shop, she'd thought over and over again about each new thing she got, pretending different places she was going to wear it. Sometimes she even got an excited feeling in her stomach that lasted for the whole day. But now they were just clothes, things she had to have.

She saw a big advertisement in the mall for a Six Flags amusement park, and remembered the only time she'd been there, the time Uncle Bryan had taken her on the roller coaster and she'd thrown up. It had still been the very best time she'd ever had. She'd always wanted to go there for a whole week and spend nights in a hotel and everything. She knew Uncle Bryan would take her if she asked him to. But she didn't want to go anymore. She didn't see what was so fun about going upside down and throwing up. She'd been such a stupid little kid back then.

They passed a drugstore, and Uncle Bryan stopped. "How about a chocolate bar to tide us over till lunch?" He named her favorite kind.

"Okay," Nicki said because he seemed so glad to get it for her. But it didn't really sound too good.

And neither did lunch when they finally finished their shopping later that afternoon. Uncle Bryan took her to the Mexican restaurant she used to beg to go to every time they came to Atlanta on a visit. And she ordered her usual burrito with extra beans, but it wasn't hard at all to wait for it to come, and she ate it because she knew she had to, not because she really wanted it. She just didn't feel hungry anymore. Besides, no matter how much she ate, it didn't make the empty feeling inside her go away.

Uncle Bryan was eating a steak, which the restaurant also had on the menu. He didn't like Mexican food. "You haven't mentioned your birth mother in a while, Nick. You giving up on her?"

Nicki's heart started to beat fast. "No. But you said you'd let me know when you found out something, and I didn't want to nag you. Mom always used to say I nagged a lot and she'd get mad about it sometimes."

"So it still means as much to you that we find her?"

Nicki nodded. It meant everything to her. She'd spent hours imagining what her other mother would be like, how their first meeting would go. Whenever thinking about her mom and dad, and never seeing them again, made her feel like she was just going to curl up and die, she'd think about finding her other mother, and the scared feeling would go away a little bit.

Uncle Bryan was paying attention to his lunch again.

"So have you found out anything?" Nicki hoped it wasn't nagging to ask, since he'd brought up the subject.

"Not yet, but they're narrowing it down." He put a big bite of steak in his mouth.

Nicki put her fork down, too excited to eat any more. "Narrowing it down" had to mean they'd found out something. And if they'd found out something, they could probably find out more. So maybe there *was* a chance she'd know where her other mother was before Uncle Bryan wanted to get rid of her.

Uncle Bryan was keeping her because he knew her mother and grandma would have wanted him to, but there were no real ties—no *blood* ties—to hold him to her when she started to bug him too much. And she would. She didn't know when, and she hoped it would take longer because she was trying very hard not to get in his way, but she knew that eventually he'd be climbing the walls. Not because he wanted to be that way, just because that was Uncle Bryan.

"You remember the time when I was really little and I asked you if you had crabs in your pants?" she asked him. It made her feel better when she thought of those days.

He grinned at her. For an uncle, he was really handsome.

"Yeah, I remember. I wondered what Lori was telling you about me."

"You got really mad at her. I've never seen you and Mom yell at each other like that."

"And all because you had big ears and a little memory," he said teasingly.

"Can I help it if I didn't know the difference between ants and crabs?" she asked.

She'd been so happy in those days. She hadn't even known how great it was—or that it could all go away so fast, either.

And that was why she had to find her other mother.

She needed to in case Uncle Bryan got tired of her before she was old enough to be on her own. Even if her other mother still didn't want her, maybe she had an aunt or a grandma someplace who did.

It had never bothered Nicki that she was adopted when she lived in Shallowbrook. Actually it had made her feel special because her mom and dad had picked her, her especially, to love. But Uncle Bryan hadn't picked her. She'd been forced on him.

There was another reason she had to find her other mother. Nicki had to know why that lady had given her away. Nicki hoped that she hadn't meant to, that she, Nicki, had been taken away without her knowing it. She was afraid, sometimes, that Uncle Bryan thought about how it wasn't fair that he *had* to keep her when even the woman who'd actually had her didn't want her.

She knew that he had to think it wasn't fair, 'cause Uncle Bryan hadn't ever wanted any children, not even his own. She'd heard him arguing with Grandma about it the last time he'd come to Shallowbrook for vacation. Grandma was always wanting him to get married and give her some more grandchildren. And he'd said he wasn't the marrying kind and he wouldn't make a good father. Nicki thought he'd make the best dad ever next to her own, and she loved him as much as any kid ever loved a dad. She just wished he felt differently about wanting kids.

JENNIFER CHATTED EASILY with him when he flew her to lunch on Monday. In fact, she spent the entire meal telling him about the celebrity tennis match she'd attended over the weekend. But her describing, in great detail, how two professional tennis players had faced off against each other with two professional basketball players partnering them wasn't exactly what he'd had in mind when he'd encouraged her to open up to him.

On the way back to her office, he'd asked her again about the television spots he wanted her to do with children. She'd still refused to do them, but he had a feeling she was weakening. The idea almost guaranteed success. And the more time he spent with Jennifer the more important it became to him to make her One Price campaign a success.

But apart from the campaign, there was another reason he couldn't let the idea die. She'd refused to do the commercials because she wasn't good with kids. That worried him.

Nicki was sound asleep when he got home that afternoon, but because she hadn't slept well the night before, he didn't wake her up for dinner. He spent the evening thinking about her birth mother, instead. The woman was perplexing. She seemed so up-front and honest, yet there were times when he sensed things simmering under her polished surface that he couldn't begin to understand. She always appeared so together, but she had a past that wasn't together at all. And what made him even more uncomfortable was how much she just plain intrigued him. Somehow he had to get her to relax enough to open up to him.

The idea came to him Wednesday morning. A picnic. A quiet intimate lunch for two. And he knew just the spot—a lush green patch of land up on Stone Mountain. Telling Jacci to cancel his afternoon appointments, Bryan checked with Mrs. Baker to make certain his cheerful neighbor would be available in case Nicki had a problem at school, then dialed Jennifer's private number.

"Have you got anything comfortable to wear stashed at work?" he asked as soon as she picked up the line.

"Bryan?" She sounded pleased to hear from him.

"Uh-huh. I was thinking about kidnapping you for a couple of hours, but you'll need to change out of that suit you're wearing."

"How do you know I'm wearing a suit?"

"Aren't you?"

"Yes."

"See?"

"Okay. Well, it just happens I do have a change of clothes here. I always keep some jeans handy in case I want to have dinner with Sam," she said, sounding sassy, egging him on.

"Who's Sam?" He pretended to sound aggrieved.

"Only the best mechanic I've ever met."

"And you have dinner with him often?"

"Fairly often. Anything else you want to know?"

"Yeah, why can't you wear your suits for Sam?"

"Because they might get greasy."

Bryan grinned. "Greasy?" He pictured a couple of black handprints on the derriere of the green linen suit she'd been wearing at lunch on Monday. "Jeez, Jennifer, have some class."

"Don't get gross on me, Chambers. Sam's almost seventy years old, and whenever we work on my car together, I bring him dinner."

That got him. "*You* work on your car?"

"Guess I'm not so predictable, after all, huh?" she asked. He could tell she was laughing, though she had the grace to do so silently.

He wanted to throttle her and kiss her at once. Except that she was Nicki's mother.

"Just change into those jeans. I'm on my way," he said, and hung up.

"IT'S BEEN YEARS since I've been here," Jennifer said an hour later as he pulled into the west gate at Stone Mountain. He'd taken the sides and top off the Jeep, and strands of her auburn hair had pulled free of their twist and feathered her cheeks and neck.

She was smiling—and beautiful.

"Not too much time in the life of a busy executive to stop and smell the roses, huh?" he asked.

"There probably should be. I just don't slow down enough to find out."

He pulled around to the service drive that led to a big parking lot by the youth camping area. "Why not?"

She'd made her way in a man's world and he admired her for it. But didn't she long for some of the things she'd passed up? Things like marriage and motherhood?

She shrugged, and he sensed another of her vague answers on the tip of her tongue. And then she looked at him, really looked at him, her hazel eyes a little unsure.

"I'm happiest when I'm busy," she said.

Bryan could understand that. He was, too.

He pulled a blanket and the deli basket from behind his seat and led her into the park. He could hear children in the distance, yelling, laughing, having the times of their lives.

She helped him spread out the blanket and divvy up the turkey and roast-beef sandwiches, chips and apples. He opened a couple of wine coolers.

"I would've figured you for a beer man," she said, taking a long swallow from the bottle he handed her.

"Usually when I drink I go straight for the hard stuff, not that it happens often, but I was trying for a more romantic effect here." He'd fought with himself when he'd purchased the bottles at the deli next door to his office. No matter how much she attracted him, he had no business pursuing a personal relationship with her. But he'd gone ahead and bought the wine, anyway.

"Romance is good." The sun-draped mountain was a perfect background for her smile.

He stretched out across from her, taking a couple of sandwiches with him. "I wasn't sure you took time for that, either."

"I don't very often."

He was curiously glad to hear that.

They ate and drank, the sound of trees and grasses

rustling in the light breeze, just enough to mute the noises of the park, enveloping them in their own little world. Jennifer looked more relaxed than he'd ever seen her, and more beautiful.

"This was a great idea," she said halfway through her second sandwich.

Looking across at her, feeling more content than he'd felt in a long time, Bryan had to remind himself of his reason for bringing her there.

"I hoped you'd enjoy getting away. You work too much."

"I know."

"So why do you? Surely there are other ways to stay busy." *God, woman, tell me what I have to know before I fall for you and hurt us both.*

She put her sandwich down, turning to look up at the mountain. The chair lift taking visitors up one side of the mountain was visible from where they sat.

"I'm in a man's world, and I've always had the feeling that if I relax too much, if I let go for even a minute, I may lose it all."

He looked at her profile, the delicate features. What a contradiction she was. So feminine, yet so driven to succeed. "You're talking about a multimillion-dollar empire!"

She turned her head, looking straight at him. "And do you know how many men are just waiting for me to make that one mistake that'll let them eat me alive?"

"Then what made you get into the business to begin with, if you feel that way?"

"I took it over from my parents."

"Couldn't you have sold it, used the money to invest in something else?"

"No, I couldn't." She shook her head, looking back at the mountain. "I needed to make a success of it, not sell it. I needed to do it for them."

Bryan sat up. "Why?"

"I was born late in their marriage. My mother was already in her forties and had thought herself beyond child-bearing age. They were good people and they loved me, but I was an intrusion in their lives, one they never really, wholeheartedly accepted."

Bryan thought of his own family, feeling the familiar pang as he remembered how close they'd all been. "It must have been rough growing up," he said, thankful suddenly for Shallowbrook and the years of his youth.

"It wasn't that bad. They weren't mean to me or anything. It just seemed like I was always trying to be perfect in order to avoid their irritated frowns. Half the time I don't even think they knew they were frowning. They just didn't know what to do with a child around."

She was still facing the mountain, but at least she was talking.

"And so you grew up and made them millionaires to repay them for making your childhood miserable?" he asked.

She looked at him then and smiled, a self-deprecating, knowing smile. "Is that what it sounds like?"

"From where I'm sitting."

She shrugged. "I don't know, maybe it was a little like that. But they tried, Bryan. They were always honest with me, and fair. They gave me opportunities, including a college education they couldn't afford. After I graduated with a degree in business, I found out what a bad state Teal Motors was in. They asked me if I could help them. Finally there was something I could do to please them, to pay them back for the twenty-year disruption I'd been in their lives, something to show them I loved them. Something I could do to make them happy again. And as it turned out, pleasing them pleased me, too. I love the car business."

He admired her determination. "So how long did it take you to learn the ropes?"

"I already knew them inside and out. I grew up at the dealership and worked there for most of my teenage years. I rebuilt my first car engine, with Sam's help, during my junior year in high school."

Before or after she'd given Nicki away? "What happened to the car?" he asked.

"Nothing. I'm still driving it."

"The Mustang?"

"Mmm."

"You wouldn't be interested in selling it, would you?"

"Never. God willing, I'll be driving that car when I'm eighty."

"Somehow I believe you will be," Bryan said, gathering up the remnants of their picnic. She really cared about certain things in her life—her parents, her business, her car. But what about her child? How had Nicki missed out on that caring?

Bryan loaded their things back into the Jeep and then suggested a walk. He wasn't any less confused now than he'd been before the day had begun. How could a woman who'd grown up as she had, who'd spent her entire life trying to earn the love of her parents, not at some point have given a thought to the child she'd given birth to? Why hadn't she at least registered someplace in case the child needed her?

The path to the petting zoo was heavily traveled and swarming with kids. A couple of little boys, around five or six years old, zoomed past, racing each other to a tree up ahead, and Bryan couldn't help but smile at their antics.

"Shouldn't their parents be watching them more closely?" Jennifer asked, frowning.

"They're probably right behind us."

"I hope so. Those boys look awfully young to be on their own."

Her shoulder brushed him and he had to restrain himself from putting his arm around her and pulling her closer. She didn't need his protection. There was nothing there for her to be afraid of.

"Have you ever thought about having children?" he asked, losing sight of the boys as they rounded a bend.

"I have no interest in being a mother."

His heart sank. "Isn't that a little strong?"

"I feel strongly about it."

She'd put more distance between them, moving closer to the side of the path. "What about Teal Motors? Don't you ever think about having an heir to pass it on to?"

"Not really."

"But girls always want to grow up and have babies," he blurted. *Great, Chambers, now there's an intelligent statement.* But he was frustrated and scared for Nicki. He just didn't want to believe that Jennifer had no place in her heart for the daughter who needed her. He'd seen her with her employees, with an old lady she didn't even know. She was compassion personified. Something wasn't adding up.

"Why is it that just because I'm a woman, I'm automatically expected to produce babies? If I were a man, would you be pressuring me to procreate? And what about you? I don't see you out there lining up to be a daddy."

Because I'm already a father, and mother, too, to your child. They fell into an uneasy silence as they continued to walk, and Bryan wondered if she was wishing she'd never set eyes on him.

They'd reached a fork in the path, and Jennifer swerved onto the different route. "Let's see what's up there," she said, glancing back to make sure he was behind her.

What was up there turned out to be a birthday party for Molly, who was just turning eleven, according to the banner strung across the path. He and Jennifer walked to the end of the path, silently passing beneath the banner, before they turned around and headed back the way they'd come.

Bryan watched the birthday girls as they passed the party a second time. The girls were gathered in a huddle, squealing and giggling, right beside a table piled high with presents. Bryan got a sick feeling in his gut as he saw a woman, probably Molly's mother, call the girls over and give each of them a slip of paper and a shopping bag. A scavenger hunt.

Nicki had had a scavenger hunt for her tenth birthday. And a tornado for her eleventh. And, dear God, her twelfth one was coming up soon. His heart froze as he realized just how soon. In a little over a week, Nicki was going to be twelve years old. In a little over a week, it was going to be a full year since Lori and his parents had died.

He had no idea how he and Nicki were going to celebrate the day, but he was pretty certain she wouldn't be enjoying it the way Molly obviously was.

"Excuse me, lady. We're having a scavenger hunt. Do you have a bobby pin I could have?" A girl stood before them on the path, looking cute and carefree as she grinned up at them. Her lips were stained purple.

"No. I'm sorry," Jennifer said. She kept on walking. Bryan stared at the pinned-up hair on the back of her head.

The pigtailed girl walked backward, staying in front of Jennifer. "Would you look at my list then and see if there's anything here you might have?" she asked.

"I'm sorry, honey, I have to get back," Jennifer said, smiling as she stepped around the child.

"Thanks, anyway," the child called as she scampered off.

The whole thing had only taken a couple of seconds, but it worried Bryan more than anything that had gone before. Jennifer had been as pleasant as always, but she'd still just brushed off that child with an ease that told its own story. A story that might well contain an unhappy ending for Nicki.

CHAPTER SIX

"MAMA? MAMA! *Ma-ma-a-a!*"

Bryan shot out of bed, pulled on his cutoffs and raced into Nicki's room as he heard the familiar cry. It had been almost a month since the last time. He'd been hoping they were past this point.

He pulled the sweating body of his niece from beneath her covers and into his arms. "It's okay, Nick. I'm here, baby. It's okay," he said softly over and over as he stroked the damp strands of her hair away from her face.

He felt her shudder and knew she'd come back to him. "Uncle Bryan?" Her voice was weak and frightened.

"I'm here, baby. Right here," he said, choking down the emotion that had been so close to the surface for the past year. As hard it was for him to accept the loss of his family, he knew it was ten times harder for Nicki.

She started to cry, sobbing against his chest so hopelessly that it hurt him just to listen to her. God, he hated the Fates that had done this to such a sweet sensitive child.

He held her and rocked her, soothing her with

words of love, and long before the storm had passed, a few of his own tears had mingled with hers.

"I'm sorry, Uncle Bryan. I didn't mean to," she said some time later, pulling away from him.

He reached out, brushing the tears from her cheeks, aching inside as he saw her swollen eyes. "Don't apologize, sweetheart. It isn't your fault. None of this is your fault."

She shivered and scooted back from him, sitting on her pillow with her knees curled up to her chest. "Sometimes I think it is," she whispered.

Bryan froze. "No! Nicki, you're not to blame for anything. Don't even think it."

She looked up at him, her soft hazel eyes filling with tears again. "But if it hadn't been for me, for that stupid party I had to have, everybody wouldn't have been together outside like that."

Bryan slid down to kneel at the side of her bed, leaning over to bring his face even with hers. "The tornado would still have come, honey, and even inside, in different houses, they would have died if it was their time. It had nothing to do with you."

She studied his face, her eyes wide. "Do you really believe that, Uncle Bryan? Really?" she whispered.

"Yes, I do, honey. With all my heart."

Nicki held out her arms and asked, "Can I have a hug?"

"Of course, sprite. Always." He sat back down beside her and pulled her into his arms, silently cursing his inability to shield her from her demons.

"I just wish it didn't hurt so much," she said after a minute or two.

Bryan felt her words clear to his soul. "I know, little one. I wish that, too."

"Do you still miss them?"

"More than ever, honey. All the time."

"Do you think we'll ever stop missing them?"

Bryan weighed his words carefully. "Not completely. I don't think we'd want to. We never want to forget them or how much we loved them. But I do think that someday we'll smile more often than we cry when we think of them."

"Sometimes I try not to think of them because it hurts too much, and then I feel bad, like I'm trying to forget them. But I don't want to forget them, Uncle Bryan. Not ever, and sometimes I'm scared I will."

"I know, sweetie. But you don't have to worry about that. There's a part of each one of them in you, and no one can ever take that away from you."

"I love you, Uncle Bryan." She snuggled into his chest.

"And I love you, Nick, more than anything."

He held her until she fell back to sleep, thanking the Lord for saving her from the ravages of the tornado that had taken the rest of his family. He'd willingly lay down his life for this child. Or his heart. She came first. No matter what.

JENNIFER SAW BRYAN twice more that week. He was still after her to do some commercials with kids and had stopped by on Thursday to show her the specs for the spots he'd reserved, including a projected return on her investment. It was impressive.

On Friday he came by to bring her the scripts. He wasn't taking no for an answer. And Jennifer found herself weakening. Probably because she knew he was right. They were a great idea.

Nevertheless, as she sat across from him in her office, she said, "There have to be other good ideas."

"Good, sure, but not great." He tapped the folder against his jeans. "At least read the scripts, and then we can talk again."

Jennifer took them. There was no reason not to. "Okay, but I can't promise to like them." But she knew she would. And maybe, after next week was over, she'd even feel better about doing the commercials. She wasn't good with children, but she didn't dislike them. It was just the time of year. She was overreacting.

"All I'm asking is that you give them a chance." Bryan rubbed his hand over his eyes and down his face, the second time he'd done it in the five minutes he'd been there.

"You look tired," she said, concerned.

"I am. My partner is in the middle of the first vacation he's had in ten years, and it's been hell at the office. I'd never realized just how much he does there."

"Maybe we shouldn't have gone to Stone Mountain the other day, huh?" She still wasn't sure why they'd gone. If he'd been after a romantic interlude as she'd thought when he took her up there, wouldn't he at least have tried to kiss her?

He stood up. "It was worth it," he said, his gaze penetrating. "I wanted to see you. Besides, I worked late last night at home."

"Do you work at home a lot?" She came around her desk to walk with him to the door, wishing he didn't have to leave so soon.

"More now than I used to." He tucked his sketchbook under his arm and pulled his sunglasses out of his shirt pocket.

"You have an office there?" She didn't even know where he lived.

He stopped at the door. "I'm working on it. I just bought the place last summer and I'm furnishing it a little bit at a time."

"It's the first home you've owned?" Jennifer didn't know why she wasn't just letting him go. She had more work to do than time to do it. And apparently he did, too.

"Yeah. Ownership always sounded like chains to me."

"So what made you change your mind?"

"It was time."

A master at issuing vague answers, Jennifer knew she'd just received one. She wondered why.

"By the way, I like the dress." His eyes moved slowly over her, lingering on her breasts, the dip at her waist, before continuing downward.

"Thank you. I guess I was kind of in a rut with the suit thing."

He looked at her lips and then opened the door. "Read the scripts, Jennifer," he said, and nodded at Rachel on his way out.

SHE WAS WORKING at home herself that evening, dressed in a short black shift that she only wore around the house, when her buzzer sounded, signaling a visitor for her downstairs. She pushed the button on her intercom. She hoped it was Bryan.

It wasn't. It was Tanya.

"I want to know why you've been avoiding me," her friend said the minute she was in the penthouse. She slid out of her sandals and plopped down on one of Jennifer's white overstuffed couches.

"I haven't been avoiding you," Jennifer said, sitting on the opposite couch.

"You know about the baby, don't you?" Tanya asked.

Jennifer couldn't escape Tanya's piercing stare. She nodded.

"Who told you?"

"Dennis's secretary, indirectly. I heard her talking about your doctor's appointment."

It was Tanya's turn to look away. "I didn't mean for you to find out that way, Jen. I wanted to tell you myself."

"Then why didn't you?"

"I just wasn't sure you'd want to hear about it— especially with next week looming so close and all."

Jennifer didn't want to think about next week. "It's

been twelve years, Tanya. I think I can handle it,'' Jennifer said dryly.

"I don't, not when you use that tone of voice. Which is just what I was afraid of.'' Tanya was as blunt as ever.

Jennifer's chest tightened, making it harder for her to breathe. "What? I said I could handle it. It's not a big deal.''

Tanya's eyes softened, but Jennifer saw the hurt in them. "Yes, it *is* a big deal. To me and Dennis, anyway. And you're not happy about it.''

"Of course I'm—'' Jennifer broke off, unable to continue lying to her friend. "It's just the time of year, Tan, like you said. You know me. I get a little weepy, the day goes by, and then I'm fine again. I'll be happy for you long before the baby comes.'' At least that was what she'd been telling herself.

"That's what Dennis and I figured at first. It's why we decided to wait until after next week to tell you about it. But I'm not so sure anymore.''

"What do you think I'm going to do—fall apart at the seams?''

"No! Of course not. You're stronger than that. What you're going to do is keep avoiding me until we drift apart, and eventually we'll only see each other at the annual Christmas party.''

"Isn't that a bit melodramatic?'' Jennifer smiled at her friend.

"I don't think so, Jen, and neither does Dennis.''

"You guys are my best friends. We see each other all the time,'' Jennifer said, doing everything in her power to believe that everything was going to be just fine.

"You see Dennis at work every day, but how long has it been since you came out to the house or even met me for lunch?"

Jennifer couldn't remember the last time.

"Next to Dennis, you're the best friend I've ever had, Jen. I'm not going to lose you because I want to be a mother."

"You're not going to lose me."

"Then why have you been avoiding me?"

Jennifer looked away. "I've just been busy at work overseeing the introduction of One Price. I'm spending a lot of extra time at the dealerships."

"So's Dennis, and I still see him."

"He lives with you."

"He also meets me for lunch."

"All right! I'll meet you for lunch. Pick a day."

"And have you cancel on me? Uh-uh."

"What is it with you, Tanya? You want me to have lunch with you, so I've said I'll have lunch with you."

"I want you to admit you're bothered by this baby."

Jennifer felt as if she was suffocating. "Why would I be bothered?"

"I was with you on her first birthday, Jen, remember?"

No! Jennifer's mind went blank. She felt numb. It was understood that that chapter in her life was over.

"I remember that day like it was yesterday. We

were both at Florida State, checking out the campus before applying.''

Pain seared through Jennifer as she remembered, too. All of it. Every painful, lonely, empty second. No. She'd come through that. It was over.

''And I got drunk and cried in my soup. I never have been able to hold my liquor worth a damn.'' She forced the words past the constriction in her throat.

''You cried because your heart was breaking.''

Jennifer jumped up. Why had she ever thought Tanya was her friend? Friends didn't do this to people. ''Okay, I was dying inside. Is that what you want to hear?''

''No.''

''What, then? What do you want from me, Tanya?'' She was nearly yelling. *Deep breaths. Calm down. It's over.*

''I want you to let go of the guilt, for starters.''

''Leave it, Tanya.''

''I can't, Jen. I'm going to lose you if I do. And you're going to lose, too.''

Jennifer sat back down, her head in her hands. ''I can't do this again.''

''You haven't done it yet. That's my point. All these years, I've thought you handled everything so well, but instead, what you've been doing is beating yourself up every year on her birthday until you're crazy with pain, and then you run from it the rest of year.''

Jennifer couldn't breathe. ''You've deduced all this because I'm not happy you're pregnant?'' Jennifer couldn't believe how awful those last five words sounded.

"No!" Tanya rubbed the slight mound of her belly as if apologizing to her baby for Jennifer's horrible words. "But when you started avoiding me, it got me thinking about a lot of things. Made me see them in a different way."

"What things?"

"Look at how you are around children, Jen. Or, rather, how you're *not* around them. You avoid them like the plague. At last year's Christmas party you even arranged it so they'd be in a different room altogether."

"I hired a Santa, Tanya! He had gifts for every one of those children. Can you imagine what a ruckus there'd have been if they'd been in the same ballroom as several hundred adults?" She went over to the wet bar and poured Tanya a glass of the sparkling water she always kept on hand for her.

"It might have been fun. There's nothing like seeing that glow in children's eyes when they're opening presents from Santa. Besides, that doesn't explain your refusal to speak to all those eighth graders at that young businessmen's convention last fall, or your insistence that we shop during school hours. And what about that time they wanted you to appear at the children's home to raise money for the new roof? You bought the damn roof yourself so you wouldn't have to go."

"I'm just not good with children, Tanya," she said, handing Tanya the glass.

"Baloney."

"I'm not. They make me nervous. I don't know, maybe I get it from my parents, but I always feel uncomfortable when I'm around kids."

"Maybe it's because you can't look at them without remembering, without all the old guilt coming back, and that makes you feel unworthy all over again. I don't think it's the children who make you uncomfortable, Jen. I think it's the relapse into low self-esteem that does that."

"Since when did you get your degree in psychology?" Jennifer asked, going back to pour herself a glass of wine. Her hands were shaking and some of the wine spilled over the rim of her glass.

"I love you, Jen. I think that counts more than a degree."

Jennifer couldn't continue to fight Tanya. She knew her friend well. Tanya had a stubborn streak the size of Georgia when she believed she was right. And Jennifer had a feeling Tanya *was* right this time. She took her wine over to the couch, needing to sit. Her legs were shaky, too.

"What do you want from me, Tanya?" she asked softly, meeting her friend's concerned gaze.

"I want you to forgive yourself for giving away your baby. I want you to let yourself grieve for your loss."

"Oh, I grieve, Tanya. More than I realized."

Tanya shook her head. "You don't grieve, honey. You just hurt. Grieving means letting go."

Jennifer couldn't hold back the tears any longer.

They welled in her eyes and rolled slowly down her face. "I wish it were that easy, Tan. But maybe it isn't possible to have a baby and then just let go." Jennifer felt alien saying the words. She hadn't talked about her daughter since the baby's first birthday when she'd poured out her soul to Tanya. But maybe Tanya was right. Maybe she hadn't recovered from that time in her life as she'd thought she had. She *should* be feeling happy for her friends' upcoming parenthood. So maybe, as Tanya said, it was time to take a close look at herself, come to terms with her past.

And suddenly, as the walls she'd built so many years before came tumbling down, Jennifer was swamped with emotions, with thoughts, she hadn't dared let herself acknowledge. And every one of them hurt.

"I never said it was easy, Jen." Tanya's voice brought Jennifer back up from the abyss. She'd forgotten, for a moment, that her friend was even there in the room. "But I'm afraid you're never going to get on with your life if you don't let her go."

Jennifer saw the love in Tanya's eyes, and it gave her the strength to continue into territory she'd thought never to visit again. "It doesn't seem right that I turn my back on my firstborn and then go blissfully on with my life."

Tanya grabbed a tissue from an end table and sat down beside Jennifer. "You didn't turn your back on her, honey. You gave her a shot at a much better life than you could have provided for her."

Jennifer sniffed, her tears still streaming down her face.

"Oh, Jen," Tanya said, holding Jennifer the way she had that day so many years ago.

Jennifer cried until she didn't have any tears left, leaning on Tanya, needing her friend's strength. Tanya continued to hold her, murmuring soothing words. At last Jennifer sat back on the couch, her mind clouded by the anguish she'd kept bottled up inside.

"You know, there're places you can go now, places you can register yourself as her mother in case she's looking for you." Tanya's soft words broke the silence. "There are even ways you can find out where and how she is."

"I've thought of that," Jennifer said, her voice still thick with tears. "During those first years, I drove myself crazy thinking about finding her. Do you have any idea how many times I've stopped in a crowd because I saw a child who looked her age and had my color hair?"

"Then why haven't you registered? What could it hurt?"

"I promised I wouldn't." But until that moment, Jennifer hadn't even realized she still put any stock in that childish promise. She had at first, of course, during those early difficult years. But she was an adult now. She hadn't thought of those hospital-bed promises in years.

Tanya frowned. "Promised who?"

"I don't know. God maybe. Or myself. I promised

I wouldn't look for her, and I wouldn't ever let anything or anyone ever take her place in my heart, if only she could have a happy life.'' She'd promised something else, too. She'd promised never to make love again. But surely she wasn't still holding herself to that vow, was she? The reason she hadn't been with another man was simply that she hadn't had the time to develop a close enough relationship.

''When, Jen? When did you promise that?''

''The night before they took my baby away. A nurse brought her in to me.'' If she closed her eyes, Jennifer could still feel the softness of her daughter's skin, still smell that new-baby smell. ''I held her.'' Her words were barely a whisper, but they conveyed twelve years' worth of anguish.

''Oh, Jen,'' Tanya said, her eyes filling with tears. ''I'm so sorry. But surely you haven't been holding yourself to a promise made under those conditions. You were only a child!''

''I know. And it's not like I've even thought about that old vow for years, but I thought about it a lot those first few years, and I guess upholding it just became habit.''

She drew a shaky breath. ''Besides, in my heart, I know I don't have the right to hunt her down. If she does have a happy life, if her family is everything I chose not to be, it would be cruel for me to breeze in now and stake my claim to her. She may not even know she's adopted. And what if she hates me for what I did? Or worse yet, what if I'm like my mother? What if I'm just not good with kids? With her?''

Tanya wiped away her tears. "You need to quit worrying about that right now, Jen. You're too good with people not to be good with kids. After all, they're just miniature adults with a huge dose of innocence thrown in. All you need to relate to kids is some compassion, and you're one of the most compassionate people I know."

Jennifer smiled through her tears. "What about that time Ralph Goodwin brought his kid to the Teal corporate offices and then got tied up with the accountant for over an hour? Rachel went home sick and I got stuck with the child. He must've told me ten times he hates me. He even stuck his tongue out at me."

Tanya laughed. "He was a brat, Jen. He stuck his tongue out at everybody."

"Okay," Jennifer conceded, serious again. "But how about that time here in the building when the electricity went out and I was in the elevator with that little girl who lived downstairs? She huddled in the corner the whole time and acted like I was the big bad wolf, ready to eat her at any second. That had to be the longest two hours of my life."

"She was scared. She wanted her mother. It wasn't anything you did."

"I wish I could believe that."

"You'll see. You'll have your chance. Just as soon as junior's born."

Jennifer didn't think so. She'd always been afraid of being like her parents, unable to relate to children, but she'd been pretty sure of it that night in the elevator. She'd been unable to reach that little girl, unable to offer any comfort. And there hadn't been a single instance since then that had proved her wrong.

But Tanya was right about one thing: it was time to stop running. She'd had no idea she'd let herself get so out of whack over the years, and wondered if that vow she'd made as a child had had other far-reaching effects. Maybe it, and not lack of time, had stood in the way of her ever developing a lasting relationship with a man. She didn't know, but it was a possibility she was going to have to face, and she would, just as soon as her One Price policy was up and flying. And until then, no matter how painful she might find the next several months, she was going to be there every step of the way for her friends, just as they'd always been there for her.

Tanya broke gently into the silence that had fallen. "Even if you don't search for your daughter," she said, "you can still register yourself as her birth mother."

The prospect was exhilarating and frightening at once. What if her daughter needed her? But what if she failed her daughter? "Maybe."

"Just maybe?"

Jennifer thought of Bryan. Of the commercials he wanted her to do. "I don't know. You may not think I'm a failure around kids, but I'm not so sure. I never know what to say to them."

But if the lines are written for me, if they're rehearsed, if I know in advance what the children are going to say...

"At least think about it, Jen. Don't be so ready to condemn yourself."

"Maybe…"

The two sat silently for a couple of minutes, absorbing the peace of the penthouse. And then Tanya got up to retrieve her glass and sit back down on the other couch.

"Now that that's out of the way, tell me about this gorgeous hunk you've been seeing," she said, typical Tanya-style.

"I'm not seeing him. We're just friends. And you can tell your husband that his big mouth is going to get him into serious trouble if he doesn't watch it," Jennifer replied, feeling more like herself again.

Tanya grinned. "Oh, my! I didn't realize this Bryan guy was such a big deal. There may be hope for you yet."

Jennifer threw a pillow at her friend, hitting her square in the face.

"Now look what you've done," Tanya said, laughing as she jumped up with the glass she'd been holding. "You've spilled water all over your pretty white couch."

Jennifer stood up, too. "Either come help me answer some charity letters or go home, Tanya. I have work to do."

"But what about the couch?" Tanya asked.

"It'll dry."

Tanya answered more than thirty letters, including checks from Jennifer in each, before she finally went home. She didn't mention Bryan or the baby again.

JENNIFER WAS BUSY all weekend, working both at home and at the office, visiting a couple of her dealerships as she usually did on weekends and holidays so her people knew that while she expected them to work the off-hours, she wasn't asking anything of them she didn't do herself. She attended a Hawks game on Saturday night with her finance managers and their spouses, and an art exhibit with Tanya on Sunday. And afterward, she had dinner with Dennis and Tanya at their home in Snellville, just west of Atlanta.

She saw the nursery her friends were setting up, picked up a tiny white T-shirt and cried all the way home. But at least she was no longer running.

She didn't hear from Bryan all weekend.

But he called her first thing Monday morning, before she'd even had a chance to pour herself a cup of coffee. "Did you read them?" His voice was wonderfully familiar and exciting at the same time.

"Don't you ever say hello?"

"Hello, did you read the scripts?"

"Yes."

"And?"

"They're good."

"And?"

He sure didn't make anything easy. "I want your word that I have the final say on anything that's aired, and that you'll destroy any tapes I don't approve of."

"So, you're going to do them." The approval she heard in his voice almost made the rough weekend she'd spent fighting with herself over her decision worthwhile.

"On a couple of conditions."

"Which are?"

"You'll be there for the filming of each and every one of them."

"Of course."

"And if I say stop, we stop."

"You're the boss. How soon can you clear a couple of days to get it done?"

She looked at her calendar. Friday—The Day—was blank. She was hoping to spend it with Bryan—but not working. It was going to be hard enough just to get through those hours.

"Is next Monday soon enough?"

"Monday's good. Calvin'll be back by then to hold down the fort here, and it'll be easier for me to spend a few days away from this place. It'll also give me time to find the kids. I'll let you know the details later in the week."

"So I won't see you before then?" she asked. She couldn't come right out and ask him for a date on Friday. Just like she hadn't been able to look up his home phone number and call him over the weekend, no matter how badly she'd wanted to. She might be a nineties woman, she might live in a man's world, but she'd been labeled "easy" once. It wasn't going to happen again.

"Would you like to?"

"Yes."

"Then I'll see what I can do to juggle things here."

Jennifer pulled out the tickets she had. They weren't for Friday, but she'd told him she'd let him know if she heard of a concert more in his style. She wasn't asking for a date, merely doing a favor for a friend.

"Boston's playing at Fulton County Stadium on Wednesday night. Somebody gave me a couple of tickets." Someone had. The girl she'd bought them from at the ticket outlet where she'd stood in line on Saturday.

"Boston. Quite a band. Now that brings back some memories."

"I don't know about blankets in the grass, but it'll be outdoors and blue jeans."

"Just my style. Okay, lady, you've got yourself a date. What time's the concert?"

"Eight."

"Then how about if I come for you at five and we can stop someplace for dinner on the way?"

"I'd like that," Jennifer said, feeling better than she had in weeks, years maybe.

Just two more days until she saw him again.

CHAPTER SEVEN

BRYAN WANTED TO KICK himself for agreeing to go to the concert. He could have gotten out of it easily. He could have simply told her he was busy all week with Calvin out of town. She'd have understood. And he would have told her that if she hadn't agreed to do the commercials, if she hadn't given him another spurt of hope.

But he still should have turned her down. Because the concert was a date. Pure and simple. He had a date with the most beautiful woman he'd known in a long time, a woman he'd been fantasizing about since he'd spoken to her in that art gallery all those weeks ago, the first woman he'd seen more than three times without getting bored. Nicki's mother. A woman who was off-limits.

A woman who might very well hate him when she found out he'd been seeing her as a means to his own ends. One thing he'd learned over the past weeks with her was that she didn't trust lightly. But she trusted *him*. She was opening up to him in ways she apparently hadn't done with a man in a long time. And he was breaching that trust at the same time he was encouraging her to open up more.

But what choice did he have? Nicki had had another nightmare over the weekend. He'd figured the recurrence was probably due to her upcoming birthday, but that didn't make it any less painful—for either of them. He wasn't sure how much more his niece could take. He wasn't sure how fair he was being to her by having the information she wanted more than anything else and not giving it to her.

And yet, could he risk the chance that Jennifer might reject her? Could he risk Nicki's falling apart on him completely? Bryan didn't have any answers, but he knew one thing: he was living on borrowed time.

THANK GOD it wasn't blankets on the grass. Bryan didn't think he'd have been able to keep his hands off her if they were lying down. As it was, he was having as hard a time keeping his mind on the show as he had at the symphony. And Boston was one of his all-time favorite rock bands.

But Jennifer was wearing one of those short shirts Nicki had wanted, minus the daisy. The tanned strip of bare waistline only inches away from him was sheer torment. Her hair was up as usual, but a few tendrils had escaped and brushed his arm every time she turned her head.

The chords from the beginning of "More Than a Feeling" blared out across the stadium, and Bryan felt the familiar rush of adrenaline he always got when he heard the song. He sat forward to watch the lead guitarist, his hand dropping to the arm of his seat.

But it didn't land on the arm of the chair. It landed on Jennifer's hand. And before Bryan's lust-fogged brain could demand that he remove his hand immediately, Jennifer's fingers curled around his.

He looked over at her silently, unable to hear or be heard above the deafening roar of the band. He wasn't sure what he had to say, anyway. She smiled at him, her eyes promising him things he couldn't have. He smiled back, wondering what it was about her that made her so different from all of the other women he'd dated.

It had been far too long since he'd had a woman. Too long since he'd felt the soft gliding of a woman's fingers on his body, pleasuring him, getting tangled in the hair on his chest, digging into his back. Too long since he'd kissed the delicate flesh of a woman's body, since he'd heard her cry out in passion and delight.

And it was going to be even longer. His first and only concern right now was Nicki. And if it turned out that Jennifer didn't want Nicki, then he would never have Jennifer.

But he held Jennifer's hand throughout the remainder of the concert, and he took it again as they walked to his Jeep afterward. "I, uh, don't have all the times set for next week yet. I'll have Jacci give you a call with them on Friday," he said, as if talking business with her somehow made the fact that he was touching her less dangerous.

"I won't be in on Friday."

Bryan helped her over a knee-high wall as they took a shortcut between parking lots.

"You're taking the day off?"

He'd wondered how she was going to spend Nicki's birthday, if she even remembered what day it was.

"We're having the carpets cleaned in the executive offices. It's an annual thing."

The carpet cleaned. Nothing more profound than that. He released her to unlock the passenger door of the Jeep. "As it happens, I have the day off, as well. I have some personal business to attend to."

"Oh. Will it take all day?"

"Uh-huh. I'm driving up to Shallowbrook."

"Isn't that where you said you grew up?"

"Yeah. It's a great little town." Or at least it was. Before a tornado swept in and destroyed everything in its path.

He told himself not to be disappointed that she hadn't remembered Nicki's birthday. He didn't expect her to have spent the past twelve years thinking about the daughter she'd given away. And she had no way of knowing how difficult this particular day was going to be for Nicki. And for him.

She didn't know because he chose not to tell her. And he was no closer to doing so. He hated the indecision. He preferred to act and deal with the consequences. But this wasn't about him. It was about Nicki. And so far, all he knew was that Nicki's mother didn't want children, and apparently never thought about the one she'd had. But how would

Nicki react if he told her he couldn't find her mother? Would she break down completely?

"Would you like to come in for some coffee?" Jennifer asked half an hour later as she unlocked the door of the penthouse.

The vulnerable look in her eyes was almost his undoing. She hadn't offered lightly. But he knew what would happen if he stepped inside that door.

"I'd love to, but I'll need to take a rain check. I have work to do with Calvin being gone."

She looked disappointed. "You're going to work tonight?"

"For a while." It might help him sleep.

"And you thought *I* didn't take enough time to smell the roses."

Bryan reached out, brushing aside the hair framing her face. He wished he'd met her in another lifetime. "I'll take time to smell them. Just as soon as Calvin returns," he promised.

It was a promise he wasn't going to keep. And he wasn't going to kiss her good-night, either. He saw the confusion in her eyes as he stepped back into the elevator. He was hurting her, but there didn't seem to be any way not to.

BRYAN WAS UP early on Friday, creeping around his kitchen furtively, trying not to make a sound as he prepared Nicki's favorite breakfast—pancakes with blueberry syrup, and grits. He piled it all on a tray he'd decorated with linen and a china plate he'd bought specifically for the occasion and topped it off with a single yellow rose. He was going to make her feel special today if it was the last thing he did.

"Up and at 'em, kid," he said cheerily as he pushed into her room.

"But it's the first day of summer vacation," came the sleepy voice from the bed.

"It's more than that, and you know it. Now open your eyes and see what I've brought you."

She turned over reluctantly and sat up, her eyes still only half-open.

Holding the orange juice steady, he set the tray down across her legs. She looked at it and then at him.

"Oh, Uncle Bryan," she said, her eyes filling with tears.

"Happy birthday, Nick."

She looked back down at the tray. "My very own breakfast in bed. Just like a grown-up."

"Just like a princess," Bryan corrected, handing her a tissue from her nightstand. "Now eat up before it gets cold. The chef'll get mighty cranky if his food goes to waste."

She ate every bite.

THEY'D BEEN BACK to Shallowbrook several times since the tornado. Nicki had insisted on it during those first months when visiting the cemetery was the only thing that seemed to give her any comfort. But it had been a couple of months since their last visit, and Bryan headed north toward his hometown reluctantly. A lot of plans had gone into the day. But he still wasn't sure he was doing the right thing taking Nicki back, especially on the anniversary of the tragedy that had changed their lives.

He left the sides and top on the Jeep for the trip, and Nicki stared silently out her window as he drove. "We couldn't have asked for a nicer day," he said after they'd been on the interstate for several minutes. The sun was shining. No clouds in the sky. No storms on the way. Thank God.

Nicki nodded warily.

"We could run across the border to Tennessee before we go if you'd like, pick up some fireworks for the Fourth of July."

"Okay," Nicki said with the same lack of enthusiasm.

"Would you rather we stay in Atlanta, Nick? We can go back to town and find something fun to do there, or we could take the plane up."

"Nah, that's okay."

They passed a billboard advertising the Gold Rush museum in Dahlonega with promises of gold-panning opportunities, reminding Bryan of the first time he'd taken Nicki off on his own. Lori and Tom had been driving down to Atlanta to stay with Bryan after Christmas one year when Nicki was about four, but instead of driving straight through, as Bryan was doing, they were going to take a detour and stop at an outlet mall on the way. Rather than travel with her parents to the mall, Nicki had begged to ride to Atlanta with him in the Jeep. He'd told her it was fine with him, certain that Lori, who never let her daughter out of her sight for more than five minutes, would refuse. He'd had the shock of his life when she'd agreed. Apparently shopping with a four-year-old wasn't exactly a picnic.

So he'd buckled Nicki in and started out for home, but Lori and Tom, in spite of their detour, had arrived there long before he did. That was because Nicki, asking questions about everything she saw, had insisted when they'd passed a colorful sign advertising the Gold Rush museum that they stop and put gold in pans, too. She'd conned him into three more stops along the way—for fudge, a hamburger and, the last, a traveling carnival she saw when he'd pulled off for her to use the rest room—before he finally got her home.

Lori had been furious, waiting in the parking lot of his condo when he pulled in sometime after dark. Crying with relief and hollering at him at the same time, she'd taken one look at Nicki sleeping soundly in the seat beside him and hit him in the chest with both fists over and over. He'd never seen his sister so angry.

What he'd give now to have her angry at him again. To have her there at all. Or even to have back that talkative little elf who'd gotten him into so much trouble. He looked over at Nicki now, trapped in her silent world of grief, and wanted to pound his fists into something, too.

"Calvin's due home this weekend, so what d'ya say we give him a week or two to get settled in and then we take a trip to the beach?"

"Okay. If you want to."

"Don't you want to go, Nick? We could do some snorkeling."

She shrugged. "It doesn't matter."

He saw a sign for her favorite burger joint. "You want to stop for lunch?"

"Okay."

Damn. I could tell her now, if I wanted to.

He bought her a hamburger, french fries and a chocolate shake, and refused to leave the restaurant until she'd finished all of it. But he gave up on conversation when they got back in the Jeep. He was too concerned about what lay ahead of them, or rather, Nicki's reaction to it, to force a cheerfulness he was far from feeling.

They'd been back in the Jeep for about half an hour when Nicki broke the silence. "Uncle Bryan? I have something to ask you...and I don't want you to get mad at me."

They were the most words she'd strung together in days. "Ask away. I never get mad at you."

"It's about my other mother. I just wondered if you'd heard anything yet."

He glanced over, expecting to see her staring out the window. She wasn't. She was looking straight at him, trying to hide the hope in her young eyes.

"I..." He couldn't do it. He couldn't just crush that hope. "We're making progress, Nick. They have her name."

"They do? What is it?" Her eyes were almost

bright, her voice sounding more like a little girl's than it had since he could remember.

What is it. He wasn't ready. "I don't know yet, honey, not until I get the report. And don't get too excited. They haven't found *her* yet—they just have her name. She could be anywhere in the country, or even out of it, and there are probably several women with the same name."

"Yeah, but if they could get this far, they just *have* to find her. I can't believe they really know her name. I wonder what it is…" She looked out at the road as if the answer was written there. "Maybe Ariel or…or Cameron. That would be neat, don't you think? Cameron sounds like a cool name."

I feel like scum, he thought. "It's probably something ordinary, honey, like Debbie or Sue." *Or Jennifer.*

"Maybe. I can't wait to find out. I wonder how soon they'll find her?"

"It's hard to say, sprite. Just don't get your hopes up too high."

"I know. I won't. And about that trip to the beach?"

"Yeah?"

"I guess it'd be good."

Just the mention that her birth mother had a name, and suddenly she *wanted* to go to the beach. She actually *wanted* to do something. It was going to be damn near impossible to tell her her mother couldn't be found. But what would happen if he told Nicki who she was and Jennifer walked away from her? Again.

They stopped for some flowers at the local florist, now set up in a brand-new shop on Main Street rather than the historical building Bryan remembered from his youth, and went out to pay their tributes to Lori and Tom and Bryan's parents.

Bryan cried inside for the young girl who knelt so carefully on her parents' grave, telling them she loved them as she left her flowers there for them, explaining to Lori through her tears that she'd brought her carnations because they smelled the best and lasted the longest. He stood back, allowing her time with them, thinking that if it were up to him, they'd never visit the graves at all. What he needed from his family he had in his heart. But he knew Nicki wasn't old enough to understand that yet.

She didn't say much else, just pulled some grass from around their stone, and then stood and turned away. Bryan put his arm around her and walked her back to the Jeep.

"I wish birthdays had never been invented," she said, trying not to cry again.

Bryan pulled her into his arms and held her, a few tears of his own escaping from his tightly clenched eyes, while she sobbed out her anguish. He held her until her breathing evened and he knew she'd spent all the hurt inside of her. For now.

"Let's go," he said.

Nicki gave him one last squeeze. "I love you, Uncle Bryan."

"I love you, too, Nick. Always."

"Do you think Mom'll be mad at me for finding my other mother?" she asked as she climbed back into the Jeep.

"No. Your mother was prepared for the time you might have questions. She knew she was your real mother, and that was all that mattered to her." Bryan had stretched the truth a little bit. It wouldn't do Nicki any good to know that though Lori had been prepared for the questions and would have encouraged the search, she'd also worried about losing Nicki to her biological mother someday. He thought that was probably a normal reaction, though.

Instead of heading to the interstate, Bryan turned the Jeep back toward town.

"Where're we going?" Nicki looked nervous.

"There's someone here who wants to see you, Nick," he said, hoping she was up for it. She hadn't wanted to see any of her old friends since she'd left Shallowbrook, but they had a surprise waiting for her. One he hoped she'd like.

"Who?"

"Just wait and see."

He turned a couple of corners and pulled onto a street that hadn't been touched by the tornado.

"Sally's house?" Nicki asked as he pulled into her best friend's drive. She didn't seem happy to be there.

Bryan turned off the ignition. "C'mon. Let's go in."

Ten girls were waiting on the covered porch, all dressed in shorts and tops like Nicki's, several of them sporting the daisies Nicki wore, and all talking at once. They stopped when they saw Nicki, probably not sure what to make of the changes in their once lively and talkative friend, and then Sally ran forward and threw her arms around Nicki's waist.

"Nicki! I can't believe you're finally here!"

Nicki stood awkwardly in Sally's embrace, looking over her shoulder at the group of friends waiting behind Sally.

Come on, Nick. You'll be okay. Bryan didn't know why he'd ever thought this might help.

The other girls rushed forward then, surrounding Nicki, and Bryan lost sight of his niece as they tried to make her feel welcome. They were all talking at once, telling Nicki about the party they'd planned for her, wishing her happy birthday. He didn't hear Nicki utter a word.

His gaze sought Betty Sanderson, Sally's divorced mother, over the girls' heads. Her eyes were full of sympathy.

"Come on, girls," Betty said cheerfully. "Let's go inside and show Nicki what we've got for her."

He waited until they'd all pushed their way through the door before walking up the steps himself. "It'll be all right," Betty said as she held the door open for him.

He'd grown up with Betty. He'd even dated her a time or two. She'd filled out a little since then, and her dark hair had a couple of strands of early gray, but she still looked great. She'd always been smart, and perceptive beyond her years, too, even back in high school, and he'd learned to trust her judgment. This time he was counting on her being right.

Nicki was sitting on the couch, the girls beside her and on the floor in front of her, their talking making up for Nicki's near-silence. They didn't seem to notice she was answering their questions with only one or two words, sometimes just a shrug.

"How are you doing?" Betty asked Bryan quietly, standing just inside the room with him.

"We're getting along."

"She's still not opening up much, is she?"

"I'm beginning to wonder if she ever will. Maybe the tornado did something to her we'll never be able to fix."

"I doubt that, Bryan. She's young yet. Give her time. Maybe our little surprise today will help."

"Or make her miss what she lost even more."

"I don't think so."

Bryan watched his niece parry questions, hating the lost look in her eyes. She used to be the noisiest one in the bunch. But she wasn't a part of their chatter anymore. Not only had she moved away physically, she'd moved away emotionally, leaving her childlike trust and innocence behind.

"Have you made any progress on your search for her birth mother?"

"I found her."

"Nicki's met her? What happened? Didn't it go well?"

"Nicki doesn't know I've found her. She thinks we're still looking."

Betty frowned. "Don't you think you ought to tell her? The last time you called you made it sound like it was all that mattered to her."

"Which is exactly why I'm waiting. Look at her, Betty. I'm not sure she can handle it if her mother doesn't want to acknowledge her."

Betty looked over to where Nicki sat, quiet and solemn, with her friends.

"She doesn't want her?"

"I don't know yet, because I haven't told her about Nicki, either, but it doesn't look good. She's uncomfortable around kids. Says she doesn't ever want to be a mother."

"Oh, no," Betty said sadly.

"Well, she's not as bad as she sounds. That's why I haven't given up on the whole thing yet. The woman's really something. She's the most honest, fair, compassionate person I've ever met. She's tough when she needs to be, she's a first-rate mechanic, though not by trade, she's got a great sense of humor and very loyal friends." Bryan stopped.

"It sounds like you've gotten to know her rather well."

"I took a job creating a new campaign for the company she owns."

Betty's eyebrows raised. "You work for her and she doesn't know about Nicki?"

"Not yet. But I don't think I'm going to be able to keep them a secret from each other much longer."

"How do you think the woman'll take the news?"

"She'll probably never speak to me again."

Betty yanked on the end of his ponytail. "Turn on some of that charm of yours, Chambers. She'll come around."

Bryan grinned at his friend, glad he'd kept in touch with Betty over the past year. "So," he said, ready to be done with what he and Betty had planned, one way or the other, "let's get this show on the road."

Betty walked back out to the hall and opened the door to the dining room. "Nicki! Look who's here," she said, releasing a furry dynamo of brown and gold and white from captivity.

A Shetland collie—a miniature Lassie—came barreling into the room, leaping and barking.

"Lucy? Lucy's here? She's alive?" Nicki jumped off the couch, stumbling over the girls in her path as she ran to meet the Sheltie. She dropped to the floor, clutching the dog to her with all her might, laughing and crying as Lucy covered her face with kisses.

"Look, Uncle Bryan! Oh, look! Lucy's alive!"

Bryan's throat was thick as he hunkered down beside his niece. He scratched the excited dog behind her ears, a little surprised by just how glad *he* was to see Lucy again. He and Nicki had conspired to get the dog for Tom and Lori for Christmas three years before.

"A farmer found her about five miles out of town," Betty said. "She was dehydrated, but not hurt. He put notices up, but everybody was too busy taking care of things after the tornado to pay much attention. Then last week, Sally and I were driving by the farmer's house, and Sally saw her. We stopped and called her name, and sure enough it was Lucy.''

Nicki's gaze was glued to the dog, her fingers stroking her pet as she listened. Suddenly she froze, squeezing the little dog so tightly Lucy squirmed to escape. "We can keep her, can't we, Uncle Bryan? We're gonna take her home with us, right?'' she asked, her young face filled with fear.

"Of course, Nick. Happy birthday, honey.''

"Oh, Uncle Bryan, thank you. Thank you. Thank you. Thank you.'' She got up and threw her arms around Bryan's neck, tears streaming down her cheeks. But for once, Bryan knew, they were happy tears.

His eyes met Betty's over Nicki's shoulder. She was crying, too, but she was also smiling. She gave Bryan a thumbs-up.

"Okay, who wants cake?'' she asked a couple of minutes later. The girls were crowded around Nicki again.

"We do!'' Ten girls screamed their approval. One sat oblivious, hugging her dog in the middle of the floor.

NICKI SLEPT most of the way home with Lucy nestled in her lap. The dog was obviously as happy to be reunited with Nicki as Nicki was to have her. Bryan breathed a huge sigh of relief. He'd been afraid seeing Lucy would make Nicki lonelier for her parents. He'd even gone so far as to think she might refuse to have anything to do with the dog. He'd never given any thought to his own reaction. He'd certainly never expected to find that he'd have any affection for the animal.

Fancy that. Bryan Chambers, bachelor extraordinaire, comforted by a family dog.

CHAPTER EIGHT

JENNIFER HAD SPENT The Day as she always had—trying to forget. She hadn't heard from Bryan all weekend and she'd missed him. A lot. Now it was Monday, and she stood in the service drive at Teal Pontiac waiting for him, nervous and worried about the upcoming filming and trying not to show it. And he was late.

"You've done it again, Jennifer. One Price Selling has only been in place for a couple of weeks, and already there's a noticeable increase in sales volume," Ralph Goodwin said from beside her. She hadn't even realized the general manager had joined her.

"It's still too early to really judge, but thanks for the vote of confidence." She'd noticed the increase herself; she'd been monitoring sales reports daily since the first commercial had hit the air two weeks before. But she was too cautious to get her hopes up yet. Advertising in general usually brought in increased business at first.

Ralph rested his elbow on his other arm, his hand under his chin. "The place is buzzing with positive feedback. The general consensus seems to be that customers are fully embracing the idea of being able to buy a car without the pressure of haggling for it.''

Where's Bryan? The film crew's already in the showroom. ''How about your sales staff? They giving you any trouble?''

''A little. Not a lot. We've had an occasion or two when a customer wouldn't buy a car unless he could dicker, not believing, of course, that we wouldn't dicker when push came to shove. When we wouldn't, the customer walked. There's a little grumbling each time it happens.''

''But the numbers the guys'll gain in the long run when people understand we mean what we say will be well worth the loss of a sale or two.''

''I know. It's just a hard concept for salespeople to swallow—letting a deal walk out the door. But none of them are quitting yet. I'd even go so far as to say that the majority are happier. We've taken away a lot of the negative pressure of the job by giving them a good product and reliable service to sell, rather than price.''

Jennifer nodded. It still sounded right to her. It could work. It *had* to work.

She saw a familiar vehicle pull onto the lot. Bryan. Finally.

She walked over to meet him as he hopped down from the Jeep.

His gaze sought hers immediately. ''How're you doing?'' It wasn't an idle question.

Okay, now that you're here. ''Better than I expected.'' He looked great. He was wearing lightweight cotton pants today, instead of jeans, and a polo shirt. The short sides of his hair were windblown, but the back was in its usual ponytail.

He studied her. "I thought you might dress a little more casually today, since we're going for kid appeal," he said, walking with her toward the showroom.

"I just felt more comfortable this way. Besides, suits are my image. I've worn them for every commercial I've ever done. I was afraid the whole thing would look fake if I wore something different now."

Bryan conceded the point. "I like your hair," he said.

It was up in its usual twist, but she'd added a couple of gold-and-black clips that matched the buttons on her suit. "Thanks."

He looked over at her again, his sexy brown eyes warm, approving. "I'd like to see it down even more."

Jennifer felt his regard all the way down to her toes, although she'd been telling herself all weekend to forget him. She'd decided he obviously wasn't interested in her—not as a woman. In all the times they'd been together, he'd only kissed her once. That time in her office. And it wasn't like he hadn't had the opportunity.

But when he looked at her like that...

"Hey, boss, we're ready to start whenever you give us the go-ahead," Jake Landers said as she and Bryan walked into the showroom. Bryan stopped to have a few words with him.

Jennifer continued on into the showroom, her gaze immediately seeking out the little boy standing with his mother by the electric red Pontiac Firebird Trans Am Coupe. About four feet tall, blond and dressed in shorts and a Hawks T-shirt, he looked harmless enough. So why did her stomach suddenly feel as if she was going off to war?

"Ready, Jen?" Bryan said, crossing to her. Nobody but Tanya and Dennis had ever called her Jen. She liked the sound of it coming from Bryan.

"Ready," she said, smiling at him. As ready as she'd ever be, at least.

"Okay, you remember Bob McKinney and Jake Landers, don't you?" he asked, leading her over to the two men.

She smiled and reached out to shake their hands. "Of course. How are you, gentlemen?" She'd liked them the last time they'd worked together. She'd liked the films they'd turned out, too.

"Just fine, ma'am," Jake said for both of them. "If we can have you right over here, we'll get this show on the road."

With one last look at Bryan, Jennifer put herself in the hands of his crew.

The morning wasn't too bad. Jennifer found that if she kept her own counsel, watching the proceedings from the side except when she said her lines, making this commercial was no different than any of the other ones she'd done. The little boy, in spite of his youth, was a professional. She wasn't expected to entertain him, or even watch out for him. He had his mother there to do that. And she didn't have to make him like her—Bryan's lines took care of that.

She'd been convincing her staff of over six hundred employees about the merits of One Price Selling for weeks. And she believed in it herself. So the part she was playing, explaining One Price to the boy's mother, felt almost natural to her. Answering his questions, in slightly less formal terms, was simply a matter of reciting the lines Bryan had written. By the end of the morning, when Jake and Bob were finally satisfied they had enough on tape, she was feeling pretty relaxed. The next few days might not be so bad, after all.

"It was nice meeting you, Ms. Teal," the boy said as he and his mother were leaving. It was the first time he'd spoken to her apart from the scripted lines.

"It was nice meeting you, too, Taylor. You're pretty good at what you do, you know." Jennifer was glad to have a chance to tell him. She'd been impressed, and she always made it a point to offer praise for a job well-done.

The little boy smiled and blushed. "Thanks. You're not so bad, either. And I love your cars."

If he were old enough to drive, she would probably have given him one. Jennifer continued with her goodbyes, all the while hearing Taylor's words ringing in her ears. *You're not so bad, either.* She could have hugged him right there on the showroom floor.

Tuesday, at Teal Hyundai, was even easier than Monday. There were two kids, a boy and a girl posing as brother and sister, and all Jennifer had to do was walk up while their parents were busy working out the financing, smile at them, offer them a Teal Automotive coloring book and walk away. A voice-over introduced One Price Selling, pointing out that the bank's financing paperwork was the only time-consuming part of buying a car at any of the Teal Automotive dealerships.

They ran through the take half a dozen times, and each time, Jennifer smiled at the children, and each time, they smiled back. She knew they'd been told to, that their smiles were written into the script, but they made her feel good, anyway.

They were about halfway through the shoot when the little girl came over and stood in front of Jennifer. "I love your earrings," she said. "My diary has hearts on it and so does my jewelry box."

Jennifer's fingers went automatically to the heart-shaped gold studs in her ears. She'd forgotten she'd put them on. "Thank you," she said, smiling at the child.

"Ready to roll," Jake called, putting an end to the impromptu conversation before Jennifer could worry about finding something to say about diaries or toy jewelry boxes. It was back to the safety of rehearsed lines and staged smiles.

But the little girl smiled at Jennifer when she came over to tell her goodbye, and that wasn't rehearsed at all.

"What were you so worried about?" Bryan asked her as they walked out to their cars afterward. He was smiling at her, too, and her heart beat faster.

She shrugged. "I'm not sure at the moment, but let's get through tomorrow before we celebrate."

"Tomorrow's going to be the easiest of all. You put a baby in a built-in car seat and you're done."

Jennifer knew that. It was the thought of picking up the baby to begin with that was keeping her up at night. Tanya's pregnancy had shown her how much she'd been fooling herself all these years. And she hadn't held a baby since...

She didn't want to think about that now. "Are you and Calvin still going over things?" she asked. He'd had to rush away the day before to meet with his partner.

"Yeah, but we got a lot done. He came to the house last night, too. One more afternoon and we should just about have it wrapped up. I'm looking forward to a little time off, I can tell you. It's been two weeks since I've been up in the air."

They reached her car. She unlocked the door, but didn't immediately climb inside. "Speaking of time off, how'd last Friday go?" she asked. She couldn't help but wonder about the personal business that had taken him back to his hometown. It had dawned on her that while he demanded she open up to him, there were parts of his life about which she knew nothing. She didn't even know where he lived.

His expression grew solemn. "Better than I expected."

"You were expecting a bad time?" she asked. She hadn't thought of that when she'd tormented herself with visions of what he might have been doing. Like seeing an old flame—or a current one.

He looked at her, as if searching for something, and then seemed to come to a decision. "Do you remember the tornado that ran through northern Georgia this time last year?"

"Of course." That part of the state had been declared a national disaster area. She'd donated heavily to the cleanup cause herself. And then it hit her.

"Shallowbrook was right in its path. It was one of the towns worst hit, wasn't it?"

He swallowed, looking out over the top of her car, and nodded. She felt a sickening sense of dread even before he spoke.

"I lost most of my family in the blink of an eye." He sounded as if he still couldn't quite believe it.

Jennifer reached out to him, uncaring for once of who she was, of where they were. She cupped his jaw with her palm. "I'm so sorry, Bryan." There was nothing else she could say.

"I was driving up when the storm hit. There was a family party at my parents' house. Everyone was there—my sister and her husband, cousins, aunts and uncles. I was two hours late and so…" He didn't have to explain any further. She could only imagine the hell he was revisiting.

"I'm so sorry," she said again, her eyes filling with tears.

He looked down at her, taking her shoulders in his hands as if touching her somehow grounded him in the present, away from visions of the past. "Thanks," he said, looking at his hands on her shoulders, then letting go of her all of a sudden, as if he'd only just realized his hands were there.

"So it wasn't as bad going back as you'd thought it would be?" she asked.

"I've been back many times, and it's always hard. But a friend of mine had found something she thought I'd want. I wasn't so sure until I got there, but she was right."

Curious, Jennifer asked, "What was it?"

"My sister's dog. The damn thing had been wandering around for several days after the tornado, and this farmer found her and took her in." He went on to tell her how Betty and her daughter happened on the Sheltie, took the animal home and called him right away.

"Did the dog remember you?"

"Oh, yeah, she remembered all right. She's been underfoot ever since."

Jennifer smiled. "So you brought her back with you?" she asked, liking the picture of this big, strong, free-spirited man driving home with a dog in his lap.

"Yeah. She's at home. She's part of the reason Calvin and I didn't finish last night. We took her out back for a game of ball that lasted longer than it should have."

"I'm glad you have her," Jennifer said. It made her feel better for him to know that he had at least a small piece of the family he'd lost.

"Me, too." He was smiling again.

Jennifer was perfectly content to bask in that smile.

BRYAN STOPPED HOME after he left Teal Hyundai. Nicki had still been asleep when he'd left that morning, and he didn't like not having shared breakfast with her before he went off to work.

She was still sleeping when he got home shortly before lunchtime, but she'd moved from her bed to the living-room couch, probably because she'd had to get up to let Lucy out back. Bryan frowned as he looked down at his sleeping niece. She'd been asleep yesterday afternoon when he'd called from the office, too.

Lucy was jumping up on his leg, and he reached down with one hand to grab the dog into his arms. "What are we going to do with her, Lucy my girl?" he asked, scratching the dog behind the ears. He was rewarded by a lick on his chin. He laughed.

Nicki sat up suddenly, disoriented. She pushed the hair out of her face. "Uncle Bryan?" she said when she saw him. "Why are you home? Is it dinnertime already?"

"No. It's not quite lunchtime," he said. He was worried about her, sure that sleeping through summer vacation was not healthy.

She rubbed her eyes. "Then how come you're here?" she asked, yawning. And then she stopped midyawn to stare at him.

"Did you find her? Is that it?" She studied his face. "Is it bad?" she whispered, looking frightened again.

He hated that look.

"I didn't find her yet, Nick. I just stopped in to take you to lunch," he improvised. He'd give her a reason to stay awake if he had to, give her hundreds of them. She wasn't going to break down on him. He dropped the dog to the floor.

"You didn't have to," she said, scooping Lucy up and burying her face in the thick fur.

"I know, Nick." Lord, he was tired of not reaching her. She'd looked so excited when she'd thought he had news. But her answers might not lie in finding her birth mother. He had to help her find the will to live within herself.

She looked at him as if waiting for something.

"Go on. Get some clothes on. We're going to the Burger Barn. And bring a swimsuit." To hell with Calvin and Innovative Advertising. He was taking Nicki to Splashtown. Even she couldn't sleep through an afternoon at the water park.

He called his partner and arranged to meet him later that evening. Calvin's family had stayed at the beach for an extra week, so Calvin didn't mind working another evening. Bryan didn't mind, either. The busier he stayed, the less time he had to think.

BRYAN DROVE to Teal Ford bright and early Wednesday morning. He'd finished filling Calvin in on the projects at hand and had cleared his schedule for the day. As soon as they wrapped up the filming, he was going to have a talk with Jennifer. He couldn't go on this way any longer. He wanted the woman so badly he went to bed aching at night, and his dreams were filled with fantasies so wild even he couldn't believe his subconscious had conjured them up.

She wanted him, too. He'd read it in her eyes. He'd known it the night of the Boston concert. If he'd gone into her apartment then, they would have made love.

But more than the wanting, she cared about him. He knew that when he'd told her about the tornado. The damnable thing was, he was beginning to suspect he cared about her, too. More than he'd ever cared for a woman before. More than just physically.

But she was Nicki's mother. And if she didn't want Nicki, then they had no future. Even if she did, they probably had no future, Bryan admitted as he pulled into the lot of Jennifer's largest dealership. Because as soon as she found out who he was, why he'd really met her, she'd never trust him again. And he wouldn't blame her. He'd knowingly abused her trust.

Of course, her wanting Nicki was a big "if." She wasn't comfortable around children, and the possible damage to Jennifer's reputation alone might be reason enough to keep her away. Especially now that she'd embarked on her One Price campaign.

Bob and Jake were just setting up when Bryan arrived, and Jennifer was talking with a couple of salespeople on the showroom floor. Bryan hoped the crew would be ready to start soon. He wanted to get this over with. He pulled his cellular phone out of his back pocket, unfolded it and dialed Nicki.

"Hello?" Her voice was groggy with sleep.

"It's me, Nick. Listen, I need you to do me a couple of favors this morning."

He listed the chores he'd invented on his way to work that morning. They should be enough to keep her up and moving around for most of the day. He and Nicki were going to beat this thing if it killed him.

The morning's filming promised to progress as smoothly as it had the previous two days. Thank God. His patience level was impossibly thin. The baby's mother was a pleasant woman, and she was delighted to meet Jennifer. Jennifer looked a little tired, but she smiled at the other woman and welcomed her to Teal Ford.

Jake ran through the take with both women, indicating just when the mother should hand her baby to Jennifer without getting into the picture herself. Jennifer hadn't looked at the baby once, as far as Bryan could tell, and she seemed a little tenser than she had the previous two days. Nevertheless she nodded at Jake and took her position by the Windstar they'd picked for the take.

Everything went as planned until Jennifer reached for the baby. Bryan wasn't sure what went wrong, but suddenly the baby was screaming and Jennifer was making a beeline for the baby's mother, getting rid of the angry little bundle as fast as she could.

"Cut!" Jake's voice rang out over the baby's wails.

Bryan walked over, noticing all the curious hangers-on. He motioned to Frank Dorian. Jennifer had introduced him earlier as the general manager of Teal Ford.

"Clear these people out, would you, Frank?" Bryan asked.

"Consider it done," Frank said, motioning to a man on the other side of the room.

"What happened?" Bryan asked when he finally made it over to the small group clustered around the squalling baby.

Jennifer stood back from the group, her hands clutched in front of her. Her face looked pinched. She didn't say a word.

"He's just scared. He'll be fine in a second," the mother assured everyone, rocking the baby against her shoulder. "He's usually pretty good about going to people, but every once in a while he gets a mommy attack."

True to her word, the baby calmed almost immediately. They waited another couple of minutes for the tears to dry on his lashes, and then Jake called everyone to their positions. Jennifer came forward, but she didn't look at all sure about what she was doing. Catching her eye, Bryan smiled at her encouragingly. He stayed closer this time, wanting to be certain they got it right. It didn't look like Jennifer was going to hold up for many more takes.

"Roll 'em," Jake called, and Bob held up the cue cards. Jennifer ran through her lines perfectly, the poised confident businesswoman, and then Jake swerved in for a close-up of the built-in baby seat through the open side door of the Windstar, giving Jennifer a chance to take the baby from his mother.

Bryan saw her reach for the child. She held him gently in her arms, about an inch from her body. But before she could get him the two feet to the van, the baby started to scream again.

Jennifer returned the baby to his mother immediately. "That's it, guys," she said to everyone present. "This one isn't going to happen. Sorry for wasting everybody's time."

Without another word to anyone, she turned and left the showroom.

Bryan made it outside just as she was pulling off the lot.

Yanking his keys from his pocket, he jumped into the Jeep and took off after her. He'd never seen her so upset, and he couldn't let her leave like that. Not as a professional, and not as a man who cared about her, either.

She was heading toward her office building, he guessed, and he pulled onto Peachtree right behind her. He couldn't figure out what had gone so wrong back there. In spite of all his weeks of getting to know Jennifer, it seemed as if he didn't know her at all. He would never have believed she'd run out like that. She was a fighter, not a quitter.

About two miles from the Teal corporate offices, she finally noticed him behind her. Catching his eye in her rearview mirror, she shook her head. He nodded. She drove for about another quarter of a mile before she suddenly cut across two lanes of traffic and swerved into a deserted parking lot. Horns honked behind him as Bryan followed, pulling his Jeep up beside her Mustang.

He jumped down and opened her car door.

"I can't do it," she said, looking straight ahead through her windshield. Her hand still rested on the ignition, as if she was prepared to take off at any second.

"I'm not going to ask you to go back there," he said. He'd already dismissed his crew. "I just want to talk."

She glanced up, the look in her eyes shocking him. It reminded him of Nicki, of the emptiness he saw sometimes when he looked at his niece. He wouldn't be surprised if she was going to refuse to discuss what had happened that morning.

"So talk," she finally said.

He leaned on the door frame of her car. "What happened back there?"

"I told you I'm no good with children. Did you think I was just making that up? I've been through this before. Oh, not commercials, but anytime I'm alone with a child, he or she either ends up huddling in a corner, crying or wrecking the place."

"You've been working with kids all week, Jen, and you did fine. They liked you."

"They were professional actors."

"They were kids! They were well behaved, yes. And they'd been taught how to memorize lines, but if little Taylor hadn't liked you, you can bet we wouldn't have had such an easy time of it on Monday. I've worked with him before. I know."

"You wrote every word I said, Bryan."

Damn, Bryan thought. What was it with the females in his life?

"That little girl yesterday worshiped the ground you walked on."

"She liked my earrings."

Patience, he reminded himself. Jennifer was one of the most confident people he knew. Yet it was as if he'd never met the woman sitting in her car. This woman reminded him a lot of Nicki—a mass of insecurities. But at least he knew what had caused Nicki's problems.

"Jennifer, that baby today was only three months old. He was hardly old enough to hold up his head by himself, let alone take an instant dislike to someone. He just didn't want to be separated from his mother."

"He didn't cry the couple of times Jake took him, when he was demonstrating the take."

He'd forgotten that. "Jake probably reminded him of his father."

"He didn't like me, Bryan. I'm not good with children. I don't understand them, and I don't know how to act around them. They make me nervous, and children can sense things like that."

"Okay, let's say for a minute you're right, but that still doesn't explain this." He reached out and took her hand off the steering wheel.

"What?" She wouldn't look at him.

"You've been gripping that wheel so tightly your knuckles are white." He held up her hand. "And you're shaking, too."

Bryan hunkered down beside her, keeping her hand in his. "Come on, Jen. What gives?"

"I don't like to be put in situations where I'm not sure of myself." Her words were almost a whisper. It sounded like tears weren't far away.

Suddenly he was no longer the professional, and he wasn't Nicki's uncle, either. He was simply a man trying to comfort a woman he cared about.

"No one does, but that doesn't explain why you're so upset. I thought we'd become friends over the past few weeks. Can't you tell me what's wrong?"

"I just...I just haven't held a baby since..." Her voice was filled with tears and she broke off, trying to compose herself.

Bryan pulled her from the car and over to his Jeep. Opening the passenger door and leaning back against the side of the seat, he settled her between his legs and held her against him.

"Since when, honey? You haven't held a baby since when?"

"Since I..." She looked up at him, her eyes full of shadows. "Since I...gave my own away."

CHAPTER NINE

EVEN KNOWING what he did, Bryan was shocked at
Jennifer's revelation. He wasn't sure what he should
say. She hadn't held a baby in twelve years? As pun-
ishment? Or because she really didn't like babies?

Finding no answers or even words to comfort her,
Bryan simply held her, rubbing her back, smoothing
her hair away from her face, just as he'd done for
Nicki so many times in the past year. So much pain.

He knew now that she hadn't forgotten Nicki.
There was no doubt that she hurt for her lost baby.
That didn't mean she'd accept Nicki, but it was time
to find out. He was beginning to hope as he held her,
as he wanted to continue holding her, comforting her,
that maybe this bizarre situation could somehow work
out happily for all three of them. Maybe.

If she ever forgave him for the deceit he'd been
practicing since the evening they'd met.

She pulled away from him, wiping tears from her
eyes. "Sorry, I didn't mean to go all blubbery on you.
I don't make a habit of it, I promise."

She was embarrassed. Bryan lifted her chin until
her eyes met his. "Don't. Don't apologize or get all
distant on me. You've had a rough morning—you

needed a friend. After the past year I can certainly understand that. I'm just glad you chose me."

She reached up and cupped his cheek. "Dear Bryan. I don't know where you've been all my life, but I'm certainly glad I finally found you."

Looking down into her beautiful face, Bryan knew he was lost. She was everything he'd ever wanted in a woman and more. He leaned over the couple of inches it took to close the distance between them and touched his lips to hers. He kissed her the way he'd wanted to kiss her for weeks, totally, intimately, the way a man kisses a woman he desires beyond all else.

She melted against him, her lips pliant and eager. She'd obviously been wanting the kiss as badly as he had.

Bryan couldn't keep his hands still. He ran them over her, down her back, up over her waist, brushing the sides of her breasts, before tilting her head to allow him better access to her mouth. He deepened the kiss.

She moaned, pressing her hips against his; he might have forgotten himself completely if a horn hadn't honked on the street behind him.

He lifted his head slowly, holding Jennifer's gently between his hands, looking into her eyes for confirmation of what he already knew. That she wanted to make love to him as much as he wanted to make love to her.

But there were things they had to settle first. And once they were done settling them, there might never be an afterward.

She leaned her head against his chest. "It's scary to think I might have lived my whole life and never felt like this," she said.

"Surely you've felt it before." *Some*one had fathered Nicki.

She stepped back. "You'd think so, wouldn't you?"

"I'd like you tell me about it, Jen."

"And I will—someday. But not today. Please don't ask me to go through it all again right now. I think I've had about as much as I can take."

"But—"

"I know I'm being unfair, Bryan. I can't lay this on you and expect you not to wonder, but I need a little time. I've never told another living soul about that part of my life, with the exception of two very special friends who helped me through it. I've only realized in the past week how much of it is still unresolved for me, and I'm just not ready to talk about it yet."

"Can you just answer one question?"

"I'll try."

"Do you think you did the right thing giving your baby away?"

"I was young, Bryan. I did what I thought was best, and, yes, I still think I did the right thing—especially after today. I'm just not good with kids. When God handed out mother's instinct, I guess he skipped me. My mother was the same way—my father, too, for that matter—and believe me, if I'm like them, my baby's better off with someone who wanted her badly enough to go through the adoption process to get her.''

If she'd been anyone else Bryan would simply have accepted that here was a woman who wasn't meant to be a mother. But she wasn't anyone else. She was Nicki's mother. And he couldn't help wondering if Jennifer wasn't good with kids because she did indeed take after her own parents, or just because she'd convinced herself she did.

Whether Jennifer *wanted* Nicki or not was no longer even the problem. If she was convinced she didn't have a knack for mothering, she probably wouldn't even try. Hell, knowing Jennifer, judging by what she'd just said about her child being better off without her, she'd probably convince herself that she'd be doing Nicki a favor by staying away from her.

He had to find out if she was right. He had to know if Nicki was better off without her, if knowing her would do Nicki more harm than good, before he even considered introducing them as mother and daughter. And the only way he could find out if they were good together was for them to meet.

''I have a confession to make.''

She frowned, looking confused. ''What?''

He had no idea how to break it to her gently. ''I don't live alone.''

She froze. ''You have a roommate, you mean?''

He'd never thought of Nicki as a roommate, but he said, ''Sort of.'' After Jennifer had spent the morning telling him how uncomfortable she was around children, how did he just blurt out that he had one?

"Male or female?"

"Female."

She backed up another step, her face draining of color.

And then it hit him how the conversation must sound to her. "She's *twelve,* Jennifer. And she's mine."

"You have a daughter?" She didn't look much less horrified.

"Technically she's my niece, but I'm raising her now. She was my sister's daughter. She's all the family I have left."

Jennifer gave an audible gasp and her eyes shimmered with emotion. "Oh, Bryan...the sister killed in the tornado. Of course. Oh, God, I'm so sorry. For both of you."

"She's mine now, Jennifer. Legally, but emotionally, too. I love that kid so much it hurts. And it hurts a lot, because she's having a really tough time of it. She lost even more than I did that day, because she lost her childhood. I'll always have great memories of mine."

Jennifer gazed at him in silence for a moment. Then she said, "You're one special man, Bryan Chambers."

"I do what I have to do," he said, shrugging off her praise.

"Still, I'd say she's very lucky to have you."

Bryan hoped so. At the moment he wasn't sure he

was doing anything right. "The reason I told you about her is because I wanted you to meet her. I have a feeling she's going to like you as much as I do. You could come and have dinner with us tonight."

She stepped back. "Uh, thanks, but I don't think so," she said, looking toward her car.

Bryan turned her back to face him. "Jennifer. Nicki and I are a package deal. I care about you more than I can ever remember caring about a woman, but Nicki and I are a team. You see me, you see her, too."

"Why didn't you ever mention this to me before?"

Good question. One Bryan wasn't ready to answer. And if she couldn't handle *his* having a child, how would she react if she knew that child was hers, as well? He needed to convince her she was good around kids first, good around Nicki, and then he'd think about telling her the rest. Otherwise he was going to lose before he'd even begun. And Nicki would lose, too. And all because Jennifer thought she'd been born without the ability to mother a child.

He couldn't believe she was right. He remembered her hand cupping his face when he'd needed comfort, the hero worship in the little girl's face as she'd followed Jennifer around the dealership the day before.

Jennifer was still watching him, waiting for an answer to her question. He might not be able to answer her honestly as Nicki's uncle, but he could as a man who wanted a relationship with this woman. "By the time I knew that I wanted to bring you home, that you were more than just a casual attraction for me, you'd already told me you weren't comfortable with children.''

''Wasn't that even more reason to tell me?''

''Probably. I just didn't want to lose you before I had a chance to convince you it might be worth your while to hang around.''

Jennifer wanted to hang around. More than she'd ever wanted anything in her life—other than her baby a long time ago. But *twelve*... The same age now as the baby she'd given away. She just wasn't strong enough to handle that. Not yet. Not when she was just discovering for herself how much of the past she had still to face.

''I'm sorry, Bryan. It just isn't a good idea,'' she said.

His stricken expression was the last thing she saw in her rearview mirror as she drove away.

It HAUNTED HER in the two days that followed, as well. She worked incredibly long hours, even for her, waiting for the moment Bryan would call to say he had the tapes ready for her to view, even while she dreaded speaking with him if it was only going to be about something so superficial. She'd never made love with the man, never shared any real physical intimacies with him, and yet she had the feeling he knew her as well as she knew herself.

Part of her couldn't believe the cruelty of fate that would allow her a taste of all life could be, all that her life had been without, only to make it all unobtainable. But the other part of her, the weak part, knew that it was only what she deserved. What right did she have to love, to be loved, to live happily ever after, when she'd withheld her love from her own child?

He finally called Friday afternoon.

"The tapes are still in the lab. They should be ready sometime early next week," he said as soon as she picked up the phone.

Jennifer smiled. It was just so damn good to hear from him. "Hello yourself." She wrapped the phone cord around her finger.

"How you doing?" His voice was softer, more personal as he asked the question.

"I've been better. I miss you."

"Enough to have dinner with me tonight?"

Her heart began to slam against her ribs. "Just you?"

A heavy silence hung over the line, as if he was only just then deciding the answer himself. She held her breath, hoping with all she was worth that his answer was yes.

"Me and Nicki," he finally said.

She thought about all the what-ifs and what-might-have-beens she'd been torturing herself with for the past couple of days. And she hadn't even met his niece. She was afraid to find out how much worse it would get if she did what he wanted.

"I can't, Bryan."

"You don't know what you're missing, Jen. Nicki's a great kid."

She closed her eyes. That was exactly what she was

afraid of. Meeting Nicki was going to make her need to have what she could never have all that much worse. And more, she was terrified that if she met Nicki, it was only going to prove, once and for all, that she was a failure with kids. Bryan wouldn't be able to make any excuses for her if his own kid didn't like her. And she wouldn't be able to make any, either.

"It's not Nicki that's the problem, Bryan. It's me. I'm sorry. I can't have dinner with you tonight."

He said, "You can't run forever, Jen. Think about it." And he hung up.

As awful as Jennifer felt, she also knew a huge sense of relief when she dropped the receiver back into the cradle. He'd invited her to dinner again. He'd had time to think about the bombshell she'd dropped in his lap on Wednesday, time to calculate the years, time to figure out what she'd been doing when most fifteen-year-olds were still having their parents drive them to the movies. And he'd still invited her to dinner.

It was then that Jennifer admitted she'd been worrying herself sick that he wouldn't. She'd been afraid, after blurting out her secret, she'd lost Bryan's respect.

Jennifer packed up her briefcase, cleared off her desk for the weekend and told Rachel she was leaving for the day. She might not be ready to face Bryan's niece, but there was something she *could* do.

She called Tanya from her car phone.

"I have the afternoon free," she told her friend as

soon as she answered. "I thought maybe we could do a little bit of shopping for that package you're carrying."

"Where are you?"

"In my car approaching Lenox."

"Phipp's Plaza is on Lenox. I'll meet you there in fifteen minutes."

Tanya hung up and Jennifer had no chance to change her mind. Not that she was going to. She wasn't about to lose the only real friends she'd ever had. Which meant she was going to have to come to terms with the new person in their lives. She could do it, too. She was a survivor. She wasn't going to live out the rest of her life running away from a past she couldn't change. But she couldn't afford to fall apart at the seams, either. Not with the One Price campaign resting in the balance. She'd just have to take things one step at a time.

Tanya pulled into the mall parking lot with two minutes to spare. She jumped out of her car with a determined grin on her face and said to Jennifer, "I'm not letting you off easy now that you dragged me over here."

Tanya needn't have worried. Jennifer wasn't about to back down. "Lead the way," she said, trying to ignore the knot in her stomach.

They walked into the department store, and Tanya headed right to infants' wear with an ease that told Jennifer she'd already been there many times.

"I've got a full layette of T-shirts, newborn through twelve months, but I haven't started on sleepers and socks yet,'' she told Jennifer as they walked past a display of cribs.

''You're *buying* clothes already?'' Jennifer asked. She'd expected they'd just look for now.

''I have to have something to do. Dennis won't let me paint until after the baby's born. He's afraid the turpentine fumes might harm it.''

Jennifer's hands were shaking as she tried to look around the department without seeing it. ''Did you ask your doctor about it?'' she asked.

''Nope. It wouldn't matter whether she said I could or not. If Dennis is worried the fumes'll hurt the baby, I won't mess with them. But if he tries to tell me I have to sit home all day and watch soap operas and knit booties, I'll have to give him a severe piece of my mind.''

Jennifer smiled as she pictured Tanya doing just that.

Tanya stopped at a rack filled with tiny garments on hangers. ''We need to start with newborns and work our way up,'' she said, pulling a sleeper off the rack. ''I want fourteen of these in each size.''

Jennifer was sweating as if she'd just jogged, not driven, to the mall. ''Fourteen?''

''I've heard that babies go through a ton of clothes, sometimes three or four outfits in a day, and I'm not gonna lose what little sleeping time I'll have to do laundry,'' Tanya said.

It made sense to Jennifer. She looked at the plastic tags along the top of the rack, searching for one that said newborn. She found it, moved toward it and grabbed a hanger off the rack. "How about this one?" she asked.

"It's cute, but we can't do pink, or blue, either, since we don't know if it's a boy or a girl."

Jennifer looked at the sleeper. She hadn't been aware she'd picked a pink one. But once she looked at it, she couldn't look away. It was so incredibly small she could hardly believe a body could be small enough to fit in it. The feet were barely two inches long. And it was such a pretty pink, soft with a white lace ruffle across the bottom. It reminded Jennifer of one she'd picked once. She used to go to stores and choose outfits she'd like to buy for her baby, back in the beginning when she'd thought she'd be strong enough to stand up to her parents and keep the child growing inside of her.

"You okay?" Tanya's voice pulled her back.

Jennifer blinked the tears from her eyes. "Yeah."

"You wanna go? I didn't mean it when I said I was going to hold you to this, you know."

Jennifer nodded, putting the garment back on the rack. "Yeah, I know. But it's okay. We can stay. And why don't you know if we're shopping for a boy or a girl? You're almost four months along." Ultrasounds were usually done as a matter of course, and when she'd been pregnant, she'd been told the sex of her baby by her fourth month.

"We don't want to know," Tanya said. "Neither one of us gives a rip what it is so long as it's healthy, and we decided to do it the old-fashioned way. Wait until it's born.'' She put a couple of little garments over her arm.

Jennifer picked up a purple sleeper. It was terry cloth, and she liked the hearts embroidered on the chest. Love was what a baby needed most.

''Here,'' she said, handing it to Tanya. Tanya took one look at Jennifer's face and added it to the bunch.

They found four sleepers in all, a couple of pairs of newborn shoes and a comforter that doubled as an activity table before Tanya announced that they'd exhausted that department. Jennifer insisted on paying for all of the purchases. It was something she wished she'd been able to do twelve years before.

''Where to next?'' she asked Tanya as the two made their way back out into the mall.

''You sure you're up for more?'' Tanya settled her bag against her hip. It was almost as big as she was.

Jennifer wasn't sure. But she wasn't giving up. ''Lead the way,'' she said, ''and give me that.'' She took Tanya's package, stopped to buy a handled shopping bag to put it in and then carried it herself.

They went through the next store, a baby boutique this time, with a fine-tooth comb, adding several more sleepers and a sterling rattle set to their pile of purchases. At last Tanya suggested they stop for burgers and malts in the food court. And the entire time they stood in line, she critiqued the children walking through the mall, or rather, critiqued their parents, telling Jennifer what she was going to do the same or, in many cases, differently with her baby.

''How do you know all this stuff?'' Jennifer asked

her as they sat down at a table for two in the old-
fashioned burger joint.

Tanya shrugged, swallowing a bite of her big juicy
hamburger with everything on it. "Common sense."

"Aren't you the least bit worried you might not be
a good mother?"

"Hell no!" Tanya said loudly enough to draw several pairs of eyes their way. "All it takes to be a good
parent is plenty of love," she said, lowering her
voice. "And that I've got in excess. I can't believe
how much I love this kid already, and I haven't even
felt it move yet."

Jennifer smiled sadly, remembering. "I know."
But she didn't agree with Tanya's assessment of parenthood at all. Her parents had loved her, yet in a lot
of ways they'd been awful parents.

"Have you thought any more about registering
someplace?" Tanya asked softly, looking at Jennifer
over her malt.

Jennifer remembered a tiny hand brushing her
cheek. "Constantly," she told Tanya, pushing her unfinished burger aside. "I want to, but I keep wondering if it's the right thing to do. Say I find her, say she
wants to meet me and her parents are even agreeable
to it, and, hell, while we're at it, let's pretend she
likes me, will I be able to handle seeing her knowing
she's not mine? Will I try to take over, not even
meaning to, or will my mere presence interfere in her
relationship with her mother? At the very least, it
would be complicated. And sometimes I think it

would be best for all of us if I just left well enough alone and got on with my life.''

"Can you?" Tanya asked, blunt as always.

Jennifer thought of Bryan, of his niece—Nicki, he'd called her. "I thought so," she said. But even if she wasn't getting on with her life, was searching for her daughter the answer?

"What if she needs you, Jen? What if something's happened and she really needs you? You have so much you could give her now. And even if she doesn't need you, even if she's perfectly happy, wouldn't you like to know that? Honestly?''

Jennifer felt a panic attack coming on just thinking about it. "Of course. But she doesn't need *me*, Tan. If I'm at all like my mother was, the last thing my daughter would need is me.''

"You're nothing like your mother, Jennifer Teal. That woman had ice for a heart. Your only problem is that you're too perfect for your own good, my dear,'' she said.

"What are you talking about?" Jennifer scoffed. Perfect was one thing she'd never been. Not even as a baby, according to her mother and the tales of colic and diaper rash she'd heard about while she was growing up.

"You are, Jen. You always have been. You're so damned good you have to invent things to worry about. Dennis says it's because you always tried so hard to please your parents, and the worst part was they never even noticed.''

"That's not true. They noticed me a lot, and always

when I seemed to be screwing something up. Dennis is right about one thing, though. I did try. And it paid off in the end. I finally did something right when I took over the business and they were able to retire in luxury."

"And did they thank you for it?" Tanya asked somewhat bitterly.

Jennifer loved her friend for her loyalty, even if it was misplaced. "They would have if they hadn't died before they had the chance."

"The car accident was six months after they left!"

"But they were in the Orient most of that time."

"I remember," Tanya said.

Jennifer wondered if Tanya also remembered that she'd been unable to cry at their funeral. It was something she'd never understood.

"So what's up with your hunk?" Tanya asked later as they strolled through the mall. They had too many packages to carry already and had decided to leave any further shopping for another day.

Jennifer thought of the relief she'd felt when she hung up from Bryan that morning. "Well, he doesn't think I'm easy."

Tanya hooted. "I don't see how he could. You're the biggest prude I've ever met."

"I am not," Jennifer said, laughing as she hit Tanya with one of the sacks she was carrying. "I remember skinny-dipping in a very cold lake with about ten other people for club initiation."

"We were all *girls*, Jennifer. That doesn't count."

"I'm not a prude, Tan," Jennifer said, suddenly

serious. "I just learn from my mistakes. Unfortunately I learned too late that you're often judged by them. No matter what I did those last two years in high school, I was treated like a...a cheap slut."

"That was all a long time ago, Jen. You were a kid. You made a mistake. No man worth his salt is going to hold that against you today. Besides, Bryan doesn't know about it, anyway, does he?"

Tanya stopped suddenly and stared at her friend. "*Does* he?"

Jennifer couldn't miss the astonished, but hopeful look on Tanya's face. "I told him about the baby."

"Well, hallelujah!"

CHAPTER TEN

SHE WAS HOLDING her baby, smelling the baby-sweet smell, gazing into her daughter's bright blue eyes, and everything was as it should be, as it always would be.... And suddenly the nurse was there, taking her baby away, and there was nothing Jennifer could do about it. Her arms wouldn't work, her hands were numb, and no matter how she cried out, the nurse didn't seem to hear her. Her parents were there, too, and the doctor, but no one saw her. They were all looking at her baby. And then, ignoring her protests, they all walked out of the room together, taking her baby with them....

Jennifer woke up feeling sick to her stomach, her tears mingling with the cold sweat on her face and neck. She lay shaking in her bed, trying to tell herself that it was only a dream, that she had to be up in just a few hours, that she should go back to sleep. But she didn't want to go back to sleep. She didn't want to dream anymore.

Getting up, she wiped her tears away, but to no avail. They kept right on falling. As if she had no will of her own, she was drawn to her wallet, to the tattered picture waiting there to torment her. She pulled it out, looked again at the image she knew better than her own face and remembered. Remembered things she hadn't thought about in years...

She'd lost her virginity on her fifteenth birthday. She'd been hoping for a quiet celebration, just she and her parents and a good meal someplace where they sang "Happy Birthday" to you and brought you a little cake with a candle in the middle. She'd had a quiet party, all right—a TV dinner at home, alone. Her parents had forgotten what day it was.

But Billy Wilson hadn't forgotten. A couple of years older than Jennifer, he'd taken her out a time or two, and while his experience had made her uncomfortable, she'd basked in his attention. No one had ever made her feel special before. Billy brought flowers for her birthday, red roses, and told her he loved her. He asked her to drive out to the lake with him, to let him make the day really special. Anxious to get out of the empty house, Jennifer grabbed a sweater and followed him to his car.

His kisses excited her at first. And though she knew it was wrong, she even liked the feel of his hands on her breasts. But when his fingers slid beneath her skirt, she wanted him to stop. He told her that she wasn't being fair to him, that she couldn't lead him on and then just expect him to stop. He said that he loved her, that he wanted to show her how much, that he wanted to marry her as soon as she turned seventeen. That if she loved him, she'd let him do what he wanted.

Jennifer wasn't even sure what love was, yet she

knew she wanted to be loved more than anything else on earth. Feeling awkward and scared, she lay down in the back seat of his car and let him climb on top of her. It hurt. A lot. But he held her afterward, so gentle with her she almost cried. And she was glad she'd let him love her that much.

She wasn't nearly so glad a couple of weeks later when she caught him out with a girl from the cheerleading squad at school. Or when, that same day, she heard some girls talking about her in the locker room. They knew what she'd done with Billy.

She wanted to die then. She went to her favorite place, the last mechanic's bay at Teal Motors, and worked on an old Pontiac her parents had given her. They'd taken it in on a trade, and even the wholesalers hadn't wanted it. She could keep it if she could get it running. She cried a bucket of tears as she worked, hating Billy Wilson, but mostly hating herself for being such a fool.

Her only comfort in the days that followed came when she'd gotten her period. Billy hadn't made her pregnant...

Jennifer looked again at the picture in her hand, wondering just when she would have atoned for the sins of her youth. If there would ever be a time. She didn't know, but one thing was for sure. Until she did, she couldn't see Bryan and his niece. She just couldn't handle it....

"DAMN!"

Nicki huddled back into the couch as she heard

Uncle Bryan in his office swearing again. He'd been working all morning, even though it was Sunday, and things didn't seem to be going too good.

He'd been a grouch all weekend, though he'd stayed nice to her—so far. She was probably what was causing his bad mood. She was bugging him, and there was nothing he could do about it.

"Nick!"

She jumped up and rushed to the door of his office. "Yeah?"

"Would you make us some lunch, honey? I think there's enough bread in there for peanut-butter-and-jelly sandwiches. That'd be easy."

"Sure, Uncle Bryan," she said, and hurried away before she did something to make him mad.

She tripped over Lucy on the way to the refrigerator for the jelly, but she didn't mind. She couldn't believe how happy she felt when she hugged the dog. It was almost like hugging her mom again.

Lucy began to bark as soon as Nicki had the jar of peanut butter open, and Nicki quickly scooped up a fingerful for the dog, telling her to hush. Lucy was a peanut-butter freak. She ate an awful lot of food, in fact, and she ran around the house a lot, too, sometimes knocking things over. She was probably part of the reason Uncle Bryan was so grouchy. He'd never had to take care of a kid before, let alone a pet. Nicki hoped they found her other mother soon. She needed some other family out there somewhere just in case Uncle Bryan couldn't stand to keep her anymore.

And she hoped they liked pets. She'd just die if she lost Lucy now.

She put two sandwiches and some chips on a paper plate, about the only kind Uncle Bryan used, not like the china ones her mom and grandma had always used, grabbed up a napkin and a glass of milk, and took it all into Uncle Bryan's office.

"You didn't have to do this, Nick. I could've come out there with you," he said when she set the plate down beside him.

"That's okay. Lucy'll share mine," she said.

He looked at her over his drafting table. "Just make sure you get the bigger share."

Nicki went out to the couch and curled up again. She'd have liked to snuggle up on her bed, but it seemed to bug Uncle Bryan when she did that. Anyway, she didn't want a sandwich. She wasn't hungry. She hadn't been feeling too good since she'd woken up that morning, and she was really afraid she might be going to start her period. She'd just die if she did. She couldn't go to the school nurse with it being summer, and they lived too far away from the store for her to go there by herself and get stuff. Besides, she didn't have any money and she wasn't even totally sure what to get. But one thing was for sure—she couldn't go to Uncle Bryan for help if it happened.

He'd probably faint if she asked for those pad things. She'd probably faint, too.

Nicki thought again of her other mother, something she did almost all the time lately. She thought about how wonderful it would be if she found her mother *before* she started her period, and if her mother wanted her, she'd have a woman there to help her through the whole yucky thing.

She thought about how happy Uncle Bryan would probably be to have his freedom back again. And she tried not to think about how sad that made her feel.

JENNIFER SPENT all day Sunday with Sam, changing the plugs and belts and oil and filter on the Mustang, and eating ribs Sam barbecued himself on the old grill he kept outside his apartment building. Sam had been living in the same six-unit building Jennifer's whole life, though he was no longer a tenant. He'd bought the building a few years before when Jennifer had promoted him to corporate mechanic, a fancy title that allowed her to pay him a lot of money to do what he loved to do. And he was worth every penny.

When she went back to work on Monday she was ready for business. The first thing she did was refuse all calls. She instructed Rachel to pick up her private line for her through the remainder of the week and to send Bryan Chambers's calls to Dennis from then on. Her vice president could handle the rest of the One Price campaign himself.

She made it through the day better than she'd expected to, and by Tuesday morning she was certain she'd done the right thing. She got a lot more work accomplished when she wasn't waiting for her phone to ring. It was also easier to pretend she wasn't missing Bryan so much when she wasn't constantly hoping to hear his voice on the other end of the line.

Dennis's familiar knock sounded on the door of her office shortly after nine.

"Come on in," she called. She hadn't seen Dennis since before her shopping spree with Tanya on Friday.

"Mornin', Jen. Did you get my message about the newest One Price films? Chambers is bringing them over tomorrow morning for us to take a look at them. He says they're dynamite." Dennis took his usual seat in the armchair next to her television set.

"Rachel told me, yes, but I can't make it. I'm meeting with Peterson tomorrow," she said. John Peterson was the architect they'd hired to put up the new truck building next to Teal Chevrolet.

"Put him, off, Jen. We need to get these commercials on the air."

"I trust your judgment, Dennis. You can okay them without me."

Dennis settled his ankle on the opposite knee. "Chambers expects you to be there."

"Then he's going to be disappointed." She tapped her pen against her desk pad. She'd made her decision.

"What happened?" Dennis asked, frowning. "I thought you two had a thing going."

Jennifer knew it would be useless to deny it, especially since his wife had almost as big a mouth as he did. "We did. But I'm having a little trouble dealing with his niece."

"I didn't even know he had a niece."

"I didn't know it, either, until last week. She lives with him."

She figured that was all she'd have to say. Dennis would figure out the rest. Tanya would've filled him in on Friday's conversation, as well as the one she'd had with Jennifer that day in her penthouse. He'd know what she was dealing with. More so than Tanya really, since Dennis had been with her since the very beginning. He'd already been working for her father when she'd met Tommy Mason. He'd watched her jump through hoops for the older boy. And he'd also been her sole emotional support in the year that followed.

"So is she a delinquent or what?" he asked, leaning forward with his forearms resting on his knees.

Jennifer looked at him, surprised. "I don't know. I haven't met her. She's twelve," she said.

Dennis's eyes filled with understanding. "I can see where it might be a little rough at first, but I still don't see that as a reason to avoid the man if you're really interested in him."

"I do."

"You're twenty-eight years old, Jen. Don't you think you've been punishing yourself long enough? Isn't it about time to forgive yourself?"

"It's a little hard to forgive someone for being irresponsible enough to create a life with no means to care for it," she said. Peace, she'd thought she'd found. Acceptance, she knew she'd found. Forgiveness, she didn't think she'd ever find.

"If you'd done it consciously, maybe, but you

didn't, Jen. And you've paid for your mistake. Tenfold.''

"I was paid for it, you mean."

"What in the hell are you talking about?" Dennis asked, getting up and sitting on the corner of her desk.

Jennifer didn't like having him tower over her. She already felt menial enough as it was. "I took their bribe, Dennis, remember? Give up the baby and get the car I'd always wanted."

"That's bull, Jennifer. Even *your* parents wouldn't offer a car in exchange for a child. They gave you that car to appease their guilt, not buy you off."

Jennifer hadn't seen it that way. "I still took it. I still gained by giving the baby up," she said.

"But you'd have given the baby up either way, Jen, because it was best for the baby. You took the car to please your parents, just like you'd been doing your whole life. You knew it would make them feel better if you allowed them to do something nice for you."

"I loved that car, Dennis."

"Sure you did. You still do. It's a great car. And it served you well back then, too, giving you the distraction you needed."

Jennifer smiled sadly. "I'd love to think you're right, my friend. I'd love to think I wasn't as awful as I've always thought, but pretty words can't change the past. If I'd been stronger, I could've fought them. There are places I could've gone where they'd have helped me find a job and take care of my baby."

Dennis leaned down, holding her gaze with his. "And what kind of life would that have been for that child, Jen? Could it have competed with the two-parent, financially secure family you sent her to? You're one of the strongest people I know, lady. It took one hell of a lot of guts to give away the one thing you loved most in the world.''

Jennifer's eyes filled with tears as she listened to her friend. He'd pulled her through some hard times in the past, taught her how to hold her head up high again when she'd gone back to high school branded a tramp.

''So you think two people with money raising her compensates for the fact that she'd been denied her own mother's love?'' she asked. She'd driven herself crazy all weekend, the questions going round and round in her head.

''I think if they love her as if she was their own flesh and blood, she's just the same as every other kid on the block.''

''Except that she knows she has a mother out there someplace who didn't want her.''

''If her adoptive parents love her enough, it doesn't matter. You wanna know what I think?'' he asked, his eyes filled with challenge.

''What?''

''I think you're getting a little stuck-up in your old age, lady, placing so much importance on yourself in that girl's life. I'd wager a guess that if she ever thinks about you, it's fleetingly.''

A slow grin spread across Jennifer's face. Dennis had always known just what to say to make her feel better. "Why couldn't I have fallen in love with you?" she asked him.

"You knew I was saving myself for Tanya," he said, grinning back at her. But they both knew there'd been a time when he'd have married Jennifer in an instant if she'd have had him.

"Yeah, and you'd better be saving your money, my friend. That woman plans to buy out the stock in every baby store in the city over the next five months."

"Yeah. I saw all the loot she bought on Friday." He sobered. "So you're really okay with our having a baby?"

Jennifer set her pen down. "It might be a little hard at times seeing Tanya go through all the stages I went through, but I'm ready for it. I have to let the past go."

"If you really mean that, why not let Chambers introduce you to his niece and see what happens?" Dennis asked. "Maybe spending some time with a twelve-year-old would help you get on with life, rather than avoiding it."

"You think that's what I've been doing?"

"Isn't it?"

Jennifer shrugged, not sure of anything anymore. "Don't press me on this, okay? Meet him for me tomorrow?"

Dennis got up. "If that's what you want," he said, heading for the door. He didn't bother to hide the fact that he thought she was making the wrong decision.

"It's what I want," Jennifer said. But she heard

the lie in her words even if Dennis didn't. She honestly didn't know what she wanted, except maybe to be fifteen again, to have the chance to do it all over—and get it right this time.

HER MEETING with Peterson took as long as Jennifer had expected, but just to ensure that she missed the meeting with Innovative Advertising, she stopped at the drugstore on her way back to the office. Walking up and down the aisles, buying an extra deodorant when she already had a spare at home, stopping for more of the toothpaste and bubble bath she'd picked up over the weekend, she wondered how strong Dennis would think her if he could see her now.

By lunchtime, having stopped at the cleaners and her favorite jewelers, as well, she figured it was safe to return to the office. She'd have Rachel order her a sandwich of some kind while she caught up on the work she'd missed that morning. She wanted to get moving on Peterson's plans as soon as possible. Which meant she had several phone calls to make to get the city permits they needed.

She spent a frustrating twenty minutes talking with the mayor's office, ten of them with the mayor himself, which only resulted in having to make more calls than she'd started with. If the pollution didn't suffocate the world, she figured the red tape would. It made no sense that she had to beg the city to allow her to spend her own money to develop a garbage dump into a valuable piece of property that the citizens of Atlanta could be proud of.

The door to her office burst open and Jennifer glanced up, her heart rate accelerating at the sight of Bryan Chambers.

"I'm sorry, Ms. Teal. I told him you weren't to be disturbed," Rachel said behind him, wringing her hands.

"I didn't figure that meant me." He held his ground as if he owned it.

Jennifer stood. "It's okay, Rachel," she said, dismissing her secretary. As much as she'd done to avoid him, she didn't have the strength to demand he leave now that he was there.

"You weren't at the meeting." Bryan strode into the middle of her office, challenging her.

"Hello to you, too," she said, stalling. She'd come to no decisions about him. About them.

Had she?

"I wanted you to see the tapes."

"I'd planned to look at them tonight. I had an appointment this morning. With my architect."

His brow rose. "You're building a house?"

"A truck building next to Teal Chevrolet."

Their eyes caught and held as they stood across the office from each other, as if neither knew where to go from there. He was dressed as usual in blue jeans and a short-sleeved pullover, his ponytail hanging down over his collar. He looked wonderful.

"Have dinner with us tonight," he said, his words soft, seductive.

She let out a breath, one she hadn't realized she'd been holding until he'd asked the question. And it was then she knew she'd made her decision. Dennis had said a lot of things the day before that had struck home. Things she'd needed to hear.

"On two conditions," she said.

He took a few steps toward her, his face slowly breaking out in a grin. "What might those be?" he asked.

"We go someplace neutral, a restaurant, and we drive there separately."

"Giving yourself an escape route?" he asked, but he didn't seem to care. He was still grinning.

"Maybe." She wished she could take this as lightly as he was. She felt like she was strangling.

"Then I have a condition, too." He was no longer smiling.

"What?"

"If you run out on us, you make certain Nicki knows it doesn't have anything to do with her. Fake a sickness or something, I don't care, but I don't want that little girl upset. She's been through enough."

"Of course," Jennifer said, hurt that he'd found it necessary to warn her, as if he wasn't sure he could trust her around his niece. But then, she couldn't blame him. She didn't trust herself, either.

She agreed to meet Bryan and Nicki at seven o'clock at a steak place closer to her penthouse than the office, and she wondered suddenly if she was doing the right thing, if she shouldn't have followed her instincts and left well enough alone....

CHAPTER ELEVEN

NICKI DIDN'T WANT to go to dinner. Bryan had thought his niece would've been eager for some female companionship for a change, but though she hadn't argued, he'd seen the resistance in her eyes. Eyes that were exactly like her mother's.

"What's up, Nick? I thought it'd be fun for us to get out," he said.

Apparently he'd said the wrong thing. That fear was back in her eyes. And he had no idea why. Hell. He'd climb a damn mountain for the child, if only she'd tell him which one.

"You can go, Uncle Bryan. You don't have to drag me along on your date."

"Who said anything about it being a date?"

"It's with a woman, isn't it? The same one you took to the symphony, you said, and out to Stone Mountain that day."

Bryan's eyes narrowed. Apparently Nicki paid more attention to what went on around here than he'd thought. "It's with the same woman, yes, but tonight's not a date. She wants to meet you, Nick."

Nicki's eyes widened. "Me?"

"Of course, you. It's the whole reason for the dinner. We're a pair now, Nick. You and me. My friends need to be your friends, too. Besides, why wouldn't she want to meet you? You're a pretty spectacular kid.''

''And you're positive I wouldn't be bugging you if I'm there?''

He grabbed her by the shoulders, holding her steady while he looked her straight in the eye. ''Positive.''

''But what would I wear?'' she asked, her expression worried again.

''How about that flowered thing we bought a couple of weeks ago, the one with the thin straps?''

Her brows came together as she considered his suggestion. ''The one that's shorts that looks like a dress?''

''Yeah. The color looked great with your hair.''

She smiled, nodding. ''Okay. When do I have to be ready?''

Bryan looked at his watch. ''A couple of hours,'' he said.

''Then I better get moving.'' She was already pulling her long hair out of its ponytail as she headed toward her room.

Bryan watched her go, well aware that she could be ready in an eighth of that time, but he'd give her all night if she wanted it, as long as she kept looking as happy as she'd looked walking down that hall. She had a purpose.

Bryan went in to change, uncomfortable with the power he unwittingly held over the two most important people in his life. He was orchestrating something between them that was highly personal for both of them, and neither one of them even knew about it. But when he considered his options, he couldn't see any other way.

And it might just possibly be the right one, too. First Jennifer had surprised him by agreeing to the dinner at all, and now Nicki actually appeared to be looking forward to it. Maybe it was meant that mother and daughter finally meet.

Nicki was as quiet as usual as they drove the couple of miles to the restaurant, and just in case she was worried about meeting Jennifer, he took the time to tell his niece a little bit more about her. He told her things he thought might interest a twelve-year-old, such as that Jennifer drove a convertible and was friends with a famous artist, but that was all.

He saw her sitting at a table as soon as he ushered Nicki into the crowded restaurant. She looked beautiful. He'd never wanted a woman so much just from looking at her. Or was it because he could only look that he wanted her so much?

With one arm around his niece, he led her toward Jennifer's table, surprised to find that his hands were sweating. So much rested on the evening. Far more than either of his guests knew.

He could tell the second that Jennifer noticed them. He saw her stiffen, saw her glance run over Nicki and then away. His heart sank. She was meeting her own daughter for the first time. Shouldn't she feel something, some connection, even if she didn't know why?

"Is that her?" Nicki whispered.

"That's her," Bryan said. He wished he could tell Nicki that the woman she was heading toward was her mother. She deserved to know that. Jennifer deserved to know it, too. It was unfair of him to walk her daughter up to her as if she was a total stranger. And yet, as he saw Jennifer's eyes shy away from the child at his side, he knew he couldn't tell her. He couldn't tell either of them. Not yet.

"Jennifer, this is Nicki," he said as they reached the table. He held Nicki's chair out for her. Waiting.

"Hi." Nicki grinned, a hint of the imp he'd once known.

"It's nice to meet you," Jennifer said, returning Nicki's smile, then looking away.

Nicki didn't seem to notice Jennifer's reticence. She sat down, picked up her menu and started to read it as if she actually had an appetite to appease.

Jennifer picked up her menu, too, and Bryan looked from one to the other of them, a man truly between a rock and a hard place. He was amazed, once he saw them together, how very much they resembled each other, with their long auburn curls and striking hazel eyes, and knew a moment's unease when he considered the possibility that someone else might pick up on the resemblance, as well.

They ordered dinner, but as soon as the waiter left, silence fell over the table again. Bryan refused to let the evening fail and spent the next ten minutes trying to keep the conversation rolling for all three of them. But between Jennifer's monosyllabic replies and Nicki's shy smiles, it seemed an impossibility. He was relieved when their dinners arrived and they could occupy themselves with the business of eating.

"My steak's great. How's your, Nick?" he asked.

"Good."

Bryan looked to Jennifer. She wasn't eating much, which was unusual. "How about yours?" he asked.

"Fine."

Silence descended again. Bryan was beginning to think he'd made the biggest mistake of his life.

"Could I have the salt, please?" Nicki's soft voice broke the silence.

The saltshaker was by Jennifer. She picked it up, passed it to Nicki with a tight smile and turned her attention back to her plate.

"Thanks," Nicki said.

"You're welcome."

Great. These two had spent nine intimate months together and now the most they could manage was polite platitudes? Bryan's appetite was rapidly dwindling to nothing as he sat between them, needing to make things right for both of them and suspecting it might be impossible.

Nicki put her fork down on a near-empty plate. "Your hair's the same color as mine," she suddenly said, looking at the twist of hair on Jennifer's head.

Bryan almost choked. Their hair color *was* unusual. Would either of them be suspicious of the resemblance? Would Nicki? She knew he'd been looking for her birth mother.

"Yes, it is." Jennifer glanced at Nicki's long auburn curls, then away.

"I guess you have to be careful with colors, too," Nicki said, her voice tentative.

Jennifer smiled at her before looking away again. "Always."

Nicki looked over at Bryan. "You know what Lucy did today, Uncle Bryan? She fell asleep in the dirty clothes," she said, a smile on her lips. It didn't quite reach her eyes, but it was a start.

The evening ended as soon as they finished dinner. Bryan and Nicki walked Jennifer to her car.

"It was nice meeting you," Nicki said, somehow making the words sound sincere, rather than merely polite.

Jennifer glanced at his niece only briefly. "It was nice meeting you, too, Nicki. Bye," she said before climbing into her car.

Bryan couldn't let her just drive away. He was afraid he'd never see her again. He leaned down and kissed her fully, if much too briefly, on the lips. He'd have liked to have spent the next several hours kissing her—and more. But Nicki was there. And Nicki came first.

"Bryan?" Jennifer's voice called him back as he turned to go. "Call me." The two words sounded ominous.

He nodded, leading Nicki away.

"Bye," Nicki said one last time, looking over her shoulder as she and Bryan headed to the Jeep.

"She's nice," Nicki said on the short drive home.

Bryan was amazed. How could Nicki say that? Jennifer had barely acknowledged her all night.

"I think so," he said.

"She eats her salad without dressing, same as me. And Mom always said I must be the only person in the world who does that."

So she'd noticed, too. "She does, huh?" *Intelligent, Chambers.*

"Do you think we can go out with her again sometime?"

Bryan glanced at his niece, seeing the interest sparking in her eyes. "I'll ask her," he said, knowing he couldn't promise any more than that, and worried he was setting Nicki up for a disappointment. He wouldn't be at all surprised if Jennifer planned to end things once and for all the first chance she got.

He'd just have to see that she didn't get the chance.

Bryan had some papers to drop off at Teal Automotive the next day, and he stopped home to get Nicki on the way to Jennifer's office.

"Are you sure she won't mind if I come to her work?" Nicki asked, already slipping into her sandals.

"I'm sure," Bryan said, though he wasn't at all. After the way Jennifer had acted the night before, he wasn't sure she ever wanted to see Nicki again. Which was why he couldn't give her a choice. She had no idea how much was resting on her learning to care for Nicki.

Not only was Nicki's happiness hanging in the balance, but Bryan's, as well, and, he suspected, Jennifer's. He'd only begun to realize how much he'd grown to feel for Jennifer over the past weeks, how much his future happiness had begun to depend on her. He'd intended to insinuate himself into the woman's life, find out what made her tick for Nicki's sake. He hadn't expected to want to stay there.

And if she didn't accept Nicki, he'd never get the chance.

SHE WAS SUCH A YOUNG LADY, so grown-up. Jennifer hadn't realized how mature twelve was. And yet, there'd been a true air of innocence about her—

"Hey, Jennifer! You in there?"

Jennifer's gaze flew from the window of her office to the man who'd been sitting across from her most of the morning. "Sorry, Dennis. Where were we?" she asked, looking at the figures in front of her.

"I've been right here. It's you who keeps leaving us. We can put this off, you know. We didn't finish this year's projected budgets until last August. Next year's can certainly wait another week or two."

Jennifer gathered up the papers on her desk. She really had it bad. There had never been a time when work didn't take care of what ailed her. "If you don't mind, I guess we better stop for now. I'm having a little trouble concentrating."

"I've noticed," Dennis said dryly, putting his copies of the Teal Automotive projected profits back into a folder. "You wanna tell me what's got you so tied up?"

"I met his niece last night," she said softly, remembering the long excruciating ordeal.

Dennis froze, his papers half-in and half-out of their folder. "And?" he asked, watching her carefully.

"She was older than I expected."

"She's not twelve?"

"Yeah, she's twelve. Twelve is older than I expected. She knew exactly what to order for herself and didn't have to be reminded of her manners even once."

"You sound disappointed."

Jennifer shrugged. "Silly, isn't it? It's just that whenever I've pictured my baby out there, growing up, it's always been with the idea that she still needed mothering. But Nicki's so self-sufficient."

"I'm sure not all twelve-year-olds are, Jen. And just because she can eat by herself doesn't mean she doesn't need a mother. You certainly could have used one at that age."

She looked up, surprised. "I had one."

"In fact, maybe, not in deed, but I'm not going to debate with you about it again. So how'd it go otherwise?"

Jennifer fiddled with the magnetic paper-clip holder Sam had given her for Christmas one year. It was in the shape of a Mustang. "It went okay," she said.

Dennis didn't say anything. He just sat watching her.

"I liked her."

"You two hit it off?"

"Not exactly, but I don't think she hates me."

"She'd be nuts if she does. What'd Bryan say about it?"

"I don't know. I haven't talked to him yet today." She'd been waiting for his call all morning.

Dennis pushed his files aside. "Was it as hard as you thought it would be?"

"Harder." Jennifer was appalled when tears sprang to her eyes. She'd thought she'd cried them all out during the long dark hours of the night.

"I'm sorry, Jen," Dennis said awkwardly, leaning forward to brush the top of her hand with his fingers.

Jennifer swallowed, then wiped her eyes, willing the tears to stop. "Her hair's the same color as mine," she said, her words barely above a whisper. "I kept watching her in my peripheral vision and wondering if my own daughter looks like that, if she smiles so sweetly, if her bone structure is as fine. If she eats her salad without dressing."

"Bryan's niece ate her salad without dressing?" Dennis asked.

Jennifer nodded.

"And I thought you were the only one who did that," he said, smiling across at her gently.

"I know. And she seems to like catsup as much as I do, too." Jennifer stopped, composing herself. She'd never been so confused in her life, but she was *feeling* again. She just hadn't decided if that was a good thing or a bad thing.

Her intercom buzzed, startling her.

She pushed the call button. "Yes, Rachel?"

"Mr. Chambers is here to see you, Ms. Teal."

Jennifer's eyes flew to Dennis. She wasn't ready to see him yet. Not like this.

Her office door opened. "Oh, but— I'm sorry, Ms. Teal," Rachel said over the intercom as Bryan stepped into her office.

He wasn't alone. Jennifer's gaze fluttered to the child hovering nervously at his side.

"Hello, Nicki, it's good to see you again," she said, her heart floating. Dear God, was it right for her to feel such an immediate bond with this child? She flooded with guilt when she thought of her own child, the one she'd abandoned, the one who had the right to expect her affection—

"Hello, Ms. Teal. Uncle Bryan said you wouldn't mind if I came along with him."

Her voice was as sweet as Jennifer remembered.

"I don't mind at all," Jennifer said, looking at Bryan. He smiled at her in that way he had that made her feel like the only woman alive.

And then, coming farther into the room, he shook Dennis's hand. "Good to see you, Dennis," he said. "I've got some schedules for you two to approve." He pulled a folder out of the sketchbook under his arm.

Nicki wandered over to the couch, and Jennifer wanted to leave the two men to their business and join the girl there. But she couldn't think of a thing to say. She didn't have any idea what twelve-year-old girls were interested in. Did they play with Barbie dolls? Or did they think fashion dolls were dumb by the time they reached twelve? Did they still watch cartoons and think boys had cooties? She couldn't remember how it had felt to be twelve. She started to get nervous.

"Let me see what you've got," she said, joining the men.

Nicki sat quietly on the couch, looking at the pictures on Jennifer's office walls.

BRYAN CALLED Jennifer later that afternoon to invite her to his place for dinner the following evening. He didn't expect her to accept, but he wanted her to know he wasn't going to give up. He was shocked when she agreed to come. His house wasn't ready for guests.

She'd never seen his home before, and picturing the cool perfection of her penthouse, he spent the entire next day at home cleaning, much to Nicki's amusement. But as much as his niece teased him about his unusual behavior, she helped him, too. She seemed almost excited herself at the prospect of company.

Nicki was a whiz in the kitchen, having learned to cook from her mother and grandma, and when she offered to make a meat loaf with all the trimmings, Bryan didn't have the heart to tell her he'd been thinking of something a little fancier.

She was wearing her daisy outfit and had been pacing between the living-room window and the kitchen for almost half an hour by the time Jennifer pulled into the driveway.

"She's here," she announced. Bryan dropped the stack of magazines he'd been trying to find a home for right back where they belonged—in the middle of the coffee table. He was what he was, blue jeans, ponytail and all.

Nicki hung back when he answered the door, but not too far. Jennifer looked beautiful as always, slim and cool in a short white dress that flared just over her hips. He brushed her lips with his and invited her inside.

"Hi," Nicki said from behind him.

"Hello." Jennifer smiled over his shoulder at Nicki before turning back to Bryan.

"I like your house," she said, looking around at the interior with its open-floor plan.

"It's not quite a penthouse." He cursed himself for saying that. Possessions didn't matter to him. And he'd be damned if he'd start apologizing for what he was just because he'd met a woman who mattered.

"It's a lot nicer than a penthouse." Jennifer walked into the living room, turning around. "You don't have to wait for an elevator to get home, for one thing," she said.

"You live in a penthouse?" Nicki asked, following her into the room.

Jennifer nodded, glancing at Nicki only briefly before looking around again. "Where's your dog— Lucy, didn't you say her name was?"

"Uncle Bryan made me keep her outside. She barks a lot when she meets someone new."

"She also jumps up on people, and I didn't want

her to get hair all over you before you even got in the door," Bryan said, leading Jennifer over to the couch.

Jennifer sat down, sniffing the air. "Something sure smells good," she said.

"It's meat loaf. Nicki made it."

"I hope you like it," Nicki added, sounding apologetic.

"I've always liked meat loaf," Jennifer told them both, jumping up to peer at the books in Bryan's bookcase.

They'd been his mother's. The wall they'd been on since before Bryan was born hadn't been touched by the tornado that had torn up most of the house.

Nicki went out to put the finishing touches on dinner, and Bryan poured a couple of glasses of wine. As tense as he felt, it was still great to be alone with her for a moment.

"Here, this is for you," he said, taking her a glass. But he didn't hand it to her immediately. He bent down to kiss her first. A kiss that exploded between them the minute their lips touched. A kiss that would have continued if Nicki hadn't called from the kitchen to say that dinner was ready.

By the time they met his niece in the dining room, Bryan had his breathing a little more under control. The rest of his body wasn't so quick to cool down. He took his seat at the head of the table, wondering if he was ever going to find out what it was like to make love with Jennifer, to have her moaning beneath him, begging for satisfaction. Somehow he couldn't picture Jennifer begging for anything.

Nicki passed around plates and bowls, and the conversation was as scarce as it had been the other night. Bryan still hadn't seen Jennifer look directly at Nicki for more than a few seconds, but at least she was eating better tonight. He hoped that meant she was getting a little bit more comfortable being around Nicki.

"You know what, Uncle Bryan? I think you've set a record for the number of times in a row you've seen Ms. Teal," Nicki said about halfway through the meal.

Bryan nearly choked on his baked potato. Jennifer offered him his glass of water, solicitous as always, but he saw the grin she was trying to hide.

"You might even fall in love with her," Nicki continued. Bryan didn't know whether to shout with glee at this glimpse of the Nicki he used to know or to strangle her.

"Finish your dinner, Nick," he said, trying to sound stern and fatherly.

"I *am* finished." Nicki motioned to her empty plate. "Grandma always used to say that it would take the love of a good woman to bring peace to your wandering soul," Nicki said.

She sounded just like his mother when she said it, too. "Having you here brought peace to my soul, sprite. Now go get us some dessert or something."

"I made brownies," Nicki said, taking her empty plate into the kitchen.

He watched the door swing shut behind his niece, hearing again the words he'd just said. Having her with him, having someone he loved at home, needing his care, did seem to have brought peace to his soul, at least for the time being. He'd been feeling a lot of uncomfortable things lately, but claustrophobic wasn't one of them. Of course, knowing himself as he did, he knew that the dreaded restlessness could attack at any time.

"She's sweet," Jennifer said, looking at the door Nicki had left through.

"She's the best," Bryan said. Now all he had to do was convince her mother of that.

AN HOUR LATER Nicki and Jennifer stood in front of the video cabinet in the living room trying to decide which movie to watch. They'd let Lucy inside as soon as the dishes were done, and Jennifer, after confessing she'd never been allowed to have a pet while she was growing up, took an instant liking to the dog. The three of them played tug-of-war with her until Lucy, finally tired out, curled up in a corner of the room and went to sleep. That was when Bryan suggested a movie. He didn't want Jennifer to leave when they were all finally starting to relax.

Nicki grabbed a movie from the cabinet, but Bryan had a feeling she didn't even know which one she held. She was spending more time looking at Jennifer than at the movies in front of her. He waited by the video-cassette recorder, watching them both. Their resemblance was amazing.

"I like your jewelry." Nicki's words were soft, hesitant.

"Thank you." Jennifer glanced at Nicki briefly before returning her attention to the triple stack of movies.

"I had a baby ring," Nicki said. She was looking at the gold chains around Jennifer's neck. "It had my name and my mom's engraved on the inside."

"Oh," Jennifer said, pulling out a movie to read the blurb on the back.

Bryan remembered the ring. Lori had bought it for Nicki for her first birthday, their first birthday together. Come to think of it, he hadn't seen it since the—

"I used to wear it on a gold chain around my neck, but I took it off to go swimming and then the tornado came and I never saw it again."

Oh, God. He should have realized. He should have remembered how important that ring was to Nicki. They could at least have looked for it in the rubble.

"Your uncle told me about that tornado," Jennifer said gently. "I'm sorry."

"Me, too." Nicki shrugged. "Have you ever seen *The Lion King?*" she asked, pulling another video out from the cabinet. Bryan was amazed. It was the first time Nicki had ever mentioned the tornado without crying.

Jennifer looked at the movie Nicki held out. "No."

"It's a great movie. You and Uncle Bryan should watch it."

"What about you, Nick?" Bryan asked. "I thought you were going to watch with us."

"I've already seen it a hundred times," she said. "I'd kinda like to go to bed."

He should consider himself lucky. Nicki had stayed up an hour later than usual already.

And it wasn't like time alone with Jennifer was going to be any hardship for him.

Grabbing Lucy, Nicki kissed Bryan on the cheek. "Night, Uncle Bryan," she said.

"Night, Nick. Be sure you brush."

Nicki grimaced at him. "I will. Night, Ms. Teal."

"Good night, Nicki. Thank you for the meat loaf. It was very good," Jennifer said, standing awkwardly in the middle of the living room.

If she'd been watching she'd have seen the glow that spread across Nicki's face at the polite praise, but she was still looking at the movie cassette Nicki had given her. Bryan couldn't figure it out. Though she was gentle about it, Jennifer continued to shy away from Nicki as if the child had some kind of disease, yet Nicki was blossoming before his very eyes simply having Jennifer around.

Jennifer seemed to relax the second they heard Nicki's bedroom door close behind her. "We don't have to watch this if you don't want to," she said, handing him the movie.

Bryan reached for the video, pulling Jennifer up against him as he did. "As good as this is, there *is* something I'd rather be doing," he said, nuzzling her neck.

Tilting her head back, she gave him better access. "Mmm. I see what you mean."

They were alone and in private, and he'd been wanting her too long to just stop. He covered her lips with his, hungry for the taste of her. She was warm and sweet, and far too sexy for his peace of mind. Her lips opened beneath his and his body quickened as he accepted her invitation, deepening the kiss.

Never had a woman affected him so powerfully. His body surged against hers, aching with the strength of his yearning to take her with him on the wildest ride of his life. She was perfect. Her slim body filling his arms was like heaven, her breasts pressing into his chest an exquisite torture.

Bryan started to shake with the effort it took him not to lower her to the floor and pump himself into her until he found the blessed relief her kisses promised. She deserved better than that. So did he. And Nicki was right down the hall.

He dragged his lips from her mouth, resting his forehead against hers. "I guess we better watch that movie, after all," he said, his breathing heavy.

"Probably." Jennifer smiled wryly. "Nice girls don't seduce their hosts when they're invited to dinner, do they?"

"Is that what you were doing, seducing your host?"

"I don't know. If I was, was it working?"

Bryan grinned at her, still holding her against him. "What do you think?"

"I think that you're one hell of a man, Bryan Chambers."

"Because I'm so hard it hurts?"

"No!" She burst out laughing. "Because you don't let your physical desires overpower your brain—"

"You haven't seen me at four o'clock in the morning," Bryan interrupted, thinking of all the cold showers he'd taken since he'd met this woman.

"—and you don't put pressure on me to satisfy those desires," she finished.

"One thing I've never done was coerce a woman into bed. Either she wants it as badly as I do, or we don't do it."

"See, that's what I mean." She looked up at him. "Why couldn't I have met you when I was fifteen?" she whispered.

Bryan tensed. "Who *did* you meet?" It was important for him to know the details, to understand.

She pulled away from him and sat on the couch. "No one really," she said, looking down at the dainty white sandals on her feet.

"You had a baby, Jen. There had to be someone."

Her head shot up. "I had a baby, yes, but I didn't say it happened when I was fifteen." She looked at him, puzzlement furrowing her brow.

Bryan froze, thinking back to the day she'd told him about her giving up a child. No. She'd never said *when* she'd had the baby. That was something he'd figured out on his own, because he knew how old Nicki was. Good Lord, what had he just done?

CHAPTER TWELVE

MORE THAN ANYTHING, Bryan hated the lies. He sat down beside Jennifer on the couch, leaning forward with his elbows on his knees. "I guess it was the way you said you wished you could've met me when you were fifteen," he replied. "I just assumed that was when you got pregnant." He tossed the truth around like a hot potato.

"Oh." That was all. Nothing else.

"I won't pressure you to tell me about it, Jen. But whenever you're ready to talk, I'll listen."

She slipped her hand through the crook in his arm, resting her cheek against his shoulder. "I was too young, Bryan. But old enough to know better. And I don't want you to know. I don't want you to think any less of me."

He couldn't promise her it wouldn't matter. It was his niece she'd given away. "The woman I care for is the woman you are today. Who you were with in the past is just that—in the past." He spoke to her bowed head.

"I hope you mean that," she whispered, raising her head, studying him, as if to determine the sincerity of his words.

"I'm more concerned with how you and Nicki get along than in how old you were when you lost your virginity."

She pulled back. "I'm not sure she likes me," she said, sounding just about her daughter's age.

"She likes you, honey. After dinner the other night, she asked if we were going to see you again."

"Maybe because she was hoping you weren't."

"Trust me. She wasn't. She almost got excited when I told her you were coming for dinner tonight."

"She barely said two words to me."

"You barely said two words to her, Jen."

"Because I don't know what to say."

"You say what you'd say to me, within reason of course. You just need to learn to relax around her a little bit. She's a great kid once you get to know her."

Somehow he had to convince Jennifer she was good with children. She was having a hard enough time sticking it out with Nicki merely being his niece. She'd bolt for sure if she knew the true significance of winning Nicki's regard.

It wouldn't be like it was the first time she'd abandoned her daughter.

"She's really strong, isn't she?" Jennifer asked, sitting back on the couch. "I'm amazed how well she's adjusted to the loss she's suffered."

"Until she met you, she spent most of her days in bed," Bryan said bluntly.

Jennifer's brows drew together in concern. "Was she sick?"

"Not unless you call the tendency to sleep your life away being sick."

"But she seems so...so...normal."

"She opens up when you're around, Jen. Maybe it's because you're a woman, I don't know, but she seems to have come out of her shell more in the past few days than she has in the whole past year."

Jennifer's eyes widened. "Really?"

Bryan grinned. She looked so naively pleased sitting there, this woman who'd given birth while still a child herself. "Yeah. Really. Listen, I promised Nicki a trip to the beach as soon as Calvin got caught up on things. Why don't you come with us? We could take a couple of days, leave the day after tomorrow. What do you say?"

"To the beach?"

"Yeah. You can even pick the beach, as long as it's on this coast."

"I haven't been to the beach since I was about ten."

"Then it's high time you went, wouldn't you agree?"

"Just the three of us?" she asked, looking excited and scared out of her wits at the same time.

"Just the three of us. It'll give us a chance to see if we've got something good going here or not." It was time to make some decisions.

"I'm not sure I want to know if it's the 'or not,'" she said.

He didn't want to know that, either. But it was time he found out one way or the other. And if, as he suspected, Jennifer was fine with Nicki once she allowed herself to relax, *then* he'd have to find out if Jennifer cared enough for him to understand when he told her who he really was, or rather, who Nicki really was.

"Don't you want to find out now if we're kidding ourselves here?" he asked.

"I guess." She took a deep breath. "Okay. I'll go. Just give me a couple of days to clear things up at the office."

"You got 'em," Bryan said, telling himself he was doing the right thing. He wasn't going to finally meet a woman who didn't make him feel like her sheets were a straitjacket only to lose her before he ever really had her. He simply wasn't going to let that happen.

NICKI WAS LOOKING FORWARD to the trip to the beach now that Ms. Teal was going with them. Uncle Bryan wouldn't get bored with his pretty girlfriend along. They were going to some private beach Uncle Bryan knew about off the Florida Keys. It only had one hotel, and Uncle Bryan had gotten a three-bedroom suite for them. Nicki spent the next two days packing, and promising Lucy that she'd have a good time next door with Mrs. Baker and that she'd only be gone a few days.

Nicki really liked Ms. Teal. She didn't talk much, but her voice was soft when she did say stuff and she always paid attention when she, Nicki, talked. And she smiled at her like her mom used to do sometimes when she came home from school. It made Nicki feel special, even if she really wasn't.

Nicki looked at the three swimsuits spread out on her bed, wondering which one to pack. They were all one-pieces. When she'd gone to Shallowbrook for her birthday, her friends had all been talking about their new two-piece swimsuits. Knowing her uncle would never go for that, especially after he'd refused to buy her the baby T she'd wanted, Nicki looked back at the suits she had. She liked the plain green one the best, but the top was a little tight, and it made her feel kind of funny wearing it, like everyone could see that she was getting breasts. But the other one-pieces had flowers all over them and made her look like a little girl. She finally threw all three of them in. Maybe she wouldn't go swimming at all.

She'd bet Ms. Teal looked like one of the ladies on TV in her swimsuit. It probably didn't have any flowers. And she'd bet that Ms. Teal wouldn't feel funny if her top fit tight, either. Ms. Teal probably never felt funny about anything. She was just about the most perfect person Nicki had ever met. Nicki'd sure love it if her other mother turned out to be someone like that.

But she wouldn't. Someone like Ms. Teal would never have given her baby away. She'd have found a way to keep it, no matter what.

They were only going to be gone for three days, but Nicki packed all her new summer stuff. She didn't want Ms. Teal to think she dressed like a dope.

She froze as a thought suddenly occurred to her.

What if her real mother dressed like a dope? What if she didn't understand about how some colors were good on some people but looked awful on others? What if she didn't know how to wear her makeup or style her hair? Omigosh! What if she didn't have any teeth?

Nicki giggled as she folded up one of her new shirts, picturing an old witch with no teeth knocking on the door, and Uncle Bryan telling her she had the wrong house when she asked for Nicki. But she stopped laughing when she thought about her other mother really showing up. Maybe she should tell Uncle Bryan she didn't want to find her other mother—now, before it was too late.

She'd been worried a lot about why her first mother had given her away, about meeting a lady who'd allowed complete strangers to take her own baby. She'd been worried about the lady still not wanting her.

And besides, if Uncle Bryan was falling in love, if Ms. Teal was going to bring peace to his wandering soul, which surely she would since Nicki had never known her grandma to be wrong, then he'd be settling down, anyway, which meant Nicki didn't need to worry about him feeling cramped and leaving her.

And Nicki hadn't been feeling so crazy these past few days, either. She even felt a little happy about going to the beach and didn't just want to stay in bed all the time. So maybe she didn't need to worry about having something wrong with her from her other mother. Maybe she didn't need her other mother at all anymore. And if she didn't need her it wouldn't

matter, then, whether her other mother wanted her or
not.

Ms. Teal would surely want her. Nicki could tell
she liked her, 'cause she smiled at her so nice. And
she'd wanted to come to the beach with them, too.
Besides, she loved Lucy. It had been her idea to get
down on the floor to play tug-of-war with Lucy's
stuffed turtle, and she didn't even say anything when
Lucy's hair had gotten all over her pretty white dress.
She'd even laughed when Lucy had jumped up in her
lap and kissed her. And if she loved Lucy she had to
be someone who wouldn't mind having a kid around.

Yeah, maybe if things went as good as she hoped
at the beach, Nicki would just tell Uncle Bryan she
didn't want to find her other mother, after all.

THEY LEFT ATLANTA early Sunday morning. Bryan
and Nicki picked Jennifer up at the penthouse before
breakfast and drove straight to the airport. Nicki and
Jennifer had breakfast there while Bryan got the plane
ready to go. He said he'd grab a couple of doughnuts
to take with him out to the hangar.

Jennifer stood with Nicki at the counter while they
waited for the food they'd ordered, and then followed
her to an empty booth, sliding in across from her.

Nicki smeared catsup on her hash browns, then
handed the dispenser to Jennifer. ''I liked your place,
Ms. Teal. It's really neat having your own key to the
elevator and everything.''

''Call me Jennifer, please. Ms. Teal makes me feel
so old. And the elevator is actually a pain a lot of the

time,'' Jennifer said, reminding herself to pretend she was talking to a miniature version of Bryan or Tanya as she, too, covered her potatoes with catsup. ''It takes forever to carry things up from the car after I've been shopping all day. And if you have to go to the bathroom, forget it.''

Nicki giggled. ''What do you do then?'' she asked.

''Tap my foot a lot.''

Nicki laughed again. Jennifer started to relax.

''You know, you're pretty when you do that,'' Jennifer said.

''Do what?'' Nicki looked down at her plate, her face flushed.

''Smile,'' Jennifer said, losing confidence. She'd bungled things already. She'd never have told Tanya she looked pretty when she smiled. And now she'd gone and embarrassed the child.

Nicki looked up, her eyes serious. ''Thank you,'' she said.

Jennifer's fork hung suspended in midair. ''For what?''

The child shrugged. ''For saying that. My mom used to tell me I was pretty sometimes, but Uncle Bryan...well, you know, he's a man. He mostly doesn't like to see I'm growing up.''

''He's giving you a hard time about it?''

''No. He just doesn't want boys to notice me, which is okay, 'cause I don't, either, but that doesn't mean I wanna look dumb.''

''You don't look dumb! But I think I understand,''

Jennifer said, trying not to smile. "Your uncle still sees you as a little girl, huh?"

"Yeah." Nicki smiled and took a bite of toast.

"That's not all bad," Jennifer said, remembering her own youth. "At least he notices—and cares." Maybe things wouldn't have turned out as they had if someone had guided *her* a little more carefully.

"That's what I thought, too," Nicki said.

Bryan came in to get them just as they were finishing. He charged their meal to his account and led them out to the waiting plane.

"Jennifer, you climb up first," he said, helping her up the steps. "Nicki's riding in front with me."

"I am?" Nicki asked, clearly surprised.

"Of course. When have you ever flown with me and not been my copilot?"

"Never. But I thought—"

"Wrong," Bryan said. "God forbid something should happen to me, but if it did, you'd know what to do with the plane. Jennifer's only been up once."

"Besides, I'm happier back here, Nicki," Jennifer said, just as she'd have done to make one of her customers or employees more comfortable. "All those dials make me a little dizzy."

"They're nothing once you get used to them." Nicki smiled, climbed into her seat and put on her headset.

Bryan glanced at Jennifer in the back, his eyes thanking her even as they glowed with a more heated emotion. Jennifer smiled and stuck out her tongue at him.

The scenery below them was beautiful as they reached cruising altitude, but Jennifer found her eyes straying to the pilot more often than not. She was in love with him. She guessed she'd known it deep inside for a while now. She'd finally admitted it to herself when she'd picked up some birth control the day before. The last time she'd made love, it hadn't been love at all, and it hadn't been because *she* wanted to. And the consequences had been devastating. This time she was prepared all the way around.

He said something into his headset, apparently to Nicki because she grinned over at him and said something back. She really was a pretty child. And a nice one, too.

So far being with Nicki wasn't as bad as she'd thought it was going to be. The pain was still there, the regrets, but they'd always been there, even if she'd tried not to acknowledge them. Being with Nicki just made them impossible to ignore.

But somehow, being around Nicki also made the pain a little sweeter, almost consoling. On and off over the past twelve years, she'd found herself wondering how her daughter would feel about something, what kind of things she'd be into at the different stages in her life. And watching Nicki, Jennifer finally had answers for some of those questions. At the very least, she had some ground upon which to base those answers.

She still didn't feel any more certain about developing a relationship with Nicki, about her own ability to be the type of person a child would be comfortable with, but she was determined to give it her best shot. She wanted this thing to work.

Bryan had a limousine waiting for them at the airport in the Keys, and he'd arranged for a technician to service his plane, too.

"Jeez, Uncle Bryan, I can't believe it!" Nicki teased as they followed their driver to the car. "You're actually going to let someone else touch your plane. Grandma would've been shocked!"

Bryan grabbed Nicki in a neck hold, rubbing his knuckles against the top of her head. "Don't bug me, sprite. I'm on vacation."

"I'm sorry already," Nicki said.

Jennifer could barely understand her through her giggles. The sound was so infectious she joined in.

She opted to wait with Nicki by the luggage while Bryan checked them into the hotel. And as she stood there, she imagined how the three of them must look to the people around them, like a normal family vacationing in the Florida sun. She hadn't seen herself in a picture like that before, and though it felt odd, it also felt good. Very good.

Maybe someday...

"Did you want to..." She turned to Nicki, only to find that the girl wasn't beside her anymore. She'd been there a couple of seconds ago.

Panicked, Jennifer flew around, scanning the massive hotel lobby. Her stomach settled back where it belonged when she saw Nicki, only a few feet away, gazing into the window of the gift shop. Jennifer looked beyond the girl to the blue plaid two-piece swimsuit hanging there. The top wasn't so much a bra as a crop top. It would look good on Nicki's burgeoning young figure. Nicki turned, and with one last glance over her shoulder, walked back to join Jennifer.

Bryan reached her at the same time.

"You can check in with Dennis as soon as we get to the room if you want to," he told her.

Jennifer hadn't given Teal Automotive a thought all morning. "Don't bug me, Chambers. I'm on vacation," she said, grinning at Nicki. "Besides, it's Sunday. Dennis doesn't work on Sundays."

"Only the chairman of the board does that, huh?" he asked. Jennifer stuck her tongue out at him for the second time that morning.

Nicki laughed. Bryan grinned at his niece and then looked back at Jennifer. "You can catch flies that way, you know."

Jennifer closed her mouth.

Bryan gave the bellboy their room number, arranging to have their luggage brought up, and then led them to the elevator.

"Who's ready to hit the beach?" he asked as they rode up to their suite.

"I could stand a few hours of that," Jennifer said. She couldn't believe how good it sounded to do something so lazy.

Nicki seemed to be way too interested in the advertisement for the hotel dining room that hung on the elevator wall.

"How about you, Nick? You ready to take on the waves?"

Nicki shrugged.

"What's the matter? You were always the one begging to get down to the water," Bryan said, frowning.

"I know." Nicki ran her fingers over the buttons on the control panel.

"You wanted to come to the beach, Nick. What'd you think we'd do once we got here?"

"I don't know."

Bryan looked at Jennifer, obviously perplexed. Jennifer started to panic. If he didn't know how to handle the situation, what were they going to do? *She* certainly had no idea what had changed Nicki's mood so suddenly, and no suggestion for how to make things better.

The elevator stopped and the doors opened on their floor. Jennifer followed Bryan and his niece to the door of their suite, feeling horribly awkward and out of place. She wasn't good with children at the best of times, but dealing with them when there was a problem was simply beyond her.

Still, she had no desire to leave. Nicki was not a surly child. Something was bothering her. Jennifer wished she had a clue as to what it might be. She wished she didn't feel so damned inadequate.

The suite was spacious and open, with a living area large enough to house a family of six comfortably. It even had a kitchenette, complete with a two-burner stove and half-size refrigerator.

Nicki opened the refrigerator. "It's empty," she

said, sounding disappointed as she shut it again and then peered into the cupboard.

"We can make a grocery run if you like, and make you the official cook," Bryan offered, grinning at her.

Nicki looked like an angel as she grinned back at him. "Don't bug me, Uncle Bryan. I'm on vacation," she said.

Jennifer started to relax again.

Her room, complete with its own bathroom, was too big for one person, but luxuriously appointed, and as soon as the bellboy delivered their luggage, Jennifer took a couple of minutes to hang her clothes and set out her toiletries.

It was as she put her swimsuit out on the bed that it hit her. Nicki had been looking at that suit in the shop window downstairs. She'd even glanced back at it as she'd walked away. And it had been Bryan's question about going down to the beach that had brought about the sudden mood change. *And just that morning at breakfast, Nicki had told her about Bryan wanting her to dress like a little girl.* Though the suit she'd been looking at in the lobby had been appropriate for a girl Nicki's age, it would definitely not make her look like a little girl. But Jennifer would bet a month's profits that whatever Nicki had brought with her would.

Jennifer remembered herself at that age. She remembered how painfully shy she'd been about the changes taking place in her body, how self-conscious she'd felt about her looks, how desperately eager she'd been for any word of praise. And how hard it had been when none had been forthcoming.

Collecting her wallet, she went back to the living room. Bryan was there, opening curtains to the ocean view.

"I'm going to run downstairs for a second," she said. "I'll be right back."

She hurried out the door before he could ask her where she was going. She had a hunch she could solve Nicki's problem, and she didn't want him stopping her.

The blue plaid suit was still in the window, and the clerk directed Jennifer to a whole rack of identical ones in various sizes. She had to guess at Nicki's size, but with her description and the clerk's help, she was pretty sure she found a suit that would fit. She handed over her credit card and didn't even bother to look at the slip as she signed it. She didn't care how much the suit cost. She could afford it. And even if she hadn't had more money than she knew what to do with, she'd have bought it, anyway. It was that important.

Barely ten minutes after she'd left, she was back in the living room of the suite, bag in hand and nervous as a wet hen. What if she was way off the mark? What made *her* think she knew what Nicki needed?

"Did you find what you went after?" Bryan asked, coming in from his bedroom.

"Yes. Where's Nicki?"

"Still in her room, I guess." Bryan walked over

and knocked on his niece's door. "You okay in there, Nick?"

The girl's "yeah" came muffled through the door.

Aware of Bryan's curious scrutiny, Jennifer walked over to Nicki's closed door. "Are you decent, Nicki? Can I come in for a minute?" The bag was slipping from her sweaty fingers and she rolled it up further, tightening her grip.

Nicki opened her door, standing to one side. "Sure," she said. She was still wearing the shorts and T-shirt she'd worn on the plane. She shut the door behind Jennifer.

"I brought you something," Jennifer said, handing Nicki the bag before she chickened out.

Nicki grinned. "Me? What is it?" she asked, looking inside the bag.

"Oh, Ms...I mean, Jennifer," Nicki said, looking from the bag to Jennifer and back again. "How'd you know? Oh, thank you!" She threw her arms around Jennifer in a hug. Jennifer felt like a starving woman brought to a feast.

Nicki finally pulled back. "I can't believe you got the one I wanted the most," she said, pulling the suit out of the bag.

"Why don't you go try it on?" Jennifer suggested, smiling at Nicki's eagerness.

Nicki looked up, her eyes alarmed. "Do you think Uncle Bryan will like it?" she whispered, as if only now realizing that her uncle was just in the next room.

"I'm sure he will," Jennifer said, crossing her fingers behind her back. She had about two minutes to convince Bryan Chambers that he had to like Nicki's new swimsuit. She figured that was about how long it was going to take Nicki to get into it.

He was standing just outside Nicki's bedroom door waiting for her. ''You heard?'' Jennifer asked.

He nodded, seeming not the least bit repentant for his eavesdropping. ''How *did* you know?'' he asked softly.

Jennifer and Bryan moved farther away from Nicki's door and into the middle of the living room. ''I saw her staring at it downstairs. But I wouldn't have figured it out if she hadn't said something to me at breakfast this morning.''

Bryan followed her over to the window, his hands in the pockets of his shorts. ''What was that?''

Jennifer glanced up at him, this man whose biggest strength was his love for the child in his care. ''She says you want her to keep looking like a little girl even though her body's starting to grow up. She thinks it makes her ugly.''

Bryan frowned, looking toward Nicki's door. ''She said that?''

''Maybe not in those exact words, but I knew how she felt. My mom was still buying me undershirts when I was fifteen.''

''So that's why she didn't want to go down to the water.''

Jennifer nodded. ''I think so. Please tell her you like it, Bryan, even if you don't. Your opinion means so much to her right now.''

Bryan ran his fingers through Jennifer's hair, then

cupped her face with his palms. "I think I could get used to having you around, Jennifer Teal," he said, and dipped his head to kiss her.

Jennifer gave herself up to the heady feeling his kisses always brought her, welcoming the thrust of his tongue against hers, wishing he could hold her like that forever.

She pulled away from him at the sound of Nicki's door opening.

"Do you like it?" The girl walked out into the living room, her arms crossed over her chest, her eyes darting everywhere but at her uncle. Her gaze finally landed on Jennifer's smiling face.

"You're going to be the death of me in that thing, you know," Bryan said. Nicki's gaze flew to him, her eyes anxious until she saw the grin on his face.

"I can keep it?" she asked him, dropping her arms.

"You can keep it."

Nicki ran to him, throwing her arms around him with the exuberance of a normal twelve-year-old. "I love you, Uncle Bryan."

"And I love you, sprite."

Jennifer swallowed a lump in her throat as she stood apart from them, knowing that the moment they shared was one forged through years of getting through the good and the bad together, as a family. A family she wanted to be a part of more than she'd ever wanted anything in her life.

THEY SPENT almost every hour at the beach that day and the two succeeding ones, taking turns playing in the waves and lying on towels on the sand. Bryan spent a lot of time with Nicki in the water, swimming out to the buoys with her, dunking her in the waves, until Nicki enlisted Jennifer's help and the two of them together did their best to force Bryan's head underwater a time or two. They were successful, sort of. Not wanting to fail Nicki and seeing failure as imminent, Jennifer finally resorted to dirty pool and grabbed Bryan intimately under the water. He was so shocked he stopped struggling long enough for Nicki to finally succeed in dunking him. Jennifer was well out of reach by the time he resurfaced.

But her body sang with anticipation when his gaze met hers across the water promising retribution. Later.

They went sailing the second afternoon and had dinner at a different restaurant in the hotel every night. Each evening they went back out to the beach after dinner to listen to the band the hotel had hired to play there. They stayed outside until Nicki was ready to turn in, and Bryan was encouraged when he noticed that each night she stayed up a little bit later.

And each night, after his niece went to bed, Bryan played with fire. He pulled Jennifer down to the couch with him, holding her in his arms, touching the body that all day, in the sleek, black one-piece suit, had driven him crazy. And when he'd nearly driven himself crazy with desire, he'd lose himself in her kisses.

All in all, Bryan figured their time at the beach was about as perfect as a vacation could be, with the exception of the constant misery his body was suffering. Holding and kissing Jennifer was not enough. He needed to make love to her. And he couldn't. Not until he told her the truth about her and Nicki.

And he couldn't do that until they were back home, where they wouldn't be forced to stay together if her reaction to his duplicity was as bad as he feared it might be. Where she'd be free to take some time away to assimilate the facts, adjust to them. He just hoped to God that when she calmed down, when she listened rationally to his explanations, she'd have a big enough heart to understand.

He was no longer worried about how Nicki would fare. Jennifer obviously adored her.

CHAPTER THIRTEEN

NICKI WAS INVITED to play volleyball during their last day at the beach, and Bryan was so delighted to see her having a good time with kids her own age that he let her stay out a bit longer than he should have. By dinnertime it appeared she'd had too much sun, and she was complaining of an upset stomach.

Jennifer helped by rubbing aloe cream on Nicki's burned skin and convincing the girl to eat most of a bowl of chicken soup. Nicki finally fell asleep around six-thirty, and knowing that sleep was the best thing for her, Jennifer and Bryan closed her door and left her alone.

Bryan called room service, ordering a bottle of wine to accompany their filets and baked potatoes. He had the waiter set the whole thing up out on their balcony, which faced the beach. He didn't want to take a chance on waking Nicki.

The hotel was having a bonfire on the beach that night, and Jennifer's face glowed from the muted light of the flames as she sat across from him at the small wrought-iron table. She was wearing a white halter dress that looked incredible against her newly acquired tan. Bryan could barely keep his eyes off her.

They ate and talked about Nicki, about places they'd traveled, about the tornado that had taken Bryan's family and the car accident that had taken Jennifer's. They even talked about some of the people they could see below them on the beach, deciding that one couple were newlyweds and another on their second honeymoon. Bryan, trying to get a rise out of Jennifer, suggested that the second couple was really a married man on an illicit tryst with his secretary, but Jennifer point-blank refused to have any part of his potentially unhappy scenario.

And before he knew it, the food was all gone, and there wasn't a drop of wine left in the bottle. But he wasn't ready for the evening to end.

"I think I saw a bottle of wine in the minibar. Would you like another glass?" he asked Jennifer.

Her slow sensual smile just about brought him to his knees. "I've probably had enough already, but yes, one more glass sounds good. It's so lovely out here. I'm not ready to go in yet."

Bryan opened the bottle and filled their glasses. "I just looked in on Nicki, and she's still sound asleep."

"I know. I looked, too, when I went in before."

Bryan wasn't sure just when their conversation filtered away, or why he was torturing himself by touching her soft silky hand where it lay on the table, but there was no mistaking the invitation in her eyes. Or the way his body was responding to it.

"I think I've had more wine than was wise," he said, his gaze locked on hers in the darkness.

"I *know* I have. But I still want to make love with you, Bryan Chambers. I have for a very long time."

His body throbbed with her words. "It's just the wine talking," he said, trying to hold on to the thin thread of sanity he had left. "It has a tendency to make you think that way."

She smiled and shook her head. "Not me it doesn't. I've tried it a time or two, you know. I've tried to get in the mood, to let myself go, to enjoy a perfectly normal adult experience, but it never worked, no matter how much wine I drank."

"Never?" he asked, his eyes intent. "Are you telling me you haven't…"

"Not since I was fifteen," she whispered. Her eyes were moist as she held his gaze, but they were full of such conviction, such pure sweet wanting, that Bryan knew he was a drowning man. And he didn't care. Satisfying the desire in her eyes was worth dying for.

He pulled her up and into the suite, turning off the living-room light as he led her into her bedroom, which was on the opposite side of the suite from his and Nicki's.

Her bare back was a golden lure of femininity as she entered her room in front of him. She took a long look at the huge bed in the center of the room, then looked back at him. He thought he saw fear in her eyes, but it was quickly replaced by the fire that had been glowing from within her all evening.

"Are you sure?" he asked, trailing his fingers down her neck.

"Absolutely sure."

He pulled her against him, letting her feel how ready his body was for her before they'd even begun. "I've never wanted a woman like I want you."

"I think I knew that," she whispered, flicking her tongue along his neck. "I've never wanted a man before, period."

Bryan knew that what she was telling him was important, that he needed to understand certain things about her, but all he could think about right then was making the night ahead everything she'd ever dreamed of. He didn't just want her to want him now, he wanted her to want him afterward, too. Desperately.

And maybe, if he could show her how much he cared for her, she'd be forgiving when he told her what he'd done, why they'd met....

He pulled the pins from her hair one by one, watching as the long auburn curls fell down past her shoulders and over his arm.

"It's a crime to keep this all tucked away," he said, running his hands through the silky strands, imagining it over him, around him, beneath him.

"Long tangly hair doesn't fit my image."

He buried his face against her neck. "It fits the image I have of you perfectly."

"Oh? And how do you see me?" she asked, leaning back to grin at him as she tugged gently at the rubber band on his ponytail.

But Bryan saw the flicker of apprehension in her eyes in spite of the grin. She really needed to know and was afraid of knowing at the same time. Incredible.

He smoothed the hair back from her face, cradling her head between his hands, caressing her cheeks with his thumbs. "I see you as a siren and an innocent, as a strong capable woman and yet one I want to take care of."

Her gaze held his as she reached up to him, running her fingers through the shorter hair on the sides and top of his head, to the longer strands in the back that hung freely past his shoulders. "You are the man of my dreams, Bryan Chambers," she whispered. "I don't know what I've ever done to deserve you, but I can't not love you. I tried, but I just can't."

His heart plummeted, and then sped up, reminding him of his first roller-coaster ride. Adrenaline surged through him. "Then stop trying," he said, and kissed her. *She loves me,* he thought. It was all that mattered in those moments as his lips laid claim to hers. *She loves me.*

Jennifer had no idea where this night might lead. She was afraid to think of the future, to consider the fact that Bryan might want to marry her, that he might even want to have other children someday. She didn't know if she'd be strong enough to turn him down; or was the real strength in accepting him? She didn't have the answers anymore, but she knew, clear to her soul, that the present was right where it should be. She was where she belonged—in Bryan's arms.

He looked like a heathen, a pirate, as he bent over her, his hair creating shadows around him in the dim light of her bedroom. His black cotton pants and T-shirt added to the illusion, and Jennifer shivered with the excitement this man could raise in her.

His lips devoured hers, his kisses different than they'd ever been before, harder, more determined, and the more he asked of her, the more she gave him, the more she took. She couldn't seem to keep her hands off him, filled with a need to touch every part of him. His warm broad shoulders, his strong back, his lean, muscled buttocks.

"Lord, woman, what you do to me," he groaned, pressing her against him.

"The miracle is what you do to me," Jennifer said, giving him more than her body. She was laying her soul on the line for this man, and she hadn't a single regret. "I know all about sex. I know what goes where, how it all works. But never, ever, have I dreamed I could ever feel like this."

Bryan led her to the bed, unhooking the neck of her halter dress, turning her to face him, watching every inch of her as it slid away. "So what's the 'this' you're feeling, Jen?" he asked, touching the tip of one bared breast with his finger, gently, reverently.

She gasped. "Like I'm on fire. Like I'm going to die right here and now if you don't stop that and make love to me," she said, pulling his hand away from her breast. She was getting the most curious sensation in the pit of her stomach, as if she was going to collapse in a heap before they'd even begun.

Bryan's hand returned to her breast and kneaded it

tenderly. "But I am making love to you, Jen, body and soul."

She sank onto the bed, naked except for her white silk bikini panties, feeling not one moment of embarrassment as she lay before him. He was her man, her love. It was right that he see her.

She didn't think she could get any more turned on for him until he started to strip off his clothes. There was no playacting, no pretense, just a steady removing of material, a gradual revealing of such male perfection that her breath was snatched away. And when he loosened the drawstring at his waist and slid his cotton pants down over his hips, she was just plain shocked.

"You're not wearing any underwear!" she said, thinking how prudish she must sound.

"It's too constricting," he told her, completely comfortable with his nudity as he lay down beside her.

Jennifer was still too rattled from the first unexpected sight of his engorged manhood to belabor the point.

Bryan Chambers was a magnificent lover. His hands were everywhere, caressing her, giving her pleasure. She tensed when he found her scar, the only thing she had left of the baby she'd given birth to so long ago, but even that he touched reverently—as if it was special simply because it was a part of her.

Jennifer had had no idea she had so many erogenous zones, but he showed her every one of them and introduced her to a few of his own, as well. She was a willing, eager, if impatient pupil, but Bryan ignored her impatience, imploring her to trust him, to hold on.

"Let me show you how good this can be," he said when she was once again urging him to complete their union.

"If it gets any better than this, I'm not going to live through it," she murmured, smiling up at him. His face was so precious to her. She'd never loved anyone as she loved this man.

"Yes, you will. You're going to live long enough to do it again and again and again..." His words trailed off as he pushed himself slowly into her.

"Oh, my God," Jennifer groaned as she stretched to accommodate him, feeling finally some measure of completeness.

"Come with me, Jen. Let me take you on the wildest ride of your life."

"Isn't that where we are already?" she gasped as he moved within her.

"We haven't even left the ground yet, lady."

He reached down between them, touching Jennifer intimately and rotating his hips at the same time.

And as he continued to love her, tension built within Jennifer, her body holding him tighter and tighter as she fought to control the sensation.

"Come with me, babe. Come with me," he said.

Jennifer thought she'd break into a million pieces. She could hardly breathe. "I can't!" she cried, wishing he would never stop what he was doing to her, yet knowing she couldn't take much more.

"Yes, you can," he said, kissing her, his tongue

entering her in rhythm with his lower body. "Let go, Jen. I'll catch you," he said. His voice sounded as strained as she felt.

She did as he bid, giving herself up to him completely, letting go of the tenuous thread of her control. And as she exploded around him, as she accepted his climax within her, her soul cried out in triumph.

She lay beside him afterward, unable to muster enough strength to speak, let alone get up. She couldn't even work up the effort to wonder what he was thinking about as he lay silently holding her. She'd finally found the peace she'd been searching for. He hadn't "taken" her or "done it" to her. He'd made love with her. And by doing so, he'd given her back a measure of the dignity she'd lost so many years before. Rather than feeling worthless, she felt beautiful.

She thought he might have fallen asleep, until his hand shifted around her, cupping her breast, his finger slowly, almost aimlessly, tantalizing her nipple. She lay still, wondering if he was indeed asleep, if he was even aware of what he was doing. And then he shifted again, his other hand cupping her other breast, his penis nudging her.

Her stomach started fluttering and she felt herself grow moist. "Again?" she asked, giggling in spite of the tension slowly building within her.

"Again and again and again..." His voice sent excited chills down her body as he leaned over and took her nipple into his mouth.

BRYAN WAS at his drafting table by noon the next day. He'd barely made it back to his own room that morning in the hotel before the phone had rung. Calvin had the flu and wasn't going to be able to keep his appointment with Wonderly.

They'd planned to sleep in and fly back leisurely that morning, but Bryan had had to wake Jennifer and Nicki and hurry them out of the hotel a few hours earlier than planned. Or at least he'd hurried them after he'd woken Jennifer properly. Lovemaking with her was as good the morning after as it had been the night before.

The Wonderly president and his executives were flying in to sign the papers that would seal a big contract with Innovative Advertising based on the preliminary campaign Bryan had done for the company a few months before. Bryan only had another hour to go over the long-term campaign Calvin had mapped out for him before the group arrived.

He tried to concentrate on the Wonderly account, but moments from the night before and the morning after, with their passion and their promise, continued to play themselves out in his mind. He was impatient to get on with it, to know that things were settled once and for all, to finally introduce Nicki to her mother.

He'd invited Jennifer over for dinner that night and he was going to tell her who Nicki was before he took her home that evening. After the past several days with Nicki, there was no longer any doubt that Jennifer was good with children, or at least with

Nicki. Even Jennifer had to be settled on that score. There was no longer any need for secrets.

He was going to ask Jennifer to marry him.

The phone rang on his desk, bringing him back to the business at hand. "It's Nicki, Bryan," Jacci called through the door connecting their offices.

He snatched up the phone. "You feeling okay?" he asked. Nicki had been better that morning, but she hadn't eaten much and her skin had still been extremely sensitive. Jennifer had found a loose-fitting sundress for her to wear down in the gift shop.

Nicki giggled. He still wasn't used to hearing that sound. "Yes, Uncle Bryan, I'm fine. Jennifer's right, you know. You never do say hello."

"Hello doesn't mean anything." Bryan smiled. Jennifer had brought Nicki back to him. He was eager to give them to each other.

"It means hello, but I don't care if you don't say it. I love you just the way you are."

"I love you, too, Nick. The days at the beach were fun, weren't they?"

"Yeah." The way she said it left a huge "but" hanging there.

"So what's up? You sound like you got something on your mind."

"I just need to talk to you, that's all."

Bryan glanced at his watch. Wonderly was due in about twenty minutes. "Shoot."

"I don't know how to say it."

Bryan's gut clenched. Was there trouble in paradise

already? "Just like you always have, Nick. Just say it right out."

"Okay. You can quit looking for my other mother. I don't want to find her anymore."

Bryan froze. "What do you mean you don't want to find her? That's all you've talked about for ages. Why don't you want to find her?"

"'Cause I don't need her." His niece's soft words stopped him before he hollered at her. She couldn't mean this. Not now.

"How's that, Nick?"

"I just don't," she said. "Besides, the more I thought about it, the more I didn't ever want to meet her. I mean, she gave me away, you know?"

He felt the blood drain from his face. "Maybe she had a good reason." *Like being sixteen and alone, with parents who were never there for her.*

"I can't think of a good enough one. And anyway, she might not even want to meet me, and if she doesn't, I don't want to know."

"But what if she does, honey? What if she's been missing you all these years and would love to meet you?"

"It's okay, Uncle Bryan. I know what you're trying to do, letting me know it's okay to find her even though you don't want me to, but I'm not just saying this to make you happy. I've really changed my mind. You can call those people and tell them to stop looking. By the way, can I cook dinner again tonight? I wanna make spaghetti. That's easy."

Bryan's heart felt like lead. Food was the last thing

he cared about. "Sure. That'd be great, Nick. We'll see you around five-thirty, okay?"

"'Kay."

"I love you, sprite."

"I love you, too, Uncle Bryan. I gotta go now. Lucy's scratching to go out."

Bryan slammed the phone down. So much for paradise. Nicki didn't want to meet her mother. But after what he and Jennifer had shared at the beach, he still had to tell her the truth. His love for her demanded it. But now he was going to have to hurt her more in the telling. He was going to have to tell her that, for some reason, Nicki had changed her mind, that she no longer wanted to meet her birth mother. It might even spell the end to their relationship. Because his first priority was still Nicki. And if she refused to accept Jennifer, then he'd have to honor that decision.

Bryan was almost relieved when the Wonderly president called to say they were going to be a couple of hours later than planned. Their flight had been delayed. Damn. There was no way he was going to be out of here in time to make it home for dinner. He called Jennifer to cancel.

"I haven't told Nicki yet—she's planning to make spaghetti," he said, more tired than he could ever remember being. Though he knew it had very little to do with the near-sleepless night he'd spent.

"Then just tell her to go on ahead with her plans, and we'll have dinner just the two of us. If you're really nice, maybe we'll even save you some," she said, her tone making her words seductive enough to heat his blood.

"You'd better save me some, woman," he growled, foolishly thankful for the reprieve. One more night of loving her before everything blew up in his face.

"You can have it all, Bryan," she returned softly. "You know that."

"I'll call Nicki," he said before ringing off. It couldn't hurt to have Nicki spend some time alone with Jennifer in the real world. If his niece grew fond enough of Jennifer she wouldn't be able to turn her away.

"YOU GOT A MINUTE?" Jennifer pushed open the door to Dennis's office.

He set aside the papers in front of him. "Sure, what's up? Did you have a good time in Florida?"

"The best." Jennifer blushed.

Dennis grinned. "I see."

She sat down on the couch. "No, you don't see. I've got a problem."

"What?" He got up from his desk, coming around to the armchair across from her.

"I just had the best three days of my life, and I'm feeling so guilty I can barely look at myself in the mirror."

Dennis frowned. "Jennifer, if anyone deserves to be happy, it's you."

"It's not that so much. It's Nicki."

"What about her?"

"I think Bryan might ask me to marry him. That would make Nicki mine, too."

"You can handle it, Jen. You'll be a great mother to her."

She smiled sadly. "You know what? I finally believe that I might not be a half-bad mother, but no matter what I tell myself, I can't help feeling like scum for wanting to love Nicki when I abandoned my own child. I made this vow, you know, that night in the hospital when I gave my baby away. And the thing is, if I believe it doesn't mean anything and I don't have to uphold my part of the bargain, then I also have to believe nobody's been watching out for my baby all these years."

She sighed. "In my head I know I was just a child when I made that promise, that it's crazy to live my life based on such a ridiculous thing, but I just can't get beyond the fact that I promised my baby I'd never replace her, as long as she grew up happy." She paused. "As long as she didn't have to grow up with parents like mine."

"That's not very likely, Jen. There aren't many parents as selfish as yours, thank God."

Jennifer frowned. "They weren't selfish. They just didn't know anything about caring for a child."

Dennis swore, shocking Jennifer with the words coming out of his mouth. "No one's born with the knowledge, Jen. It's something you work at, learn as you go. Your parents were too wrapped up in themselves to even try. Maybe it's because you came so late in their lives, or maybe they were just too set in their ways, I don't know, but for whatever reason, they never made any concessions to having a child in their house.''

Tears sprang to Jennifer's eyes. "It wasn't like that.'' *Was it?*

"It was exactly like that. They always came first. Did they ever once take part in anything you did? Girl Scouts, dance recitals, birthday parties, anything where they had to do something just for you? Were you ever even allowed to laugh and make noise when they were home?''

"They were busy. They had the business to run. And when they were home, they were tired. They couldn't help being older than most parents.'' Her protests sounded weak even to her own ears.

Dennis shook his head in dismay. "When are you going to open your eyes, Jen? They failed you over and over again, and you always blamed yourself. And what about when you really needed them, when you gave birth? Hell, you were doing what they wanted— you were giving away the baby you already loved— and they still wouldn't take the time to help you through. After they signed the papers for you to have the C-section, they didn't even stick around until the baby was born. They went straight back to work. They never came to see you. They sent *me* to pick you up and take you home. It wasn't you who was lacking, honey, it was *them*.''

"They left? They didn't stay when I went into surgery?'' Jennifer was aghast.

"I thought you knew that,'' Dennis said, coloring.

"They left before I had the baby?"

"The doctor told them they wouldn't be allowed to see you for a while, and their manager had just walked out on them at the dealership," Dennis said, as if by trying to excuse them he could take away the pain he'd unwittingly caused her. "They left the dealership's phone number at the hospital with orders to call if they were needed."

Her face streaming with tears, Jennifer finally heard the things Dennis had been trying to tell her for years. Her parents had let *her* down, not the other way around.

Dennis crossed to the couch and put his arm around her. "You see?" he said. "It wasn't your fault you'd always been in their way. It was theirs."

"You really think so?" she asked.

"I know so, Jen. I was there, too, remember? I'd been working at Teal for over a year before you ever took up with Billy the Bastard. You were a victim back then, honey. It's time you saw it all like it really happened and forgave yourself for something you couldn't help. You were just a kid looking for love, trying to be happy in the only way you knew how."

Jennifer took the tissue he handed her. "But what about my baby?" she asked, tears still streaming down her face. "I can't love another woman's child or even have another child of my own until I know that my firstborn has all the love she needs."

"She's probably happy as a clam."

"I hope so. I've been counting on it every day for

twelve years. But I still don't feel free to love another child until I know for certain. It's crazy, isn't it?"

Dennis squeezed her shoulder. "So what're you going to do?"

"I don't know." She couldn't look at him.

"I think you do, Jen. It's time to quit running."

She turned to face him, sniffling and smiling at the same time. "I'm going to look for her, aren't I?" she asked. "I'm finally going to look for my daughter."

Dennis smiled, standing up and pulling Jennifer with him. "Yes, my friend, you're finally going to do what you've been aching to do since the minute you left the hospital without her."

Jennifer gazed warmly at Dennis. "You've always known, haven't you?"

He nodded.

"The reason I'm not married yet wasn't because I didn't have time. It was because I couldn't go on, I couldn't break that promise, until I was sure she had a happy life," she said, seeing things so clearly now.

"Probably."

Jennifer wiped her tears away and walked toward the door. "I've got some calls to make." She stopped with her hand on the doorknob and looked back. "Thanks, friend."

"Don't thank me, Jen. You figured it out all by yourself."

"I don't just mean now. I mean for always."

"Go make your phone calls," Dennis said, stepping back behind his desk. She'd embarrassed him, but she'd pleased him, too. She could tell by the color in his cheeks. It gave him away every time. But she kept the knowledge to herself as she left to go call her lawyer. *Baby Doe, here I come.*

CHAPTER FOURTEEN

"IS THERE ANYTHING I can do to help?" Jennifer asked as Nicki led her into the kitchen later that afternoon with Lucy underfoot. Bryan's house smelled like an Italian restaurant.

"Nope. We have to eat in here 'cause Uncle Bryan's model stuff is all over the dining-room table."

Jennifer grabbed the plates and silverware Nicki had put out on the counter and placed them at the table. "What kind of models?" she asked, bending down to scratch Lucy behind the ears.

"Toy ones. Radio-controlled airplanes mostly." Nicki pulled a pan of bread sticks out of the oven. "He says it helps him think and he has to do that a lot for his work. Sometimes they get really big. You should see the thing he made when he first started working for you." Her smile was infectious.

"Mammoth, huh?" Jennifer asked with a grin, glad to know she'd been important to him even then.

Nicki nodded. "I'll say. It's in his bedroom and it takes up half the room."

"He keeps it in his bedroom?"

"Yeah, that's when I knew you were different.

Usually he flies them a little bit and then gives them away to the children's hospital or to families who don't have enough money at Christmastime or something. But he kept this one. And Uncle Bryan never keeps anything,'' she said, sounding conspiratorial. ''Until he got me he never even owned any furniture.''

Nicki tossed the spaghetti noodles with a little butter, put them in a casserole dish and ladled sauce over them, then carried the dish to the table.

''You do that very well,'' Jennifer said, impressed.

''Thanks. My mom loved pasta. We used to have it almost every night.'' She took the salad she'd prepared earlier out of the refrigerator. Jennifer looked at the bowl as Nicki set it on the table. It was nothing but lettuce. She hid a smile, glad to see that Nicki still did some things like a kid.

''You must miss your mom a lot,'' she said as Nicki sat down across from her.

''Yeah, I do. My dad, and my grandma and grandpa, too. But Uncle Bryan's great. I used to wish sometimes I could live with him, you know. He'd come and visit us, and I'd have the best time ever and then miss him like crazy when he left.''

''I can understand that. He's not someone who goes unnoticed, is he?''

''Nope. He's the best. But sometimes...'' Nicki hesitated, looking down as she wound spaghetti around her fork.

''Sometimes what?'' Jennifer asked, smiling, encouraging Nicki to confide in her.

"Well, sometimes it's hard, you know, just living with an uncle. I mean he's a *man*."

Jennifer thought of the little-girl swimsuit Nicki had been embarrassed to wear. "Men don't always catch on to things, honey, but your uncle has a great set of ears. You just need to talk to him."

Nicki looked up at Jennifer, her eyes filled with conviction. "There are some things a girl just can't talk to a man about."

"I think your uncle's pretty open-minded." Jennifer was surprised how important it was to her to defend Bryan.

"It's just that…" Nicki hesitated again.

"What?"

She set down her fork. "I'm twelve years old now. My mom started her, you know, monthly stuff, when she was twelve."

Ah. Jennifer felt rather obtuse when she finally realized what Nicki had been trying to tell her. And thrilled that the girl felt comfortable enough to talk to her about it. She just wished she had a single clue about what to say. Her own mother had never talked about such things. Jennifer had learned it all from her friends' somewhat exaggerated accounts, and what they hadn't told her, she'd found out for herself.

"I guess it would be kind of hard to bring up with your uncle," she conceded.

"I'll say." Nicki took a big bite of salad—without dressing.

Jennifer did the same, taking comfort in the fact

that she and Bryan's niece had something in common besides Bryan.

"I mean, I can't ask him to pick up stuff for it on his way home from work."

Jennifer smiled as she imagined just that. "Have you been feeling any different lately?" she asked, still not sure how to proceed. Should she offer to buy Nicki her supplies? Should she tell her how to use them?

"Nah. I had a stomachache one day, and I was a little scared...but it went away. And it's not like just because my mom had it when she was twelve that *I* will."

"You're right to wonder, though. A lot of times girls do take after their mothers."

"Not me. I guess Uncle Bryan didn't tell you. I was adopted."

Jennifer dropped her fork. *Adopted? This child was adopted?*

"You were?" she asked, picking up her fork, trying to rebalance herself.

"Yep."

Jennifer's mind reeled with questions. There were so many things she wanted to know. "Did you like it? Being adopted, I mean?"

"Yep. It was great. I never had to wonder if my parents really wanted me, you know? They picked me out specially. I have this friend back in Shallowbrook, Sally Sanderson. She was a mistake, and her parents had to get married because of her and everything, and all they did was fight all the time until her dad finally just walked out. And Sally always thought it was her fault and if only she'd never been born her mom would be more happy. *My* mom always used to say that my birthday was the best day of the year because if I'd never been born she'd never have been so happy. We used to have a big party every year, and Mom and Dad would make a toast to the woman who gave me to them, thanking her for our happy family..." Nicki's voice wobbled and she took another bite of spaghetti.

"It's okay to cry, honey. It's okay to miss them," Jennifer said, rubbing Nicki's arm, praying her own daughter had found such a loving family.

Nicki sniffled and nodded. "I try not to because it gets Uncle Bryan mad at me."

"Oh, no, Nicki! Not mad. He doesn't want you to keep everything bottled up inside. Men are just funny about tears. Especially if they're crying inside themselves."

Nicki looked up. "You think Uncle Bryan cries?"

"I'm sure of it, Nicki. He lost his family, too, and he hurts every bit as much as you do."

"But he seems so strong all the time, just goes on making jokes and stuff."

"What else would you have him do? Curl up and die? Your mom and dad and grandparents wouldn't want that, would they?"

"No. I guess not."

"And besides, he's got *you* to think of. He wants to make your life happy."

"Did he say that?" Nicki's fork hung suspended in midair.

"He talks about you all the time, Nicki. You're his life now. He'd do anything for you, don't you know that?"

Nicki shrugged. "I guess. I just don't want to bug him."

"You make him happy, Nicki. Never doubt that."

"I think *you* do, too," Nicki said, taking her empty plate to the sink. "Hey. You wanna see some pictures of my mom and stuff? The albums are in a cupboard in Uncle Bryan's office."

"Sure. Let's just do these dishes first so your uncle doesn't come home to a mess."

"Now you sound just like my mom," the girl grumbled, but she was grinning as she cleared the rest of the table.

Half an hour later they sat on the couch with the photo album open between them. Jennifer was anxious to see Bryan's family, the people who meant so much to him, the people she'd never get to meet. There were pictures of him, too, as a baby, a toddler, a schoolboy, a young man. He looked a lot like his dad.

"Grandpa was a doctor," Nicki said, pointing to a picture of Bryan and his father on the steps of a hospital. "That was taken when they named the new wing at the hospital after him."

Bryan had never told her his father had been such an important man. But then, he wouldn't have. He'd only told her what he'd found significant, the good man, the good father, he'd been.

"Uncle Bryan dated every girl in school," Nicki

confided as they looked at yet another picture of Bryan, in blue jeans and tennis shoes, standing next to a beautiful girl all decked out in prom finery.

"It looks that way," Jennifer laughed, telling herself her pang of jealousy was absurd.

"Don't worry. The school was really small. Besides, Grandma said it was just because he liked to date, but he didn't want any of the girls getting any ideas about tying him down, so he never took any of them out more than once or twice. It used to drive her crazy. I wish she could've met you," Nicki said, smiling shyly at Jennifer.

Jennifer put her arm around the girl's shoulders and gave her a squeeze. "I wish I could meet her, too, Nicki, but at least I got to meet you."

"Yeah. Look, here's a picture of the Christmas we got Lucy for Mom and Dad."

"You and your grandparents?"

"Nope." Nicki shook her head, her long auburn hair tickling Jennifer's arm. "Me and Uncle Bryan. He flew me to Atlanta one Saturday when Mom thought he was taking me to the movies in town, and we picked Lucy out together. He had to keep her, though, for a whole week before he came for Christmas. She chewed a hole in the wall of his apartment and he had to pay to have it fixed." Nicki giggled.

"I'll bet he wasn't too pleased with Lucy then."

"I don't think he minded too much. Uncle Bryan doesn't care about *things* that much. At least he laughed when he told Mom and Dad about it. 'Course, Lucy was theirs then."

Nicki turned the page and was silent for the first time since Jennifer had walked in the door that evening. It was obviously Lori's wedding picture. She'd been a beautiful bride with long hair, dark like Bryan's, and big brown eyes. Her dress looked like something out of a designer shop with its layers of silk and lace and beads. She was also obviously very much in love with her husband, and he with her.

A single tear fell onto the page.

"Oh, sweetie," Jennifer said, her throat thick as she hugged the girl.

"It's my m-m-mom," Nicki said, and started to sob. "I m-m-miss her so much."

"I know, honey, I know," Jennifer said, rocking the child back and forth.

She didn't even try to offer any platitudes to soothe Nicki. There were none.

Nicki's sobs tore at Jennifer's heart. She wished there was something she could do, some way to make it better. She felt so helpless sitting there, allowing the girl to hurt so badly. And all the while Nicki cried, Lucy paced worriedly around the couch.

"Sorry," Nicki finally said, wiping her face with the back of her hands.

"Don't apologize, honey. Anytime you need a shoulder, I'm here."

Nicki set the photo album back on their laps. "It's just that she was always so happy, you know, so bouncy and stuff. I never thought of her not being here." She bent over to pull Lucy up on the couch beside her.

"Of course you didn't, sweetie. No one did. But I meant what I said. Anytime you want a woman to talk to, you can come to me, okay?"

"But you're so busy, being so important with your work and all."

"My business is just that, Nicki, business. It isn't life." And for the first time since she'd taken over her parents' business, Jennifer knew that to be true.

"Okay," Nicki said.

She turned the page and giggled again. "Look, here's a picture of me as a baby. It was taken in the hospital right after I was born. They gave it to my mom when she came to get me..."

Nicki continued to talk, but Jennifer couldn't hear her for the roaring in her ears. She felt like she was going to be sick.

She stared at the picture on her lap in total disbelief. How had it gotten there? That wasn't Lori's picture. It was hers. Only hers. She'd cherished that picture for twelve years, carried it with her everywhere she went, every hour of every day.

"Are you okay, Jennifer?" Nicki asked. "You don't look so good."

Jennifer didn't know if it was the concern in the girl's voice or the way Nicki jumped up off the couch that made her realize she wasn't alone. But she needed to be alone. Immediately. She couldn't believe that picture in that album. She had to leave. To breathe. To think.

"I'm sorry, Nicki. I—I'm not feeling well. I think maybe I better go home."

"But you don't have to leave! You can lie down on Uncle Bryan's bed."

Uncle Bryan's bed. Bryan knows. He's probably always known.

"Excuse me..." Jennifer ran for the bathroom and promptly lost her dinner. Her stomach heaved with such spasms she thought she might die, she hoped she might, but when it was finally over, she was left with nothing but numbness. Blessed mind-healing numbness.

When Jennifer finally emerged from the bathroom, Nicki was pacing worriedly outside the door, Lucy right beside her. "You okay? It was the spaghetti. I just know I did something to it."

Jennifer couldn't look at the child. She wasn't prepared. She wasn't ready. God help her, she wasn't strong enough to handle it. But neither was she going to allow the girl to blame herself for something completely out of her control. She'd done enough of that herself.

"It wasn't the dinner, honey, or you'd be sick, too. I wasn't feeling very well this afternoon, but I thought it had passed. I just need a good night's sleep and I'll be fine in the morning." Jennifer grabbed her things and headed for the door.

"Do you really have to go? I know Uncle Bryan would want you to stay," Nicki said, still sounding worried.

Bryan. He had so much to answer for. Had it all been an act, then? And for what? What had driven him to use her like this? To be so cruel. And she'd hoped he *loved* her. Just as she'd hoped Billy had, and Tommy. Oh, God, she couldn't go through it all again.

"I'll call him when I get home, honey. Promise me you'll lock up after me?" She had no idea where she got the composure to answer the child.

"I promise." Nicki was standing just inside the door. "Hope you feel better."

"I will," Jennifer said, all but running to her car.

Two blocks from Bryan's house she stopped to put down the top on her convertible. She needed more air.

The picture was in someone else's photo album. Nicki's photo album. Her picture. Of her baby.

She pulled onto the expressway, pressing the accelerator to the floor. The warm night air hit her skin, numbing her as she drove, going somewhere, anywhere, she didn't care. She didn't care about anything. She couldn't care. She didn't dare.

Until she found herself in the parking lot of Innovative Advertising. Then, suddenly, when she knew she'd be facing Bryan in a few short moments, she cared. Far too much. The pain rose to choke her again as she thought of his duplicity. But only for a second. Then the familiar numbness was back, sealed into place.

The outer door was unlocked and Jennifer pulled it open, welcoming the cool air as she stepped into the deserted lobby. She heard Bryan talking and headed toward the sound of his voice, the only door with a light shining beyond it. She walked into the room, his office, judging by the sketchbooks lying around. He was on the phone. He turned when he heard her, his face lighting up when he saw who was there.

His face lit up for *her*. As if she really mattered to him. She saw his eyes skim over her body, saw his look change from welcoming, to slumberous, to the heated sensuality that had melted her blood. A sudden mind-destroying pain ripped through her. He'd used her.

"She's mine," she said, grasping for the numbness that was going to get her through the next hours, the next years.

Bryan spoke hastily into the phone.

"Nicki's mine." She hardly dared say the words. She approached Bryan's drafting table. "Tell me."

He hung up the phone, his eyes worried as he tried to take her in his arms. But it was the guilt she saw flash across his face that was her undoing. Standing right there, in the middle of his office, she fell apart.

Tears streamed down her face as she lashed out at him, hitting him on the shoulders, the chest. "She's mine, isn't she?" she cried. "Isn't she?" She didn't even recognize the shrill voice that screamed at him.

Bryan grabbed her arms, but she kept hitting him. "Yes."

He spoke softly, yet the word slammed into her with the force of a blast. Burning up with pain, she slapped him and then turned to run back out the way she'd come.

Bryan grabbed her before she made it to the door. He tried to hold her, to soothe her.

"Don't touch me." Her voice was cold, foreign.

He dropped his hands immediately.

It was that more than anything else that finally reached Jennifer, the way he did as she said without question, as if he respected her right to be left alone. She sank onto the only chair in his office, put her head in her hands and sobbed. It just didn't make sense. The world had lost its mind. Nothing went together.

Nicki was hers. That adorable, precious, beautiful girl was hers. Her *daughter*.

And Bryan had betrayed her. He'd used her. In the basest way possible.

He stood in the middle of the room, silently. She sensed him there, but she couldn't reach him. He was outside her personal storm. He'd caused it.

"She has my hair," Jennifer finally said. She looked out the window behind his drafting table.

"And your eyes." His voice was thick, hoarse.

Jennifer's gaze flew to him, her heart aching when she saw the raw emotion he wasn't bothering to hide. But he'd betrayed her.

"Why?" she finally whispered.

"She wanted to find you, *had* to find you. She was losing her grip and no one could reach her. I had her to doctors, to counselors—nothing helped. I was afraid of suicide. She wasn't interested in anything— except finding you."

Jennifer swallowed as a fresh flood of tears trickled down her face. Her poor baby. She'd suffered so much. And she was so young.

"So you found me."

"It wasn't easy, but yes, after six weeks of professional searching, I found you."

Six weeks of professional searching. He'd been mighty determined. But then, so would she have been in his position.

"That night at the gallery..."

He nodded. "I knew."

"And the campaign..."

"My 'in' with you."

At least he wasn't trying to worm his way out of any of it. Jennifer remembered how easily she'd fallen in with his plan, how easily she'd fallen, period. She felt sick again.

"Why?" she asked.

She saw by the look on his face that he knew exactly what she was asking.

"A rejection would very probably have been the last straw for her. I saw how you avoided kids. Listened when you told me you weren't any good with them. I didn't have a choice but to wait until something changed."

"You could've told me."

"What, and have you go to her? Have you explain who you were, let her know it was nothing against her, it was just you, but that you didn't want her? Hell, as conscientious as you are, I could see you setting up some bank account for her, providing generously for her, while withholding the one thing she really wanted—you. And all because you didn't believe in yourself. You'd have thought you were doing her a favor. But she wouldn't have seen it that way at all.''

Jennifer felt the blood drain from her face as she realized the truth of his words. He knew her well. And a month or two ago, she really might have done what he'd just said. Because she hadn't believed in herself, not outside Teal Automotive. Until their trip to the beach, she probably *would* have thought she didn't have anything to offer Nicki but her money.

He took a step toward her, but stopped when she drew farther back in the chair.

''Think about it, Jen. If I'd told you from the beginning who I was, what I wanted, would you have agreed to meet Nicki and get to know her?''

His hands clenched inside his pockets. She stared at the bulge of his knuckles, focusing on them, as if seeing only them could make the rest go away.

''I don't know,'' she finally whispered. But she had a feeling she did know. As much as she'd have wanted to be there for Nicki, she wouldn't have believed herself capable of helping any child, let alone an emotionally disturbed one. But she'd have insisted on providing for Nicki, just as he'd predicted.

''I wasn't sure, either, and I couldn't take that chance. You didn't know her then, Jen. She did nothing but sleep and cry and have nightmares. She couldn't have handled another blow. I could've lost her. She was putting everything on the hope of finding her birth mother.''

And Jennifer had believed herself to be anything but mother material.

"I guess I should thank you for hanging in there long enough to show me that I could be for her what she needed me to be."

"It's what you needed, too."

Jennifer conceded the point with a bowed head.

Bryan knelt in front of her, close, but not touching her. "I intended to tell you, Jen, tonight when I picked you up for dinner. I want to marry you. I want for the three of us to be a family."

Jennifer couldn't bear to hear the words. They were a mockery of all she'd been foolishly hoping for such a short time before. "That would be convenient, wouldn't it?" she asked.

Bryan looked taken aback. "What do you mean?"

"If you really loved me, *me,* not Nicki's mother, how could you make love to me without truth between us? The rest I can understand, but not that."

"I didn't intend for that to happen."

Rather than soothing her, his words only deepened her wound. *She'd* intended so much for *that* to happen that she'd cold-bloodedly walked into a store and purchased the birth control that would allow it to happen. He hadn't intended it at all.

"What was it—the wine?" she asked. "No, don't answer that. It's bad enough that our relationship had so little significance that you were willing to risk it like this. You know me well, Bryan, very well. Did you honestly think I wouldn't care about having sex when there were still lies between us?"

"No."

"But you made love to me, anyway, making a

mockery of what we were sharing." She stood up, brushing by him. "Damn you!" She turned, her look strong enough to kill. "I gave you everything…" She was horrified when she started to cry again. The man didn't deserve her tears.

He had no words to defend himself. He stood before her, proud, tall—and guilty as hell.

"It's all so clear to me, you know," she said, her voice soft now, sad. *He can't help what he is.*

"Then maybe you'll explain it to me, because I can't think of a single way to help you understand that what I feel for you is completely separate from the fact that you're Nicki's mother."

He almost got her with that. Almost, but not quite. Even then, even when everything was resting on it, he hadn't told her what, exactly, he *did* feel. He still hadn't told her he loved her.

"You're a rebel, Bryan, a wanderer. You need your freedom like the rest of us need air to breathe. When you got Nicki you lost that, didn't you? You were cramped beyond your imagination by having the sole responsibility for an emotionally distressed child. So you meet me, you find me attractive and, bingo, you have your solution. Marry me, and you've got an instant mother for Nicki, someone who'd obviously feel bound to take on that responsibility since she's partly mine, and in the process relieve you of some of the responsibility that's choking you."

"It wasn't like that."

"Then how was it?" She wished she could believe it was anything else.

"I don't know," he said.

Bryan racked his brain for something, anything, that would prove the lie to her words, but he couldn't find it. He was ashamed to wonder if maybe there was an iota of truth in Jennifer's words. Maybe the reason he'd never felt claustrophobic with their relationship was because, subconsciously, he had seen it as a means to an end all along. He didn't believe he was capable of such a course of action, but she'd hit a raw spot. His track record gave too much truth to her words.

"Answer me this," Jennifer said. "If you didn't have Nicki, would you still be asking me to marry you?"

He could tell her yes. He might even be able to convince her. But could he live with her, could he live with *himself,* if he wasn't sure? His life had changed so much in the past year he wasn't sure of anything anymore.

"I don't know," he answered honestly. She deserved the truth. She always had.

She didn't say a word.

Weary, and feeling more alone than he'd ever felt in his life, he cleared up his office, wondering as he did if he'd ever see her there again, or if this was it, the one and only time she'd be there, standing silently, hating him. He didn't know how it had gotten so out of hand. He only knew that he felt it all slipping away.

CHAPTER FIFTEEN

"SO NOW WHAT?" Bryan looked at Jennifer in the darkness of the parking lot. She'd been silent the entire time he'd closed up his office and they'd walked down to their cars.

"I want to meet my daughter."

Bryan nodded. "I'll tell her tonight. Why don't you come by first thing in the morning?"

"I'm coming tonight."

He watched her open the door of the Mustang. Not only was it unlocked, she'd even left the top down. Damn! He'd never wanted to hurt her.

And he might not be done yet. "I'm not so sure that's a good idea, Jen. You're upset. She's bound to be upset. Let me talk to her first, and I'll give you a call tonight, no matter how late it is."

"She's my daughter. I'm coming with you."

I don't need her anymore, Uncle Bryan.

"Children don't take these kind of surprises well, honey. It threatens their security to have any major changes in their lives. They say things they don't mean—"

"And they have a million questions," Jennifer said, smiling bitterly. "See? I'm learning already. But in this case, Nicki has a right to her questions, and I'm the only one with the answers. It's not me I'm thinking of Bryan, it's Nicki. I'm coming with you."

"Okay. I'll follow you," Bryan said, unlocking the Jeep.

He pounded his hand on the steering wheel as he watched her pull out of the parking lot. He cursed the Fates that had brought him to this point, that had brought the two people he cared for to this point. His sense of foreboding was so strong it was strangling him, and there wasn't a damn thing he could do about it. He was following the woman he wanted to marry into hell, and he couldn't stop her.

Nicki met them at the front door. "Oh, Jennifer, I'm so glad you're back. Are you feeling better?"

"A little." Jennifer smiled weakly in Nicki's direction. She still looked sick and worried and scared out of her wits.

Banking on the fact that she wouldn't make a scene in front of Nicki, Bryan put his arm around her and led her into the living room. She needed someone to lean on whether she wanted to admit it or not, and at the moment, he was it.

"Come in here, Nick. We need to talk to you," Bryan said after settling Jennifer on the couch.

"What?" Nicki came in. That damn look was back in her eyes, the "frightened fawn with nowhere to run" look. "What's the matter with her? Is she going to be okay, Uncle Bryan?" Nicki's voice wobbled with tears.

"She's going to be just fine, honey." Leaving Jennifer, he crossed to Nicki, gave her a quick hug and led her to the couch. He sat her next to Jennifer. *Please, God, if you never hear another word I utter, hear these. Don't let this be the end. They need each other. And I need them.*Nicki looked from Bryan to Jennifer's bent head and back again. ''What's wrong?'' she asked, her fear evident.

And now that the moment was upon him, Bryan didn't have any idea what to say. How did you tell a twelve-year-old child that the woman she thought was her friend was really the mother she no longer wanted to meet?

''Well, Nick, it's like this. Remember when you asked me to—''

''I'm your mother.''

The bald words fell into the room, leaving a deafening silence in their wake.

Bryan watched Nicki, ready to grab her up and take her away from a situation she wasn't ready to handle. He wanted to take her to a place where only good things happened and children were always happy. She sat frozen, staring at Jennifer, a look of disbelief on her face. Jennifer's head was bowed, as if she couldn't bear to see the shock on her daughter's face. Nobody moved. Nobody said a word.

As if sensing that something was horribly wrong, Lucy ambled over to Nicki, nudged the girl's limp hand, then raised her paws to Nicki's knees.

Slowly, almost unconsciously, Nicki started to stroke the dog. Her movements grew faster, harder, until she buried her face in Lucy's fur and started to laugh.

What the hell?

Bryan's gaze met Jennifer's, their eyes identical pools of worry.

"I thought you said you were my mother," she said, speaking to Jennifer, but looking at the dog.

"I did." Jennifer's words were as gentle as a spring breeze.

But they didn't have a gentling effect on Nicki. "No!" the girl cried, jumping up. "You're not! You're wrong!" She burst into tears.

Bryan pulled the distraught child into his arms, rubbing her back, soothing her with the meaningless platitudes he'd spoken over and over to her during all the nightmares of the past year.

She looked up at him, her face streaming with tears. "Please, Uncle Bryan. I don't want her to be my mother. Please make her go away."

"Shh. It's okay, Nick. Calm down. It's okay." His gaze sought Jennifer's over Nicki's head. He'd never seen such raw pain. Dry-eyed, Jennifer was dying right before his eyes, and there was nothing he could do to help her.

"Come on, Nick, calm down," he said, his voice low.

"Make her go away, Uncle Bryan! I thought she was my friend. Make her leave. I don't ever want to see her again." Her words cut into Bryan. He could only imagine what they were doing to Jennifer.

"Shh. You don't mean that, honey. I think you half love her already."

"I don't. I hate her!"

"Nicki! Don't talk like that." His tone was rough now, reprimanding. No matter how upset she was, he couldn't allow her to go that far.

She jerked away from him. "Why not? It's true. And I hate you, too!" She turned and ran from the room. Bryan stood there in shock until he heard her bedroom door slam.

He looked over at Jennifer. She was staring at the hallway where Nicki had fled.

"I'm sorry," he said. "She's never acted like that before."

"It's not her fault." Jennifer's eyes were dead. "I don't blame her for hating me. It's what I expected."

Bryan sat down beside her, warming her cold hands between his own warmer ones. "She doesn't hate you, Jen. She loves you. She just needs some time."

Jennifer looked straight at him. "I gave her away." Her words, delivered in a lifeless monotone, cut him to the quick.

"You were barely sixteen!"

Jennifer shrugged off his defense of her and got to her feet. "She deserves to know the truth. If it's the only thing I can give her, at least there's that. I'll leave as soon as I'm finished."

"Jen, wait," Bryan said, but she'd left the room.

Dread filled his heart as he followed her down the hall.

"Go away." Nicki's muffled voice reached Bryan as he watched Jennifer enter her room.

"As soon as I've told you a few things." Jennifer's voice was firm, strong. He had a feeling it was the only thing about her that was.

Nicki was lying on her bed, her head buried under her pillow when he entered the room.

Jennifer was sitting on the bed beside her. She reached out, her hand hovering over Nicki's back before it slowly descended. Nicki flinched as Jennifer touched her. Jennifer's hand stilled, but she didn't remove it from Nicki's back. After a couple of seconds, she started to move it again, rubbing it slowly up and down the child's spine. Just as slowly, she started to speak.

"I made some major mistakes when I was growing up, Nicki, but none that I regretted as much as I did giving you up. But I was little more than a child myself when I had you. And a pretty mixed-up child at that."

Nicki lay as still as a statue, obviously listening to every word. Bryan swallowed, his throat thick as he watched mother and child, as he listened to the woman he loved lay herself open to the child who had just rejected her.

"You see, I didn't have the same kind of childhood you did. My parents didn't love me like yours loved you. I never felt special—just in the way. I was a mistake, like your friend Sally. My parents were already in their mid-forties when I came along, and I grew up as little more than an intrusion in their lives.

I spent the first fifteen years of my life trying to please them, but what I didn't realize was that my mere presence was displeasing to them, no matter what I did.'' Jennifer's voice wavered, and she stopped speaking for a moment, but she didn't stop touching her daughter.

Bryan watched that contact, suspecting that they both needed it more than either of them would be willing to admit.

"My parents forgot my fifteenth birthday. There was no celebration waiting when I got home from school, not even a card propped on the counter. So I waited for them to come home from work, thinking they were planning to take me out to dinner. I hoped it would be to one of those places where they bring you a little cake and sing 'Happy Birthday.' I really wanted that little cake.''

She smiled ruefully. "They didn't come. But Billy Wilson did. He was one of the most popular boys in school and we'd gone out a few times. I could hardly believe it when he said he actually wanted me to be his girlfriend. I had no idea what he saw in me. My clothes weren't fashionable, my face was plain, my mother was constantly telling me I was too tall—I kept growing out of my pants. But here was Billy, on my birthday, with a bouquet of flowers just for me.

"He told me he loved me, and I was so starved to hear the words that I believed him.''

Jennifer stopped, tears brimming in her eyes, but she blinked them away. Bryan stood by the wall, his hands clenched behind him. He didn't want to hear any more.

"He told me that if I loved him back, I'd do whatever he wanted me to do..."

Bryan ground his teeth together.

"Two weeks later he was spreading it around school what I'd done. The boys all looked at me differently, made nasty remarks. The girls shied away from me. What little bit of faith I'd had in myself was gone. I felt completely worthless."

Nicki turned over, her eyes accusing. "So that was my *father?*" she asked. "A stupid selfish boy who wasn't even very nice?"

Bryan could cheerfully have gagged his niece. Jennifer had been through enough just in retelling the story. She'd obviously already judged herself a million times and come up wanting. She didn't need her daughter's condemnation on top of that.

"No."

What? Bryan straightened in the doorway.

"Then who was?" Nicki asked, still accusing.

"His name was Tommy Mason. He worked for my father. He was Billy's best friend. Or at least he was until Billy turned on me. Tommy came to my rescue. He told me how beautiful I was, how sweet to have cared so much for Billy, to have trusted him so much. After a while we started dating. Tommy had a lot of money for a boy his age, and he spent most of it on me. He was always doing little things to make me feel special. It was only later that I learned he was just like Billy, except that he'd invested more into getting what he was after because he had more at stake.''

Jennifer stared into space, and Bryan knew that he and Nicki had lost her to a time before either of them had been a part of her life. Her face was twisted in a grimace of self-loathing so strong it was hard for Bryan to believe she was the same woman he'd known all these months.

Nicki just sat silently, a one-child jury who'd already convicted the defendant.

''They had a—'' Jennifer stopped as a single tear slid down her cheek. She closed her eyes. ''A bet. If I'd *do it* with Tommy, Billy would give him ten dollars. If not, Tommy owed Billy.''

Bryan's dinner was about to come up on him.

''Why'd he spend all that money on you if he was only gonna win ten dollars?'' Nicki asked. Her eyes were softer, not forgiving, exactly, but more like the Nicki he knew.

''It wasn't the money that was at stake, it was his ego. He had to win to prove to his buddies that he was as much a man as Billy was.''

''So what'd he do when you told him, you know, about me?''

Jennifer smoothed the hair away from her daughter's brow. ''He said he wasn't your father. He told my parents that he hadn't been the first boy I'd been with, and that he was sure he hadn't been the last. He claimed that there was no way even *I* could know who your father was.''

''What did they say?''

''They believed him.''

Bryan left the room. The anger surging through him frightened him. He didn't want to do something he'd regret, especially in front of Nicki. His fists ached to smash into something, preferably this Tommy Mason's face.

Pacing out in the hall, he heard his niece ask, ''Was it the truth?''

''No,'' Jennifer said firmly. ''After Billy, there was only Tommy, and only that one time.''

Bryan had to stop himself from putting his fist through the wall.

''That still doesn't explain why *you* couldn't keep me.'' Nicki wasn't ready to forgive her for that. Bryan wasn't sure she ever would be. In her eyes, Jennifer had abandoned her, regardless of how happy Nicki had ultimately been.

He couldn't stand by and let her torture Jennifer anymore. ''Let's give it a rest, eh, Nick?'' he said, coming back into the room.

Jennifer shook her head at him. ''It's okay. She has to know the truth if she's ever going to understand.''

Bryan didn't like it, but he leaned against the doorjamb and let her continue.

''I gave you away because I loved you, Nicki.''

''How can you say that?'' Nicki's look was hard again.

''Because it's true.'' The peace that settled across Jennifer's face surprised Bryan almost as much as her next words did. ''I nearly changed my mind, you know.''

"You did?"

She did?

"Uh-huh." Jennifer smiled sadly. "I'd given in to my parents early on in my pregnancy, agreeing to give you up before you were more than a speck in my belly. They wouldn't give me a second's peace, telling me they wouldn't have any part of my baby—"

Bryan could just imagine the terms they'd probably used to describe the child Jennifer had been carrying.

"—and they weren't going to have any part of me, either, if I didn't do what they said. I was scared. I was young. I wasn't even old enough to get a work permit or drive a car. I didn't see how I could take care of myself, let alone a baby. So I did just what I'd always done. I gave in to them and agreed to give you up for adoption.

"But a funny thing happened during those months I carried you. You became the light of my life, the best thing that had ever happened to me. You taught me what love was all about for the very first time. Every time you kicked me, I'd feel like smiling, and when you moved in the middle of the night, waking me up, I'd sit up and play with you, trying to get you to move some more. You were mine. And I wanted to take care of you and protect you for the rest of my life."

"So why didn't you?" Nicki asked.

"I did," Jennifer said softly. "I had to have you by cesarean, and so I was unconscious when you were born, but that night, the night before I was due to leave the hospital, I talked a young nurse into bringing you in to me. I hadn't signed the papers yet that would release you to someone else, and I didn't intend to ever do so. But when I held you in my arms—'' tears filled Jennifer's eyes, but she was still smiling at Nicki ''—you were so small, so defenseless, so precious, I knew I couldn't take you home to that unhappy house. You deserved so much more. I couldn't bear to think of you growing up the way I had, with my parents frowning their disapproval upon you. And secretly I was afraid that maybe I'd be like them. I didn't know any more about raising a baby than they did, and I might be just as awful at it. After all, I'd failed at everything else I'd ever tried. It was then I knew I couldn't keep you. So I made a promise, instead.''

''A promise?''

''I promised God that if He'd give you a happy loving family, I'd let you go. I wouldn't look for you, or bother you, and I wouldn't ever replace you, either.''

Bryan finally understood. More than just a fear of being a bad parent had kept Jennifer from registering to find Nicki. She'd made a pact with God, and if she broke her half, He might not uphold His. Bryan had never felt such a surge of love for the woman he wanted to make his wife.

Nicki looked at Jennifer, as if not quite sure how she felt anymore. ''So when did you get rich?''

''After I got out of college. I took over my parents'

business and for the first time in my life I did something right.''

Nicki nodded. She still didn't look at Bryan—she hadn't since she'd run out of the living room—but she'd certainly calmed down.

''Can I ask you something?''

Jennifer brushed her fingers along Nicki's arm as if she couldn't get enough of touching her. ''Sure.''

''How long have you known who I was?''

''I just found out tonight.''

''You did? You mean you didn't know when you were nice to me at the beach, when you bought me that swimsuit? You did that just because you liked me?''

''Just because I like you, sweetie. You're a pretty special young lady.''

Nicki shrugged off Jennifer's praise, as if not quite sure how much weight it carried. ''So Uncle Bryan just told you tonight?''

Bryan suddenly wondered how she *had* found out. He'd been so concerned about her reaction to the news that it hadn't dawned on him to wonder how she'd come by it.

''No. This did.'' Jennifer pulled a picture out of the pocket of her dress and handed it to Nicki.

''It's me!'' Nicki said, gazing in awe at the battered photo. ''It's the same picture we have in the album.''

Jennifer nodded, tears in her eyes again.

''You mean you didn't know until I turned that page and you saw this picture?''

''That's right.''

"Omigosh," Nicki said, looking at the picture again. "How come it's so beat-up?"

"It's been through twelve years of my life with me, honey, every hour of every day."

"Always?" Nicki asked, her expression defense-less all of a sudden.

"Always."

Nicki's gaze was glued to Jennifer's; Bryan had a feeling they didn't even know he was still there. "You must have loved me an awful lot."

Jennifer smiled. "With all my heart, Nick."

"Is it okay if I hug you?" Nicki asked, suddenly awkward as she finally looked at Jennifer in a new light.

"I thought you'd never ask," Jennifer said, gathering her daughter into her arms for the first time in twelve years.

Bryan slipped from the room.

THE DINING-ROOM TABLE was strewn with the mak-ings of a miniature double-winged biplane, similar to the one the Wright brothers flew. Bryan had always admired them, not only because their early experi-mentation had opened up the skies, but because of their quest to have their freedom no matter what the cost.

Freedom had always meant that much to him, as well. More than a home, more than a wife or children, more than possessions. He left Nicki in with Jennifer, left them to forge a relationship that didn't include him, and went out to work on his plane. It was ridiculous for him to feel left out. He had no reason to feel threatened. And lonely wasn't a feeling he'd ever had time for. There was always that unknown something beckoning him from just over the next hill. So why couldn't he hear its call now?

He split a piece of balsa with his razor-blade knife. He could finish the plane with just a few more hours' work. He was anxious to see how it flew. Maybe he and Nicki could take it to the coast over the weekend and send it up over the ocean. A day alone with Nicki sounded good to him. He had a plan. With renewed purpose, he set to work.

NICKI FOUND HIM in the dining room after spending an incredible hour getting to know her birth mother. He was so intent on the little piece of wood he was shaping he didn't even notice her. Figured.

She moved closer to the table and picked up a packet of glue.

His head shot up. The wood in his fingers cracked into two pieces. Nicki held her breath. She'd heard him swear before when that happened. And this time she'd caused it.

"Where's Jennifer?" he asked.

Nicki felt funny having him refer to her mother by her given name, and yet, she didn't know what else to call her. She couldn't call her Mom. Not ever. She already had a Mom. She felt guilty even thinking about it, like she was hurting Mom by even *knowing* Jennifer.

"Nicki? Did Jen leave?" he asked, getting up from the table.

"No. She's still in my bedroom. She said I had to come talk to you." Nicki hadn't wanted to, she'd just wanted to leave, but Jennifer hadn't budged.

"I'm sorry this was all such a shock to you, honey. I wouldn't upset you for the world, you know that, don't you?"

Nicki shrugged. She didn't know what to think.

He came around the table and put his arm around her. It felt so good to have him hold her, but something made her shrug his arm away.

"Hey!" He knelt down in front of her. "What's going on here, Nick? We're a team, you and me, remember?"

"If we're a team, then why didn't you tell me the truth about her?"

He hesitated, and Nicki knew he was trying to think up something to tell her. Which meant he wasn't going to tell her the truth.

"I was going to tell you, honey. I just wanted to make sure you liked her first. I planned to tell both of you tonight, except that I had to work late."

He'd known she was her birth mother for months. Even back when all that mattered had been finding her other mother, he'd already known who she was. And he'd told Nicki he was still looking. Even on her birthday he'd said that.

He'd lied to her. And that hurt so bad she didn't even want to look at him.

"I want to go stay with her."

"What? Why?" He jumped up, clutching her shoulders as if he could keep her with him by sheer force. "You don't need to leave here. We live close enough for you to visit her every day if you want to."

"You're hurting me!" Nicki said, trying to pull away.

"Sorry." He loosened his hold, but he didn't let go of her. He rubbed her shoulders softly with his fingers until they felt better. But *she* didn't. He'd lied to her.

"I don't want to *visit* her, I want to *stay* with her, find out what she's like."

"You can spend a couple of nights with her, I guess, if that's what you want. It's summer and you wouldn't be missing any school." He went back to the table, picking up a new piece of balsa wood and his littlest pair of scissors.

He'd given in so easily Nicki almost started to cry. But she wasn't going to do that. Not in front of him. She'd promised herself she wouldn't. It wasn't like she hadn't known, anyway. Uncle Bryan was a free spirit; he was used to being on his own. She'd thought maybe he'd changed, that with Jennifer around he'd want to settle down, but her birth mother had just told Nicki that she and Uncle Bryan weren't going to be seeing each other anymore. She hadn't said why, but Nicki figured it was because Uncle Bryan wanted it that way. He was always the one who broke things off.

Nicki figured she'd better go before he broke things

off with her, too. She couldn't stand to stay, worrying about when he'd do it. She'd been worried for months about cramping him. And now she had Lucy, too. But she also, finally, had someplace else she could go.

"I don't want to just visit her," she said again. "I want to move in with her. Lucy, too."

He didn't even look up. "You can't do that, Nick. You belong with me." His voice sounded strange. Faraway. Was he paying attention to her at all?

"No, I don't. I'm not really a Chambers. Or a Hubbard, either. I'm a Teal. I want to go live with my *real* mother." It killed Nicki even to say the words. She held her breath, waiting for Uncle Bryan to tell her she was wrong, to take her in his big strong arms and tell her he'd never let her go.

He was quiet for so long Nicki wondered if he'd forgotten her. He worked on his little piece of wood until he got it just right and then glued it to the front of the model he was building. It was another airplane—an open one with two wings on each side. It would probably be fun to fly. They could put a little man in the cockpit and then they'd have to fly it almost perfect or the man would fall out.

"Is it okay with Jennifer?"

She jumped when he finally spoke. He'd never used that voice with her before, like she was someone he didn't know very well. Was he already that glad to be rid of her?

"Yes." At least she hoped it was. She'd only asked her birth mother if she could spend the night with her.

"Then I won't stop you."

CHAPTER SIXTEEN

I WON'T STOP YOU...I won't stop you...I won't stop you...

The edge of the razor slid into Bryan's finger. "Damn it to hell!" he said, sucking on his finger as he went into the bathroom. He swore out loud the entire time it took him to stop the flow of blood and get a bandage on his finger. It didn't matter what he said or how loud he said it. There was no one around to hear him.

I won't stop you. What an incredibly asinine thing to tell her. What in hell had he been thinking? He could have at least tried to stop her. What did he have to lose by trying?

So why hadn't he?

Turning off the bathroom light, Nicki's bathroom light, he wandered into her bedroom. It was surprising how much stuff she'd been able to pack up in the half hour it had taken her to leave him. The room looked so vacant. Sure, her magazines were still stacked on the shelf. Her little jewelry box was still on the dresser. He opened her closet. Her winter clothes still hung there, and some dresses. There were even a couple of pairs of shoes.

He glanced back at the bed. But there was no Nicki. The room mocked him with its emptiness. Hell, the whole house mocked him. He'd bought it for her.

But if she didn't want to be with him...

Bryan went back to his airplane.

He could have tried to stop her, but what good would it have done? He couldn't make her want to stay. And deep down, he wondered who had more right to her, he or Jennifer. If he fought them, if they fought him back, if Nicki went to court and testified that she wanted to live with her biological mother, how much chance did an adoptive uncle stand?

Or was there another reason he hadn't fought any harder to keep her? Deep down, had he welcomed the chance to hand over the mammoth responsibility of looking after Nicki, of dealing with her ups and downs? Had he, per chance, wanted his freedom, as Jennifer had accused earlier that evening?

He looked at his watch. It had only been four hours ago that Jennifer had appeared in his office, but it seemed like days. Then again, Nicki had become his in the space of five minutes, the time it took a tornado to destroy half a town. Why shouldn't he lose her just as quickly?

He'd become a father overnight. The question was, could he resume his old life just as rapidly? Did he want to?

He finished the model at three o'clock in the morning. He'd have gone outside to try it out, but he didn't want to wake the neighbors. So instead, he wandered around the house again, thinking of the things he'd been planning to do, the dark paneling he wanted to rip out in the den, the tile he wanted to lay in place of the outdoor carpet on the covered porch, the wall of windows he wanted to put in in his bedroom. He'd promised Nicki a pool for the backyard, and he'd figured he'd throw in a Jacuzzi for himself, as well.

He'd planned to landscape the whole backyard around the pool, building a fountain made out of rocks that would empty into the deep end of the pool. And he'd wanted fruit trees, too, and lots of lush green grass so Nicki could run around barefoot.

But what did he know? A pool was probably a pain to take care of. And grass had to be cut. Maybe he'd just sell the house.

He was behind his drafting table at Innovative Advertising two hours later, chased out of the house by something he didn't understand. He'd showered and changed his jeans for a pair of shorts, his polo shirt for a bright red tank top, and he'd left his hair loose over his shoulders. He was going to go to the batting cages as soon as they opened at ten o'clock, and then maybe he'd try to catch a Braves game. And surely there was someone he could call for a date that night, even at this late notice...

Anything was better than going home to that house again. He couldn't stand another evening there.

JENNIFER BARELY SLEPT all night. She missed Bryan.

And her daughter was asleep in bed right on the other side of the wall. Jennifer shivered with disbelief just thinking about it. She got up out of bed three times to make sure Nicki was really there. And she watched the clock until she knew Tanya and Dennis would be up. Maybe when she told her friends about Nicki it would begin to seem real.

Damn him. Damn him for using her, for making her believe in love again, for showing her how wonderful love could be. Damn him for not being there to share Nicki with her, to share her excitement—and her fear that it was all just an incredible dream. To hold her until she believed.

Damn him for not loving her.

But he'd given her Nicki. He'd given her back her daughter. So try as she might, she couldn't hate him.

Nicki was still sleeping soundly at seven o'clock. Jennifer stood in the doorway of her guest room, Nicki's room as of last night, and watched the covers rise and fall with her daughter's breathing. Nicki's hair was tangled and spread all over her pillow. Lucy was curled up to her chest, almost as if Nicki had been cuddling her before she'd fallen asleep.

Tears filled Jennifer's eyes and slid slowly down her face as she stood there watching, trying not to think of the years she'd lost, thankful beyond comprehension for the years she'd just gained.

She'd been through so much, this poor baby of hers, but Jennifer was set to shower Nicki with enough love to ease the pain that had taken over the child's life. She was going to do whatever it took to help Nicki be happy again.

It wasn't going to be easy, Jennifer knew. Nicki had barely said a word since they'd left Bryan's house the night before, in spite of the fact that she'd insisted she wanted to come live with Jennifer more than anything else in the world. And even though Jennifer had already suspected Bryan had planned all along to ease his own responsibility to Nicki by bringing her, Jennifer, into the picture, she was still surprised by how easily he'd capitulated to Nicki's request. Surprised, and hurt.

And Nicki must have been hurt by it, too. No matter how much she thought she wanted to live with her birth mother, she still loved her uncle—and she'd already lost so much.

Leaving Nicki's door open a crack, Jennifer went out to the kitchen and phoned Tanya.

"Are you free for lunch?" she asked her friend as soon as they'd said hello.

"I think so." Tanya sounded sleepy.

Jennifer wrapped the cord around her finger. "I have something to show you. How about meeting me at Max's?" She named one of their favorite restaurants.

"Sure. What time?"

"Noon."

"Fine. Now what're you not telling me?" Her friend was definitely awake now.

"Why does there have to be something I'm not telling you?"

"Because I've never heard you sound so, I don't know, excited, maybe."

"I'll see you at lunch," Jennifer said, intending to hang up before Tanya could worm her surprise out of her. She wanted to see Tanya's face when she walked in and saw Nicki sitting there with her. She wanted to see if Tanya noticed the resemblance between them, or if she was only imagining it.

"It's Bryan, isn't it? He's asked you to marry him."

"No. As a matter of fact, I don't think I'm going to be seeing him as much."

"You're not... But Dennis said your trip to the beach was a miraculous success. He said you and Bryan even, you know..."

"I never told him that!"

"I know. He just said he could tell."

Jennifer felt stupid, blushing on the telephone. "Well, it doesn't matter now. It's over."

"Oh."

"Don't sound so disappointed in me. I didn't do it this time. *He* did."

"Oh. Oh-h-h." Now the word was filled with sympathy.

"Yeah," Jennifer said, promising herself she wouldn't cry again. She'd been a fool to think she could have it all. And at least Bryan hadn't left her all alone. He'd given her the one thing she'd wanted more than anything else in life—a second chance with her daughter.

And she wasn't going to ruin it by wanting his love, too. She just wasn't.

"What happened?" Tanya finally asked.

"Wait until after lunch, and then I'll answer any questions you have left."

"It's not nice to drive a pregnant woman crazy, Jen."

"Lunch, Tanya. Oh, and tell Dennis I won't be in today, okay?"

"You sure you're all right?" Tanya asked, sounding concerned again.

"I've never been better," Jennifer said, though it was only partly true. She yearned for Bryan. As much as he yearned for freedom.

"HAS UNCLE BRYAN ever met your friend?" Nicki asked Jennifer as they sat at their table at Max's later that morning waiting for Tanya to arrive. It was the fourth time she'd mentioned her uncle that morning.

"He met her once at one of her art shows. But he knows her husband pretty well. Dennis works for me."

"So she's the artist Uncle Bryan told me about you being friends with?"

"She must be, 'cause she's the only artist friend I have."

Nicki was wearing the same flowered culotte dress she'd worn the first night Jennifer had met her. She looked beautiful. Jennifer felt like everyone in the restaurant was looking at them, recognizing them as mother and daughter. She wanted to introduce Nicki to every last one of them.

"Do they...know about me?"

Jennifer covered her daughter's hand with her own. She hated that frightened-doe look in Nicki's eyes, and wondered what it was going to take to help Nicki feel secure again.

"They don't know yet that I found you, if that's what you mean."

"But they know you had me? Had a baby, I mean?"

"Dennis brought me home from the hospital after I had you."

"Where was your mom?"

"At work."

"But you said you had stitches and stuff."

"Uh-huh."

"Jeez," Nicki said. Jennifer nodded. That just about summed it up.

"Tanya spent your first birthday with me."

"She did?" Nicki brightened. "You mean you celebrated it, too?"

Jennifer wasn't sure how much to tell Nicki, how much the child needed to hear or should hear, about that time in her life. "Sort of," she said.

"You remembered at least," Nicki said, making the words sound more like a question, an important question.

"I never forgot, Nicki. Not for a second. That night I cried almost the whole night. I'd just lost the first year of your life and I knew I was never going to get it back," she said, listening to her instincts.

Her stomach tightened when tears sprang to Nicki's eyes. She'd made her daughter cry. "I'm glad," Nicki said. "I mean, I'm not glad you were sad, but I'm glad you remembered, like you really cared and all."

"I always cared, Nick. Always."

"Jennifer?"

Jennifer turned at the sound of her friend's voice. Tanya was coming toward them like the building was on fire.

"You found her? Why didn't you tell me?" Tanya asked, staring at Nicki. "I can't believe you didn't tell me!"

Nicki looked as if she was ready to bolt.

"Sit down, Tanya," Jennifer said, concerned for Nicki, but so full of pride she thought she'd burst.

"Where did you find her?" Tanya was still looking at Nicki as she slid into her chair. "I can't believe how much she looks like you."

Nicki stared at her plate.

"You'll have to excuse Tanya, Nick. She never did have any manners, but she's nice enough once you get to know her, I promise," Jennifer said lightly.

Nicki glanced at Jennifer, an uncertain smile flickering across her face.

"Tanya Bradford, meet Nicki Hubbard. Nicki, this blabbermouth is my friend, Tanya."

"Hi," Nicki said.

"Hello yourself, sweetie," Tanya said, embracing Nicki with her smile. "I've been waiting a long time to meet you, and you're even more beautiful than I imagined."

Nicki blushed.

Their waitress came over, having seen Tanya arrive, and they were soon taken up with the business of ordering lunch, all three of them deciding on turkey croissants. Nicki was having hers with french fries.

Tanya looked from Nicki to Jennifer again as soon as their waitress walked away. "Boy, your lawyer sure works fast."

Jennifer put down the water glass she'd been sipping from. "My lawyer?"

Tanya frowned. "Isn't that how you two found each other?"

Jennifer shook her head. "I haven't heard back from him yet."

"You were looking for me?" Nicki gazed at Jennifer with glowing eyes.

Jennifer nodded. "I had to find you before I could love your uncle and the child I thought was just his niece."

"You did?"

"I couldn't give my heart to you until I knew for sure that my own child was happy."

"Oh." Her daughter was smiling the biggest smile Jennifer had ever seen. "I thought you didn't want to find me. Uncle Bryan told me you hadn't registered," her daughter explained.

Jennifer covered Nicki's hand with her own, afraid to tell Nicki the truth—but more afraid not to. There had already been too many lies in their relationship. "I didn't until just a week ago. I didn't want to interfere in your life, honey." That part was easy. "And I was afraid to know where you were, knowing I couldn't be a part of your life, afraid of how badly it would hurt."

Nicki pulled her hand away. "But I needed you."

"I'm sorry, Nicki. So sorry. But the truth is, until very recently, I believed that even if you needed me, I'd just fail you again, like I had when I was sixteen. That's why I didn't register to find you sooner. Not because I didn't love you."

"Wait just a minute here," Tanya said, looking from one to the other of them. "Are you saying that *she's* Bryan Chambers's niece? The one you went to the beach with?"

Jennifer and Nicki looked at each other and nodded.

"And you didn't know... He didn't... Oh, my G— Oh. But why?"

"He wanted to make sure we got along before he introduced us. He didn't want Nicki to be hurt any more than she already had been."

Nicki's gaze flew to Jennifer. "He didn't?"

"Didn't he tell you that?"

Nicki shook her head.

"That's why he didn't let you know who I was, Nicki. He was trying to protect you the best way he knew how."

"Well, if she's his niece and your daughter," Tanya asked, confused, "then what's the matter with you and him?"

"It wasn't me he wanted so much as a mother for Nicki," Jennifer said, choosing her words carefully in front of Nicki.

"You don't know my uncle," Nicki said, sounding far more mature than her twelve years. "He's always taking off for places, and you can't do that when you have a kid around. I guess you can't do it with a girlfriend around, either, only he didn't show it with Jennifer because of who she was.''

Tanya looked at Jennifer. ''This is true?''

''Maybe. A little,'' Jennifer said.

''Well, what happens now?''

Jennifer took her daughter's hand, gave it a squeeze and held on to it. ''We live happily ever after....''

''How is she?'' His voice jolted Jennifer out a sleep-induced haze.

''Bryan?''

''Of course. Is everything okay?''

She pushed herself up in bed, willing her heartbeat to settle back to its normal pace. He was calling about Nicki.

''Fine. We're fine. She's fine. She's asleep.''

''I figured she would be. That's why I waited so late to call. I don't want her to think I'm checking up on her or anything.''

''Then why are you calling?'' His voice sounded so good to her, too good.

''To check up on her, of course. I... Oh, never mind. I'll call you tomorrow.'' He made it sound like a chore.

''You don't have to do that, you know. We're doing fine. I'd call you if we weren't.''

''You're telling me not to call you anymore?''

Did he have to make it sound so final?

''I'm telling you it's not necessary.''

"Have you been reminding her to brush her teeth? She just got her braces off six months ago."

"She's brushing her teeth, Bryan, and eating, and she even took a shower today." *You're free to get on with your life. Now let me get on with mine.*

"Lucy's not getting in your way, is she?"

What did it take to ease this man's conscience? If he needed to be free, they weren't going to hold him back. She and Nicki had discussed it over dinner.

"Lucy's fine, though she's missing her yard, of course. I'm thinking about looking around for a house someplace. Right after I look into schools."

"It sounds like you're taking to motherhood just fine."

She was. It was the womanhood she was still struggling with. He'd been her lover for one night, and she felt like she'd lost a limb.

"I guess I'm better at it than I thought."

"Good. Good." Was that relief she heard in his voice? Was he now going to take off into the sunset? She'd told herself that she wouldn't hold him back, that she didn't want a man who couldn't be happy by her side, a man she'd constantly have to worry about leaving her. And yet she'd never thought saying goodbye would hurt so much.

"I never meant to hurt you, Jen."

"I know." But that didn't stop the tears from springing to her eyes. Again.

"Maybe we could—"

"I don't think so, Bryan." She cut him off before he talked her into settling for less than she really wanted. She'd been doing that all her life, believing that she wasn't worthy of more, that she was weak-willed, and she wasn't going to do it ever again. She wasn't looking at herself through her parents' eyes anymore.

"I'll call you tomorrow night." He hung up before she could beg him to leave her alone, and she didn't trust herself to call him back. She lay down, but the sleep she needed so badly eluded her. She was counting the hours until she heard his voice again. And torturing herself with images of just what he might be doing with his newfound freedom.

"UNCLE BRYAN called me today," Nicki said over dinner almost a week later. She and Jennifer were still living in the penthouse, much to Lucy's disgust, but Jennifer had seen a couple of homes she liked and was thinking about making an offer on one.

"He did?" she asked now, more disappointed than she should have been. Did that mean, then, that she wouldn't be talking to him that night as she had every night since Nicki had come to live with her? She waited all day for those nightly calls.

"Uh-huh." Jennifer's throat caught at the sight of her daughter's happy smile. Nicki missed her uncle more than she was letting on.

"So what did he have to say?"

"He went to the ocean over the weekend to fly his new model plane. He says he might keep it, too, if he doesn't sell his house."

He's thinking about selling his house? "Sounds like he had a good time."

Nicki shrugged. "I guess."

"You know, honey, if you need to move back with him, or even just go visit him, it's fine with me."

The frightened-doe look was back in Nicki's eyes. "You don't want me here?"

"Yes! Of course I want you. You can live with me until you're old and gray if you'd like. But it's more important that you be happy, Nick, and Bryan is all the family you have left. It's natural you'd need to see him. I just don't want you to feel like you'd be disloyal to me or hurt my feelings by going back."

Nicki shrugged. "It doesn't matter. Like we said my first night here, he can't help how he is. He can't help it if I get in his way over there. But it was still fun to talk to him."

Jennifer let the subject drop, but she was troubled by the unhappy look in Nicki's eyes. Whether Bryan's blood flowed in Nicki's veins or not, he was her family and she needed him.

"Can I ask you something?" Nicki asked later that evening as she sat with Jennifer in the living room. Lucy was curled up on the floor by Nicki's feet.

Jennifer looked up from the work she'd had Dennis drop by for her that afternoon. "Of course, honey. What's up?"

"Remember that talk we had that night at dinner at my...at Uncle Bryan's house? The one about it not mattering about my mom being twelve and all when she...you know."

"Uh-huh," Jennifer said, suddenly nervous.

Nicki dog-eared the pages of her magazine. "Well, I was wondering...how old were you?"

"I was twelve, too, so you probably are right to think you might be getting close. Why don't we stop off at the drugstore tomorrow on our way to Phipp's Plaza and get you stocked up on stuff so you're ready when the time comes?" It wasn't nearly as hard as she'd thought it would be. It actually felt right to be talking to her daughter about such things.

Apparently Nicki felt so, too. "Okay." She grinned. "But I really don't know what I'll need for sure."

"I think between the two of us, we can figure it out..."

"YOU KNOW, NICK, it's okay if you leave some of your stuff lying around if you want to," Jennifer said the next evening. She'd been signing some letters while Nicki watched her favorite sitcom on TV. But her attention had wandered again and again to her daughter, to the wonder of actually having her there in the same room with her.

Nicki laid her head back against the couch, her legs curled up beneath her. "Uncle Bryan said the same thing when I came to live with him, but I just like to put things away. I don't really even think about it. Uncle Bryan says it's my dad's fault. The first game he taught me was one where we raced to pick up my toys."

Jennifer smiled at the contented look on her daughter's face. "Who won?" she asked.

"Him mostly, but that was okay 'cause that meant he picked up the most toys."

"Aha, so you were a conniver even as a little tike, huh?"

Nicki laughed. "Not really. It was just fun watching him crawl real fast all over the floor. He'd do tricks and hide toys and stuff and then I'd find them in my toy box. He was really good at magic stuff."

They spent the rest of the evening as they'd spent most of the previous ones, talking. Jennifer wanted to hear every last detail of Nicki's first twelve years. She was getting to know the entire Chambers family through Nicki, and the more she heard, the more she grew to love them. They'd given Nicki a wonderful childhood, raised her in a safe, secure, but most important, *loving* environment. They'd shaped her into a beautiful young woman, inside where it counted. The only thing to which Jennifer could lay claim was the outside.

"HEY, THERE, you want some company?"

Bryan squinted up through his sunglasses at the scantily clad, dark-skinned Bahamian beauty who was dripping water all over his beach towel.

Hell, yes, he wanted company. Badly. "Not today, but thanks for the offer."

His gaze followed her all the way down the beach. Had he lost his mind? The woman was gorgeous, her walk so sensual, her bottom so tempting, he should be drooling into his umbrellaed drink.

But she wasn't Jennifer.

He finished his drink in one gulp, jumped up with his towel in hand and headed back to the hotel lobby. Maybe he'd take a course in skin diving. It was something he'd always wanted to do, and he had all the time in the world at his disposal.

Back at the hotel he was halfway to the concierge desk to sign up for skin diving when he turned around and headed for the elevators. Once in his room, he packed his duffel and called down for a ride to the airport. There were lots of skin diving classes offered in Atlanta. He'd check into it as soon as he got home.

He called Nicki from the airport before he left the Bahamas. The conversation was the same as it had been every other day over the past week. She sounded happy to hear from him, but when he asked her how she was doing, when he tried to get her to talk to him, her voice cooled, like he was some friend of the family, rather than family itself.

He'd blown it, plain and simple. Like an idiot, he'd tried to play God. And he'd lied to Nicki. By omission, he'd lied to her mother, too. He'd betrayed their trust. Oh, he'd told himself he'd been doing it for Nicki, that he'd had no other choice, but as he flew above the clouds, more alone than he'd ever been in life, he wasn't sure Nicki had been the only one he'd been thinking about. As much as he loved her, having the sole responsibility for a fragile twelve-year-old was an incredible burden, especially for a confirmed bachelor like himself. So had he, as Jennifer had accused, been biding his time, wooing her, simply as a means to an end? Had his desperate need to show her that she could love a child, love Nicki, been not solely for Nicki's sake as he'd thought, but for himself, as well?

He wished to God he knew.

CHAPTER SEVENTEEN

SCHOOLS. SHE'D SAID she was going to look into schools before she bought a house. But she couldn't register Nicki for school. Only *he* could do that. He'd already *done* that. Because Nicki was his. *His.*

The front two legs of Bryan's chair slammed back down to the floor. Damn it. What in the hell was he doing sitting here in his office missing her?

He cleared off his desk. "Jacci!"

"Yeah?" His secretary's head popped inside the door.

"Clear my calendar for the afternoon. I'm leaving for the day." Checking his back pocket for his wallet, he put his sunglasses on and grabbed his keys out of his in tray.

"You finally going after her?"

Bryan looked back at his secretary. "Yeah, you wanna make something of it?"

"Nope. But you might want to comb your hair—it's a mess," she called after him.

Bryan grabbed a comb from the dash of his Jeep, pulled it through his hair and found a rubber band to secure it into a ponytail. For the first time in two weeks he had a reason to look responsible.

He called Jennifer's apartment from his cellular phone as he pulled out onto Peachtree. Nicki was home alone, but Jennifer was on her way home for lunch. That was fine with him. He wanted to see her, too. He rang off without telling Nicki he was coming.

The doorman recognized Bryan and let him upstairs when Bryan explained why he was there, wishing him luck as the elevator closed behind him. Bryan didn't stop to think about needing a little luck. He was on a mission.

Jennifer pulled the door open when he knocked. "Bryan!"

He walked past her and into the apartment, with Lucy jumping at his heels. "Where's Nicki?"

"She's—"

"I'm right here," Nicki said, coming into the living room. She approached him slowly, watching him strangely. But he wasn't going to be deterred. Not anymore. He strode across the room and grabbed her up into a hug that lifted her right off the floor.

"I've missed you, sprite," he whispered as he kissed her on the neck.

Nicki looked at him, nose to nose. "You have?"

How could she doubt it? "I have." He remembered his mission. "I've come to take you home." He set her down, raising his hand to forestall her reply. "Don't bother arguing with me. You're legally still mine, and I'm taking you back where you belong. You're a Chambers whether you want to believe it or not. We raised you, we taught you everything you

know, we loved you. *I* love you. Now go get your
things. You're coming home." He paused. "Okay?"

Bryan had no idea how much her acquiescence
meant to him until she nodded and scampered off. He
told himself he'd have taken her even if she'd argued,
but it sure eased some of the loneliness of the past two
weeks to have her agree to come back to him almost
as easily as he'd agreed to let her go in the first place.

He bent down to calm Lucy. "How about you, girl?
You ready to come home?" He was surprised how
good those words sounded to him. His family was
coming home. All of it, he hoped.

He felt Jennifer's gaze on him and he turned, knowing he had yet to fight the toughest part of this battle.
Her eyes were dry, but filled with anguish.

"I'm not taking her away from you, Jen. I want you
to come with us." She looked so good to him, like a
glass of cool water in the middle of the desert.

"I can't."

He should have expected the words, but he hadn't.
He'd hoped she'd been as miserable as he had, hoped
she'd be as eager as he was for them to be a couple
again.

"I want to marry you. I want us to be a family. All
three of us."

He couldn't believe it when she shook her head, her
eyes flooded with tears. He could have sworn when
she'd opened the door to him that her eyes had flashed
with relief—and longing.

He strode over to her and pulled her into his arms.
It was what he should have done to begin with. What

he'd been wanting to do since she'd walked out of his house two weeks before.

She leaned into him, shuddering as she laid her head against his shoulder. Her arms wrapped around his neck, squeezing him against her. Finally. His world was righting itself after spinning out of control for two long weeks.

But then she pushed him away. "I can't go with you, not until I know why you were interested in me in the first place, not until you can tell me that your feelings for me don't have anything to do with my being Nicki's mother."

"You're asking the impossible, Jen. You *are* Nicki's mother. Giving her up, loving her all these years, has made you the woman you are today."

"I asked you this two weeks ago, Bryan," she said, "and I'm going to ask you again. If you didn't have Nicki, would you still be asking me to marry you?"

Bryan's answer was still the same. He honestly didn't know. Now he looked in her eyes, her loyal, trusting, anguished eyes, and said nothing.

She turned away from him. "There's your answer." Her shoulders shook. He knew she was crying.

He reached out and turned her to face him. He had to make her understand. "I'd still care this much, honey. Having Nicki doesn't change the way I feel. It just changes what I do with it. Before Nicki I simply would never have thought to ask you to marry me, at least not right away. But I would've been everything to you a husband should be. I would've been faithful to you."

"But for how long?" she whispered. "Don't you see, Bryan? Marrying you would be like playing the lottery. I may win it all, but chances are, after all the hoopla dies down, after Nicki grows up and doesn't need us anymore, after *you* don't need me anymore, I'll be left empty-handed. You aren't the marrying kind, and I can't get married knowing in the back of my mind that the day may come when you won't be walking in the door at night. Or that someday the phone may ring and it'll be you telling me you're in Fiji or climbing a mountain somewhere. Or just plain on the other side of town, needing your freedom."

She couldn't do this. He'd had it all in the palm of his hand. "Life doesn't have the kind of guarantees you're looking for," he said, swallowing the emotion threatening to choke him.

"I'm not looking for guarantees, Bryan. I only want a fighting chance. I've made enough foolish choices in my life. I can't make another one."

So taking a chance on him was a foolish choice. There didn't seem to be much more to be said. He nodded, shoving his hands into the pockets of his shorts before they could betray him and take her with him against her will.

"You're welcome to Nicki any time you want her," he said.

"Thank you." Her eyes filled with tears. "You'll call me, won't you, if she needs anything? If you, uh, need a woman's advice?"

"Of course. We can work out some kind of visitation, too, where you'll have her on a regular basis. If you want to, that is.''

"I'll take her any time. If you feel crowded and need to take off for a day or two, you call me. I'll keep her for you.''

"If I take off I'll take her with me, but I mean it about the visits, Jen. You're a part of her life now.''

He couldn't believe how civilized they sounded, like some couple after an amicable divorce.

Nicki came back into the living room, carrying the suitcases she'd taken with her. "I left some things here for when I come visit,'' she said, looking at Bryan. She wouldn't look at Jennifer.

"We were just talking about that. We're going to set up a regular schedule for you to spend time with Jennifer, every other weekend or something, and other times in between, too, if you want.''

Nicki nodded, still not looking at her mother.

Jennifer walked over to the girl, pulling her into her arms. "It's okay, Nicki, honey. You belong with your uncle. I've known that all along. I'm just glad I had this time with you, and we'll have lots more time together in the future, too, I promise.''

"But I said I wanted to live with you. You were going to buy a house and everything.'' Nicki's voice was loaded with guilt.

"I know, sweetie, but I also know how much you missed your uncle. And he's right. You *are* a Chambers, through and through, and that's the way it should be.''

Nicki pulled away to study her mother's face. "You're not mad at me?"

Jennifer shook her head, smiling through her tears. "Not even the tiniest bit, sweetie. Now, take Lucy back to her yard where she belongs, okay?"

Nicki nodded, smiling through her tears. "Can I call you?" she asked.

"You better."

"Every day?"

"Twice a day if you'd like."

Nicki stared at Jennifer for a long moment, as if weighing her thoughts. "I love you," she finally said, so softly Bryan could hardly hear her.

"I love you, too, Nicki. With all my heart."

And with one last hug between mother and daughter, Nicki was Bryan's again. But he left a vital part of himself behind when he walked away.

Jennifer stood in the doorway, holding back her sobs until she saw the elevator doors close behind them. If only he'd said, even once, that he loved her…

DENNIS CALLED BRYAN at home two days later. "There's been an accident. Jennifer was broadsided—"

"When? Where? How is she?" Bryan asked, his skin cold with dread. She wasn't going to leave him. Not like this.

"They took her to Oldike Memorial, but nobody'll tell me how she's doing. The cop that called just said her car was totaled. I'm on my way to get Tanya and head over to Oldike now."

Her car was totaled. "I'll meet you there," Bryan said, hanging up the phone and grabbing his keys.

"Nicki?" he called, his stomach a sick knot of fear. He had to tell her. As much as he wanted to leave her in blissful ignorance, he couldn't do that to her ever again.

"Yeah?" She was wearing her daisy outfit, and her smile as she came into the room was like a ray of sunshine, warming him.

He took her into his arms, needing to shelter her even as he needed her comfort. "Jennifer's been in a car accident, honey. We don't know how badly she's hurt yet, maybe not badly at all, but I have to go to the hospital where they've taken her. Do you want to come?" he asked.

Nicki's body went limp against him as she absorbed the words. He waited for the sobs he knew were to follow. Damn the Fates that hurt this child so unfairly. She was everything that was good and right. Why in the hell did she have to keep getting stomped on?

Hold on, Jen. I'm coming.

Thirty seconds passed before he realized Nicki wasn't crying. "Nicki?" he asked. Had she passed out? "Nick, you okay?"

She pulled out of his arms and straightened her shoulders. "I guess." She *was* crying, just not hysterically.

"Do you want me to call Mrs. Baker to come over and stay with you while I go?"

Nicki shook her head and wiped her eyes with the back of her hand. "No. I want to come. And we better hurry so she knows we're there,'' she said, charging ahead like the Nicki of old.

Bryan wasn't going to question the miracle that had just happened, wasn't going to wonder how or when Nicki's inner strength had returned to her. He was only going to hope there were two miracles in store for him that day.

"Let's go," he said. Jennifer was going to be okay. She had to be okay. Because he finally had her answers. He finally knew why she had to marry him.

HER HEAD HURT. She wished someone would turn off that bright light. And turn down the noise, as well. Couldn't they see she was trying to sleep?

"Shh," she finally said, pushing aside the hand that had just touched her eye. Couldn't a person get any rest around here?

"She's come to!"

The speaker obviously hadn't heard Jennifer's command for silence. "Can't you guys be a little quieter?" she mumbled, trying not to wake herself up. Her head still hurt too much. She needed to sleep a while longer.

"Ms. Teal? Can you hear me?"

Who was that? Bobby? The mechanic at the Ford store whose son had been hit by a car? "Of course I can hear you," she said, trying not to bite his head off. She tried to open her eyes, as well, but they were too heavy. She'd apologize to him later. If he'd just turn off that damn light...

He could fix the car later. Couldn't he see she was sleeping?

The voice came again. "Ms. Teal? I'm going to look in your eyes now." Look in her eyes? What on earth for? And why, come to think of it, was she sleeping in a mechanic's bay?

"My head hurts," she said, hoping he could shed some light on the situation for her or at least leave her in peace.

"I imagine it does, ma'am. You've been in an accident and you have quite a shiner where you hit the windshield."

"An accident?" Her mouth felt as cottony as her brain, as she finally forced her eyes open.

She recognized the stethoscope around the doctor's neck immediately, and the IV-drip tube. Fear engulfed her, threatening to put her under again as she tried to sit up.

"Is everyone okay? Nicki? Was she with me?" No. Of course not. Bryan had taken her away two days before.

"Calm down, ma'am." The doctor's hands pushed her gently back down. "You were alone in the car, and you weren't hurt, other than that bump on your head. You're going to have a doozy of a headache tomorrow, I'm afraid."

"I have a doozy of a headache now," Jennifer said, wishing she could just go back to sleep. Except that there was a terrible ruckus on the other side of the curtain surrounding her.

"Where is she? This is her daughter here. We have a right to see her."

"Bryan?" she called. This time she succeeded in

sitting up. She didn't know why he was there, how he'd known to come, but she'd never wanted to see anyone more in her life.

"Jennifer?" The curtain around her moved, and then he was there, standing beside her bed looking as if he'd been the one in the car accident, not her.

"Your hair's a mess," she said, reaching up to smooth back a loose strand.

"I tried to tell him he should comb it before we came in, but he wouldn't listen."

Jennifer's head swiveled, stars filling her eyes for a second at the sudden movement. "Nicki?"

"Yeah." The girl's voice was a balm for Jennifer's sore head. Nicki came forward and took Jennifer's free hand. The one that Bryan wasn't clutching.

"You should've seen Uncle Bryan. They told us you were okay, but they wouldn't let us see you, so he just pushed past the nurse and came, anyway. It was really cool even if we do get in trouble," Nicki said, smiling.

"You really shouldn't be in here, sir." The doctor spoke for the first time.

"How is she, Doctor? How soon can I take her home?" Bryan asked.

The doctor shrugged. "Now seems like as good a time as any. Just give me a few minutes to get a nurse in here to remove the IV and help her dress."

"You mean she's really all right? There's nothing the matter with her?" Bryan asked, his sharp tone making Jennifer's head hurt all the more.

"Nothing that a couple days' rest won't cure. She's

pretty bruised up and she's bound to be sore for a few days. She also suffered a slight concussion, but other than that, she's just fine.''

"My car..." Jennifer only just remembered. She'd been driving the Mustang that morning.

Bryan leaned over her again, trailing his finger across her lips. "...is just a car, honey. You've got the real thing now."

SHE'S JUST FINE. She's just fine. Bryan kept repeating the doctor's words to himself while he watched Jennifer sleep later that night. She was lying in his bed, in spite of her protests, and he was keeping an eagle eye on her, waking her every half hour just as the doctor had instructed. Her long amber hair was a riot of tangles around her, a hint of the fire he knew she harbored inside. He didn't know what he would've done if he'd lost her. But he knew what he was going to do now. He was going to marry her. He wasn't going to waste any more time.

"Bryan?"

He jumped up from the chair he'd pulled next to the bed when he heard her voice. "I'm right here, honey," he said, sitting down on the bed beside her. He gently smoothed back the hair matted against her forehead. She had one hell of a bruise there, but no cuts. She'd gotten lucky.

"I'm thirsty," she said, licking her lips, her eyes still closed.

Bryan poured some water from the pitcher on his nightstand and lifted her up as he held it to her lips.

She drank half a glass before lying back down with a sigh. "Thanks."

"How's your head?" Bryan had a lot to tell her, but he wanted her coherent when he did so.

"Still hurts," she said, drifting off again. When he was certain she was sleeping soundly, he went back to doze in the chair by the bed.

Bryan kept up his vigil through the night, undressing sometime just before dawn and climbing in beside her. The next time he woke up, she was snuggled against him. He willed his starved body to behave.

She moved, her hip brushing against his groin, and he lost his battle. His body filled with wanting. He was going to have to get up.

"Feels a little dangerous down there," she said.

Bryan froze. Was that laughter he heard in her voice? "Depends on what you consider dangerous," he said, not daring to move.

She lay still against him. "Loving someone who doesn't love you back." She'd spoken so softly he almost missed it.

Very gently, careful of her tender body, he rolled over, holding his weight on his arms as he lay above her, gazing into her troubled eyes. "Then there's no danger here at all, lady, because I love you more than life itself."

She closed her eyes. "You don't have to lie to me, Bryan. I'm ready to give in, anyway. The past two days have been hell."

"You don't have to give in. I do love you. I have for a long time. It just took me a while to trust myself with the feeling. But when Dennis called, when I thought I might never see you again, I was filled with such panic I knew for certain that this feeling I have for you wasn't something that was going to go away in the morning.''

Her beautiful hazel eyes widened. ''You've loved me for a long time?''

''Probably since the first time I kissed you. You were different, Jen. Instead of looking for ways to escape you, I just kept coming back for more. But you hit a sore spot when you started talking about forever. I didn't know if I could promise it or not. Not because I didn't want to, but because I'd never been able to before.''

She smiled, reaching up to brush her fingers against his neck. ''So what changed?''

''When faced with the fact that I might never see you again, I realized it didn't matter *why* I'd fallen in love with you, only that I had. I don't know if, in the beginning, I pursued you as a means to relieve some of my responsibility to Nicki. Maybe I did. But there's nothing wrong with that. Being a parent isn't easy. Being a single parent is damn near impossible sometimes. Wanting a partner to share the load is only natural.''

''But what about your freedom? How do you know you won't be choking to death on your wedding vows a year from now?''

''I had my freedom, honey, for two whole weeks, and it damned near killed me. Life changes people. It changed me when it took away my family in one swoop of a wind cloud. I suddenly had a whole new perspective, a whole new set of needs that aren't any less valid because they're new. What's around the bend doesn't matter to me anymore. It's what's right here that counts." He lowered his head to kiss her, tenderly, reverently.

He could wait until she felt better to make love with her; he was going to have her in his bed for a lifetime. Now was the time for giving her his love with his heart, not his body.

As SHE WAITED for Jennifer and Uncle Bryan to get home, Nicki hummed a tune her mother used to sing to her when she was a little girl. She'd just come in from school and found Jennifer's note. They were due home any minute.

She couldn't believe how happy she was. Jennifer and Uncle Bryan had been married for just over three months, and Nicki didn't feel the least bit disloyal about loving Jennifer anymore. Her mother would be so happy to see Uncle Bryan married she'd be friends with Jennifer just because of that. And she'd be mad at Nicki if she wasn't friends with her, too. Besides, the way Nicki figured it, lots of people had two moms. Like when you got married and got your husband's mom, as well as your own.

"Nick? You home, honey?" she heard Jennifer call as the front door opened.

"I'm in here," she said, plopping down on the living-room couch. Jennifer came in, frowning like she was worried about something.

Uncle Bryan came in behind her. He was grinning from ear to ear.

"Are we?" Nicki asked, holding her breath. She wanted it so bad it hurt to even think about it.

"Yep!" Uncle Bryan said, giving a silly whoop.

Jennifer frowned at him, then crossed to Nicki and sat down beside her. She took one of Nicki's hands in hers, rubbing it gently like she'd done a couple of months before when Nicki had gotten her period for the first time and had such terrible cramps.

"Are you sure you're all right with this, Nicki? I don't want you to feel like we're pushing you out of your place here. You're still our first, and you always will be."

Nicki giggled and hugged Jennifer. "If you knew how badly I've wanted a brother or sister, you wouldn't ask me that," she said. She could hardly believe it. She wasn't going to be an only child anymore. "Besides, the way I figure it, this is just about perfect."

"How's that?" Uncle Bryan asked, coming over to sit with them.

"Well, it'll be my half brother or sister biologically, right?"

"Right."

"And it'll be yours biologically, too, right?" She looked at her uncle.

"Right."

"So that means our blood's finally connected."

Uncle Bryan's face got all tight for a second, like he was going to cry or something, but then he grinned at her just like he had when she'd finally beat him at one of his arcade games. "You're absolutely right, Nick. Our blood's finally connected."

A FEW HOURS LATER Nicki waited for Jennifer to come in to kiss her good-night, butterflies wrestling themselves in her stomach. There was only one thing bothering her about the new baby, and she needed to get it settled.

"Can I ask you something?" she said to Jennifer when she'd straightened from kissing Nicki's cheek.

"Of course, sweetie."

Nicki wasn't sure how to say it without sounding jealous or something. "Well, it's just that, even though I had Mom, you're still my mother, too, right?"

Jennifer sat down on the bed. "Yes."

"Just as much as you'll be the new baby's mother."

"I thought you were okay with that, honey." Jennifer stroked Nicki's cheek with a finger.

"I am. It's just that it doesn't seem right that he or she will get to call you Mom when I just call you Jennifer—like you aren't really related to me or anything."

Jennifer's finger stilled. "I guess we can teach him or her to call me Jennifer, too," she said. But she didn't sound very happy about it.

"Or...I could, maybe, call you Mom—to make it easier," Nicki said, holding her breath.

Jennifer's eyes shimmered with tears as she gathered her daughter into her arms, against her heart where she belonged—and so did Bryan's as he watched from the doorway. Lori's baby had finally made it home again.

NICKI'S NEW BABY SISTER came home from the hospital on Nicki's thirteenth birthday. Bryan didn't know who was the happier of his women as he walked behind them out of the hospital. Nicki was fairly bouncing as she pushed Jennifer's wheelchair, craning her head so as not to lose sight, even for a second, of the baby in Jennifer's arms.

Jennifer's face was radiant as she glanced back at him. Bryan could only imagine the emotions surging through her as she finally left the hospital with her babies—her new one, and her firstborn.

"Do you have it?" she asked him.

"I thought we'd wait until we got home." His arms were full of flowers.

"No. It has to be here. Nick, stop a minute, would you, honey?"

Nicki rolled her eyes at Bryan, a grin on her face. "I thought she was supposed to quit being weird after the baby was born."

Bryan grinned back, then glanced at his wife. Her lovely eyes were filled with sudden tension.

He set the pots of flowers down and reached into his pocket for the jeweler's box Jennifer had given him before she'd gone into labor. "It's right here, honey."

Jennifer took the box, handing him the baby, and pulled Nicki onto her lap.

"This is for you, love." She gave Nicki the box.

Nicki looked at the box and then up at Bryan.

"Go ahead, sprite."

Slowly Nicki opened the box, her hands shaking when she saw the tiny gold baby ring nestled there on a shiny gold chain. It wasn't identical to the one she'd lost, but it was close. Jennifer had spent months looking for just the right one.

Bryan put his free hand on her shoulder. "It's beautiful, Nick."

Nicki picked up the ring and turned it over, reading the inscription engraved on the inside as tears dripped down her cheeks.

"Thanks, Mom," she said, throwing her arms around Jennifer.

Jennifer squeezed her daughter close and then took the chain and fastened it around Nicki's neck. "Don't take this one off even to swim," she said through her tears.

The ring settled against Nicki's throat, back where it belonged, and when Nicki smiled, Bryan knew that his family, wherever they were, were smiling with her.

The inscription read "Nicki and Lori, forever."

Another Man's Child

CHAPTER ONE

THE WOMAN HAD A BODY that practically begged a guy to come out and play, a glint in her eyes that dared him to win.

And she was looking at Marcus. There was enough money among the businessmen she was addressing to buy the eastern United States twice over, but it was Marcus with whom she made eye contact.

He shifted in the cushioned armchair he'd chosen midway around the table. He knew Julie Winters. Had always admired her genius. She had a helluva mind for numbers and for manipulating those numbers, making her one of the most successful forces on Wall Street.

"In summary," she concluded, "independents are the businesses of the past. Diversify your assets. Scratch your own backs before someone else scratches it for you and leaves you bleeding."

She caught Marcus's eye. *I'd like to scratch your back, but I'll be gentle,* her glance seemed to say.

He had a sudden vision of Lisa's eyes when she'd looked up at him from the paper that morning. They'd had that sad, troubled, faraway quality he'd seen all too often in the past eighteen months.

The meeting was over. And Marcus had a question or two for Julie. She'd quoted some figures he hadn't heard before, pertaining to the future of electronic advertising. Standing at the back of the room while he waited for her to finish, he admired the confidence with which she was dealing with one of his more overbearing peers.

That glint was back in her eyes when she finally approached him.

"Marcus! It's good to see you again." She placed a perfectly manicured hand on his forearm, her red nails glistening against his sleeve.

"You, too, Julie. Got a few minutes? I'd like to hear more about your predictions regarding warehouse to the consumer."

"I have another session to get to," she said, "but we could talk about it over dinner."

The woman's smile promised more than just dinner, and his body surged to life. *Tell her no, jackass. A few minutes to pick her brain is all you're after.*

He looked at his watch, the Rolex Lisa had given him when he was still the man of her dreams. "We could meet back here in the lobby at six."

"I'll be here."

Her bright red lips promised to make the evening one he'd remember. With one last look up and down his suited frame, she left the room.

He tried his damnedest not to carry the vision of her lush breasts and womanly hips, encased so seductively in that black-and-red business suit, with him as he headed to the last session of the day. He was a married man. Very much in love with his wife.

Except that every time he thought of Lisa, he saw again the disappointment, the sadness he'd brought to her eyes—to her life. He'd always been a doer, a problem-solver, but there wasn't one damn thing he could do about that look in Lisa's eyes.

At five o'clock he was back in his room to shower and change from his suit to slacks and a sport coat, trading his staid navy tie for one a little more colorful. He couldn't quite meet his reflected gaze as he took one quick look in the mirror, but he refused to feel guilty. He was going to a business dinner. That was all.

He also avoided the picture of Lisa he'd set out on his nightstand when he'd checked in that afternoon. And he didn't call her as he'd promised when he'd kissed her goodbye in their garage that morning, either.

He'd come to the convention, not only to deliver his paper on multiple diversification, but to garner enough space from his lovely unhappy wife to consider the consequences of his inability to give her what she wanted most in the world. He'd sacrifice his life to save his marriage. But there were some things he just couldn't change.

The door of his hotel room slammed behind him as if sealing his fate, even while he knew that there was no earthly pleasure worth selling his soul for. But as he walked down the hall, his mind flashed back to the way Julie had looked at him, the way Lisa *hadn't* looked at him since that diagnosis eighteen months ago. These days all he saw in her eyes was that damn sadness and disappointment. He pushed the button for the elevator.

Julie was waiting for him as he stepped off the elevator, and her smile was as bright as the sequined halter dress she was wearing. Her eyes, dancing with pleasure, made another slow seductive tour of his body.

"Do I pass?" he asked, smiling as he took her arm to lead her to the glass-sided elevator that would whisk them to the top floor restaurant.

She rubbed her elbow against his side. "More than ever."

One soft breast brushed against him, and his body throbbed with sudden desire. She wasn't looking at him with the embers of a dying happiness in her eyes. He could give her exactly what she wanted without even trying.

Julie smiled politely as the maître d' led them to an intimate table for two alongside a wall of windows in the glass-enclosed revolving restaurant. Marcus felt carefree, full of anticipation, virile again, as he escorted her, knowing she was turning the heads of the other patrons. He'd always felt like that with Lisa, too, back when they spent enough time together to accommodate dining out.

"I have to admit, I'm surprised you agreed to have dinner with me," Julie said an hour and a half later. They'd finished the lobster he'd ordered, their conversation almost entirely business and even more stimulating than he'd expected, and had moved into the lounge area of the restaurant. His body was humming with the wine he'd consumed.

"You're a very beautiful woman. I find it hard to believe you'd ever question a man's desire to be with you." For just a moment his gaze caressed her. Down over her gleaming bare shoulders, her lush breasts to her slim waist, and back up to a mouth made for kissing.

"The last time we met, you didn't seem the least bit interested."

The last time. That conference in New York two years before. He and Lisa hadn't known then. "Times change." Marcus stared at the liquor he was swirling in his glass before setting it back on the table decisively. "You want to dance?" he asked abruptly.

"Yes." If she minded his brusque tone, she certainly didn't let it show as she took his hand. Along with desire, Marcus felt a surge of sympathy for her, this woman so cloaked in the aggression necessary to take her success from a man's world that she scared off the suitors she also craved.

The band was playing a romantic ballad, the perfect background for seduction. Marcus led Julie to a shadowy corner of the half-empty dance floor and brought her into his arms. Her skin was like satin as his hands came to rest on her bare back, her breasts soft mounds against his chest, tempting him. The sequins on her dress glittered under the muted lights. One dance. Just one dance.

They moved naturally together, swaying skillfully

to the music. Marcus tried not to notice when her nipples hardened against him, or to see the smoky knowing look in her eyes. He'd have to stop if he acknowledged them. He wasn't the type of man who could cross that line.

Julie's lips parted, inviting his kiss. He pulled her closer, instead, even though he knew she could feel his arousal. She moaned, pressing her pelvis against the hard resistance of his, burying her face against his neck. Her passion was so honest it threatened his control.

She was his for the taking. He could lose himself in her, bring her the satisfaction she so obviously hoped for. He didn't have a single doubt he could give her what she desired. That alone was the biggest temptation.

But still a forbidden one.

He'd known it was going to come to this. Julie had made no secret of the fact that she wanted him. So why had he accepted her invitation to dinner? Why had he asked her to dance? Why was he torturing himself?

He adjusted her body against him, trying to mold her softness so that she fit him better, to find that feeling of protectiveness that would come when she settled her head on his shoulder. He craved that feeling. Craved that surety that he could make everything right for her. That he could take care of her.

Marcus adjusted the woman in his arms again, but to no avail. She just didn't fit. She wasn't ever going to fit.

She wasn't Lisa.

And no matter how badly he wanted the release, he couldn't take it at Lisa's expense. He'd promised her his loyalty, and that, at least, was something he could still give her.

With a feeling of inevitability, he pulled back from the beautiful woman in his arms. He couldn't do it. He couldn't take the pleasure she was offering. He loved Lisa too damn much.

"HEY, DOC, HOW'S IT GOING?" Beth Montague stopped outside Lisa Cartwright's office door in the medical complex connected to Thornton Memorial Hospital.

Lisa looked up from her desk and met her friend's searching gaze with a shrug.

Coming in and closing the door behind her, Beth planted one plump hip on the corner of Lisa's desk. "The kitten didn't help, huh?"

Lisa shook her head. "No more than the cruise, the summer home at the beach and the season's tickets to the theater." Instead of filling up empty holes, the cat's presence had pointed out what bottomless pits those holes had become. She and Marcus had both tried so hard to make the cat a reason to come home that they'd smothered it with attention. "The poor thing ran from us every time we walked in the door," she said, shaking her head again.

"Cats are that way sometimes," Beth replied. "Remember I told you about Corky, the cat we had when I was growing up? He'd only come out from behind the furniture at night. I used to wait up for him some-times, and after he got used to me sitting there in the dark, he would crawl up into my lap and purr so loud I was afraid it would wake up my little brothers and sisters.''

Lisa smiled. She'd heard a few stories about Beth's favorite childhood pet.

''Of course, he got a lot bolder as he grew up. Anyway, maybe you guys just needed to give the kit-ten more time. Cats are great companions.''

''It wasn't the cat, Beth. It was us.'' She hesitated, almost loath to admit the rest. ''One night last week Marcus and I spent half an hour talking baby talk to the thing, trying to coax it out from under the bed to play with this new squeak toy Marcus bought. Sud-denly we looked at each other, sitting on the floor in our work clothes acting like a couple of idiots, and it hit us what we were doing. And the worst part was, we couldn't even smile about it. It was just too... pathetic. So Marcus found another home for the cat the next day. A home where it's allowed to just be a cat.''

Beth's cheerful blue eyes filled with sympathy. ''Okay, so you haven't found what works yet, but you will.''

''I wish I could be so sure.'' Marcus hadn't called after his meetings in New Jersey the day before as he'd promised. He'd phoned, instead just as Lisa was climbing into their big empty bed that night, and he'd been different somehow. Nothing she could name ex-actly, just a little distant, evasive, as he'd answered her questions about the day. She'd hung up with the unsettling knowledge that no matter how much she loved her husband, no matter how solid their friendship was or how completely she believed in them as a couple, their marriage was in serious trouble.

"Have you tried to talk to him again about the possibility of artificial insemination? It's the perfect answer, you know." Beth was a doctor, too, though not a pediatrician like Lisa, and she ran a fertility clinic at Thornton. Not only was she Lisa's friend, she was also the doctor who'd overseen the months of testing she and Marcus had been through in their attempts to have a child.

"I'm not going to mention it to him again," Lisa said. Her stomach became tied in knots just remembering what had happened the first time she'd broached the subject with Marcus. She'd already tried talking to him about adoption, she'd brought home pamphlets on fostering a child, and both times Marcus had refused even to discuss the issues with her. But he'd discussed artificial insemination, all right. She still remembered the stricken look on his face.

Beth's brow furrowed. "It sounds as if nothing else is working, hon. What could it hurt to talk about it to him again? The clinic's *designed* for couples in your position." Tragically widowed while still in her early thirties, Beth had never had children of her own. Now she spent her life helping others to do so.

"I can't, Beth. He'll just tell me that if I'm dissatisfied with what he can and cannot provide, then I'm free to leave him for someone who *can* satisfy me.

The worst part is, I think he really means it. As much as he loves me, he would just let me go. He's so eaten up with self-hatred he can't even look at things with an open mind. And *I* can't hurt him anymore. He sees his sterility as his ultimate failure, and I can't continue to rub it in his face."

"Do *you* think he's failed you?" Beth asked.

"No!" Lisa had no doubts about that. "I'm a doctor. I *know* he had nothing to do with the fever that rendered him sterile. I love him, Beth, flaws and all. But..."

"But?"

"But I just can't see either one of us being happy without a child. It's what we both want more than anything on earth, what we've always wanted. Hell, Marcus and I were planning a nursery before we even planned our wedding. Every big decision we've ever made, every goal we've set, has been influenced by the family we'd planned to raise. I just don't see how we can keep a union that's been built on such a foundation from toppling over."

"Answer one question for me." Beth's eyes were piercing.

"Sure. If I can."

"Who do you love more, need more—your husband, or the baby he was supposed to give you?"

"That one's easy. My husband. He's my best friend. I can't imagine a life without Marcus."

Beth stood up, nodding. "Then you'll find your answer, Lis."

"Even though there's a part of me, a part that's

been there as long as I can remember, who needs to be a mother, too?'' Lisa asked the question softly, almost afraid even to say the words out loud.

Beth's eyes warmed with concern. Lisa knew how much her friend was pulling for her and Marcus. The three of them had formed an unshakable bond that first year after Beth's husband had been shot waiting in line at a fast-food restaurant. She and Marcus had insisted that Beth move in with them, and for six months they'd both taken turns sitting up with their friend on those nights when the demons had become too fierce for her to face alone. That had been more than five years ago.

''I understand your reluctance, Lis,'' Beth said now, ''but you need to talk to him again. Have him come visit me. Maybe if he sees how much he'll be involved in the process, if he understands how scientific everything is, he'll come around.''

Lisa smiled and nodded as her friend left, but she knew she wouldn't do as Beth suggested. She'd never known Marcus to look so beaten as he had the night she'd tried to talk to him about giving him a child through artificial insemination. She'd never seen him so angry. Or so hurt. No, she couldn't do that to him again.

TWO DAYS LATER when she unpacked Marcus's suitcase and found the shirt rolled in with his other dirty clothes, she was tempted to change her mind. She picked up the shirt slowly, staring blankly at the lipstick-stained collar for a moment, her mind masked with disbelief. It couldn't be.

Standing there, unable to move, to look away, she felt frightened—and stupid. Had Marcus...? Surely he hadn't... No. Of course not. He wouldn't. Not ever.

And then she remembered his phone call from New Jersey. Not only had he not called when he'd promised, he'd been strangely evasive.

She blinked, surprised when a tear splashed onto the incriminating collar. Had they come to this, then? Had they really come to this? Were their ties of friendship, their loyalties to each other, in jeopardy? Was the love she'd cherished for more than a decade going to slip through her fingers right along with her dream of having a child? She dropped the shirt as if she'd been burned.

And then just as suddenly picked it up again. The lipstick was still there. She could see it through the blur of her tears. She just couldn't believe it. And didn't know what to do about it. This happened to other women, other couples. Not to her and Marcus.

"Nothing happened."

Lisa jumped. She hadn't heard Marcus come upstairs.

"*Something* apparently did," she said, throwing his shirt in his face. It was too much. To lose Marcus on top of everything else was just too much.

He grabbed her arm as she pushed by him. "Nothing happened, Lisa."

She looked up at him, this man of her dreams, and even blinded by tears of anger and disappointment, she knew she still loved him. After ten years of marriage, after eighteen months of anguish, even after finding another woman's makeup on his clothes, she felt the impact of him clear to her soul. "Her lipstick's on your collar."

Marcus dropped her arm and bowed his head. "We had dinner—and one dance. That's all."

It was enough. She knew him that well. Wrapping her arms around her middle, she warded off the darkness that threatened to consume her. "You wanted her."

"*She* wanted *me*. And yes, I guess part of me wanted her, too, wanted to be with a woman who didn't know I could only do half the job."

A sob broke through the constriction in Lisa's throat, and she backed away from him.

"Who was she?" She willed herself to speak calmly.

Marcus swore and strode over to her, grabbing her arms, forcing her to look at him. "Nobody. She was nobody, Lis. Just a woman. Any woman who'd looked at me the way she did would probably have had the same effect. Which, in the end, was no effect at all. Because she wasn't you."

"Was she pretty?" Lisa couldn't let it go.

"She was pretty, sure, but so are you. And you're the one I want to be with. You're my best friend, Lis."

She studied his face, his blue unblinking eyes. "Are you sure about that?"

"Absolutely."

His gaze bore into her, telling her things mere words couldn't, and suddenly some of the tension that had held her rigid, barely able to breathe, drained away, leaving her feeling weak and helpless. She sank against his chest.

He held her silently, his hand rubbing the back of her head soothingly as she soaked the front of his shirt with her tears. He was still wearing his business suit, and Lisa burrowed her arms beneath his jacket, taking comfort in his lean hard strength, letting his love console her, just as it had done for well over a decade. She needed him more than life itself. And she felt it all slipping away.

"I love you, Lis." His voice was thick through the whispered words.

"I love you, too."

But she knew that love might not be enough, not if he refused to believe in the strength of that love, not if he continued to blame himself for something he couldn't help and was convinced that she blamed him, too.

MARCUS LAY FLAT on his back, staring at the shadows the moonlight made on the ceiling as he listened to Lisa breathing beside him. He'd made love to her that night, giving her everything he had to give, and she'd been smiling when she fell asleep in his arms. But still, he knew that what he had to give wasn't enough. It was never going to be enough. Because no matter how often or how expertly he made love to her, he was never going to leave behind the seed of that love.

He was never going to impregnate his wife. He wondered how long it was going to be until she started to think about leaving him for a man who could.

She stirred in her sleep, snuggling up against his chest, and Marcus automatically put an arm out to pull her close, settling her head in the crook of his shoulder. He used to love these moments in the night when he lay awake and cradled her, glorying in the knowledge that this gorgeous, intelligent, caring woman was his. Until he'd met Lisa, the only kind of affection he'd known had come in terms of discipline, respect and loyalty—necessary, but so cold. It had taken years before he'd really believed that Lisa's body curled warmly and lovingly into his was something he could count on for the rest of his life.

Now the feel of her against him was merely a reminder of how he'd failed her, of what he couldn't do, of things he couldn't make right.

Being careful not to disturb her, Marcus got up from the bed and went downstairs, hoping to dispel his demons with a shot of whiskey. But after the second shot, he knew the hope was in vain. He sat alone in the living room of the home where he'd grown up, where his father and grandfather had grown up before him.

He had it all. He'd taken the family shipping business and turned it from a solid respectable venture into an enterprise that far surpassed even his father's vision. Cartwright Enterprises had been through many transitions since its inception almost two centuries before. His early ancestors had made the family's first millions in whaling and sealing, and the generation following them were glorified Yankee Peddlers. His grandfather had expanded into imports and exports. Marcus's father had doubled the Cartwright shipping fleet before a car accident had taken his life—and his wife's, as well.

But in the eight years since Marcus had taken over, Cartwright Enterprises had become a business of the nineties. It owned several of the companies it had once shipped for. It was no longer just the middle man.

And like his father before him, Marcus had done it all for the son to whom he would one day pass his heritage. He was a Cartwright. One of *the* Cartwrights. His ancestors, English gentry with everything but money, had come to the New World with dreams and determination. Through the early battles with Indians, the revolutionary war, the Civil War and both world wars, the Cartwrights had remained strong, determined and successful, each generation continuing and surpassing the achievements of the one before. And from the time he was old enough to understand, Marcus had worked hard to fulfill his responsibility to his birthright, to ensure that the breath of his ancestors, when he passed it on, would continue to thrive.

But unlike his father, who'd worked for financial power, Marcus had worked like a madman for another reason. He'd done it to buy his freedom, to have the time to be at home with his family when he had one, to make it to every school play, to watch each and every game, to attend all recitals, birthday parties and Christmas pageants. He wanted to make enough babies with Lisa to fill the rooms in the home he was born to, and to dispel forever the emptiness of his boyhood.

He didn't look back on those lonely years with any fondness. His parents had been interested in raising the Cartwright heir, not a child.

Marcus reached for the bottle and poured another inch of scotch. His mind turned to his sterility, and he tried for the millionth time to think about the alternatives Lisa had talked about soon after his diagnosis. But as hard as he'd tried, and God knew he'd tried, he just couldn't consider them rationally. He felt the rage coming, felt it in the sudden heat in his veins, in the tenseness in his muscles. *Why?* By what cruel twist of fate did *he* have to be the one to end the Cartwright line, to silence forever the voices of his ancestors? He who wanted children more than wealth, who understood their value in a way his father never had?

He'd worked hard all of his life, earning an honest living when, in his position, it would have been surprisingly easy to do otherwise. He gave to charities. He upheld the faith of his ancestors and never balked when there was a task to do. He'd never left a job unfinished in his life.

So why had he been robbed of the ability to do the one thing he wanted most to do? There were plenty of men out there who didn't want children, who fathered them without even knowing or caring. Yet it was Marcus who'd had that privilege revoked. *His* wife who had to look elsewhere to get his job done.

Marcus strode around the living room, trying to outdistance his demons. And as always, as the rage within him continued to boil, he was seized by the desire to just pack his bags and leave this town for a place where the Cartwright name meant nothing, where he could hide from his shortcomings—and his heritage. Where he could live out the rest of his days, if not in happiness, at least in peace. He'd have gone, too. If it wasn't for Lisa.

Marcus took one last swallow from the crystal shot glass, then hurled it into the fireplace where it shattered into a thousand glittering pieces, reminiscent of the dreams he had once been foolish enough to have.

CHAPTER TWO

DREAMS. LISA HAD always had two of them. One was to grow up, get married and have babies as sweet as her little sister, Sara, had been. Lisa had been an only child, a somewhat lonely child, until she was ten years old. And then Sara had come along, surprising them all, like a ray of sunshine that continued to shine in Lisa's heart long after her baby sister was gone.

Lisa's second dream, also a by-product of Sara, was to become a pediatrician. So at least she had realized one of the two. And as the weeks passed, she immersed herself more and more in her work. Marcus was never home anymore, and on the rare occasions when he wasn't working late, he kept busy in his den or out on the grounds, rarely smiling and hardly looking at Lisa at all.

So Lisa volunteered for an extra shift on call. She added to her already full patient load; she offered to cover for whatever physicians were on vacation or taking a long weekend to spend with their families. Anything she could do to stay busy, to keep her mind occupied, to ignore the fact that Marcus was slipping away from her. He still made wonderful love to her— Marcus had always had an incredible sexual appetite—but he didn't gaze into her eyes while they were making love anymore, nor did he linger in her arms afterward.

Pushing away the fear that had become her constant companion, Lisa pulled some recently delivered X rays from their folder, placed them up on the view box beside her desk and flipped on the light so she could study the results. Her heart sank.

Little Willie Adams's back was broken; he wouldn't be playing Little League any more this season, and probably not next, either. Depending on the damage to his spinal cord, he might never be playing it again. Reaching for the phone, she punched in the number for one of the best neurosurgeons she knew, all the while thinking of the little redheaded boy lying so still in the hospital bed across the street. Willie was one of the patients Lisa saw gratis, courtesy of state welfare. He was one of six kids, the only boy, that his mother was raising single-handedly. His father had run off before Willie was born. The one good thing in Willie's life was his success in Little League.

Lisa pulled into the gate at home two hours later, weary in body, but even wearier in soul. She'd spent an hour with Willie until Dr. Shea had come; she'd told Willie and his mother Willie's prognosis, she'd answered all of his mother's questions and watched Willie's face turn to stone, but she'd never seen him shed a tear. Considering the amount of pain he was in, that was amazing in itself, but to have just had his one hope of getting out of the ghetto snatched away...

Lisa left her Mercedes in the circular driveway,

then trudged up the steps, her briefcase weighing on her exhausted muscles as she let herself in. It was late, long past dinnertime, and she knew Hannah, the part-time housekeeper who saw more of Lisa and Marcus's home than they did, had left hours before. She started to call out for Marcus, needing him desperately, but closed her mouth before she wasted her breath. He'd been out until midnight or later most every night lately, attempting to keep Blake's, a family-owned chain of department stores in Rhode Island, from going bankrupt. She didn't begrudge him the time. Not really. She knew her husband well enough to know how good it made him feel to be able to help save someone else's dream. Especially since he couldn't seem to save his own.

But that didn't stop her from needing him.

Taking her briefcase into the home office she shared with Marcus, she shrugged out of her suit jacket and rubbed the stiff muscles along the back of her neck. Sometimes she wondered if she was *meant* to be a doctor. She'd never been able to develop that impenetrable shell they'd talked about in medical school.

"Rough day?"

At the sound of Marcus's voice she whirled around, filled with the instant warmth that still came to her every time he walked into a room.

"Yeah." She didn't elaborate as she once might have, rubbing at her neck again.

He looked relaxed, wearing slacks and a polo shirt, instead of one of the suits he always wore to work.

She wondered how long he'd been home and was instantly disappointed that she hadn't been here with him. The gorgeous Connecticut June weather was perfect for evenings sitting out under the stars, sharing a drink. Or more.

His eyes were loving, sympathetic, as he moved closer to her.

"You want to tell me about it?" He pushed her hands aside and began massaging her tense muscles with the expertise born of experience.

Lisa bowed her head, giving him easier access to her neck. "A patient of mine, an eleven-year-old boy, broke his back today playing baseball. He was sliding into home and the catcher fell on top of him."

"God, the poor kid." Marcus's hands continued to work their magic.

"He'd just had an offer from a city team. He's good, Marcus. And he's inner city. Baseball was his one shot out."

"He's young, Lis. He's got time to mend." Marcus pulled her fully into his arms and Lisa soaked up his strength, nestling her head into her usual place on his shoulder.

"He's paralyzed. The damage may be permanent." As she said the words out loud, words she hadn't yet had the heart to tell Willie or his mother, the dam inside her broke and she started to sob, not only for the stalwart little boy lying so still across town, but for the man who held her, for the permanent damage that long-ago fever had done to him, for the damage it was still doing to *them*.

Marcus held her until her emotion was spent. And then he started to kiss her, long, slow, tender kisses. The healing kind. Offering her forgetfulness in the one way that always worked. She clung to him desperately, and when they moved upstairs to their bedroom, arms wrapped around each other, she gave him all the love within her, all the passion only he could raise. He was her husband, her lover, her best friend. And just as she was going to do everything in her power to help Willie Adams, including footing his bills anonymously if she had to, she was going to do whatever it took to fix the problems between her and Marcus.

Her life's work was saving lives, but her life was nothing if she didn't have her soul mate beside her, sharing it with her.

WITH HER NEWFOUND RESOLVE still burning inside, Lisa approached her tenth wedding anniversary the following week with optimism. She checked in on Willie that morning, satisfied that he'd come through his second surgery better than they'd hoped, and then took the rest of the day off. She had some primping to do.

Stopping at the mall on the way home, she wandered through a couple of exclusive lingerie shops until she found just what she was looking for—a black pure-silk teddy. Marcus was a sucker for silk.

"Will there be anything else, Mrs. Cartwright?" the saleswoman asked when Lisa handed over her charge card.

"Is that lavender bubble bath?" Lisa gestured toward the display beside the counter.

"Yes, ma'am. It's not too overpowering, though, and it's full of moisturizers. I use it myself. Would you like to try some?"

"Sure, why not?" Lisa said, feeling a little decadent. These days she rarely had time for more than a quick shower, let alone a leisurely bubble bath, but her husband had always liked the scent of lavender. And she'd bet he could think of a few interesting things to do in a lavender-scented tub. He was wonderfully inventive.

She hurried home and stayed there only long enough to pack a few things for herself and a bag for Marcus. Telling Hannah not to bother with dinner, she jumped back in her car and headed out of New Haven. She knew exactly where she was going. Haven's Cove, the beautiful private resort on the coast between New Haven and Milford. It was the perfect place for her and Marcus to celebrate. If the memories they'd find there didn't remind them of all that they were to each other, nothing would.

She spent half an hour or more reacquainting herself with the grounds, glad to see that little had changed since the last time she'd been there, and then whiled away the afternoon in the salon, treating herself to the works. She was going to bring the hungry look back into Marcus's eyes.

At five o'clock on the nose, she sent a telegram to Marcus: MEET ME AT HAVEN'S COVE. I NEED LOVIN'. And then she waited.

Some of the best hours in Lisa's life had been in the cabanas at Haven's Cove. It was where Marcus had first told her he loved her. Where, months after they'd become lovers, she'd finally seen the knowledge of her love for him dawn in his eyes. Where he'd asked her to marry him.

And now she hoped he still believed in them enough to join her.

MARCUS WAS BEAT when he arrived back at his office. He'd just come from an afternoon meeting that had lasted twice as long as it should have. The Rhode Island department-store venture had to be pulled into the nineties if it was going to have any hope of surviving, and George Blake, the old gentleman who sat at the helm of the family business, while seemingly agreeable to every suggestion Marcus and his team made, was having a hard time letting go of the only way of life he'd ever known.

Marcus didn't *have* to take the time to consider the man's feelings. Not legally. But he couldn't just take over a man's life's work and leave him with nothing. He wanted Blake to understand the changes, to be able to continue to sit at the helm of his company after Marcus had him set up and running again. So he was taking the time to teach the man what it had taken himself four years at Yale, and three times as many in business, to learn. Or at least an abridged version thereof.

He'd realized halfway through the meeting what day it was. He'd been putting in so many long hours for Cartwright Enterprises the past couple of weeks that the days had all started rolling into one. Not that he minded. To the contrary. The only time he didn't have doubts about himself these days was when he was working.

But he still didn't know where the first half of the month had gone. Someone had mentioned a golf date when they'd taken a break for lunch, and it had suddenly dawned on Marcus that it was the middle of June. The sixteenth to be exact. His anniversary.

Or maybe it hadn't suddenly dawned on him. Maybe he'd been unconsciously trying to forget. He wasn't sure there was much to celebrate. Not for Lisa, anyway. Not anymore.

He'd had coffee with his wife early that morning and she'd read the paper just like every other morning, not giving any indication that she'd remembered what day it was. She sure as hell hadn't wished him happy anniversary as she had all the other years since they'd been married. And when he'd tried to call her at lunchtime, he'd been told she wasn't expected in her office at all that day. Which meant she was either out exhausting herself in the free clinic or volunteering her time at the hospital. Anything to stay away from home. Not that he blamed her. The emptiness there mocked him, too.

"A telegram came for you about an hour ago, and your other mail is there, too," Marge, his secretary of thirteen years, said as he let himself into his suite of offices on the top floor of Cartwright Tower in downtown New Haven. She'd been with him since his sophomore year at Yale, when he'd begun working his way up the ranks at Cartwright Enterprises. She'd been working for him the year he'd met Lisa; had been at his wedding, too. "There's also a stack of letters for you to sign, and Paul Silas wants you to give him a call."

"Thanks, Marge. Give yourself double overtime this week and go home. You don't owe me all these late nights."

"It's okay, Marcus. The twins left a couple of weeks ago to take summer jobs at the University of Connecticut—they're getting ready for their freshman year—and the house is so quiet it's depressing. I'd just as soon be here as home."

"Where's James?" Marcus asked.

"He's in Florida for a month, overseeing the construction of a new shopping complex outside Orlando. I almost wish he hadn't been promoted to project manager."

Marcus smiled at his middle-aged secretary's uncharacteristic grumbling. "You don't mean that, Marge. You'd have to give back that boat he bought you last summer."

Marge grinned. "You're right. I don't mean it. But I'm telling you, Marcus, for once I think you and Lisa have the right idea."

"About what?"

"About not having children. It hurts bringing them into this world, they take years off your life with all the worry they cause, and then they just up and leave home, not caring that they're breaking your heart as they go.''

"And if you could, would you trade away any of the past eighteen years with them, Marge?" he asked softly.

She smiled, her pretty features lighting up. "Of course not. Don't mind me. I guess I'll go home and bake some cookies. I promised the boys I'd send them some before the weekend.''

"So why not take tomorrow off and deliver them yourself? Storrs is only an hour away, and you'll feel a lot better once you've checked up on them.''

"Am I that obvious?''

"Maybe I just know you better than most,'' Marcus said, envying her sons. He wasn't even sure his folks had known he was gone when he left the family home for a dorm room at Yale.

"But what about the Rhode Island group?" Marge asked, frowning. "Aren't you all meeting here to-morrow?''

Marcus shook his head. "We postponed it until after the weekend. George wants a couple of more days to study the manuals for the computer system we're installing at Blake's. So take the day off.''

"Yes, sir!'' She was grinning from ear to ear as she tidied up her desk and gathered her purse.

Listening to her humming, Marcus headed on into his office and the tasks waiting there for him. Maybe the telegram was something urgent. Anything to take him away from New Haven and the empty house he knew he'd find if he went home. Of course, with all the time he'd been spending on the Blake venture, he had enough pressing work on his desk to keep him busy well past midnight. With that comforting thought, he opened the telegram.

MEET ME AT HAVEN'S COVE. I NEED LOVIN'.

Marcus stared at it, hardly daring to believe the words. But there they were, all neat caps, teasing him with long ago memories. Good memories.

He read it again. MEET ME AT HAVEN'S COVE. I NEED LOVIN'. What full-blooded man could turn down an invitation like that?

Especially when the woman issuing it was Lisa?

The love of his life.

And when the man was feeling such incredible relief that the woman wanted to celebrate their anniversary, after all. He broke every speed limit in Connecticut as his Ferrari ate up the miles to Haven's Cove.

THE CABANA SMELLED of Lisa. It amazed him that after ten years of marriage, he could be aroused merely by the scent of his wife.

"Lis?" he asked, letting the door close behind him. He was eager to see what she had planned for them, prepared to change her mind if it wasn't bed in the next ten minutes.

"In here," she called from the direction of the bathroom.

Marcus shed his jacket as he headed across the room, the splashing of water luring him on. It sounded as if she was in the bath. As he recalled, the bathtubs at Haven's Cove were huge. He'd played out a few fantasies in one of them on their honeymoon.

They'd been so filled with dreams back then. Dreams that had turned to ashes. He stopped outside the door. Maybe this wasn't such a good idea.

"Marcus, come on. The water's wonderful," Lisa called, her voice husky with desire. It was all the invitation Marcus needed. All the invitation he'd ever needed. His wife to want him.

Lavender. The air was filled with lavender. Lisa was sitting in the enormous porcelain tub surrounded by bubbles, a piece of skimpy black silk hanging haphazardly from the towel rack above her. Her dark hair was pinned up on her head, with a few wispy tendrils, damp on the ends, falling down around her face and shoulders. The glistening skin of the tops of her breasts was just visible above the white foam.

She'd never looked so desirable in her life. Not even the first time he'd seen her naked, when her young ripe body had been much more beautiful than he'd even imagined.

"Hi," he murmured, staring at her.

Her big brown eyes were sultry-looking, telling him she was his to command, to do with her as he willed. There was no sadness in them now. No disappointment lurking in their depths.

Marcus stepped out of his shoes and dropped the rest of his clothes in a pile at his feet in one quick move. Lisa's eyes widened, and for the first time in a long time, Marcus was proud of his body. Sexually, he knew no other man could please her more than he did. Because no man could love her more.

"I hope you didn't call for room service," he said, lowering himself, facing her, into the warm water.

She shook her head, her eyes filled with a hunger room service couldn't assuage. "I waited for you."

"Good." He slid his hands up her calves to thighs that were still as smooth as the day he'd married her, holding her gaze with his own. "Your skin's like satin."

She smiled slowly, the smile that had brought him to his knees the first time he'd seen it and kept him there ever since. For a woman who had come to him almost innocent, she had the art of seduction down to amazing perfection.

Skimming his hands over the sides of her hips, he found her waist and almost circled it with his big hands. Every time he felt her slenderness, her femininity, he was filled again with a need to cherish her, to protect her from whatever hurts life might throw her way.

He'd just never counted on being one of those hurts.

His fingers continued their exploration, up her rib cage to her breasts. He cupped their exquisite softness, knowing the feel of them, and yet finding their familiarity wildly exciting. They were his. *She* was his. Right here. Right now.

"You're as beautiful now as you were the first time," he said.

She reached for his swollen penis and caressed it.

She chuckled softly, a sweet husky sound. "You remember that first time? I wanted you so badly it was driving me crazy, but I was scared to death you'd think I was easy."

Marcus smiled, too, remembering. She'd been such a contradiction, seducing him and crossing her knees at the same time. "All I could think about was getting between those gorgeous legs of yours. You'd been tempting me all summer, running around in shorts so short they revealed more than they concealed."

"They did not!" she said, pretending to take offense.

"Oh, yes, you were a little tease," he returned, and then he immediately availed himself of the treasures the shorts had promised that long-ago summer.

Her hand had fallen away from his penis, and now she reached for him again. "Oh, Marcus, please..."

He gently pushed her hand away, completely caught up in his memories of the past, the invincible feeling he'd had the day he'd married her. "Not yet, my love."

"But..." She frowned up at him as he placed his finger against her lips.

"Let me." He spent the next hour, in the bath and then out on the bed, showing her how much he adored her.

Her eyes were slumberous with passion, with a peace he hadn't seen in months, when he finally entered her and found his own bit of paradise.

"I love you," she whispered in the aftermath, her

body still clinging to his. Her words warmed his heart as thoroughly as she warmed his body.

"I love you, too," he said. He looked at her and saw she was smiling. And at that moment, Marcus had all he wanted. "Happy anniversary." They fell asleep, locked in each other's arms.

MARCUS STAYED IN BED with Lisa for most of the next twenty-four hours, loving her, laughing with her, debating with her about everything under the sun—except the life awaiting them outside the door of their cabana. They explored each other in ways they never had before, made love in ways that were achingly familiar and ordered whatever outside sustenance they needed from room service. He wanted to draw out their time at the cabana forever. To never let the honeymoon end. Because he was afraid of what came next.

As long as they were in the cabana, he was everything Lisa wanted. It was only outside those doors that he failed her.

"Can I ask you something?" Lisa said, looking up from the crossword puzzle she'd found in the morning paper that had been delivered along with their breakfast. She was dressed in his shirt from the day before, propped on a mountain of pillows in the middle of the bed.

He set the business section of the same paper down on the table beside him. "Sure," he said, but he *wasn't* sure. The shadows were back in her eyes.

"If you'd known ten years ago that we couldn't have a family, would you still have married me?"

"Does it make a difference?" He wished he was wearing more than the sweats Lisa had packed for him. He had a sudden urge to head back to the city.

She shrugged, laying aside her puzzle. "I think it might."

"I suppose, if you'd known then what you do now, if you'd been content with that knowledge, then yes, I'd have asked you to marry me."

"Why?" Her beautiful brown gaze bore into him, telling him how badly she needed answers, allowing him no choice but to give her the truth.

"Because even back then you were the best friend I'd ever had." He moved over to the bed, taking her hands in his. "I've never been able to talk to another person the way I can talk to you, Lis. I've never cared as much about another person's happiness as I do yours."

She smiled, but her eyes brimmed with tears. "Then where are we going wrong now?"

"It's not a perfect world, Lis. And you didn't marry me at peace with the idea of never having a family."

"But I would have, Marcus. You have to believe that. I care the same about you as you do about me. You're right, it's not a perfect world, and our lives aren't turning out to be the perfect fairy tale we envisioned, but we still have each other. Why can't that be enough?"

"Can you honestly tell me that you're content facing the rest of your life childless?"

Her gaze dropped to the covers across her knees. He had his answer. And so did she.

But she was looking at him again when she finally spoke. "I can tell you this, Marcus. I can't bear to face the rest of my life without my best friend." She began to cry.

Her tears broke his heart and he wiped them away with the pads of his thumbs. "Shh."

"I'm scared, Marcus. I'm so scared I'm losing you."

If truth be known, Marcus was more than a little afraid himself. "I'm right here, honey. And I love you more now than ever. We'll get through this, Lis. Trust me." Even as he said the words, he feared how empty they might prove to be. He loved her. More than life. But he was no longer sure he could make her happy.

AT TEN THAT EVENING Lisa's beeper sounded. One of her welfare patients had acute appendicitis, and Lisa had to rush back to town to perform an appendectomy.

But she took the memory of the past twenty-four hours with her, along with a large dose of hope. The bond between her and Marcus was too strong to be ripped apart. Somehow they were going to find a way to be happy together again.

She grabbed a couple of hours' sleep on the couch in her office after the surgery and then started her morning rounds. But only after calling Marcus and telling him how much she loved him. He was on his way into work, as well, but said he'd be home early that evening.

And he was. That evening, and several after that. But as the days passed, it was getting harder and harder for him to pretend he was happy there in that huge house. Its emptiness taunted him with what would never be. She knew it must, because it taunted her.

"Let's move," she said one night almost two weeks after their anniversary. They were both in their home office, working at their respective mahogany desks on opposite sides of the room, but Lisa had a feeling Marcus wasn't concentrating any better than she was.

He looked up from the page of figures he'd been studying when she spoke. "Move? Move where?" he asked, frowning at her. "I've lived here all my life. Why would I want to move?"

Lisa told herself not to be intimidated by that frown, nor by his logic. They *had* to do something.

"That's exactly why. You've lived here all your life. Maybe we need a change."

He set his pen down on top of the papers in front of him. "What kind of change?"

"I saw this new development out on the edge of town today—you know where the old whaling museum used to be?" Lisa couldn't look at him as she continued, feeling herself starting to sweat. "It's called Terrace Estates and it's a beautiful gated community. The condominiums are larger than most single-family homes, and they're all set back from the street about a hundred feet, some more, with separate gated yards. There are three community sports complexes, a PGA golf course and even a couple of fine restaurants all within the community walls. And there's twenty-four-hour security, too.''

''I didn't realize you had a problem with our security. Why didn't you tell me you're nervous here alone?''

''I'm not!'' Lisa said, afraid to tell her proud husband the real reason she'd gone to see the new community. And even more frightened by the fact that there were things she could no longer discuss with him.

She and Marcus seemed to have made an unconscious agreement after they'd left Haven's Cove two weeks before to stop talking about what ailed them. It was as if by ignoring the problem, they could pretend it didn't exist. But it did exist, and Lisa feared that if they didn't do something soon, she was going to lose Marcus.

''What is it, Lis? I always thought you loved this place.''

He sounded disappointed. ''I *do* love this place. I always have. But Terrace Estates might suit us better.'' She sneaked a peek at him. He was still frowning, obviously confused. ''It's an adult community, Marcus. I just thought we might be happier there.''

He didn't say anything. But the tightening of his jaw told her he now understood her motive. He sat silently at his desk, his fingers steepled in front of him, his chin so rigid it could have been carved from stone. Lisa longed for him to look at her, to give her some hint of what he was thinking, what he was *feeling*. Day by day, he was closing himself off to her. And day by day, her heart was breaking.

"I'll take a look at it." She jumped when he finally spoke, his voice without inflection, and his eyes, when she met them, were just as empty.

"Tomorrow?" she asked, desperate enough to keep pushing.

"Fine. Set up a time."

They were the last words he said to her that night. Although he reached for her when he finally climbed into bed beside her sometime after midnight. And while she went willingly into his arms, she didn't find the joy she'd found there two weeks before. And once again, when he reached his peak, his gaze was locked, not on her, but on the wall behind her head.

CHAPTER THREE

"THE WALLS ALL HAVE double insulation to insure your privacy, in spite of the common wall between you and your neighbor. Of course, since we're all adults here, we find we have little problem with noise..."

The woman continued with her friendly sales pitch, but Marcus had a hard time concentrating on what she was saying. The four-bedroom unit she was showing them certainly appeared to live up to her praises, but for the life of him, Marcus couldn't figure out why anyone would want to live there. The Cartwright mansion might be empty, it might be quiet, but at least there he could breathe. The moment he'd driven Lisa through the ornate gates of Terrace Estates, he'd felt like he was suffocating.

They'd been stopped by a security guard immediately. Their names were on the visitor list and the guard sent them on through, but if they lived there they'd have to show a pass to the security guard every time just to get to their own home. Their guests would have to do the same. It reminded Marcus of a prison.

But if this was what Lisa wanted.

He looked at his wife as she followed the Terrace

Estates representative into a double walk-in closet. Lisa had come straight from work and was wearing the soft yellow suit he'd bought her last Christmas. The cropped jacket showed off her slim waist, and the short skirt complimented her long gorgeous legs, reminding him of the last time they'd been wrapped around him. She'd cradled him lovingly, but without ecstasy. He was losing her, slowly but surely.

"Marcus! Look at this closet! It's big enough to be another bedroom." Lisa sounded almost as enthused as the Realtor. Didn't the place seem as barren to her as it did to him? Had they really grown so far apart?

"It is large," Marcus replied, glancing inside. It seemed like a lot of wasted space to him. And it was along the wall the unit shared with the place next door. He couldn't imagine listening to some stranger scraping hangers along the clothes bar every morning. Couldn't imagine why anyone would want to.

"Oh, and come see the bathroom!" Lisa called from the other side of the master suite.

Marcus made the proper noises as she pointed out the sunken bathtub, the separate Jacuzzi and shower stall. Very nice, very modern, but he just didn't see how any of this was going to help things. Their problems went a lot deeper than empty rooms. Lisa was only fooling herself if she didn't see that.

"What do you think?" Lisa whispered to him as he peeked into the ceramic-tiled shower stall.

"We'll buy it if you want it." He'd never been good at telling her no.

With her hand on his shoulder, she turned him to

face her. "Do *you* want it?" she asked, her big brown eyes filled with love—and doubt. The Realtor had tactfully disappeared.

"I want you to be happy."

Lisa's eyes filled with tears. "I *am* happy, Marcus. As long as I'm with you," she whispered.

Looking down into her lovely face, Marcus could almost believe her. "Then let's go home," he said, putting his arm around her as he walked her out. Her hand slid around his waist, pulling him closer, and he tried to convince himself that she wasn't ruing the day she'd fallen in love with him.

"Disappointed?" he asked, glancing over at her as they left Terrace Estates behind them.

She shook her head. "Relieved. I love our house. I'd have hated living there."

"But you'd have done it."

"Yes. But, oh, Marcus, it's just…I miss you. I miss the time we used to spend together." She stared out the windshield.

They'd been together almost every evening for the past couple of weeks, but Marcus knew what she meant. They were together in body, but in the ways that mattered, they were more apart than ever. Since their anniversary, they'd been hiding from each other—thinking before they spoke, weighing every word to make certain they didn't voice the thoughts that were tearing them up inside.

"Let's go to the club," he said suddenly. "We haven't gone dancing in months." He needed to hold her. Just hold her.

She turned to him, her face alight. "What a good idea! I'd love to."

He grabbed her hand, holding it under his on the gearshift between them. "Dancing it is," he said, and he turned the car along the road toward the country club. Disaster had been averted once more.

But as he drove her home later that night, as he took her upstairs, undressed her and made slow intimate love to her, Marcus was stabbed again with the guilt that was corroding everything good and dear in his life. What right did he have to deprive her of the family she wanted, the family she'd always dreamed of having? What right did he have to deny that family the chance to thrive under her great store of love? What right did he have to keep it all for himself?

None. No right at all. He simply wasn't ready to face the alternative. To live his life without her beside him. He'd been taking care of Lisa since the first day he'd met her, when she'd been trying to carry too-big boxes into her sorority house the August before her sophomore year at Yale. He'd taken one look, relieved her of her burden and decided then and there that she needed watching over. By him. He'd been watching over her ever since, this gorgeous woman who was physically weaker than he and therefore in need of his protection. But he'd known almost from the first where the real strength in their relationship lay. Within her. He drew his strength from the love she gave him so freely. And, God help him, he wasn't sure he could give that up.

He held her long into the night, listening to her

breathe softly beside him. But sleep eluded him. His own selfishness left too bitter a taste.

LISA'S THIRTY-THIRD birthday fell on a Sunday in the middle of July, and for once she wasn't on call. Marcus woke her with a kiss when the sun was peeking over the horizon. He set a warming tray laden with two covered plates, a single red rose and an envelope on the night table beside her.

"Happy birthday, sweetheart," he said, kissing her once more before he straightened.

He was wearing nothing but a pair of cut-off sweats, and desire pooled in her belly as she ran her gaze up his long muscular thighs.

She lifted the comforter and smiled at him. "Come back to bed, Marcus..."

The omelets Marcus had made for them were still warm, if a little tough, by the time they got to them, but Lisa enjoyed every bite. Hannah provided enough deliciously cooked meals to get them through the week, but they cooked for each other on weekends. Lisa always enjoyed those meals the most.

She and Marcus sat across from each other on the unmade bed, the warming tray a table between them. Or rather, she sat. He was sprawled on his side, propped up on an elbow, taking up the whole length of the bed, and still naked.

"You're beautiful, you know that?" he said, munching on her last piece of toast.

"I'm glad you think so."

"I know so." He motioned to the envelope still

propped against the bud vase on the tray. "That's for you."

Lisa reached for the envelope slowly, excited, but just a little afraid to see what was inside. Marcus wasn't a card man. In all their years together, he'd only given her two. One on their first anniversary and one for Valentine's Day. She still had them both.

The intent way he was watching her as she slid the card from the envelope only increased her trepidation.

The front was simple, an airbrushed picture of a sailboat. She opened the card.

Every day of my life, I celebrate the day you were born. Love, Marcus. He'd written the words in his familiar scrawl. The rest of the card was blank.

Tears filled Lisa's eyes as she read the words again. She hadn't realized how much she'd needed that reassurance.

She looked across at her husband, smiling through her tears. "Thank you."

Removing the tray from the bed, he tumbled her onto her back and showed her the truth of his words.

"HOW ABOUT WE MOVE this party to the shower? We have exactly half an hour before we have to be somewhere," Marcus said almost an hour later.

Lisa glanced at the clock. "Where could we possibly have to be at nine-thirty on a Sunday morning?"

Marcus just grinned and headed across the room to her dresser, pulling out a pair of white shorts and a blue-and-white crop top. "You ask too many questions. Now get your pretty rear into the shower and then into these clothes." He tossed them on the bed.

Two minutes later she heard him singing in the shower. With one last sip of coffee, she went in to join him. In spite of her efforts to draw him out, Marcus remained closemouthed about where they were going as he hurried her out to his Ferrari. Lisa giggled, enthralled with this playful side to her husband. Marcus hadn't been so lighthearted since before—

No. I'm not going to think about that. Not today.

"We're heading toward the ocean. Are we going to Angelo's?" she asked, naming her favorite Italian restaurant.

Marcus shifted the Ferrari into fourth and grinned at her.

"But, Marcus, we just ate breakfast."

He kept his gaze on the road, still grinning.

She thought about Angelo's succulent pasta. The bottomless basket of freshly made Italian bread. "I suppose we could walk on the docks awhile and work up an appetite."

If anything, his grin grew wider. The man was infuriating. Didn't he understand that she didn't want to spoil a perfectly wonderful meal by being too full to eat it?

"You don't want to walk on the docks?" she asked.

"I didn't say that."

"That's the problem. You aren't saying anything.

Going to Angelo's is a wonderful idea. I *want* to go. I'm just not hungry yet.''

''Did I say anything about going to Angelo's?''

He'd stopped the car at the marina. And right in front of her, bobbing in the deep blue ocean, was a sleek beautiful sailboat with a huge red ribbon blowing from the masthead. But the name, written in large gold print across the stern, was what finally reached her. *Sara.*

The name she'd chosen for their firstborn, in memory of her little sister.

''She's ours?'' she asked, still staring at the boat. She'd always wanted to learn to sail. And Marcus had always promised to teach her. But somehow they'd never found the time.

''Happy birthday, Lis.''

Excitement bubbled up inside her. Excitement and hope for the future. Their future. This was something they could do—together.

''Are we going to sail her today?''

''Unless you'd rather go straight to Angelo's,'' Marcus said, his eyes twinkling.

Lisa punched him in the arm, then threw her arms around his neck, kissing him full on the mouth. ''Thank you, Marcus.''

''You like her?'' he asked, and she heard the hesitation in his voice. There it was again, his questioning his ability to please her. She just didn't know how to convince him that he still made her happier than any other person on earth. That it was something he did just by loving her. She cursed his parents for teaching him that he had to earn affection, for showing him that if he was ever cause for disappointment, he'd lose that affection. For convincing him that he was responsible for everything—even those things beyond his control. For making him doubt that he was worthy of his wife's love.

Lisa looked at the *Sara* again, the shiny white bow trimmed with royal blue. "It's perfect," she said, giving him another hug. She'd just have to keep showing him until he believed again.

"In that case, Dr. Cartwright, let me teach you how to sail."

They didn't go far, they didn't go fast, and at times, Lisa was more of a hindrance than a help, but she loved every minute of it. The boat was just the right size for a two-man crew, and Lisa was delighted when she discovered the cabin below, complete with a tiny kitchen, an even tinier bathroom and a queen-size bunk.

"We'll christen it soon," Marcus called down from the deck where he was busy maneuvering them toward Long Island Sound. Lisa smiled. He'd read her mind—as he often did.

She was exhausted but happy when they finally docked the boat in the slip just before sundown. She couldn't remember a day she'd enjoyed more. The Connecticut shoreline beckoned them, the lush green banks blending into the vivid blue sky as if rendered on canvas by a painter.

Lisa's skin was a little tender from so much time in the sun, her cheeks and hair were filled with salty ocean spray, her clothes were damp and wrinkled, and she felt great. She watched as Marcus went forward and secured the *Sara* to the dock. The wind had blown his hair into casual disarray, his polo shirt had come untucked from shorts that were no longer white, and his skin had a healthy golden glow. A secret little thrill washed through her as she watched him. He was gorgeous—all man—and he was hers.

A pretty young woman standing with a baby on her hip on the deck of the boat across the dock from the *Sara* smiled and waved when she saw Lisa on the deck. Lisa waved back just as a toddler came running up and clutched the woman's leg, saying something Lisa couldn't hear.

With a shrug and another little wave, the woman took the child's hand and led him away. Probably to the bathroom, Lisa thought. She wondered if the woman knew how incredibly lucky she was.

And she was so young. She couldn't have been more than twenty-two or -three. A whole decade younger than Lisa. And she already had two children. Lisa blinked back the tears that sprang to her eyes, quickly wiping away the couple that spilled over, cursing herself for her weakness. She lived a blessed life, with a man she adored. It was enough.

"Let's get this thing bedded down," Marcus said, his voice clipped. He'd come up behind her.

Lisa swung around, stricken. Marcus looked from her tear-filled eyes to the other boat, where the woman and her children had been standing only seconds before, and then turned away. His shoulders were as stiff as his Puritan ancestors'. Lisa knew he'd seen the whole thing.

Cursing herself again, Lisa ran her hand along his back. "Marcus—"

"Leave it, Lis."

He didn't look her way again as he instructed her on furling the sails.

Lisa helped Marcus secure the *Sara* in the slip, eager to learn everything she could about caring for their new boat, but much of the glow had gone from her day. Marcus was beating himself up again, and this time it was her fault. Suddenly thirty-three felt ancient.

A MONTH LATER Marcus gave Lisa another surprise, though he wasn't there to share it with her. She went in to see little Willie Adams again, the eleven-year-old ball player with the broken back. She'd talked to Marcus about the boy weeks before, and he'd agreed that they would finance the boy's treatment, but so far, Willie's physical-therapy sessions had been a complete waste of time. She'd been particularly worried because the boy's lack of progress stemmed more from his defeated attitude than it did from his injury.

But when she entered his room at the hospital that morning, he was wearing a baseball glove and tossing a ball between it and his free hand, in spite of the cast that kept most of his torso immobilized. His red hair was combed into place for the first time since she'd admitted him, and he was grinning from ear to ear.

"How you doing today, Willie?" Lisa asked, taking the chart from the end of his bed to see what could have brought about such a miracle. Had the boy regained some more feeling in his legs? And if so, why hadn't she been called? She'd left instructions to be informed the minute there was any change.

"Hi, Doc. Watch," Willie said. He shoved the covers down past his toes, and slowly began to rotate his right foot. And then, a bit more quickly, his left.

Lisa watched, her heart thumping. *Finally*. Now he had hope.

"That's great, Willie!" she said, as the boy started on his right foot again. "How does it feel?" She ran her hand over the boy's leg.

Willie shrugged, his freckled face breaking into an embarrassed grin. "I guess I can feel it a little better," he said. "It kinda hurts."

Lisa helped him settle the covers back over his partially paralyzed limbs. "Well, don't overdo it, buster," she said. A week ago she'd been begging him to try to sit up.

"But I gotta work hard, Doc. Danny Johnson says that if I'm better by next summer, I can come to his Junior League training camp."

"Danny Johnson?" Lisa asked, suddenly understanding—and falling in love with her husband all over again.

"He's a pitcher for the Yankees, Doc, the best, and he runs a camp for promising teenage baseball players every summer."

He'd also gone to college with Marcus. "Teenage

players?'' Lisa smiled at the boy. ''You won't be thirteen until the summer *after* next.''

Willie grinned. ''I know. Ain't it great? I'll be the
youngest guy there, but Mr. Johnson talked to my
coach and he says I'm ready.''

Lisa replaced the chart at the end of Willie's bed.
''Then we'll just have to make sure you're better by
next summer, huh?'' That gave them a year. And as
there was no longer any sign of permanent damage
to Willie's spine, she figured they could just about
make it.

Lisa tried to wait up to thank Marcus that night,
but by midnight, she knew she was going to have to
go to bed without him. Again. She was on call starting
at six the next morning, and her young patients deserved to have her well rested. It wasn't their fault
that her husband would rather be in meetings with
strangers than at home with her. In the month since
her birthday, he'd hardly been home. And he hadn't
touched her at all.

''SOMETHING TELLS ME this is more than just a
friendly visit,'' Beth Montague said when Lisa took
a chair in Beth's office late the next afternoon. The
office was light, airy, with a white carpet and a lot of
blond wood. And comfortably cool, despite the August heat.

''I'm losing him, Beth.''

Beth was silent for a moment, her gaze darting toward the framed picture on the corner of her desk.
Lisa knew it was a picture of John, Beth's late hus-

band, and that her friend could fully understand the
pain of losing the man you loved. "Have you tried
talking to him?" Beth finally asked, her eyes unusually somber.

Lisa shook her head. She'd been reading a pam-
phlet about artificial insemination when he'd come in
late one night a little over a week ago, and the frozen
look on his face had been haunting her ever since.
"It's a little difficult to talk to someone who's never
around." Her throat thickened with tears. For weeks
he crawled into bed at night long after she was asleep
and was up before she awoke.

"John and I couldn't have children, either. Did I
ever tell you that?"

Lisa's head shot up. "No! I thought you'd just been
waiting until the clinic was up and running."

Beth shook her head, glancing again at the picture
of her husband. "We were genetically incompatible.
I miscarried a couple of times after we were first married, but neither one of us expected to hear the doctor
tell us that I'd probably never carry a baby to term,
and that if I did, chances were it would suffer severe
defects."

Lisa was shocked. She'd never guessed. Beth and
John had always been so cheerful, so obviously happy
with their life together. "How did you get over it?"
she asked.

Beth shrugged. "It was hard at first, of course. But
we'd both come from big families, and neither one of
us had ever had a burning need to produce a child.
Quite the opposite, as a matter of fact. We appreciated

the peace we found alone together. But still, having a family was the natural course of things, so we'd decided to do it while we were still young—that way we'd have a lot of golden years afterward. Naturally, when we were first told we couldn't have children, we suddenly wanted them a lot. But once we got used to the idea of a whole lifetime of golden years, it wasn't so bad. We had more time for each other than our friends did—their time was taken up with feedings and diapering and pacing the floor with crying infants. As it turned out, I'm thankful for every moment of that time.''

Lisa gaped at her friend. ''You amaze me, you know that? You've been through so much, but you're one of the most cheerful and optimistic people I know.''

''Well, look at my life.'' Beth waved a hand at the room around her, the walls adorned with plaques, commendations and many many baby photos—Beth's success stories. ''How can I not be happy? I have a job I love, friends enough to chase away the loneliness, enough money to do what I want to do—and I have memories of a love most people are never lucky enough to find. But then, you know all about that once-in-a-lifetime love. You and Marcus are in with the lucky few.''

Lisa nodded.

''And that's why I can't just sit back and watch you two fall apart.''

''I can't watch it, either, Beth. Which is why I'm here.'' Lisa smoothed a wrinkle from the skirt of her pale blue suit. "I've got to do something. A lot of Marcus's problem is that he knows how badly I wanted to have a child, and he thinks his inability to give me one is cheating me out of my life's dream. I'm sure that's why he won't consider adoption. He seems to think that would be shortchanging me, raising another woman's child when I'm perfectly capable of giving birth to my own."

"I guess that makes some sort of sense," Beth said. She leaned her forearms against the edge of her desk and folded her hands in front of her ample chest, just as she had the day she'd told them that Marcus was sterile.

"He's against artificial insemination, too, of course, but you know Marcus," Lisa rushed on. "He'd make a wonderful father. And with insemination he wouldn't have to feel guilty anymore. He wouldn't have to feel like I've been cheated."

Beth spread her hands wide. "That's what I've been telling you all along, Lis. I've thought artificial insemination was your answer from the first, but it's not me you have to convince."

Lisa sat back hard in her chair. "I know. So how do I convince my husband that it's a good thing to impregnate myself with another man's seed?"

"You're a doctor, Lis. You know that part of it is little more than a medical procedure, like getting someone else's blood. We have blood banks. We have sperm banks. Legally, and every other way that really counts, the baby would belong to Marcus."

Lisa knew that. She crossed one leg over the other. "How is the donor selection actually made?"

Beth pulled what looked like a homemade catalog from a pile in front of her and tossed it to the outside edge of her desk, just within Lisa's reach. "You look through there and you pick one."

Lisa took the catalog, opening it slowly. She scanned the first couple of entries. "These listings are incredibly thorough," she said, glancing up at Beth. She'd expected to see physical characteristics, medical history, maybe even an IQ, but the records also contained notations of schooling, of likes and dislikes, habits.

"But remember, they only represent the final product of one particular genetic toss-up, mixed with an unknown environmental upbringing. There are no guarantees."

"No, of course not." Lisa continued reading. If only she could find one with eyes of Marcus's particular shade of blue, with his rich brown hair and quick mind.

"The one on page forty-nine is probably what you're looking for. If I didn't know better, I'd say Marcus was the donor."

Lisa shut the book. "I'm not really in the market."

Beth rocked back in her chair. "Fine. But if you ever decide you are, page forty-nine's there."

Shaking her head, Lisa tried to make herself think clearly, to not let herself hope for—or want—something she couldn't have. "Page forty-nine. It's really that impersonal, is it?"

"Yep."

"But what about the donors? Couldn't one come back looking for his child?"

Beth shook her head. "Not here they can't. In the first place, a donor must sign a waiver before the process is ever begun. And then, as soon as all medical tests are administered and the man is cleared for donation, all records are destroyed."

"Destroyed? They aren't locked in some cabinet somewhere or sent out into cyberspace?"

"We destroy them, as is the common practice at most fertility clinics."

Lisa folded her hands, rubbing her thumbs together. Back and forth. Back and forth. "So what happens after a donor is chosen?" She was just curious. It was fascinating what medical science could do.

"The mother has a physical, blood tests for HIV, rubella and so on."

"I just had my yearly last week, and I've been having that blood work done each year since Marcus and I first started trying to have a family," Lisa said.

Not that it mattered. She couldn't seriously consider any of this. Not without Marcus's support. She folded her arms across her chest.

Beth smiled. "I thought you weren't in the market."

"I'm not." She couldn't be.

"Well, if you were, you'd need to get out your ovulation kit again, back to the old basil thermometer every day. And as soon as you begin ovulating, you have an ultrasound done and a blood test to show your hormone level. Then come to see me within the next twelve to thirty-six hours. But remember to give me at least an hour to thaw page forty-nine.'' Beth grinned.

''That's really all there is to it?''

''For you it is. The important forms have already been signed.''

''They can't be.'' She knew Marcus had to sign a waiver, allowing her to have the procedure done. Because, legally, married to her, the baby would be his responsibility, too.

Beth pulled a thick folder from a cabinet behind her. ''Remember that first time you two came in here—professionally, that is?''

Lisa remembered back to the day she and Marcus had first come in for testing. They'd been so full of hope. Beth had asked them if they were willing to do whatever it took to have a baby. They'd both replied with an emphatic yes. And she'd given them each a stack of papers to take home, red tape that could slow down the process if they had to stop and sign for each procedure. They'd signed them all that night and Lisa had returned them the next day.

''There wasn't anything about...''

''Yes, there was. I have his signed waiver right here.'' Beth pulled a sheet of paper from the file.

Frowning, Lisa leaned forward. It was Marcus's signature all right. ''But he wouldn't have...''

Lisa thought back to that night. Marcus had gone into the office the minute they'd arrived home. He'd come back out with the completed stack of papers in record time and tossed it on the hall table, as if it wasn't the least bit important. He'd just wanted to be done with it, so sure that they weren't going to need anything but the basic tests to set their minds at ease, certain they'd conceive as soon as they quit trying so hard. He hadn't read the papers.

"It's notarized," was all she could think of to say, still staring at the form. The other information had been typed in. Marcus had simply scrawled his signature across the bottom.

Beth was nodding. "I had it done here, along with a stack of other things. At the time, I really didn't think we were going to need it."

Lisa remembered Beth saying much the same thing that first day. She'd thought that having the tests would simply help them relax and let nature take its course. It was probably the only thing Marcus had heard that whole afternoon. The only thing he'd wanted to hear. Which was another reason it had hit him so hard when they'd finally learned the truth. Until that point he hadn't even allowed the possibility of sterility to enter his mind.

"He didn't read what he was signing," Lisa finally said.

"Were you with him?"

"No." She'd been in the bathroom, drying tears she didn't want him to see. Because she'd had a feeling, even if he hadn't, that they had a problem. She was a doctor, and her instincts had been crying out for months. Oftentimes a couple couldn't conceive while trying too hard because they made love strictly to have babies. She and Marcus had always made love because they couldn't stop themselves.

"Then you don't know that he didn't read it, Lis. It's possible that he read what he was signing and, dismissing it as an impossibility, signed it, anyway, just to avoid further discussion. Marcus has always thought he could control the world, or at least his part of it."

Lisa smiled sadly. "He's always been able to until now."

Beth's eyes softened. "So what's it going to be, Lis? Are you going to pull out that ovulation kit?"

Lisa looked at the paper again. At Marcus's scrawl across the bottom. Unable to speak through her tears, she shook her head.

CHAPTER FOUR

OLIVER WEBSTER was worried. His thirty years as a professor of law at Yale had in no way prepared him to deal with the problems facing his daughter's marriage. He had no idea how to help Lisa and Marcus, what to even suggest to them. But he knew someone who might have more answers than he did. Lisa's friend, Beth Montague. He had a hunch just talking with Beth would make him feel better. It usually did.

He stopped by her office on his way home from his volunteer shift at the hospital. He'd been taking a stint every week since Barbara had died, having found during his wife's prolonged illness how badly the hospital was in need of volunteers. Helping other people who were suffering as she had made him feel a little closer to Barbara. But lately he'd been looking in on Beth on a fairly regular basis, as well.

Her office door was open and she was sitting behind her desk engrossed in a textbook that looked as big as his law tomes.

He tapped lightly on the door. "Am I interrupting something?"

"Oliver!" Her head shot up, her studious expression replaced with a welcoming grin. "I was wondering if you were going to stop by. How were things on the ward this afternoon?''

It pleased him that she remembered his schedule. ''Rosie Gardner's back in. She's developed an infection at her dialysis sight, but they've got it under control.'' He shoved his hands into the pockets of the tweed jacket he wore even in the heat. ''I, uh, wanted to talk to you about something. Do you mind if I sit down?''

''Of course not. Have a seat.'' She came around the desk and joined him. ''What's up?''

''I'm more than a little concerned about Lisa and Marcus. The last time we had dinner together, all three of us, was two months ago. They're both working themselves to death.''

Beth grimaced, her round features serious. ''I know.''

''The thing is, I know what the loss of a child, or the loss of the ability to have a child, can do to a marriage.'' It chilled him even to think about that time in his life.

''I know you do.'' Her eyes brimmed with sympathy.

''Eighty percent of the marriages that go through it fail afterward, did you know that?''

''I didn't, but I'm not surprised. I also don't think Lisa and Marcus are in that eighty percent.''

Oliver smiled, feeling better already. ''Somehow I didn't think you would. And I remember John saying that once you'd made your mind up about something, everyone involved may just as well accept it as fact.''

Though Beth's husband had been several years his junior, he'd enjoyed his conversations with his younger colleague. It was through Oliver's connection with John that Beth and Lisa had first met. During one of her mother's bad spells, Lisa had accompanied Oliver to a university function where John and Beth were in attendance. Lisa had just started her residency at Thornton Memorial Hospital at the time, and Beth had immediately taken her under her wing.

"So, are we going to have dinner or do you have to hurry off?" Beth asked. Her plump cheeks had a way of dimpling when she smiled that made him feel like smiling, too.

"Dinner, most definitely," Oliver replied, offering her his arm. He refused to dwell on the twinge of unease he felt as he escorted Beth out to his car. There was absolutely nothing wrong with the friendship he and Beth had developed over the past year. Neither of them was looking for passion; each respected that the other had already had that once-in-a-lifetime privilege. But neither had mentioned the friendship to Lisa, either. Oliver wasn't sure how his daughter would feel about his befriending a woman almost young enough to be his daughter.

Almost, but not quite, Oliver reminded himself as he sat across from Beth at their favorite Chinese restaurant. At fifty-three, he still had a lot of years ahead of him. And if dinner once a week with a woman who made him smile made those years happier ones, where was the harm in that?

"I GOT ALL THE FIGURES you needed, Mr. Cartwright. A couple of the properties look promising for Cartwright warehouses. The rest I'd leave alone."

Marcus glanced up from the report he'd been studying to find his long-haired executive assistant at the door to his office. "Thanks, Ron. Leave them there on the table, will you please?" He returned his attention to his report.

"Yes, sir." Ron Campbell did as he asked and then hesitated by the door.

Marcus looked up again. "Was there something else?"

"Not really, sir. It's just that, I hope you don't mind my asking, but you and Mrs. Cartwright aren't planning on moving, are you, sir? That property you had me check in Chicago is residential."

Marcus swore silently, tired to the bone. He should have done that investigating himself. He knew how thorough Ron was, too thorough to simply call for terms as Marcus had asked him to. Which was the reason Ron had reached such an elevated position within Cartwright Enterprises at the tender age of twenty-five, in spite of his ponytail.

"We're doing a lot more business in the Midwest. I thought it might be beneficial to have a home there," he said. "Even the nicest hotels get old after a while."

Ron nodded and left, not looking completely satisfied, and Marcus couldn't really blame him. He traveled to Chicago once, maybe twice, a year. Certainly not enough to warrant a home as nice as the one he'd had Ron check on. But Ron didn't need to know that Marcus wanted the house so that he'd have a place to go when he gave Lisa her freedom. A man of action, he wasn't sure he was going to be able to exist in their current stalemate much longer. More importantly, he didn't think Lisa could, either.

LISA COULDN'T SLEEP. She'd been restless ever since she'd stopped by Beth's office earlier that day, but the restlessness solidified into guilt as soon as she climbed into bed and turned out the light. Rolling over to Marcus's empty side of the bed, she flipped on his bedside lamp and flopped back down to hug his pillow to her breasts. She kept thinking about page forty-nine, and every time she caught her mind dwelling on that anonymous specimen, she felt as if she was being unfaithful to her husband.

Where *was* Marcus, anyway? It was almost one o'clock in the morning. She needed his arms around her to chase away the uneasiness of the day, to surround her with his love and convince her they weren't falling apart.

Beth and John had overcome childlessness quite successfully, happily, even. Surely the love she and Marcus shared was every bit as strong. Still clutching Marcus's pillow, she rolled over and looked around their room. Elegant to the core, it could have been showcased in *House & Garden* magazine, and probably had been when Marcus's parents were still alive.

But her gaze didn't fall on the matching Queen Anne furnishings or the professionally decorated walls and floor. She glanced, instead, at the little gold jewelry box Marcus had bought for her at an antique fair on their honeymoon, at the Norman Rockwell original she'd surprised him with for his thirtieth birthday, at the numerous photos on her dresser and his. At the *his* and *hers* rocking chairs they'd laughingly picked out together when they'd gotten engaged. They'd planned to rock their babies in those chairs—and grow old in them together.

But there weren't any babies to rock. And Lisa wasn't putting much stock in their growing old together, either. Not lately.

The light was still on and Lisa was lying awake in their bed when Marcus finally came in, pulling off his tie, almost an hour later.

"Hard night?" she asked softly.

"This dragging George Blake into the nineties—I don't know who it's hurting more, him or me," Marcus said with a self-derisive chuckle, sitting down to untie his shoes.

"He's still fighting you on things?" Marcus looked like he'd aged ten years in the past twelve months. There were new lines on his forehead and around his eyes.

"Sometimes. But it's even worse when he doesn't. Today he was as docile as a lamb, and I hated to see it. The man built an empire from a single five-and-dime store. He didn't do that by sitting back and taking whatever comes. And every time I have to tell him that his way won't work anymore, every time he nods and gives up without a fight, I feel like I'm killing part of a legend.''

Lisa watched him unbutton his shirt. She loved Marcus for caring about an old man's feelings, but she hated seeing him beat himself up over it. ''He didn't work his entire life to have the Blake's department stores go bankrupt.''

''You're right, of course.'' Marcus stepped out of his slacks and tossed them on the valet. ''It's just been a long day.''

Padding naked to the bed, he clicked off the light and slid in beside her.

''Thanks, Lis. I was beginning to feel like the big bad wolf.''

''You're a good man, you know that, Mr. Cartwright?'' Lisa asked, taking him in her arms automatically, before she remembered that they weren't doing that anymore. She tensed, afraid he would push her away.

''I bet you say that to all the guys, don't you?'' he teased, reminiscent of the old days when he'd been completely confident in his ability to give her whatever she wanted. But tonight, as he leaned over to kiss her, there was no sign of the arrogance that usually accompanied the remark.

It had been so long since Marcus had touched her that Lisa's entire body responded to that first stroke of his lips. The blood surged in her veins. Her nerves sang in anticipation—and relief. She'd obviously misread the last month of abstinence. Marcus still wanted her; he'd just needed her to come to him. Another first. But one she could live with. Pushing the thoughts of the day from her mind, she gave herself up to the magic that only Marcus could bring her.

This was all she needed. All either of them needed. They could make it through anything else when they shared a love this passionate.

It took her a moment to realize that Marcus wasn't sharing her passion. His body was ready, she could feel his rigid penis against her thigh, but he'd stopped kissing her and was pulling her gown down where it had ridden up over her hips.

"What..." Her voice trailed off as he pulled away from her and lay back, his shoulders propped against the headboard.

"I'm sorry," he said.

The words sounded so final.

She sat up, facing him. "Marcus? What's wrong?" Had something terrible happened that he hadn't told her about? Something more than George Blake's coming-of-age? She wanted to turn the light back on, to see his expression more clearly than the moonlight coming through the window allowed, but fear held her paralyzed.

"We can't go on this way, Lis."

She wasn't ready. "What way? What are you talking about?"

"Us. Our lives. Both of us working ourselves to death, neither of us happy."

Lisa had to touch him, to draw her strength from him, just as she always did when life looked as if it was going to be more than she could bear. "I love you,'' she said, putting her hand on his thigh, soaking up his warmth.

"And I love you." His hand covered hers, his fingers wrapping around her knuckles. "But don't you sometimes wonder what your life would be like with someone else? Honestly?''

Lisa snatched her hand away, attacked by a vision of that lipstick on his shirt collar. Did he think *his* life would be better with someone else? That his need to fill his empty house with a passel of children would just vanish?

"No," she finally said slowly, firmly. "I've known since the moment we met that you were the only one for me." There was no room for pride in the desperation she was feeling; maybe that would come later, but for now she wasn't going to give up on all that they were together without a fight.

"But back then, we thought I could give you everything," he said. "And while I *can* still provide your creature comforts, we've got to face the fact that I'll never be able to give you the one thing you want most to have.''

Relief flooded through her; another woman wasn't the problem. "You're wrong, Marcus," she said softly, rubbing her hand along his thigh again. "*You* are the one thing I want most to have. You always have been. That hasn't changed. And it never will.''

With a muffled oath Marcus stood up and pulled on a pair of sweatpants. "We can't keep avoiding the issue here, Lisa. You can't tell me you're happy, that you've been happy these past months. I know you too well. And I can't continue to get up at dawn every morning to avoid the sadness I know I'm going to see in your eyes.''

Lisa sat frozen. Feeling nothing. "What are you suggesting?"

He ran his fingers through his hair, his frustration spilling over into the room he paced. "I don't know what to suggest, or I'd have done something long before now. It looks to me like we've tried everything there is to try, Lis. And it's just not working. Maybe it's time to face the fact that there's nothing *to* do, nothing that will make this better for both of us. Hell, I didn't want to get into this tonight." He strode over to the window, a lion caged.

"Are you telling me you want a divorce?" she asked. She'd never felt so numb.

"No! Yes. I don't know, Lis." He turned to look at her, his blue gaze piercing. "How *do* you know when it's over?"

Somehow she held his gaze without flinching. "I'm not sure. I never thought it would be."

"Every time I look at you, I know I've failed you," he said, finally coming back to sit on the edge of the bed beside her.

She cupped his face. "Oh, no, Marcus. Never. Never have you failed me. Not in any way that matters. What's happened is not your fault."

He took her hands from his face, then held one on his leg between both of his. "It's not just my sterility, Lis." He tapped their hands against his thigh, accenting each word. "It's the rest of it, too. My in-

ability to consider any of your options. I wanted to.
God knows I've tried to consider adoption, but I just
can't get past the rage I feel every time I think about
your having to just make do. I just can't accept a
lifetime of pretending, not for me, but especially not
for you.''

"Adopting a child wouldn't *be* pretending. We'd
be his real parents, Marcus. He'd belong to us, just
like we belong to each other.''

"You can try to make it sound pretty, Lis, but it
wouldn't be the same as having a baby come from
your own body, feeling your belly swell with his
growth, nursing him. Those are the things I'd be denying you. Things I know you want so badly that not
having them makes you cry.'' He paused. "Things
you're perfectly capable of having with someone
else.''

Lisa cursed all those times she and Marcus had
dreamed aloud together about the family they'd have,
cursed the intimate longings she'd confessed to him.
"I only wanted those things with you, Marcus, not
with anybody else. It wouldn't mean anything with
anybody else.''

He stood up again. "Of course, you think that now,
honey, because you have no idea who might be out
there. You haven't looked. But how long do you think
it will be before you start to wonder? How long before these empty rooms start getting to you like
they're getting to me?''

Telling herself to stand, to be strong, Lisa slid off
the bed and faced the man she couldn't live without.

"Can you tell me, honestly, that you want your freedom?" she asked. "That this...this thing between us has killed your love for me?"

She could see his self-deprecating smile even as he hooked his hand around her neck and pulled her to him. "Sometimes I wish it had, honey. It would be much easier to leave you to the life you deserve if I didn't love you so damn much. But I guess you can add selfishness to my list of shortcomings, because, God help me, so far I can't seem to walk out that door."

The knot in Lisa's stomach loosened a little. "Thank God," she said. Her eyes filled with tears, which overflowed and spilled down her cheeks, wetting his chest.

He crushed her to him and held her tight. "If I were any kind of man, I'd let you go. I'd free you to find someone else." The words sounded as if they were being dragged from him.

Lisa looked up at her husband, took in his strong handsome features despite the shadows and the blur of her tears. "You are the best kind of man, Marcus Cartwright. Don't you ever doubt that."

"So what are we going to do, Lis? We're right back where we started."

"I don't know," Lisa said. But deep inside, she did know. She knew what she was going to have to do—not just for herself, but for Marcus. Because she knew her husband, his sense of honor. Eventually he would let his misplaced sense of failure convince him to leave her, to release her to what he saw as a happier life for her. But she also knew that when he did that, he'd have no life at all. He'd never have the chance to be the father he was meant to be. The father *he* wanted to be as much or more than she wanted to be a mother. He'd never have the family he'd been dreaming about all his lonely life.

Not unless she took the decision out of his hands.

SICK WITH ANXIETY, with guilt, with the million doubts that had been whirling around inside her all week, Lisa once again walked into Beth's office. She was ovulating. According to the results of the blood test, her hormone level was optimum. It was time.

Beth glanced up as Lisa came in, took one look at her face and came around the desk. "Hey, there's no reason to rush into this if you aren't ready, Lis," she said, placing a hand on her arm. "It's not too late to back out, try again next month if you want to. Or not."

Lisa thought of Marcus's death grip on her that night a week ago. She didn't know how much time she had left.

"What? And waste poor thawed-out page forty-nine?" she joked. She had no intention of backing out on what might be Marcus's only shot at the life he'd worked so hard for.

Beth smiled, but her eyes were filled with concern. "Seriously, Lis. I'm starting to feel as if I've pushed you into this. It has to be something you want deep in your heart. I don't need to remind you we're talking about the possibility of another life here."

The thrill that shot through Lisa at the mention of that life was all the incentive she needed. "I'm ready, Beth. Now quit being a mother hen and hurry up and make me a mother before I have a premature bout of morning sickness."

Beth nodded. "Okay. Everything's ready. Right down the hall. But if you want to change your mind, just say the word."

Lisa found it oddly amusing that Beth was the one getting cold feet.

LISA LOST HER lunch. But not until she'd waited the obligatory couple of minutes after Beth, clad in a white lab coat, had finished injecting her with the seed she hoped would create a new life for her and Marcus. She'd even managed to get herself back into the pale peach suit she'd donned that morning, in spite of the row of tiny buttons on the jacket. It was when she'd slipped the paperwork Beth had given her into her purse that she'd had to dart for the bathroom.

She wished she could lose the memory of the past half hour as thoroughly as she'd lost the contents of her stomach. She felt as if she'd betrayed the vows she'd made to Marcus on their wedding day.

She'd almost yelled at Beth to stop when Beth had told her she was about to pass the specimen. But her mind had been too filled with Marcus's desperation when they'd finally gone back to bed that night a week ago, as if, through sheer strength of will, he could make everything right for them. The frenzy with which he'd made love to her had convinced her more than anything that he knew it was only a matter of time before he forced himself to leave her.

But the same sense of honor that would force him to go would also force him to stay once he learned she was pregnant. Wouldn't it? He'd stay long enough to fall in love with their baby, to see that Lisa was right, that what she'd just done was their route to happiness. Wouldn't he?

Lisa's stomach turned over again as the panic she'd been holding at bay all week finally got the better of her. What if she'd just made an irrevocable mistake? What if Marcus didn't accept this baby as his own? What if he couldn't forgive her for what she'd just done? Oh, God, what if she lost him, anyway?

Leaning over the toilet bowl in the clinic's bathroom a second time, Lisa held her hair back and was sick again.

"Lisa? You okay in there?"

"Fine." Lisa tried to inject some conviction into her voice. Being sick had always terrified her.

A key scraped in the lock and Beth's face appeared around the edge of the partially open door. Apparently Lisa hadn't been convincing enough.

Her friend was inside the lavatory with the door shut behind her in a flash. She felt for Lisa's pulse.

Lisa smiled at her friend's show of concern. "I really am fine, Beth. Just not used to handling the big stuff on my own. Marcus is usually around to carry half the burden." Beth checked her pulse, anyway. "I hadn't realized just how much I'd come to depend on his opinion when I'm making a decision. I really like having him there to confide in.''

''So you still haven't told Marcus about this,'' Beth said.

Lisa shook her head.

''And you're sick with guilt.''

''That and a few other pressing emotions. Like panic.''

Beth nodded. ''A little bit of panic is to be expected, even when a couple has been planning this together for months. Having a baby's a big step.''

There it was again. That tiny thrill that was like nothing else Lisa had ever felt. A baby. A new life. A son or daughter to fill the empty rooms in Marcus's house. In his life. And hers.

''Do you think it'll take?'' she asked Beth, rubbing her hand over her flat belly.

''The first time? Maybe. Chances are, though, it won't.''

Lisa didn't think she could go through this again. ''It won't?''

''Only twenty percent conceive the first time out.''

Twenty percent. Lisa started to feel sick again, though for an entirely different reason. Did she have enough time to wait another month? Would Marcus give her that long before he did the gentlemanly thing, the honorable thing, and walked out on her?

Could she live with him for another whole month without telling him what she'd done? Could she go through this again?

''How long till we know?'' she asked.

"We can do an early detection in a couple of days. It'll be two weeks before we'll really know for sure. But, if you're so inclined, you can have a blood test done each day, since you're here, anyway. That way you'll know for certain the first second it's possible to tell."

Two weeks. Could she wait two weeks? Lisa didn't think it was possible. She also didn't see where she had any other choice.

THAT AFTERNOON Lisa did something she'd never done before. As soon as Hannah was finished for the day, Lisa called Marcus at work and left him a message to come home. Then she showered and changed into a sexy black lace nightie and waited for him to arrive. Twenty minutes later she heard him at the front door.

"Lisa?" he called the moment he stepped over the threshold. "What's wrong—" He stopped abruptly as soon as he caught sight of her coming into the foyer. She was barefoot and practically naked, her hair a wild tangle around her shoulders.

Wrapping her arms around his neck, Lisa pulled his head down for a scorching kiss before he could ask any more questions. She'd startled him. Good. She could feel his confusion in his kiss, in the way it took him just a fraction of a second to respond. She poured every ounce of passion she had into that kiss, giving him all her love, promising him it had always been, and always would be, his alone.

His briefcase dropped to the floor at their feet as

he scooped her up into his arms and carried her into the living room, falling with her on the thick velvet couch.

"I think I'm glad you called," he murmured into her ear as he worked his way around her neck, leaving hot little kisses in his wake.

"Me, too." He had no idea how glad, how badly Lisa needed to wipe away the thought of another man's seed in her body.

Their lovemaking, there on the couch, was more intensely passionate than Lisa had ever known. It was almost as if Marcus sensed her desperate need for him, and it triggered an answering need in him. And when, sometime later, he finally exploded inside her, Lisa knew it was then that their baby had been conceived. Because it was only after Marcus's love had mixed with that tiny bud of life inside of her that she could relax enough to accept the seed of another man into her womb.

He had a second orgasm before he finally led her upstairs to their bedroom, and while Lisa rode the waves with him every inch of the way, she couldn't help being aware, that second time, of a difference in Marcus's touch, an edge that had never been there before. She wasn't sure what it meant.

"I could get used to coming home early," he said later, holding her against him in the middle of their bed.

"Mmm. Me, too. 'Course the neighbors might begin to talk about the steam coming off our roof every afternoon."

Marcus chuckled, a warm rumble beneath her ear. "People have always talked about us, Lis. They can't figure out why I prefer to spend my free time with you rather than out hitting a little white ball around a bunch of manicured grass."

"Hey! I take my share of it, too. I'm always the odd one out when the girls get together in the cafeteria to complain about picking up their husband's dirty socks."

He pulled her closer. "I guess we're luckier than we think sometimes, huh?" he asked, but he didn't sound convinced.

"We sure are," Lisa said, believing the words, but knowing full well that luck, like their love, may not be enough to save their marriage.

She lay awake in his arms long after he'd fallen into an exhausted sleep. She continued to be besieged with moments of sheer panic, when she imagined the disgust, the breach of trust she'd see in Marcus's eyes once he knew what she'd done. She prayed over and over, in those moments, that the seed hadn't taken, that Marcus would never know how she'd betrayed him.

But as her mind grew weary, her thoughts drifted to her old dream, the one where Marcus was holding their baby in his big strong arms, cradling it against him, protecting it. And always in the dream, Marcus's eyes were filled with love, his voice echoing with laughter.

The dream vanished suddenly when, out of the darkness, it finally came to her what had been different about Marcus's lovemaking that second time. He hadn't held her as if he was protecting her, but more as if he was letting her go.

As if he'd been saying goodbye.

CHAPTER FIVE

RON CAMPBELL stuck his head into Marcus's office one afternoon almost two weeks later. "The house is yours, Mr. Cartwright."

"Thanks, Ron." Marcus hated the place already.

The young man came into his office and sat down in one of the huge maroon chairs in front of Marcus's desk, handing Marcus a fax with the final figures on it, along with a copy of the deed.

"They're overnighting the keys. You should have them sometime tomorrow."

"Fine. As soon as they arrive, I'd like you to fly out and get it furnished for me." He'd live with whatever choices Ron made, though judging from the ponytail hanging down the young man's back, Marcus had a feeling their tastes were very different.

"Of course. I can do it this week if you'd like. Should I consult Mrs. Cartwright on her preferences?"

Marcus shook his head, already feeling the overwhelming loss that was going to leave him incomplete for the rest of his life. "She's got a lot on her mind right now. Just go ahead and use your own judgment.''

Oh, Lisa. How am I ever going to live without you?

MARCUS LEFT WORK early that Friday. He'd just received a telephone call from Ron telling him the house would be ready the following day. He couldn't stall any longer. He waited only until he knew the housekeeper would be gone for the day and then packed up his briefcase. He wasn't sure how soon he'd be back.

"You okay?" Marge asked, a concerned frown marking her matronly brow as Marcus told her he was leaving and wouldn't be back before Monday.

"Fine." Truth was he'd never felt worse in his life. But he was finally doing something. It beat these past months of procrastinating.

Marge couldn't seem to let it go, and her words stopped him as he was about to step through the door. "You're sure nothing's wrong, Marcus?"

He sighed. "Nothing a day or two of rest won't fix."

"So why the new house in Chicago?"

He opened his mouth to tell her. She'd know soon enough, anyway. But the words just wouldn't come. "We've doubled our Midwest holdings in the past two years. It's time to have a base there."

"You haven't kept me here all these years for being stupid, Marcus. I just want you to know that I'm here if there's anything I can do."

Warmed by his secretary's words, he nodded and left. There wasn't anything Marge could do. There wasn't anything *anybody* could do.

Meaning to go straight home and get it over with, Marcus found himself heading toward Yale, instead. With Oliver Webster only a couple of blocks away, it wouldn't be right if he left without saying goodbye.

Walking across the sixteen-acre village green, bordered on three sides by churches as old as New Haven, and by Yale on the fourth, Marcus was surrounded by monuments of his ancestors. Straight in front of him was Center Congregational, the church his great-great-great grandfather had helped build with his own hands.

And when Marcus turned, Yale yawned before him, a huge testimony to the few men, Harvard graduates, a Cartwright among them, who'd had a dream, and the determination to see it through. Not only had they founded a new university, they'd fought the battle to see Yale permanently settled in New Haven, rather than one of the larger towns in the new Connecticut territory.

That was the stock from which Marcus had come, doers all. They'd passed on their determination from generation to generation, producing heirs to carry on the tradition of excellence. Each generation of Cartwrights had fulfilled that responsibility. Until now. Until Marcus. The Cartwright line was going to end with him.

Striding across campus as if he could outdistance the voices of his disappointed ancestors, Marcus hardly noticed the bustling students around him, the comfort of the warm late-summer day, the beauty that the coming fall promised to be with the abundance of huge maple trees surrounding him. He reached his father-in-law's office in record time.

Oliver's door was windowed, and looking in, Marcus couldn't help but smile, though it was a smile tinged with sadness. Oliver was sitting behind his huge oak desk surrounded by books of every shape and size—on the floor around him, lining the shelves along the walls, even on the chairs across from him. With his spectacles on, his brow furrowed, Oliver looked like every student's worst nightmare of an intimidating college professor. Few people knew just what a softy Oliver Webster really was.

Marcus knocked on the door.

"Come in," the older man called gruffly, not looking up from the volume in front of him.

"You got a minute?" Marcus asked.

"Marcus! Of course, son, come in. Have a seat."

Oliver was dressed as usual in a tweed sport coat, slacks and a skinny tie that had been out of fashion for more years than it had been in. Marcus felt a rush of affection for his father-in-law, unlike any feeling he'd ever had for his own father.

"This is difficult," Marcus said, seated in front of Oliver's desk, his elbows on his knees. He looked up at his father-in-law, at the understanding in Oliver's eyes, and suddenly felt a dam burst inside him. "I'm making your daughter miserable, Oliver. I can't remember the last time I saw joy in her eyes. These days they're either unhappy or attempting to mask unhappiness."

"Give her time, son. She'll come around."

Marcus shook his head. He couldn't allow himself to buy into false hopes any longer. "Time isn't going to change our problem. It only seems to be making it worse. These past couple of weeks Lisa hasn't just been unhappy. She's been edgy, nervous. She's hiding her thoughts from me." That was what had finally convinced Marcus to give Lisa her freedom. He couldn't bear it that his wife no longer felt she could confide in him, that he was losing her friendship along with everything else.

"Come to think of it, she's been that way the few times I've seen her, too," Oliver said, frowning. "Maybe we should have a talk with that girl, huh?"

"She and I have done all the talking we can do." Marcus shook his head a second time. "Talk can't change what's ailing us, Oliver. You know that as well I do. Lisa was meant to be a mother, and she's not going to feel fulfilled and happy until she is one."

"Have you two talked more about adoption, then?"

"Again, there's no point. I have no intention of forcing Lisa to settle for someone else's child when she's perfectly capable of having her own. I won't rob her of the experience of feeling her baby kick inside her, of having him nestled at her breast or seeing herself when she looks in his eyes."

"The way my daughter feels about you would more than compensate her for missing those things."

"I'm not so sure about that. But even if it does now, for how long? What if we find out, too late, that it doesn't compensate at all?"

Oliver spread his hands wide. "Do we ever have such guarantees?"

"It's a moot point, regardless," Marcus said, standing. "Because while Lisa needs to be a mother, I am not meant to be a father."

"What nonsense is this?" Oliver stood, too, facing Marcus. "You'd make a wonderful father."

"Apparently the good Lord doesn't agree with you." Marcus held up his hand, warding off Oliver's next words. "Say what you will, Oliver, but I've thought about this long and hard. Hell, sometimes it feels as though I think of nothing else. And the only conclusion I come to is that I'm not meant to be a father. It's the only thing that makes my sterility bearable—the thought that maybe I'm sparing some poor kid a bad life."

"I'd be more willing to bet that any child you fathered, by any means, would live a blessed life," Oliver said softly.

Marcus forced himself to look the older man straight in the eye. "I've failed Lisa. Our plans together have become impossible dreams. I do not intend to go on failing her."

"What are you saying, son?" Oliver asked, his brow furrowed.

"I've bought a house in Chicago. I plan to stay there until the divorce is final—maybe forever if Lisa wants our house. I certainly have no need for it."

Oliver fell back into his chair, stunned. "You're walking out on her?"

"Of course not," Marcus said quickly. "I'll be

there for her until the day I die, if she needs me to be. I'm simply giving her the freedom to find another man to build her dreams around. I hope, in the long run, I'll be making her happy again.''

''And this is what you want? For another man to father Lisa's children? You trust another man to teach them, to provide for them, to love them?''

Marcus sat back down, knowing he'd lost, even while Oliver was still fighting for him. The thought of Lisa in another man's arms made him want to kill. But what kind of man would he be to deny her the chance? Didn't loving her mean making her happy? And if that meant freeing her to find the dreams he couldn't give her, what choice did he have?

''I trust Lisa to choose a man who would be worthy of her children,'' he said, the words cutting a wound clear to his soul.

''You're determined to do this?''

''I am.''

''What about your own happiness, son?''

''I'll be a lot happier than I am now just knowing she's happy again.''

Who the hell am I kidding? he thought. *If I get through the next twenty-four hours, it'll be a miracle.*

FEELING LIKE A MAN convicted for a crime he didn't commit, Marcus walked slowly up the front steps of the house he'd grown up in. The late-August heat was sapping his strength, but he wouldn't take off his jacket. He couldn't afford to get comfortable. Just a little bit longer, and he could crawl away and begin the long arduous chore of healing his wounds. One thing was for sure. He was going to be healing them alone.

The house was silent when he let himself in. He was glad he'd waited until Hannah was gone before confronting Lisa. He couldn't stand to think of someone else overhearing the demise of his marriage.

"Lis? You home?" he called, dropping his keys into the little brass tray on the side table.

"In here," Lisa called from the living room.

She was sitting on the couch, her legs tucked up under the skirt of her pale blue suit, hugging one of his mother's brocade throw pillows to her chest. She avoided his eyes when he walked in, killing his last hope that there was another way. His decision was right. It was necessary.

"Our time's up, isn't it, Lis?" he asked, forcing himself to sit down and handle this calmly.

Her gaze flew to his face, stricken, but she looked away again immediately, still hiding from him. He wondered if it was relief she was hiding. She'd probably been ready to do this weeks ago, but knowing Lisa, she'd never be the one to leave him. She'd stand beside him until the end if he asked her to. And as soul destroying as Marcus knew that would be, he was tempted, even now, to ask. If she'd just look at him.

"I bought a house in Chicago," he said. "I can move in anytime."

"What?" she cried, her expression shocked. He

had her full attention now. "You're moving? You can't move."

"I thought you'd want this house, but if not, we'll get you another. You can have whatever you want, Lis. What's mine will always be yours. The divorce won't change that." Even as he said the words he wondered if he was trying to hold her with the one thing he'd always known people wanted from him—his money. "Unless you want it to, that is," he added. *Smooth, Cartwright, real smooth.*

"Divorce?" The blood drained from her face. "You're asking for a divorce?"

She wasn't supposed to take it so hard. He wanted her to be thankful for her freedom, to make this just a little bit easy on him. "It's the only answer, Lis."

She jumped up from the couch. "It's no answer at all! You can't divorce me now. I'm pregnant!" she hollered, throwing the pillow she'd been holding at him.

The pillow hit Marcus in the face and dropped into his lap. Did she say pregnant? Lisa was pregnant? He saw the confirmation in the still way she held herself, the strained look in her face. Relief rushed through him. Profound relief, leaving him weak. He didn't have to leave.

And then it hit him. The baby wasn't his. Couldn't possibly be his. Nor could it be some anonymous donor's; he knew he had to sign a waiver for that to happen, and he hadn't, had he? Somewhere in the back of his mind he wondered if he'd make it to the bathroom in time to be sick. He'd known Lisa wasn't happy. And he'd have bet his life on her fidelity. *Who the hell is this man who'd laid his hands on my wife?* He'd not only lost Lisa's friendship, he'd lost her loyalty. And suddenly nothing mattered. Nothing.

"Who's the father?" he asked, because it seemed like something he should say, not because he ever wanted to know. The deed was done. The whos and whys no longer mattered.

The part of him that was outside the entire scene, watching dispassionately as his life crumbled around him, saw Lisa fall to her knees in front of him. And that same part felt her clutch desperately at his hand with both of hers. It saw the pain in her eyes and wanted to reach out to her, make her pain go away.

But he sat frozen. His love for Lisa, his marriage of ten years, had been a mockery. He'd thought these last couple of weeks of living with Lisa and knowing he was losing her had cost him more emotionally than anything else in his entire life. He'd been wrong.

"Oh, Marcus, I'm so sorry," Lisa was saying. She was crying, too. His slacks were becoming damp with her tears.

He watched her silently, saw her wrenching display of emotion, afraid of how much he was going to feel if he allowed himself to feel.

"I...I didn't mean for you to find out this way," she said brokenly. "I had everything all planned. Oh, Marcus, I did it for you. I love you so much. Please believe me—the last thing I wanted to do was hurt you."

"I'm not hurt," Marcus said. It was true. He wasn't feeling anything at all.

"When you said that about a divorce, the news just came tumbling out. I'm so sorry, honey. There is no father other than you. I haven't been with anybody but you." She looked up, and her big brown eyes, so full of love, implored him to understand. "I was artificially inseminated, Marcus."

He didn't react. All he felt was confusion. She did this without his knowledge or agreement? Or had he... Numb, Marcus just stared at her.

"After my birthday and that horrible conversation we had about knowing when it was over," Lisa went on, "I knew it was only a matter of time before you convinced yourself I'd be happier without you. But you're wrong, Marcus. You're the other half of myself, and no other man, and no baby, either, is ever going to complete me the way you do."

She paused, still gazing up at him, as if waiting for his reaction. When Marcus continued to stare at her silently, she started to speak again, but had to pause when fresh tears choked her. Marcus watched as she blinked them away, swallowed and began again. "I also know that if you left, *you'd* never be happy again, either."

Marcus flinched, almost overwhelmed by a pain that was frightening in its split-second intensity. And then it was gone. His happiness wasn't her problem.

"I know you, Marcus," she said, her voice firm for the first time since he'd walked in the door. "You'd have lived out the rest of your life alone, never knowing the greatest of joys, only the greatest of sorrows. And I love you too much to see that happen. So I went to see Beth.''

He said nothing.

''I chose a specimen that matched you completely—brown hair, blue eyes, six-one, 186 pounds—''

''I weigh 180,'' Marcus said. It mattered somehow.

''—even the same blood type,'' she continued, as if he hadn't interrupted. ''It was just one little vial in a bank, Marcus, sort of like blood in a blood bank...'' Her voice trailed off, her eyes still pleading with him to understand.

Rage consumed Marcus, blurring the sight of his wife on her knees in front of his chair. She had another man's seed in her womb. She was his wife, but she had another man's child growing inside of her. He clenched every muscle in his body, willing himself to remain controlled, to keep a hold on the violence shuddering inside of him.

''Say something, Marcus. Please say something.'' She was crying again. And begging. And no matter what she'd done, he couldn't bear to see her like that.

''You went to Beth,'' he said, concentrating on that piece of information. His wife had betrayed him, but he was apparently still the only one who knew the delights of her body. At the moment, that small victory hardly seemed to matter.

''She's the only one who knows,'' Lisa said, her voice contrite.

''What about Oliver?'' Marcus asked, thinking of

his visit to his father-in-law that afternoon. Had Oliver known?

Lisa shook her head. "Only Beth."

Marcus nodded. He didn't know what else she wanted from him.

"It's our baby, Marcus. Yours as much as mine."

No! his mind screamed. The seed she was carrying had nothing to do with him. He couldn't pretend otherwise.

"You're as much a part of the reason for this baby's existence as I am, Marcus."

She wasn't going to rationalize this one away with pretty words. There was too much at stake.

He heard her crying again, but he didn't look at her. He didn't dare look at her.

"Th-that night I called you home. We made love. That's when our baby was conceived, Marcus. I know. Until *your* love was inside me, I couldn't accept the sperm Beth had given me. My body was rejecting it. Until you."

More pretty words. Marcus didn't trust himself to speak. He stared straight ahead, wishing she wouldn't touch him, wishing she'd leave him to his numbness. He didn't think he could hold on much longer.

She ran her hand along his forearm. "Eighty percent of women who are artificially inseminated by a donor don't conceive the first time. But I *knew,* Marcus. That night I knew we'd made a baby."

Thinking back to that night, to the intensity with which he'd made love to her, remembering how he'd poured his heart and soul into her, Marcus felt used.

And betrayed.

And jealous.

He stood up abruptly and headed for the door before he gave himself another reason to hate himself. *Jealous.* What kind of man did that make him, that he was jealous of his own wife's *ability* to conceive. Jealous because she was having the baby they'd always wanted, that she wouldn't have to *pretend* that she, not someone else, had created their child.

He heard her call after him, but he couldn't slow down. He had to get out of there before he did something he'd regret.

HE DROVE FOR HOURS with no idea where he was going. He didn't care. He just kept driving. Thoughts whirled through his mind, torturing him. Lisa's dream was coming true and his was not, never would. She was moving on without him. They were no longer part of the same whole. He thought he'd prepared himself to face that eventuality. But nothing could have prepared him for the agony that ripped through him now, making him yell out into the silence, bringing tears to his cheeks.

He was surprised to find them there. He hadn't thought himself capable of tears. Hadn't cried since he'd been a young boy, forgotten at boarding school during the first two days of summer vacation one year. It had taken the school that long to locate his parents in Europe and for them send someone to pick him up.

Lisa was having a baby. *Another* man's baby. A

stranger had been able to do for her what he could not. No matter how he looked at it, the fact was like acid, eating him up inside.

He drove faster and faster, until the roads became blurred and he was skidding around corners. Finally he checked himself into a run-down motel for the night. It had everything he needed. Which meant no phone.

LISA SPENT THE NIGHT alone, wandering through the rooms of Marcus's family home, touching his things, looking at pictures of the many generations of Cartwrights and worrying herself sick about the man she loved more than life itself. She needed desperately to lean on her best friend, to talk to him, to try to make sense of a world spinning too rapidly out of control—but he'd just walked out on her and she didn't know if he was ever coming back.

When the minutes stretched into hours and it became obvious that Marcus wasn't coming home for dinner, Lisa showered, changed into a pair of jogging pants and one of his Yale sweatshirts, fixed herself some toast and made herself eat it. She was having Marcus's baby, and she was going to take care of it for him, even if he didn't want it. This child would be a Cartwright just like all the other Cartwrights who had left their mark on this town. He would have the same strength of character, the same determination, the same ability to dream. She would make sure of it.

BETH MONTAGUE stayed late at the office on Friday. She always had things she could do, lab reports to go over, dictation to finish, but the work on her desk wasn't what was keeping her there. Oliver was in a meeting at the hospital. He was lobbying for new dialysis equipment for the ward where Barbara had spent so much time during the last years of her life. Beth wondered if it was wrong of her to hope he was still going to stop by after he was done fighting for his wife's cause.

And she worried about what he was going to think when he found out what she and Lisa had done. Would he blame her for her part in Lisa's decision?

The phone on her desk was eerily silent. She'd been waiting all afternoon to see how things had gone between Lisa and Marcus. Why hadn't Lisa called?

Beth picked up the phone to call her friend, but then put it back down. This was a special time for Lisa and Marcus, to be shared by just the two of them. If things went as well as Lisa had hoped, that was. And if they didn't…

Beth's gaze alighted on the picture of her husband. Dear, sweet, absentminded John. How she'd loved him! How she missed him! What would he think of her, interfering like this in her friend's business? She glanced at her watch and then at the door again. What would he think of her sitting here like an adolescent on the off chance her friend's father would stop by?

John's image seemed to be looking at her. She knew he'd say she should have left Lisa and Marcus to deal with their problem on their own. And as usual, he'd have been right. Oliver was going to think the same thing.

John would also consider her kind to befriend his lonely colleague. Though he'd wonder why, if she wanted Oliver to stop by, she hadn't just asked him to. Funny how much older Oliver had seemed than she and John when John and Barbara had been alive.

Barbara. Lisa's mother would have been thrilled to learn she was finally going to be a grandmother. She wouldn't have given the artificial means of conception a thought, other than to be thankful that the option was available. And eventually, with Barbara's help, Oliver would have seen things that way, as well—

"Hi, am I interrupting?"

Beth jumped guiltily at the sound of Oliver's voice. "No, of course not. Come on in. How'd the meeting go?"

Oliver shrugged his broad shoulders. "These things take time. But we're making progress."

He smiled at her and Beth smiled back, telling herself it was natural to feel that little flutter in her stomach. He was an attractive man, that was all. Any woman would find him so. Besides, she was still in love with John.

"Are you free for dinner?" Oliver asked, coming farther into her office.

"As a matter of fact I am." Beth collected her purse, glad to have what time she could with him before he found out about Lisa. She was too keyed up to be alone, in any case. And Oliver was safe. He'd never see her as more than his daughter's plump cheerful friend.

"Has Lisa been to see you again?" Oliver asked. He was looking at his daughter's folder on the top of Beth's desk. "I thought all that was done."

Damn. She'd had the folder by the phone in case Marcus called her. He was bound to have questions once he knew. "Uh, just the usual follow-up," she said now, grabbing the folder. It wasn't her place to tell him what was inside. Oliver was as old-fashioned as the tweed jacket he was wearing. She wasn't sure he'd approve of what his daughter had done or of Beth's role in it. If she had her way, he'd never have to know—except that, of course he would. Oliver knew Marcus was sterile.

Oliver frowned. "What follow-up? It's been more than a year and a half. Is something wrong with her? Something she's not telling me?"

"No! She's fine," Beth said, speaking with her hands, as well as her voice. And as she did, a single piece of paper, the only one not yet fastened in, today's lab report, slipped out of the folder in her hand and fluttered to the floor.

She and Oliver both went for the report, their fingers colliding as they reached it at the same time. Startled at the warmth of his touch, at her inappropriate response to it, Beth snatched back her hand. Oliver picked up the report.

He slumped down in the chair in front of her desk, reading. "Oh, my God."

Beth sat down beside him, looking at the paper still

in his hands, wishing she'd been more careful. "It looked like their only hope, Oliver. She seemed convinced it was the right thing to do."

"You don't understand," Oliver said, glancing up at Beth, his brow furrowed. "This makes it all so much worse." He paused. "Because he's leaving her."

"What?" Beth's stomach knotted with dread. And guilt.

"He came to see me this afternoon. He bought a house in Chicago. He wants a divorce. He said he was freeing her to have a family with someone else." Oliver glanced again at the paper in his hand. "He never said—"

"When this afternoon?" Beth interrupted.

"Midafternoon. It was before my three-o'clock class."

"He didn't know." Sick at heart, she thought of the child she'd helped to create, a third life that was now going to suffer—unless Lisa's news would be enough to stop Marcus from leaving. Or would it just send him from her faster?

"He didn't know?" Oliver frowned down at the report.

Beth was surprised at the tenderness that welled up inside her as he struggled to assimilate the truth. She reached over and squeezed his free hand. "She came to see me. We did it all right here."

"Ah." Oliver glanced away, obviously embarrassed, but he didn't look angry. "And it worked?" Was that hope she heard in his voice?

"It worked the first time. I don't know which of us was more shocked."

"I'm going to be a grandpa."

Relief flooded Beth as she heard the boyish wonder in his voice. She sent up a silent prayer that Marcus had been even half as glad to hear the news.

CHAPTER SIX

LISA WAS AFRAID to leave the house. Afraid she'd miss Marcus, afraid he might clear out his things and be gone when she wasn't there. But by Saturday noon, after phoning both the police and every hospital she knew of in a two-hundred-mile radius of New Haven and reassuring herself that Marcus hadn't been in an accident, she was just plain afraid. Where was he? And worse, was he going to even come back?

She didn't call Cartwright Enterprises. She didn't want to hunt him down. She also didn't want to know if he wasn't there.

Forcing herself to keep busy, she spent the afternoon baking and decorating sugar cookies, made from her grandmother's recipe. They were Marcus's favorite kind, and cookies were one thing Hannah never baked. She took a couple of cuts of beef tenderloin filets out to thaw. Marcus loved her filet mignon.

And all the while she worked, the vacant look in Marcus's eyes as he'd sat frozen in their living room the day before haunted her. After more than ten years of loving him, she couldn't begin to guess what he was going to do. She'd hurt him. In his eyes, she'd betrayed him. She'd hoped his finding out that they were finally going to have a baby would make up for the fact that she'd had herself inseminated without telling him. She'd thought it would make a difference to him once he understood that she'd taken another man's seed out of her love for *him*. She'd been wrong. Dreadfully wrong.

And yet, she couldn't regret the tiny life that was even now forming in her womb. Because she knew, in the depths of her soul, that this baby was a product of the love she and Marcus shared. That it was *their* baby, conceived in love.

She talked to Beth on the phone, assuring her friend that everything was fine. She couldn't bring herself to admit that Marcus was gone. That she had no idea when or even if he'd be back. But she couldn't keep up her pretense for long, so she told Beth she'd call her on Monday. Beth sounded delighted for Lisa and Marcus, eager to let her friend go, obviously believing that Lisa and Marcus wanted to be alone. And they were. Just not together.

Oliver called her early Saturday evening, just as she sat back down on the couch after looking out the window, watching for Marcus, for the hundredth time that day.

"Everything okay there?" he asked.

"No." She'd eaten the filet herself, although she'd had to struggle to swallow every bite. "But it will be." *It had to be.*

"Marcus came to see me yesterday, Lisa."

"He did? When? What did he say?" Did her father know where Marcus was?

"That he'd bought a house in Chicago. That he was leaving you to find someone else, someone who could make your dreams come true."

Oh. Tears blurred Lisa's eyes. "I'm already pregnant, Dad."

The silence on the other end of the line was unnerving, but Lisa pushed on, anyway, telling her father about the artificial insemination and that she'd had the procedure without her husband's consent.

"Don't you think he had a right to know beforehand?" She hadn't heard reprimand in her father's voice since she'd been a teenager.

"Of course he did." She held back her tears, afraid that once they started falling, they'd never stop. "I can't believe what a mess I've made of everything. But I knew he was thinking about leaving. He'd convinced himself it was the honorable thing to do, to free me to have the life I always wanted. I tried to talk to him about artificial insemination before, several times. He wouldn't even discuss it." Suddenly all the frustration from her unsuccessful attempts to convince her husband of the truth, that he gave her the life she'd always wanted, came pouring out.

Her father listened to her silently.

"Marcus is a proud man, honey," he said when she'd finally emptied herself of pent-up anguish. "A man used to providing whatever is needed. He's having to take a whole new look at himself, at who and what he is—and what he isn't. He's doing what he thinks is best."

"So you think he's right to leave?" Lisa asked, incredulous.

"No, honey, I don't. That man loves you to distraction, and I know how happy he makes you."

"Happier than I've ever been in my life. Which is why I went to see Beth. I had to do something, and that seemed like the only answer left. This way Marcus wouldn't feel as if he was cheating me out of anything, and he could still have the child he's always wanted."

"I take it he didn't see it that way."

"He didn't really say *how* he saw it. He just got up and walked out." She twisted the phone cord around her finger, watching her fingertip turn red.

"So what happened when he cooled down and came home?"

"He hasn't come back yet."

Lisa heard her father take a deep breath. "Lisa, are you certain Marcus wanted to have children, that he wasn't just trying to have a family for your sake, to please you?"

"I'm positive." She unraveled the cord from her finger. "Marcus talked about wanting children almost from the time I met him. He's a Cartwright, Dad. He feels it's his duty to have children. But it's also something he wants very badly. He needs to fill this house with the laughter he never heard growing up here. Which is why I know he'll be a wonderful father."

"He doesn't think so."

Lisa sat up straight, suddenly cold. "What? Whatever gave you that idea?"

"He told me so himself yesterday. His sterility has left him feeling inadequate, maybe even a little insecure. And the way he's compensating for that is to assume that perhaps he wouldn't have been any good as a father. This way, by his not having children, he's saving some poor kid from an unhappy childhood."

"But that's ludicrous!" She felt sick to her stomach, and it had nothing to do with morning sickness.

"Sterility can do strange things to a man, honey. Especially a man as proud as Marcus. In order to accept it, he needs to understand why this has happened, and the only conclusion he's been able to reach thus far is that he isn't father material."

"Oh, my God!" Lisa gasped, reeling from the ramifications of her father's news. *What have I done?*

"Marcus is strong, Lis. He'll come around. Give him some time."

"I never would have had the insemination if I'd known that. Never. I did this for him, Dad. Because I couldn't bear the thought of him leaving me to have my wonderful life with someone else while he sentenced himself to a life of loneliness. But now it sounds like all I've done is sentence him myself." She wiped at the tears streaming down her face. She couldn't stop them now.

"Did you tell Marcus all that?"

"Of course."

"And?"

"It didn't seem to make any difference."

"What did he say, honey?"

"Nothing." Lisa's voice broke. "I explained everything. I told him how much I loved him, and he walked out, anyway. I haven't heard from him since.''

''And you've been there all alone since yesterday?''

''I don't know when he'll be back, and I don't want to miss him.'' She sniffled and wiped her eyes. ''I'm just glad I'm not on call.'' For the first time in years, Lisa hadn't even been thinking about her job.

''I'm coming over,'' Oliver said, sounding the way he had when she was a kid.

Lisa smiled in spite of her tears. ''It's okay, Dad. I'm a big girl now. I made this mess, and somehow I'm going to have to live with it. Besides, I'd rather be here alone when he comes back. I might only get this one chance to turn him around. But thanks.''

Oliver harumphed and then fell silent for a few moments. ''He'll be back, you know,'' he finally said.

''I know.''

''But I can still come over and stay with you until he gets there. Lord knows you have enough rooms in that house of his.''

''Maybe. If he's not back by tomorrow. Just for dinner or something,'' Lisa conceded. She'd be grateful for her father's presence.

''You'll call if you need anything?''

''Of course.''

''So...I'm going to be a grandpa?'' Lisa heard the emotion in his voice. At least *someone* was happy about her news.

''Yeah.''

''And you're feeling okay?''

"Beth says everything looks great."

"Congratulations, sweetie." His soft words brought a fresh wave of tears to her eyes.

"Yeah. You, too."

"Lisa? For what it's worth, I think you did the right thing. Marcus had already made up his mind to free you, give you a chance at your dreams. Now you've given him a chance to have his, too."

LISA MADE IT through the second long night comforting herself with her father's words, but as the weekend wore on with still no sign of Marcus, no word at all, she finally called his office only to find out from security that he hadn't been in all weekend. She could no longer hold her panic at bay. What if something had happened to him? What if she'd hurt him so badly he'd done something foolish? What if he hated her so much their marriage was over? What if he never came back?

By Sunday afternoon Lisa was sitting on the bathroom floor in their master suite, dressed in a pair of jean shorts and one of Marcus's old T-shirts, her stomach tormenting her as thoroughly as her rambling thoughts. She prayed she wasn't going to be sick, not while she was alone. She knew her fear of being sick was irrational, that it was a direct result of the days of her little sister's illness, the many times she'd watched helplessly as the medicine they'd given Sara had made the four-year-old violently ill.

She'd watched—hiding in the bedroom closet—as her baby sister died. And she'd sworn to herself then that she was going to be a pediatrician when she grew up. She was going to cure little kids like Sara so they didn't have to suffer so. And she was going to have a house full of children, too, so she could hear Sara's laughter again.

But as much as she wanted this child, as thrilled as she was every time she thought about the life growing inside her, the pregnancy meant nothing without Marcus....

HE FOUND HER in the bathroom, asleep on the floor, when he finally returned home just after three on Sunday afternoon. She looked so fragile to him, so waif-like, that he knew he'd made the right decision. The only decision.

A stab of guilt shot through him as he realized how exhausted she must have been to have fallen asleep on the cold tiles. He should have phoned.

"Lis?" he said softly.

"Marcus..." She sat up, instantly awake.

"I just wanted to tell you I'm home."

Her beautiful eyes were shadowed as she stared up at him. "To stay?"

Marcus nodded. He wanted to tell her that he wasn't angry with her anymore, to take away the fear in her eyes, but he couldn't lie to her.

"You're sure?" she asked, still sitting on the floor.

He nodded again.

She leapt up and threw herself against him, her arms wrapping around his neck. "Thank you, God," she whispered. "Thank you."

Marcus held her close to his heart, where he knew she belonged. She still fit him perfectly, as if the child she carried was nothing more than a bad dream. Then her slender frame began to shudder, and the shudders turned to sobs. His arms tightened. He'd been wrong to leave her hanging all weekend with no word from him. He knew how emotional Lisa was, how deeply she felt everything. How much she'd worry.

But she'd been wrong, too! Even as he held her, he felt the bitterness of her betrayal. The pain of her deception. The jealousy. She'd accepted another man's seed into her womb.

Anger surged through him anew, and it took everything he had to continue holding her. He tried to concentrate on his love for the woman in his arms, wondering how much time would have to pass before the destructive emotions he felt would be gone, dreading the possibility that he would be living with them for a very long time. Perhaps for the rest of his life.

Surely loneliness and empty walls would be better than that.

He knew why Lisa had turned to artificial insemination, understood that her intentions, if not her actions, were honorable. She'd been trying to save him from himself. He could hardly fault her for that when he'd been presumptuous enough to attempt to do the same thing with his plans to leave her. But his plans would still have left the opportunity for them to live their lives together if she'd ultimately chosen to come back to him. He had been going to free her, yes, for a time. Free her to find out if he was what she still wanted, sterility and all. His plans had left the choice up to her.

But her plans had taken away *his* choices.

Which was one of the reasons he'd come back to her. She was pregnant. He was her husband. He would stand by her. Because he was an honorable man. Because she needed him. And because he loved her so damn much that, even pregnant with another man's child, he still wanted her. But he would never accept her baby as his own. He couldn't. It wasn't his. Not in thought, and certainly not in deed.

"I did it for you," she said against his neck, her voice wobbly with her tears.

"I know."

"I love you so much."

"I know."

She pulled away to gaze up at him. "I never meant to hurt you like that, Marcus. Never. I'm so sorry."

"Shh." He pulled her close again and kissed the top of her head. "It's okay, Lis. I understand. Everything's going to be all right." He wanted it to be. He was going to try his damnedest to make it be. Except that, deep inside, he was afraid nothing was ever going to be right again.

OLIVER HAD IT BAD. He wondered if fifty-three was too old for a midlife crisis. He was thrilled at the thought of being a grandfather, of holding Barbara's grandchild in his arms. But maybe the fact that he was going to be a grandfather was *bothering* him, too—subconsciously. Maybe that was why he was suddenly finding himself thinking about the woman across the table from him at odd times during the day.

She looked so cute in her short-sleeved red dress, like a juicy ripe tomato.

"Lisa was in today. It's great to see her so happy," Beth said, devouring her salad.

"It is," he agreed, though he suspected his daughter had some rough times ahead of her yet. "I haven't seen much of Marcus, though, have you?"

"No." She frowned. "Come to think of it, the last couple of times I stopped over, he was nowhere around."

Oliver's heart sank as he nodded. He'd noticed the same thing. He'd just been hoping it had been coincidental, a matter of bad timing. "Has she said anything to you about him?"

Beth put her fork down. "No. Why? Is something wrong? I thought he was happy about the baby."

"Well, he left her when she first told him she was pregnant." The confidence just slipped out naturally, as if he were sitting here with Barbara and they were discussing their daughter, just as they'd done through every other crisis in Lisa's life. Except that he knew full well that the woman across from him wasn't Barbara. And he wanted to confide in her, anyway.

"He what?" Beth said, her eyes wide with shock.

"He was only gone for a weekend, and according to Lisa, everything's been fine since he came home. But I know my son-in-law. He's honorable, he loves my daughter, and he's also one of the most stubborn individuals I've ever met. And if he's still got it in his head he isn't meant to be a father..."

Beth paled. "He doesn't want to be a father? Then why did he put himself through all those tests?"

"It's *because* of the tests. The results, I mean. Men like Marcus tend to approach the crises in their lives logically, and he's determined that maybe he wasn't meant to be a father at all, that perhaps it's best he's sterile because he may be inadvertently saving a kid from an unhappy childhood."

"But that's so wrong." Beth frowned. "He had a fever when he was a child that wasn't attended to quickly enough. I told him that. His parents had left him with a nanny who was more interested in her boyfriend than in Marcus, and by the time his parents returned home from a trip they were on, his fever had been too high for too long."

Oliver put down his fork. "I knew nothing of this."

"I don't think Lisa knew, either, until I asked Marcus if he ever remembered having a high fever. He made it sound like it was no big deal."

"I suspect that my son-in-law learned very early on not to expect much from his parents."

They were both silent for a minute, and Oliver wondered why it was that some parents never understood that children were gifts to be cherished, not brushed aside. And why some people who were meant to be parents had that chance snatched away. He thought of his little Sara, of the few precious years they'd had with her, and couldn't imagine having

missed a single moment of her life. How he still ached
for a glimpse of her laughing eyes.

Beth touched his hand, bringing him back to her.
"You think Marcus is still working himself to the
bone?"

His hand tingled where she'd touched it. "Probably."

"So the baby hasn't helped their problem at all."

Oliver hated to hear her sounding so despondent.
"It's helped. It's helped Lisa. She's smiling again,
dreaming again. And if nothing else, seeing Lisa
happy will help Marcus."

"But how long is she going to be happy if *he*
isn't?" Beth asked.

That was a question Oliver couldn't answer.

"I SAW THE GREATEST MOVIE over the weekend,"
Beth said later, over dessert. By some unspoken understanding, they'd steered away from the conversation of Lisa and Marcus through the rest of dinner.

"What'd you see?" he asked, pushing aside the
guilt that accompanied his thoughts of Beth more and
more these days, guilt that grew with his eagerness to
hear whatever details of her life she wanted to give
him.

But all the while she told him about the movie,
Oliver was wondering who she saw it with and then
wondering why it mattered to him. He must be crazy.
Beth Montague was almost young enough to be his
daughter. She was the wife of his dead colleague. His
daughter's best friend. She hadn't even had children

yet, and he was going to be a grandfather. And she wasn't Barbara.

So why, when she smiled at him, did he feel like kissing her?

BETH SHOWED UP at Lisa's office the next afternoon, interrupting Lisa's dictation.

"I thought Wednesday was your early day," she said, propping her hip on the edge of Lisa's desk.

Lisa put down the mike from her dictaphone and shut off the machine. "It is, but Marcus is working late tonight, so I'm taking the time to get caught up on all this." She motioned toward the charts and correspondence littering the top of her desk.

"He's working late again? He was working on Friday night when we went looking for baby cribs. I thought the idea was that you'd both stop working yourselves to death."

Lisa shrugged. "I have. And he will. Just as soon as he gets this Blake deal done."

"I don't know, Lis." Beth frowned. "There will always be other deals."

"Of course there will, but this one is far more than just business to Marcus. He really cares about the old guy." She filled Beth in on the difficulties Marcus was having with George Blake.

"You sure that's all it is?" Beth asked.

Lisa loved her friend, and she was glad Beth cared, but sometimes she wished she didn't care quite so much. "He just needs time, Beth. I knew it would take him a while to come to grips with the baby, and

I'm willing to wait. *I* had a chance to prepare, but it came as a complete shock to him.''

"I kind of expected to hear from him."

Lisa, too, had hoped that Marcus would contact Beth. He usually liked to have a handle on everything. She sighed. "He doesn't say much about the baby yet, but he's fine with it."

Which wasn't entirely true. Marcus never said *anything* about the baby. And he hadn't completely forgiven her yet for her duplicity in conceiving it. He also hadn't made love to her since she'd told him she was pregnant. But she was completely certain that he was as committed to their life together as she was. The rest would come with time, just like her father said. It had to.

MARCUS WAS HOME for dinner the very next night. Hannah had left a casserole in the oven, and Lisa served it in the kitchen. She and Marcus had been eating in there for years, preferring its homier atmosphere to the formal dining room Marcus's parents had insisted on using for every meal when they were home.

"Do you remember Sue Carrin, that ditsy blonde who pledged my sorority our senior year?" Lisa asked Marcus over dinner.

"The one with the big—"

"Marcus!" Lisa laughed, cutting him off.

Marcus looked up from buttering his roll to grin at her. "Well, if she was going to make out with her boyfriend where someone could trip over them, she should have kept her top on."

"And if you were going to try to sneak in my window after curfew, you should have been watching where you were stepping."

"How was I supposed to see them? She and Skinny were behind the bushes! He was panting so hard the lenses in his glasses were all steamed up. Poor Skinny, it was probably his first real kiss, and I had to go and ruin it for him. I wonder what ever happened to him."

"He married Sue. I ran into her at the hospital today. She was bringing her mother in for cataract surgery."

"I'll be damned. Little Skinny Whitehall married Big Bazookas—"

"Stop it!" Lisa said in mock outrage. "Sue's a very nice woman. You're just mad because you got caught trying to besmirch my virtue. And I guess Skinny's not so little anymore. He's made quite a name for himself as a computer-systems consultant, with a couple of nationwide firms on his client list."

"I ought to put him in touch with George Blake," Marcus said, no longer smiling.

Lisa pushed her plate aside. "George is still holding things up?"

"Yeah, but I don't blame him, Lis. I'd do the same thing if our positions were reversed. Still, he questions every move we make. It's so damned frustrating. A merger that was supposed to take weeks is taking months."

Lisa reached across the table to lay her hand over his. "George Blake is lucky he found you."

"I'm not sure he'd agree with you, but it's too late to pull out now. So, what's for dessert?"

They had their choice of chocolate cake or apple pie. Neither sounded good to Lisa, but she sat with Marcus while he had a piece of each. She wanted to ask him which one of them was eating for two, but wasn't sure he'd see the humor.

"By the way, our two-month obstetrical appointment is next Thursday morning at ten o'clock," Lisa said as she cleared the table after dinner. "Is that okay with you?"

Marcus was rinsing dishes at the sink where they'd leave them for Hannah to do in the morning. He stopped and turned to look at Lisa, his expression blank.

"I just..." she said hesitantly, "that is, you always said you wanted to be a part of things..."

Marcus turned back to the dishes. "That was a long time ago, Lisa. I'm not a part of what's going on with you now."

Lisa's stomach knotted. "'What's going *on* with me?' I'm having a baby, Marcus. *Our* baby."

He turned off the water with such force Lisa was surprised the faucet didn't break off in his hand. "We need to get something straight here," he said, facing her again.

Lisa backed up a step. She'd never seen him this angry.

"The child you are carrying is not, and never will be, *ours*," he said through clenched teeth.

Lisa stared at him, her world teetering dangerously.

"When I said I wanted to be a part of every aspect of our child's birth, that included the conception."

She fell back another step. He hadn't forgiven her. He wasn't *ever* going to forgive her.

"I'm sorry," she said, anyway, feeling his pain, as well as her own.

"I spent the first twenty years of my life pretending that I had a father, Lisa. I cannot spend the next fifty pretending that I *am* one."

"What're you saying?" she asked, feeling a chill, afraid for the baby growing inside her.

"The child you're carrying is yours. I want no part of it."

He couldn't mean that! "Then why are you here? Why'd you come back? What have these past weeks been?" she cried.

"I'm here because you are my wife, and because, in spite of everything, I find that I still love you as much as ever."

She felt the blood drain from her face. This couldn't be happening. Never in her worst nightmares had she considered that Marcus would want her but not their baby. That he would continue to live with her, love her, but reject the child she was carrying.

"You're his father," she whispered, still not quite believing that she wasn't misunderstanding Marcus somehow.

His eyes filled with a pain so intense Lisa felt it

clear to her soul. ''No, Lis, I'm not,'' he said, his shoulders slumping as he turned and walked out of the room.

Lisa sank into a chair at the kitchen table, cradling her stomach, and the tiny life it harbored. It would have been better if Marcus had left her. Because as long as he was coming home to her, caring about her, she didn't think she could leave him. But neither could she bring her baby into a home where he wasn't wanted, where his own father could ignore him as if he didn't exist.

''It's okay, little one,'' she whispered, rubbing her stomach soothingly. ''Your daddy'll come around.'' *Please God.* ''He'll love you more than any daddy ever loved a child.'' *He will. I know he will.* ''See, there's something about your daddy I haven't told you yet. He's never had much love in his life, so the one thing he's always wanted more than anything is a family to love. And you're it, little one. So hang in there. And don't worry, your daddy never stays angry for long.''

CHAPTER SEVEN

"DAMN!" MARCUS SWUNG the Ferrari around and headed back toward home. He'd forgotten the marketing textbook he'd promised to bring with him when he met with George Blake later that day. Impatient with his lapse, with the lack of concentration that had been plaguing him all week, he pulled around the circular drive to the front of his house, barely looking at the lushly landscaped lawn in front of him. Although fall used to be his favorite time of year, this year the leaves had changed colors without him even noticing. The crisp October morning was wasted on him.

Work had always been able to distract him, if not heal what ailed him. But ever since Lisa had asked him to accompany her on her first prenatal checkup, he'd been eaten up with corrosive emotions. All of a sudden the pregnancy was a reality, something he could no longer ignore.

He hated the anger that burned within him—and the panic. Lisa was going on with her life without him, and there was nothing he could do about it, no way for him to catch up. He knew it and she knew it. She watched everything she said around him these days, choosing her words so carefully it made him ache. He could feel their closeness deteriorating, knew they were in danger of becoming nothing more than wary house-mates and yet was powerless to prevent that from happening.

Because he couldn't involve himself in Lisa's changing life. He was already so plagued with if onlys he wondered sometimes if he'd ever again know peace of mind. He might just as well have gone with her to the damn doctor's appointment the day before. He'd done nothing but sit in his office and torture himself with wasted dreams the entire time he'd known she was there.

Lisa's pregnancy had become a constant reminder to him of everything he'd always wanted, everything he could never have. He was so damn envious he couldn't think straight.

And he was scared to death that Lisa's baby was going to look nothing like Lisa.

Unlocking his front door, he hurried into the office he shared with his wife, hoping to be in and gone before she heard him. He made it a practice to leave the house before she was up and around these days. It was just easier that way. Easier to keep his emotions under wraps, easier to ignore the changes in his wife's body, his wife's life.

He hadn't made love to Lisa, either, not since the day she'd told him she was expecting a child. He didn't trust himself to touch her. He was afraid of what might happen if he let his guard down, if he let himself be vulnerable, if he let himself feel everything he always felt when he made love to her. He wasn't sure what other emotions might be unleashed or what he might do if they were.

He was also unsure how much lovemaking she could do in her condition, and he didn't want to ask. It just seemed better not to talk about that.

Grabbing the textbook from a shelf behind his desk, he was on his way out the door when he heard the sounds of retching upstairs. Lisa was sick.

Taking the stairs two at once, he made it up to the master suite just in time to hear Lisa throw up a second time. How long had she been suffering like this?

Without thought, Marcus dropped the textbook on his dresser, tore off his jacket and hurried into the bathroom. He wet a washcloth at the sink, then crossed to her and hunkered down, wiping her face and forehead, holding her hair back when the spasms came again.

"I'm sorry," she finally said, tears wetting her lashes. She took the cloth from him and buried her face in it.

Marcus rubbed her back, admiring her strength. He knew how frightened she was of being sick to her stomach. "Shh. You don't need to apologize, Lis. It's me, remember?"

She nodded, saying nothing, only looking at him. He hated the uncertainty he read in her eyes.

"This happen often?" he asked.

She shrugged. "Not so far."

But maybe later. As her pregnancy progressed. There it was again. The wall he slammed into every time he was with his wife these days.

"Are you gonna be okay now?" he asked, feeling awkward. After all, this had nothing to do with him.

Lisa nodded.

Marcus got to his feet. "I, uh, guess I'll be going then. I just came back to get a book I forgot."

Lisa stood up, as well, and moved to her sink. "Have a good day," she said, reaching for her toothbrush.

Marcus stood there for a second longer, wishing there was some way he could make everything right again. He missed her so much. "Yeah, you, too," he finally said, stopping in the bedroom to shrug back into his suit jacket.

"Marcus?" Lisa poked her head around the bathroom door.

"Yeah?"

"Thanks."

Marcus nodded and left, his day suddenly a little brighter.

LISA WAS SICK again that evening after dinner, and several more times during that next week. The violence and frequency of her vomiting started to alarm Marcus. He'd been waiting to leave with her in the mornings since the first time he'd found her sick, and after the fourth morning of nausea in a row he was an old hand at soothing her through the episodes. But while he quieted her fears, his own grew. It seemed to him that these bouts of nausea were far more than normal morning sickness.

"I want you to talk to Dr. Crutchfield today when

you get to the hospital, Lis,'' he said on Wednesday morning while they both got ready for work. It was the middle of the last week in October, Lisa's ninth week of pregnancy. ''You're sick all the time now.''

''It's perfectly normal,'' Lisa said, chuckling. She opened her eyes wide to apply her mascara.

He couldn't tell, looking at her now, that she'd been so violently ill only half an hour before. She looked healthy. Better than healthy. She was glowing. Still...

''I can't believe that every woman goes through this every time she's expecting, Lisa.''

''Some women just have it worse than others,'' she said, continuing with her lashes.

Why was she taking this so lightly? Few things in life scared him, but the thought of something wrong with Lisa, seriously wrong, scared the hell out of him.

''I'd still feel better if you talked to the doctor,'' he said.

Lisa met Marcus's gaze in the mirror, her eyes amused. ''I *am* a doctor, if you...'' She stopped midstream when he stared, stone-faced, back at her. ''You're really concerned, aren't you?'' she asked, surprised.

''Yes,'' Marcus admitted, refusing to apologize for that.

''I'll stop by and see her this morning, Marcus. I have office visits until eleven, but I'll go over straight after. Okay?'' She smiled at him, looking about sixteen in her slip and bare feet, with her makeup only half-on.

"Okay." Marcus smiled back. God, how he loved her.

"IF LISA CALLS, put her right through, no matter what," Marcus told Marge as he walked into his office later that morning.

"Nothing's wrong, is there?" Marge asked, getting up to follow him. She stood in his doorway, a mother's worried frown on her brow.

Marcus had not yet told anyone about Lisa's pregnancy. He hadn't wanted to face the inevitable questions, the role he'd have to play in order to protect his wife's privacy. And his own.

But no matter how much he resented the position Lisa had put him in, her condition wasn't something he was going to be able to hide much longer. "No. As a matter of fact, she's pregnant," he said, trying to sound happy about the situation.

Marge was so effusive in her congratulations Marcus felt more like a fraud than ever, but he accepted them because he had no other choice. He tried to measure up to her expectations of a happy father-to-be. And by the end of the morning every other member of his immediate staff had been in to congratulate him. He found it increasingly wearing to keep up the pretense, but it warmed him to see how much genuine affection his coworkers seemed to have for Lisa and him. He hadn't expected everyone to be so excited. His paychecks guaranteed their loyalty. Not their well wishes.

It warmed him far more when, shortly after eleven,

Lisa called to say that everything was just fine with the baby and her. He brushed right by the part about the baby, giddy with relief to hear that Lisa was in perfect health. He'd been more worried than he thought.

He forgot himself long enough to go out and share the good news with Marge.

"It sounds to me like you need to read up on the next seven months, Marcus, if a little morning sickness throws you so off kilter," Marge said, grinning at him.

Marcus considered her suggestion. Maybe he *should* find out just what the next months were going to bring. He'd had nothing to do with creating Lisa's condition, but her bouts with morning sickness had brought home to him how precarious an actual pregnancy could be, the risks it posed to the expectant mother's health. Lisa's health. He wanted to know more about it.

"Could you recommend some good books about it?" he asked his secretary. Having something to concentrate on, something positive he could contribute, something he could *do,* felt good.

Marge picked up her purse and headed for the door. "I'll stop at the bookstore when I'm at lunch," she said, still smiling at him.

Marcus grinned back. Finally. He had a purpose, a way to regain some of the inner balance he'd lost when his wife had become pregnant with another man's child.

BETH KNEW where Oliver lived. She wished she didn't. That it wasn't so easy for her to find him on this, the darkest of days, made even darker by the Thanksgiving holiday that followed so soon after.

It wasn't right that she reach out to him this way. Lisa would probably be expecting her to call, maybe even expecting her to spend the day with her as she had the year before and the year before that. Nothing had been said this time. But Lisa knew.

Beth almost turned her BMW around to head back to New Haven. It was a gorgeous Indian-summer day, a gift she should be thankful for. She could drive up to East Rock, spend the day at Eastrock Park, as she used to do all those weekends when John was glued to textbooks. Surely she could outdistance her memories among the 650 acres of gorgeous Connecticut countryside. She had no business dropping in on Oliver. None whatsoever. Except that she was certain he could make her feel better. Beth's eyes blurred with tears. She blinked them away so she could see the road in front of her.

When had she come to rely on Oliver for her emotional equilibrium? How had she come to need him without even knowing it? And could she take comfort from him without making a mess of things?

She turned into the neighborhood where Lisa had grown up, finding the rambling house easily. She'd been there last Christmas, guests of Lisa and Marcus. It had been then, celebrating that emotional holiday, that she and Oliver had first connected. They'd both been celebrating with only half a heart, having lost a part of themselves when they'd buried their spouses.

Which was why, on this day in particular, Beth was

drawn to her best friend's father for comfort. Oliver wouldn't just sympathize, he'd *know*.

Pulling up to the garage behind Oliver's house, Beth parked, grabbed her purse and got out of the car. There was nothing wrong with her coming here like this. It meant nothing more than a person seeking comfort from a friend who understood.

So why had she not told Lisa where she was going? Why had she purposely not gone home to change after church in an effort to avoid Lisa's phone call? And why had a swarm of butterflies taken up residence in her abdomen?

"Beth! What a wonderful surprise," Oliver said when he answered her knock. "I was just deciding what to fix for lunch. Come join me."

That was it. No questions asked.

Following him back to the kitchen, she dropped her purse on the counter, then looked over his shoulder as, together, they inspected the contents of his refrigerator. She felt better already.

Deciding on cheese-lettuce-and-tomato sandwiches, they prepared lunch together and ate it out on his covered patio, enjoying the unusual warmth of the day. The lush green acre of his backyard, lined with the spectacular autumn foliage of dogwood, was enchanting. In the spring the yard was filled with the pink and white blossoms of mountain laurel, as well as colorful rhododendron shrubs, the perfect accompaniment to the orchids that had been Barbara Webster's pride and joy.

"This was just what the doctor ordered," Beth said, finishing the last of her sandwich.

"Kind of convenient, don't you think, to be able to give your own orders?" Oliver smiled at her.

The pleasure he was taking in her presence was almost enough to soothe her tattered emotions. Almost.

"John was killed six years ago today." The words came out of their own accord, as if they'd been fighting for release. And she supposed maybe they had, going by the number of times they'd repeated themselves over and over in her head since she'd awakened, alone, early that morning.

"Ahh." Oliver's expression, his voice, was filled with instant understanding, and warmed with a huge dose of empathy. "I remember when we got the call at the university... Come." He reached for her hand. "Why don't we sit in the gazebo. I go there sometimes when I'm feeling blue. It seems to help."

Beth walked with him to the gazebo in one corner of his backyard. She'd been there before, of course, but always with Lisa. Surrounded with flowers except in the cold winter months, it had a slatted roof open to the sun and to the many birds that came to perch on the feeders Oliver had built. It was the most peaceful place Beth had ever been.

"Were you with him when it happened?" Oliver asked, sitting with her on one of the benches along the inside of the gazebo. Though the little building allowed in the sun's warmth, Beth's hands were cold, and Oliver rubbed them gently with his.

She'd had no idea how much she'd needed the contact, the touch of another person. "Uh-huh," she said, watching a couple of birds hover around one of the larger feeders hanging from the ceiling of the gazebo, but seeing, instead, her husband's blood on the tile floor of the hamburger place. They'd only stopped there for a quick bite before heading out to the country to look at homes. That day had been filled with sunny promise, too, just like this one.

She could still hear the shrieks of the women and children around them, the shouts of the men who'd tried to help, still feel the frantic flurry as everyone ran, trying to escape the gunman's next bullet. They needn't have worried. He'd turned the next one on himself.

Beth hadn't even realized she'd been speaking out loud until Oliver put his arm around her, pulling her into the comfort of his embrace. "I'm so sorry, my dear, so sorry. Shh. Don't cry."

It had been a long time since Beth had been cuddled, since she'd had someone to lean on. Burying her face against the solidness of Oliver's chest, she clung to him, allowing the sobs she'd been holding in check all day to burst free. The nightmare of that day would be with her always, but it almost felt as if she'd be able to bear it as she sat there with her head against Oliver's chest, listening to the strong steady beat of his heart.

"Thank you," she said, pulling away just enough to lift her head, to gaze into his warm brown eyes.

"Hush." He placed a finger against her lips. "You don't need to thank me. You've helped me more than I can ever say."

His gaze left hers to travel down to where his finger was still touching her lips. With no thought to what she was doing, Beth wet her lips, tasting the saltiness of his skin.

She saw the look in Oliver's eyes change, recognized the intentness of his gaze. Dazed, she watched his head lower and knew only that she wanted him to move closer, that nothing had felt so right in years.

Still, she was shocked by the first touch of his lips, by the warm connected feel of a man's mouth against her own, caressing her own. It had been so long. Too long.

Unable to deny him, to deny herself, Beth parted her lips to his. Her heart beat a passionate tattoo, and her belly flooded with wanting. Losing every ounce of the maturity of her thirty-eight years, she felt like a teenager again.

She gave kiss for kiss, clinging to him as he caressed her back with sure hands. Her senses swam with the taste of him, the bristly feel of his beard against her skin, his musky scent.

She wasn't ready when he slowly pulled back from her.

"I'm not going to apologize," he said, looking into her eyes, desire smoldering in his.

Beth melted under that gaze, felt cherished and alive. She wanted to lean her head against him again, but wasn't sure she should.

She shook her head, instead, bringing herself back to reality. "You don't have to apologize," she said, surprised to hear how breathless she sounded. "I needed comfort. You offered it.'' She told herself that was all it had been. That was all it *could* be. They'd both already given their hearts—to someone else.

''And I'm almost old enough to be your father,'' Oliver said, setting her away from him. ''I can assure you, Beth, it won't happen again.''

Beth nodded, glad for the reassurance. He was her friend's father. And she loved John. The feelings Oliver had evoked in her were just an outcropping of her longing for her dead husband. A natural emanation of her emotional neediness.

And his. Because as much as she missed her John, he missed his Barbara, too.

THE DAYS GREW SHORTER. Thanksgiving arrived, a quiet affair spent with Marcus and her father, eating out at the country club as Marcus's family had always done. Beth spent the day with her cousin in upstate Connecticut.

Willie Adams took his first steps the day after Thanksgiving, well on his way to recovery; but when she ran over to share the good news with Beth, her friend seemed almost distant, as she'd been ever since the anniversary of John's death. Lisa had tried to reach her all day that Sunday, knowing how difficult the anniversary was for Beth. But to no avail. When she'd asked Beth about it afterward, Beth had been evasive.

Lisa was thrilled about the changes in her body, evidence of the baby growing inside her. She'd tried to set up a dinner date alone with her father, needing to gloat over her progress with the only other family member who cared to hear about it, but Oliver was unusually busy, unable even to meet her for lunch. She'd had to satisfy herself with a shared coffee break at Yale the afternoon after Thanksgiving, and then only because she'd shown up at his office unannounced.

She was no longer on call at the hospital, agreeing with Debbie Crutchfield that it would be much healthier for her baby if she got her full night's rest. Nevertheless, she missed the excitement of administering emergency aid.

And then there was Marcus. The man made her happier—and sadder—than she'd ever been in her life. He also infuriated her, frustrated her and sometimes just plain made her laugh. He'd become a mother hen, watching her every move, denying her even the simple privilege of rinsing the dishes with him, insisting, instead, that she sit at the table while he did the task himself. He monitored every bite she ate, which meant her occasional hamburger and french-fry binges had to happen during the workday when she was usually too rushed to savor them. And he locked the doors and turned off the lights at nine-thirty every night to ensure she got her sleep.

She hated the unnecessary inactivity he was forcing on her, but she loved the attention he was giving her, or rather, giving her pregnancy. If only he'd be as attentive to her other needs. Because each night, after he saw her settled into bed, he went back downstairs to the office to work, sometimes not coming to bed until the early hours of the morning. Many nights Lisa lay there alone, awake, waiting for him to finally join her,

her body taut with need, wanting nothing more than to feel her lover's arms around her, his body hard and demanding inside hers.

But she waited in vain. Marcus always eventually climbed in beside her, but he never took her in his arms. Other than the chaste kisses he gave her when he left her in the morning and returned home at night, he didn't touch her at all.

In the old days she'd have talked to him about it, just as she'd have argued with him about most of the constraints he was putting on her activities. Now she was just so damn grateful that he was taking any interest at all that she kept her dissatisfaction to herself. She was afraid to rock the boat, afraid that she'd push him right out the door again. And that the next time he wouldn't be back.

She missed his friendship most of all.

Lisa stumbled getting up from the kitchen table the night after Thanksgiving. Marcus's arms shot out, catching her against him, and her senses flamed. She wanted him so desperately she was almost embarrassed by her need. Rather than stifling her desires, pregnancy seemed to have heightened them. The instant hardening of Marcus's body told her in no uncertain terms that he still wanted her, too.

Acting purely on instinct, Lisa moved against him, silently inviting him to make love to her. It had been so long.

He pushed her away.

"I have work to do," he said, retreating to the office.

Only the fact that he'd left the dishes for her to rinse told her she hadn't just imagined his shudder of desire. For some reason, Marcus was denying himself something he wanted as badly as she did. He'd had to run away to stop himself for taking her up on her unspoken invitation. But the knowledge did little to ease the ache inside her.

"WHEN'S YOUR NEXT doctor's appointment?" Marcus asked the following night over dinner. They were at their favorite pizza parlor, sharing a cheeseless pizza, because Marcus said cheese had too much fat.

Lisa froze, her slice of pizza six inches from her mouth. "Why?" she asked, remembering his reaction the last time she'd had an appointment.

"I think I ought to accompany you."

Excitement spun through her. "You're sure?" she asked him. They'd had a wonderful day aboard the *Sara,* although it was too cold to take her out for a sail—and too dangerous, according to Marcus, for Lisa. They'd spent the day bundled up in sweaters and jeans, picnicking and playing cards in the cabin down below, almost as if nothing had ever come between them.

He nodded. "There're a couple of things I want to ask her."

"I have my end-of-first-trimester check on Thursday morning at ten," she said, too relieved to further question his change of heart. But the moment pointed out to her just how far from each other she and Marcus had strayed, that she was so giddy over so mundane a thing. The question was, had they become so adept at hiding from each other that they'd lost their closeness forever, or were they finally on their way home?

"I'll meet you at your office. We can walk up together." His blue eyes met her brown ones and he actually smiled at her.

For the first time in a long time, Lisa allowed herself to believe in their future.

"HOW MUCH REST is enough?"

Lisa lay on the examining table and bit the sides of her cheeks to hold back her smile. Marcus had been grilling Debbie Crutchfield ever since she'd entered the examining room.

Debbie exchanged a glance with Lisa, hiding her grin behind the clipboard she took a sudden interest in. "Everyone's different, Marcus," she said, obviously used to the vagaries of expectant fatherhood. "Lisa's body will tell her when she needs to rest. I suggest you lay off those books a little. Having a baby is a completely natural process. Just let nature do its job."

"Books?" Lisa asked. *What books?*

Marcus looked a little sheepish. "I'm going a little overboard, huh?" he asked the doctor.

"What books?" Lisa asked again. Debbie slid Lisa's top up almost to her breasts and stretched a tape measure across the slight mound of Lisa's stomach.

"I assumed you and Marcus had bought out the local bookstore with all the questions he's been asking,"

Debbie said, stretching the tape across Lisa's stomach at another angle.

"My secretary picked up a couple for me," Marcus admitted.

Lisa grinned up at him then. He was reading books about pregnancy. "You told Marge?" she asked.

"A few weeks ago," he replied absently, his eyes on what the doctor was doing. "What's the purpose of that?"

"We monitor the baby's growth by the growth of Lisa's stomach." Debbie went on to explain to Marcus the different ways they'd be keeping track of Lisa's condition throughout her pregnancy, while Lisa lay between them, a spectator at her own party.

She stared at her husband, wondering if she was reading too much into his announcement to Marge, into his willingness to be a father, at least publicly. Was she only lying to herself by believing that his reading all those books pointed to a more private commitment? Happiness bubbled up inside her, in spite of her warnings to herself to wait and see. Happiness and a relief so powerful she felt light-headed as she lay there, grinning from ear to ear.

"What about intercourse?"

Lisa's grin vanished and she felt herself turn ten shades of red. She was a doctor, too, for God's sake. Couldn't he have saved that question for her?

"What about it?" Debbie asked, her hand hovering over Lisa's exposed belly.

"I was under the impression it might be slightly, uh, risky."

Lisa wanted to pull the paper on the examining table up over her head.

"Not normally. I would think the risk of dying of frustration would be the more serious one," Debbie said, smiling. She was obviously used to such questions, unlike Lisa who didn't discuss sex much on the pediatrics ward.

Marcus looked down at Lisa, his eyes sizzling with a heat she hadn't seen there in weeks. "Good."

Is that why he hasn't touched me in all these weeks? He's been worried about the baby?

"Are you taking your vitamins?" Debbie asked Lisa.

Lisa nodded, struggling to pay attention to what the doctor was saying. All she could think about was getting her husband alone.

"And how's the morning sickness?"

"Better. The soda crackers helped."

Debbie pulled a pair of double stethoscopes from her pocket. "By the size of things I suspect we might just get to hear this determined character today," she said.

"Really?" Lisa popped up.

"Lie still and we'll see," Debbie said, pushing gently against Lisa's shoulders until she was flat on the table again.

Lisa barely felt the chill of the stethoscope against her stomach as she studied the concentrated look on the doctor's face, waiting while Debbie listened for the baby's heartbeat. She held her breath, afraid the sound of her breathing would drown out the fainter sound Debbie was seeking.

The doctor froze suddenly, holding the stethoscope just to the left of Lisa's belly button. "Don't move. It's right here," she said, sounding excited. "Here, Marcus, let's put your mind at ease. You come listen first." She held out the other set of earpieces.

Lisa looked over at Marcus, impatient for him to hear their miracle, to share with him the most exciting moment of their lives. Hoping to see her favorite smile lighting his features, warming his serious blue eyes, she was shocked at the brief glimpse she caught of his face before he turned, and without a word walked out of the room, closing the door behind him with a definitive click. Her new, oh-so-foolish hopes shriveled and died right there in the examining room, to be replaced by the fear that had become too common a companion these past months. Fear for herself, for her baby, but most of all, fear for Marcus. Was he never going to allow himself the happiness she was trying so desperately to give him?

At Debbie's urging she listened to the faint steady beat of her baby's heart, but rather than the elation she'd expected to feel, she felt only despair. What had she done? Dear God, what *had* she done?

CHAPTER EIGHT

LISA GOT THROUGH the rest of the doctor's appointment as people usually get through a crisis, simply because she had no other choice. She made some inane excuse for Marcus, something about his being embarrassed showing emotion in front of people, and while she was sure Debbie didn't buy it, the woman was too kind to say so. And while she listened to Debbie's orders for more exercise and vegetables over the coming month, her mind was on Marcus, on the depth of despair she knew that frozen look of his hid, on whether or not he'd be waiting for her on the other side of the door—or anywhere.

She almost wished he'd just leave her and get it over with. The thought panicked her, devastated her, but she honestly didn't know how much longer she could go on walking on eggs, afraid to upset the fragile peace under which they'd been going about their days, wondering when he might reach his threshold of endurance and walk out on her again.

She held her breath as she left the examining room, hoping Marcus would be waiting for her, ready to tell her he'd just become so overwrought with joy that he'd needed a moment to compose himself. Or that he'd had an instant of panic as it finally hit home what a mammoth responsibility they'd undertaken by bringing a new life into the world. Anything. She'd accept anything. As long as he was waiting there.

He wasn't waiting outside the door. Bracing herself for whatever the next hours might hold, Lisa said goodbye to Debbie, avoiding the pity she knew she'd find in the doctor's eyes, and took the elevator back downstairs to her office, telling herself to hold it together at least until she got home. She'd think about Marcus then. Just let her get home.

He was waiting for her in her office, his overcoat already on, but unbuttoned. He looked so solid and male and dependable. Relief flooded through her in that first second when she saw him standing there, but one glance at his face, and the knot in her stomach returned, tightening painfully.

"Can you leave?" he asked, his jaw clenched with the effort it was taking him to contain whatever emotions were roiling within him.

Lisa nodded, collected her keys and slipped into her winter coat. Picking up the phone to call her receptionist, she cleared her calendar for the day, with orders to send any emergencies to the pediatrician on call, and followed her husband's forbidding back out to the parking lot, where they climbed into their respective cars.

She drove home dry-eyed, a cloud of dread pervading her, and pulled the Mercedes into the garage beside Marcus's Ferrari, closing the automatic garage door behind her. She felt trapped as she sat there, not wanting to follow him into the house, not wanting to find out how bad things really were. And she was trapped by her own body, too, by the life growing within her from which there was no escape. Trapped by the dreams that made this child so essential to her happiness.

He was sitting in the middle of the velvet brocade couch in the formal living room, his overcoat tossed carelessly over the back of the matching Queen Anne chair. The coat frightened her. It was unlike Marcus to leave anything lying around.

Unless he was planning to go out again.

He stared up at the portrait of his father that hung over the fireplace. His face was no longer a frozen mask. He looked sad, defeated. Lisa felt physically ill, watching him.

She'd done this to him.

He reached out his arm to her as soon as he noticed her standing there. "Come. Sit with me," he said, helping her off with her coat.

He didn't sound like Marcus at all, lacking the pride, the self-assurance, that had first attracted her to him all those years ago, when he'd informed her that day outside her new sorority house that he'd carry in the rest of her boxes.

She thought of those few crucial seconds in Beth's examining room and wished there was some way she could undo them. She'd meant to give her husband back his dreams. Instead, she'd taken away his self-respect.

"I'm sorry." The words weren't enough, not nearly enough, but she meant them with all her heart.

Marcus slid his hand beneath hers, curling his fingers around her palm. "No, I'm sorry, Lis. I'm sorry I can't give you the children you need but—"

"No, Marcus," she interrupted, needing to make him understand once and for all. "You can't take responsibility for what happened. You can't keep blaming yourself for the negligence you suffered as a child. *I* don't blame you. *I* don't love you any less for it. Your sterility is something that happened to both of us, equally, just as if our house burned down, or we lost all of our money on Wall Street. It was just a piece of bad luck."

His jaw clenched, and Lisa wished she could know what he was thinking.

"—but I'm sorrier still for what I'm about to say," he continued as if she'd never interrupted him.

Lisa went cold at his words, her hand still locked with his.

"I love you, Lisa, far more than anyone or anything else in my life. And I'll stand beside you until the day I die, as long as that's where you want me to be."

"Always, Marcus. I want you there always," she said, running her free hand along his cheek. How she loved this man!

He pulled away from her caress. "Let me finish," he said, then paused, as if composing himself.

She sat still, the silence agonizing while she waited for him to go on.

"We can't keep skirting around each other, Lis. I don't want hiding from each other to be our way of life." He took his hand from hers.

"Neither do I. You don't know how much I've missed sharing your thoughts."

She needed to touch him, but wasn't going to make the mistake twice. He was talking about bridging the silences between them, yet he'd never seemed farther away.

"I understand, you know. I know why you enlisted Beth's help, and I've long since forgiven you for what you did, though I'm not even sure that it required forgiveness, that your going to Beth was in any way wrong. I just know I'm okay with it now. I want you to have your baby, Lisa. I want you to be happy."

Tears pooled in Lisa's eyes for the first time that day. There was more. She heard it coming. And she wasn't ready for it. She didn't want to know.

"But I cannot, and never will be, a father to that child."

No! Lisa sat silently beside him, holding back sobs with every ounce of strength she had left.

"I can't have you expecting it of me, Lis, or hoping that someday I'll change my mind. You'd only be setting yourself up for disappointment, and it wouldn't be fair to either of us, or to your child."

He sounded more like himself, in control again. And it was that more than anything that convinced Lisa he meant what he said.

"Do you want me to leave?" she asked.

"Not unless you want to. Our marriage can continue just as it always has."

"You're saying you want us to live together, all three of us, only one of us gets ignored by another one of us all his life?" She was incredulous.

Marcus was silent, staring straight ahead, obviously digesting her words. Surely he'd see how unfair that was, how deplorable to bring up a child that way. Surely he'd—

"I won't ignore the child, Lisa, any more than I'd ignore anybody living in our household. I just can't be a father to it. I can't rejoice in the little things parents get happy about. I can't take pride in the child's accomplishments. They aren't mine to take pride in.

"I went to your doctor's appointment today because of you, because I want to know everything you're going through, because I want to help keep you safe and healthy—not because of the baby."

Lisa couldn't stand it. "You're cheating yourself out of so much, Marcus. It's like you're punishing yourself for your sterility, denying yourself a joy you've wanted all your life. You could have listened to that heartbeat this morning. You would have felt the wonder. I *know* you would have, if you'd only given yourself a chance."

Marcus stood up, walking over to stand with his back to the fireplace, to the portrait of his stern-faced father. Lisa was frightened by how much the two of them looked alike at that moment.

"I've discovered something these past few months,

Lis. First, I was presumptuous enough to think I was doing what was best for you by making plans to move to Chicago. And then you had yourself inseminated, partially because you thought you knew better than I what was best for me. But the truth is, we were both doing each other a grave injustice, taking away each other's basic rights to decide for ourselves. Only *you* know what's best for you, honey, and if you think having your baby and having me, too, is your best shot at happiness, then I'm behind you one hundred percent. But *I* have to do what's best for me, too, and that's to accept that some things will never be. I can't claim what isn't mine. I can't spend the rest of my life pretending. Not even for you.''

His gaze was filled with his love for her, and it broke her heart. ''I want us to grow old together, Lis, just like we planned, but only if you can be happy without a father for your baby.''

Tears filled her eyes, but she blinked them away as she continued to hold his gaze, truly seeing inside him for the first time in months. Marcus was such a proud man, a man who stood by his convictions. She'd always loved those things about him. She'd never dreamed they might put an end to his dreams.

She ached for him, for his inability to allow himself the happiness that was his for the taking, for the insecurities that made it so hard for him to accept anything he didn't provide for himself. And she ached for the child she was carrying, who might never have all the benefits of his father's great wealth of love.

''I love you, Marcus, with all my heart. And if this

is what you need, we'll find a way to make it work,"
she said, falling apart inside.

His eyes narrowed as he looked at her from across
the room. "You're sure?"

"I'm sure." But she wasn't. Not at all. Not for
herself. Not for their baby. But most of all, not for
the man she loved. Marcus was meant to be a father;
he was a natural care giver with a heart bigger than
the state of Connecticut. And she feared that he'd
never be happy if he continued to deny himself this
chance.

"YOUR FATHER-IN-LAW is returning your call on line
six, Marcus." Marge's voice on his intercom interrupted Marcus's reverie about his wife. In the week
since he and Lisa had talked, he seemed to spend
more time thinking about her than about the work at
hand.

He pushed a button on the intercom. "Thanks,
Marge," he said. He picked up the phone. "Hello,
Oliver."

"Marcus? Is something wrong? Is Lisa all right?
And the baby?"

Marcus chuckled. "Everything's fine. We're just a
little concerned about you. We haven't heard from
you since the day after Thanksgiving. Lisa's starting
to get worried."

"Ah, you know how it is, Marcus. I always lose
touch a little bit as finals draw near."

"That's what I told Lisa, but she worries, anyway.
Especially now. Was Barbara emotional when she
was pregnant?"

"I'll say she was," Oliver said. "I came home one day when she was pregnant with Lisa and found her crying because I'd bought a green teddy bear for the nursery, instead of the yellow one she'd wanted. I tried to convince her that one was just as nice as the other, but she wouldn't hear it. Said it didn't match the wallpaper."

"So what'd you do?" Marcus asked, thinking of Lisa's disappointment when he'd accidentally brought home chocolate-chip ice cream, instead of the fudge ripple she'd asked for the previous night.

"I returned the green teddy, of course."

Marcus settled further into his chair and smiled. He'd gone back for fudge ripple, too.

"Seriously, son, things okay with you two now?"

"They're better. We've reached an understanding that I'm confident will work."

"An understanding?"

Oliver was family. He was going to have to know. "We're staying together, but not pretending I'm the child's father."

"So what are you?"

"Lisa's husband."

"And the child?" Oliver sounded doubtful.

"Her child."

"And you're sure you'll be able to handle this? Sharing her with the baby but not sharing the baby with her?"

Marcus wasn't sure yet, but he was working on it. "I love her, Dad. I want her to be happy."

"I know, son. But it isn't wrong to want a little happiness for yourself, too, is it?"

Marcus didn't know what happiness was anymore. "I'm happy," he said.

"You want to tell me how you do that?"

"Do what?" Marcus picked up the gold pen Lisa had bought him when he'd graduated. They'd had so many dreams back then.

"Convince yourself to be happy with what you have when you want more. I'm thinking I could use the lesson."

Marcus sat up, concerned. "Why? What's up?"

Oliver chuckled, but there was no joy in the sound. "I've just been thinking about the next twenty years of my life and wondering which part I'm looking forward to."

"Meaning?"

"I've had the love of my life, Marcus. I've reached the pinnacle in my career." He paused. "I've been starting to question where I go from here."

"Where do you want to go?"

"I'm not certain yet. Let me ask you this. Do you consider fifty-three too old to begin thinking about starting over?"

Marcus couldn't think of a career that suited Oliver better than the one he had, but he knew it wasn't for him to make that determination. "Not if that's what you really want to do."

"You wouldn't think I was just being an old fool?"

"Never. You're the least foolish person I know,

Oliver, and if there's something out there you want, then go get it.''

''I'm not sure I can, son, but, thanks. You've given me something to ponder.''

Marcus wasn't at all clear on what they'd just been talking about, but he was glad to have been able to help someone else, since he couldn't seem to find a way to help himself.

Shortly after hanging up the phone with Oliver, Marcus packed it in. Wednesday was Lisa's early day, and he'd been driving her to and from work most of the week. They'd often traveled to work together back before Marcus's diagnosis. It was something he'd missed when they'd started working such crazy hours. Something he was enjoying doing again when he could.

He also enjoyed the massages he gave Lisa each night before dinner to help ease the cramps in her muscles. And he looked forward even more to the lovemaking that always came later. He'd made love to Lisa every night since the doctor had given him the okay to do so, and he still couldn't get enough of her. All she had to do was look at him in that way, or he at her, and they started undressing. He'd wondered a time or two if maybe they were falling into bed so much because that was the only part of their relationship that was working, but decided that if that was the case, he was just grateful that *something* was working.

Surprisingly enough, he was even finding himself turned on by Lisa's expanding belly. Regardless of how the baby came to be inside her, she looked so womanly to him, so sexy, growing big with child. He was awed by her physical ability to do that which he, a mere man, could never do.

And he was awed by the things he was finding out he could do. It was hard to feel like a failure when all it took to make his wife stop crying was for him to walk into the room.

He arrived at the medical complex a few minutes early, and not wanting to bother Lisa while she was working, decided to pay a visit to little Willie Adams while he waited. The convalescent center was at one end of the medical complex, and he'd been in to see Willie a few other times during the boy's long recuperation, finding himself drawn to Willie's cocky self-assurance against all odds.

"Hi, Mr. C. I just saw Dr. C. this morning. It's pretty cool, you two having a kid and all," the boy said as soon as Marcus walked into his room. He'd offered to pay for a private room for Willie, but the boy preferred to have the company of other children, and so shared a room with two other long-term orthopedic patients. He was alone that afternoon, however.

"Dr. C.'s been wanting one a long time," Marcus said. He was learning to think of the baby only in terms of Lisa, hoping that would eventually make the whole thing easier somehow.

"Yeah, she'll prob'ly be a great mom, too, for a woman." Willie grinned, his red hair and freckled skin standing out against the stark white sheets of the hospital bed.

"I hear you've been doing pretty well yourself," Marcus said, sitting down on the end of the bed. "Dr. C. tells me you've taken a few steps without any assistance."

"I got to if I'm gonna be runnin' by next summer," Willie said, his chest expanding importantly.

"Just don't overdo it, fella. Dr. C. and your other doctors are doing everything they can to get you ready in time, so don't go messing up all their hard work by rushing things." Lisa had told him just the other night that Willie had been caught trying to get out of his bed by himself over the weekend to practice walking.

"I only did it once, Mr. C., honest. They canceled my therapy Saturday morning, and I didn't want to waste a whole day of getting better."

"They canceled your session because of some swelling in your muscles, Willie. I guess you pushed yourself a little hard on Friday, huh?"

"I guess." The boy looked contrite for all of two seconds and then grinned up at Marcus. "But I was awesome, Mr. C. You shoulda seen me. I made it all the way across the bars, only stopping once." Marcus knew a lot of Willie's workouts consisted of forcing his legs to move forward in walking motions while he supported his weight with his arms on the bars on either side of him.

"I'm proud of you. Keep up the good work, and you and I'll hit the batting cages before you go to camp next summer. Can't have your hitting rusty when you're playing with those older guys.''

"Cool! You mean it, Mr. C.?''

"Yep. Just as soon as Dr. C. says you're ready.'' He glanced at his watch. "And now I've got to get over to her office before she gets mad at me for being late.''

Willie's eyes opened wide. "She really gets mad at you?''

"Yeah, but I can handle it,'' Marcus said, ruffling the boy's hair affectionately.

"Hey, Mr. C.?'' Willie called just as Marcus reached the door.

"Yeah?'' he looked back at the boy, thinking how small and defenseless he looked in the bed.

"Your new baby sure is gonna be lucky, having you for a dad and all.''

Marcus felt the sting of the boy's words clear down to his soul.

THE FOURTH MONTH of her pregnancy was both the best and the worst time of Lisa's life. In some ways she and Marcus had never been closer. She cherished their love, knowing what an incredible gift it was.

And she was pregnant, soon to have the baby she'd always wanted. Her morning sickness had subsided and she felt great. She was even starting to show enough to need some of the maternity clothes she'd already purchased, with Beth's help, one Saturday afternoon. And she spent a lot of time daydreaming about the months to come. She was scheduled for her first ultrasound during her four-month checkup and might even then know the sex of her baby.

Everything would have been perfect if Marcus had shown any interest whatsoever in the life her body was busy creating for them.

She'd chosen the bedroom across the hall from them to use as the nursery, instead of the room Marcus's parents had used farther down the hall, and by the fifteenth week of her pregnancy, she was well under way with plans for decorating it. She and Marcus had always said they'd decorate the nursery themselves, piece by piece, rather than hire a professional as his mother had done when she'd been expecting him. And though Lisa longed for Marcus's help, she settled, instead, for remembering as best as she could the opinions he'd had when they used to talk about the nursery they'd have someday. He'd wanted colors, lots of them, all primaries, and balloons, too. He'd also wanted a race-car motif, but she was holding out on that, waiting to see whether the baby was a boy, or a girl who might prefer something a little softer, like the teddy bears she'd always wanted.

Marcus had also always wanted a Raggedy Andy doll. It was something he'd confessed to her one night after they were first married, and only after having had a couple of drinks. One of his earliest memories was of wanting the doll because of a cartoon he'd seen where the boy, Andy, had saved a little girl's life. And that was one of the few times he'd received his father's complete attention. The old man had blasted Marcus for wanting a doll, any doll. Cartwright boys didn't play with dolls.

Lisa's first purchase for the nursery was a pair of two-foot Raggedy Ann and Andy dolls.

She'd looked through scores of books of wallpaper samples and had settled on a pattern of red, yellow, blue, orange and green balloon bouquets, all floating on a background of soft white clouds. She bought her supplies, but waited until Marcus was at the office one Saturday to begin the actual transformation. She wanted the conversion to be as painless for him as possible.

She managed to sand down three of the walls rather quickly, but was having trouble getting the old wallpaper down from the fourth wall. Turning off the electric sander, which just seemed to be smoothing the wallpaper into the wall, she grabbed a hand sander and started in on the wall with good old elbow grease. Twenty minutes later, she was blinking back tears of frustration, mingled with drops of sweat. She was only about a tenth of the way done with the wall.

"What in hell do you think you're doing?"

Lisa jumped, dropping the sander on her toe.

"You scared me," she accused, standing before him in her plaster-spattered leggings and one of his old shirts, her hair pulled back in a ponytail.

"I'm sorry," he said. But he didn't sound it. "With all this racket going on, you must not have heard me come in. What are you doing, Lis?" He asked the question as if he thought she'd lost her mind.

"Decorating the nursery. What's it look like?"

"It looks like you're in danger of hurting yourself. What were you thinking, tackling a job like this all by yourself? You're pregnant, Lisa. You're smarter than this."

Lisa resented his high-handedness. And she'd had enough of sanding a wall that didn't want to be sanded, of carrying a baby that its own father didn't want.

"And who was I going to ask to help me with it, since the father of my baby has refused to have anything to do with him?" she hollered at Marcus.

She wanted to take the words back the minute they were out of her mouth. Marcus's face froze into that awful mask again.

"I'm sorry," she said, leaving the mess behind her as she walked over to her husband. She laid her head against his chest, sliding her arms beneath his jacket. She hadn't wanted to hurt him. Hadn't meant to hurt him. But she was hurting so damn badly herself the words had just slipped out.

"I'm truly sorry, honey," she said again as his silence rent the room. "I'll hire someone on Monday to do the job."

He didn't put his arms around her, didn't reach for her at all, except to push her away from him. "Give me time to get changed and I'll do it," he said, turning to leave before she could read what was in his eyes.

But she *could* read the posture in his back as he crossed the hall into their bedroom. His shoulders were slumped, his gait slow, as if he'd just fought an important battle—and lost.

CHAPTER NINE

THE NURSERY GOT PAINTED. And papered. Marcus tried not to look at the colorful balloons when he pasted them up, which was a little difficult since he had to match the strips as he hung them side by side. He tried not to care that Lisa's choices were making a room so like what he'd pictured for his own children back when he'd thought he'd have some. He tried to concentrate on her satisfied smiles, instead, as they worked on the room together every evening that week. And was never so thankful in his life as he was the day he finally put the supplies away for the last time. The job was done, and now they could get back to normal—at least for the few normal months left to them.

He took Lisa to dinner Friday night to celebrate.

"Here's to a finished nursery," she said, smiling across their intimate table for two at one of New Haven's elite restaurants. It was a place frequented more by his parents' generation than his own, but it was quiet.

Marcus tapped the edge of his glass of whiskey to the apple juice she held up to him. "To a finished nursery," he said wholeheartedly.

"Marcus! Lisa! Goodness, we haven't seen you in months!"

Marcus cringed when he heard the voice of his mother's best friend behind him. Soon after his parents' death, he'd cut most of his ties with the superficial society they had flourished on, but Blanche Goodwin kept reappearing once or twice a year, like a flu bug he couldn't shake.

He stood, holding out his hand to Blanche's silent husband. "Blanche, Gerald. It's good to see you again." Gerald's handshake was slightly unsteady.

Blanche bobbed her silver head importantly. "You're looking good, Marcus. We read in the paper that you'd acquired Blake's department stores. Your father would have been proud of the way you've taken charge of the business." She spoke before her husband could get a word in edgewise.

"I hope so, Blanche," Marcus said politely, angry with himself for the immediate pleasure he felt at her words, for the fact that his father's approval still mattered.

"Are you still toiling down at Thornton, Lisa?" Blanche asked next, making it sound as though Lisa scrubbed bedpans.

"I am," Lisa said, smiling graciously at the older woman.

"Let's leave the kids to their dinner, Blanche," Gerald said, his words a little slurred. Marcus was pretty sure he was drunk.

"Oh, my, yes, of course. I'm sorry. Your food must be getting cold. It was good to see you again, Marcus,'' she said, shaking Marcus's hand. "And Lisa…'' She held out her hand to Lisa, far enough away that Lisa would have to stand to reach it. Marcus recognized the sort of power play meant to make Blanche feel superior.

The bitch, Marcus thought, watching Lisa stand. She looked beautiful in the dark blue maternity dress she'd donned for the occasion. Beautiful and—

"Oh, my God! You're pregnant!'' Blanche said, loudly enough for all the tables around them to hear. Marcus had actually managed to forget for a few brief minutes.

"Yes, I am. Sixteen weeks today,'' Lisa said gently, looking at Marcus.

He smiled at her. He'd prepared himself for the fact that their many acquaintances would naturally assume that Lisa's baby was his. He could handle having to claim the child in public situations. After all, he'd been handling Marge's questions for weeks, and had managed to relay information about his wife's child just fine without thinking about it in terms of himself.

Blanche inspected Lisa's stomach once more before looking at Marcus as if he'd just amassed another million. "Oh, Marcus, congratulations. A Cartwright heir! Your mother and father would have been so pleased.''

He felt like he'd been slapped. He wasn't ready for this. Not by a long shot.

"Thank you,'' he said, forcing himself to continue smiling as Lisa answered Blanche's questions about the due date and late-night feedings. And watching his wife's animated face, it came home to him just how much he was missing. Lisa was living their dream. He was on the outside looking in. And always would be.

HE HAD TO WORK the next morning, but remembering the trouble Lisa had gotten herself into the previous Saturday, he handled only what absolutely had to be done before Monday morning's meeting with his executives. He drove home with his head full of plans for a drive up the coast that afternoon. Maybe he and Lisa could stop at some seaside place for a late lunch and then spend the night at Haven's Cove. Remembering their anniversary, the glorious idyll of forgetfulness they'd found in the little cabana there, he called from his car phone to make a reservation. And maybe they'd even get some snow while they were there, making it impossible for them to return.

Recognizing in his high-handed approach to planning their lives a hint of desperation, Marcus pushed it away. He and Lisa were talking again. And though they were facing a very unorthodox situation, somehow they would make their marriage work. They loved each other too much not to.

"Lisa?" he called, shrugging out of his overcoat and pulling off his tie as he walked in the front door. He'd left the Ferrari out front. It should only take him a couple of minutes to change into jeans and help Lisa pack an overnight bag.

"I'm up here!"

Marcus took the steps two at a time, eager to share

his plans with her. The more he thought about it, the more he knew that a weekend away was just what they needed.

"Pack a bag, Lis. We're—" She wasn't in their bedroom.

"Lis?" he called, back out in the hall.

"In here."

Marcus looked at the door across from him. The door he'd been avoiding. What was she doing in there now? He'd finished everything up in there so they wouldn't have to go in again. At least not for a while. With reluctance, he approached the nursery.

His good spirits evaporated when he saw what was inside. An entire room full of boxes—and his wife standing in the midst of them, dressed in a new pair of designer maternity jeans and a silk-embossed sweatshirt, grinning from ear to ear.

"I knew you'd be mad if I tried to put this all together by myself, but please hurry and change, Marcus. I can't wait to see how it all looks in here. I think we should put the crib over there. What do you think?"

Marcus blanched, his plans for the weekend fading as he surveyed the number of boxes in the room. There was barely room to walk.

"If that's where you want it, Lis," he said, calculating the hours it was going to take him to get all that stuff put together. "I'll be right back."

Swallowing his disappointment, Marcus canceled the reservation he made for the night. Lisa was trying hard to make their marriage work. To allow him to help her, even though she knew he was only doing it for her, not for the child she carried. He couldn't afford to waste her efforts.

Pulling on a pair of sweatspants and a T-shirt, he decided to tackle the crib first, sensing his wife's impatience to see it assembled, in spite of the fact that she'd never mentioned the furniture to him. Other than when she'd answered Blanche Goodwin's questions the night before, she hadn't mentioned the baby since last week, when he'd caught her sanding the nursery all alone.

"I already brought up the electric drill and all the screwdriver bits," she said. Marcus hoped he remembered how to use it. They had a shed full of tools, but they were for the gardeners and whatever handymen Hannah occasionally hired.

Lisa's excitement was contagious, and as they pulled the various pieces of the crib from the box and slowly put them together, Marcus started to relax.

"Remember that waterbed we bought when we were first married?" he asked, grinning as he thought back to those invincible days.

"What a mistake *that* was," Lisa groaned, sliding the long plastic covering on the top bar of the crib. "It would've been nice if they'd told us beforehand that it was really nothing more than a million pieces of plywood."

"Or if we'd had any idea that the only real stability the thing had was *after* it was filled with water. But it was still kind of fun putting it together, wasn't it,

Lis? You were so damn cute strutting around with that tool belt on.''

Lisa slid the plastic tube on the top bar of the other side of the crib. ''I probably would've enjoyed it a whole lot more if I hadn't just started medical school. All I could think about was how many hours it would be until I could get some sleep,'' she said.

''I wish I could've helped you more, honey. You practically killed yourself that first year, and I was so busy climbing my own ladder I didn't even notice how tired you were half the time.'' He tightened a bolt on the bottom of the crib.

''Oh, no, Marcus! You were wonderful! Most of my classmates were working, and some were even raising families. Compared to them I was spoiled rotten. I had a wonderful home, no financial concerns, all the time I needed to study—and a lover who could always be depended upon to take my mind off whatever ailed me. You were what got me through medical school.'' She handed him another bolt.

''That's not the way I remember it. You wore yourself out.''

''I was a woman in a predominantly male class. Whether it was true or not, I always felt like I had to do everything better than the rest, to prove I deserved the place I was taking up.''

Marcus glanced at her, loving her more than ever. ''It wasn't just that. You had to learn everything there was to know, didn't you, hon? So you could save all the little Saras in the world.''

''I just needed to do my best,'' Lisa said, rubbing

her belly protectively. *Soon,* he could almost hear her saying. Soon her home would be filled with childish laughter again. And Marcus understood, more than ever, how much his wife needed the child she was carrying.

"Hold this while I get the bar to slide into this end," Marcus said suddenly, cursing himself for reminding her of painful times.

Lisa's breast brushed against Marcus's hand as she moved to the other side of him. He fondled her nipple between two of his knuckles almost subconsciously for a second before she grabbed the edge of the headboard where he'd indicated. Her eyes were smoky as they met the sudden question in his.

"Later, buster. We've got work to do," she said, but she was smiling again.

"Slave driver," Marcus grumped cheerfully, filled with new incentive to get the job done. He could think of nothing better than losing himself in Lisa's lovemaking.

Inspecting the sides of the crib before he attached them to the frame, he assured himself that the bars were close enough together that a baby's head couldn't slip through.

"How come you're setting those springs so low?" Lisa asked as he was about to screw the bed together.

"There's going to be a mattress on top of them, Lis. You don't want the baby to fall over the top when it starts to stand."

She grinned, warming the cold spots within him. "We can lower the springs later, as he grows. See, they're adjustable. And at first, when he'll only be lying down, I'll need the mattress higher so I can reach him to lift him in and out.''

Marcus looked over the crib again, picturing, for a second, a newborn baby lying there and Lisa trying to get to it. He raised the springs. For Lisa.

He finished tightening the last screw and stood up, releasing the catch on the side of the crib to make certain that it lowered and raised as it should. Lisa pulled the mattress over and stood with it propped up against her leg.

''It looks great. And you didn't even swear!'' she said, admiring his handiwork.

Marcus glanced over at his wife. ''Was I supposed to?''

She grinned again. ''I don't know. It's just that I always hear people talking about how guys swear putting cribs together.''

''Oh, but I'm not 'guys,''' Marcus said, coming over to relieve her of the mattress. ''I do a lot of things differently from most.''

''I'm holding you to that,'' Lisa said, her voice husky.

He lifted the mattress easily, laying it on the springs he'd just fixed into the bottom of the crib, and was shocked by the surge of strange emotion that struck him. He was leaning over the crib just as he'd pictured Lisa doing a moment before. Except that this crib wasn't his for leaning over. He wouldn't be lifting a baby off this mattress. He'd never have a child of his own to tend to in the middle of the night.

Clamping down on the raw agony that shot through him, he was filled with the old anger again, the cancerous rage that was as irrational as it was hopeless.

"I'm going down to get a beer. You want something to drink?" he asked Lisa, straightening abruptly. He had to get out of there before he ripped the damned mattress apart.

She was opening the package that contained the crib sheet. "Ice water would be nice," she said, smiling her thanks. Her smile turned to a frown when she saw his face.

"What's wrong?" she asked, immediately concerned. Her hands stilled.

"Nothing. I'm just thirsty. I'll be right back." He wiped the sudden sweat from his brow as he headed for the stairs. He hadn't had such a destructive surge of anger in weeks. He'd thought he was done with all that, that he'd come to terms with himself, his place in Lisa's life. Now he was beginning to wonder if he ever would.

"MARCUS!" LISA WAS calling, and Marcus reached out, but there were too many people around for him to get to her. All he could see was a flash of white. There were too many lights. The flurry of people made him dizzy with fear.

Someone screamed. Lisa, he thought, but as he pushed forward, knocking over the people in his way, he heard the doctor calmly order him outside. It took three sets of strong arms to arrest his progress, but they couldn't get him to leave.

"I need to operate," the doctor said, *and the flurry increased. The noise was too loud, hurting his ears, and then suddenly all he could hear was crying. Lisa crying. Or was it him?*

Marcus sat up, his body drenched with sweat, which cooled his skin in the night air. His gaze flew to Lisa. She was breathing softly, regularly, her lovely face nestled in a corner of his pillow.

His gaze strayed to the mound Lisa's belly made beneath the covers. *Please, God, let us get through this. All of us.*

LISA WAS IN THE DEN, reading literature she'd just received on a new strain of flu virus, while Marcus was on the telephone in their office. They'd both been in the office until Marcus's conversation with George Blake had distracted Lisa to the point where she couldn't concentrate.

It was Monday, one week before Christmas, and she and Marcus were planning to go Christmas shopping. But first she had a presentation to prepare. She was going to be speaking at the free clinic staff meeting on Tuesday about this new strain of flu, and she wanted the staff well-informed. There had only been a couple of cases in New Haven thus far, but in other parts of New England the virus was rampant. The free clinic was bound to be hit the hardest.

It usually started with a headache followed by— Lisa stopped reading as she felt a peculiar jolt in her belly. Her heart rate practically doubled as she sat completely still, waiting to see if it would happen again. It did. Another little jolt. And then another.

Grinning from ear to ear, Lisa ran down the hall toward the office, bursting with joy at this, the first definite movement of her baby. She had to tell Marcus.

He was still on the phone, but she rushed in, anyway, hoping he'd get a chance to feel the miracle, too. He looked up at her, a question in his eyes, and it was in that second it dawned on Lisa. He wouldn't want to know her news. Marcus didn't want to be his baby's father. He wasn't going to share in the little joys that parents share. Shaking her head at him, she turned and left the office, the rumble of his voice on the telephone nearly drowned out by the roaring in her ears.

She couldn't stand it. Dear God, she couldn't live a lifetime of having every cause for celebration turned into a moment of sadness. What would happen when her child said his first word, took his first step, made the school play or hit a home run? When he came running into the house to share his news only to have his bubble burst by an indifferent father?

Lisa wandered upstairs, telling herself it wouldn't be like that, it wouldn't be that bad. Marcus wasn't heartless the way his own father had been. He'd come around. She went into the nursery, the room she and Marcus had built together—so much like they'd planned that she'd actually forgotten for a time that Marcus had done it all for her, not for their baby.

Sitting down in one of the rockers they'd brought

over from their bedroom, she picked up the Raggedy Andy doll and hugged it against her.

"Don't worry, little one. Your daddy's a good man, a fair man, and a very loving man. He'll come around for you. You'll see."

The baby chose that moment to kick her again, harder than the first couple of times. Hard enough that Marcus would for sure have been able to feel it if he'd put his hand there. Lisa buried her face in Andy's soft cloth chest, using the toy to stifle her sobs.

BETH HADN'T SEEN much of Lisa in the weeks since the anniversary of John's death. True, her professional services for Lisa were done. And she was really very busy, with more and more couples seeking the services of the fertility clinic. Furthermore, she knew how important it was that Lisa and Marcus have as much time as possible alone together as they passed through this crucial adjustment period in their marriage.

But she was avoiding Lisa.

Beth sat in her office late on Friday, the Friday before Christmas, and faced a few more home truths.

Oliver wasn't coming. The holiday was only two days away. She'd already told Lisa she wouldn't be spending the day with them, that she was driving upstate to see her cousin again, but she'd bought something for Oliver, anyway. It was nothing momentous, just a tie she thought would look good with the tweed jackets he favored, one that was just a little bit wider than the ones he had. She pulled the gaily wrapped package out of her desk drawer, staring at it as if it had answers to the questions that were eluding her. Oliver had missed two out of the last four Fridays. Both of them since they'd sat together in his gazebo.

She was disappointed. More disappointed than she had any business being.

Oliver had been John's colleague. He was her best friend's father. He was fifteen years older than she was. He was still in love with his wife. And Beth still tingled whenever she thought of the way he'd kissed her.

Which was often. More often than she cared to admit.

She looked at the clock on her wall one more time. It was an hour past the time Oliver usually stopped by. No. He definitely wasn't coming.

Picking up her purse, Beth shrugged into her coat, locked up and headed home. To the memories of her dead husband.

She was glad Oliver was backing off from their friendship. He wasn't right for her. Not at all.

"MERRY CHRISTMAS, sweetheart."

"Merry Christmas, Lis. I didn't hurt you, did I?" Marcus asked, concerned that he'd been a little too inventive. He wasn't sure what had gotten into him lately. It was almost as if, now that the pressure was off him to give Lisa the baby she wanted, now that he didn't have to feel guilty for his inability to give her that child, he was free to really let his passion loose.

"Uh-uh." She shook her head lazily, her eyes slumberous as she smiled up at him, her long dark hair in disarray across both pillows. There was a blizzard outside, making their large bedroom seem almost cozy. "Not that I have much to go on, mind you, but you've got to be the best lover in the world."

"I'll bet you say that to all the guys," he murmured softly, gazing down at her naked body. They'd shared most of the holiday with Oliver, and Marcus had enjoyed every minute of it, but it was these moments alone with Lisa that he'd been waiting for.

"You *are* all the guys in my life." She looked as if she wanted to say more, but wasn't sure she should. "Can I tell you something?"

"Of course, Lis."

"I lied to you."

His heart started to pound with dread. "When?"

"Remember that first time we made love?"

"At the cabin? Of course. I'd thought I'd died and gone to heaven."

Lisa smiled, though a little nervously. "Remember, right before, when you asked me if I was a virgin?"

"Sure." Marcus wondered if this was another one of those pregnancy things, where she got a little irrational for no reason he could figure out. "You explained about that other guy, Lis. It was only once. You were of age. I've never thought anything of it."

"There *was* no other guy, Marcus." She looked away again, as if embarrassed. "I lied to you. I was afraid you'd go all noble on me and stop if you knew it was my first time.''

Marcus propped himself up on one elbow. ''You should have told me, Lisa. I wouldn't have stopped—we'd come too far for that—but I could've made it easier on you. I must've hurt you.'' He didn't know whether to feel angry with her for putting herself through that, or elated that she'd never been with another man.

Lisa shrugged. ''It hurt a little, but at that point, I didn't care. And you made me forget about the pain soon enough.''

He leaned over, wondering what he'd ever done to deserve this woman. ''I'm still sorry I hurt you,'' he said, running his hand along her brow and down over her cheek. ''But, God, Lis—I'm the only one?''

Her tentative nod freed something inside of him, a sense of security he'd never known before. His fingers brushed the sensitive spot on the side of her neck. She'd just given him the best Christmas present he'd ever had.

Lisa shivered, and Marcus continued the caress, down over her shoulders to her breasts and below. Lisa's belly had expanded to the size of a small basketball, and he caressed the taut skin. She was his Madonna. She was his angel sent from above.

Marcus began to make love to Lisa again, his movements more careful than usual—as if she were a virgin, showing her how it should it have been for her all those years ago. When it was time, he entered her slowly, with the ease of familiarity, but also with a hesitant exploration, learning her anew.

He loved her as slowly as he could, until he was certain he wasn't going to last another second. And then he plunged into her fully. But just as he reached his hilt, something jerked against him, from within her, as if protesting his invasion.

Marcus flew off Lisa and away from the bed so fast he almost hurt himself, staring at his wife as if he'd never met her before. He couldn't believe what had just happened.

Lisa's baby had kicked him. Where it counted. Another man's baby was inside his wife telling him to go away.

What if the baby did that after he was born, too? Told him to go away? Would it come in between him and Lisa? Force her to choose between the two of them?

"Marcus?" She sounded close to tears as she sat up, staring back at him.

Lisa's baby had kicked him.

There really was a little human being growing inside her. One she was going to give birth to in the not-too-distant future. And he'd felt it move. In the most intimate way possible.

He knew her baby in a way no other man ever would.

Yet…it changed nothing. Still didn't make Marcus the father of Lisa's baby. But suddenly he found that he was no longer jealous of the man who *had* fathered her child. Envious as hell, yes. Definitely. Always.

But no longer jealous. Marcus knew that baby far more intimately than *that* man did.

LISA SLEPT LITTLE that night, tormented by the look of horror she'd seen on Marcus's face when the baby had kicked him. He'd come back to her, finished what he'd started, tenderly drawing a response from her as he always could, but the minute he'd fallen asleep, her tears had come, sliding silently down her cheeks to sink into the pillow beneath her head. So much for a merry Christmas.

Lying in bed beside Marcus, listening to his steady breathing, she despaired of their future. How could she raise a child with a man who hated it? What would it do to their son or daughter to live in a house with a man who was repulsed by the child's touch? What right did she have to subject *any* child to that kind of life?

Getting out of bed, Lisa wrapped herself in the big furry bathrobe Marcus had given her for Christmas that morning and sat in the bathroom trying to make sense of the tangle that had become her life. The man she adored hated her baby. What was she going to do, torn as she was between the baby she'd come to love so dearly, the baby she needed so badly, and the man who was her other half? How could she possibly keep all three of them happy?

She didn't know, but she could no longer hide from the fact that something had to be done. She couldn't raise her baby in a house full of resentment or indif-

ference. The poor child would grow up feeling un-
loved.

Much as Marcus had done.

And as confident as he was, when it came to loving,
Marcus still blamed himself for the fact that his parents hadn't loved him enough to find time for him.
He believed that he was lacking, that he was unlov-
able. And, God help her, she didn't think she could
ever leave him and, in his mind, confirm that belief.

CHAPTER TEN

OLIVER WAS CONCERNED about Lisa. She'd invited him to dinner one Sunday in the middle of January, and by the end of the afternoon, she looked awful. Her skin was white, her eyes dull, and she had almost no energy at all.

"I'm just tired, Dad," she said when he became too worried to keep silent about it.

"Dr. Crutchfield said to expect this," Marcus added later as he walked Oliver to the door.

Oliver wasn't a doctor. And after losing one daughter and a wife, he knew he tended to overreact a bit sometimes, but he'd still rest better with the reassurance of someone who would know just what she was talking about. Someone who wouldn't sugarcoat things for him if, indeed, there *was* something wrong with his daughter.

He hadn't seen Beth at all over the holidays and was certain he'd recovered from whatever middle-aged foolishness had overcome him. At least that was what he told himself when he made a detour by Beth's office on his way home from the university on Tuesday.

"Oliver! Come in!" She sounded happy to see him. He'd been half-afraid she'd show him the door.

"You busy? I can get back to you another time," he said, noticing the huge stack of files on her desk. She looked tired, too. Maybe it was just something that was going around.

"No! No. Come on in. Have a seat. I've missed you these past several Fridays. Not that you have to come by or anything. It's just that I'd gotten kind of used to seeing you."

She was babbling. Oliver liked it. A lot.

"I've been pretty busy lately," he lied, shrugging out of his overcoat. He hated lying, but even more, he couldn't stand to hurt her with the truth. He'd been out with another woman the last Friday, a volunteer at the hospital like he was, a woman his own age. "There's always so much to do when the new semester starts up."

She smiled, looking relieved. "That's all right. I probably wouldn't have been much company, anyway. I've been busy, too. Last Friday I was asleep by eight o'clock."

He could just picture her all curled up in bed. He'd bet she wore a nightie, not pajamas. "Have you seen Lisa lately?" he asked, reminding himself of the reason for his visit.

"Not in the last week or two. She's been spending all her free time with Marcus. But I've spoken with her doctor. Why?"

Oliver shrugged, feeling better already. "I had dinner over there Sunday. She looked tired. Wan."

Beth grinned. "Wouldn't you be feeling kind of

tired yourself if you were lugging around all that extra weight? She's gained almost ten pounds.''

Oliver considered the grandbaby his daughter was going to present him with. ''I guess I would,'' he said. He was suddenly happier than he'd been in weeks. ''And Lisa's small-boned, too, like her mother. Though I don't ever remember Barbara looking so sickly.''

''I'll take a look at her, Grandpa. Would that make you feel better?''

''It would,'' Oliver said, feeling deflated. *Grandpa.* What would a woman Beth's age ever find of interest in an old codger like him?

And why was he even thinking such things again? He'd been cured of all that.

LISA WAS ANEMIC. Debbie Crutchfield recommended that she cut down her working hours to part-time until she was fully rested and had regained her strength.

''I think you should quit working altogether, Lis. At least until after you have your baby,'' Marcus said as soon as they left the doctor's office. He helped her into her coat, pulling it up over the sleeves of her suit jacket before he tied the belt across her expanding belly.

She was glad he was there. He'd missed one of her checkups because he hadn't wanted to accompany her to the ultrasound that immediately followed the appointment.

''I'll see what I can do,'' Lisa said, her arm through his as he walked her back to the car. If she had to quit work, she would. She was willing to do whatever it took to have a healthy baby. She just didn't know what she was going to do after the baby was born. She was almost into her seventh month. That gave her three more months. Three months to decide what would happen when she had another life to consider before her own. Would she still be able to lean on Marcus then?

He'd just said it again. *Your* baby. Not *our* baby. He couldn't make it plainer that the baby she was carrying was hers and hers alone. And she was growing more and more afraid that was just how she was going to be raising it. Alone.

"We haven't talked about afterward, Lis," Marcus said later that night. They were in the den, sitting in front of a roaring fire, waiting for the eleven o'clock news.

"What do you mean?" she asked, her heart leaping. Had he read her mind? Did he know that he and her baby couldn't live as strangers in the same house? That she might be forced to choose between the two of them?

"Your work, for one thing. Do you plan to go back after the baby's born?"

Oh. "I guess I just assumed I would, once he's old enough for me to leave him."

Marcus's eyes narrowed. "You keep saying 'he.' Do you know you're having a boy?"

"No." Lisa shook her head. What an insane conversation to be having with the father of her child. If he'd been with her during the ultrasound, he'd know.

Or if he'd cared enough to ask her at any time during these many weeks since. "The baby was lying on his stomach and it was impossible to tell."

Marcus nodded, looking about as interested as if they'd been discussing the weather. "So you plan to hire a nanny to care for it?"

It. Not him or her. *It.* "Yes. I've already made some inquiries at the hospital." She plucked at the bottom of the lounging pajamas she'd put on as soon as they'd arrived home.

"I think that would be preferable to day care," he said.

Lisa froze, not certain she wasn't reading more into his casual statement than was there—as she had a tendency to do these days. But it had sounded like Marcus had just expressed a personal opinion where *her* baby was concerned.

"I thought I'd only work part-time, for the first year at least," she said tentatively.

"That sounds like a good plan. A child should have its mother with it as much as possible during those first years."

As he, Marcus, had not. Lisa heard what her husband wasn't saying. *Oh, Marcus, please let yourself be loved as you were meant to be loved. Not just by me. But by your new family, too.*

"I don't think I'll be able to leave him more than that, anyway," she said, chuckling. "I'm finding I have some rather possessive motherly tendencies."

Marcus smiled. "I'm glad."

He reached for the television control and flipped on

the news, which effectively put an end to the conversation. But Lisa was smiling when she went to bed that night. Was Marcus finally starting to thaw? Could it be that she'd be able to have her baby and her husband, too? Was it possible she'd gambled—and won?

SHE WAS STILL ASLEEP when Marcus left for work the next morning. He left her a note on his pillow, telling her good-morning, rather than waking her. He was happy to see that she was finally getting some rest. With her nights constantly interrupted by trips to the bathroom, getting up at the crack of dawn had become too much for her.

He'd be relieved when the whole thing was over, he thought as he drove through the old and elegant streets of New Haven, beautiful even with the gray skies overhead and the slush on the ground. As much as he enjoyed watching Lisa's body blossom, he was growing increasingly more worried about her as her pregnancy progressed.

Of course, he had his share of apprehensions for afterward, too. Would Lisa still have time for him? Would her baby resent his place in Lisa's life? She was going to be a very devoted mother, which pleased Marcus, but would she need him around once she had her baby to love?

Disgusted with himself for harboring such fears, Marcus attacked his work that day with a vengeance. He had another meeting with George Blake, and he was going to get the deal done. It was time to quit being Mr. Nice Guy.

Blake and his team arrived fifteen minutes early, but Marcus was ready for them. He led them to the executive conference room down the hall from his office then waited only until Marge had served coffee before beginning the meeting.

"Gentlemen, I think what we've worked out here together should just about take care of the future of Blake's department stores," Marcus said, cutting to the chase. He held up a copy of the latest proposal for a fifty-one/forty-nine percent merger, allowing Blake's the fifty-one percent and Cartwright Enterprises the management privileges, all of which were specified in minute detail.

"I have just one suggestion about page fifteen, item one, young man," George Blake said, "under software implementation for inventory control."

Marcus stifled a groan. He'd known the old guy was going to find a way to make this difficult. It was time to play hardball. "What would that be, George?"

"I'm not sure that it's fiscally wise to invest so heavily in a system that will be outdated by the end of the year."

Marcus's rebuttal died in his throat. "Oh?" he said. He'd had to fight for months to get George to allow him to put computers in the Blake's enterprise at all because the old man hadn't known the first thing about them and, thus, didn't trust them.

"CD-ROM, all of that, will be a thing of the past

before we know it," George said, tapping the pages in front of him. "If we were buying this two years ago, I'd agree that it would be worth the investment, but at this late date, I say we buy a system that will allow us to move into the future, a system that we can expand on, rather than replace."

Marcus felt like giving the old man a hug. He grinned, instead. "I'd say that's sound advice, George. I'll have my team on it first thing in the morning."

OLIVER WAS BUSHED. He stopped by Beth's office after volunteering on Friday, needing to see her in spite of the anger tamped down inside of him. They'd lost another kidney patient that week, one who probably could have been saved if they'd had the new dialysis equipment he'd been campaigning for. Thornton had the money. They just chose to spend it in other places. Such as Beth's clinic. A few lives gained for one lost, he thought with uncharacteristic bitterness.

"You up for dinner?" he asked, poking his head around her door.

"You bet." She turned off her computer, grabbed her coat and locked up behind her, watching him all the while.

"What's wrong?" she asked.

They were walking briskly out to their cars, hunched over against the cold.

"Rosie Gardner died today."

He could see the instant understanding in her eyes as she slowed to look at him. It was hard to blame her for taking the dialysis-equipment money when she looked at him like that.

"I'm sorry." She linked her arm with his so naturally that he shouldn't even have noticed. Except that he did. His whole body noticed.

"If we'd just had that damned equipment," he said, reminding himself that it was better if he stayed at least a little bit angry with her. Except that he wouldn't have a grandchild on the way, an extension of Barbara, if it wasn't for Beth's clinic.

"Have you asked Marcus for help?" she asked, standing beside her car while he unlocked the door for her. He could see her breath in the frosty air.

"Of course not. I'd never ask Marcus for money. Too many other people do that every day of his life. The boy already thinks his money is the only reason most people care about him. I certainly don't want him thinking that about me."

Beth smiled, her full dimples twinkling up at him. "I didn't mean personally. I meant Cartwright Enterprises. If you get your money from a private source, it has to buy only what it was donated to buy. The hospital no longer has a say in designating how the funds are spent. And it's not unheard of for private companies to donate to hospitals, though the way hospitals have become big businesses themselves, it's not done as often anymore. Still, it's a great tax write-off."

"You're sure the hospital has no means to direct the spending?" Oliver asked. He'd understood that everything that was used in the hospital had to be hospital-sanctioned.

"They can direct only insomuch as determining which machine they deem most suitable to their needs, but all the money either has to be used for the designated purpose or returned."

Oliver followed Beth to a steak house around the corner from the hospital, mulling over her suggestion. It might work. It just might work.

Beth was one smart woman. Which was one of the reasons he enjoyed the time he spent with her.

It had nothing whatsoever to do with the fact that her lips were made for kissing.

"OH, LOOK AT THIS ONE! It's so tiny." Lisa held up the cutest little T-shirt she'd ever seen.

"I think your baby's already too big to fit into that," Beth said, grinning at her.

"Nah," said Crystal, a maternity nurse from the hospital. "She's hardly showing yet. Just wait another couple of months. Then he'll be too big."

"Don't even talk about it." Lisa rubbed the front of her navy blue maternity dress. "Another couple of months and I'm not going to be able to walk."

Everyone laughed and Lisa was suddenly glad Beth had arranged the baby shower for her. She'd missed her friends.

"Have you guys picked out names yet?" Nancy, a doctor from ER, asked.

"Sawyer if it's a boy," Lisa said. "Sara Barbara

if it's a girl.'' The names had been picked so many years ago she didn't even have to think about it.

She opened another gift, a pair of tiny designer tennis shoes. And looked up just in time to see Marcus standing in the doorway. He was supposed to be in Storrs at a meeting for most of the afternoon. Which was why she'd agreed to Beth's suggestion that the shower be at her, Lisa's, house.

He was gone before anyone noticed him, before Lisa had a chance to call him back, but not before the look on his face had torn her heart in two. Raw longing had blazed from his eyes as he'd looked at the tiny pair of shoes she held. Longing and agony. Her husband still wanted a child of his own. And it was killing him that she was having one without him.

SHE TRIED TO PULL AWAY from Marcus, to make herself, and her condition, as scarce as possible after seeing his face that day of her shower. She just couldn't bear to hurt him anymore.

But staying away was almost impossible. Everywhere she went, everything she did, he was right beside her, watching over her. Protecting her. Loving her. And her foolish heart began to hope again. Marcus's pain would vanish if he could only allow himself to believe that the baby she was carrying was his.

But how did she make him believe?

''LET'S GO FOR A WALK,'' Marcus said one Sunday during the seventh month of her pregnancy. It was one of those sunny February days, still cold but dry,

514 ANOTHER MAN'S CHILD

and perfect for walking. He looked disgustingly energetic in his jeans and corduroy shirt.

"I'm too tired." Lisa was lying on the couch reading the paper and perfectly content to stay that way.

"Come on, Lis. You heard Debbie. The more walking you do, the easier the birth will be on you."

Lisa threw down the paper. "Fine. We'll walk," she said, hauling herself up to go put on some warmer clothes and some shoes. She was getting tired of everyone else knowing what was better for her than she did.

Marcus waited more than fifteen minutes before he started to get concerned and went up to check on her. What could possibly be taking her so long?

She was in the bedroom, stomping her foot on the carpet and crying like a baby. She only had one tennis shoe on.

"Lisa? What is it, hon?" he asked gently.

"Nothing," she said petulantly, sounding more like a child herself than a woman preparing to give birth to one.

He crossed to her and took her in his arms. "Something must be wrong, Lis. Please tell me what." He wasn't sure he was ever going to become accustomed to her unpredictable mood swings.

Laying her head against him, she sniffed noisily, then muttered something inaudible.

"Hmm?" he asked, stroking her hair.

"I can't tie my shoe," she said more loudly.

He had to use every muscle in his face to hold back the grin that threatened to burst forth as he took stock of the situation. His beautiful talented wife could no longer reach her arms around her expanding belly to get to her feet.

"Then I guess it's my job to do it for you, huh?" he asked once he was sure he had his smile under control.

She pulled back from him. "I guess," she said, holding her foot out dejectedly.

She teetered a little when Marcus bent to his task. "Maybe you better sit down." He nudged her backward to the bed.

Kneeling, he tied the shoe and then slid the other shoe onto her other foot, tying that one, as well. Just as he was finishing, he felt her foot quiver, spasms that were repeated throughout her body, even shaking the bed.

Damn. If she was sobbing that hard she really had it bad.

"It's okay, Lis," he said, running his hand gently along her calf. He glanced up at her, wishing he could do more to help her—and couldn't believe what he saw. She wasn't crying. She was laughing so hard her whole body shook.

"I'm s-s-sorry," she said, through her mirth. "It's just…seeing you down there…" She broke into another peel of laughter.

Feeling alive and in love, and very relieved to see his wife had regained her sense of humor, Marcus took her into his arms, sharing her laughter and her love.

Their walk was postponed until later in the afternoon.

THE SHOWER WAS RUNNING. Marcus could hear it when he came in from work one Thursday during the last week in February. Dropping his briefcase in the office, he climbed the stairs, a grin on his face, one he could definitely share with his wife. It must not have been one of Lisa's more energetic days if she was only just getting around to showering at four o'clock in the afternoon. It amused him how much a lady of leisure she was becoming as each day seemed to add another pound for her slight frame to carry around. He loved having Lisa pregnant.

There were still times when his laughter stuck in his throat, when he thought about what might have been if Lisa's pregnancy had been as real for him as it was for her. But he'd learned to ignore those moments. Most of them.

He could see her through the steamy glass door of the shower enclosure. Her head was back, her hands running through her hair as the water ran across her face and down over her shoulders. Marcus's gaze followed the route the water was taking, stopping at Lisa's ripe breasts. Her nipples pebbled as the water caressed them and then streamed over her rounded belly.

His own body hardened with desire and with sheer male pride as he watched her. *His woman.* The baby she was carrying wasn't his, but the woman was. He was the only man who would ever know this particular sight of her, naked and wet and swollen with child. Marcus had never been more grateful for anything in his life.

Stripping off his clothes, he joined her in the shower, greeting her with a wet heated kiss.

"Nice greeting," she said, wrapping her arms around him. "I'm glad you're home."

He licked a drop of water off from her chin. "Had a rough afternoon?"

"I seem to have slept most of it away," she said, grinning at him.

Marcus took the bar of soap from its dish and began a leisurely exploration of Lisa's curves, caressing her shoulders and then her breasts.

"Mmm. This was worth getting up for." Lisa's eyes were closed, her lips smiling and moist. Marcus bent to kiss them as his soapy hands moved down to caress the stretched skin of her belly.

He touched her so tenderly, his big hands almost reverent in their attention, that Lisa thought she'd die of love for him. The water grew cold and Marcus turned it off, never missing a beat as he continued to kiss her. Wrapping her in a big fluffy bath towel, he lifted her and carried her to their bed.

But later that night, when the loving was done, she couldn't help wishing that the wealth of tenderness Marcus was showing her included the child she carried....

BETH STOPPED to see Lisa the next day on her way home from work.

"How ya doing, Mama?" she asked, giving Lisa a hug.

"I don't know," Lisa said, returning the hug.

Beth's stomach sank. "You're not feeling well?" she asked, searching Lisa's face for any sign of pain, pallor, anything she might have missed when Lisa had opened the door. Lisa looked great, every bit the healthy mother-to-be in her maternity blouse and slacks.

"I feel as well as can be expected physically." Lisa shrugged. "You want some tea?"

"Sure." Beth followed her friend to the back of the house, to the huge homey kitchen she knew Lisa adored. Oliver had told Beth that Lisa and Marcus were doing fine. Better than fine, according to Marcus. So what was up?

"I'm glad you stopped by," Lisa said. "I've missed you." She put water on to boil and pulled a couple of herbal teabags out of a canister on the counter.

Feeling uncomfortably guilty, Beth reached for the cups. "I've missed you, too. It's not the same not having you at work."

Lisa gave a small grin. "I don't miss it as much as I thought I would. Of course, that's probably because it's such an effort just getting out of bed in the mornings I can't imagine having to handle a crisis."

Beth smiled. Maybe the normal fatigue that went with pregnancy was all that was bothering Lisa. "Get your rest now, while you can. 'Cause in a couple of months, you'll be lucky to look at your bed, let alone get in it.''

Lisa poured hot water over the teabags, still grinning. "I know. I can't wait.''

The two women sat down at the kitchen table, sipping their tea, and Beth couldn't help being a little envious. Not of Lisa's beautiful home. Not even of her baby. But of her happiness, her surety of where life was leading her, the closeness she shared with her husband.

"It's probably not going to be all that bad for you, anyway,'' Beth said. "Knowing Marcus, he'll insist on taking all the middle-of-the-night feedings.''

Lisa frowned, looking down into her cup. "I'm planning to breast-feed.''

"So he'll get up and bring the baby in to you, always changing his diaper first, of course.''

Lisa was silent for a minute before looking up at Beth. "He's not going to have anything to do with this baby,'' she said softly, her eyes suddenly filling with tears.

Beth covered Lisa's hand with hers. "What makes you even think such a thing?''

"I don't just think it, Beth. I know it.'' The conviction in Lisa's voice was chilling.

"He's said so?'' Beth asked.

Lisa nodded, the tears spilling from her eyes and rolling down her cheeks. "Many times. I thought he'd change his mind, even after he told me not to hope that he would. I thought I knew Marcus. But I guess

I don't. As far as he's concerned, my baby doesn't exist.''

"Oh, Lisa, I'm so sorry. What are you going to do? Do you want me to try talking to him?''

"Yes. No. I don't know anymore. It wouldn't do any good. I've talked until there aren't any words left. Dad's talked to him, too, though I don't think he has any idea how bad it really is.'' Beth saw utter despair in Lisa's eyes. "I can't even imagine a life without Marcus,'' Lisa went on, "don't know where I'd ever find the strength to leave him. But how can I bring my baby into a house where he'll be ignored, treated as if he doesn't exist?''

"Does Marcus know? That you're thinking about leaving him, I mean?''

Lisa shook her head, looking more miserable than any pregnant woman ought to look. Beth got up and took her friend into her arms, her heart breaking in two. This was her fault; she'd ripped apart the lives of her best friends with her meddling. Her tears slowly mingled with Lisa's as she held her, wondering when it was she'd forgotten that she was a doctor and started playing God, instead.

CHAPTER ELEVEN

BETH COULDN'T GO HOME that night. She couldn't face the silence, the recriminations, the "I told you sos" she'd hear every time she looked at John's picture. He'd been after her for her meddling since the day they'd met, telling her to leave other people's business alone. But it was a habit she'd developed early on, growing up with a bunch of younger siblings. She'd been the one to take care of everyone, to prevent whatever disasters she could, to make certain everyone was tended to. She'd had to meddle to keep everyone safe—and she'd been good at it.

But it was an asset that had become a liability as she reached adulthood. This wasn't the first time she'd caused someone heartache because she couldn't leave well enough alone. If only John were still alive. He'd have stopped her from pushing Lisa into this last irrevocable step.

Beth didn't make a conscious decision to seek out Oliver, but found herself pulling into his driveway just after dark, anyway. She wasn't sure how he'd react when he found out how awful things really were between Lisa and Marcus. He'd probably never forgive her for sticking her nose in where it didn't belong. Remembering Lisa's broken sobs, she didn't think she'd ever forgive herself.

"Beth! What is it, my dear? Come in. What's happened?" Oliver asked as soon as he answered his door and saw her face.

Beth knew she must look a wreck. But it didn't matter. Not when her friend's life was falling apart.

"I've made the biggest mistake of my life and there's no way to fix it," she said bluntly, standing in the foyer of Oliver's home.

Oliver's eyes darkened with concern. "I'm sure it's not that bad. We'll think of something. Come in and sit." He put one arm around Beth's shoulder and led her into his living room.

I don't deserve his concern, Beth thought.

"Marcus refuses to accept Lisa's baby and it's all my fault. I talked her into it. I was so sure it was the perfect answer. But I had a feeling she hadn't told him, and I went ahead and inseminated her, anyway. And now it looks like she's going to have to choose between the husband she adores and her baby. Where do I get off thinking I know what's best for other people when I don't even know what's best for myself?"

"Shh. Slow down. What's this about Marcus and the baby? He told me himself just two days ago that things were great between him and Lisa. He looked happier than he's looked in years."

Beth shook her head. "He *is* happy with Lisa. But he's got some cockamamy idea that he and Lisa can be married while she raises her child herself. Even *I* know that's no way to bring up a child.''

Oliver shook his head, sadness mingling with the worry Beth saw in his eyes. ''She's got to give him more time. Wait until he sees the baby. Until she brings it home. I suspect he'll come around then. Marcus has a wealth of love to give. I'm laying odds he'll make the right decision when the time comes.''

''And if he doesn't?''

''I'm not ready to consider that possibility. It would kill my daughter to lose Marcus. I know that as surely as I know my own name.''

To her chagrin, Beth felt tears fill her eyes. ''Oh, God. What a mess I've made of things,'' she said. How could she have ruined the lives of the two people she cared about most in the world?

''What do you mean? You did your job. That's all.''

Beth shook her head. ''I wish that was all. I'd been after Lisa for months to consider artificial insemination. I was just so sure it was the right answer. The only answer for them. I couldn't have been more wrong.''

''But the final decision was Lisa's, my dear. She wanted this baby, make no mistake about that.''

Beth wished she could be so sure. ''She said no for months, Oliver. She wouldn't even consider it, because she knew Marcus would react this way. I see that now. But she was so unhappy, getting unhappier every time I saw her, so I kept at her. The week before we did the procedure she came to see me. I'd even picked out a donor for her and told her all about him. She still said no.''

Oliver put his arm around her shoulders again. Beth couldn't believe how badly she wanted to snuggle into his embrace, in spite of how wrong that would be. ''She didn't come to you against her will, Beth. Lisa's a big girl with a mind of her own. You, my dear, seem to have a tendency to be a bit too hard on yourself. You're not to blame for Marcus and Lisa's current situation any more than Marcus is to blame for his sterility.''

''It's just that I meddle sometimes. I know I do. I try not to, I really do, but before I know it, I'm up to my elbows in someone's problems.'' Oliver might as well know.

He pulled her against him, right where she so wanted to be. ''That's called caring, dear Beth, not meddling,'' he said softly.

Beth glanced up at the odd tone in his voice, and her blood started to race the minute she met his gaze. He was looking at her with complete honesty, holding nothing back, and the desire she saw in his eyes took her breath away.

''Oliver?'' she whispered, knowing they were crossing a line never meant to be crossed, yet unable to prevent herself.

''Ah, Beth. Life's too short, happiness too fleeting, to let this slip away. You feel it, too, don't you? This thing between us. It's not just a silly fantasy of a wishful old man, is it?''

"You aren't old, Oliver. Not by a long shot. And yes, I feel it, too."

As he bent his head and kissed her and she lost herself in the blissful experience of his touch, she hoped John would forgive her for falling in love with another man.

HER BACK ACHED. Drugged with sleep, Lisa rolled over, burrowing into Marcus's side as she tried to get comfortable. But the pain came again, sharper this time, bringing her fully awake. And instantly afraid.

"Marcus?" she said, scared to move, to sit up.

"What is it, Lis?" He flipped on the bedside light, concern in his eyes.

"It's the baby, Marcus. He's coming and it's way too early." Tears stung her eyes, but she was afraid to cry. She lay perfectly still, hoping against all the logic of her doctor's training that if she didn't move, she could keep the tiny life inside her a little while longer.

Another pain gripped her, and Lisa cried out. Something was wrong. Drastically wrong.

"Lis? Do you need to get to the bathroom?"

"No!" she cried. "No. I don't want to move. I'm not going to lose my baby. Not now. Please, God, no." She started to sob softly, as yet another pain shot up her back. She'd been feeling twinges in her back for just over a week, but she'd thought they were perfectly normal.

Marcus was a blur in her haze of pain as he reached for the phone on the nightstand and dialed Debbie

Crutchfield. He spoke quickly, then just as quickly hung up the phone and got out of bed.

"I'm going to have to move you, Lis. Debbie's meeting us at the hospital in fifteen minutes."

He pulled on a pair of jeans and a sweatshirt while he talked, shrugging into his jacket and pulling on his shoes in record time.

"Here we go. Just lie still, honey," he said, wrapping the comforter from the bed around her and lifting her, still in her nightgown, into his arms.

He sped down the stairs with her, not even stopping to lock the door behind them as he stepped out into the garage and settled her into the Ferrari.

Lisa felt a rush of warm liquid between her thighs when he lay her back in the seat. "Oh, God, no!" she cried.

"What?" Marcus looked down at the blanket around her, saw the spreading stain. "Okay, Lisa. Just hang on, love. We'll beat this yet. Just hold on."

His words did little to ease the ache in her heart. She was a doctor. She knew what was coming. With her water broken, they wouldn't be able to save the pregnancy. And she was barely seven months along.

She bit her lip and groaned as another pain consumed her. She was losing her baby.

"Hold on, sweetheart. Just hold on another few minutes. We're almost there, and then everything's going to be fine. You'll see, it'll be fine..."

Marcus's soothing words filled the car during the entire trip to the hospital, but Lisa barely heard them as she fought the pain. It was constant now, and building in such intensity she was afraid she was going to tear apart.

Don't go, little one. Please don't go. She repeated the words over and over, as if somehow they could manage to accomplish what she knew medical science could not. She couldn't bear to lose this baby. She couldn't.

A stretcher was waiting for her at the hospital, and Lisa looked up into Debbie's worried face even before she was inside the emergency-room doors.

She heard Debbie's brisk command. "Take her into delivery, stat."

"No! Not yet. Let's wait and see—"

"It's too late, Lisa," Debbie said, hurrying along beside the stretcher. "It's you we have to be concerned about now. You're losing a lot of blood."

It was *her* they had to be concerned about now. Did that mean...? No. It couldn't. She'd felt the baby move only a couple of hours ago. He'd kicked her hard, twice, when she'd climbed into bed. She'd rubbed her hand over him, soothing him, until he'd fallen asleep. She'd whispered good-night to him, just as she had every night since she'd found out she was pregnant.

She was rushed into a room filled with bright lights and people. Things were happening so fast, orders coming so quickly, Lisa couldn't keep track of it all. She was in agony, both mentally and physically, and soon the only thing she was conscious of was Marcus standing beside her bed, dressed in surgical greens.

"We'll make it through this, Lis. You just hang on

for me, you hear?'' he said, holding her hand while the doctor and nurses got an IV going, examined her and hooked her up to a couple of different monitors. In one part of her brain, Lisa knew everything they were doing. And she knew why. She knew she'd have given the same orders Debbie was giving were their positions reversed.

Yet she hated the doctor for taking away her dream.

As the minutes passed and the pain didn't relent, Lisa focused more and more on Marcus. On his steady strength. His hopeful words. He was telling her what she wanted to hear. What she needed to hear. That everything was going to be all right. And because he was saying it, she tried to believe him.

Marcus thought that this was what it was like to lose one's mind. He was finding it increasingly difficult to concentrate. To focus. As the medical personnel rushed around Lisa, peeling the bloodstained blanket away, he sank further and further into a blind panic.

''Get me the blood, stat,'' Debbie Crutchfield hollered at one of the orderlies. ''She may be hemorrhaging.''

It was his worst nightmare coming true. Lisa was in trouble. And all he could do was stand by and watch as the team of professionals tried to save her. And pray. Marcus had never prayed harder for anything in his life as he did then, standing beside his wife, horrified as he watched the blood flow out of her.

Only Lisa kept him sane. Lisa and her need of him.

Marcus refused to let her see his fear or hear the worry in his voice. He reassured her over and over, knowing how desperately she needed the words of encouragement. He would pull her through this with his strength alone if he had to. He wasn't going to lose her. Not now. Not like this.

Lisa gave a sharp cry and Marcus's heart missed a beat. He glanced at Debbie, looking for reassurance, but Debbie's face was a study of intense concentration as she worked between Lisa's legs.

And suddenly Marcus knew a new fear, an unfamiliar fear, as he considered the life his wife was trying so desperately to save. Not her own. But the life inside her. For the first time he noticed the mirror set back behind the doctor. And as he glanced up, he saw a flash of a tiny head, a swatch of hair, and then the full head, as Lisa started to push the baby from her body.

Her fingers were clutching his so tightly he lost circulation, but he continued to hold her, to soothe her, his eyes glued to the mirror behind the doctor.

There were the shoulders. And with one last groan from Lisa, the tiniest body he'd ever seen emerged into the brightly lit room. Marcus's gaze flew to Debbie's face. Waiting.

"She's alive."

He hadn't even realized he'd been holding his breath until he heard the words. *She's alive.* His gaze darted from the too-tiny body to his wife's face, and then, medical personnel be damned, he gathered Lisa into his arms, holding her against him.

LISA HAD BARELY a glance at her daughter before Debbie snipped the cord and they whisked the little body away. She didn't even get a chance to see if the baby had all her fingers and toes, seeing only that she had a full head of dark hair, this child she'd waited so long to have, yet had way too soon.

She buried her head against Marcus, no longer able to hold back the sobs that tore through her. She was a doctor. A children's doctor. She knew.

The baby couldn't have weighed more than two pounds. And she hadn't cried, indicating that her lungs weren't fully developed—if at all. Her chances of surviving were slim.

There were so many things that could go wrong, that could already be wrong. Lisa wished she could still the voices in her head.

She knew what she'd tell the parents if she was the attending pediatrician. And she couldn't bear to hear the words. This time she was the parent. And that hopelessly tiny silent baby was her daughter. Sara Barbara Cartwright. She had a daughter. Who was to have had a perfect life.

And suddenly Lisa knew that any decision she had to make had already been made. If Marcus could not be a father to their daughter, she couldn't live with him. Because if the baby survived—and she would if Lisa had to breathe life into her every day until she could breathe on her own—she was going to be raised in a house of love.

Debbie finished with Lisa, making way for the

nurse to prepare her to go to her room, and Marcus stood aside while they did what they had to do.

"You came through this just fine, Lisa. Much better than I expected, as a matter of fact. I suspect you'll be released sometime tomorrow." The doctor didn't smile, didn't attempt to sugarcoat her words. She was fully aware that Lisa knew exactly how grave the situation really was.

Lisa could go home the next day. The baby wouldn't be going home for a long time. If ever.

Tears streamed down Lisa's tired face and Marcus wiped them away. Turning her face into his palm, Lisa kissed him. In spite of the decision she'd made, she needed him desperately. Needed his strength. His warmth. She wasn't going to get through the next hours without him.

"I've ordered something to help you sleep as soon as you get settled in your room," Debbie said, pulling off her gloves.

"I don't want to sleep. I have to see her, see what they're doing. I have to know."

"Listen to the doctor, Lis," Marcus said, his hand on her shoulder.

"You have to be sensible, Lisa." Debbie stood on the other side of Lisa's bed. "For the baby's sake, as well as your own. You just came through a rough birth, you came close to hemorrhaging, and you need your rest if you're going to do that young lady any good later. And they won't let you in with her right now, anyway. You know that. Randal Cunningham is with her. He's the best there is. Let him do his job."

Marcus stayed with Lisa until she fell into an exhausted sleep. It was more than an hour after the birth, and she'd fought sleep with every bit of strength she had, waiting to hear about her baby, but the sleeping pill Debbie had prescribed had finally done its work, allowing Lisa the rest she so desperately needed.

Marcus rubbed his hands down his face as he sat beside Lisa's bed, more exhausted than he'd ever been in his life. What a night. The most frightening night of his life.

He shuddered when he saw again all that blood soaking the blanket around Lisa. He'd never been so afraid of anything as he'd been during that trip to the hospital and the minutes immediately following.

Standing, he took one last look at his wife, and then headed out into the silent corridor of the sleeping hospital. He needed to get home, get some rest, if he was going to make it back by the time Lisa awoke in the morning.

Stopping only long enough to notify the night nurse that he was going home and that he expected to be called if Lisa so much as turned over in bed, he continued on down the hall toward the elevator. Most of the rooms he passed were in darkness or lit only by a soft night-light, but there was a window down by the elevator that was glaring with so much light it spilled out into the hospital corridor.

Marcus found out why when he reached the window. It was the nursery. He told himself to keep on walking, that there was no reason for him to glance that way, but as he passed he heard the plaintive wail

of a newborn baby and turned his head instinctively.
It wasn't Lisa's baby he heard.

Hers was the one everybody was working on in a
separate part of the nursery. Marcus could barely see
the tiny body in the sea of medical personnel surrounding the funny little crib in which she lay. It was
a box not more than two feet long and maybe eight
inches wide, with huge bright lights hanging above it.
He winced as he saw the many hands, which looked
so big next to such a small body, working over it so
quickly.

Marcus moved around the corner, entering a viewing room with a couple of couches and chairs that
had another window into the nursery, a window closer
to the peculiar bed with the miniature baby. From
there he could see the card that hung at the end of
the crib. *Cartwright Girl.*

His gut clenched as he looked again. *Cartwright
Girl.* That tiny baby girl had his name.

He knew he needed to go, that he had to get some
rest before he collapsed, but he couldn't make himself
leave the window. Lisa's baby was barely the size of
his hand. He didn't see how it could possibly have
all the working parts necessary to sustain life. He
knew the baby was still alive. There would be no
reason for anyone to be working over her if she
wasn't. But that bit of news didn't tell him anything
about her chances to survive.

One of the nurses moved away from the crib for a
moment, reaching for something on a tray, and Marcus had a clearer glimpse of the baby. A tube wider

than her arm was taped to her mouth with what looked like a big Band-Aid. The other end of the tube was connected by a series of contraptions to a ventilator machine. She wasn't breathing on her own.

He had no idea what the rest of the many tubes and wires applied to her minute body were for, but knew it wasn't good that they took up more room in her bed than she did. Other than the medical paraphernalia attached to her, the baby was naked, her diminutive bottom lying on an open disposable diaper. Her tiny head wore a blue-pink-and-white-striped cap, covering up the thatch of hair that was the first sight he'd had of her. Her eyes were closed. He wondered if she was actually sleeping through all of the ministrations, or if she simply couldn't open her eyes.

She appeared to have all her fingers and toes.

The nurse returned to the crib, blocking Marcus's view, and he slumped back into the chair closest to the viewing window, watching as the specialists worked. *Cartwright Girl.* He'd kept himself so apart from the life Lisa had been creating these past months that he'd never even considered there would be a name for the child. His name.

He wondered what else Lisa planned to call her baby. But he already knew. Sara, for her beloved little sister. And Barbara, after her mother. Sara Barbara Cartwright. The name had a familiar ring to it. Sara. He hoped Lisa was calling her Sara. They'd always said they'd name their first girl Sara.

Personnel came and went from the baby's crib for most of the night, and as the hours passed, Marcus continued to sit, to watch. He wondered about the baby's father. Was he a young college student who'd given a donation to the sperm bank for a quick buck? Or a good samaritan who wanted to make dreams possible for women who couldn't have children any other way? Maybe he was in the medical field. If so, Lisa's baby was going to be one smart little girl. If she survived.

And suddenly Marcus knew without a shadow of doubt just how badly he wanted the child to survive. Lisa would never be the same if her baby died. After all she'd been through, after all the lives she'd saved and the ones she'd lost, she deserved this chance for herself. And the baby deserved it, too. She was Lisa's baby. That alone made her the most special child in the nursery.

The tall silver-haired doctor who hadn't left the baby's side all night finally turned away from the crib, stripping off his gloves. Marcus's heart caught in his throat as he waited for some sign that the battle had been won—or lost. The doctor spoke to a nurse who'd remained beside the crib, and the nurse nodded several times before pulling a chair up to the side of the crib and sitting down to watch the baby's monitors. It was then that Marcus noticed what he thought was some kind of heart monitor, set way off behind the baby. The marks he saw were wavery. But they were there.

Marcus heaved a huge sigh of relief. He thought again of the father of Lisa's baby, wondering if the guy would care that his daughter was lying there, so tiny, fighting impossible odds for her life. The guy was a first-class bastard if he didn't.

Marcus was appalled at all the gadgets surrounding the tiny body, the IV taped to her skull, the catheter in her right arm, which was strapped to a board. He hated that someone so small had to endure so much discomfort. And aside from all the wires and tubes, her entire body was wrapped in what looked like a big piece of cellophane. She lay there silently, her eyes still closed. Marcus hoped she was sleeping peacefully.

He was still there early the next morning when Beth came in to see the baby.

"Beth!" He shot upright. "Oh, my God. I never even called Oliver. How'd you know where to find us?"

Beth didn't turn from the window, her gaze glued on the box that was Lisa's crib. "Crystal called me an hour ago. Lisa was awake and asking for you, and they couldn't reach you at home, but she's asleep again now," she said. Crystal was the night nurse working Lisa's floor. "Crystal said Lisa had the baby shortly after one. Have you been here all night?"

"I didn't realize how much time had passed," Marcus said, turning toward the baby again. She hadn't moved a muscle in all those hours. He knew. He'd been watching every second for any sign that she was taking control of her life.

"Has anybody been out yet to tell you anything?"

"No."

"Crystal said she's holding her own."

"But she's not breathing on her own."

"Not yet. But that's to be expected for now."

"What're her chances, Beth?" He'd spent the night avoiding the question, but he had to know.

"Twenty-five percent. Maybe thirty."

"That's all?" His heart sank.

"Her lungs aren't developed. But the machine can do their job until they are," she told him.

"Is everything else all right?" he asked.

"It's too early to tell," Beth said, still watching the baby. "Her digestive system isn't fully developed yet, either. But again, that's expected. There's a fairly good chance of brain damage and deafness. Mental retardation, too." Her voice caught in her throat and Marcus knew she was feeling a lot more than she was letting on. Her bedside manner could only cover so much. And Marcus knew Beth well.

"But isn't there a chance she'll be perfectly normal once she grows up to size?" He was asking for all their sakes. Including the baby's. The baby's most of all.

Beth shrugged. "A slight one."

"What about her kidneys and other organs?" he asked, wondering for the hundredth time how a body so small could actually sustain life.

"It's too early to tell. She'll be fed intravenously for now, glucose only. After a few weeks, if they can, they'll begin tube-feeding her. It'll be a while before they know if her excretory system's working."

Marcus heard the qualifier. *If* the baby lived. They both stood silently, keeping their vigil.

"It killed her to do this without you, you know," Beth said.

It took Marcus a second to understand what she meant. He didn't reply. He couldn't. He'd put all that behind him now.

"I found her in the bathroom afterward, being sick to her stomach. She said she was going home to seduce you, that her baby was going to be conceived in love one way or the other, and that you were going to be the one to provide that most necessary ingredient. The love."

Marcus remembered that night, remembered the way Lisa had met him at the door. Desperate for him. For his love. He'd given it to her, too. Just as he'd always given her everything she wanted. Except the one thing she'd wanted most.

"How long's the baby going to be in that special crib?" he asked, looking at the child Lisa and Beth had created that day, needing to make Beth stop talking about things that were past.

"It's a warming bed, and that depends completely on her. One of the reasons she's there is so they can get right at her, but also because her body's unable to maintain enough heat to stay alive. The warming bed simulates the mother's uterus, maintaining a temperature of ninety-eight point six rather than normal room temperature of seventy. And based on her size, I'd say she could be in there for six weeks or more before she's moved to an incubator."

If she lives. Damn. She *will* live. Watching the still

form in her bed of plastic wrap, he said, "She's going to make it, Beth."

"I hope so, Marcus. I sure hope so." Beth turned from the window to face him.

It was then that Marcus saw the tears running slowly down her face. He pulled Beth into his arms, offering what comfort he could, taking from her the silent solace she had to give.

CHAPTER TWELVE

LISA AWOKE with a feeling of dread and she reached for Marcus automatically, thinking even through her groggy confusion that whatever was wrong was manageable with Marcus beside her. Her hand bumped against the cold rail on the side of her hospital bed, instead. And it all flooded back to her. Her baby! Oh, God, was she…

Fumbling frantically, she found the call button for the nurse among the covers on the side of her bed, depressing the lever immediately and continuously. A young nurse she barely knew flew into the room, her short dark hair framing a no-nonsense face.

"Yes, Dr. Cartwright? Do you need help?"

"My baby. How's my baby?" Lisa asked, clutching her bedcovers.

"She's alive, Doctor."

Lisa released the breath she'd been holding. "She made it through the night. That's a good sign," she said almost to herself, while visions of underdeveloped lungs and kidneys filled her mind. There was so much that could be wrong, that could take her baby from her at any moment. Her chest tightened.

The nurse smiled shyly, her features softening into

prettiness. "You've got a fighter there, Doctor," she said.

Lisa nodded, trying to smile. Trying to be strong.

"Your husband brought some clothes for you. I can help you get ready to go if you like. Dr. Crutchfield will be here to release you shortly." The nurse picked up an overnight bag from the floor at the foot of her bed.

Lisa heard one thing through her panic-induced haze. "Marcus is here?"

The nurse nodded. "Dr. Montague's been here, too. Your husband just left to get some coffee, at her instigation, and I'm willing to bet he'll wish he hadn't. He really wanted to be here with you when you woke up. I wish my husband were half that besotted with me," she confided.

Lisa smiled, barely hearing the nurse's small talk. Marcus was here. She just had to hold on a few more minutes and he'd be with her. And then she'd face whatever news was waiting down the hall in the nursery. She'd find out what kind of battle her tiny baby was fighting.

There was a knock on the open door, and Lisa turned her head to see her father standing there, holding the biggest teddy bear she'd ever seen.

"Hi, honey," he said, his eyes only for her.

"Let me know when you're ready to get dressed," the nurse said softly, and slipped out the door as Lisa opened her arms to her dad.

"Oh, Daddy..."

Dropping the teddy bear on the end of the bed,

Oliver pulled her into his arms and held her tightly, wordlessly, telling her with his touch what no words could convey. They'd both lost so much. They needed Lisa's baby to fill the voids left in their lives.

"Have you seen her?" Lisa asked when Oliver finally pulled away to sit on the side of the bed.

He nodded. "She's the prettiest one in there," he said. But his eyes, moist with unshed tears, frightened her.

"She's going to make it, Dad," Lisa promised. She'd been too young to save his Sara, but she'd save her own. Somehow.

Oliver nodded and patted her arm. "I know, honey. Now, did I hear the nurse say you could get dressed?"

Lisa nodded. "They're letting me out of here. It's supposed to be better, you know, under the circumstances, for me to be at home as soon as possible."

"Then I'll leave you for now, sweetie. Call me when you get home, okay?"

Lisa nodded, and he bent to kiss her head. "I love you."

"I love you, too, Dad."

Lisa called for the nurse again the minute Oliver left. She couldn't stand the silence in her room that allowed her medical knowledge to torture her. A body that small fighting against the world of disease into which it had been born. Why, even a simple cold could—

"You ready to get dressed?" The nurse was back. Thank heaven.

At Lisa's nod, the young nurse helped Lisa lift herself from the bed.

"You okay here, or would you like me stay?" the nurse asked as she let go of Lisa in the bathroom.

Lisa swayed on her feet for a moment and then took a step, moving cautiously as she felt the pull from her stitches. "I'm fine," she said as soon as she knew it was true.

"Feel free to take a shower, then, and call if you need me." The nurse closed the door behind her when she left.

Lisa was just soaping down in the shower when she heard the door open again.

"Lis? You okay?"

Marcus. "Yes." *Now that you're here.* "Would you mind waiting, though, just in case?"

"I'm right here, sweetheart. How do you feel?"

"Physically a lot better than I thought I would," Lisa called back. She finished rinsing and shut off the water. Marcus handed her a towel as she pulled open the shower curtain.

His blue eyes warmed her instantly. "She's alive, Lis."

"I know." She wanted to ask him if he knew any more than that, but she couldn't. Not now. Not yet.

Debbie Crutchfield came in as Lisa was pulling on the loose denim jumper Marcus had brought her, and after a quick look at Lisa's stitches, announced that Lisa could go home whenever she was ready.

"I've ordered an injection to dry up your milk," she said, as she was signing off Lisa's chart.

"No!" Sara was going to need that milk.

"It's going to be quite a while before your baby's even able to suck, Lisa, if ever. You'll be miserable."

"I'll pump six times a day if I have to. My milk will be better for her than anything else once she's ready for oral consumption."

Marcus walked over, putting his arm around Lisa's shoulders. "Will it cause Lisa any harm to do as she wishes?" he asked.

Debbie shrugged. "No harm. Just a lot of discomfort."

"I have a feeling," Marcus said, "that the discomfort you refer to will be nothing compared to what it would do to Lisa to miss this chance."

Lisa smiled up at him. Her knight in shining armor. She could only imagine what this was costing him, being a part and yet wanting no part of the tragic events of the past hours. But he was here for her. Just as he said he'd be. How was she ever going to find the strength to send him away?

Just as Debbie was leaving, Randal Cunningham arrived. The silver-haired doctor gave Lisa a report too detailed for her mother's heart to handle. Not her baby. How could he just sit there and discuss her little Sara's chances, or rather, lack of them, like that? Like she was just another case.

Except that, even as her soul protested, Lisa's doctor's mind understood that Randal was handling things in the only way he could—impartially, professionally. He couldn't allow himself to become emotionally involved with his patients. It could mean the difference between life and death, the making of a tough decision that could save a life—or lose one.

And so Lisa listened to the things she needed to know, her mind already jumping ahead to probable crises and ways to fight them.

"Because of the risk of infection, it's best that only the few personnel taking care of her be near her right now, but I'm not going to tell you you can't go in there, Lisa. I will ask, however, that it not be for more than an hour twice a day."

Lisa nodded, realizing the necessity for Randal's request. But one hour twice a day! It seemed like a prison sentence.

Please, dear God, don't let it be a lifetime one.

Marcus helped Lisa gather her things together as soon as Randal was gone, putting Oliver's teddy bear in her lap as she got settled into the wheelchair the nurse had left outside the door. He began to push her slowly down the hall.

"I need you to take me to her, Marcus," she said, afraid he'd freeze on her again. But her need to be with her baby was too great.

"I know. That's where we're headed."

He wheeled her down to the nursery window and then turned the corner, entering the nursery viewing room. He let go of her chair, and Lisa panicked, afraid he was going to leave her. She needed to draw on his strength to help her through whatever she might discover when she looked through that window.

"Don't go." She was breaking his rules.

"I'm right here." But he was looking at her, not the window.

Lisa held his gaze for another second and then slowly turned. Her eyes found her daughter instantly, knowing just which part of the nursery housed the neonatal babies. *Cartwright Girl,* she saw. *Sara. Her name is Sara.*

They were going to have to change that card.

And then she brought her gaze to the minuscule body lying so quietly in the cellophane-wrapped warming bed.

Forgetting everything, even, in that moment, her husband standing behind her, Lisa rose from her chair, motioned for a nurse to let her in and went through the door into the overly warm nursery. She saw nothing but the baby in front of her. Her baby. Her Sara.

Mindless of her own discomfort, she scrubbed at the sink by the baby's crib and tied a mask over her face, her eyes still on her daughter. She had a daughter. She was finally a mother.

With tears in her eyes, gloves on her hands and more than nine hours after giving birth to her, Lisa finally touched her baby. She couldn't hold her, couldn't take her away from the healing warmth of her crib, but she touched her.

"Hello, my precious," she whispered through her tears, running one finger lightly along the baby's side.

Sara was lying on her back, completely still, breathing only with the help of the tube taped to her mouth.

Careful of the various wires and vials attached to the baby's body, Lisa lay her hand against Sara's belly, needing the contact, needing her daughter to feel her touch, despite the gloves she wore and the plastic covering the baby. Her baby. Her Sara. Lisa had never felt such an overwhelming rush of love in her life.

"Mama's here, my Sara," she said, her voice stronger. "You be a good little girl and do just what the doctor tells you, you hear?"

Lisa stood beside the crib for the entire hour she'd been allotted, rejecting the rocker a nurse brought over to her. She wanted to be as close to Sara as she could possibly get.

And throughout the hour, one eye on the monitors attached to Sara, she talked to the baby, bonding with her new daughter, not in the usual way, but bonding with her just the same.

The nurse told her when her hour was up, and Lisa nodded, running her hand along Sara's side one more time. "You're going to be just fine, Sara. Just fine. Mama's going to be watching over you every second now, so don't you worry."

"She's a strong one, Doctor. If ever a preemie had a chance, it's this one," the nurse said, smiling down at Sara.

"She hasn't opened her eyes, has she?" Lisa asked, still watching her daughter.

She knew the answer even before she heard it. "No. It could take weeks."

Lisa nodded. "I know," she said. But they'd be

blue when she did. They were meant to be blue. Like Marcus's. Except that he couldn't allow himself to claim them.

"Her pulse and blood pressure are fluctuating," Lisa said, glancing again at one of the monitors attached to her little darling.

The nurse nodded. "It's something we expect at this stage."

Glancing at the monitors, the nurse took a small blood-pressure cuff from a tray beside the crib and lifted the plastic around the baby enough to fit the one-inch-long cuff around the baby's arm. Sara's arm was barely as thick as the nurse's middle finger.

Lisa couldn't bear to watch anymore.

"I love you, Sara," she said one last time, bending to brush her masked face against the tip of the cap covering the baby's head. Sara didn't respond.

Stopping only long enough to ask that the baby's nameplate be changed, Lisa stripped off her sanitary garb and went out to find Marcus, more afraid than she'd ever been in her life.

She practically fell into the wheelchair he had waiting for her, only then becoming aware of how much she ached, thankful she didn't have to make it down to the car on her own. She wasn't sure she had the strength even to make it out to the hallway. Nor the will. She'd just left her heart with a tiny bit of humanity who couldn't so much as open her eyes. Or cry when she was hurt.

Marcus didn't once look toward the nursery as he helped her into her coat and wheeled her out, and all during the drive home, Lisa waited for him to say something, anything, about the child they were leaving behind.

She waited in vain.

MARCUS DROVE Lisa back to the hospital that evening for her second hour with her baby. He hated the toll this premature birth and resulting vigil was taking on Lisa, the panic that came to her eyes every time the telephone rang. He hated, too, his helplessness to make things better.

This was supposed to have been a happy time for her. One of the happiest times of her life. Instead, she'd cried when Hannah had met her at the door with an uncharacteristic hug. And she'd cried over the cards and flowers and gifts that had been arriving steadily all day—from her colleagues, from his, and from the matriarchs of the families on New Haven's social register.

She'd cried when she'd talked to Beth on the phone. And she'd cried when he'd carried her by the door to the nursery they'd decorated, too. Her heart was breaking, and there wasn't a damn thing he could do about it.

He waited outside the hospital nursery while Lisa visited the baby, though a well-meaning nurse had invited him in, too, with the provision that he scrub and dress as Lisa had in the sterile garb. He saw the look of hope in Lisa's eyes, but she didn't ask him to come. He wanted to be there for her, to fulfill her wishes, but he just couldn't cross that final line. He'd be there for her, but outside the nursery.

The entire time Lisa was in with her baby, he watched the child, as he had the night before, thinking that her color looked a little better, though she was still awfully red. Most of the tubes and wires were just as they'd been that morning. Marcus didn't know if that was good news or bad. Still, he prayed for the child. Prayed she had what it took to win with the impossible hand she'd been dealt.

He noticed, too, that her nameplate had been changed. *Sara Barbara Cartwright.* She still had his name.

OLIVER PICKED BETH UP from work the next evening. After spending most of the afternoon with Lisa, he needed a means of forgetfulness. They drove straight to his house and she was barely in his door before he took her in his arms. Not with passion, that would come later, but with warmth, seeking and giving comfort.

"I've needed this since the hospital called yesterday," he said.

"Me, too. I'll bet you barely made it home in time to get Marcus's call. We're going to have to tell them about us, you know," Beth said.

"Yes. But not yet." Oliver was afraid to trust the happiness that had begun to bloom in him again. It seemed so delicate, so fragile.

"Not until we know more about Sara's condition?"

"Right."

"You think Lisa's going to take our relationship hard?"

"Maybe. What do you think?" Oliver had been wanting to ask her that since the first time he'd kissed her. Beth was Lisa's best friend. In some ways she knew his daughter better than he did.

"I think she's going to be shocked," Beth said. "And I'm sure she doesn't need to hear about it now."

"Then we'll have to be careful for a while."

"Right." She kissed him gently, almost innocently.

"I'm a grandpa."

She smiled at him softly. "I know. She's beautiful."

"She is, isn't she? Prettiest one there. And the strongest, too. She'll be making more noise than all the others combined before we know it."

Beth pulled out of his arms, turning her back as she moved to the front window and looked out. "Her chances aren't very good, Oliver. You realize that, don't you?"

He stood his ground. "I hear what they're saying."

"This is one time I wish I didn't know even half of what I learned in medical school." She shivered. "The things that could go wrong... I can't even imagine the hell Lisa must be putting herself through."

Oliver hated to think of the anguish his own little girl must be suffering. He'd watched her torture herself all afternoon. It was just too much. First she'd lost her baby sister. And then her mother.

They weren't going to lose Sara Barbara, too. They just weren't.

SARA'S HEART CONTINUED to beat. As the hours turned slowly into days, the baby lay in her warming crib, relying on a respirator for her every breath, but still alive. Her oxygen level fluctuated, her body temperature fluctuated, and she slept constantly. But she was alive.

A week after the baby's birth, Lisa's doctor ordered Lisa back to work. Part-time only, and nothing but office calls, but back to work. Debbie was worried about Lisa's mental state and said that working would not only give Lisa something to do other than anticipate what could go wrong with Sara, it would also bring her closer to Sara for more hours during the day.

Marcus agreed with Debbie's reasoning, knowing that being near her baby would bring its own measure of comfort to his wife.

He returned to work himself, though only part-time, as well. He wasn't going to leave Lisa home alone any more than he had to. Nor was he going to have her sitting in the nursery viewing room for hours every day letting her fears eat her alive. Instead, he bought her a ship-to-shore radio and took her to the *Sara*. He picked up several romantic comedies at the video store and sat through them with her, although he had to take cold showers after every one of them. He missed making love to his wife.

And daily, he told her how strong she was, how

capable, hoping that if she ever needed to rely on that strength, she'd know it was there.

He also held her when the anguish was too much for her and she could no longer hold back her sobs.

As the days passed, one after another, he found himself thinking about the tiny little girl lying across town in her funny little bed. He worried about her. Almost constantly. And almost every evening, on his way home from work, he stopped by the hospital and stood at the nursery window watching Lisa's baby wage her battle for life.

The baby was eight days old when he noticed a new catheter in her foot. He knocked on the nursery window, getting the attention of Regina, Sara's personal night nurse.

"You want to come in, Mr. Cartwright?" she asked, peeking her head out the door that was always kept secured.

He shook his head. That was always her first question. "What's the new catheter for? The one in her foot?"

"It's not new. It's just been moved. Her veins are too fragile for us to use any one site for too long."

Marcus didn't know what Regina thought of his refusal to get close to Sara and he didn't care. All that mattered to him was that the woman keep his visits there to herself. If she found his request that she do so odd, she was professional enough not to say anything, and professional enough, as well, to agree to keep whatever gossip his visits might at some point incur away from Lisa's ears.

"And what about the longer vial?" Marcus asked now.

"We've upped her fluid intake."

"A step forward?" he asked, his hands in his pockets as he rocked back on his heels.

The nurse shrugged. "Her diaper weighed almost an ounce more this morning. That means her excretory system's working. Your daughter's a fighter, Mr. Cartwright."

She wasn't his daughter. Marcus wasn't even sure why he had this insatiable need to know every little thing about that tiny life lying just beyond the window. But if he was somehow going to give Lisa's baby the strength to live, he had to know what they were up against.

LISA KNEW SOMETHING was wrong the minute she walked off the elevator. There was too much commotion in the nursery. Praying that her baby wasn't the cause, even though she knew she was, Lisa rounded the corner, her gaze straining frantically for her first glimpse of Sara's crib.

All she could see were the medical personnel surrounding it.

Lisa ran the last couple of yards to the nursery door, pounding on the secured entrance with all her might. She had to get in there. Her baby was in trouble. And she was a doctor.

The door opened immediately when one of the nurses inside recognized Lisa.

"She's developed some congestion in her chest,

Dr. Cartwright. They're giving her a treatment right now.''

Lisa scrubbed quickly, donning her garb faster than she'd ever donned it before, never taking her eyes from the figures bending over her daughter's crib.

She almost cried out when she finally got to the side of the bed herself and saw what they were doing to her child. The mask on the baby's tiny face was bad enough, but when they had to start chest percussion, someone had to lead Lisa away. There was nothing she could do to help, and if she stood there any longer, she was going to stop everyone from doing anything. It was too terrible to watch. By the time she reached the nurses' station, the mask she was wearing was soaked with her tears.

"She's so tiny!" she wailed. "Too tiny to have to endure so much!"

"It's her only hope, Doctor," one of the nurses gathered there reminded her.

And with that, Lisa was silent, her gaze once again glued to the mass of bodies surrounding Sara. Her only hope. *Oh, please, God, let it work. Don't take her from me now.* But even as she prayed, Lisa wondered if she was being fair to the tiny being she'd brought into this world. How much suffering was too much? When was life no longer worth the agony?

Lisa sat there for another fifteen minutes, every muscle in her body tensed against the pain Sara must have been in. Until finally, one by one, the therapists and nurses surrounding Sara moved away, pulling off their masks, until only one nurse remained, resealing the cellophane that was Sara's only blanket.

Lisa felt the constriction in her chest loosen just a little. They'd finished. For now.

"She's better, Dr. Cartwright," Jim, one of the therapists, said, stopping by the station where Lisa sat. "That's one tough cookie you've got there, ma'am."

At Jim's words, Lisa felt the rest of her strength drain out of her. They'd made it through another crisis. Everything was okay. For now. But as she drove home later that afternoon, she couldn't help wondering how many more crises there'd be. And how many more she could ask her child to survive.

CHAPTER THIRTEEN

MARCUS DIDN'T TALK to Lisa about her baby. Her father, Beth, and all her colleagues did that, he knew. His job was to distract her from the trauma just enough to keep her going. But he continued to visit the child, although he did so without Lisa's knowledge. Not because he wanted to keep secrets from her, but because he couldn't let her get her hopes up that he was in any way seeing himself as a father to the child. He wasn't.

He wanted the baby to survive. He wanted to bring her home. For her sake, and for Lisa's. Not his own.

They didn't talk about the baby, but Marcus could always tell, even without having visited the hospital himself, when Sara had taken a turn for the worse or not gained the weight Lisa had hoped or not made any of the other progress Lisa watched for daily. He could tell the minute she came in the door, and his heart ached for her. And for the baby trying so valiantly to live.

"Let's have dinner at Angelo's," he said one night almost four weeks after the baby's birth. He knew the child had lost a couple of ounces over the past day and a half, and Lisa was worried sick. She'd dropped her briefcase by the front door as she came in from work, barely looking at him.

Lisa shook her head. "I'm not hungry." Continuing on through the house to the kitchen, she fell into a seat at the kitchen table, staring aimlessly into space. Just as she'd done the night before. And the night before that. She didn't even kiss him hello anymore.

"You ready to give up your fight, Lis?" he asked softly from the doorway behind her. Her apathy alarmed him.

"No!" She swung around, jumping up out of her chair. "Why would you even say such a thing? Is that what you want? For me to give up? Let her go? That would suit you just fine, wouldn't it, if it was just you and me again. Isn't that what you really want?"

Her words stung. "Of course I don't want that, Lisa. I'm not heartless."

"Aren't you?" she cried. "Aren't you? What do you call it, then?" She stepped closer. "Our daughter's barely big enough to fill your hand, let alone a cradle. She may be dying. She's certainly hurting, and still you don't claim her. Damn you! Why don't you claim her?" she screamed, hitting him in the chest with her fists.

The pain her words inflicted far surpassed that of the physical blows. "I can't, Lis. I've tried, but I just can't." Grabbing her wrists, he held her hands still against him. "She isn't mine to claim."

She could have no idea just how much he wished, every minute of every day, that the tiny baby fighting so stalwartly was his to claim. But that choice had been taken out of his hands long ago.

"She is so yours! She's your daughter, Marcus, just as much as she is mine." Her voice broke. "You're just too damn stubborn to see it." Tears dripped slowly down her cheeks, the fight going out of her as she gazed up at him.

"I wish she was, Lis. More than you'll ever know, I wish she was," he said, wrapping his arms around her to hold her close to his heart. He wanted to make love to her, to sink into her velvety depths and find forgetfulness for both of them. To reaffirm that they were still part of the same whole. But she wasn't ready. It was still too soon after her baby's birth.

The child was less than a month old, and already she was coming between them.

LISA HAD THOUGHT, back when they'd first found out Marcus was sterile, when her marriage had been disintegrating right before her eyes, that things couldn't get any worse. She'd thought she'd reached the depths of despair and couldn't hurt any more than she'd been hurting. She'd been wrong. Because these days she'd discovered a whole new realm of despair where the pain was so fierce, so frightening, it rendered her powerless.

Never in her worst nightmare could she have imagined anything like the situation she was facing. Her life's dreams were warring against each other. Eventually one had to lose.

"I figured I'd find you here."

Lisa turned away from the window of the nursery viewing room to see Beth sit down beside her. "I'd be in there if I wasn't so damned worried about infection," she said, looking back at the familiar two-foot box, the only home her daughter had ever known.

Beth's arm slid through hers. "I know."

"She's not gaining like she should," Lisa said, forcing herself to face the truth.

"I know."

"I've been pumping my milk four times a day for a month, sure that she'd soon be needing every drop. My freezer's so full that yesterday I had to throw some out."

"Are you thinking about drying up?" Beth's question was hesitant.

Though no one talked to her about it, Lisa figured it was what everyone wanted. Debbie Crutchfield thought Lisa was making things harder on herself, but this was one time that Debbie Crutchfield didn't have a clue. "No."

Beth surprised her by nodding. "Good. Your daughter's held on too long to be robbed of any single chance she has. And once she's ready to digest it, your milk will be the best thing for her."

Lisa blinked away sudden tears. "Thanks, friend," she said, squeezing Beth's hand. "You know, I'm a mother, but I'm not. It's like I'm still pregnant, waiting for her to be born, but instead of feeling my baby growing inside me, I have to watch her development through a maze of wires and tubes and plastic, watch other people taking care of her, changing the diaper underneath her, doing the things I should be doing. About the only time I feel like a mother is when I sit by myself with my breast pump. And someday, she's going to be ready for all those nutrients I'm providing. I have to believe that.''

"You bet you do,'' Beth said, squeezing Lisa's hand back. "That little fighter in there deserves to have all of us believe in her. She's already come farther than anyone predicted. And she's going to need the support from all of us even more in the months ahead. There'll be a lot of lost time to make up for.''

Thinking of what lay ahead, the least of which was the developmental catching up her baby, her fatherless baby, faced, Lisa felt a fresh surge of tears. "I know.''

"Lisa?'' Beth looked at her, her brow lined with concern. "What is it? What'd I say?''

Lisa shook her head. "It's nothing you said.'' She met Beth's gaze, knowing she had to face facts if *she* was going to survive. "If Sara lives, I have to leave Marcus.''

"No!'' Beth shook her head in confusion. "I thought he'd finally come around. He's been wonderful through all this, anticipating your every need, cutting back so much at work...'' Her voice trailed off.

"I know,'' Lisa said again, smiling sadly. "He's been the best. Which just makes everything worse. I love him so much it hurts, Beth, but he isn't going to accept Sara. Not as his own. And if I ever get to bring her home, it can't be to a father who rejects her. It just can't. Can you imagine how awful that would be for her?''

She paused, then went on, ''In every way that matters, Marcus is her father. She was born into our marriage. She has his name. Can you imagine how much his neglect would hurt her? Because she'd know, if we were living with him, that it was *her* he didn't want. But if we're divorced, she'd be just like any other kid in a single-parent home. Not the best situation, God knows, but at least she wouldn't feel personally rejected.''

Beth stared at Lisa, obviously shocked. ''But I thought… I mean he…the night she was born, he…''

''He what?'' Lisa asked. She and Marcus had never talked about that night, other than for Marcus to tell her how awful he felt for her, how sorry he was this had happened.

''He was here, sitting right on that chair, all night.''

''Marcus was here?''

''Uh-huh.'' Beth nodded. ''Watching Sara. I found him here about four o'clock in the morning just staring at her crib. And other than when he left me to go call your father, we sat here together until the six-o'clock shift change. He left then just long enough to go home and get your bag.''

Hope bubbled up in Lisa as she listened to Beth. Marcus had been here. He'd watched over their daughter for the whole night. He *did* care. He *was* the man she'd thought him to be. She'd gambled on him and won, after all. Her thoughts sprang ahead to the dreams that might yet come true, the years of living and loving that might be waiting just around the corner.

But they slammed to a halt when she remembered his words to her in the kitchen several nights before.

"That must have been what he meant when he said he'd tried," she said softly, sadly, almost to herself. She hadn't thought it possible for her heart to break any further. "He told me he'd tried to accept her, but he just couldn't."

She looked through the window at Sara, still sleeping silently in her odd little bed, seeing her as Marcus must have seen her that night. Knowing him as she did, she could just imagine the torture he must have put himself through as he watched his wife's baby, unable to get beyond the fact that her tiny features, her little fingers and toes, genetically belonged to another man.

Remembering the agony she'd seen on his face that day he'd walked in on her baby shower, she could almost feel the anguish he must have suffered sitting through an entire night of watching her baby. And as she sat there suffering in sympathy, she finally understood that Marcus wasn't ever going to come around, not because he didn't want to or wouldn't let himself, but because he *couldn't*. He had as little choice in the matter as she did. And knowing that, she couldn't go on hurting him. She couldn't force him to live the rest of his life watching from the outside. Bringing Sara home to him wasn't only unfair to Sara, it was unfair to Marcus.

"Maybe if he had some counseling," Beth suggested somberly, her gaze fixed, like Lisa's, on the infant on the other side of the glass.

Lisa shook her head. "Marcus isn't confused. He sees things clearly. Too clearly, really. It's just that his vision is different from mine. I think being a father starts with the heart. He thinks it starts with the body. It's an argument no one can win."

"I can't believe this." Beth rubbed her hand down her face.

"Me, neither," Lisa whispered. "Every time I pray for Sara, I know that the answer to my prayer means the death of my marriage. If my baby lives, I lose the other half of myself." Lisa started to cry. "Oh, God, Beth, what have I done?"

Beth's arms wrapped around her, and Lisa lay her head against her friend's shoulder, taking the comfort that Beth gave so willingly, the same comfort Beth had taken from Lisa those months immediately following her husband's death.

"It's not what *you've* done, Lisa. It's what *we've* done. I'm so sorry I ever talked you into this."

Lisa pulled back, shaking her head. "Don't be sorry, Beth. Don't ever be sorry." She looked toward the nursery again and the tiny baby lying there. "I wouldn't trade her for anything," she said, swiping at the tears spilling from her eyes. "I just wish Marcus could feel as I do. I wish he could find a way to accept the gift I've tried to give him."

"The man's a fool," Beth said, but Lisa could tell she only half meant it. If Marcus was a fool, if he was wrong, if she could be angry with him, it wouldn't be so hard to do what she had to do. But he wasn't wrong. He was simply a man who had strong convictions and who lived his life as his conscience dictated. Even now, even in this, he was the man Lisa had fallen in love with.

She and Beth watched the baby silently for a moment, both women considering the magnitude of what they'd set in motion that morning so long ago.

"Have you told Oliver that you're leaving Marcus?" Beth asked a few minutes later.

Oliver? He'd always been "Dr. Webster" or "your father" in the past.

Staring at her friend, Lisa shook her head. "I haven't even told Marcus yet. Sara's still got a long way to go, and I'm just not strong enough, or maybe it's that I'm not unselfish enough, to leave him before I have to," she said, wondering if there was something *else* going on she should know about. She'd been so wrapped up in Sara these past few weeks that she'd barely been aware of a world outside home and the hospital.

Beth nodded, saying nothing more, but Lisa had the most uncomfortable feeling that she was missing something. It was the way Beth had said her father's name, the *familiarity* in it. Lisa didn't like it. She didn't like it at all.

A nurse came in to put a new diaper under Sara's bottom, and Lisa and Beth watched as the young woman took the diaper over to the counter to weigh it. But Lisa sneaked a couple of surreptitious glances at her friend, as well. The years of missing John had taken their toll on her friend, adding lines around her eyes that hadn't been there before, lines that had nothing to do with the smiles Beth wore so easily.

Lisa shook her head. She was really losing it if she thought Beth had any interest in her father. The two hardly knew each other. And not only was her father a generation older than Beth, but her friend was still in love with the husband she'd lost so tragically. Thinking of her father and Beth together was ludicrous. Ashamed of herself, she apologized silently to both of them.

But as she walked back to her office later that day, her thoughts drifted to her father once again. Was it possible he would someday take an interest in another woman? Lisa had never really thought of him as a man before, only as a father, and she found it unsettling to do so now. She supposed a lot of women would find him handsome. And, in his early fifties, he was still relatively young. Certainly young enough to have sexual interests. Except that he was still so in love with her mother.

Thinking of Barbara, of the mother she'd lost too soon, Lisa felt the familiar pangs of loss and regret. And she knew her father felt them, too. He might be young enough to begin a relationship with another woman, but Lisa knew he wouldn't. He'd already had the best.

SARA BARBARA CARTWRIGHT was one day short of five weeks old when she finally opened her eyes for the first time. Marcus heard all about it the minute he got to the hospital that night. Regina rushed over to him as soon as she spotted him outside the nursery window.

"Dr. Cartwright was here when it happened," she said, grinning as she recounted the joyous moment.

"Lisa was in the nursery with her?" he asked, wishing he could have been there to see Lisa's face. To share her elation with her, just as, together, they'd shared so much sorrow.

"Yep." Regina nodded. "From what I heard, she was standing there talking to her like she usually does, and suddenly the wee one just opened her eyes and stared straight at her."

Looking at Lisa's baby through the window, Marcus could feel Lisa's excitement almost as if it had happened to him. "Was she awake long?"

"I guess it was only for a minute or two, but Dr. Cartwright carried on like her kid had just graduated from Harvard. Not that I blame her, of course. I'd have done the same thing, and the mite isn't even mine." She leaned her head a little farther out the nursery door. "I've been watching her ever since I came on shift, hoping to catch a glimpse of it myself. But so far she's sleeping tight. My luck, she'll wake up when I'm at dinner."

Marcus chuckled, but his eyes never left the baby in her funny little bed. He, too, had a surprisingly strong urge to witness the phenomenon. To look into the child's eyes, to see the little person who'd been living so silently in a world of her own.

He stayed an extra half hour that night, on the off

chance the child would wake up. He knew he should go, that Lisa would be waiting at home for him, but like a gambler mesmerized by the gaming table, Marcus couldn't seem to tear himself away. He kept thinking that the next minute would be the one.

He took one final look as he was turning to leave, and as if she'd known this was her last chance, the baby opened her eyes. Just like that. With no warning, no fanfare, her little head turned, and she was staring right at him. His breath caught in his throat as he returned her stare, feeling exposed, as if she was taking stock of him, maybe finding him wanting, even though he knew she couldn't be, that she probably couldn't even focus yet.

She was more beautiful than he'd even imagined. But there was something odd about her eyes. Marcus continued to stare at her, unable to put his finger on what was wrong. Their shape was perfectly normal, amazingly normal considering the circumstances, nice and round and big. But something wasn't right.

He felt sick to his stomach when he realized what it was. All along, he'd assumed that Lisa's baby would one day look at him with Lisa's warm brown eyes. But Sara didn't have brown eyes at all. Hers were clear blue, like a bright summer sky. They were someone else's eyes. Another man's eyes. Because she was another man's child.

Marcus turned and left.

AT LISA'S SIX-WEEK checkup, Debbie pronounced her well, even going so far as to say she didn't expect there to be any problem if Lisa ever wanted to have a second child. Nevertheless, Lisa left the doctor's office feeling vaguely out of sorts.

Debbie had suggested again that Lisa allow her milk to dry up. And she was beginning to wonder if maybe the doctor was right. Sara was six weeks old and still not taking any nourishment other than the glucose they continued to shoot into her veins. Lisa was throwing away more milk than she was keeping. And while she'd known all along that Sara's good days would be mixed with bad ones, the ups and downs were getting harder and harder to take.

Debbie also told Lisa that she and Marcus could make love again. Lisa couldn't believe how much she missed the intimacy with Marcus. Not just physically, though she was certainly hungry for her husband's body, but she missed the emotional connection their lovemaking provided. She missed that feeling of oneness, a togetherness so intense it seemed nothing could come between them. A time when only the two of them existed.

A time she knew was slipping away.

Needing a pick-me-up, she detoured from the route between Debbie's office and her own for a quick stop at the nursery. She'd already spent her hour with Sara earlier that morning, but another dose of her darling baby was just what she needed.

"Dr. Cartwright, we were just calling your office," one of Sara's day nurses said when she arrived at the nursery door.

Lisa's stomach dropped. "What's wrong?" She

knew they'd been toying with the idea of removing the baby's ventilator for a trial period, but surely they wouldn't have done it without notifying her.

The nurse grinned at her. "Nothing's wrong, Doctor. They're about to take Sara off the ventilator, and Dr. Cunningham said to get you up here."

"He'll let me be there?" Randal was a tyrant when it came to playing things his way. And having a mother standing next to him when he was facing a life-and-death situation with a child was something he never allowed. Not even if the mother in question was a damn good pediatrician in her own right.

"Just as soon as you're scrubbed," the nurse confirmed, standing aside as Lisa rushed by her.

Lisa's hands were shaking as she scrubbed them, and she had to accept the help of one of the aides to get into sanitary garb. She'd never been more nervous in her life.

She approached the familiar crib on rubbery legs, for once wishing she could make use of the rocking chair that was kept beside Sara's bed. Standing where Randal instructed, she watched as a technician pulled the cellophane away from Sara's body and carefully, slowly, removed the tape holding the tube to the baby's mouth.

Lisa held her breath, her gaze glued on her daughter, waiting to see if the infant lungs would take over for the respirator. The air surrounding the warming bed was filled with tension as the seven adults watched that tiny body, waiting...

Sara shuddered, her muscles protesting against the

hands holding her down. Her big blue eyes were wide open at first, and then they scrunched closed as she objected, silently, to the attention she was receiving.

The tube was taken away, and the machine wheeled backwards. At the sudden silence, Sara opened her eyes again and uttered a small sound. Sara's muscles twitched, as if she'd surprised herself, and the sound came again. A little louder. A thin wail of disapproval, followed by a sigh.

Sara was breathing on her own.

A nurse slipped a rocker behind Lisa, and she sank onto it, tears blinding her to the smiles on the faces of the other adults. But she heard the relieved sighs of all of them.

Wiping her tears, Lisa looked around her at the staff of medical professionals that had been helping her daughter to sustain life for these six long weeks. There wasn't a dry eye among them.

"Well, Mama, you ready to hold her?" Randal asked, wiping his arm suspiciously across his own face.

Lisa's heart thumped heavily. "You'll let me hold her?"

Her stern colleague actually smiled. "Her temperature's been steady all week. I think it's safe." He reached into the bed, careful of the catheter in the baby's foot, slid his large hands beneath her and gently lifted her.

With quivery arms, Lisa reached for her baby, her heart soaring with a joy she'd never known before, in spite of the danger she knew Sara still faced.

The little girl weighed less than four pounds and was more a warmth than a weight against Lisa's breast as, six weeks after she'd given birth to her, she held her baby for the first time. The baby snuggled against her, her little chest shuddering again with the unfamiliar burden of breathing. And then, tired out by her new chore, she fell promptly asleep.

THE NURSERY WAS STILL buzzing when Marcus arrived before dinnertime that night. Regina was just coming on shift, and she met him at the viewing-room door.

His glance shot immediately to the box that served as a crib for Lisa's baby.

"Where's the ventila— She's breathing?" He stared in astonishment at the almost steady rise and fall of the tiny chest.

"Yep. Has been all afternoon. You can come on in and hold her, but the doctor says only for ten minutes at a time until he's more confident that she's maintaining her body temperature on her own."

Marcus felt something closing in on him. He could hold her. He could take that little body into his arms and make certain that nothing ever harmed it again. Regina said he could.

"Come on, Mr. Cartwright. You'll do fine. Fathers are always a little timid at first. Especially with the preemies."

Fathers. He wasn't one of those.

"I'll pass."

"Okay, but I'll leave the door unlatched in case you change your mind," she said, turning to go.

He'd disappointed her. "Regina?" he called.

"Yeah?"

"Has Dr. Cartwright held her?" Suddenly it was very important that she had. That the child know she had a parent who loved her unconditionally.

"Yep. She was here when they removed the respirator. They said she just broke down and sobbed, poor thing."

Marcus stared at the baby, concentrating on containing the emotions that threatened the control he'd been maintaining so carefully since he'd recommitted himself to Lisa and their marriage. "Thanks, Regina," he said. The nurse nodded and left.

The baby moved her head, looking in the direction of the door as it closed behind Regina. He wished he'd been there that morning, sharing those first moments with Lisa. He wished they were his moments to share. And he was angry with himself for doing what he'd promised himself he'd never do again. Wishing.

The baby moved again, flinging her unobstructed arm up, and Marcus found himself moving to the window for a closer look. He couldn't tell if she had fingernails yet. He looked at the nursery door. The unlatched nursery door. And looked away. Why did he have to torture himself with what could never be? Was this his fate, to be always on the outside looking in?

Cursing at himself, or the fates who'd played such

a cruel joke on him, he yanked open the nursery door, strode to the nurses' station and asked for instructions on how to sanitize himself enough to be near Lisa's baby. He didn't yet look at the child. He didn't ever intend to touch her. But he wasn't going to be afraid of her, either. She was going to be living in his home.

He had to know whether or not she had fingernails.

Regina appeared from a small room off the nurses' station. "Here, put this on—" she handed him a gown "—and come with me."

She led Marcus over to the sink he'd seen Lisa use the day after the baby was born, waited while he washed his hands, then showed him how to apply the elastic gloves that covered not only his hands, but his wrists. "I'm glad you changed your mind," she said now, leading him to the baby's part of the nursery. "It's really not so bad once you get used to it. Holding her isn't that much different from holding a football. Did you ever play football, Mr. Cartwright?"

Marcus nodded, though he wasn't sure what she'd asked. His attention was on the impossibly small body squirming around not six feet in front of him. He couldn't believe she was that small.

"How on earth does she stay alive?" he asked Regina as they drew nearer to the baby's box.

The nurse shrugged. "That's for God to determine. Medical science has no explanation for how she's managed to accomplish as much as she has so far."

"Does this mean she's out of the woods?" Marcus asked. Was this it, then? Had they really made it?

Regina shook her head. "I wish I could say it did,

Mr. Cartwright, but there's still so much that can go wrong. She's not even eating yet.''

''What's that she's listening to?'' They'd reached the crib. ''That sounds like my wife,'' he said, recognizing the soft soothing voice. ''Where's it coming from?''

''Here.'' Regina showed him a small tape recorder tucked in among the baby's other technical paraphernalia. ''Shortly after the baby was born, Dr. Cartwright recorded stories and songs on cassettes, and we play them for Sara twelve hours a day. We use it to help set her biological clock so she'll know the difference between night and day, but more importantly, so that she'll learn to recognize her mother's voice first and foremost, and to bond with it.''

Marcus nodded, his gloved hands stiff at his sides.

''Would you like to hold her now?'' Regina reached for the baby.

''No! I'd rather not, no,'' Marcus said. ''I'd just like to stand here a few minutes, if I may.''

''Certainly, Mr. Cartwright. You can stay an hour if you'd like,'' she said, pushing a rocking chair closer to the bed before she moved away.

Marcus ignored the chair. He ignored his own longings. He ignored everything but the baby girl lying stark naked in front of him. She'd been alive six weeks and still hadn't had so much as a diaper around her bottom.

''You just wait, little one,'' he said softly, leaning over just enough to be sure she could hear him. ''Your mother is a clotheshorse, and she's already got a closet full of designer duds for you. Just as soon as you split this joint, she'll be changing you so often you'll wish you could go around naked as a jaybird again. Don't worry, though. She's got great fashion sense. You'll be the prettiest little girl on the block.''

At some point over the next half hour he pulled up a stool, which allowed him to sit very close to the baby. She'd fallen asleep in the middle of his recitation, but he kept talking to her, anyway.

"You have to be strong. Your mama needs you so much. More than she needs me, I think.'' He stopped, looking over his shoulder to see if anyone had heard him make such an asinine comment. It probably wasn't something a grown man should say to a kid. Even if it was true.

To his relief, the nurses were all keeping a respectable distance.

"I know this is all kinda rough right now. I know you must really hurt sometimes. But your mama will make it up to you. No little girl will ever be loved more than you are. But your mama won't smother you with it. Not her. Nope. She's really good about that. She'll be there for you, supporting you, always trying to understand, doing what she can to make your dreams come true. But she won't be one of those parents who try to live their own lives vicariously through their children's. She'll let you have your own. 'Cause she has her own, too, you know. She's a doctor. A fantastic one. She takes care of sick kids, too. And she's also my wife. But don't let that bother you any. We've got that all worked out.''

Marcus continued to prattle on to the baby, unconsciously relieving his mind of things that had been running around inside it for months, until a full hour had passed and he knew it was time to go. Pushing the stool back into the corner where he'd found it, he stood over the crib one more time to say goodbye, then dropped his hospital attire in the basket Regina had shown him earlier and let himself out the door.

CHAPTER FOURTEEN

"I DON'T THINK this is going to work."

Beth's heart froze. She'd been a fool to believe that anyone as experienced, as distinguished, as Oliver Webster would take more than a passing interest in her. A fool to think she could find love more than once in a lifetime. "Why not?" she said anyway.

They were sitting outside on his patio, barely finished dressing from the latest of their afternoon rendezvous. Oliver leaned forward in the lawn chair he'd pulled up close to hers and took her hand in both of his.

"Because, my dear, it's getting harder and harder to let you go each day. I don't just want stolen moments with you. I want to share dinner with you every night, to see your face next to mine when I wake up in the morning."

"And that's bad?"

"I find myself wanting more than I can have, and I think we should stop before things get out of hand."

They'd been lovers for weeks. Wasn't it already out of hand?

"So you want us to stop seeing each other." She'd been prepared for this from the beginning, hadn't she?

Oliver was endearingly old-fashioned, and they had too many strikes against them.

He nodded. "It might be for the best."

"Do I get any say in this?"

He looked at her, his eyes sad. "Of course."

"Well, good," Beth said, something deeper than reason driving her on. "Because I think we'd be fools to walk away from the happiness we've found. I know you feel guilty about Barbara sometimes. I feel guilty about John, too, but do you really think either one of them would begrudge us a little more happiness and love? Are we supposed to walk around half-dead because they're no longer with us?"

Oliver frowned, deepening the lines around his eyes. "Of course not, but—"

"I'm not ever going to take anything away from Barbara, Oliver. The part of you that she has she'll always have, just as the part of me that I gave to John will always be his. But I have other parts of me, some I'm only just discovering. I'd like to give them to you, if you want them."

"Oh, I want them, honey. Don't ever doubt that." His eyes were fierce now with self-condemnation. "I want them so much I've acted like a dirty old man."

Beth smiled in spite of the tears forming in her eyes. "You aren't old, Oliver. You're twenty years younger than Ronald Reagan was when he ran for his first term as president. And what about Charlie Chaplin? He was fathering children in his seventies."

"But that's just it, my dear. I've fathered my children. I've raised my family. You haven't even started yours.''

"I raised my family when I was still a child, Oliver. My mother died when I was eight, leaving me five younger brothers and sisters to care for. When the last one finally made it into college, I knew I'd be hard-pressed to give up my freedom again. I figured out a long time ago that I'm much happier being an aunt than I would be being a mother.''

"But I'm a grandfather!''

"So?''

"I know that a lot of people today are happy to just live together, but I can't do that, Beth. Not to you or to myself. It leaves too many doors open.''

"I understand,'' Beth said. And she did. She just didn't like it. She was tired of living alone. Of eating alone. Of waking up alone.

"I guess we're just going to have to be patient a little longer until I can talk to Lisa. I can't ask you to marry me until I've at least warned my daughter that I've rejoined the living.'' His sheepish grin charmed Beth—and then his words sank in.

"What?'' she squeaked. Had he said *marry* her? She hadn't even dared consider such a thing. Whenever she'd looked into their future, she'd just assumed Oliver would want her as a long-standing "friend.''

"She's my daughter, Beth. I have to tell her.''

"Did you just ask me to marry you, Oliver, or did I miss something?'' Beth asked, hoping she didn't sound as young as she felt.

"Not yet. But I intend to. Just as soon as I have a

talk with my daughter. Little Sara's getting better every day, so we shouldn't have to wait too much longer.''

Beth worried a moment as she thought of Lisa's likely reaction to the news. She was not at all sure her friend would be happy for them. Especially when her own marriage was in so much trouble. She hadn't told Oliver about that last conversation she'd had with Lisa in the hospital, when Lisa had said she was planning to leave Marcus as soon as she brought her baby home. But in any case, she knew her own happiness wasn't worth causing Lisa more distress.

''Maybe we should wait at least until Sara's home.'' She entwined her fingers with his.

He nodded. ''You're right. Lisa's a strong woman, as was her mother, but everyone has a breaking point and I can't risk putting any more on her shoulders just now.''

''Lisa always said her mother could handle anything. She envied that,'' Beth said, looking out over the lawn that still showcased the gardens Barbara Webster had cultivated.

Oliver squeezed her hand. ''Thank you, my dear.''

Beth smiled. ''What for?''

''For allowing me my memories.''

And suddenly Beth understood. ''You never have to worry about mentioning Barbara around me, Oliver. No more than I ever want to have to worry about talking to you about John. I can't go through life being threatened by the past. Nor do I want to lose the beautiful memories I have of it.''

"I love you, Dr. Montague," Oliver said. He leaned over to kiss her, and for the first time since John's senseless death, Beth felt real hope for the future.

"Tell me something," Oliver said several minutes later as he walked her out to her car.

She grinned up at him. "Anything."

"When I do get around to asking, is your answer going to be yes?"

"THIS IS BETH MONTAGUE. I can't come to the phone right now, but if you'll leave a message, I'll—"

Lisa hung up the phone with a frown. That was the fourth time she'd tried to call Beth in the past week and found her out. Not that Beth wasn't free to go away, of course she was, but over the years, Lisa had become so familiar with Beth's schedule that she almost always reached her friend on the first try. She called Beth's office to make certain Beth had been showing up there, to assure herself that Beth was at least all right. Then she put a call through to her father, asking if he was going to be home for the next hour because she wanted to stop by. She knew he had a faculty meeting that evening, but Sara had been breathing on her own for almost four hours. She had to share her news with someone!

Oliver looked great when he opened his door to her fifteen minutes later. "How's our little one?" he asked immediately.

"She's breathing on her own, Dad! Has been for

over four hours now." Lisa could barely contain her excitement.

"She's off the respirator?" he asked, pinning her with his no-nonsense gaze.

Lisa nodded. "Yes!"

"And she's getting enough oxygen?" Oliver was well versed on every aspect of Sara's progress.

"Her counts have been out of the danger zone."

"Well, I'll be damned!" He grabbed Lisa up and swung her around.

She noticed a new bounce in his step as she followed him out to the enclosed back patio for a quick cup of tea. It had been years since she'd seen her father look so happy. She was glad to see that he was finally getting over the loss of her mother.

"Guess what else?" Lisa asked, sipping her tea.

"What else?" her father asked, mimicking a game they used to play when Lisa was a little girl.

"I held her today."

Oliver's mouth fell open and he sat forward, taking Lisa's hands in his own. "You took her out of her bed?"

Lisa's eyes brimmed with tears as she nodded. "For ten whole minutes."

"That's great, honey. That's just great!" His eyes were moist, too, as he shared her joy. Other than herself, Oliver was Sara's only living blood relative. It did her battered heart good to know that he cared for her daughter as much as she did.

"I imagine Marcus was standing in line to hold her," Oliver said thirty minutes later as he and Lisa walked back through the house to the front door. He had his meeting to get to, and she had a husband who'd be waiting for her at home.

Lisa stopped, unwilling to face that part of her life, but knowing she couldn't put it off any longer.

"Marcus doesn't know, Dad. He hasn't had a thing to do with the baby since the day she was born, or even before, really."

Oliver stopped in his tracks. "Nothing?" He frowned.

"He says he can't pretend." Fresh tears gathered in Lisa's eyes.

"Oh, honey, still?" He pulled her against him. "I'd hoped he'd worked his way through all that after Sara was born. Why didn't you say anything?"

"I kept hoping he'd come around, too," she said. It sounded so feeble when she said it aloud, but that tiny thread of hope had been keeping her going for months.

"I'm sorry, honey. So sorry."

Lisa squared her shoulders. "If Sara lives, I think I'm going to have to leave him, Dad."

Oliver nodded, the happiness in his eyes dimmed. "I understand. You can't bring the baby home to his house if he doesn't accept her."

Hearing her father say the words made them all that much more real to Lisa. Had she been hoping he'd disagree with her, try to talk her out of it?

"Can I bring her here, Dad? Just at first? Just until she doesn't need round-the-clock supervision?" Lisa hated even having to ask. Moving home was the last thing she wanted to do.

"You bring her here and stay here, young lady. I'll not have you off someplace caring for her all by yourself. You, me and Sara, we'll make a great family."

"I'll need to get a place of my own at some point."

"We'll worry about that later," Oliver said, dismissing her concern. But Lisa promised herself she'd start looking for a home for herself and Sara right away. She'd stay with her father as long as the baby's safety depended on having extra ears and eyes around, but she was going to have a home waiting for them when they were ready. She had to if she was ever going to believe that her marriage to Marcus was over.

"I can't imagine that Marcus is taking this sitting down," Oliver said, walking with her out to her car.

She took a deep breath. "I haven't told him yet."

Again Oliver nodded as if he understood. "Time's getting close, though," he said, echoing the thoughts she'd been trying not think ever since she'd left the nursery several hours before.

"I know." Lisa was filled with a sudden urge to get home to her husband, to grasp whatever last minutes she could with him.

"YOU OKAY?" Lisa asked Marcus over the pizza they shared later that evening.

He'd had the idea on the way home to take her to their old stomping grounds, the pizza parlor they'd frequented during their years at Yale. They had something to celebrate, even if she didn't know he knew that.

"I'm fine. Why?" He smiled at her. She really was a beautiful woman.

"I don't know. You just seem different."

He felt different. "I'm fine," he repeated, unable to explain to her what he couldn't understand himself. Nothing had happened. Nothing had changed. He just didn't feel quite his usual self.

She took another bite of her pizza. "Anything happen at work today?"

"Nothing out of the ordinary." He wanted to tell her about his trip to the hospital. He wanted her to tell him how it felt to hold Sara. He wanted to know how significant she thought it was that they'd removed the respirator. But he knew it wouldn't be fair to her. She'd accepted the situation as it had to be. He mustn't let her get her hopes up, allow her to start expecting things from him he wouldn't be able to give.

"I saw Debbie today," she said casually.

"You did?"

"Uh-huh."

He watched her through narrowed eyes. Could Lisa really not have any idea how desperately he'd been waiting for her to be ready for him again? How hard it had been to lie beside her each night these past weeks and keep his hands to himself? Did she not know that he'd have had her *before* dinner if he'd realized he could?

"And?"

She grinned at him, and Marcus dropped the piece of pizza he'd been about to devour. The minx knew exactly what she was doing to him. He gestured at her plate. "Are you done there?" he asked.

She continued to grin. "That depends," she said.

"On what?"

"On how quickly you can get me home."

"Good answer, woman." Marcus threw down a wad of bills, then took his wife's hand and practically dragged her from the restaurant.

FOR ALL HIS HASTE, Marcus took his time making love to her. He undressed her slowly, then caressed every inch of her while she lay beside him on their bed. He forced himself to be patient while she reacquainted herself with his body, as well.

"You turned every college boy's head in that joint tonight," he whispered, his lips against her neck.

Touched by his nonsense, Lisa laughed softly. "I did not. To them I'm an old lady."

He nipped her earlobe. "Hardly. I'm telling you, honey, every male eye in the place was on you as you sashayed your sweet butt out of there tonight."

"I did not sashay."

"Sure you did, Lis." He moved to her other ear. "You always do."

He captured her lips, and she returned his kiss passionately. She was desperate for Marcus. For his touch. For his tenderness. For him. Desperate because even while she made love to him, she knew it was all slipping away.

Her swollen breasts ached beneath his tender ministrations as he ran his fingers lightly over them, discovering their new hardness. A drop of milk leaked
out, rolling down one side of her breast. Marcus
caught it with his fingertip.

"Are you saving all of it?" he asked, staring at the
path the drop of milk had taken.

She shook her head, oddly embarrassed. "Not anymore. There's too much."

"How long does it keep being produced?"

She tried to turn over, afraid that he found her milk
repulsive, but he was half on top of her now and
didn't move. "As long as I keep pumping," she finally said. He was still her husband. He had the right
to an answer.

He ran his hand lightly over her again. "Does it
hurt, this pumping?"

"Not much. It's supposedly a lot worse than nursing, but I don't really mind."

Her breast dripped again, and Lisa bit her lip. She'd
had no idea that being with Marcus would stimulate
her milk glands. Again Marcus caught the drop on his
finger, and this time he brought it to his mouth.

Marcus cherished her that night, loved her in ways
he never had before, and when he finally entered her,
bringing them both to a climax that seemed to go on
and on, Lisa gave him more than her body and heart.
She gave him her soul all over again. At least for one
more night.

And later, when he lay sleeping beside her, she
gave him her tears. Because for everything she'd

given him that night, she'd lost just as much. She couldn't fool herself any longer. Marcus wasn't going to come around. Sara was breathing on her own. It was time for Lisa to find her daughter a home.

MARCUS DIDN'T EVEN STOP at the viewing-room window the next afternoon on his way home from work. He proceeded right to the door, and then on to a set of scrubs as soon as Regina answered his knock. He had business to attend to.

"Hello, Sara," he said, settling himself beside the warming bed on the stool he'd used the night before. "My name's Marcus."

A nurse he'd never seen before walked by, and Marcus leaned down a little closer to the crib. "I'm married to your mama."

The baby was awake, but she appeared to be studying a scratch on the side of the bed opposite Marcus. He fought the urge to turn her little face toward him. He wasn't going to touch her. Only the medical professionals and her parents were supposed to be touching her. He was neither.

"Here's the thing. I love your mama very much. And pretty soon, as soon as you get to know her, you're going to love her, too. And she loves both of us. So you and me, we're going to have to share her."

He paused, giving her time to digest his words. One of her inch-long feet kicked in the air.

"Well, I just wanted you to know that I'm okay with that now, sharing her with you, I mean. I'm sorry it took me so long to come around. But it'll work out fine, you'll see. I have an office at home, and I can always work in there on the nights you need her to help you with homework, or if she's teaching you to sew or something. And then she can get a sitter some nights and go out with me, too.''

It wasn't ideal. But it could work.

''But, uh—'' Marcus looked around him before leaning in just a bit closer ''—unless you're sick or something, I get her nights.''

The baby didn't cry. Marcus decided that was a good sign. ''Okay. Now that that's done, I'll go get someone over here to change that diaper for you.'' He looked around for Regina.

Marcus backed up while Regina moved the cellophane covering Lisa's baby and slipped a dry diaper beneath her. She plopped the old diaper on a scale, wrote something on the baby's chart and came back with a doll-size pacifier in her hand which she attempted to place in Sara's mouth. The baby spit it out, and Regina put it back in, all the while watching a bottle of milky solution drip into the baby's catheter.

''Should she have that thing if she doesn't want it?'' Marcus asked. He'd read that pacifiers were bad for babies' teeth.

''Before she can nurse, she has to learn how to suck,'' Regina said, patiently forcing the pacifier back into the baby's mouth. Sara spit it back out.

Marcus grinned. The baby was as stubborn as her mother. ''Maybe it'd be better to try her again later,'' he suggested.

Regina shook her head. "We give it to her only when she's eating so she'll learn to associate sucking with the full feeling in her stomach."

Marcus looked at the baby's apple-size stomach. "She's eating?"

"Yep." Regina nodded toward the bottle she was watching. "She's taking about an eighth of a cup every four hours. We're just about ready to try her on breast milk."

Thinking of the night before, Marcus had a sudden urge to go home and make love to Lisa again.

"My wife will be glad to hear that," he said, instead.

"She was. We called her about an hour ago. She's going to bring in the first four ounces in the morning and hold Sara while we feed her."

Marcus felt a pang as he thought about being there to watch Lisa feed her baby for the first time, but he knew better than to torment himself—or Lisa. So he settled for watching the nurse continue to offer the baby the pacifier, until Sara finally gave in and accepted the unfamiliar object in her mouth. She sucked for about a minute and then fell asleep.

"I'm a little concerned about her temperature," Regina said, feeling the baby's face with the back of her hand. "She's getting feverish."

Marcus's stomach tightened. "Is that normal?"

Regina frowned and called out to another nurse. "See if Dr. Cunningham's still in the building, Susan." She kept looking from the baby to the dials on one of the machines beside the warming bed. "Her temperature's climbed a full degree in an hour. And no, that's not normal,'' she said to Marcus.

They were the last words anybody said to him during the next fifteen minutes as a full team of medical personnel went to work on Lisa's baby. Marcus watched from the viewing-room window, just as he had for all those weeks. And when the team finally came away from the baby's bed, Sara was once again hooked up to the respirator.

They were right back where they'd started.

CHAPTER FIFTEEN

URGENCY FUELED his blood as Marcus drove home. He wanted to be with Lisa in case the hospital called. He didn't want her home alone when she heard the bad news. When he walked in the door, he could smell Hannah's crab Alfredo coming from the kitchen. Lisa was in their office, working at her desk. She looked up at him when he came in, saw his worried expression.

"What's wrong?" she said, rising. Her face got that pinched look he'd come to dread.

With his arm around her shoulders, Marcus led her to the leather couch that dominated one wall of the office. "Sara's got some kind of infection, Lis. A nurse noticed her temperature rising when she was feeding her dinner. They had to call Randal Cunningham."

"Oh, my God. Oh, no. Not now." Lisa started to get up from the couch. "I've got to go."

Marcus pulled her back down beside him. He was giving himself away, but seeing Lisa through this crisis was the only thing that mattered right then. "It's okay for now, honey. They managed to stabilize her. The nurse said she'd call immediately if there was any change. The soonest they'll let you in to see her is tomorrow morning, anyway, until they're sure the antibiotic is working.''

Lisa's big brown eyes stared at him, begging for reassurance that it wasn't worse than he was telling her. He looked away.

"They had to put her back on the respirator, Lis.''

"No!" she cried, tears brimming in her eyes.

Marcus hated having to be the one to bring that frightened look back to her eyes, and he hated being powerless to make everything better. "She wasn't getting enough oxygen, honey. I'm sorry.''

Lisa jumped up and began pacing in front of the couch. "She was doing great this morning. I can't stand this. I can't stand that her life is in question from minute to minute. She's fine one minute and then in terrible danger the next. There's never a time when the worry quits.''

His hands hanging uselessly between his knees, Marcus watched her pace. "I know, Lis. But you of all people know that as quickly as infections crop up, they go away, too.''

She nodded, and Marcus saw the exact moment she switched from the baby's mother to an award-studded pediatrician. "Did they say what it was?" she asked brusquely, stopping in front of him.

"They didn't know yet. When I left, Randal was sending blood to be tested.''

She nodded again, assimilating God only knew what in that quick brain of hers, but whatever it was, it panicked the mother in her. Her face crumpled and

Marcus grabbed her hand, pulled her down beside him and into his arms.

"She's beaten all the odds so far, Lis. Don't give up on her now."

"I'm n-not. It's just so...so hard." He felt the sobs that racked her body as he held her, the tears that wet his shirt, and could only marvel that she'd held up as long as she had. She was one helluva strong woman to be able to go to that nursery every day, to sit with her baby, to see the catheters they'd inserted into her scalp, her tiny feet, knowing all of the things that could easily go wrong.

Her tears stopped suddenly, and she pulled slightly away from Marcus, staring at him.

"How did you... Why were *you* there?" The hope in her eyes clawed at him.

"I, uh, only stopped by because I assumed you were there. I called here before I left work and you didn't answer." It was weak. He knew it was weak. But he still couldn't allow her to hope for something he couldn't give her.

"I was in the shower," she said, studying him like a specimen under a microscope.

"I was going to offer to take you to dinner, but it smells like you've already put Hannah's casserole in the oven." *Smooth, Cartwright.* Why did he suddenly feel like he'd been caught with his hand in the cookie jar?

"It's almost ready," Lisa said, linking her arm through his and laying her head against his shoulder.

Marcus allowed himself to relax a fraction. She was going to let it go.

"Is it really all that bad that she's back on the ventilator, Lis, other than that she's lost some of the ground she gained? Ground she can regain?" he asked. He'd wondered about it all the way home from the hospital. And since Lisa knew he'd been there, anyway, he didn't see the harm in asking her a couple of things.

She hugged his arm to her side. "I wish it was that simple," she said, her voice small and worried. "But the longer Sara's on the ventilator, the more chance there is of other things going wrong. Not only is there increased risk of brain damage, but her hearing and internal organs can be affected, too."

He digested her words in silence. Did the worrying never stop?

"There comes a point when she's just plain been on the machines too long."

Brushing back her hair, he kissed her gently on the top of her head. "That's not going to happen, Lis. You have to believe that, believe in her."

"Did you see her, Marcus?"

He nodded, and then realized she couldn't see him with her head pressed against him. Swallowing the lump in his throat, he answered, "I saw her."

"She's so tiny."

"But she's strong."

"I don't know the night staff well, other than the brief phone conversation or two I've had with them. I think I'll call now, just to make sure they know what they're doing.'' She started to get up, but Marcus put a hand on her arm, restraining her.

"They knew what they were doing, Lis. They had Randal Cunningham there within minutes. Save your worries for the real stuff. They said they'd call if anything changes. And they will.''

Lisa was silent for a couple of minutes. "They must've thought it odd that you were there,'' she finally murmured, and Marcus felt another prick of guilt. He wondered how she explained his supposed absence in the nursery to her colleagues. Or how she would explain it at other functions in the years to come.

His chest constricted, leaving little room for him to breathe. He needed to go out, get away, not just out of the room or the house, but out of her life. Except that he couldn't. Lisa was his life.

"I've been there before, Lis.'' He cursed when he heard his words. He was only going to hurt her more in the long run.

"You have?'' Her neck practically snapped in two when she looked up at him, and the hope he saw in her eyes confirmed his doubts. Because at some point, if not tonight, then tomorrow or next week, he'd only succeed in killing it again. She wanted something from him he didn't have to give.

"Like I told you before, Lis, I'm not heartless. I love you. And she's a very important part of you. I've been keeping tabs on her progress.''

Confusion clouded her eyes. "Then why did't you ever say anything? Do you have any idea how many times I've needed you, needed to be able to talk to you about her, to know that you care?''

His heart was heavy as he pulled her closer. ''You've always known how much I care for you, Lis. I didn't say anything about the visits because I knew you'd start hoping again, and I couldn't let you do that to yourself. Nothing's changed. I'm not deluding myself into thinking I'm the child's father. I go there merely for you, honey, not for myself.''

She leaned against him silently, and Marcus would have given the Cartwright fortune to know what she was thinking, what she was feeling. More than anything, he hated the way she'd learned to close herself off from him. The barrier that came up between them terrified him. His life wouldn't be worth a nickel if he lost Lisa.

''Since you've been going, anyway, will you go with me to see her in the morning? I'm so scared for her, Marcus. Please come. For me?'' Lisa broke the silence with her soft question.

The next day was Saturday. He didn't have to work. And Lisa was at the end of her tether. Looking at the frightened expression still marring her face, he sensed that she didn't just want him there, she needed him there. ''All right,'' he said.

But he was going for Lisa. Period.

IT WAS WORSE going the next morning than Lisa had thought it would be. She was trembling even before she got off the elevator. Though she'd known all along it could happen, she wasn't ready to face Sara's setback.

"She'll be fine, Lis," Marcus said, taking her free hand as they headed together toward the window in the nursery viewing room. "She's got you to rely on."

His words gave her the strength it took to look through the window. But even so, her stomach churned and she felt a wave of nausea as she saw the ugly tube once again taped to her baby's mouth. She didn't know how much more Sara could take.

The nurses hadn't noticed her yet, hadn't come to the door to let her in. Clutching the sterilized bottle of breast milk she'd brought, Lisa watched her daughter, looked at the unbelievably long lashes against Sara's tiny cheek. Lisa's lips quivered as she fought back tears.

"Her color's good, Lis. She was kind of flushed yesterday."

Unable to speak, Lisa just nodded, holding on to Marcus's hand for all she was worth. Almost immediately her stomach started to settle down. It still amazed her, even after more than ten years of living with Marcus, how much his mere presence was able to calm her.

The nurse finally noticed them standing there and came to the door to meet them. "I'm sorry, Dr. Cartwright, but Dr. Cunningham said no visitors for twenty-four hours. Not until he's certain we've got the infection under control."

Lisa nodded. She'd half expected as much, but still

she'd hoped. Yesterday she'd held Sara against her heart. Today she couldn't even be in the same room with her. She felt Marcus's arm slide around her shoulders. "Can we see her tonight?" he asked. "That would be twenty-four hours since she started the antibiotic."

The nurse shook her head. "The doctor said twenty-four hours this morning."

"Can we speak with him?" Marcus asked.

"It's okay, Marcus," Lisa said before the nurse had a chance to reply, though she appreciated his willingness to go to bat for her. "We don't want to put Sara at risk." She turned to the nurse. "Can we still give her this?" she asked, holding out the bottle.

The nurse smiled and nodded as she took the bottle. "We've been waiting for it. She hasn't had her eight-o'clock feeding yet." It was almost eight-fifteen.

They watched the nurse take the bottle of breast milk away. "I'm sorry you can't be in there sharing it with her, honey," Marcus said, moving with her back to the window.

Lisa hooked her arm through his. "I'm just glad I have you here with me." If she couldn't be with her daughter while the baby took her first mother's milk, there was no place else she'd rather be than with her husband.

The nurse came back into the nursery with a vial filled with Lisa's breast milk and hooked it up to the tube that would send the milk into the baby's stomach. Lisa stared at the vial as the milk slowly disappeared.

"She took it all!" Marcus exclaimed a short while later.

Lisa smiled for the first time that morning. She was thankful for every small victory she had. And she'd just had two. Sara had had her first real feeding. And Marcus had exclaimed over his daughter's progress just like the proud papa he was supposed to be. It wasn't much. But it was enough to keep Lisa going. At least for another day.

SHE WASN'T SURE just when she knew she wouldn't give up her husband without a fight. The knowledge just seemed to grow in her over the next few days as Marcus continued to share her visits with Sara. They were allowed into the nursery on the second day after the baby had been put back on the ventilator, and Lisa sang to her daughter through her morning feeding that second day. Sara was taking four ounces of breast milk every four hours. And digesting every bit of it. Lisa could tell that Marcus was pleased at this small bit of progress by the satisfied expression on his face, but that was the only indication he gave. He never involved himself with anything that went on in the nursery, never got close enough to the baby to touch her.

But he was always there.

Marcus was the most heroic man she'd ever met. He was the spice in her life, the warmth of the sun on her face. He was also the father of her child. Somehow she had to get him to believe that. For all of them.

They stood together in the deserted nursery viewing room one evening, having stopped by the hospital for another quick peek at Sara after they'd gone out for dinner.

Lisa saw the way his gaze flew immediately to their baby as they entered the room. Saw the way the lines around his mouth relaxed when he saw that she was resting peacefully.

"You care about her," she blurted, frustrated beyond endurance with his inability to allow himself the wealth of love Sara would bring to him.

His face froze, a look Lisa hadn't seen in months, but she ignored it. She wasn't wrong about him. She couldn't be wrong about him. "I saw you looking at her just now, Marcus. You were worried that she wouldn't be all right."

He shoved his hands into his pockets and hunched his shoulders defensively. "I worry for your sake, Lisa, for hers, not for my own. Don't read any more into it than that."

"I see you look at her, Marcus. You watch everything they do to her so intently. I see you tense when they're hurting her, as if you're taking on her pain yourself. I know you, Marcus. You care about her."

"I care for you, Lisa. Period. Don't do this." His jaw clenched.

"Look at her, Marcus! How can you look at her and not love her?"

"She's not mine to love." His words were clipped, his eyes shuttered.

"She's not those nurses' in there, either, but I can

guarantee you that every last one of them have fallen in love with her.'' Lisa couldn't let it go. Too much was depending on making him see this her way.

Marcus was silent for so long that Lisa dared hope she'd finally won. Until he pinned her with a stare she didn't even recognize. It was hard. Unrelenting.

''You promised, Lisa. There was to be no more of this. Yes, I care about the child, just as those nurses do as outsiders. That's what I am—an outsider.''

Her heart splintered into a million fragments. She hadn't won at all. She wasn't ever going to win.

She sensed rather than saw the softening in him. ''But we can be happy, Lis. I know we can.''

''Just you and me?'' she asked, bitterness the only thing she had to give him in that moment. Was he so blind that he couldn't see the writing on the wall?

''The three of us.'' He rocked back on his heels, his hands still jammed in his pockets. ''I'll never begrudge you the time you spend with her, the days and evenings that will belong to her alone, as long as I have your love. I'll always be good to her, Lis, treat her with gentleness and respect.''

She felt herself giving in, even though she knew it would never work.

''It might be unconventional, but so was flying when the Wright brothers decided to give it a try. So was talking over wires before Alexander Graham Bell thought it was possible. And now look—everybody's doing it.''

There was wisdom in his logic, but he'd missed one key factor. Emotion. Particularly the emotions of a little girl who'd never know her father's love. Gentleness and respect just weren't enough.

"At least give it a try, Lis. Give us a chance. Let me show you it'll be all right. If you aren't happy or you think for one second that Sara's not happy, I'll leave. But please, give us a chance."

Too choked up to speak, Lisa nodded, but she knew she'd never be able to follow through on his request. She couldn't gamble with Sara's well-being. If she did as Marcus asked, if she brought Sara to live with him and the child suffered from his indifference, his leaving would be too late. The damage would already be done.

But neither could she handle sending him out of her life tonight. She stood beside him for another fifteen minutes while their daughter slept, oblivious to the turmoil going on in her parents' lives. She stood there thinking about the expression she'd caught on his face when they'd first come into the viewing room that evening, and she stubbornly hung on to a thread of hope she knew in her heart had already been severed.

IN SPITE OF the breast milk she was consuming four times a day, Sara lost three ounces that week.

Lisa's heart sank when Randal Cunningham told her about it Friday morning, Sara's seven-week birthday. They were in the nursery, the baby sleeping in her bed between them. Lisa had just tied a Happy Birthday helium balloon to the baby's blood-pressure monitor. Marcus was at work.

Randal tapped Sara's chart against his hand. "She's still under four pounds, Lisa. I'd hoped to have her in an incubator by now, but she's got to hit the four-pound mark first."

Lisa nodded, biting the inside of her lip as she tried not to cry. "The breast milk isn't helping?" she asked. All her determination to help her baby, all those hours of pumping, just weren't enough.

"Oh, it's helping," Randal said. "It's the infection that caused the weight loss. I suspect she'd have lost a lot more if not for your milk. Now's not the time to be getting discouraged on me, Doctor. If she remains stable over the next twenty-four hours, I intend to try taking her off the ventilator again sometime before the weekend's out."

Worry clutched Lisa anew. If Sara didn't make it the second time off the machine, chances were she never would. "Are you sure?" she asked. As much as she wanted the baby off the hateful machine, she wasn't ready to risk a failure.

The brisk Dr. Cunningham's eyes filled with compassion. "Sometimes we know too much for our own good, don't we, Lisa." He looked at the sleeping baby.

Lisa stood next to him, watching her silent little girl, and nodded.

SHE KEPT HERSELF busy for the rest of the morning, taking the few office calls she'd had scheduled for well-child exams and inoculations, dictating charts, even rearranging a shelf of reference books in her office. Anything to keep her mind occupied and not on Sara. What if they took her off the machine and she didn't make it? There'd be no going back a second time. At least not without certain damage to the baby's vital organs.

By noon she couldn't stand herself any longer. Her stomach was turning inside out, and every breath was more of a labor than it should have been as she pushed the air past the constriction in her chest. Her panic eventually grew to the point of dizziness, forcing her to do what she always did when her head was running away with her. She called Marcus.

"Hi, hon," he said as soon as he heard her voice. "Is everything okay?"

"She's lost a little weight, but Randal says it's due to the infection and nothing to worry about."

"But you're worried, anyway."

"He wants to take her off the ventilator again this weekend."

"Lisa! That's great, honey." He sounded far happier than "merely for her" should entail.

"I'm scared, Marcus. If she doesn't make it this time, chances are she won't make it at all."

"She's outrun all her other odds, Lis."

Lisa twirled the phone cord around her finger. "I know, but it's dangerous to take her on and off life support. It damages all kinds of things—the respiratory system, the brain, the heart. Deafness is already a concern, and mental retardation, too."

"And we could be struck by lightning the next time it rains."

"I'm serious, Marcus. You have no idea how many very real dangers she's facing. I'm not overreacting here."

"I'm serious, too, Lis. I'm fully aware of the dangers, but you're worrying about things you can't control. Save your energy for handling whatever comes."

"But what'll I do if—"

"You'll do whatever you have to do, Lis," he interrupted her. "You always have."

She felt better after she hung up the phone, though she'd been disappointed to hear that Marcus wouldn't be able to make it for her afternoon hour with Sara. He had a meeting with George Blake.

And by the time her second hour that day with Sara was ending, her panic was back. Determined to fight it, to take what control she had left to her, she walked down to the kidney ward, hoping to find Oliver still there. With the exception of her visits to Sara, she hadn't been at the hospital on Friday afternoons in years, since that was one of the days she volunteered at the free clinic downtown, and she wasn't even sure what her father's hours were anymore.

She was disappointed to hear that she'd just missed him, not more than ten minutes before. Thinking he might stop to see Sara again on his way out, she rushed back upstairs, only to find she'd missed him there, too.

"Damn!" she said, punching the elevator for the bottom floor. She couldn't go home. Hannah was still only working part-time, though she'd offered to come full-time after the baby was home, and Marcus wouldn't be out of his meeting with Blake yet. She knew better than to go home and sit by herself. The empty rooms would only torment her.

Cool April air filled Lisa's lungs and the sunshine warmed her face as she walked across the compound to Beth's office. Just being out of the sterile antiseptic-filled air that permeated the hospital corridors helped. Hopefully Beth was done for the day and could go out for a drink or something. She could use a dose of Beth's cheer. She missed her friend. Missed being an everyday part of Beth's life. Something she hoped would change after she brought Sara home.

If she brought Sara home.

Wherever home was going to be.

Her stomach started to churn again, and Lisa picked up her pace, determined to outdistance her demons. The door to Beth's office was closed, but her light was on, which meant Beth was still working— but not with a patient. Beth never closed her office door with a patient inside.

Relieved far beyond what she should have been, Lisa knocked lightly once and opened the door.

She started to speak, words of greeting on her lips, but no sound came out. Beth wasn't alone. And she wasn't working.

Lisa closed the door before either person in Beth's office even knew it had been opened, so involved were they in what they were doing. Cold all over, Lisa walked away as quickly as she could without attracting attention to herself. She felt like a fool. And alone. And heartsick. She couldn't believe what she'd just seen. She kept trying to convince herself that it wasn't true, that it wasn't what it seemed.

Except that there was no way it could have been anything else.

She tried not to think about it, tried to concentrate on finding her car in the parking lot, counting how many red cars there were in the row in which she was walking. Or blue ones. Or green. But all she could see, over and over again, was Beth, sitting on her desk, her blouse halfway undone, kissing a man.

A man Lisa had thought she knew very well.

Her father.

CHAPTER SIXTEEN

"YOU'RE A GOOD MAN, Marcus Cartwright. If I'd ever had a son, I'd have wanted him to be just like you," George Blake said, shaking Marcus's hand as the two men left the conference room long after everyone else on Friday afternoon. They'd just finished going over the best quarterly reports Blake's had ever known.

"I imagine I'd have grown up a little happier if I'd had you for a father," Marcus said, uncharacteristically open with the older man. He'd had a soft spot for George Blake since the moment he'd met him.

George walked with him down to the elevator, as straightbacked as a much younger man. "Your father was a little rough on you, huh?" he asked.

Marcus shook his head. "He never lifted a hand to me. He just wasn't ever there."

George nodded. "He had a business to run."

"Something like that."

"Yeah, me, too. If I regret anything in my life, it's not taking the time to watch my daughters grow. Girls are baffling little creatures, but they'll leave a mark on you that you'll cherish till the day you die."

Marcus reached out and pushed the button for the elevator. "My wife just had a little girl a couple of months ago. Her name's Sara."

"Well, congratulations, boy! Why didn't I hear anything about it? It wasn't even in the paper, was it?"

"We've kept things quiet for Lisa's sake. The baby was more than two months premature. It's been touch and go. I'm on my way to Thornton Memorial to see her now."

George's brows drew together in a frown, and his eyes filled with compassion. "I'll be praying for her, son. For all of you," he said, clasping Marcus on the shoulder just as the elevator doors slid open.

"Thanks, George."

"I'd like to keep in touch, Marcus, other than to discuss Blake's, if you can find the time."

Marcus didn't hesitate. "I can find the time."

George nodded again and Marcus watched the elevator close on his new friend. He couldn't remember a time when he'd felt so contented.

LISA HAD ONLY BEEN HOME a few minutes when Marcus called from his car to say he was on his way and asked that she put on a pair of jeans and a warm sweater. But he wouldn't say where he was taking her. It had been so long since he'd planned one of the mysterious dates she'd always loved that she'd forgotten how magical they could be. It was just what she needed to take her mind off the rest of her life.

She was ready and waiting when he strode through the door and even had *his* jeans and pullover sweater laid out on the bed for him. She called the hospital with instructions to call her on her cellular if there was any change in Sara's condition, while he got ready. She was looking forward to whatever diversion he had in mind.

When she climbed into the Ferrari beside Marcus, Lisa caught sight of a couple of bags from Berelli's. Her favorite deli. Things were looking better every minute.

"So where we going on our picnic?" she asked, grinning at her husband.

He merely grinned back, put the Ferrari in gear and roared out of the drive. But Lisa knew where they were going almost immediately. She couldn't have chosen better herself.

She followed him across the dock to *Sara*'s slip, then took his hand as he helped her aboard. It was a beautiful evening, not cold, though there was a nippy breeze blowing in from the ocean. The water was too rough to take the boat out, but Lisa wouldn't have wanted to be away from shore and the hospital, anyway. She was content to sit with Marcus, enjoying the night, with the waves lapping at the boat, away from it all, and yet close enough to not be away at all.

"I went by Beth's office on my way home this afternoon," she said once they were sitting together on the deck, a blanket from down below wrapped around her. Marcus had a glass of wine for his pre-dinner drink. He'd brought her a couple of nonalcoholic wine coolers in deference to her breast feeding.

"How's she doing?" he asked, his arms crossed in front of him as he toyed casually with his wineglass.

"She was making love with my father," Lisa blurted. She still couldn't believe her father would get involved with a woman young enough to be his daughter. It upset her every time she thought about it.

A full minute had passed before she realized that Marcus wasn't saying anything. He was looking out to sea, and Lisa could almost envision the wheels turning around in his head.

"Define making love," he finally said.

"Her shirt was undone. He was…touching her. They were kissing." It embarrassed her to talk about it.

She was shocked when Marcus turned to her and grinned. "Well, I'll be damned," he said.

"You aren't appalled?"

"I think it'll take some getting used to for sure, but think about it, Lis. They've both already had, and lost, their mates. In spite of their age difference, they're at about the same point in their lives, settled in their careers, their homes. They're practically perfect for each other."

"She's young enough to be his daughter," Lisa said. She kept picturing herself with Beth's father, or Marcus's had he still been alive, and she shuddered.

"Not technically," Marcus said, reaching under the blanket for her hand. "She's five years older than you, Lis."

"There's an entire generation between them."

"But if it's not a problem for them, why should it be for us?"

"He loves my mother," Lisa said softly, and suddenly knew where her shame should be directed. Not at her father, but at herself. She was jealous.

"And Beth loved John every bit as much, honey. I suspect they both understand that. It's probably why they were drawn to each other in the first place."

Lisa sighed. "I'm being a jerk, aren't I?" she asked, not at all proud of herself.

"Just being human, love," Marcus said. He leaned over and kissed her.

"Well, it *is* going to take some getting used to," she said when she could finally think coherently again.

Marcus nodded. "It all makes sense now, though."

She frowned. "What makes sense?"

"A conversation I had with Oliver a while back. I thought he was talking about his career, but he must have already been seeing Beth. He was saying something about looking at the years still stretching out in front of him and wondering where to go from there. He asked if I thought he'd be acting like an old fool if he started over."

Lisa's eyes pooled with tears. Marcus's words gave her a whole new insight into the man she'd taken for granted all her life. He was much more than just a father. He was a man with needs and desires, a man who still had a lifetime stretching out in front of him. A man who, despite his loss, was still capable of finding love with the right woman. It was time she recognized that. And loved all of him.

"So you think we should tell them we know?" she asked, suddenly just wanting to get it over with.

"They don't know you saw them?"

Lisa shook her head.

"Then I think we ought to let it be until they come to us. It should be their call."

"I just don't want them to feel as if they have to hide from us," Lisa said, understanding now the change in her friend over the past months, the times when Beth had avoided her. Although, when Lisa had needed a friend, Beth had still been that friend. Lisa was ready to return the favor.

THE HOSPITAL CALLED the next morning. They were removing Sara's ventilator. Randal wanted Lisa present.

Marcus held her hand all the way to the hospital and during the minutes standing next to Sara's bed while the technician removed the tape that held Sara's life support secure. As before, the baby protested the attention, but she didn't seem to Lisa to be putting up as much of a fight. Her little arms and legs weren't squirming quite so energetically. Lisa broke out in a cold sweat while they stood there watching. And waiting.

Marcus stood silently beside her. Lisa wondered if he realized how crucial the next moments were. She wondered if he allowed himself to care at all. And suddenly she didn't want him there. Not if he wasn't there for Sara's sake. She didn't want anybody in the room who wasn't pulling for her baby. Sara deserved a supportive family, not a disinterested bystander.

But before she could do more than release her grip on Marcus's hand, the tube was gone. Sara blinked at the sudden need to pull in her own air. The room was silent. There were no little wails like the last time. Nothing to indicate that the baby was going to help herself.

Until suddenly Sara's little features scrunched up into the ugliest face Lisa had ever seen, and she let out a wail that reverberated throughout the entire nursery.

"Thank God." The words were Marcus's.

LISA DIDN'T WANT to leave the nursery. She was afraid to go home, to let the baby out of her sight, in case something went wrong. Marcus agreed without any argument and sat with her in the nursery viewing room once their allotted hour with Sara was through. He left just before noon to pick up some lunch.

They'd barely finished the hamburgers he'd brought back when Oliver walked in the door to the viewing room, an apprehensive look on his face. Beth was right behind him. Her eyes darted to Lisa and then away. She looked like she was going to cry.

"Hey, you two," Lisa said, "don't look so glum."

Beth did start to cry then. "I'm so sorry, Lisa," she said. "I had no idea you'd come by."

Oliver coughed and looked down. Lisa looked at her husband. "You called them."

Marcus grinned sheepishly. "I called your father. Beth was there."

"So what was all that about waiting for them to come to us?" she asked, standing up.

"I was wrong. The more I thought about it, the more I realized you were right. I didn't want them hiding from us, either. Besides, I knew you were missing them. That you wanted them beside you today."

Oliver crossed to Lisa, brushing a strand of hair back from her face as he'd done when she was a child. "I'm sorry, baby. I'll always love your mother, you know."

Lisa threw her arms around her father, proud to be loved by him. "I know, Dad. And don't ever be sorry about being happy."

He crushed her to him, and for the first time Lisa was at peace with her mother's passing and her father's moving on. He'd had too much anguish in his life.

And so had Beth. Lisa reached out and hugged her friend as soon as her father let her go. "I love you, Beth. Be happy," she whispered for Beth's ears alone.

"I've missed you, friend," Beth whispered back.

"So when are you going to make an honest woman out of her, Dad?" Lisa asked, one arm still around Beth.

Oliver laughed, a hearty outburst that Lisa hadn't heard in years. She'd missed it. "I guess we have nothing to wait for anymore, do we, Beth? So what do you say? Are you going to marry me?''

"You mean you haven't asked her?" Lisa gasped.

"He was waiting to talk to you first," Beth said, smiling up at her lover.

Lisa hadn't expected such consideration, but she appreciated it. She wasn't losing a father or memories of her mother. She was gaining a new closer relationship with her best friend. It still felt a bit odd. And it would definitely take some getting used to. But she was happy for her father and Beth.

And then she saw Marcus, standing away from the three of them, gazing through the window into the nursery with a frown on his face. Her gaze flew to Sara. The baby was sleeping peacefully, her heart monitor beeping reassuringly. But Marcus's frown remained. Was he, in the face of the love she shared with her father, reminding himself that he'd never have a daughter with whom to share a similar love? His face froze when he caught Lisa looking at him, and she knew she was right.

BETH AND OLIVER stayed for more than an hour, holding hands while they watched Sara breathe. Lisa saw the love brimming in their eyes as they watched her daughter, and she knew that whether or not Sara grew up in her father's house, the child was going to be surrounded by a family who adored her.

Marcus was silent most of the afternoon, frowning more often than not, but when Lisa tried to talk to him after Oliver and Beth left to go inspect the new dialysis equipment Cartwright Enterprises had purchased for the hospital, his replies were nothing more than one or two syllables.

"You don't have to stay if you don't want to," she finally said. They'd been sitting there for more than four hours.

"I'll stay," was all he said.

Lisa didn't speak again until she heard a commotion in the hallway outside the nursery viewing room. They'd been lucky to have the room to themselves so far, though she knew that the room was rarely used except by the families of preemies. The full-term babies could be seen better from the viewing window around the corner out in the hall.

"So where's this kid I been hearing about?"

Lisa turned her head, recognizing the sassy voice instantly. "Willie Adams. What're you doing up here?" she scolded. She'd dismissed the boy from the hospital a month ago, but he was supposed to be down in physical therapy every afternoon for several hours.

"Look at you, Willie!" Marcus said, turning to watch as the boy walked slowly into the room. His left leg was still dragging a bit, but Lisa could see that his motor coordination had much improved, even from the previous week.

"They say I gotta do stairs, and I figure the real kind are better than that stupid machine they want me to go on. At least this way I get somewhere." His grin went straight to Lisa's heart.

"Besides, I gotta see this kid. Which one is she?"

Marcus put his arm around the boy's thin shoulders, pointing to Sara's warming bed. "She's right there. See, her name's on that plate at the bottom of the crib."

"What's she in that funny-looking bed for?"

"It helps to maintain her body temperature."

"Why don't she just do that for herself?"

"Give her time, Willie, she will. She just has to grow a bit more."

Lisa wondered if Marcus had any idea how much he sounded like a papa defending his young.

"She don't look big enough to grow."

"She's almost four pounds now. You should've seen her when she was born."

Willie nodded, apparently satisfied. "We can skip the batting cages if you want, you know, since you got your own kid to think about now."

Lisa braced herself as she heard the words. Did it hurt Marcus every time people referred to Sara as his, or did he just freeze out their words as he did hers? And how could he possibly think they could go through life living this way?

"I'll have time, Willie. We'll go as soon as you're ready."

Of course he would. Willie wasn't a threat. He expected nothing. Marcus was able to be more of a father to Willie than he was to his own daughter.

SARA'S OXYGEN LEVELS began to drop around four o'clock. She'd only been breathing on her own for just over six hours. Lisa watched as her little chest continued to rise and fall, as her lungs labored for air, worried that each breath might be the baby's last. In spite of the capable medical staff attending to Sara, Lisa was afraid to take her eyes off her baby even for a minute.

"I'll watch her, hon," Marcus said shortly before five. "Why don't you go down and get some fresh air?"

Lisa shook her head. It could all be over before she got back.

"Would you like me to call your father?" he asked.

Again Lisa shook her head. It might be hours yet before they knew anything for sure. Lisa wanted her father to have what unrestricted happiness he could. She was glad that Beth was with him, that if the unthinkable happened to Sara, her father wouldn't be alone.

Sara slept on. The baby hadn't opened her eyes in more than four hours.

Marcus went in with Lisa while she sat through Sara's eight-o'clock feeding. Lisa sang to the child, as she always did when she fed her, but while the baby's body was continuing to accept nourishment, Sara slept through her entire meal.

"She's going to have to go back on the ventilator," Lisa whispered as Marcus led her back out to the viewing room.

"Let's just be patient, Lis. Randal hasn't given the order for that yet," Marcus said. Though his face was pinched, his brows tight with worry, Lisa just ac-

cepted that he was worried on her account. The
baby's, too, but only in the way anyone would be
concerned about another in a life-threatening situation. She wasn't going to read any more into it than
that, couldn't afford to waste any more energy hoping
for what would never be. For as much as she believed
in Marcus's ability to be a father to her child, he
didn't believe in himself, and there was nothing she
could do to change that.

Randal arrived in the nursery at nine. He checked
Sara carefully, not only watching her readings, but
listening to her chest and looking under her eyelids.
Finally, straightening, he motioned for a technician to
bring back Sara's life support.

Lisa started to cry as the machine was wheeled over
beside the baby. She just couldn't let them do it. She
couldn't put her baby through more pain if it was all
going to be for naught.

Randal caught sight of her sitting out there, and
Lisa didn't even bother to wipe away the tears that
were streaming down her face. She wasn't a professional. She was a mother.

"We're not hooking her up just yet, folks," Randal
said, poking his head out the nursery door. "Her levels have been fluctuating a little more this past hour.
We'll wait for one more reading."

Lisa nodded, but she knew that at that point the
chances of Sara's breathing normally on her own
were slim to none. Marcus stood silently behind her,
his hands on her shoulders. She leaned back against
him, soaking up his warmth. He'd been a rock

throughout the entire day, never leaving her side, watching her baby intently, as if he could actually will his own breath into the baby's lungs. She knew, without a doubt, he would if he could.

"Can we sit with her?" Lisa asked. Surely, given the circumstances, Randal would break the rules this once.

The doctor nodded.

"Let me help you with that," Marcus said a few minutes later. Lisa's hands were shaking so badly she couldn't get into her scrubs. Marcus was already dressed and masked.

He was being a wonderful father. If only there was some way to make him see that, believe it.

Lisa could feel every beat of her heart as Randal approached Sara's crib half an hour later, checked the baby over and then checked her a second time, finally turning to face Lisa and Marcus. His face looked grim.

"Her oxygen levels are up. She's breathing well enough on her own again." He stood by Sara's bed, looking down at the baby. He appeared to be struggling for words.

"What's wrong, doctor?" Marcus asked. He slid his arm around Lisa's waist, pulling her against his side.

"She's not responding to..." The doctor looked at Lisa, his eyes filled with sorrow. "She's in a coma, Lisa."

Marcus caught Lisa as her legs gave way beneath

her. A rocker appeared behind him and he lowered Lisa's limp body into the chair.

"What happens next, Doctor?" Marcus asked.

Lisa heard the conversation. There was nothing they could do but wait. She already knew that. The medical team had done everything possible. It was up to God now. They could wait hours. They could wait days. They could wait forever.

Marcus talked Randal into allowing them to remain in the nursery with Sara for the rest of the night.

Lisa dozed on and off that night, her head settled back against the bars of the rocker on which she sat. And Marcus was in a rocker right beside her, holding her hand, dozing off only when she woke up.

She prayed for all she was worth, but as time slid slowly by with no change from the baby lying so still in her bed, Lisa stopped asking for anything at all. She looked at her baby, all trussed up with wires and tubes and laboring to breathe. Was it right to let her baby suffer so?

She saw Marcus stir, exchanged tired sad smiles with him as they silently changed guard, and settled back to try to get some sleep. She honestly didn't know which was worse. Her sleeping nightmares or her waking ones.

Marcus's soft murmuring woke Lisa sometime in the early hours of the morning. Disoriented and frightened, Lisa struggled to sit up, only to realize that she was already sitting up. And that her neck ached horribly. The shaft of pain she felt when she tried to straighten brought her back to full consciousness. *Sara.*

Her eyes flew open immediately, seeking reassurance that her baby was still alive. Sara's monitors were bleeping, but Lisa couldn't actually see her for the man who was leaning over her crib.

"YOU'VE GOT TO BE strong now, Sara," he said. "It's up to you. Everyone's pulling for you, ready to catch you, but you have to take the jump, Sara. Just take the jump."

The baby's eyes popped open.

Marcus's heart catapulted into his throat when he saw Sara stare straight at him. He was afraid to move, afraid those beautiful blue eyes were a mirage, a cruel twist of his exhausted mind.

Sara blinked.

He straightened, still watching the baby, holding her gaze with his own, as if he could somehow make her consciousness real by sheer will. She blinked again, and his heart started to pound in double time. The baby was really awake.

"Lisa!" He turned, intending to wake his wife, but the minute his eyes broke contact with Sara's, the baby started to cry, soft thin little wails.

Marcus turned back, frightened, thinking something was wrong. "What is it, little one?" he asked.

The baby stopped crying as soon as he spoke.

Freezing beside the crib, Marcus was aware of Lisa behind him. He knew she was awake because he'd heard her sharp intake of breath when Sara had cried out. But he couldn't go to her, couldn't leave this tiny little girl.

He heard a nurse approach and he shook himself. He was being ridiculous. He had nothing to do with the baby's crying. It was mere coincidence that the child had woken up right when he'd started to speak to her, that she'd stopped crying when he'd turned back to her. Forcing himself to face reality, he backed slowly away from the funny little crib. Sara's eyes followed him until he was no longer in her sight.

And then she started to cry again.

Vaguely aware of the crowd gathering in the nursery, of his wife sitting and sobbing in her rocking chair behind him, Marcus approached the crib again. As soon as Sara saw him, her wails turned into pitying little hiccups. Instinctively, before he even realized what he was doing, Marcus reached down into the warming bed and slid his hands beneath the naked little body staring up at him so trustingly. Careful of the catheter in her foot, he lifted her up to his chest. Sara snuggled against him, obviously not the least bit daunted by his awkwardness.

And in that instant, Marcus suddenly understood what being a father was all about. Just like that, he had his answers.

He'd been such a fool.

He'd allowed his sterility to shake his confidence in himself to the point where he actually thought that if he didn't have what it took to make a child, then he didn't have what it took to care for one. But being a father wasn't about perfection or the ability to do everything. It wasn't even about biology. It was the willingness to struggle, to worry. It was the intense need to provide. To protect. The willingness to give up one's own life, if need be, for the little being dependent on him. Being a father was about loving. And somehow this tiny baby snuggling against him so trustingly had known how much he loved her even before he'd known it himself.

LISA SAT UNMOVING in her chair, tears streaming unchecked down her face as she waited for Marcus to turn around. She wanted to get up, to go to him, but she was trembling so much she wasn't sure she could stand. So she sat. And waited. For what seemed like hours, but was probably only a couple of minutes, while Marcus held his baby.

He turned around slowly and Lisa choked on a fresh wave of tears as she caught her first glimpse of her big strong husband holding their tiny daughter in his hands for the first time. Marcus's palms were resting one on top of the other, supporting Sara's body, but it was his eyes that told her they'd finally found their dream together. His eyes were glistening with tears—and awe.

He walked toward Lisa slowly, lifted the baby away from his chest, kissed her tiny head and slowly lowered her into Lisa's arms.

"I'm a father." His gaze met Lisa's briefly before going back to the baby in her arms. He reached out and ran one finger lightly down the baby's cheek, as if, now that he'd finally held her, he couldn't touch her enough. "I'm a father," he said again.

Too moved to speak, Lisa nodded, as cheers broke out around them.

Marcus watched his wife brush her lips across their baby's brow, and his heart was finally at peace. He'd given Lisa what she'd always wanted, after all. Her dream had not been to have a baby with her husband, but to share one with the man she loved.

And by some miracle, that man was him.

EPILOGUE

THREE-YEAR-OLD Sara Barbara Cartwright was not a
happy camper. She kept watching out the window like
Mommy had told her, but Daddy's car wasn't coming
like Mommy'd said it would. She stomped her foot,
trying to make someone notice she wasn't happy, but
the sound just went right into the carpet. Mommy
didn't even glance up.

Sara looked over her shoulder at Mommy and Aunt
Beth, kind of glad they hadn't heard her. She didn't
like being naughty. Mommy saw her and smiled and
took Sara's mad away.

"You keep watching, Sara baby. Daddy'll be home
in just a few minutes."

Sara turned back to the window.

She wondered what "few minutes" was. She'd
thought Daddy was coming *now*.

Aunt Beth had her hand on Mommy's tummy,
waiting to feel the new baby kick. Sara had gotten to
feel it first, so she didn't mind when other people
wanted to feel it, too. Especially Aunt Beth. Aunt
Beth was married to Grandpa. And she made babies.
She made her, Sara. She made her new sister, too.
Except she made her new sister bigger than Sara. She
was staying in Mommy's tummy longer.

Sara didn't remember being in Mommy's tummy, but she sure wished her new baby sister wouldn't stay in there so long. Mommy couldn't play on the floor so much now. And she slept a lot. One day Sara had even seen Daddy have to tie Mommy's shoe. She wasn't sure why having a baby in your tummy made you forget how to tie your shoes.

She wished the baby would just come out so she could play with her. It wouldn't be so hard to wait for Daddy to get home if she had somebody to play with. Sara stuck her thumb in her mouth, staring out the window. She didn't like "few minutes." It was making Daddy take too long.

Then she heard his car. She couldn't even see it yet, but Daddy drove a really loud car that sounded like the big truck on cartoons. Sara ran to the door.

She started to jump up and down when she heard his key in the lock. "Daddy!" she shouted, barreling toward his legs as soon as the door opened.

"Hi, pumpkin!" he said, swinging her up over his head, and then back down to straddle his stomach. "Did you have a good day?"

She played with the buttons on his shirt. She loved his buttons. They were all the same size. Not like Mommy's, which changed every time she wore different clothes. "I drawed and made cookies," she told him, hoping she wasn't leaving out something else good.

"Cookies? That's great! Did Hannah help you?"

She nodded. "Hannah buyed me gum," she told him, remembering the other good thing.

Daddy carried her into the living room where Mommy was with Aunt Beth. He kissed Mommy hello, and his voice got all soft and gooey like it always did when he talked to her. He said hi to Aunt Beth, too, and then carried Sara with him into the kitchen. They were going to have cookies.

Really, he was going to have some. Mommy wouldn't let her have any of her own because they would spoil her dinner, but Daddy would share his with her. Daddy's cookies didn't spoil dinners.

"You promise to eat all your dinner, pumpkin?" he asked her as he reached into the cookie jar.

"Yes, Daddy." She always had to finish every bite so she'd grow up big and strong.

Mommy came into the kitchen just as Daddy popped the last bite of cookie into his mouth. Sara giggled, trying hard to keep her own mouth shut so Mommy wouldn't see the cookie in it.

"What're you two doing out here?" Mommy asked.

"It's a father-daughter thing," Daddy said. Sara wasn't sure what that meant, but she was glad she had it with Daddy.

"You're the best daddy in the whole wide world," she said, hugging his neck.

Daddy squeezed her. "You've sure made me the happiest one, Sara."

Sara wasn't sure why Mommy got tears in her eyes when he said that, but she supposed it must just be from having a baby in her tummy.

Sara just wished it would hurry up and get borned.

Shotgun Baby

PROLOGUE

SOMEBODY'S WITH HIM. Con took another swallow of whiskey, trying to drown the memory of the sergeant's words.

They'd had to go in. They'd been out of time. As soon as Nick Ramirez heard about the bust he'd have vanished. And they'd have been back to square one. Again. The drugs would be on the streets and kids would be dying.

Somebody's with him.

He lit a cigarette and motioned for another drink. "Make it a double."

The bartender grunted.

Con paid for the drink, downed it quickly and slid his empty glass back across the scarred wood of the bar. "Again," he said.

Hell, he wasn't the one who'd screwed up. He wasn't the one who'd panicked, who'd arrested members of Ramirez's organization before Ramirez himself had been brought in. One thing Special Agent Connor Randolph did not do was panic. Ever.

Somebody's with him.

Con shook his head. The words wouldn't leave him alone. "Another one," he said, concentrating on his enunciation. "Better start a tab."

How could he have known? Hell, anyone in the same room as Ramirez had to smell as rank as he did. The slimy lawyer had been stinking up Phoenix for years. But they hadn't nailed him on drugs; check fraud was the charge they'd finally been able to hang on him. And they'd been damn lucky to do that. Ramirez filled his organization with his own kind, and they stuck together.

Somebody's with him.

Con tipped the whiskey glass to his mouth again. So somebody was with Ramirez. Two for the price of one, he'd thought. A deal.

A deal. The somebody with him was a woman. A young blond beauty. Wearing a blue dress. Con squeezed his eyes shut, but that didn't obliterate the images that tormented him. How much more alcohol was it going to take?

"May I sit down?"

Opening his eyes, he slowly turned toward the voice. Could it be her?

"May I?" she asked a second time.

He nodded and the woman took the stool beside his. It sure looked like her. The alcohol was finally working.

"How come you're all alone?" she asked.

He shrugged and glanced at her. At least she wasn't wearing blue. His cigarette had burned itself out in the ashtray and he lit a new one.

"I'm all alone, too," she said. "I don't like being alone. Do you?"

He shook his head. "Buy you a drink?"

Of course, he could understand why she'd changed her dress. Red splotches had messed up the blue one.

"Sure, if you want to. A glass of wine, please," she told the bartender. "Red."

That could have been what was spilled all over her pretty blue dress. Red wine. There was something drastically wrong with this theory, but he didn't have the energy to figure out what. Con sipped his drink, welcoming oblivion.

"You don't mind if I sit here, do you? I'm not bothering you or anything?"

Hell no, she wasn't bothering him. She'd just saved him from his demons. He shook his head again.

"It's just...I didn't want to be alone, but when I came in here, most of the men looked at me like I was good for only one thing, you know what I mean? But *you* didn't. You don't see me like that, do you?"

To tell the truth, Con couldn't see her clearly at all. The lighting in the bar wasn't that great to begin with, and things were getting blurrier by the minute. He gave her his standard answer, a shake of the head. It was just about all he could manage. It seemed to satisfy her.

"I guess you broke your nose sometime, huh? It's okay, though. I like the rugged look. How about you? What do you like?"

Con shrugged. He couldn't think of anything at the moment. He lit another cigarette.

"You sure are big, even for a man. I mean I can see you're in fantastic shape, but I don't know if I've ever sat beside such a big man. You're sitting down and all, but there's hardly room for your legs under the bar.''

Con nodded.

"I know I chatter a lot. Does it bother you? I can leave you alone if you want.''

"No!'' Anything but that. As long as he didn't question things too deeply, she was keeping the demons at bay. He needed her to stay right there beside him. "Don't go.'' And then, just to make certain, he added, "Please.''

"Sure. Don't worry. I'll stay. For as long as you like. I got no place to be. You got someplace to be?''

He didn't want to think about life outside the bar or even off the stool. "Nope.''

"So, whatcha wanna talk about?''

He shrugged, took a drag on his cigarette. Talking meant thinking, didn't it? He didn't want to talk.

"That's okay. I can do most of the talking if you want. It won't hurt my feelings if you just wanna sit there. I know what. You want me to tell you the story about how my dog—Estelle, that was her name—you want me to tell you how Estelle got into the movies?''

A dog in the movies. "Sure,'' he said. She wanted to tell him about a dog in the movies. Nobody had ever talked to him about dogs in movies.

Slouched silently beside her, he half listened to her ramblings, smoking his cigarettes and drinking his whiskey. As long as she kept talking he was going to be all right.

"I have a cat now. They're so much more inde-

pendent, know what I mean? How about you? You
got a cat?''

''Nope.'' No cat would want to live with him.

''You should get one. They're lots better than living alone.''

Con wasn't so sure. He liked living alone. Most of
the time. It was a helluva lot better than just making
do with someone or knowing that someone was just
making do with you. Alone meant there was no one
around to disappoint.

''You do live by yourself, don't you? I mean you
aren't wearing a ring or nothing, not that all men do
even these days, but if you were married or, like, had
someone, you wouldn't be sitting here all alone on a
Friday night, right?''

What? Con was having difficulty concentrating. He
nodded, because that seemed to be the response she
wanted, and raised his glass to his lips once more.

''Me, too, I been living alone for a whole week,
ever since that rat Joe threw me out,'' she said. ''And
all because I like to watch the soaps. Lotsa wives
watch the soaps, and even though we weren't married
yet, I was sure we would be, so keeping house and
watching the soaps was a real job even if Joe said it
wasn't.''

Something pricked at Con's conscience. ''What
about your son?'' he asked. His tongue felt like it had
doubled in size.

''My son? I don't have a son.''

He looked at her, but couldn't quite focus. ''You
sure?'' They'd said she had a fifteen-year-old kid.

"I'm sure. I don't have *any* children, even though I'm almost twenty-seven. I haven't even been married."

So they'd been wrong about her kid. He felt like crying with relief. And she hadn't been married, either. He drained his glass to celebrate.

"You mind if I have another drink?" the woman asked.

"Have whatever you want." He owed it to her.

"Really? Like, I can get a burger, too? You want something to eat?"

Con's stomach churned. There'd been a half-eaten burger on the desk that afternoon. "No." He just needed another drink.

She ordered her food and a carafe of wine. He was glad she planned to stay around a bit longer. Maybe after a while he'd get himself some food.

"I bet you have a job. An important one, too, just like Joe. He owns ice-cream shops and he wears a suit to work every day. You just get off work? That why you're still in your suit?"

He'd changed suits. The one he'd put on that morning had been soaked with blood.

"Don't get me wrong. I think it's great you're still wearing your suit. I like men in suits."

With painfully clear vision, Con saw a man in a suit. A dark-haired man wearing a light gray suit. A man who put a gun to an innocent woman's head and held it there, fully intending to blow her brains out if Con didn't get out of his way and let him go free—

"You okay, mister?"

"Huh?" Turning to look at the woman beside him, Con found his focus blessedly blurry again. "Fine."

"I didn't mean to turn you off by saying I liked you in your suit. I'm not after you or anything. At least, not unless you want me to be. But it can only be for tonight, anyway, because I've already got a date for tomorrow night. And he's a really nice guy. I met him standing in line at the bank. It was kind of funny, really. I've only ever been with Joe, and there I was cashing the check that Joe gave me when he kicked me out, and I meet someone else. Life's weird, huh? Anyway, I'll just move down a seat if you want."

"No! No. Stay." He gulped the last of his drink. *Please, God. Make her stay. Let her be okay for a while longer.* Let him pretend...

The woman in the blue dress had been in Nick Ramirez's office to do some redecorating. She'd had no connection to the lawyer's organization at all. She'd been clean, innocent. And her perfume had lingered in the air even after the gun had gone off when she'd tried to pull away from Ramirez.

"You sad about something, mister? You keep getting a funny look on your face."

Her concern pulled Con back from the abyss. She was sitting beside him. Healthy and alive. He'd never been more grateful for the presence of another human being in his life. "I'm fine," he said, because there was nothing else he could say.

She ran her fingers along the back of his hand. He was almost too numb to feel the light contact, but he saw the whiteness of her skin against his. There was a gentle quality to her touch, something Con had known little of in his life. The only person who'd ever shown him any gentleness at all, and only when she thought he wasn't looking, was Robbie, and he couldn't think about her right now. She was going to be pissed off that he hadn't called her. She always got first dibs on the story when he closed a case.

The woman patted his hand.

"You shouldn't do that," he felt compelled to tell her. "Might get dirty." But he didn't pull away.

"I'll wash my hands." She giggled.

Yeah. If you got dirty, you could wash. Maybe he just needed to wash.

Her burger arrived and she ate as if she hadn't had a meal in days. He was glad she was enjoying herself. He didn't have to feel so guilty for needing her to stay beside him.

"You want dessert?" he asked. Anything to prolong her visit, to keep the truth at bay.

"Sure, if you don't mind."

"Have whatever you want." It took all his concentration to form a coherent sentence. His head was swimming, his brain muddled. Another drink or two and he'd stumble next door where the pink neon motel sign was blinking, to the room he'd rented. Just as soon as he was sure the voice in his head wouldn't follow him there.

An hour passed. Then two.

"It's time to close up." Con didn't like the

bartender's tone of voice. It reminded him of another warning.

Somebody's with him.

The images assaulted him again. He shook his head and looked at the woman beside him. Her eyes were awash with fear. The look was too familiar, and he knew he had to make her fear go away. He had to get it right this time.

"Wha's wrong?" he asked her.

"I don't wanna go home. I've only been living alone for a week and I get scared at night."

He reached out an unsteady hand, intending to stroke her hair. His hand landed around her shoulder, instead. "You don' have to be scared."

"It's just that I never knew how thin the walls of a trailer are. I can hear every sound, every car that drives by, and I lie there all stiff until I'm sure it's passed. Joe won't let me in at home. But I don't wanna go back to the trailer he bought me, not when it's dark out."

Con took another look at the woman beside him. *A second chance.* He had to help her before it was too late.

"You can come with me if you want," he heard himself offer, although he had no idea what he'd do with her if she did. He could hardly entertain a woman when he was passed out on a motel bed.

"Can I? You really don't mind?"

The fear was fading from her eyes. He'd saved the day, after all. "Sure," he said, leaning on her just a little as he slid off his stool and threw several bills down from the wad in his money clip. He pulled the motel key from his pocket and stumbled out of the bar, then across the parking lot beside his guardian angel. The night air cooled his skin, lessening his stupor, allowing the dark images to fill his mind once again. It didn't hit him until they were inside the motel room and she flipped on the light. Something was very wrong. A reason this woman couldn't make anything better.

She wasn't the same blonde who was haunting him. She couldn't possibly be.

Somebody's with him.

"She died." His words cracked like a gunshot in the tiny room.

Coming out of the bathroom, a bar of soap in her hand, she said, "Who died?"

Pain exploded through Con's head. He sank down on the side of the bed, burying his head in his hands to try to still the pounding.

"Who died?" Her soft voice wafted across him, as feather light as her hand on the back of his neck.

"I tried to get to her, to stop him, but there was no time. She stumbled when she pulled away, and the gun went off."

She snatched her hand back. "You killed someone?"

"No!" He couldn't stand the accusation in her voice. It was too much like the echo in his head. "I'm the good guy." At least that was what he'd been in the beginning. He wasn't sure when all that changed, when getting his man became the most important thing.

"You're a cop?" Even through his alcohol-fuzzed mind he heard the hope in her voice.

"Yeah," he said. Sort of. He had a license to carry a gun.

"Well, it's okay, then." The soothing touch returned to his neck. "You were only doing your job."

And what exactly was that? To make the bust? To close the case? Or to protect the innocent? The hammers were pounding so fiercely in his head he couldn't be sure of anything.

Except that as the woman sat down beside him, as her fingers continued to caress him, the vision of blood soiling a pretty blue dress faded just a little.

"Here, let's get you out of this jacket, OK? And loosen your tie. There, that's better, isn't it? Now just lie down here and I'll rub your back. Joe used to love it when I rubbed his back."

Before he realized it, Con found himself stretched out on the bed, his angel of mercy sitting beside him working magic on his tortured muscles. When he was sober enough to think, he was going to make this up to her. Somehow he would find a way to thank her for saving him.

But when he awoke late the next morning, alone, naked and sick as a dog, the only thing to tell that she'd been there was an empty money clip, and his FBI badge lying open on the table beside it.

Holding the badge, looking toward the unmade bed, he hoped to God he hadn't done anything else to hate himself for. The last thing he remembered was a woman's cool hand running gently along his back, and him wanting to thank her for something. But he couldn't thank her. He didn't even know her name.

CHAPTER ONE

Fifteen months later

IT WAS DONE. And done right. He should care.

"Congratulations, Randolph."

Con nodded at FBI Special Agent Orlando and continued on his way out of the bowels of the Tyler building in downtown Phoenix. Orlando's job was just beginning; he had cleanup detail—documenting every shred of evidence so that when operation Dogtags came to trial the government could nail these bastards.

"You did it again, Randolph. Thanks." Maricopa County Sheriff Tom Whitcomb was standing just inside the front door of the building with a couple of his men, waiting for William Tyler to appear.

Con nodded again, shoved his hands into the pockets of his slacks and headed silently out into the blistering June heat. The sun felt good. He barely noticed the flashing lights of the police cruisers surrounding the area. After fifteen years with the FBI very little fazed him.

"I'll get you for this, Randolph!"

Con turned just in time to see William Tyler make a complete ass of himself as he was escorted out of the building that, until today, had been an institution, a monument to the Tyler dynasty in Phoenix. William Tyler, the epitome of the American dream, a classic case of a good man making good. He'd been a poor itinerant preacher who'd started with one small investment. And he'd donated his first million to the church. The sedately suited man was hollering loudly enough to be heard on the next block. "I'll hunt you down and cut your—"

Con turned his back. He'd really expected the man to go quietly with a measure of class. During the past several months of investigation, he'd found Tyler to be a crook, but a gentleman just the same.

Or maybe he'd just wanted to find something good in the ex-preacher. Something redeemable in one of the shady characters he dealt with day after day, year after year. What he'd found, instead, was a foul-mouthed villain.

Con lowered himself into his nondescript sedan, government-issue blue, and cursed as his knee hit the dash. Turning his key in the ignition and setting the air conditioner to high, he reached for his cell phone and the cigarettes on the console at the same time. He dialed first.

"Newsroom." Her voice was like a welcome blast of fresh air.

"OK, Robbie," he said, pulling a cigarette from his pack. "It's public now. It's Tyler."

"William Tyler? *He's* the investment broker you've been after?"

Con took a long satisfying drag on his cigarette. "He's on his way downtown now."

"This is good news."

"Uh-huh."

"So how come you sound so whipped? What's the matter with you, Randolph?"

Trust Robbie to jump right into his personal minefield. Nobody else would dare talk to him like that. Nobody else would get away with it. "It's just a job."

"It didn't used to be." Her voice was soft, unusually tender. "I'm worried about you."

Yeah. Lately he was getting a little worried himself. "Don't be. Now get your butt down here or you'll lose an exclusive."

"I'm on my way."

The phone was almost back in its holder when Con heard Robbie call his name.

"Yeah?"

"Take care, friend."

TWO HOURS LATER Robyn Blair was back at the TV station. She'd just spent the afternoon covering the arrest of one of Phoenix's pillars of society, a man who'd been charged with insider trading. Tyler had a beautiful wife of thirty-five years, three great kids, all college graduates, a couple of grandchildren and was an ordained minister. Go figure.

She was looking forward to a nice cold beer in a frosted mug. Hearing voices coming from the newsroom at the end of the hall, she prepared to join the guys for their Wednesday-night jaunt to Coyote's.

"Come on, let's get going. Robbie may not be back for hours," she heard Tom Richards, a staff writer for the six-o'clock news, say. "I think maybe she's gone back to police headquarters."

"I'm ready," Darrin Michaels boomed. He was one of Channel Four's star photographers. "Going without Robbie might be nice for a change. At least I won't have Alysse harping at me when I get home. Why that woman has a problem with Robbie joining us for a beer I'll never know."

"You, too? I thought Joan was the only one who had a screw loose where Robbie's concerned."

Robbie stopped in her tracks as Rick Hastings, her producer, jumped into the conversation. Joan had a problem with Rick having drinks with her? She couldn't believe it! Hell, she'd baby-sat their kids just last weekend so Joan and Rick could go to the movies. Joan had said she didn't know what they'd do without her.

"Connie, too." That was Tom again. *Connie, too?* Robbie sagged back against the wall, her notebook hugged against her chest. She'd considered all three of those women her friends. How could they not have faith in her—or in their husbands? It was ludicrous.

"I don't get it. It's not like I'd be interested in Robbie even if I were free," Tom continued.

Robbie was glad to hear it.

"Me, either," Darrin seconded. "If you took her dancing, she'd probably want to lead."

"I wouldn't go that far, but Robbie is a bit too aggressive for my taste," said Rick.

Rick's words hit her harder, probably because he was right. But a woman in her profession *had* to be aggressive.

"It's not just that she has the tenacity of a pit bull," Tom added. "Can you guys honestly say you'd ever want to get into bed with a woman whose hair is as short as yours and who wouldn't know what to do with a tube of makeup if she had one? I'll bet she even wears boxer shorts for underwear."

The other guys laughed.

Robbie had never been overly fond of Tom Richards, and she was liking him less and less. Short hair was easy to manage. And so what if she'd never understood why smearing goop on her face was supposed to be a good thing; at least, she'd been blessed with a complexion that didn't need any covering up. And she most certainly did not wear boxer shorts.

"And she'd insist on being on top all the time, too," Darrin added, causing another round of male laughter. Robbie stood frozen outside the door. She'd thought these guys were her pals! But she had to admit—in her one brief relationship, she *had* rather enjoyed being on top.

"Come on, guys, Robbie's all right," Rick said. "Besides, have you ever taken a look at her legs? They're the best pair I've seen since Christy Brinkley's. I can tell you, under different circumstances, I wouldn't mind having them wrapped around me."

"Yeah, but only if the package was different."

Robbie didn't know whether to slink away quietly

or to barge into the room and strangle Tom Richards with her aggressive hands.

"Oh, I don't know, her boobs aren't so bad, either," Darrin said. "Come to think of it, when you get past the way she acts and dresses, her body's worth taking a second look at."

"And a third."

Robbie gritted her teeth at the newly appreciative tone in Tom's voice.

"OK, guys, we better go have that drink before we get ourselves in too deep to pretend we never had this conversation," Rick said, suddenly serious. "Robbie is Robbie, aggression and all, and she's saved our butts more than once. Let's just hope she never learns how to shop for clothes, or our wives'd really start harping. And I don't know about you, but if I'm going to be nagged, I'd just as soon it be over someone who turned me on."

The men approached the door and Robbie slipped into the women's room across the hall. She'd never been so thankful to find the place empty in her life. It would have been the last straw to have had to explain the tears streaming down her cheeks.

As Con PULLED into his driveway that evening, he saw a woman at his front door. Which would have been fine with him if his professional eye hadn't already cataloged her in detail. This was not one of his occasional female acquaintances.

This woman had to be pushing sixty. Her posture was stiff and her clothing prim. With that manila folder clutched in her fingers, she looked just like his fourth-grade English teacher, old sourpuss McLaughlin. He had no idea who she was, and he wasn't in the mood to find out. It didn't appear, however, that he'd have much choice. She'd seen him pull into the driveway.

Opening his automatic garage door, Con drove inside and closed the door behind him. When he entered the kitchen, he dropped his keys on the ceramic-tiled counter, pulled a beer from the refrigerator, uncapped it and took a swig. With his free hand he picked up the pack of cigarettes he'd left on the counter that morning. One long satisfying drag later he walked, beer in hand, to his front door and swung it open. "Yes?"

The woman's face took on an even more sour look as she appraised Con. "Are you Mr. Connor Randolph?"

"Who wants to know?" he asked, purposely allowing his cigarette to hang out of the corner of his mouth. He'd had to put up with snobs like her throughout his adolescence, but he wasn't a kid anymore.

He leaned against the doorjamb, allowing himself the satisfaction of forcing her to take a step backward. He was always conscious of his intimidating stature and normally tried not to take unfair advantage of it unless he was working, but at the moment he didn't give a damn about fair.

"The state wants to know."

The state? He was the state.

Flicking the ashes of his cigarette outside the door, he took another long drag. What he really wanted was to finish his beer, strip off his clothes and dive into his backyard pool.

"You collecting money or signatures?" he asked, resigned to giving her either so she'd go away and leave him alone.

"Are you Connor Randolph?" she repeated.

Stepping back, he nodded.

"Then if I could just get your signatures here, I'll be on my way." She pulled some forms from her folder and thrust them at his chest.

Con stubbed his cigarette in the hallway ashtray and reached into his suit jacket for his pen. "What is it this time—higher taxes or better neighborhoods?" he asked, barely glancing at the papers. If she wanted something from him, she sure wasn't going about it the right way. But then, it was probably hard to get people to go door-to-door collecting signatures anymore.

"It's your son, Mr. Randolph." She practically spit the words.

He froze, his pen poised above the papers. "What did you say?"

"Your son. We've found a family who wants to adopt your son. A fine proper family. The only thing holding us up now is your signature. So if you could just sign these preliminary forms, we can get the formal proceedings under way. Of course, the state will also be petitioning you for child support for the three months he's been with us."

Con lowered his pen. "I don't have a son."

She didn't bat an eye. "My name is Sandra Muldoon, Mr. Randolph. I work for social services. And according to our records, you do have a son. Now if you could just sign there on the line marked with a star—"

Con's back was suddenly as stiff as hers. "I don't have a son."

"I realize you refused responsibility for the child, Mr. Randolph, but that doesn't negate his existence. However, we're prepared to sever all connections just as you wish. You need only to sign the forms."

She had the wrong man. Con had no interest in having a child, in fact had decided quite unequivocally that he would never bring a child into such an ugly world. But neither would he refuse responsibility for one he'd created. Not ever. This woman had the wrong man.

"Who's the mother?" he asked.

"Cecily Barnhardt," she said, as if he already knew full well who the mother was and was wasting her time.

It was all the confirmation Con needed. "I've never heard of her."

The woman's mouth fell open. "Never heard of her? Well—" the scorn was back in her voice "—I must say you might at least try to learn the names of the women you, uh, consort with in the future, Mr. Randolph, especially if you aren't going to consort responsibly. Now, if you'll just sign these forms..."

Con turned to the hall table and set down the beer

he'd been holding. Hard. It foamed up and over the mouth of the bottle. "I've never 'consorted,' nor had sex, with a Cecily Barnhardt," he said, enunciating very clearly, though softly, as he reached to close the door in the woman's face.

"She says you did. And we have proof."

He pulled the door back open and glared.

"It's all right here." She shook the manila folder in front of his face. "The baby was conceived at the Pink Lagoon Motel the night of March sixteenth last year. In room 173—a room registered to you. He was born at Phoenix Baptist Hospital on December twentieth and abandoned at the same hospital three months later with his birth certificate and a letter from his mother begging that someone give him a good home. You, sir, are the father named on the birth certificate."

Con felt the blood drain from his face. Anyone could be named on a birth certificate. He knew that.

But he had been at the Pink Lagoon. He'd never forget that seedy motel. Or, no matter how hard he tried, that date. Just as he'd never remember what did or did not happen after he'd reached his motel room the night he'd deliberately drunk himself into a stupor.

"Now, if you will just sign these papers..." The woman said again.

"No." Nausea roiled inside of him.

"Excuse me?"

"No." He couldn't be much clearer than that.

"But you said you didn't want to have anything to do with the child."

"I said nothing of the kind."

"It's all here, Mr. Randolph. We found Cecily and she told us how she couldn't care for the child herself and that the baby's father had refused to help her. She signed him over to the state."

Con stood to his full six-foot-five height. "Let's understand one thing. I would never have turned my back on a child of mine if I'd had any idea that it existed. If, as you say, this child is mine, *I* will take him. *I* will raise him," he insisted—though he had no idea how he could possibly do such a thing. He knew only that he couldn't *not* do it.

"But you can't!"

Her reaction didn't surprise him. He'd been getting it all his life.

"Can't I?"

Her gaze raked him, stopping for pointed moments on beer splattered on the hall table. "Well, look at you. You can't possibly care for a baby."

He felt as if he were back in the seventh grade and his teacher was telling him he couldn't possibly expect to run for class president. He was, after all, nothing but a troublemaker, a loser.

"*Is* the child mine?" His steely gray eyes held her gaze.

"Y-yes. It would appear so. But—"

"Then *I* will care for him. Where is he?" Con looked behind her, almost as if he expected the child to appear.

"He's in a foster home in Gilbert, but—"

"Then let's go get him," he said.

"You can't just go get him!" Sandra Muldoon cried, shocked.

"Of course I can. He's mine."

"Th-there will have to be tests. We'll need proof. Besides, you can't really mean to raise him yourself."

"Why not?" The more she pushed him, the more desperate he became to rescue his son from the same system that had made his own childhood such a mockery.

"You aren't even married!"

"There's no law against that." Finally, something in the whole mess he was sure about.

"But you can't—" She broke off when Con's gaze turned steely again. "This is highly unexpected," she said.

"I want my son."

Putting the forms back into her folder, she clutched it to her chest. "Yes, well, there will be procedures."

"Such as?" Procedures. Something he was used to.

"Blood tests, for one."

"But you said he's my son. You're not sure?"

"One can never be certain about these things."

"You were certain enough when you wanted my signature to give him away. And certain enough to take my money for his back support."

"There will have to be blood tests, Mr. Randolph. We can't just hand over an innocent baby—"

"Not even to his father?" The words made him quiver inside.

"He's a ward of the state now," she said, as if that changed the child's parentage.

"So I'll get a blood test. Where can I pick him up?"

"I'm telling you, Mr. Randolph, you can't just go get him. We'll have to send someone from social services over first."

"Why?"

Her eyes grew wide. "To see if you're a fit father of course!"

"And you do this every time people give birth?"

"No," she said impatiently. "But you chose not to be present when Cecily gave birth."

"I wasn't informed she was pregnant."

Mrs. Muldoon didn't look like she believed him. "You also chose not to support him when she came to you asking for help."

"She never came."

"She says she did," the social worker snipped, still clutching her folder. "And which of you is telling the truth is something for the courts to decide. In the meantime, if you're serious about this, you'll need to call this number to set up an appointment with social services." She handed him a business card and turned haughtily, her back ramrod straight as she headed out to her car, parked at the curb.

"Wait a minute," Con called. But he wasn't sure what he wanted to say when she turned back to him, her eyebrows raised in irritation.

"He's normal, isn't he?" he asked, suddenly

scared to death that there might be something wrong with his son, something he couldn't fix.

"Does it make a difference to your wanting him?" Her voice was like an icicle dripping down his spine.

Of course she'd believe the worst of him. "No."

"He's perfectly normal, Mr. Randolph. And happy, too, for that matter. He's been well cared for. And will continue to be well cared for if he's adopted. I suggest you think long and hard before you decide to change the course of his young life. Even if you succeed in this foolishness, what could you possibly give him that would make up for his losing his rightful place in the bosom of a loving family?"

Con never moved a muscle as she delivered her last verbal slap, then strode to her car, climbed in and sped away.

Long minutes later he shut his front door, went into the living room and fell onto the couch.

He had a son. *My God, he had a son.*

CHAPTER TWO

HE WAS STILL HALF LYING there, holding the telephone receiver in his hand and staring off into space when Robbie burst through his front door an hour later.

"Hey, what's with the beer here?" she called by way of greeting.

When she didn't get an answer, she picked up the bottle from the front-hall table, took a swig and choked. "Yuck! How long's that been sitting there? I can't get a cold beer tonight to save my soul."

It was then that she looked into the living room and noticed Con on the couch. His face was ashen, his gaze vacant. "Hey, what's wrong?" she asked, her heart pounding in fright as she came in. "What happened?"

"I have a son." He didn't even look at her.

She stopped in her tracks, feeling the shock of his words all the way to her toes. She must have heard him wrong.

"You have a son," she repeated. This was some kind of cruel joke, just like the conversation she'd overheard at the station. It had to be.

"Yeah." His vacant gaze slid over her as he finally

hung up the phone. "*I* have a son. Kinda hard to get used to, huh?"

She stared at him, seeing the truth in his shell-shocked eyes. She'd always told herself this day would come. When she'd be faced with the final evidence of Con's love for a woman who wasn't her. But she'd expected to have survived the pain of his marriage first.

"Who's his mother?"

She prayed that Con wouldn't notice the jealousy in her voice. He'd never had any idea how she felt about him. And she intended to keep it that way.

He shrugged. "Cecily something or other."

"You don't *know?*" Con's flings were always premeditated. He was never careless, would never allow the possibility of repercussions.

"It was that night at the Pink Lagoon." He said the words so softly she barely caught them. And suddenly she understood.

"I thought you said nothing happened." She stood in the middle of the living room, her arms wrapped around herself.

"I hoped nothing had. I can't remember."

Her heart twisted inside out, her limbs as weak as her stomach had suddenly become. She was a tough woman. She could handle anything. So why was she falling apart at the seams?

And why, if he was going to make love and not remember it, couldn't it have been with her?

"So that makes him what, five, six months old?" she asked, still unable to convince herself the child was real. *She* was the one who craved parenthood, not Con.

"Six months tomorrow, the twentieth. He was born December twentieth."

She sank onto the opposite end of the couch before her legs gave out on her. Con even knew the birthdate.

"So, are you going to see his mother?" She detested the woman, everything about her.

Con glanced at Robbie. "I don't know."

She couldn't hold his gaze, couldn't trust herself to hide the tumult of emotions raging inside her. She loved him. She hurt for him—and for his child. She hurt for herself. Her worst nightmare had always been losing Con.

"Don't you think you should?" She could barely get the words past her lips.

"I didn't even know her name until an hour ago. Besides, she doesn't have the kid."

"Then who does?"

"He's in a foster home at the moment."

Oh, God. Her heart filled with the same hopeless desperation she'd felt as a teenager trying to understand the unfairness in Con's life. She knew there were some wonderful foster homes, some children who lived better lives because of loving foster parents, but Con only knew what could go *wrong* with the system. He'd grown up in a foster home. Right next door to her. He'd lived with people who called him their son but never adopted him because of the support they would lose from the state for his care.

And they'd never let him forget that he should be grateful to them for taking him, someone else's bastard, either.

He'd always hated his biological parents for subjecting him to that, for not standing by him, and had always sworn he'd never do the same to any kid of his.

Just one more reason to hate himself.

"What's his name?" she asked.

Con looked at her blankly for a moment. "I don't know," he finally said.

She ached to hold him.

"I didn't even think to ask," he added, as if he was lower than dirt.

"So you'll ask."

Con has a son. A baby. It was suddenly frighteningly real. And maybe even a bit exciting.

"How soon can you see him?" *And can I go with you?*

He shrugged. "It's not that simple." Reaching into his jacket pocket, he pulled out an empty cigarette pack, tossed it, then grabbed a new pack from the end table. He opened it, shook out a cigarette and lit it.

Robbie waited.

"He's a ward of the state," he finally said. "I have to go through social services."

"Even to see him?"

He took a long drag on the cigarette. "Apparently."

Even back when she'd first met Con, he'd been a boy of few words, having already learned not to trust his thoughts and feelings to those around him. But if she'd done nothing else in the twenty-five years since, she'd proved to him that she was the one person in the world he could count on.

She took his cigarette from his fingers and had a puff, then put it out. She was trying to get him to quit.

"Talk to me, Randolph," she said.

He lit another cigarette. "Want a beer?" He was off the couch and heading for the kitchen, taking his pack of cigarettes with him.

What she wanted was for him to stop shutting her out. "Sure." She followed him to the kitchen and sat on a stool at the ceramic-tiled breakfast bar.

Con grabbed two beers from the refrigerator and joined her, dropping his cigarette in the ashtray on the bar. Robbie picked it up, took another puff and put it out.

"I want my son." The words were raw, shattering the silence.

She resisted the urge to reach for his hand and hold it, a form of comfort she knew he wouldn't accept. "Of course you do," she said, raising her bottle and taking a swallow of the cold brew.

He lit another cigarette. "I want to raise him," he said, his look challenging.

"OK." If he'd hoped to shock her, he'd failed. That he'd want to be a father to his child didn't surprise her in the least.

"I'm not father material." The stark words hung between them.

"Baloney." She eyed his cigarette, but took a sip of her beer, instead.

"That social worker, Mrs. Muldoon, couldn't have made her horror at the thought of my raising the child plainer," he said, his voice low. "When she arrived I had a cigarette hanging out of my mouth, a beer in my hand, and I'd just come away from a man who was threatening to cut off my balls."

Robbie smiled. "You don't need 'em, Randolph, you already made the kid."

Con didn't return her smile. He took another swallow of beer, then proceeded to scrape off the label with his thumb. "I should've answered the door before getting the beer."

"Lots of fathers have an occasional beer. Ever since you've been old enough to drink, you've been drunk a total of one time. I hardly think anybody can condemn you for that."

He shrugged.

"And besides, since when do they do a character check before allowing a man to see his son?"

"Since the state only wants a man to give the kid away."

"They what? To whom?"

Con shrugged again. "There's a family…"

"Why would they look for a family to take him without consulting his father first?"

"They're under the impression I already knew about the child and refused support." He pushed the beer-label scraps into a neat pile.

"Why would they think that?"

"Cecily said so."

None of this was making any sense. Getting answers out of Con was difficult at the best of times. When his emotions were involved, it was damn near impossible.

"Why would Cecily say a thing like that?" she asked. "And come to think of it, why didn't she tell you about the baby?"

Abandoning the scraps, Con took another drag on his cigarette. "I've been asking myself the same thing. She knew I was with the bureau. It wouldn't have been hard to find me. Maybe she didn't want to keep the baby, and my support would have given her less excuse to give him up," he said, the look in his eyes empty.

"Or maybe she was afraid to tell you."

Robbie could understand someone's being afraid of him. His size alone was pretty intimidating. And this Cecily couldn't have known him very well, couldn't have known about the tender vulnerable man beneath the rock-hard protective shell.

"So what's going to happen?" she asked, wondering about the baby, Con's son. The closest thing she was probably ever going to have to a child of her own—her best friend's son.

"I called social services and they're sending someone out tomorrow afternoon to ask questions and fill out some forms. Then I can meet him."

"And then what?"

Con took another drag on his cigarette. "They'll run blood tests to make certain I'm really his father," he said, his gravelly voice subdued. "Then we go to court."

"Why court?" That didn't sound good. She took a sip of her beer.

"I have to petition for custody and there'll be a hearing. The judge decides whether or not I'm fit to be a parent."

He stared at the glowing tip of his cigarette as if it held some sort of wisdom. Clearly, were he the judge presiding over the case, he'd lose.

Robbie hated it that Con saw so little worth in himself, but then, with the lessons life had taught him growing up, she couldn't blame him. Still, he was a good man with a loving heart if he'd only learn to trust himself enough to believe that.

"I don't know anybody else more fit to be a parent," she said, as sure of that as she was that the sun was going to shine in Phoenix the next day.

"I've never held a baby." There was no emotion in his voice, none apparent in his face. He was all agent, just stating the facts.

"What about Pete and Marie Mitchell's son, Scotty?"

"Marie laid him on my lap once when he was asleep. And she was right there beside me the entire five seconds."

Robbie wasn't about to give up. "So you'll learn how to hold a baby. We can run out to a store and buy a doll that's the right size to practice on. We'll get one that comes with diapers and learn that, too, while we're at it."

She finished her beer and grabbed Con's cigarette for one last puff. She put it out. "Come on, let's go now before they close." All at once she couldn't wait to get started, to make certain they were prepared. He wasn't going to lose his son, certainly not to the same institution that had failed him so miserably.

He didn't budge. "Most of what it takes to be a parent can't be practiced on a doll."

The hollow look in his eyes almost made Robbie forget twenty years of hiding her love for this man. But now, more than ever, he needed her friendship—something that would be lost forever if he knew her real feelings. She was his anchor. Always had been. And that was far more important than any physical love she might crave.

She looked at him now, resisting the urge to run her fingers through his hair. Buddies didn't touch each other that way. "You're a good man, Con Randolph. You know what's important, what matters in life. And that's all it takes to be a good parent. The rest you learn as you go."

"What matters, Robbie?" He frowned. "I don't have any idea what matters. Not anymore."

She wasn't buying it. "Yes, you do, Con. You just stopped listening to your heart. But it's still in there." She tapped his chest. "And maybe this baby is just what's needed to get you listening again."

He lit another cigarette. "I smoke like a chimney."

"So quit."

"My job's dangerous."

"So's driving a car, breathing the smog, having me for a friend." She grinned at him.

Life was dangerous. He knew that more than most. But he was also doing something to try to make the world a safer place. Who better to be trusted with the life of a youngster than one trained to protect?

He looked over at her, his glance unusually personal. "Having you for a friend has never been dangerous, Robbie. It's the one thing I've done right."

Tears sprang to her eyes and she couldn't hold his gaze. She reached for his cigarette, took a puff and then started to grind it out in the ashtray.

"Hey, don't!" Con said, grabbing the cigarette from her.

"You're trying to quit, too, remember?" she said as she tried to snatch it back.

"Right." With one last puff he put out the cigarette. "Let's go to the store."

Robbie wasn't about to give him a chance to change his mind. She pulled her keys from the pocket of her pants. "We can take my truck," she said.

He immediately grabbed the keys. "I'll drive."

And for once Robbie let him. Her mind was elsewhere.

A baby. Con's flesh and blood. A child I didn't even know existed an hour ago, and yet I feel like I already know him. I'll be an auntie. I can take him to the newsroom, maybe even on a job or two when he gets older. We can take him to the zoo, teach him to swim....

"Hey, Robbie, you doing anything tomorrow af-

ternoon?'' Con asked as he locked his front door behind them.

She was pretty certain she had an interview with
the governor. ''Nope.''

''You wanna be here when the social worker
comes?''

''Sure.'' She wanted it more than anything else
she'd ever wanted, except maybe for Con to love her
the way she loved him.

They climbed into her truck. ''I want you to meet
him, Robbie.''

Already half in love with this child she'd never met
simply because he was Con's, Robbie's heavy heart
lightened just a little. ''Good.'' *A baby. We're gonna
have a baby....*

ROBBIE PULLED UP in front of Con's house the next
afternoon with a stomach full of butterflies. She'd
wanted a baby of her own to love ever since she could
remember, and now at thirty-three, with no one even
calling her for a date, playing auntie to Con's son was
probably as close as she was ever going to get.

Climbing out of her truck, she smoothed her hands
down her favorite cotton top, making sure it was still
tucked into the matching cotton shorts she'd hardly
ever worn. She could do this.

Con was in the kitchen when she let herself in,
leaning over the breakfast bar. She'd left him in the
exact same position the evening before.

''You been at that all night?'' she teased, trying to
see around him to the plastic toy on the counter.

"Lay off, Robbie. I just want to be ready in case the woman from social services puts me to the test."

Robbie came around the bar and climbed onto a stool so she could judge his progress. "She's not bringing the baby with her."

"It doesn't hurt to be prepared."

He held the tiny plastic feet between his thumb and forefinger, raising the doll just enough to slide the diaper beneath its bottom. She was impressed. The night before he'd stood the baby on its head trying the exact same maneuver.

"If only Pete Mitchell could see you now," she said, grinning.

"Shut up, Robbie."

Con looked so right, tending to the make-believe baby. This huge rugged man diapering a child's toy.

As soon as he'd finished, she took the doll, inspecting his work, holding on to her composure by a thread. "You've improved."

He grabbed the doll back by the hair on its head, ripping off the diaper and starting the process again, concentrated intent in every move.

Robbie grinned. "We'll have to work on the rest of your handling there, Randolph," she said just as the doorbell rang.

Her heart leaped. Were they ready?

Con shoved the doll in the oven.

It was only as they were walking together to the front door that Robbie noticed the absence of a cigarette in Con's vicinity. There were no ashtrays around, either.

SOCIAL SERVICES HAD SENT Sandra Muldoon again. Par for the course, Con thought, that the state had seen fit to send the same uptight woman to his door after he'd spent half the night hoping for a more amenable sort.

"So you see, Mr. Randolph," she was saying, "you're asking the impossible if you hope to convince the court that the child would be better off with a man in your position than with a normal loving family."

Con's blood burned at the woman's words, even as his doubts grew. By what right *did* he think he deserved to disrupt the child's life? Especially when he knew he couldn't hope to provide for him the way a married couple could. He needed a cigarette.

"I would think the state would have its work cut out trying to convince the court why a son should *not* be with his biological father," Robbie jumped in. "Especially when that father is not only law-abiding, but law-enforcing. A man who's given his life to making the world a safer place for his son to grow up. And one who, I might add, is financially more than capable to provide for a child," Robbie finished, glaring at the woman.

As much as he appreciated her spirited defense, Con hated being talked about as if he wasn't there. And he preferred to fight his own battles.

"I'm sure we all recognize the importance of Mr. Randolph's job," Sandra Muldoon said. "But that doesn't take away the threat of danger his job poses to the child. And a child needs far more than financial support.'' Her tone continued to be as prudish as it had been the day before.

"You're talking about love, ma'am,'' Robbie said, leaning closer to the woman, ''and how can you possibly measure the love a father has for his son?''

"What's his name?'' Con blurted out. He didn't do love. And he still needed a cigarette.

"His mother called him Joey.'' The woman's lips pursed disapprovingly. "His adoptive family will probably rename him when he goes to live with them.''

"Rename him?'' Con was taken aback. "We're talking about my son here, not a possession. You don't rename people.''

"Nonetheless an adoptive family has the right to change the child's name. In the case of babies, most do.''

"I like 'Joey,''' Con said.

She ignored that. "I've set up an appointment for the baby to have a blood test tomorrow morning. I suggest you do the same for yourself.''

"Fine.''

She slipped her papers back into the folder. "That's it, then.''

"When can I see him?''

"You must understand, Mr. Randolph, things don't look very promising for you. The boy's mother swears you abandoned him. If she hadn't put your name on his birth certificate, we wouldn't have contacted you at all. You're a bachelor, and I gather, from what you and Ms. Blair have told me, you're not dating anyone seriously. You don't even have a mother you can turn to. And your way of life is in no way conducive to raising a child. There doesn't seem to be much point in dragging this out any further. For anyone."

Con's jaw tightened as he struggled for control. "When can I see him?" he repeated, enunciating each word.

The woman stood, her ever-present manila folder clutched to her chest. "I would at least suggest waiting until after the blood work comes back. There's no point in upsetting the child's schedule until we know for sure."

Robbie stood, too, ready to do battle. Con read the determination in her eyes.

"It's okay, Robbie," he said, moving to stand beside her. "I disagree," he told the social worker. "There's every point. Since the United States government trusts me with their highest security clearance, I think your court can find me worthy of a visit to my son."

"But—"

"You've questioned me, seen my home. Now I want to meet my son."

"Very well." Sandra Muldoon's face puckered with displeasure. "I'll check with his foster mother and see when a visit can be arranged."

"What about right now?" Robbie asked. "We have the rest of the day free, and most babies are up from their naps by late afternoon. Wouldn't this be as good a time as any?"

The social worker frowned. "I don't know what the foster mother's plans are for the day, and we have no right to disrupt her schedule."

Con didn't see it that way. As the boy's father, he had every right. He had a son to meet.

"I was under the impression that arrangements would already have been made, that this initial interview is only a formality preceding the visit."

"In normal cases, yes…"

"So it wouldn't hurt to call her and ask, would it?" Robbie piped up.

"Well, I…"

Robbie grabbed the telephone from the coffee table. "Here, you can use Con's phone and see if she'd mind just a short visit."

"He can't go to her house. For the baby's safety the foster identity is confidential."

"I solve crimes. I don't commit them." Con kept his rising temper in check, a result of years of training. It was a responsibility that came with being a man his size.

"Then you can bring the baby here, or we'll meet you somewhere else," Robbie said hurriedly, glancing at Con. "That won't be a problem. Con just wants to see his son, Mrs. Muldoon. Surely you can understand that."

"All right. I'll call, but I still don't think we'll be able to do it today."

The woman dialed, hanging up the phone almost immediately. "The line's busy. I'll try again tomorrow." She began to leave.

Con wasn't going to get this close and give up. He wanted, needed to see the boy.

"Why not wait right here and try again in a few minutes?" he asked, stepping between the woman and his front door.

Before she had a chance to reply, Robbie joined him. "Can I get you something to drink while you're waiting? Iced tea, maybe?"

"Just what exactly is your relationship with Mr. Randolph?" the social worker asked her, then looked from one to the other.

"Like Con told you, we're childhood friends," she said.

"Too bad," Mrs. Muldoon sniffed. "He'd at least have a chance of convincing the courts to take him seriously if he got married."

Robbie's gaze flew to Con's face, and he couldn't believe what her eyes were telling him. She'd been trying to bail him out since the first day they met, when she was eight and he was ten, but surely even Robbie wouldn't go as far as to tie herself to a loveless marriage just to help him out. As for him... marriage? To Robbie? There was no way. She was his best friend. His only friend.

He wasn't even aware that she'd moved away from him until he heard her speaking to Mrs. Muldoon.

"So can I get you that glass of tea?"

Marry Robbie? No way in hell.

CHAPTER THREE

IT WAS GOING to have to be the woman. He'd been watching Randolph's house for more than a month now, and the only person who'd come over was the woman with the short blond hair, and an old saleslady or something, who didn't count. He was kind of disappointed. It wouldn't work unless Randolph really cared about the woman, and the two of them didn't seem close like a guy and girl should be close. They hung out together a lot, but Randolph never touched her or even looked at her as if he *wanted* to touch her.

He would have liked it a lot better if Randolph was getting into her pants.

But she was going to have to do. He couldn't wait any longer. A plan was formulating in his head, occupying the space that was too filled with bitterness to let him sleep nights. Yeah. It was time.

THE SKY WAS A BLUE SO vivid it made your eyes water. Sunshine splashed on the rocks in Con's front yard, turning them into nuggets of gold. A day this perfect was meant for good things. Except that practically every day in Phoenix was this beautiful, and bad things happened all the time. And the June temperatures made those golden rocks hot enough to fry eggs.

Con was sitting in his car waiting for Robbie to get off her truck phone and join him. He was sweating like a pig. He probably could have gotten away with something a little less formal than a suit, but he always felt more in control in his standard agent attire. *They'll probably take one whiff of me and call the health department.*

He honked his horn impatiently, then cranked up the air-conditioning, turning the vents so they all faced him. He was tempted to go without Robbie. Except that he was strangely reluctant to leave her behind. After all, it wasn't every day a man met his kid for the first time.

He saw Robbie's head bob and her free hand gesture wildly in the air. She was getting pretty adamant about what she was saying. Con felt a little sorry for the poor bastard on the other end of the line, whoever he was, but only briefly. Why didn't the guy just hurry up and give in to her so they could go?

The Muldoon woman had tried for almost an hour the day before to reach Joey's foster mother, but to no avail. The woman either had the phone off the hook or spent way too much time gabbing to be caring for an infant. Con had extracted a promise from the social worker that she'd keep trying the woman periodically throughout the evening. And true to her word, Sandra Muldoon had called just as he and Robbie were starting in on the pizza they'd ordered to say that he could meet his son this morning.

He honked the horn again, twice this time for good measure. Robbie had parked her truck in its usual place in front of his house, and now she glared at him through the windshield, flashed him the finger and went right on talking.

Thrumming his fingers on the steering wheel, he glanced at his watch and thrummed some more. He'd told Robbie to be here at nine o'clock sharp. Technically she had five more minutes. And then he was leaving. With or without her.

He pulled a cigarette from the fresh pack on his console, lit it and took a long satisfying drag. He'd give her until the end of his cigarette, and then he was leaving. It was 110 degrees outside. His engine was going to overheat if he sat there much longer.

He took another puff, holding the smoke in his lungs until they felt as if they might burst, and then slowly exhaled. The neighborhood was quiet as usual. Rows of white stucco homes with tile roofs, expensively landscaped yards, mostly desert, though there were a few diehards who paid heavily for the water it took each week to keep a patch of green grass.

Con flicked the ashes off his cigarette and took another long drag.

A couple of yards down from him a kid was raking gravel. The boy had been around for a while now, doing odd jobs for anyone who'd pay him, and from what Con could see, he did a pretty good job. The kid had knocked on Con's door several weeks back, offering to trim his bushes; but working in his yard was something Con enjoyed, took pride in. Still, he was glad to see the kid had found some customers.

"Sorry. That was Rick," Robbie said, climbing into the car. "He wants me to have another shot at Cameron Blackwell." She was wearing a denim skirt with some pink top he'd never seen before. He hadn't even known she *owned* a skirt.

"When is Hastings going to figure out that Blackwell wants to be left alone?"

She buckled her seat belt and reached for Con's cigarette. "Not as long as Blackwell's living here. Can you just imagine what a coup it would be to get the nation's most talked-about recluse cartoonist to actually give an interview? We'd be picked up by all the wires."

"How you gonna get to him to even ask for an interview?" Con maneuvered his way out of his neighborhood and turned south on Hayden. It was a twenty-minute drive to the social-services office where his son would be waiting for him. Twenty minutes to keep his mind off the upcoming meeting. He wished Robbie hadn't finished the damn cigarette. He'd promised himself it would be his last until after he saw the kid.

She shrugged. "I haven't figured that out yet, but I'll come up with something."

"You've been after him for more than a year."

"So, I'll keep after him for another ten if that's what it takes. All I want to do is talk to the guy. He's got a lot of fans and has gotten mighty rich because of it. People want to know more about him."

"They paid for comics. They got comics. Can't they be satisfied with that?"

She reached for his cigarettes, helping herself to one. "Honestly, Con, aren't you the least bit curious about Blackwell?"

He might have been if he wasn't so sympathetic with the cartoonist's desire for privacy. "Nope. And why don't you buy yourself a pack of cigarettes, for God's sake, and leave mine the hell alone?"

She grinned at him. "I can't. I quit."

He grunted, applying the brake as the light up ahead turned yellow. He could wait for the red light. Now that he was finally on his way, he was in no hurry to get there. What if he made the kid cry? Or, God forbid, what if they handed the boy to him? Expected Con to hold him? He couldn't do that. Not in front of them. He'd just have to make sure Robbie was the one they handed him to.

"Did you get downtown for your blood test?" she asked, taking her time about enjoying his cigarette.

"Yeah." He'd been at the forensic lab at six o'clock that morning.

She was oddly quiet as he sailed through green lights at the next couple of intersections. At this rate he'd be there five minutes sooner than he needed to be. Where were red lights when he needed them? Or Robbie's chatter, for that matter?

She continued to puff on his cigarette. He was going to buy her a damn case of them for her birthday. Exhaling, she lifted the cigarette to his lips.

"I'm going to say something here," she began,

"and I don't want you to answer or argue. Just listen, OK?"

Con nodded, fortifying himself on nicotine.

She stared at the road in front of them, a frown on her face, and he braced himself. She was powering up for something, but if she thought he was going to move that damn water bed for her one more time, she could think again. He'd told her the last time that she'd better make up her mind once and for all whether or not she wanted to sleep beneath the window or across from it, because he wasn't tearing down the bed again.

"I just want you to know," she said at last, "that if it comes to it, if they really push you about being married, you can say we're engaged."

He almost dropped the cigarette.

"You hungry?" he asked. "I'm driving through for a burger."

"I mean it, Con."

"You hungry?"

She shook her head. "I ate breakfast before I left. So you'll tell them? If you have to?"

Con looked around for a burger joint. He needed something to sink his teeth into. And while he was at it, he kept his eye open for a bank robbery, a shoot-out, a gang war. Something he knew he could handle.

"Answer me, Con."

"You told me not to."

"Okay, I'm *un*telling you."

"You're crazy." There wasn't a burger joint on this part of Hayden, so why the hell was he looking?

"I knew you'd say that, which is why I told you not to say anything. It's not crazy, Con. According to old sourpuss Muldoon, it may be the only way you can get little Joey."

"He's my son. I'll get him."

"He's a ward of the state, Con. You know how sticky the rules get sometimes."

He wasn't going to think about those years. Not now. "Right. Like they'd believe an engagement without the wedding."

"I don't have a problem with a wedding."

Con swore. Why in hell had he wanted her to come with him? He knew she never shut up. "But you'd sure as hell have a problem with what comes afterward."

"I would not."

"You're crazy," he said again.

Her blue eyes flashed. "I'm perfectly sane, Connor Randolph. And obviously the only one of us here who is. There's a little boy waiting whose whole life could depend on your being married. I'm not involved with anyone. You don't date any women long enough to be involved. We get along OK most of the time. There's no reason we couldn't cohabitate."

"You're outta your mind."

"I'm tired, Con." The depressed tone in her voice grabbed him. Robbie never got depressed, she just got tougher. "I'm tired of putting up with crap from the guys. Tired of being the odd one out all the time. Tired of being alone. I'm thirty-three years old and there's still no knight in shining armor coming around to sweep me off my feet." She paused, took a deep breath. "I want to be a mother, Con. If I marry you, I get Joey, too."

He felt like he was coming unglued. He'd never heard her talk this way before. He had to shut her up. Fast. "You can mother the boy all you want, Robbie, but there's no chance in hell of our getting married."

"Why not, if it's the only way to get Joey?"

"It won't be."

"But what if it is?"

He refused to answer. He should definitely have done this without her.

"What are you afraid of?"

Her words were nothing but challenge. He knew that. And had it been anyone else but Robbie issuing them, he'd have let them go. "Nothing. I'm afraid of nothing." But he knew it wasn't true. He was scared that they weren't going to let him have his son.

"Then what's the problem? You got some hot broad I don't know about?"

He was silent. She knew he didn't.

He always told her about the women he dated, if for no other reason than to allow her common sense to keep him from finding himself making do, getting trapped in a loveless relationship. Because as far as he was concerned, that was the only kind there was.

"Once we're married, the courts would be out of it, Con," she said, talking like it was a done deal. "They wouldn't have any say in how we conduct the marriage. We could carry on just like we are except I'd give up my apartment and rent one of the empty rooms in that big house of yours. I'd probably help with the dishes a little more, and if you're nice, you might even be able to talk me into going to the grocery store for you."

"No," he said flatly. If she thought she was going to bulldoze her way through this one, she was wrong.

"I've thought about this all night, Con. It can work."

"*Enough.*" Marriage with Robbie? No way in hell.

They'd arrived. Con stubbed out his cigarette and pulled into a parking place by the entrance. He'd say one thing for Robbie. She'd certainly managed to distract him from the job at hand.

"Just remember," she said softly, walking beside him to the door of the social-services office. "They give you any flak, you tell them we're engaged."

As they entered the building, Con broke out in a cold sweat.

A BLUE-CARPETED HALLWAY lined with closed doors on either side stretched before them. Most of the doors had white-lettered plastic signs pasted on them, and Robbie strode forward, reading each one they approached. If she left it up to Con, they'd be back in the car. She'd seen the hunted look in his eyes the second he'd stepped into the building.

"Here it is," she said, finding the door marked *playroom*. Karen Smith, the social worker who'd volunteered to supervise this meeting, had thought it best to have Con see the baby in an impersonal atmosphere. So far, the social-services representatives were treating Con like a headache they knew would eventually disappear. If Robbie hadn't been so angry for Con's sake, she'd have felt sorry for them. They didn't have a clue who they were dealing with.

Con stood frozen beside her, so she reached for the doorknob.

"Wait." His jaw was tense, his body tight as if poised for battle. Her heart twisted. How many times had she stood by and watched Con fight for what should have been rightfully his? Fight—and lose. She wasn't going to let him lose this time.

"Putting if off isn't going to make it any easier, Randolph," she said.

Con nodded and opened the door himself.

She saw the baby almost immediately. His carrier seat was in the middle of a small table that was rimmed with an army of empty miniature wooden chairs.

"Ms. Blair? Mr. Randolph? I'm Karen Smith. It's nice to meet you."

Robbie was only vaguely aware of the tall young woman who came forward to shake Con's hand. She couldn't pull her gaze from the baby sleeping just a few feet in front of her. So small. So defenseless.

Con's son.

"Ms. Smith." Con's voice rumbled beside her, as terse as always. No pleasantries there.

She needed to run interference for him, to show some social graces before they blew this altogether, but still she stared at the child, feeling as if she'd been poleaxed. The baby was too precious for words.

She glanced over at Con, wondering if he felt the same strange attachment she felt to the little being, who was completely unconscious of their presence. Con was staring at the baby, too. She'd never seen him look scared before, but she suspected that was just what she was seeing in his tense wide-eyed expression now.

"May I hold him?" Robbie asked the social worker, afraid for Con, afraid for the baby he'd unknowingly given life to. Would either of these two Randolph males have the chance to give each other the love they both deserved?

"Of course." Karen stood aside as Robbie moved toward the sleeping infant.

She slid her hands beneath his little body and lifted him gently into her arms. His warmth, his weight as he settled against her, was immediately soothing.

Nothing had felt so right in her life.

"Oh, my God, Con, he looks like you!" she cried softly, studying the baby's perfect little features, his dimpled chin, his tiny baby nose. She wasn't ever going to be able to let him go. She looked at his father again and had to consciously restrain herself from going over and holding him, too.

Con remained just in front of the closed door, staring at the child in her arms, his eyes smoldering with emotion. He swallowed, once, with an effort.

"Come, Mr. Randolph. Meet Joey," Karen said, reaching for Con's elbow.

He moved away from her, instead, taking a seat in one of the armchairs in the waiting area of the playroom, his gaze never leaving the baby Robbie held. He'd wrapped himself in control.

Robbie could see the doubt in Karen's eyes as she watched Con, could almost hear the negative thoughts whirring through the social worker's mind. But Karen didn't know Con like Robbie did. She had no idea how fiercely Con felt those things that touched him, how difficult it was for him to deal with those feelings. She didn't know, as Robbie did, that Con would give up his life to protect this child he couldn't yet approach.

She walked over to Con, perched on the arm of his chair and willed him to stay put.

"Look at him, Con. He's got your chin."

Con looked. And swallowed again. His hands gripped the arms of the chair as if he was ready to push off. But he didn't. His gaze never left the baby.

Robbie picked up one limp little hand. "Look at his fingernails!" she exclaimed in hushed tones. "They're so tiny." She could hardly believe how perfect this small being was, or how fiercely she felt the need to protect him from whatever life had in store.

"He's got all ten fingers—" she looked down "—and toes."

Con nodded.

"He's perfectly healthy, though he does top the size charts," Karen said, coming over to join them. She sat in the chair across from them, leaning to rest her forearms on her knees. Robbie felt like a fly under a microscope beneath her watchful eye.

"When's his blood work due back?" Con asked abruptly.

"We should have the results sometime next week."

Con nodded again. "I'll have his room ready."

"Slow down there, Mr. Randolph. There's no guarantee you're going to get the child even if it turns out he's yours."

"He's mine." Robbie heard the anger in Con's voice, though she doubted the social worker did. Con had perfected the art of concealing his feelings by the time he was ten. Just as she'd learned to read what he kept hidden. Most of the time.

"It would really be best if you didn't keep telling yourself that. Not until we're certain," Karen said. "And like I said, even if he's yours, there's still no guarantee you'll get him."

Robbie knew Con wouldn't thank her for it, but she couldn't sit quietly by while Karen hurt him. "Joey's his," she said, looking from Con to the baby she held. "You can tell just by looking at them. Joey's got the same dimple in his chin that Con does."

The social worker looked from Con to the baby. "Maybe so, but it's important that you both understand. Being Joey's father in no way means Mr. Randolph will get the child. There are many other things to consider."

"Such as?"

Karen noticed the steel in Con's voice that time. She looked a little less sure of herself as she answered him. "There'll be a thorough background check on you, for one."

Con nodded, undaunted.

"You'll have to be able to prove an ability to support the child."

Con nodded again, holding Karen's gaze unwaveringly.

"And most importantly your lifestyle will be examined. The judge will want to be certain that the life you have to offer this child is the one best suited to him."

Robbie sensed Con's barely perceptible flinch. How she wished there was some way she could take away his pain. As hard as he'd tried, Con had never measured up, not in the eyes of his foster parents, not in the eyes of the school system and most especially, not in his own.

"And quite frankly, Mr. Randolph," Karen continued, garnering confidence again, "from what we've seen so far, I don't think you should count on getting the child. As far as the courts are concerned, you abandoned him. And we have a family, a two-parent family, already approved to adopt him."

"I did not abandon my son."

"So you say. That's for the court to determine." Karen paused. "And the fact still remains that you do not appear to have much to offer the child. Certainly not when compared to the childless couple whose whole lives will revolve around him."

"I'm his father. I offer him that."

"*If* indeed you are his father, you'd be a single

father at best. I'm sorry, Mr. Randolph. If you were at least married, maybe you'd have a better chance, but as things stand..."

Here it comes, Robbie thought, her chest tightening. She'd feared that it would. But could she really do it? Could she tie herself to Con knowing he'd never love her the way she loved him? Could she risk his finding out how she really felt?

"There's no law against single parenting." Con wasn't backing down. Robbie breathed a small sigh of relief. Maybe they wouldn't need her drastic solution.

"No," Karen said. "But statistics do show that a child has more opportunity to prosper in a two-parent home. And that's not the only issue here. You're an FBI agent, Mr. Randolph. Your job is incredibly dangerous. What becomes of Joey if anything happens to you?"

Con was silent and Robbie could tell Karen knew she'd scored. The woman's features relaxed as if her battle was won.

"But even danger aside, you work long hours, odd hours. You're gone for days at a time. Who'd watch your son then?"

"A sitter."

Robbie held Joey closer. The sleeping baby sighed and nestled contently against her breast.

"You're asking the judge to place the child with a sitter, rather than a complete family unit who'll love him, who'll be there for him?" Karen asked.

"He's my son."

Karen sat forward, clutching her hands together, her eyes worried again. Robbie realized that the woman truly cared about little Joey, about his future. "Please try to understand, Mr. Randolph," Karen said. "If indeed Joey is your son, you've got to want what's best for him. That's all the court wants, too."

"A boy needs his father."

"Yes, sir. But he needs a mother, too."

They were going to lose him. Robbie could see the writing on the wall as clearly as if it had been emblazoned there. Suddenly the baby stretched in her arms, opening his innocent blue eyes to frown up at her. *Who are you?* his gaze seemed to ask. But he didn't cry.

"He'll have a mother," Robbie said. There was no more time to think about it. She couldn't let Con lose his son. *She* couldn't lose this precious child.

"He will?" Karen said, glancing from her to Con. "I understood from Sandra Muldoon that you weren't currently involved, Mr. Randolph."

"I'm n—"

"He is with me," Robbie blurted, before Con blew things once and for all. He'd never be able to live with himself if the courts gave his son away. "Con asked me to marry him just this morning." Robbie couldn't believe she was saying the words even as she heard them come out of her mouth. Marriage to Con would be sheer torture, loving him as she did. But she just didn't see any other way. Without a wife, Con wasn't going to get Joey.

She was strong. She'd been loving Con for years

without anybody's being the wiser. She could handle this marriage. She was sure she could. Especially with compensation like Joey. She'd be a mother. And half a dream come true was better than none, wasn't it?

Yes, she was positive she could handle it.

Until she glanced over at Con. He was looking at her through the eyes of a stranger. A stranger she'd just committed herself to marry.

"Congratulations," Karen said, smiling for the first time since they'd entered the room.

Joey started to cry.

CHAPTER FOUR

No! CON KNEW he had to stop this craziness. Now.

But how? Karen Smith was right. He had nothing to offer the child. At least nothing of any merit—unless he married Robbie. She was the only good in his life. Always had been.

But he couldn't marry her. He couldn't even *think* about marrying her.

The baby was working himself up into a real squall. Robbie held him higher and started bouncing him.

"Here, let me have him," Karen said, coming over. "He's probably hungry."

Con looked at Robbie, saw the pleading in her eyes, and realized his entire life hinged on this moment. He had to come through—whether he thought he could or not.

"I'll take him," he said, staking his claim, his right to be the one to see to the boy's needs. He reminded himself over and over of the plastic toy he'd practiced on for all those hours. He could do this. He reached for his son.

A slow smile broke out across Robbie's face, and if he didn't know better, he'd think there was a hint of tears in her eyes as she handed the baby to him.

"You've got a ball player there, Randolph," she said, her words as tough as ever.

His kid was a little heavier than the plastic one; squirmy, too, but Con forced himself to concentrate on getting it right. He kept one hand under the baby's head, just like Robbie had shown him the other night, and used his other to support the body. The little boy's face was red and all scrunched up as he howled his displeasure.

"You got a bottle?" he asked Karen as if he'd been doing this all his life. But he was sweating. And shaking, too. His kid sure had a healthy set of lungs.

"His foster mother left one. I'll get it," Karen called, pulling a bottle from the diaper bag on the table beside the baby's carrier seat. "It's still warm." She handed the bottle to Con.

"What kind of formula is he on?" Robbie asked, raising her voice to be heard over the baby's crying.

Con took the bottle. Formula. Right. He remembered Marie Mitchell talking about that once.

"He's on soy milk," Karen said, taking her seat across from them. "He was pretty colicky there for a while, but the soy milk seems to have helped."

Con looked at the wailing baby in his arms. The kid's face was still all screwed up and red, but suddenly, out of nowhere, Con felt like grinning. He was doing it. He was holding his son.

"You might want to give him that bottle." Robbie said, leaning over to try to guide the nipple into Joey's tiny mouth.

"Wait for it to cool," Con said, jerking the bottle

back. Warm milk was disgusting. He wasn't going to force it on his kid.

The baby continued to cry, though he quieted for a moment when Con started to bounce him gently.

"It's supposed to be warm, Randolph," Robbie said, smiling. "He'll get stomach cramps if it's not warm. Now feed the poor thing."

She reached over again, guiding the bottle to the baby's mouth. Con just held on.

The baby latched on to the nipple, pulling it into his mouth with a strength that amazed Con, and the room was instantly silent except for the loud sounds of Joey's sucking. The kid had an appetite. Almost as if he'd stepped outside himself, Con saw what was happening. Saw and was filled with the strangest conglomeration of feelings.

He was feeding his son.

"WE CAN'T GET MARRIED." Con sat at his breakfast bar, smoking a cigarette, a cold beer on the counter in front of him. They'd been at it for more than an hour, ever since they'd returned from downtown.

"We're getting married, Con. Get over it." He'd given Robbie her own pack of cigarettes, but she was sharing his, anyway. What was it with the woman? Did she really think it made a difference to her lungs whose cigarettes she smoked?

"It'll never work."

"It has to work."

"Just because you think something is best doesn't make it so."

"It does if I refuse to believe anything else. Joey needs us, Con. Can you honestly sit there and tell me you're going to let him down?"

Here we go again. They'd been traveling in circles and Con was getting nowhere but dizzy. She was leaving him no choice—he had to be blunt.

"You're my only real friend, Rob."

"And you're mine." Her eyes went soft on him. He hated it when they did that.

"What better basis for a partnership?" she asked.

"And how long do think we'd stay friends?" he shot back.

Robbie shrugged, fiddling with her cigarette in the ashtray between them. "I guess that depends on us, doesn't it?" She looked up at him with her "I mean business" look.

Con sighed. He was in for a long day.

"We can do this, Con. It's because we're such good friends that it *will* work. We understand each other. We're going into this with our eyes open. Neither of us has false expectations."

Con didn't come up with an immediate counterargument, and that bothered him. He wasn't going to let her talk him into this. He couldn't marry her.

"This is a big house, friend," she said. "I think we can manage to share it without killing each other."

Sharing the house with her wasn't the problem. Marriage was. "For how long?"

She blinked. "I don't know. I hadn't thought about it. As long as it takes, I guess."

He pinned her with a relentless stare. "What? A year? Two, maybe?"

"Is that what you want?"

"I don't want. Period."

"If it would make you feel better, we can put a time limit on it, but I think it might work better if we just say we'll stay together until one of us isn't satisfied anymore."

Again Con didn't have an immediate counterargument, only a gut feeling that this was all wrong. They smoked silently for a couple of minutes. Both of them regrouping, he was afraid.

"Why?" he suddenly blurted, finding that he had to know.

"Why what?"

"Why are you doing this? You've always had dreams of your big white wedding, your knight in shining armor. Why ruin that by tying yourself to me?"

"My knight stood me up."

Her mouth smiled, but her eyes didn't. He wished he hadn't asked.

"He could be waiting on your doorstep tomorrow," he told her awkwardly, rusty in the platitude department.

She shook her head. "I'm not the type of woman a knight rescues, Con. He wants someone soft and feminine. Someone who needs rescuing, makes him feel like a man. Someone who wears makeup."

Con took a long swig of beer. He was getting in way over his head. "You don't want me, Robbie."

"I want to help you. I want to be Joey's mother."
She looked up at him. "And I want a wedding ring.
I want the guys at work—and their wives—off my
back. I want to be invited to parties again, parties that
you have to be part of a couple to attend. I want
someone around to help me move the TV when I'm
tired of where it is."

"You never said you were having troubles at
work."

"I'm not. Not really. You can't blame the guys,
Con. Their wives just don't like it that they hang out
with a woman all the time. A single woman."

He still couldn't marry her.

"What about sex?"

She blushed, looked away. She didn't say a word.
Con had never seen Robbie speechless. He might
have enjoyed the moment if he wasn't hating it so
much.

"I'm a man, not a monk." He pushed his advantage.

"I know that." She still wasn't looking at him.

"We can't get married, Robbie."

She lit another cigarette, watching the tip of it
glow. "Could you be discreet?"

"What?"

"When you have your women, couldn't you be discreet? You know, make sure no one I knew ever
heard about it?"

"This is asinine." He was talking about his sex
life with Robbie. They'd talked about everything else

in their lives, but they never ever talked about sex. Now he knew why.

He took another swig of beer.

"Okay." She gave him an awkward grin, obviously finding the conversation as embarrassing as he did. "I'll be discreet, too."

Con almost choked on his beer. *She'd* be discreet? She was planning to sleep with other men while she was married to him?

And then another thought occurred to him. Robbie had sex? He felt pretty damn foolish, but he'd never seen her in that light. He hadn't pictured her as virginal, exactly, he just hadn't pictured her that way at all.

"So when you think we should do it?" she asked.

Do it? She wanted to have sex with him? Robbie and him?

"How about July third?" she continued. "That would give me two weeks to arrange enough of a wedding to convince Karen Smith we're legit. And I have that long weekend off over the Fourth so we could use those days to get me moved in before I have to be back at work."

The wedding. She was back to the damn wedding. Not sex. Which was just as well. He couldn't even think about Robbie and—

"What about your parents?" he asked, suddenly figuring out how he was going to talk her out of this craziness. They'd never in a million years convince her parents that he and Robbie had suddenly fallen in love.

"They'll be there of course. It would kill them if we got married without them."

"It would kill them to hear what you're suggesting."

Con could just imagine her father's reaction when he heard that Robbie wanted to marry him. Phoenix Police Captain Stan Blair knew what a messed-up kid Con had been, knew how little he really had to offer. Which was why Con had never given the man any reason to worry about him and his daughter. Con had always been welcome in their home, which meant more to Con than anyone would ever know, and he didn't want to lose that.

Robbie laughed at him. "Sometimes you're so obtuse, Randolph. Mom'll be ecstatic. She's always hoped we'd get married. And Dad'll just be glad to know we're finally getting on with it."

The nicotine must have gone to her head. "You're crazy, Rob. Lying won't work with me and you know it. You tell your dad you're marrying me and he'll be at my door with his gun pulled."

"He retired from the force last year, Con, you know that. He doesn't carry a gun anymore."

"They aren't going to like it, Robbie."

"You leave them up to me. Trust me. It'll be fine. Now is July third OK for you?"

Con had no idea whether July third was OK for him. He couldn't consider this. He just couldn't.

"They'd have to know the truth," he said.

"No! No one's going to know." She was sounding her bossiest. "In the first place, the truth *would* bother them, and in the second place, social services is going to be questioning everyone before they give Joey to us. We can't take any chances.''

God. The woman had an answer for everything. Every damn thing. Except one. He couldn't marry her.

''You going to let them take Joey, Con? You going to let them give him away?''

''No.'' That was the one thing he was absolutely sure of. The boy was his. He was going to raise him.

''Then clear your calendar for July third. And next time Karen Smith calls, invite her to the wedding.''

STAN AND SUSAN Blair lived in Sedona. They'd moved to the small Arizona artists' community shortly after Stan's retirement from the Phoenix police force. Robbie had missed having her parents close by at first, but she always enjoyed the two-hour drive to Sedona. Or she had until this time.

This Sunday, the barren desert land that stretched for miles and miles between Phoenix and Sedona failed to occupy her imagination. Instead of the pioneer gold miners and Indian families who'd once traipsed across the unforgiving land, all she could think about was the news she had for her parents. And the cigarette she wanted.

She was going to marry Con. Oh, he hadn't agreed yet. But he would. Because of Joey. Her parents would be delighted of course. She hadn't been lying when she'd assured Con of that. But only if they believed she and Con were in love. Which was why she was making this trip alone. Con would have insisted on coming along if he'd known what she was up to. He'd never have left her to face her parents alone, especially when he really expected the scene to be ugly.

But it was going to be hard enough to reveal her love for Con to her parents. She didn't want to do it in front of him. She wanted him as far away as humanly possible. Because while he'd see her act loving in the coming weeks for Joey's sake, he'd think it was only that—an act. But today, while she was convincing her parents, there would be no pretending.

She was actually going to marry Con. There were times in the past few days when she'd had to pull herself right down out of the clouds at the thought. Marriage to Con was what she'd wanted more than anything else since the first stages of puberty had hit her.

But not like this. Never like this. Yes, she would wear his ring. Have his name. Share his home. But not his bed. Instead, she'd be home alone in his house when he went to other women's beds. And she'd have to pretend that she didn't care what he'd done when he came home.

And she'd do it because she couldn't face the alternative. She couldn't offer herself to Con and have him turn her down. It wasn't his fault she wasn't attractive to men. She was too aggressive, too bossy. She didn't wear the right clothes, didn't laugh at the right things. She didn't giggle at all. And she liked being on top.

His friendship was one of the most important things in her life; he brought her more happiness than anyone else ever had. And she'd lose it all if she was ever stupid enough to ask him for something he couldn't give her, if she tried to give him something he didn't want.

If she'd had her choice, she'd rather never marry Con than marry him under these circumstances. She wasn't a complete fool. She knew she was letting herself in for a load of hurt. But what choice did she have? She couldn't let him lose Joey. *She* couldn't lose Joey. Sure, Con had said she could mother the baby without marrying him. But that might prove difficult when Joey belonged to another family.

Besides, as much as the marriage would hurt at times, it would help, too. Not only would she feel comfortable in the social circle at work, but she'd never again lie in bed at night, knowing that if she got sick, or heard a strange noise, there'd be no one around to call out to.

Life was good.

Her parents owned a condo that backed on the foothills of the breathtaking Red Rock Mountains. Pulling into the driveway, Robbie thought how lucky her parents were to have been able to retire in such a gorgeous area.

Little Joey would be lucky, too, coming here for visits during his growing-up years—

Robbie froze, her hand still on her keys as the ramifications of what she was doing really hit home. She was not only going to be Con's wife, she was going to be a mother. Excitement ran through her, giving her goose bumps. Only to be chased away by a surge of panic.

In a few short weeks, if all went well, she was going to have a child to raise. She'd often imagined herself as a mother, had woven wonderful dreams of how it would be. But this wasn't pretense or make-believe. She and Con were going to be *parents*. With another life to consider, to care for, every moment of every day.

And she was not only about to tell her parents she was going to be married, she'd be telling them they were going to be grandparents. She rested her forehead on the steering wheel as the enormity of what she'd set in motion finally sank in. Could she do it? Could she change so many lives simply because, to her, it seemed the only way?

"You OK, girl?"

Robbie jumped as her father opened the door of her truck and peered in, his weathered brow creased.

"Fine, Pop. Just getting up the guts to tell you something." She'd always been straight with her father, just as he'd always been with her.

"Best way is just to say it, girl," he said, leaning both hands on the edge of the door and continuing to watch her. "But it might be good to come on in out of the heat. Let your mother get you a glass of iced tea. Is this something she can hear, too?"

"Yep. And you're right. Let's go get it over with. What's Mom doing?"

"Sitting on the porch with her sewing. Making some fancy tablecloth or something."

He held the door for Robbie as she grabbed her fanny pack and climbed out of the truck.

"You're not sick or anything, are you?" he asked, taking a closer look.

She'd done what she could with her hair and put on her best tank top with a pair of khaki shorts, but she'd had a couple of sleepless nights. She knew she didn't look her best. "No, Pop. I'm not sick. Let's go find Mom."

She followed her father through the cool tiled house to the enclosed air-conditioned porch in back. Robbie had loved the room from the first. It had a great view, and now she looked out over the expanse of land, hoping to catch a glimpse of a coyote or roadrunner or even a family of quail. Anything to avoid her mother's knowing eyes for one last second.

Susan Blair jumped up, dropping her stitchery in a pile on the couch behind her. "Robbie, dear! You're early." She gave her daughter a kiss on the cheek and a hug before stepping back to examine her.

"You look tired, Robbie. You haven't been getting enough sleep, I bet. What's wrong?"

It never changed. Susan's self-appointed role in life was to look after her husband and only child, and while the attention had sometimes felt suffocating during her teenage years, Robbie adored her mother. She adored both her parents. Always had. Maybe because she'd always had Con's to compare them to.

"Mom. Pop, come sit down."

They sat. Her mother beside her on the couch, her father in his recliner across from them. But he didn't recline. He sat forward, his elbows resting on the arms of the chair.

"What is it, girl?" he asked. They both looked at her, worry lining their faces.

"Con and I are getting married."

Shock held them immobile. They stared at her as if waiting for more. She didn't know what else to tell them.

The few seconds of silence that met her announcement seemed interminable. Robbie was sure they could see straight into her heart, that they knew Con didn't love her, couldn't possibly ever love her. How had she ever thought people, especially her parents, would actually believe this charade?

"Well, it's about damn time," Stan said finally as a slow grin spread across his sun-lined face.

"Married, Robbie? You're getting married? To Con?" Her mother's voice broke and suddenly she was laughing and crying at once, pulling Robbie into her arms. And then sitting back to search her daughter's face once again. "You love him, don't you, Robbie, love him with all your heart?"

"I do," Robbie said, feeling like crying herself as she finally admitted aloud what she'd known most of her life.

"When's the wedding?"

"Where's Con?"

"Where will it be?"

"Why isn't he here with you?"

Her parents clamored to know everything. Robbie laughed and answered them as best she could.

"The wedding's July third and Con's working today. But I didn't want to wait any longer to tell you…"

They continued talking about the wedding until lunchtime. Susan had a lot of suggestions, as Robbie had known she would, and she gladly turned over the many details to her mother's capable hands. With only two weeks to plan the wedding, the ceremony would have to be very basic, but with any luck it would be enough to convince social services.

She just wasn't sure Con would agree to the white wedding her mother was insisting on.

As they finished their enchilada feast Robbie said, "There's something else I need to tell you." She'd put it off as long as she could.

Both of her parents looked up expectantly.

"Con has a son."

"He has a what?"

"Who?"

"Con has a son," Robbie replied. "He's six months old and his name's Joey."

"Why didn't he tell us?" Susan asked, obviously hurt.

"He didn't know himself until a week ago." She wasn't sure how her parents were going to react to this part, but there was no way to hide the truth from them. They loved Con. They'd understand, just as she had. And take little Joey into their hearts.

"Remember that case of his I told you about a year ago last March?"

"The one where the woman was killed," Stan said, nodding.

Robbie proceeded to tell them, in a little less detail than she'd heard it, about the circumstances leading up to Joey's conception and subsequent appearance in Con's life.

"The poor little dear," Susan said when at last Robbie fell silent. "Have you met his foster mother? Is she taking good care of him?"

"We haven't met her, no. But I think she's looking after him just fine. He was clean, well fed…"

They all knew that Joey was probably getting the finest of care, but still, it couldn't be enough. Not nearly enough.

"I can't imagine Con took it well, having the child in foster care," Stan said.

Robbie thought of the stupor she'd found Con in last week—one that had nothing to do with alcohol.

"No. But you know Con. He'd holding it all inside. Though he's making sure no time is wasted until he has custody."

"When will you get the child?" Susan asked, her eyes full of warm concern—and a bit of grandmotherly anticipation.

Robbie shrugged. "There's a lot of red tape to get through. Sometime in July, we're hoping," she said. There was no reason to worry her parents with the battle that still awaited them regarding Joey's guardianship. She and Con were going to get the baby. There was no other alternative.

ROBBIE'S FATHER followed her back out to the porch after Susan shooed them away from the lunch dishes.

"You sure you're happy, girl? You aren't just doing this for Con's sake?"

Robbie plopped down on the couch and nodded. "I'm sure. I love him, Pop. I always have."

"It's going to be different being his wife. You know that, don't you?"

Robbie blushed. Was her father fixing to give her "the talk" at the tender age of thirty-three? "Mom told me about the birds and the bees when I was ten, Pop," she said, grinning at him.

"You need a light?" he asked, grabbing his lighter off the table.

Robbie shook her head. "I quit."

"Good for you!" Stan reached for his pipe, his alternative to the three packs of cigarettes a day he used to smoke, packed it and lit up.

"I need to say this, Robbie." He paused, looking more at his pipe than at her. "I raised you to be like me, to have the courage and the conviction to know your own mind and to stand by it, but sometimes I wonder if maybe I did too good a job."

Robbie frowned. "I don't understand."

"Con's going to want a *woman* in his bed, Robbie. Not one of the guys."

They'd always been straight with each other. But it had never hurt like this before.

"You don't think I'm a woman, Pop?"

"Of course I do. You're one hell of a woman. But you're a lot like your old man, too. I'm just saying that maybe you should tone down a bit now that you're getting married. You'll have a man to stick up for you now."

"You want me to change who I am?"

"Don't get me wrong, honey. I love who you are. I'm proud as hell of what you've become. I just want to see this marriage work."

"So all that stuff you told me about being my own person, about not being afraid to be who I am—even if that's different—about fighting for what I feel is right, about speaking my own mind—all that was just until I found myself a man to take care of me?" She couldn't believe this was her father talking.

"I want you to be happy, Robbie," he said, his eyes glistening.

Even her own father knew she didn't have what it took to attract and keep a man. But she'd been who she was for thirty-three years. She couldn't change that now. Not for anyone. Not even for Con.

"I'm happy, Pop," she said. But she wasn't sure either one of them believed that.

CHAPTER FIVE

HE NEEDED A CRIB. The baby had to have a place to sleep. Diapers, too. Joey probably wouldn't come with them, like the doll had.

Con sat at his breakfast bar Tuesday night after work making a list. He hadn't seen Robbie since Friday. Hadn't heard from her all weekend. Not that either of them were in the habit of checking in with each other, but they hadn't gone this many days without talking since he'd returned to Phoenix after his stint at the FBI academy in Quantico, Virginia.

Damn. He was probably going to need a load of stuff. Bottles, something to go in them, clothes. He added all that to the list. Was regular soap OK for babies? And he'd need something disposable to wipe Joey off with, too. The doll had come with a little cloth, but he sure as hell wasn't going to be using anything he'd have to clean afterward, and paper towels were probably a little rough. But maybe they'd do at first, if he wet them down. He put disposable cloths down, anyway, just in case he happened to run across some.

He hadn't heard a word from social services since Friday. If he had, he'd have had a reason to call Robbie.

He wasn't kidding himself. He knew why she hadn't shown up on his doorstep all weekend. The marriage thing. It was already messing things up.

Con looked over his list again, sure he was missing stuff. He wasn't a stupid man. He just had no experience with babies or their needs. So how in hell did he think he could raise one by himself?

He could learn. But was that fair to the boy? When Robbie was so willing to be there to help the two of them muddle through? But was it fair to Robbie to allow her to sacrifice so much?

He picked up his list. Where did one go to get a crib? Back to the store where they'd bought the doll? Or was there a baby store that would have everything he needed? Was there more than one kind of crib? Were some better than others?

And what about a stroller? He sure saw enough of those around. Everyone with a little kid seemed to have one. He added a stroller to his list.

He needed Robbie.

In the past he'd have picked up the phone and called her. Told her to get her ass over here and show him what to do.

But that was then and this was now. Now Robbie thought they should get married. Shopping for stuff with a friend was one thing. Picking out cribs with his potential wife was something else entirely. And way too intimate for him and Robbie.

They weren't even married and he was losing her.

He thought about calling Pete's wife, Marie. She'd know everything he needed, as well as the best place to shop. And Pete could probably give him a few pointers, too. But they weren't too happy with him these days. Not that they'd ever really seen things his way, but once upon a time he'd saved their lives and they'd been grateful. Of course, that was only after he'd put Marie at risk in the first place, believing she'd been involved in some pretty nasty international sabotage.

And ever since that deal with Ramirez went sour a year ago last April, ever since it became public knowledge that an innocent woman had died, Con had been avoiding Pete and Marie Mitchell. Pete had tried to warn Con, way back when they'd been partners on Marie's case, that he was losing it; and he accused Con of going after his man at any cost. Con didn't need to see the condemnation in their eyes to know that Pete had been right. He hated himself enough without that.

What the hell. As long as he was hating himself already...

He lit a cigarette, picked up the phone and called Robbie.

"OK, WE'LL GET MARRIED," he said as soon as she answered.

"Con? Glad to see you've come to your senses. I already told Mom and Pop."

The cigarette shook in his fingers. He wished she hadn't done that. No matter what Robbie said, he knew her parents couldn't have been happy about her announcement. He stood to lose everything in this marriage. Everything but his son.

"You couldn't wait to let me speak to your father?" he said a little more sharply than he intended.

"When would that have been, Con? When Joey was twenty-one? We have a wedding to plan, and if you're going to bring your son home anytime soon, we did need to do it now."

"Plan? What's to plan? We go to the justice of the peace, say a few words and it's done."

"I'm not cheating my parents out of a wedding, Con. Besides, if we want everybody to believe this is the real thing, we have to do it right."

"Meaning?"

"You're going to have to wear a tux."

Hell. He took another puff on his cigarette. The tuxedo wasn't a problem. The wedding was. He couldn't believe Robbie was willing to go through all this for him and Joey. He couldn't believe he'd actually let her.

"Fine."

"Fine?"

"Yes, fine. Now get your ass over here. I need some help getting ready for the kid."

"How do you know I'm not busy?"

"Are you?"

"No."

"You're pushing me, Robbie."

"You're pushing *me,* Randolph. You quit smoking yet?"

He looked at the cigarette burning in the ashtray,

wishing he could tell her that at least he'd done that much right.

"No."

"Good. I'm on my way."

HE NEEDN'T have worried. Robbie was as much a pain in the ass as ever. But she took care of the whole shebang. He followed her from store to store, observing and handing over his credit card. It was all relatively simple. Robbie argued with him about everything. Apparently he was a Neanderthal when it came to decorating. He just wanted stuff that worked. She wanted it all to match. He approved of the race-car pattern she picked out for the nursery, as she called the room where the boy would be sleeping, but he gave her a hard time about it, anyway. He liked matching wits with Robbie, always had.

They went for a beer afterward, smoking half a pack of cigarettes. Con was between cases at work and didn't have much to say, but Robbie filled him in on her plans to approach the cartoonist Cameron Blackwell, bouncing ideas off him. And by the time she drove away that night, he'd almost convinced himself that things were back to normal.

Sex hadn't been mentioned all evening. Not once.

THE BLOOD WORK came back inconclusive. There was a seventy percent chance that Con was Joey's biological father.

"What the hell is a seventy percent chance?" Con

asked Karen Smith the morning she called to report the results.

"It means you *could* be Joey's father, but it's not enough to prove it. We look for a ninety-eight percent or better to determine conclusive paternity."

"So now what?"

"I'm going to ask you again to reconsider your position, Mr. Randolph," Karen said, speaking to him as his high-school teachers used to when they wanted him to admit to doing something he hadn't done. "If you would only sign the papers, Joey would be out of foster care by the end of the week and into his new home."

"You have a home ready for him?"

"We have prospective parents chosen. They won't be told they have a baby until it's official."

"By official you mean my signature."·

"Yes, sir."

"Then why will my signature not gain *me* access to the boy?"

"We've been through all this before, Mr. Randolph," Karen said wearily. "Won't you please reconsider and sign the papers? Let Joey begin his new life?"

For a split second Con considered doing as she asked. He could return all the baby things filling one of his spare rooms upstairs. Get back to his life. Let Robbie get back to hers. Smoke to his heart's content.

But could he send his son the same messages his biological parents had sent him? *We didn't want you.* Could he risk the chance that someone might raise his

son to the tune he'd always heard? *You owe us.* Or
how about his favorite? *You're a major disappointment.*

"I will not abandon my son."

"You may not have any choice."

"Let's leave that up to the judge," Con said. He
wasn't about to get into it with a state employee. Especially one he might need on his side. "What happens next?"

"We'll need more blood work—a DNA screening
this time. If you're the boy's father, the DNA will
show a more conclusive match."

"Fine."

"Assuming you are the father, we'll also need to
send someone back out to your home to see what kind
of setup you have there for the baby." She paused.
"You do know you'll need to provide a crib and personal things for Joey, don't you?"

"Done."

"He'll need clothes, bottles, blankets, lotions,
toys—"

"Done."

"All of it? What about a baby thermometer?"

"That, too." Con jotted it down on a piece of paper. If he didn't have one yet, he would before the
day was through. "Come see for yourself."

"You can be sure we will, Mr. Randolph, probably
early next week."

He was getting married next week.

"Fine."

"Well, then, if that's all…"

It wasn't all. Not by a long shot. "How soon before we hear back on the DNA?"

"It's hard to say, Mr. Randolph. Sometimes it takes weeks. Of course," she added, softening, "with your connections, you could probably get the lab-work results a lot faster than the state will."

"Consider it done." He told her where to send the baby's blood sample.

"OK, well, after the blood work comes back and all the social workers' reports are turned in, a date will be set for you to appear before the judge. He'll make his determination at that time."

"And I pick up Joey there?"

"*If* you get him. And *if* he's there. It's more likely you'd be instructed to pick him up from his foster home. I'm sure his foster mother will have instructions. In the meantime," she continued, her tone softening again, "you can rest assured he's being very well cared for."

"I want to see him."

"Yes, I rather thought you might. Tell me, Mr. Randolph, when are you and Ms. Blair getting married?"

"Next Wednesday. Robbie's sending you an invitation."

"Oh!" she sounded impressed, pleased. "I mean, I didn't expect it to be so soon. Are you going away for a honeymoon?"

Honeymoon. There wasn't going to *be* any honeymoon in this marriage. "Not until after we have the boy."

"So you'll be home over the Fourth of July weekend?"

"Yes."

"Do you think your people could have the DNA results to us by then?"

"They'll have it as soon as humanly possible once they get the sample."

"Oh. Good," she said, drawing out the *good*. "The thing is, Mr. Randolph, Joey's foster parents have made plans to take their children to Disneyland over the holiday weekend. They'd expected Joey to be with his adoptive parents by then, and they've already made all their reservations. I'm meeting with the judge this afternoon to make other arrangements for Joey that weekend."

Anger burned his gut. His son was in the way. Why in hell was she telling him this when he was helpless to do a damn thing about it? "So?"

"Well, in view of the situation and since you say you're already prepared—and of course because you're going to be married by then—I thought maybe I'd suggest to the judge that, if the DNA comes back positive, Joey be released to you for that weekend."

Something that was wound tight inside him relaxed. He was being given a chance. "I'd like that," he said, warning himself not to count on too much. They were letting him baby-sit. That was all. "I'd like that very much."

"HERE, SPRAY THE HOUSE." Robbie handed Con a can of disinfectant. He was hovering. She couldn't

scrub toilets with him hovering. And they only had
an hour before Karen Smith arrived for her inspection.
It was Monday, the day before Con's cleaning lady
was due. And two days before their wedding.

"You spray. I'll clean my own bathrooms."

Robbie laughed. "Have you ever cleaned a bathroom, Connor Randolph?"

"Don't call me that. My foster mother used to call
me that. And yes, Miss Priss, I have." He grabbed
the cleaning powder, sponge and toilet brush from her
arms and handed her the can of disinfectant.

"Make sure you spray the kitchen. I smoke too
much in there," he said.

"You smoke too much everywhere."

Her wedding was only forty-eight hours away, and
Robbie could almost convince herself she was going
to be a real wife as she sprayed the house, doing her
best to kill the stale cigarette-smoke odor that permeated everything Con owned. Karen Smith's visit
was twofold. She was coming to inspect the nursery
and to bring little Joey for Con's second supervised
visit with him. The DNA work had not been done
yet, since Joey's foster mother had been remiss in
getting Joey in for the second blood test. So they
couldn't have him to themselves, but at least they
were going to get to see him.

There were moments over the past week, dangerous
moments, when Robbie had almost let herself believe
that her dreams were coming true. In two days she
was going to be Con's wife, the mother of his child.
She looked around the unusually spotless kitchen and

pictured herself there in the early hours of the morning, wearing nothing but a robe she'd pulled on hastily when she'd had to leave Con's bed because their baby had cried. She was heating a bottle of soy milk for Joey and thinking about the glorious hours she'd just spent in Con's arms....

"That should be it," Con said, coming up behind her with his cleaning supplies.

She jumped guiltily, her heart pounding, afraid he'd know what she'd been thinking. Stooping down to hide the flush she could feel rising up her throat and into her cheeks, she swiped at the baseboard.

"Did you get the safety corners on the tables in the living room?" she blurted.

"Done."

"How about the trash?" She berated herself for being a fool. She was going to have more out of life than she'd ever dared hope, and if she allowed her stupid hormones to blow her friendship with Con, she'd never forgive herself.

"Emptied." He put the supplies on a shelf in the laundry room. He was wearing jean shorts and a polo shirt today, looking far more casual than she was used to. His long muscled legs seemed to go on forever.

"You taking the whole day off?" she asked.

"The whole week. I'm between cases."

"Good, you need a break."

"I do not need a break."

Robbie knew better than to argue with that tone. "Whatever," she said.

He reached into the drawer for his pack of cigarettes. ''Not now, Randolph,'' she admonished him. He was the one who'd forbidden smoking in the house at all that day.

He nodded, but when he began pacing like a caged animal, instead, Robbie almost wished she'd let him have his cigarette. He moved about the house, inspecting every spotless room, stopping to look out the living-room window and then beginning his tour again.

She didn't know who was more relieved when the doorbell finally rang.

Con took the baby's carrier from Karen before he even let her in the door. He carried his son into the living room and set him carefully down on the newly polished coffee table. Joey was sleeping.

''Why does he sleep so much?'' he asked Karen.

It was only one of many questions Con asked that morning. By the time the social worker left, Robbie had fallen in love with him all over again. He was so determined to learn everything he could to care for this child. A child he'd taken into a heart he didn't believe he had.

And Robbie had fallen in love with Joey all over again, too. She'd held his tiny body against her breast and known she'd made the right decision. The only decision. Unrequited love for Con was a small price to pay for the right to call this baby her son.

THE DNA RESULTS still weren't in by his wedding day. Con was glad he hadn't told Robbie about the possibility of having the boy for the weekend. She'd have been hugely disappointed. And one of them with dashed hopes was enough.

Con thought about canceling the wedding. There was no reason to put Robbie through this mess until he knew for sure Joey was his. Except that he *did* know. The boy had his chin.

And Robbie knew, too. Aside from the other reasons she'd listed for wanting to get married, she had her heart set on being Joey's mother. And he couldn't think of anyone he'd rather have help raise his son.

She was already at the church when he arrived. He knew she was there because he heard her swearing when he walked by the room she was using to change. Her colorful tirade was followed by a soft admonition from Susan. A half grin cracked Con's usually austere features as he continued on his way to the vestibule. Robbie was still Robbie. Even on her wedding day. He found something very reassuring about that.

He made it through the half hour before the wedding with relative ease. When he'd donned his rented tux that afternoon, he'd cloaked himself with the same numbing control he wore to work every day, and it stood him in good stead. This whole affair was merely a formality. Another undercover operation. He was confident he'd get through the day just like he did any other.

Until he was standing alone with the minister at the front of the church, that is, and saw Robbie and Stan coming up the aisle toward him. He didn't know which threw him more—Robbie looking radiant in her stunning white suit, or Stan, dressed in a black tux similar to Con's, smiling at him encouragingly. Robbie was going undercover with him—he could almost overlook her disguise—but Stan didn't know they were only playing a game. The older man's consummate acting could only be attributed to the great wealth of love he had for his daughter.

"Ladies and gentlemen, we are gathered here today..." The ceremony began.

Con answered the right questions in all the appropriate places, holding himself apart, an outside observer. Other than one glance at Susan, he didn't look at the audience—comprising, he knew, a few colleagues and friends—and he didn't look at Robbie again. He couldn't stand the pretense between them.

But he did make a vow during those moments that he intended to keep till death did they part. He was going to protect his friend; he was going to make damn sure that this marriage didn't hurt her, that she'd have whatever freedoms her heart desired. And he was going to ensure that the marriage ceremony his drunken one-night stand had forced on them was not going to ruin the only good relationship he'd ever had.

"You may kiss the bride."

Con froze. He couldn't kiss Robbie. He couldn't even look at her.

Why hadn't they thought of this, prepared for it? Scratched it from the ceremony?

"Go ahead, Mr. Randolph," the minister whispered, accompanied by a few snickers from behind them.

He turned his gaze to Robbie and was thrown by the vulnerable look in her eyes. For some reason this mattered to her. And then it hit him. Her friends and loved ones were all watching. They thought this marriage was for real. And he *needed* everyone to believe it was for real.

Keeping his mental distance, his professional impartiality, Con lowered his head to hers.

And for a split second forgot they were Robbie's lips beneath his. Surprised at how soft, how womanly she felt. He moved his mouth against hers automatically, deepening what he'd intended as an impersonal gesture into something far more intimate. Her lips parted and he took her invitation instinctively, until he heard the minister's discreet cough.

This is Robbie! What in the name of God am I doing?

He jerked his mouth from hers. "I'm sorry," he whispered, unable to meet the shocked look he knew he'd see in her eyes.

He couldn't believe he'd done that. Robbie was his friend.

He escorted her down the aisle, stood beside her in the small reception line, accepted the congratulations of his colleagues and hers as they filed by. He even managed to be cordial to Karen Smith, to put his arm around his new wife and pretend that he and Robbie had married for the usual reasons. But he never looked at Robbie.

Until he saw the couple at the end of the line, speaking with Susan and Stan. Then he leaned over to ensure that his words reached only her ears. "You invited Pete and Marie."

"You never actually said not to."

"I told you I didn't want them here." It was hard enough getting through this charade, putting Robbie through it, lying to her parents, allowing her to lie to them, without this. *Yeah, Pete, my man, you're absolutely right. I'll sacrifice anyone, including my only real friend, in order to get my man. Or in this case, my son.*

"But you never came right out and said don't invite them."

They were heading toward him, a striking couple with Pete towering over his petite dark-haired wife. Con held out his hand to his sometime partner, thankful to Robbie for one thing. She'd made him angry as hell, wiping out all traces of the bizarre moment in front of the altar.

"Con. It's good to see you, man," Pete said, his grasp firm. Pete was a professional arbitrator, and Con had to hand it to him. He did his job well. Con almost believed Pete meant the words.

"Congratulations, Con. I'd hoped the love bug would get you," Marie said, standing on tiptoe to kiss his cheek.

"You're looking good, Marie," Con said, focusing on her pretty features rather than her words. She looked nothing like the tense unhappy woman she'd been when he'd first met her.

"Yes, well—" she glanced shyly up at Pete "—we're expecting again."

"Congratulations!" Robbie said, hugging Marie. The two had met only once before. It was at Pete and Marie's wedding when Con had had to show up as part of a couple or be assigned to some bridesmaid, but they'd hit it off right from the start.

"Wait'll you hear Con's news—" Robbie began.

"Not now, *dear*," Con interrupted, jabbing Robbie in the side. He wasn't ready to hang out more of his dirty laundry. *Hey, Pete. You know the night I got that woman killed? I also impregnated a woman whose name I didn't know, a woman I don't even remember screwing.*

Robbie glared at him—he'd probably bruised her ribs on top of everything else—but she let the moment pass, smoothing things over for him as Pete and Marie promised to talk with them later.

Robbie saw them through the small reception following the ceremony, as well, showing everyone that theirs was a match made in heaven. She made jokes about his terser-than-normal attitude, convincing their guests he was simply a very impatient bridegroom. He played along as best he could—and was eternally grateful to her.

Not that he told her so. He didn't know how.

CHAPTER SIX

IT WAS OVER.

Back in shorts and a tank top, her wedding suit safely tucked away, Robbie looked around her empty apartment one last time. Her truck was loaded with everything she was keeping, and Con was waiting outside to drive her home.

Home.

Why was it that Con's place had always felt like home—until today? She searched the floors of her bedroom closets. Empty. She knew they were. Con had already double-checked everything for her—every cupboard, every shelf. She was stalling. There was nothing of hers left here.

It was just that she wasn't sure there was anything for her at Con's house, either. She felt awkward moving in there, having no place of her own to run to when she needed to regroup.

And all because of that kiss. The second Con's lips had touched hers, everything had changed. She knew that was what was bothering her. Knew, also, that she couldn't talk to Con about it.

She used to be able to talk to him about anything. But she couldn't talk to him about that kiss, couldn't bear for him to learn that it had mattered so much to her, couldn't bear to see his pity. The only way she was going to get through this was to pretend she hadn't responded to him with such embarrassingly obvious passion, to act as though the kiss had been as meaningless to her as it had been to him.

If things were normal between them, she could have made him laugh about it, treated the whole thing like the joke it should have been. But she had a scary feeling that things weren't ever going to be normal between them again. They'd only been married a few hours and already there was a chasm between them, forcing them apart.

She needed a cigarette.

SHE WASN'T ALONE again until much later that night when she was in her room, furiously making her bed. Con had helped her carry in all her things. He'd set up her water bed without complaining once. Moving and filling that bed was something he'd done for her many times before, though not usually without cursing her and her taste in mattresses a time or two. Even something so mundane was no longer normal. But she was moved in; she had her stuff in her own bathroom—and they'd accomplished everything without once mentioning that kiss.

Their wedding supper was nothing to write home about, but by the time they'd made it to the kitchen for some sustenance, she'd been ready to eat. They'd had tuna-melt sandwiches followed by a companionable after-dinner cigarette. They were both still wearing the shorts and shirts they'd put on for moving.

"I found a way to Cameron Blackwell," Robbie had told him. She'd been so caught up in wedding plans she'd forgotten to tell Con about her coup.

"Yeah?" He didn't sound like he believed her.

"I made friends with his dog."

"You what?"

"I spent part of the weekend hanging out in front of his place, you know, just thinking, getting the lay of the land, trying to figure out the best way to approach him—"

"You were trespassing, just waiting for him to show so you could pounce on him," Con interrupted.

"Yes, well, his dog showed," Robbie continued, "and we got to know each other."

The look Con sent her was piercing. "Where'd he bite you?"

She was enjoying the cigarette much more than she should be. But at least it had come from Con's pack.

"That part's not important, Con. It wasn't deep. It just bled a lot. And while I was waiting for the bleeding to stop, we got to talking. Cameron's really a funny guy, Con. I liked him."

"Of course he's a funny guy. He writes comics."

"Just because he knows what's funny doesn't mean he's funny himself. Anyway, the main thing is, I'll get my story."

"He agreed to an interview? Because you got caught trespassing?"

Robbie fiddled with her cigarette on the edge of the

ashtray. "Not quite," she admitted. "He wasn't too happy about that. And I had to promise him the interview would be strictly regulated by him, that I wouldn't exploit him, but rather just get to know him a little better. Oh, and I promised not to tell anyone that he reads romance novels by the dozen."

"He what?" Con's gaze shot to her, a hint of humor in his usually somber eyes.

"He came running out of the house so quickly when he heard me scream that he still had the book he'd been reading in his hand. There was a whole wall of them in his study, too."

Con studied her. "And you threatened to make something of it."

Robbie shrugged. She was a reporter. She had an obligation to the citizens of Phoenix. "I simply told him he had a choice. I'd tell my story, which was definitely going to give the wrong impression as I had so little to go on—or I'd tell his."

Con's mouth quirked into the half grin she loved so well but saw so infrequently. "You're something else, Rob. I almost feel sorry for Blackwell."

Warmth spread through her at his approving tone. And she blasted herself for the response. How would she get through years living with this man if she was going to go around reacting like a besotted idiot to every little thing he said?

"Where'd the dog bite you, Rob?" he asked, suddenly serious.

Damn. She'd hoped he'd forgotten about that.

"It doesn't matter, Con. Really. It's fine."

"Then why avoid the question?"

"Look. I told you it doesn't matter. Now drop it."

"You don't play around with dog bites. Did you have your doctor take a look at it?"

Damn his persistence. She wasn't one of his suspects. "He had to look when he stitched it up, now, didn't he?" she snipped.

Con ground out his cigarette. "God, Rob. It needed stitches? Show me where he bit you."

She put out her cigarette, too. "No."

He stood up, towering over her. "I assume the dog had all his shots?"

"Yes."

"The wound could still get infected. Show me where he bit you." He'd come closer.

He wasn't going to give up. She knew that.

"Show me." He was standing right over her.

"Here. It's right here," she said, touching the underside of her right breast.

If she'd thought the location would shock him, embarrass him, get any reaction out of him at all, she was wrong. He didn't miss a beat. "Show it to me," he said, his eyes filled with nothing but concern. They could have been talking about her big toe.

Except they weren't. And she was too aware of it—even if seeing an intimate part of her body apparently moved him not at all.

"Come on, Rob. Let me look."

"Forget it, Randolph. My tits are my own." She got to her feet, pushed past him and ran to her room, closing the door behind her.

She needn't have bothered. He hadn't followed.

Angrily Robbie forced the sheet corners around the bulky water-filled mattress.

How dare he think, even for a second, that he had any right to see her breast? For *any* reason.

How dare he think his first intimate sight of her was only going to be because of a repulsive little wound? How dare he not even realize it *would* have been his first sight of her?

How dare he not have passion in his eyes?

Robbie's hands went limp, the sheet slipping away as she sank slowly to the floor. That was the real problem. Had been all day. She'd seen the distaste in Con's eyes when the minister had asked him to kiss her that afternoon. And the memory was killing her.

It was one thing to assume she didn't turn him on. It was another altogether to have proof.

She was hurting like hell and she didn't have a clue how to deal with it. Con had never hurt her before. Because she'd never before allowed herself to want something from him he couldn't give, never before allowed herself to hope he might someday want her.

She couldn't blame Con. He'd die for her if she needed him to.

She just didn't turn him on.

"Robbie?" His call was followed by a knock on her door.

Leaping up, she grabbed a sheet corner. "Come on in," she called. The best way to get through this was just to pretend nothing had changed between them. She had to go back to looking at Con without feeling the touch of his lips on hers, without thinking about his taste, without imagining his passion.

She just hoped it wasn't too late.

"I think we need to talk," he said, leaning against the doorjamb.

Not yet. She wasn't done forgetting yet. "Go away, Randolph."

"You just told me to come in." His head almost touched the top of the doorway.

She yanked her bright yellow comforter out of a box. "Now I'm telling you to go."

"I'm sorry, Rob. I screwed up. Big time. I just want you to know it won't happen again."

She couldn't look at him, couldn't let him see how much his words were hurting her. It wasn't his fault she hadn't been honest with him about the way she felt. It wasn't his fault she was in love with him. And it certainly wasn't his fault she was such a turnoff to men. "Forget it, Con. I have."

"Thanks," he said. "And, Rob? Keep a close eye on that bite," he added, and was gone.

To spend his wedding night alone. Robbie spent the night trying to pretend that it was sweat and not tears soaking her pillow.

CON WAS UP EARLY the next morning. By the time he heard Robbie's bathroom door open, the homemade biscuits were just coming out of the oven, and the bacon and potatoes were done. It was time to put on the eggs, stay busy, not think about her somewhere in his house getting ready for the day. She'd spent the night here before—such as that time he didn't want her driving home in a monsoon and one night when she'd had too much to drink. And each time, she'd gotten up the next morning, too. There was nothing to it.

Except that she had stitches on the underside of her right breast. She'd have to be careful not to get them wet when she bathed. He spent the next several seconds thinking up different ways to keep them dry. Because he was worried about infection. That was all.

Breaking a yoke, he swore, then lit a cigarette, reminding himself of his game plan once more. He wasn't sure what he and Robbie were going to do with the day, but whatever it was, he would make up for the ass he'd been the day before. Starting with breakfast.

Susan had invited them to drive up to Sedona for a cookout later in the day, and Con wasn't averse to that. He'd be just as happy at home, working in the yard, but he'd made up his mind to do whatever Robbie wanted to do—and to be a good sport about it. Anything to get that hurt look out of her eyes. To get things back to normal. He should never have kissed her the way he had at the wedding. It was unforgivable.

And he could hardly stand to think about his moronic insistence she strip in front of him. When he'd heard that the dog had bitten deep enough to require stitches, he'd gone a little nuts. Dog bites were serious. He'd seen a guy with rabies once. He sure didn't want to lose Robbie that way. Or any other way.

"Mmm, smells good," she said, coming into the kitchen, her hair still wet from the shower. She picked up Con's cigarette, helped herself to a puff, then put it out. "If I had time, I'd make you give me some of that." She was watching him flip the eggs he was making for her.

"You going somewhere?" he asked.

She snatched a piece of bacon. "I'm covering the Fourth of July celebration at Patriots Square."

"I thought you had the rest of the week off."

"I called Rick this morning. Told him I could work." She chewed on the bacon as if she hadn't a care in the world.

Con's eyes narrowed. "Didn't he find it odd that you'd want to work the day after your wedding?"

"He assumed you had to go in."

Con lit another cigarette. "What about your parents' cookout?"

"I called them, too, told them we'd try to make it up there over the weekend."

She didn't want to spend the day with him. Maybe that was best.

"When do you expect to be back?"

She shrugged. "I don't know. Later."

Con ate their breakfast alone.

HE WAS THE ONLY ONE in the neighborhood doing yard work. Not many people celebrated the holiday that way. Which was fine with him. He had the world to himself as he clipped and trimmed, no friendly neighbors coming over to chat. Con hated it when they did that. He never had anything to chat about.

He finished trimming the bougainvillea bushes lining his wall, checked the irrigation on the fruit trees and wondered if Robbie would be home in time for dinner. Then berated himself for caring. He'd been eating dinner alone most of his life. If Robbie happened to stop over, it was no big deal. He'd never counted on it. Never needed it. He wasn't about to start now.

"I figured I'd find you back here."

Con swung around to find Stan Blair standing there. A good four inches shorter than Con, Robbie's father was still a big man, an intimidating man. Especially if you happened to have just married his daughter.

"Stan! Something wrong?" Con asked, his sheers hanging from his fingers.

"Not that I know of. I just wanted to talk. You got a few minutes?"

Con dropped his sheers on the growing pile of brush and headed toward his back door, grabbing the towel he'd left on a lounge by the pool on his way.

"Come inside," he said, wiping the sweat off his face and neck. "Where's Susan?"

"I left her at the mall. Dilliard's is having a sale."

He'd gotten rid of Susan. This talk was going to be serious. Con pulled a couple of bottles of beer out of the refrigerator and handed one to Stan.

"Thanks." The older man took the beer, but didn't

open it right away. Setting it down on the breakfast
bar, he excused himself to go to the bathroom.

Con watched as Stan left the room, a hard knot of
regret in his gut. If this were a perfect world, if a kid
had the right to choose his father, Stan would have
been a good choice for him. Not that Stan would have
seen it that way. Con had always been a pain in Stan
Blair's ass.

He'd known that Robbie's father wouldn't have
been happy about the wedding. But what could he
possibly have to say about it now, after the fact?

Taking his beer with him, Con headed to the back
of the house, as well, thinking he'd use this chance
to clean up a little, at least change his sweat-soaked
T-shirt.

His heart sank when he rounded the corner. Stan
was in the doorway of Robbie's room looking at his
daughter's unmade bed. Con's door was open across
the hall, leaving a clear view of his own unmade bed.

Though Con would have liked to turn around and
head right back to the kitchen, it was too late. Stan
had heard him. So he continued down the hall, beer
in hand, and stopped beside his father-in-law, staring
at the incriminating bed, the single head print on the
feather pillow.

"I'd hoped that things had changed," Stan said
sadly, his gaze not leaving the bed.

Con wasn't sure what Stan meant. But he was
pretty damn sure he didn't want to know. He stood
silently, waiting.

"The wedding was for the boy, wasn't it?"

"Yes."

"You don't love her."

"I care for her."

"You've always cared for her, son. But she needs to be loved."

Con stood there looking at that lonely bed and nodded. He couldn't argue with Stan. The man was right.

"I'd hoped you'd learned to love her."

"Don't." Con took a swallow of his beer. There was no point in any of them setting themselves up for disappointment.

Stan shook his head. "She's special, my Robbie. Strong as they come, but soft and warm underneath. She'll make a good wife."

"I know."

They continued to stare at the bed. Con figured it was better than looking at each other. Stan had more to say.

"She deserves better than this."

Con nodded. So far, Stan wasn't telling him anything he hadn't already told himself.

"Did you ask her to marry you?"

"What do you think?"

Now it was Stan's turn to nod. "How long's it for?"

"As long as it takes. Maybe sooner."

"How long does *she* think it's for?"

Con didn't want to answer that. He didn't like the answer. "Forever, maybe."

Stan gave Con a sharp look. "I thought you were a better man than to use her like this."

Con doubted that, but the accusation still stung. "They're giving her a hard time down at the station, not including her in things. The guys are all married now. Their wives don't like them hanging out with a single woman."

Stan only grunted.

"She says she's lonely."

"So how's she going to find a husband to take care of that when she's married to you?"

Con didn't have an answer.

"The minute she called today, I knew there was trouble," Stan said, shaking his head. "I thought maybe you two had had a spat, figured it might take her a little while to adjust to having a man around telling her what to do. I had no idea it was this bad."

"I don't tell Robbie what to do." Con wanted that clear.

"Yes, well, maybe you should. Maybe if you had to make decisions for her, you'd love her."

Con could have told Stan that he liked Robbie just the way she was, that any man who tried to change her didn't really love her, that pushing Robbie around would not only be futile, but wrong. Except that the information was irrelevant. All Stan really cared about was whether or not Con loved Robbie.

But Con didn't love anybody. Stan knew that. God knows he'd tried. His birth parents had never even given him a chance. When he'd been young and na-ive, he'd done everything he could to please his foster parents, to love them as they'd expected him to. It had never been enough, though. They hadn't been able to love him, not after the years of trouble he'd given them.

"I want a promise from you, son," Stan said, as if reaching some conclusion.

Con stood silently, bracing himself to disappoint Robbie's father again.

"I want you to stay away from her."

What kind of request was that? "We live in the same house," Con said, tamping down his anger.

"You seem to have managed it last night." Stan's tone was testy as he motioned toward his daughter's bed and then to Con's own unmade bed across the hall.

Con's jaw tightened as understanding dawned. Robbie was thirty-three years old, and Stan was still worried about Con getting into her pants. Because of Stan as much as Robbie herself, Con had never even thought of Robbie in those terms. She was too special to him. But Stan had never understood that. Con was done hoping he ever would. And it was no longer any of Stan's damn business whether or not Con had sex with his daughter.

"We're married," he said at last.

Stan turned, pinning Con with a glare that had been intimidating criminals for decades. "You touch her, you'll hurt her. I want your word, boy."

It was when he saw the despair in the older man's eyes that Con capitulated. Stan Blair adored his only child. He was trying to protect her from the pain of a loveless marriage; sex added to the equation would only intensify the pain.

The words stuck in his throat, but he finally said, "You have it."

Stan continued to study him doubtfully. Con thought he knew why.

During Con's junior year in high school the football coach's daughter had accused Con of forcing her to kiss him. The truth was Mitzy had gotten drunk at a party, thrown herself at him and been furious when he'd refused her. But the coach, a man Con had admired almost as much as he'd admired Stan, had believed otherwise. Con had been cut from the football team. And warned about the penalties for sexual assault.

"I never touched Mitzy Larson," he said through gritted teeth.

"I know that, son." Stan's leathery brow was still creased. "I was just thinking about Susan. I don't want her to know about this." Stan motioned to Robbie's room once more. "I don't want her worrying."

"Fine," Con said, wondering if Stan was telling the truth.

Stan's gaze fell and he seemed to study the toes of his tennis shoes. "I, uh, would rather Robbie not know I know, either. I'd like at least to salvage her pride."

"Fine," Con agreed again. He had no intention of talking to Robbie about sex again. Ever.

Without another word, Con turned and headed into his room. He was going to shower. Stan could wait or let himself out. It was no concern of his. All he knew was that he couldn't shake the image of that single imprint on Robbie's pillow.

CON WAS JUST SITTING DOWN to watch the ten o'clock news that evening when Robbie got home.

"Oh, good, just in time," she said, kicking off her sandals before she curled up on the opposite end of the couch.

He bit back a sarcastic remark. It wasn't her fault he'd been worried about her, or that he'd rather have had her company for dinner than eat alone. It wasn't her fault he was strangely aware of her bare feet on the couch between them. "Tough day?" he asked.

"Not too bad." She sounded too damn cheerful. And was that all she was going to tell him about what she'd been doing for the past twelve hours, after he'd spent the entire day thinking about her?

She reached for his cigarette, but he pushed her hand away, taking a drag himself.

"My, my, aren't we testy?" she drawled.

The news was just coming on and Con turned up the volume. He lit a second cigarette and handed it to her before he settled back to watch. It felt good having her home.

ROBBIE WATCHED the news as intently as she always did, but instead of listening to the stories being reported, which she already knew, anyway, she concentrated on the female announcer, Megan Brandt, noting her every expression, every nuance in her voice, every tilt of her head. Now there was a woman.

"I could do that," she finally said, leaning forward to flick the ashes off the end of her cigarette.

"I never knew you wanted to." Con was staring at her, his gray eyes curious.

Robbie shrugged. "Sure I want to. I hadn't planned on doing the grunt work all my life."

"You don't do grunt work." He turned back to the television and Robbie breathed a sigh of relief. Another few seconds under his penetrating gaze and she was going to forget that he wasn't supposed to have the ability to fire her blood.

"How're the stitches feeling?" he asked in the middle of a story about a car chase that had resulted in the arrest of two teenagers.

"Fine." Oh, Lord, they weren't going to start that again, were they? "I get them out Saturday." There, that should take the concerned look off his face. She could have told him they itched like hell, too, but she was damned if she'd discuss the condition of her breast with Con!

He nodded, his gaze on the TV again.

She turned her attention back to Megan Brandt, as well. She was going to concentrate on a dream that was feasible—to someday be the one reporting the news, not the drone collecting it. She couldn't make it through too many more days like the one that had just passed, picturing Con's face every time she closed her eyes, feeling his lips against hers every time she took a drink, driving herself crazy wanting to hurry home to him.

Only fools wasted their lives hoping for something they'd never have. And Robbie Blair Randolph was no fool.

CHAPTER SEVEN

HE EMPTIED his carton of milk in two swallows, never taking his eyes off Randolph's house as the woman came outside just after dawn Friday morning. She was wearing an old pair of cutoff sweatpants and a Phoenix Suns jersey. And she had legs that reminded him of the women he drooled over in magazines. Things were looking up.

He hadn't thought Randolph was screwing the woman all these months, although truth be told he didn't know a lot about screwing. Not nearly as much as he'd like to. But he'd seen them move a bunch of stuff in Wednesday night. And he'd been watching the house ever since, even slept in his car just around the corner the past two nights so he could stay close. He wanted to make sure he wasn't jumping to conclusions. And his vigilance had paid off. He'd been right. She'd moved in. They must be screwing.

This changed things of course. It would be longer than he'd originally figured before he could make his move. He'd have to work out another plan, take things real slow. Getting her out of Randolph's house was going to be tough. He couldn't afford any mistakes.

But he could wait. Now that he'd found a way to nail it to Randolph, to make him bleed, to hurt him so badly death would seem like a blessing, he could wait.

The woman bent down to get the newspaper on Randolph's driveway, and for a moment all he could see was her ass, pointing right at him. Now there was an ass Randolph would miss. A lot.

He could already taste victory. And it was sweeter than he'd imagined.

THE CALL CAME at seven o'clock Friday morning. Con and Robbie were in the kitchen, sharing the newspaper, a cigarette and a pot of freshly brewed coffee. He was already dressed for the yard work he'd left undone the day before, in cutoff jeans and a T-shirt. She hadn't yet changed out of the cutoffs and jersey she'd slept in.

Robbie was in the process of reminding herself that Con was her husband in name only, that the way his chest filled that T-shirt was no business of hers, when the phone rang.

"I'll get it," she said, dashing into the living room. It was probably Rick. After the way she'd been ogling Con for the past half hour she *hoped* it was Rick. She'd told her boss to call her if he came up with anything else she could cover during the remainder of her days off.

"Mrs. Randolph?" Robbie's stomach fluttered when she realized the person on the other end of the line was addressing her. That she *was* Mrs. Randolph.

"Yes?"

"This is Sandra Muldoon, from social services."

"Yes?" she said again. Oh, God, it sounded as if Mrs. Muldoon had bad news. Had something happened to Joey? Please, let their baby be all right!

"We just received the results of the DNA testing, Mrs. Randolph." The woman paused. Robbie's skin went cold.

"And?" she asked, forcing her voice to remain calm. What if, after all they'd been through, they told Con that Joey wasn't his? Whether he acknowledged it or not, Con already loved that boy. And, Robbie suspected, loved having a son. A family he could call his own.

"Mr. Randolph is the boy's father."

Tears stung Robbie's eyes and her body went limp. It took everything she had to remain standing, to remember that Sandra Muldoon was still on the line, to keep from running back in to Con, throwing herself in his arms and bursting into sobs of joy. They had their proof. Nothing had gone wrong with the test. The court could not contest Con's fatherhood.

"Are you there, Mrs. Randolph?"

"Yes, ma'am. Thank you so much for calling. How soon can we see him?"

"Today," the woman said crisply. "The court approved an unsupervised visit for the weekend dependent on conclusive DNA results. I'd like to bring him by within the next hour. I trust you can arrange your schedule accordingly?"

"Great!" she cried. *Today! Our baby's coming to-*

day! "I mean, yes, our schedule is fine!" And then more calmly, "We'll be ready."

SHE DROPPED the phone back in its cradle just as Con came into the room. He'd heard her holler.

"What's up?"

Robbie hurled herself at him, her arms encircling his neck. "We get him for the whole weekend, Con!" Her eyes shone. "The tests are back. Joey's your son!"

Con felt the shock of her words clear to the bone. And then was hit by a joy unlike he'd ever known before. The boy was his.

"He's mine." He needed to say it aloud.

Robbie was still hanging on to him. "Congratulations, Daddy!" she said.

He froze. *Daddy.* He had a son. A family. For the first time in his life he really belonged to someone.

Unfamiliar with the feelings drowning him, unsure what to do with them, Con pulled Robbie close, gazing down into her smiling face, her smiling eyes. And filled with self-hatred and despair, with selfish pride and joy, he lowered his mouth to hers.

WAVES OF PLEASURE coursed through Robbie as Con's lips touched hers.

Yes! her heart cried. Pent-up desire flooded her, almost frightening in its intensity.

Her mouth opened to him automatically, inviting him to deepen the kiss, allowing their tongues to mate. And then, in a flash, her befuddled brain remembered what had happened that last time he'd kissed her—the distaste she'd seen in his eyes.

For a split second, wanting him so badly she hurt, she considered ignoring the memory. But not at the risk of having him reject her again. She pulled out of his arms before he came to his senses. Because come to his senses he would, and she couldn't stand a repeat of their wedding day. Not today. Today was too perfect, too precious. Today they'd have Joey all to themselves.

"He's going to be here in an hour," she said, rushing over to pick up the FBI newsletter he'd left on the coffee table. She carried it to the desk he used to pay bills.

Con remained where he was, a dazed look in his eyes, and if Robbie hadn't been having such a hard time keeping her own emotions under control, she would have run right back to him.

"Robbie, about just now, I'm—"

"Forget it, Randolph. I'm happy, too," she interrupted him before he could say he was sorry a second time for kissing her. She straightened the cushions on the couch.

"He'll be here in an hour?" Con asked. She could feel him watching her, but he'd covered himself with his cloak of control again. It was in his voice, in the stillness of his body, as he stood in the doorway.

Robbie nodded. "There's nothing out in the kitchen he can hurt himself on, is there?" she asked. This would be a whole lot easier if Con would get busy, get away from her, give her a few minutes to recover.

She didn't know which was worse—only imagining his kisses, or these brief incomplete tastes of them. She just knew she needed his big sexy body out of her sight.

It wasn't to be. "Look at me," he said.

Robbie did as he asked, praying that she appeared convincingly unaffected.

"I didn't pull your stitches, did I?"

"No." She forced herself to meet his gaze. If discussing her breast didn't affect him, it certainly shouldn't affect her. Except that it did.

He studied her, frowning. "You sure you're okay?"

"Positive. Just a little nervous," Robbie admitted, surprised to realize that last part was true. She might not be much in the wife department, but she was going to be a mother in a little less than an hour. And that she was going to get right.

Con nodded, apparently satisfied. She wasn't sure if that was because she'd done a good job of hiding her feelings, or because he was distracted by Joey's impending visit. Either way, she was thankful.

He went around the room picking up ashtrays—from his desk, the coffee table, an end table beside his recliner.

"Does this mean you won't be smoking this weekend?" she asked, wishing he'd have one last cigarette before Joey arrived. She could use a puff.

"*We* won't be," he said on his way out the door.

"What do you mean *we?*" Robbie called after him. "I quit."

CON FELT LIKE he was setting off for the Academy all over again. He figured they were going to find him wanting, knew they'd be right in their assessment and was determined to make it, anyway. He'd conquered the Academy. But somehow he knew that fatherhood was going to be a much bigger challenge.

"That's everything, then," Mrs. Muldoon said, clearly not very happy about leaving Joey in their care. "His schedule's written out there for you—" she gestured at the papers she'd handed Robbie "—along with the name of his doctor. And his foster mother packed a couple of jars of food along with a list of things he likes and doesn't like."

"Thank you," Con and Robbie said at the same time. Robbie began reading the schedule.

The social worker glanced again at the baby carrier Con held, her eyes wary as she watched the child sleeping inside. "Make certain you keep his blanket with him at all times," she said, turning toward the door.

"This dirty rag?" Con asked, indicating the dingy scrap of white material clutched in the baby's fist. He planned to throw the damn thing out the first chance he got. And then go out to buy his kid a real baby blanket—something blue.

"It's clean, Mr. Randolph," Mrs. Muldoon said defensively. "Just well washed. It's been with Joey since he was born."

Which is far more than you've been. Con heard what the woman wasn't saying.

"No matter what changes life brings him, the blanket is one thing that doesn't change," the social worker explained, her face tight.

"It's his security blanket," Robbie said, looking up. "No problem. We'll take it with us everywhere we go."

Sandra Muldoon's back stiffened. "I hope you aren't planning to do much running around, Mrs. Randolph. Babies tend to be fussy when their schedules are disrupted."

"We'll take proper care of him, ma'am," Con said, moving toward the front door. He wanted the woman out of his house. Still holding the carrier with one hand, he opened the door with the other and wished Mrs. Muldoon a good weekend.

"You'll need to launder that outfit and send it back with him on Sunday. It's not his," she said as she stepped off the front step.

Looking at the one-piece green terry thing the boy had on, Con didn't see where it would be any real loss either way. But he'd send it back where it came from—along with an entire collection of outfits his son could call his own. It sickened him to think of the boy dressed in state hand-me-downs. Con had worn enough of the poor-fitting donated castoffs for both of them.

"We'll make sure you get it back," Robbie said politely just as Con was ready to tell Sandra Muldoon what she could do with her damn clothes.

"Be sure you drop him off at his foster parents' by six o'clock on Sunday." The social worker's parting words were clearly a warning. Almost as if Con was on probation. And in a way he supposed he was.

He'd just have to show Muldoon and her crew the stuff he was made of. And hope to hell the judge found something there that pleased him.

"What should we do with him?" he asked Robbie as soon as they were alone. "Just let him sleep?"

She glanced from the baby to Con and then back to the baby. "Yeah, but let's try and lay him in his crib," she said, leading the way.

For once, Con was satisfied to follow her, careful not to jostle the carrier against his leg as he walked.

Robbie kept glancing back at them, grinning. "You're really loving this, aren't you?" Con asked. It was hard to feel guilty about using her when she looked so damned happy.

"Yep. Now let's get our son to bed, Mr. Randolph."

He held the carrier over the crib mattress as Robbie slid her hands carefully beneath the baby's body and transferred him to the bed. His small chest shuddered, his chin puckering like he was going to cry, and Con held his breath. He didn't think it would be a good omen if the first thing they did was make Joey cry.

"Ssshhh," Robbie crooned, lightly rubbing the baby's back while she tucked his old scrap of blanket under his cheek.

With a huge sigh coming from one so small, the boy settled back to sleep. Con held his breath for another few seconds, waiting, watching. And feeling such a mixture of hope, pride and insecurity it was almost scary. He couldn't let his entire life depend on the boy, didn't dare count on making a home with his son no matter how much he wanted to. Because to count on it and lose would probably kill him.

"He's beautiful, isn't he?" Robbie whispered, resting her hand on Con's shoulder as she stood beside him looking down at the baby.

"Boys can't be beautiful, Rob," he said.

"He's too young to be handsome," she persisted.

"He isn't beautiful."

"How about gorgeous?" She was grinning down at the baby, her eyes glowing with love, and Con could have told her what gorgeous was. It was a woman with a heart so big she'd tied herself to a man who'd never love her, to a child she might never get to keep, and was happy, anyway.

"Or there's precious," she said. "A guy can be precious when he's still a baby, can't he?"

Con nodded, her nonsense working its magic. He might not be a particularly nice man. He might not be a lovable man. But he was going to try his damnedest not to fail this new family of his.

"Having him here makes it all worth it, doesn't it, Con?"

He didn't answer. As much as he would have liked the cop-out, he didn't believe that having a son of his own was worth irresponsibly impregnating an emotionally unbalanced woman. It certainly wasn't worth the death that had started this whole chain of events.

And he wondered if being sent a son was God's way of making sure he never forgot how badly he'd sinned.

The good Lord could have saved himself the effort. That woman's cries of fear, the blood soaking her blue dress and the role he'd played, were things that, with or without Joey, Con would remember every day of his life.

"He's family, Con. We're a family now," Robbie said. She was no longer looking at the baby. She was looking right at him, and Con didn't have to wonder what she was thinking. He could tell by the steely determination in her eyes.

"Don't count on it, Rob," he warned. What judge was going to give a child over to a guy who "got his man at any cost?" A guy so heartless he'd see an innocent woman die to close a case?

A guy who'd kissed his best friend not once, but twice? And the second time after promising her father, a man he greatly admired, that he wouldn't touch her.

"It's over Con. The past is over and done," Robbie said, her voice laced with the steel he'd seen in her eyes. "We've been given a chance for a new life here. All three of us. Let yourself take the chance, Con, please, or we'll all lose, you most of all."

If only it was that easy. To take a chance at happiness when he'd brought others so much pain. How could that possibly be right? He wished to hell he knew.

But he'd lost track of right and wrong a long time ago.

"Please let this work, Con. Let us be a family. For my sake and Joey's, if not for yourself," Robbie pleaded when he remained silent.

And suddenly Con felt the weight of his sins lifting a little bit. Robbie had done it again, had known just what to say to free him enough to reach for that elusive brass ring, after all. Not because he deserved it himself, but for Joey. And for Robbie. His son. And his wife.

As HIS TRUCK ATE UP the miles from Sedona to Phoenix, Stan Blair chewed one of the antacids he'd given up when he'd retired from the Phoenix police force. Susan was humming and knitting beside him, transforming a ball of light blue yarn into a tiny sweater. She'd been humming ever since Robbie had called this morning, telling them they had the baby for the weekend. Susan couldn't have been happier. She was so eager to meet her grandson she asked Stan again and again how much longer it would be until they got there.

She'd made the trip countless times and certainly knew how long it took to get from Sedona to Phoenix. She was just urging him to drive a little faster. And had Robbie's marriage been normal—one based on mutual love, both physical and emotional—had he been on his way to meet the son of his daughter's loving husband, the son his daughter hoped to adopt, he'd have been pressing a little harder on the accelerator himself.

But he was filled with trepidation, instead. All he saw ahead was heartache. For everyone. Con and Robbie were crazy if they honestly thought they could make a celibate marriage work. And when it fell apart, they were all going to suffer. Susan, Robbie, himself. And Con and the boy, too. No one had a hope in hell of winning this one.

So why was he driving Susan straight into the biggest heartache she'd ever known? Why wasn't he turning their truck around, taking her back to Sedona and the emotional safety of their own home?

And telling her what? How could he explain any of this to her?

How could he tell Con Randolph he didn't believe in him? Because that was the message he'd be sending his reluctant son-in-law if he didn't show up on his doorstep as Robbie had asked.

It was a message he couldn't deliver. Because he did still believe—always had—that Con Randolph was a good man. He just didn't hold out much hope that Con would ever believe it.

"Come on, Stan, the speed limit's fifty here," Susan said when they turned north on Scottsdale Road from Bell. They were almost there. The antacid didn't seem to be working.

"I know what the speed limit is, dear," he said, reluctantly pushing the truck up to fifty.

A guy worked hard all his life, protected his family from harm, raised his kid to be a contributor to society. Was it too much to ask that he grow old with his family gathered around him happy and whole?

"Oh, Stan, she's outside waiting for us," Susan cried as he pulled onto Con's street. "And Con's with her. He's holding the baby. Oh, Stan, doesn't Con look happy?"

He didn't want to see. He didn't want to worry anymore. He didn't want to be there. Con didn't love Robbie. Their marriage wasn't made in heaven. And if something didn't change, they were all going to drown in a pool of tears before the year was out.

"Look, Stan!" Susan said again.

He pulled into Con's driveway, and Susan was out of the truck in a flash. This was it. He looked.

I'll be damned. His wife was right, or at least close to it. Con did seem happy as he held out his son to Susan's eager arms. At least as happy as Con ever seemed. His son-in-law wasn't smiling, but his eyes were filled with a gentleness he'd never seen there before.

Not as reluctant now, Stan got out of his truck.

CHAPTER EIGHT

CON WAS GLAD to have Stan and Susan around that first afternoon with Joey. With Susan oohing and aahing over the boy, it was a little easier for him to stand back, to distance himself enough to keep his bearings. It was a little easier to remember that Robbie wasn't a real wife. That they weren't the real family she was pretending they were. How could he forget with Stan there, watching with eagle eyes?

That was what Stan had always done. Con thought of the way he'd grabbed Robbie earlier that day, the way he'd kissed her to escape from himself. Just once he'd like to be worthy of Stan's trust.

Still, when the Blairs left shortly after dinner, he wasn't happy to see them go.

"You've got a boy to be proud of there, son," Stan said as they all walked out to Stan's truck. Robbie and her mother were trailing slowly behind, Susan holding Joey right up to the last minute. The boy had hardly cried all day. Which wasn't really surprising considering that he'd had two women hovering over him every minute, anticipating his every need, giving him more love in one afternoon than Con had probably had in his entire life.

"I can hardly take credit for him, Stan. I've just met him myself," Con finally said.

Stan stopped by the hood of his truck. "Part of you went in to making that boy, son. Nobody can take that away from you," he said before moving to the driver's-side door.

Con followed him, holding on to the door as the older man climbed inside. "I'm not going to let them take him," he said. He wanted Stan to rest assured that Robbie wasn't going to lose the baby she'd so clearly given her heart to.

"I know that, son," Stan said, putting his key in the ignition. "I'm not saying I condone any of this or that I take back what we discussed the other day, but you've made my daughter happy, and I thank you for that."

He pulled the door from Con's grasp and slammed it shut.

"Come on, Sus, I want to get off the highway before dark," he hollered, leaning over to open the passenger-side door.

Con stood beside Robbie as she waved her parents goodbye, Joey's arms and legs flailing against her.

"It's time for this little guy's bath," she said when her parents' truck was out of sight, forestalling any conversation Con might have had regarding their visit. Which was fine with him. There was no reason to tell her that her father had just thanked him for something for the first time in his life. Nor did she need to know how good that made him feel. He was sure it would pass.

ROBBIE AWOKE with a start and sat straight up in bed. She still wasn't used to sleeping at Con's house, and it took her a moment to get her bearings. Her gaze shot to the illuminated numbers on her digital clock. It was three in the morning.

The house was quiet. Maybe she'd only been dreaming. She was just lying back down, settling in to the soothing embrace of her water bed, when she heard it again. Con was talking to someone.

And that was when she remembered Joey. The baby was sleeping in his nursery across the hall from her. Or he was supposed to be. Was something wrong? Had Con had to call for help? Why hadn't he come for her?

Heart pounding, she was out of bed and across the hall in a flash. The baby's crib was empty.

She heard Con again, speaking softly, and followed the sound to the living room. She stopped at the doorway when she realized he wasn't talking on the phone after all. He was talking to Joey.

Robbie watched him with his son. The baby was in a corner of the couch propped up against a couple of pillows, probably from Con's bed, his blanket clutched in one tiny hand. And Con was standing behind the couch in the shirt and shorts he'd had on that day, holding a bottle to the baby's mouth. From where she was standing, Robbie could hear Joey's lusty sucking, could see, too, his wide-open eyes as he gazed up at his father.

Con's size didn't seem to intimidate Joey at all.

"You're a good boy, Joey," Con said, not in the

tone an adult usually used with a baby, but as if he expected him to understand. "It's not your fault your life started off on the wrong foot. And don't you ever let anyone tell you any different. And don't you ever let anyone tell you I abandoned you, either. Because that's one thing I'll never do. You can count on it."

The baby continued to gaze up at him, his free hand resting alongside Con's on the side of the bottle. Robbie wasn't sure she'd ever heard Con string so many words together at once. He was anything but verbose.

He'd have been a lot more comfortable sitting on the couch with the baby in his arms, but she wasn't about to tell him so. He'd figure it out when he was ready. In the meantime she reveled in the pleasure of the moment. Seeing her husband bond with his son.

SATURDAY DAWNED an average Phoenix summer day, brilliant blue skies and temperatures expected to reach 120. Con and Robbie both awoke before the baby and were showered and waiting for him.

"I'll go check on him again," Robbie said when Con looked up from his newspaper for the third time in one article.

He nodded, having done the last check himself.

"He's still out," she said when she came back into the kitchen. "But I checked his breathing and it's fine."

Con nodded again, taking a sip of his coffee. He'd rather have had a cigarette.

"Joey was up awhile in the night," he finally said. He wasn't sure why he'd admitted that, because he'd been thinking he'd keep their middle-of-the-night session between him and the boy.

"That explains the extra bottle in the dishwasher," Robbie said, surprisingly nonchalant.

Trust her to notice. "He was crying. I figured he might be hungry."

"He was probably wet. Did you change him?"

Did she honestly think he'd trust himself to do that on his own the first night? The boy was a hell of a lot different from the toy he'd practiced on. "No, but you put an overnight diaper on him."

Robbie picked up the baby's schedule Sandra Muldoon had left the day before. They were keeping it out on the breakfast bar where they could refer to it easily.

"It says here he's usually awake by seven. That's almost an hour ago," she said, reading on.

Con didn't like the sound of that. Was the kid coming down with something?

"But he doesn't normally eat in the night anymore. Maybe he's just sleeping late because his tummy's full."

Con sincerely hoped so. But he decided to go in and feel the boy's skin, anyway, just to make sure he wasn't hot.

When he slipped quietly into the nursery, Joey was wide awake and gazing up at the mobile Robbie had hung over his crib, following the brightly colored race cars as the air-conditioning blew them gently in a circle.

The boy turned his head when Con approached, his

fat cheeks dimpling as he grinned up at his father. Before he knew what was happening, Con felt himself grinning back.

"So you were playing possum with us, eh, boy?" he asked, lifting the baby out of the crib.

Joey kicked his feet against Con's stomach, gurgling at him.

And Con had thought *Robbie* was irritatingly cheerful in the morning. It seemed he was going to be surrounded with cheerfulness. In the years to come he'd probably have to get up at five in the morning just to have his few minutes of grouchiness in peace.

"Robbie!" he bellowed, carrying the baby to the changing table. Joey's sleeper was soaking wet. And now Con's shirt was, too.

Joey's chin puckered, his lips pursed, and his little face turned a mighty shade of red. And then he let loose with an ear-piercing wail.

"You scared him," Robbie said, running into the room.

"So it seems," Con snapped, picking the baby back up from the changing table.

"It's okay, guy, Daddy's just got a big voice." He held the boy to his chest and rubbed his back like he'd seen Robbie do yesterday.

And before he knew it, Joey was quiet, his hiccups the only evidence of the storm.

"He's soaked," Con told Robbie unnecessarily. She couldn't help but see that the entire back of the baby's sleeper was wet.

"Into the tub with you, young man," she said, taking him from Con.

Con followed her to the kitchen, where he set the plastic tub up in the sink and collected the tear-free soap and hooded towel. He had this down pat at least.

"He was wide awake when I went in," he told Robbie as he watched her bathe the baby. He didn't know how she managed to hold on to all those squirming slippery appendages.

"We need to get a monitor," she told Con over her shoulder. "Yes, that's a good boy," she cooed to the baby in the same breath. "You like that, don't you? Is Joey a happy baby? Say yes. Say yes. Come on..." Con wished the guys she worked with could see her now.

Except that he was kind of glad he was the only one seeing her this way. She was going to be a wonderful mother. To *his* son.

If they got custody.

Joey slapped his hand on the water, splashing Robbie, the counter and a brand new roll of paper towels.

Robbie laughed. "Oh! He's a strong boy, a very big boy to splash like that..."

Con found himself grinning again, whether at the baby or the woman he'd married, he wasn't sure. He fetched an extra towel and soaked up the puddles.

But he didn't feel at all like grinning a few minutes later when she lifted Joey from the bath. The baby's foot caught on the edge of her T-shirt, jerking it up above her breasts. The first thing he noticed was that she wasn't wearing a bra. And the second was that his best friend had incredible breasts. He suddenly couldn't breathe—and couldn't look away.

And then he saw the painful-looking gash on the underside of her right breast. It wasn't large, only an inch or so, but it angered him to see it there. He'd like to get his hands around the neck of the dog that did that to her.

"Let me take him," he said, lifting the baby from her arms. "Your stitches are getting wet." He didn't mean to sound so harsh, but dammit, she should be more careful.

And so should he about where he looked.

"It won't kill me," she snapped, turning her back on him as she yanked her shirt down.

Even as he held the squirming wet baby, Con couldn't get the sight of her out of his mind. He pictured himself touching her, tasting her. And castigated himself for his body's hot response. Robbie was his friend, and his son's mother.

He of all people had absolutely no business thinking of her as a woman.

Not only because he'd promised Stan he wouldn't or because he'd led Robbie to believe he wouldn't, but because he couldn't. When Con went to a woman for sex, sex was all it was. Period. To him, women were like a shot of bourbon. A quick fix, nothing more.

And he was damned if he'd reduce Robbie to that.

Joey's sudden wail brought his parents' attention back to him.

"He's cold," Robbie said, reaching over to wrap

the towel more firmly around him. Her movements were jerky, awkward.

Holding the ends of the towel together, Con carried the baby into the nursery and placed him on the changing table.

"Let's see if I can get *this* right," he whispered to the boy, hoping Robbie was behind him to back him up.

She was. She was his coach, his judge and his part-time cheering section as he fumbled with flailing arms and legs, struggled with tape closures that insisted on sticking before he got both sides of the diaper around the baby's leg. But eventually he managed it. And eventually he dressed his son.

Almost as if sensing the importance of the occasion, Joey was a gracious participant, amusing himself with his toes throughout the entire event.

"What time's your doctor's appointment?" Con asked Robbie an hour later as he rinsed Joey's cereal bowl. Robbie was wiping the baby's face and hands for what seemed the hundredth time.

"One o'clock." She felt the blood suffuse her face at the reference to those damn stitches. He'd seen the gash she'd been trying to keep from him, after all. And a whole lot more.

"We can pick up a monitor beforehand," Con said.

She pulled the baby from his carrier. "What do you mean, we?"

"I thought Joey and I would go along." His back was still to her. He seemed to be taking an awfully long time to rinse one little bowl and spoon. And suddenly Robbie understood.

"You're afraid to be here alone with him."

His back stiffened and his hands stilled. "I'm not afraid."

She held the baby up to her shoulder, rubbing his back. It wouldn't hurt to have them come along with her. "You'll have to keep him in the waiting room," she said. She wanted it clear that Con wasn't following her in while she had the stitches removed. He'd gotten the one good look at her breasts he was going to get in this lifetime.

"Fine." He turned around, suddenly done with his chore. "We should take your truck. It's bigger."

And that was when it hit Robbie that they had a problem, after all, in spite of their preparations. "We don't have a car seat."

Con stared at her silently for several seconds. "I'll go get one." He grabbed his keys from the counter, checked to see that he had his wallet in the pocket of his shorts and started for the door.

Robbie waited.

He didn't even make it out of the room. "What am I getting?" he asked, turning back around.

"Just make sure it's a full-size infant seat, Randolph. Ask someone at the store to help you. And keep in mind that I'm going to be lifting the thing, too." She grinned at him.

Con nodded, then said, his jaw tense, "I am not afraid to be alone with him."

She turned the baby around, sitting him up on her

lap. "Sure you are, Randolph, but it's okay. Most dads are at first. It's perfectly normal."

He left without another word.

"MRS. RANDOLPH?"

"Yes?"

Con's gaze flew to Robbie. *Mrs. Randolph?*

"The doctor will see you now."

He didn't have time to fret about being left in sole charge of his son. He was too busy thinking about Robbie as Mrs. Randolph. Besides, with an office full of nurses and a waiting room full of women, he had plenty of backup.

Joey was sleeping in his new carrier-cum-car-seat, clutching his scrap of blanket. "Just pick him up if he wakes," Robbie whispered to him as she stood to go.

Con nodded. He knew what to do. He was the one who'd heard the kid cry during the night. Well, Joey hadn't actually made it to the crying stage, but only because Con's senses were acute from years of training, and the whimper that would have become a cry had woken him from a sound sleep.

He'd been unsure what to do, unsure of his ability to give the boy what he needed. But considering the alternative—going into Robbie's room to wake her, being in the same room with her while she was in bed—he'd decided to deal with Joey himself.

At least Robbie was in the house, a sort of safety net. He could always go for her if he couldn't figure

out what to do. But to his surprise, he'd done just
fine.

Give him another couple of years and he might
even be ready to tackle the kid without anyone else
within yelling distance.

He glanced at Joey and then looked again. His son.
His flesh and blood. He'd never met another soul in
his life who had his bloodline, his genes. The boy
was family.

Mrs. Randolph. He thought again of the nurse calling out the name. Of Robbie answering. He'd never
given enough credence to the brief ceremony they'd
enacted for their "undercover operation" to acknowledge that it had actually changed Robbie's name.
Changed it to his. He supposed she was family now,
too.

Joey was still sleeping when Robbie returned a few
minutes later. Con's brows raised in question, his
gaze on her breast.

Robbie frowned at him, busying herself with the
baby's things. "I'm fine. All healed. He doesn't even
think there'll be a scar," she said, reaching for Joey's
carrier.

"I'll get that," Con said, standing, as well. No
scar. Maybe not, but he'd always know where one
might have been.

Ten minutes later Con waited in the car with a still-
sleeping Joey while Robbie ran into the store for the
baby monitor. He turned the air conditioner up to
maximum. It was 115 outside. He didn't want the boy
sweating.

"It's freezing in here," Robbie said, shivering as she climbed back in the passenger side. They'd decided to take his car, after all. The car seat required a shoulder strap, which, in the truck, would have required Robbie to sit in the middle next to Con. They'd both reached the realization at the same time, and without either acknowledging why, they'd moved to the car, instead.

Con turned down the air, wondering if they'd ever regain the easy camaraderie they'd had before the wedding, before he'd blown things by kissing her. Before Stan had made such an issue of her big lonely bed.

Before someone had called her Mrs. Randolph. *Mrs. Randolph.* His wife.

He needed a cigarette. "You feel like a burger?" he asked.

"Sure." She fastened her seat belt, glancing in the back once more to check on Joey.

"You think he'll be okay if we eat it there?"

Robbie shrugged. "I don't know. Mrs. Muldoon said not to take him out too much. What do you think?"

They both looked at their sleeping charge. "I think we need to start as we mean to go on," Con said. He planned to take his son with him everywhere. At least, everywhere a kid could go.

"Then let's go get burgers. I'm starved."

ROBBIE FOUND CON leaning against a pillar outside by the pool that night after dinner. Smoking a cigarette.

"Damn," he said, putting the cigarette out when he saw Joey in her arms.

Robbie grinned. "Don't talk like that in front of the baby."

Con grimaced. "Sorry."

He looked grouchy. But he was trying so hard it broke Robbie's heart. She wished he trusted himself a little more.

"You want to go swimming?" Con asked suddenly.

A dip in the pool sounded like heaven. She'd been feeling too warm and clammy all day. "Yeah, I do," she said. "Here, take him while I change." She handed him his squirming son.

"We didn't get a suit for him," Con said, automatically settling the baby on one hip.

Robbie felt tears threaten as she watched him handle the baby. In just twenty-four hours he'd grown so much more comfortable with his son. "He can go in his diaper," she said.

Robbie ran inside and slipped into her sleek one-piece racing suit. She and Con hadn't swum together in ages.

Because the last time you did you drove yourself crazy lusting over his powerful chest, his hard-as-rock stomach, his long muscular legs, she reminded herself. But that wasn't going to happen tonight. She'd have Joey to concentrate on. She wouldn't even know his father was there.

And pigs fly.

CON AND JOEY had been in the water for quite a while when Robbie finally came out and dove into the pool behind him.

"How does he like it?" she asked, surfacing.

"He likes it just fine," Con said as she stood up in the shallow water. *And so does his father,* he thought. Why in God's name had he never noticed before what a great body Robbie had? And why was he noticing now? She, and her firm luscious breasts were off-limits. Period.

"Did he cry when you put him in?" she asked, watching as he bobbed the baby up and down.

"Nope."

She reached out to tickle the baby and Joey giggled.

"Omigosh! He laughed!" she cried, tickling the baby again.

And suddenly Con felt like laughing, too. Joey's delight in Robbie's attentions was contagious.

She grabbed the baby under his arms, swung him up in the air and brought him down to splash in the water. Joey shrieked with pleasure, and she did it again. And then again, both of them laughing.

Con had never found a woman so sexy.

He backed slowly away, into deeper water, hiding his erection. Robbie's breasts, straining against her suit as she lifted the baby, were a sinful temptation. He crossed to the other side of the pool and started to swim laps.

She was still playing with the baby when he'd exhausted his body to the point of numbness. But at least he'd be able to get out of the pool without embarrassing himself.

"I'm going in," he said, reaching the shallow end.

"Then take him, would you, so I can swim." She held the baby out to him.

He reached for the boy, unaware that Joey had a hold on the strap of Robbie's swimsuit. The baby's grip was strong, and when Con grasped him, together they pulled Robbie off balance. Her thigh brushed Con's, smooth as silk, firm, feminine.

And just like that he was on fire again.

She gasped and started to laugh again, grabbing Con's arm to steady herself, but Joey wouldn't let go of her. She fell against them, instead, her hips bumping Con's. He knew the very instant she felt his hardness.

The laughter died in her throat, her fingers dug into his arm, and her expression closed. She pried the baby's fingers off her suit.

Joey's little hand found a new target almost instantly—the mass of hair on Con's chest, which he clutched and pulled. Hard. Con had never been more thankful for pain in his life.

"No, no, Joey, you'll hurt Daddy," Robbie said softly, releasing the baby's fingers one by one.

Con's chest constricted beneath her tender touch, his nerve endings taunting him. Testing him. She knew what she was doing to him. And she was still doing it. She wasn't backing off.

But she had to. There was a very good reason she had to.

"You're a little rascal." She chuckled seductively as Joey, having discovered the fun to be had, tried for another handful of hair.

Her voice was husky, her fingers lingering against Con's skin suggestively as she once again loosened the baby's hand.

She was still the Robbie he'd always known. And yet she wasn't. She was his wife. But not in the way that mattered. She couldn't be. He'd given his word.

He thought of the promise he'd made Stan. Of the reason he'd made that promise. He'd agreed to Stan's stipulation for one reason and one reason only. Because the old man was right. Robbie deserved much more than he could ever give her. She deserved love.

And all he had to offer her was sex.

"Enjoy your laps," he said abruptly, then twisted away from her, the baby in one arm, and climbed out of the pool. Joey's fingers found their mark again, yanking harder than he'd have thought a sixth-month-old baby could. Con didn't even flinch and continued on into the house.

He didn't place the baby in his crib, because he didn't trust himself not to head right back outside to his mother.

CHAPTER NINE

IT WAS QUARTER after five Sunday afternoon. The time Robbie had been dreading since she'd gotten up that morning. She looked at the big face of her men's digital sport watch again, hoping for a few extra minutes. But it was five-fifteen, not five-ten. They needed to leave by five-twenty at the latest if they were to have the baby back on time.

Con was asleep on the couch, Joey napping on his chest. Con's arm curved around the baby, his hand resting on the baby's back. They'd been that way for more than an hour, and the last thing Robbie wanted to do was disturb them.

But she was going to have to wake them, or wake Con, anyway. This was one instance when being late could mean life or death—at least for their dreams.

She arose from the chair she'd been sitting on for most of the past hour, tucking her T-shirt back into the blue-jean cutoffs she'd had on all day. She'd been strangely comforted by the steady rise and fall of Con's chest, the stern set of his chin, even in sleep.

As she approached the couch, her gaze traveled lower, to his long muscular thighs. She remembered the feel of those hair-roughened legs pressing against her in the pool yesterday, the rock-solid hardness of him as the water rippled sensuously around them.

He'd wanted her. For one brief moment he'd found her desirable. Until he'd looked at her. Until he'd realized whose body was pressing so intimately against his own. Then he couldn't have made it clearer that his response wasn't for her. But she already knew that. Had known it for years.

She'd swum forty laps before she'd followed him into the house, attempting to dispel the pain his rejection had left behind, to numb her buzzing nerve endings, to convince herself she wasn't as starved for the feel of a man's body as she thought she was. Con's body.

"Con?" she called softly.

He was instantly awake, his eyes alert, searching.

"It's time to go." She bent to take the baby, hoping to keep Joey asleep for a while longer. She didn't want him crabby when they returned him. She didn't want to give his foster mother any room for complaint.

Con stood up, his gaze averted from the baby. "I'll get his things," he said, leaving the room. Robbie watched him go, saw the stiffness return to his back, to his entire being.

This wasn't going to be easy. Not for any of them. She hugged the baby to her breast, breathing in his sweet scent. *We'll miss you so much, little Joey. If only there were some way for you to know how much we love you. And please, oh, please, don't forget us before we see you again.*

"Let's go." Con was back, his face a study in control.

They took his car again and the forty-minute drive to Gilbert was accomplished in total silence. Con was at his most unapproachable, his eyes flinty, his body more like a marble sculpture than flesh and blood. She wished there was some way she could reach him, ease the hurt and frustration that was causing him to retreat into the armored shell he presented to the world.

As each mile passed, the knot in her stomach grew, the pain in her chest making it harder and harder to breathe. After only two days she couldn't bear the thought of waking up without Joey, sitting down to eat without feeding him first, going to sleep at night without hearing his steady breathing on the monitor beside her bed.

She couldn't imagine having him in her arms one second and gone the next.

They passed the Gilbert city-limits sign, and Robbie closed her eyes. She didn't want to see the neighborhood, the peeling billboards and unmanicured lawns, to see pictures of the places Joey might already be familiar with, places he would recognize more easily than Con's home. Tears burned behind her eyelids and she willed them back. Tears weren't going to help.

Joey was still asleep when Robbie pulled him from his car seat and carried him up to the door of the faded-wood house. Con followed silently with Joey's things, carrying an extra knapsack that contained a wardrobe of new outfits they'd picked up after their burgers on Saturday.

She'd wanted Joey to sleep, but now she hoped he'd wake up before they had to leave him so they'd at least be able to say goodbye to him. She hated the thought of his falling asleep with them and waking up with someone else. She didn't want him to think they'd abandoned him.

Betty Williams, Joey's foster mother, took the baby from Robbie's arms as soon as she opened the door.

"Good. You're right on time," she said, smiling as she looked down at Joey. "And he's sleeping, too. Hopefully it'll last another half hour. My family's right in the middle of dinner."

"Let's go," Con said to Robbie, setting Joey's things by the door before turning and heading back to the car.

Robbie couldn't just walk away and leave her little boy with this total stranger. "He's got some new clothes," she told the woman.

"Oh! Thank you." Mrs. Williams glanced over her shoulder, her hand on the front door. She obviously wanted to get back to her family.

"Well, if you have any questions about anything, call us. Our number's in there with his stuff."

"Fine," Mrs. Williams said.

"Mama!" A child's cry came from the interior of the house.

"Just a minute!" the woman called back.

Joey shifted, but he didn't wake up, as if sleeping through bouts of loud noise wasn't all that unusual.

"I'll let you get back to your dinner, then," Robbie said. She knew she had to go.

"Thanks for baby-sitting for us," Betty Williams called just before her door closed.

Robbie flinched as the words lashed her. *Baby-sitting?* Was that all she and Con were? Baby-sitters? People with no authority whatsoever in the decisions made in Joey's life? With no rights?

No! She refused to accept that. No matter what the state said, what the courts thought. They'd been a family this weekend, a real family. A mother, a father, a son.

The car was already running, with Con sitting impatiently behind the wheel. He threw it into reverse before Robbie even had her door closed. As much as she hated to cry, hated the weakness, the run-down neighborhood was blurred by her tears as they sped past. She'd just left a big piece of her heart behind.

Accelerating, Con pulled a pack of cigarettes out of the console, snapped open the ashtray and lit up, taking a long drag before offering the cigarette to her. Robbie accepted it gratefully and wiped away her tears with the fingers of her free hand. Con lit another cigarette for himself.

Angry control was in every movement he made. He drove well, but not smoothly, accelerating more quickly than necessary, taking corners sharply, yielding to no one.

He said nothing about the child they'd just left behind.

A car with a bunch of teenage boys pulled out in

front of them, forcing Con to brake or hit them. "Bastards," he said, slowing down.

Robbie held her tongue. She was sitting beside a stick of dynamite that was dangerously close to exploding.

"At least you can smoke again," she said lightly, worried about him. They had to get through this. They were probably going to have to get through a lot more before it was all over.

Con grunted.

Robbie fell silent again, watching the neighborhoods whiz past, the seemingly endless miles that were taking them farther and farther from Joey. In an emergency it would take them forever to get to him.

If he has an emergency, will we even be called?

The car jerked to a halt behind a woman in a blue minivan in the right-turn lane. The light was red, but there was no oncoming traffic. No reason the woman couldn't turn. Except that she was reaching behind her to an infant seat in the back. "Go," Con muttered, scowling.

Robbie fought a fresh welling of tears. "You had no choice, Con. You had to leave him there."

"Tell Joey that." He passed the blue minivan, accelerating from zero to the speed limit in seconds.

"I know it's hard, but we have to remember that the system is there to protect him," Robbie said. The system helped children every day, made their lives better, didn't it? Joey would be all right. He'd already survived six months without them.

"The system can go to hell."

In that moment Robbie had a hard time not agreeing with him. What kind of system would force a man to do something that went against every responsible bone in his body? Force him to turn his newfound infant son over to total strangers?

No matter how hard she tried to look for the positive, she just kept thinking about what Joey was going to think, how he was going to feel, when he woke up to find they'd gone. Would he be scared? Would he miss them? Cry for them? Or would he just shrug them off as another couple of the temporary adults who had passed through his young life?

Would he care that there'd be no race-car mobile for him to watch when he awoke in the morning?

JOEY'S THINGS mocked Con when he followed Robbie through the garage door into the kitchen half an hour later. Clean bottles stood upside down on a towel by the sink, a can of soy-milk powder beside them. A blue teddy-bear rattle had been abandoned by the refrigerator. And a soiled bib still lay on the breakfast bar.

"Why in hell didn't you put that in the laundry?" Con snapped, pointing at the offensive garment.

"I forgot. I'm sorry," Robbie said softly, picking up the bib, quietly sliding open the doors concealing the laundry closet and dropping the tiny garment into the washing machine.

"And what about the bottles?" he asked, glaring at them.

"I'll get them." She quickly removed the bottles and all other evidence of the baby from the kitchen.

What in hell was she doing? What in hell was *he* doing? *He'd* left those bottles there.

"No. I'm sorry, Rob." He ran his fingers through his hair, trying to make sense out of a world gone mad. "I just can't... It's not... I feel so..." He broke off, not knowing what he even wanted to say. He just knew that if he allowed himself to feel the waves of despair crashing around him, he'd drown. He had to keep fighting to keep them at bay.

"It's okay, friend," Robbie said, moving to him and squeezing his hand briefly. "I understand."

Which was more than he did.

"That still doesn't give me the right to take it out on you." She'd just changed her entire life for him, and he repaid her with a display of bad temper.

"That's what friends are for," she said, trying a grin that didn't quite work.

She was hurting, too. He could see the pain in her steady gaze, in the tremble in her chin. He put his arms around her and pulled her against him.

"Ah, Rob, what have we gotten ourselves into?" he asked.

"Just another one of life's little challenges, I guess." Her words were muffled against his chest.

Resting his chin on the top of her head, the short blond tendrils of her hair tickling his face, he told himself to set her away. But her warmth was too soothing. "We have to face the fact that the judge may not give him to me. To us."

She shuddered, pulling back to look up at him. "He has to, Con. And he will."

She must have seen Con's doubt. "Look at all we have to offer Joey," she added. "How could he not?"

Con grimaced. She'd never really seen him for what he was. "*You* have a lot to offer, maybe. *I* fathered a child with a woman I didn't know."

"You were drunk, Con."

"Oh, that makes it all right, then," he said sarcastically. He had to make her see the truth.

They might very well not get the boy. Con had a lot of strikes against him. Always had. And he couldn't have Robbie resting all her hopes and dreams on the chance that the judge was willing to overlook his mistakes, the flaws in his character.

"It makes you human, Con. Once you have a chance to explain the circumstances—"

He cut her off. "He'll certainly find it commendable that I was so bloodthirsty for Ramirez I allowed an innocent woman to die just to get him."

"You didn't know—"

"I knew *someone* was there," he said harshly.

She reached up and traced the lines on his forehead with gentle fingers. "But you thought it was an accomplice."

He needed to let her go. Out of his arms. Out of his life. He had nothing for her. Not even the baby she wanted so badly to mother.

"It doesn't matter what I thought," Con said. "I should have waited."

"And let Ramirez get away?"

"Why not ask the question of the family who loved that woman? Why not ask the teenage boy who had to make his mother's funeral arrangements, instead of attending his high-school prom?"

Robbie sighed and laid her head back on his chest. "You're a good man, Con Randolph. You have a good heart. Someday, somehow, I'm going to make you see that."

Con took Robbie's shoulders and held her away from him. Her belief in him was a burden he could no longer bear, not when it was leading her into pain and unhappiness. He couldn't let her stay another minute if she wasn't going to do it with her eyes open.

"I have no heart, Robbie. None."

Tears flooded her eyes as her lips formed a trembling smile. "Oh, yes, you do. You're just not listening to it yet."

Her refusal to see the truth was one frustration too many. "You're the one not listening, Robbie. It's time to give up the pretense." His grip on her shoulders tightened. "I'll never have these great qualities you think you see in me. And if you can't accept that, you need to get out."

Her eyes continued to shimmer with tears. "You have them, Con. I see them every time you risk your life to right an injustice. I feel them every time you look at me, every time I need a friend and you're there, every time you get mad at me for doing something a little dangerous."

God, the woman was obtuse. "I'm *using* you,

Rob,'' he said brutally. He had to get her away from him, to protect her.

''You aren't using me. We're using each other. Otherwise known as caring. It's what being friends is all about.''

Friends. Right. If he was any kind of friend, if he *cared*, his body wouldn't be on fire for her. Maybe, he thought next, that was the *only* way to get her see the truth. To *show* her how badly he could use her.

Even while his brain told him it was wrong, he gave in to the temptation that had been driving him mad for days. He hauled her to him and crushed her lips beneath his own. He didn't ask for a response, he took one, forcing her lips open. She wasn't his friend anymore. She was just a woman who had something his body wanted.

His tongue plundered her mouth, showing her none of the respect that had defined their relationship since they were kids. He let his desire lead him and didn't even attempt to soften its force. A part of him, some small speck left over from his boyhood, cried out, knowing he was destroying the one good thing he'd ever had in his life—Robbie's affection for him.

Her mouth was warm and soft, so deliciously soft. And her tongue was doing things to him that had never been done before.

He continued to ravage her mouth, trying to consume her. Except that she wasn't letting him consume anything. She was giving what he demanded and taking as much in return. Her tongue matched his thrust for thrust. She was a formidable opponent, better now than during the best of their verbal battles.

And suddenly Con couldn't do it. Couldn't take that final step that would make her hate him—and maybe herself, as well.

Confused, he pulled away. Something was happening. He just had no idea what. His body was still hard and throbbing, still wanting to drive into her, to seek satisfaction in the only way he knew. But his mind had suddenly taken a different route; he was thinking of the woman he held, not of the body he'd been about to plunder. He had no idea what was wrong with him, with her. He only knew he had to stop.

He moved back another step, steadying his breathing, willing his heart to resume its normal pace, until all that was left of the moment was the bitter aftertaste of shame.

"I've never forced a woman," he said. It was suddenly imperative she know that.

"I didn't think you had."

Her voice was husky. His body started to throb again. He had to put a stop to the insanity.

"What just happened," he said, "don't go thinking it meant something. It didn't."

She stood in front of him, her chest heaving with the effort it took to breathe. "It meant you want me."

Her boldness turned him on even more, making him desperate. "It meant I want sex. Who with isn't important. When it's time, I take what's offered."

He took no satisfaction when his barb hit home. She flinched and retreated a step. "I didn't offer."

"What do you call last night in the pool?"

She stared at him, stricken, speechless for the first time since he'd known her. For all her toughness she was as tender as they come, no match for him at all. He was winning hands down. So why did he feel so awful?

"Your nipples were hard as pebbles, babe, and you were playing with my chest like a woman in heat," he taunted, purposefully cruel—and hating himself for every word he said. But someday she'd thank him. Someday she'd be grateful he'd saved her from him.

"Why are you doing this?" she asked. Again her eyes shimmered with unwashed tears.

They were almost his undoing. Except that too much was at stake. Her own father knew she needed saving. "Why shouldn't I take what's offered if I feel like it? As I recall, you're my wife."

"Because this isn't how you do things, Con Randolph," she said, her chin trembling. "You may really be a cold, hard man, but you've never been cruel."

She was supposed to be running from him in tears, not sounding like some damn righteous know-it-all. And his shorts weren't still supposed to be so painfully tight.

She stepped close to him again, her gaze steady as she looked into his eyes. "You're trying to save me from myself, aren't you. It'd be just like you to do something so ridiculously outrageously noble—and stupid."

Con issued a string of expletives. She knew him too damn well. No one should know him that well.

"Sorry it didn't work, but welcome back, friend," Robbie said with a wobbly grin.

And then it was Con who found himself retreating. It was either that, or haul her into his arms again. Only this time it wouldn't have been to teach her a lesson. If it ever had been.

Grabbing a pack of cigarettes out of the kitchen drawer, he headed for the door.

"Con?"

He turned around reluctantly. He needed some space.

"Don't touch me again," she said, her voice steadier than it had any right being. "Not until you can do it without apologizing. Not until you can do it with more than just your body."

Which meant never. "I won't," he promised her. It was a promise he wasn't sure he could keep.

CHAPTER TEN

CON TOOK ONE MORE DRAG on his cigarette before crushing it in the car ashtray. Once he went inside, he wouldn't have another one. He hadn't smoked in the house in five days. Not since Friday when his son had arrived.

It had been three days since they'd seen Joey. It seemed like another lifetime. His gut had been eroding ever since.

Throwing his keys on the breakfast bar, Con headed straight for the fridge and a beer. God, he was tired. Tired to the bone. He'd been back to work for three days and already he was beat. The case he was working on was a local check counterfeiter, nothing big—not like Ramirez's organization had been. He'd be able to get the guy within the week. Too bad he didn't care.

The phone rang just as he was enjoying his first sip of beer.

"Randolph," he snapped into the receiver. If it was Robbie telling him she was going to be late again, he was going to wring her neck. She didn't have to avoid him, didn't have to worry that he was going to try to jump her bones again. That had to have been the all-time dumbest thing he'd ever done.

"Mr. Randolph? This is Karen Smith from social services."

"Yes?" Con said, bracing himself.

"There're a couple of things I need to discuss with you, sir," the woman said in a rush. "First, we've got a court date for the placement hearing. It's set for July thirtieth at ten. Is that all right for you?"

"I'll make sure it is," Con said, grabbing his pen and jotting down the date and time.

"Will your wife be attending with you?"

"Of course." He hoped Robbie was still around by then. Hell, he was beginning to hope she'd be around a lot longer than that. Though, after what he'd done Sunday night he wouldn't blame her if she'd already filed for divorce.

"Oh, good," Karen said, her relief apparent. Con heard what she wasn't saying. If Robbie wasn't there, they were all wasting their time.

"You said you had two things to discuss?" Con reminded the woman. There was something she didn't want to tell him. He could sense it.

"Yes, sir. It's just that...the baby's mother has come back into the picture."

Con felt the blood drain from his face. "Meaning?"

"Probably nothing," Karen was quick to assure him. "Except that she claims she's sorry and she's willing to do whatever is necessary to get custody of Joey."

"Is that possible?"

"Anything's possible," Karen said in her usual

noncommittal way. "But personally I'm not sure she really means it. How well do you know Cecily Barnhardt, Mr. Randolph?"

He thought of the woman who'd sat beside him in the bar that night. He'd never even gotten a good look at her. "I don't know her at all," he said, though he suspected Karen knew that.

"She's very immature," Karen said calmly. "She appears to be looking for someone to take care of her, not someone to take care of. It's possible she heard you were back in the picture and has somehow assumed that if you want Joey, you'll take her in, too."

Con listened intently, drawing up a composite of Cecily Barnhardt in his mind, prepared to outthink the woman if necessary. "I'm married," he reminded Karen. At least for now.

"She may not know that," Karen replied. "In any case, the state is obligated to allow her time to prove herself a fit parent."

"How much time?"

"At least six months."

Con slammed down his beer. "The hearing's only three weeks away."

"That will be a placement hearing, Mr. Randolph, at which time you and your wife may be appointed as Joey's caregivers, but he'll remain a ward of the state until his custody is determined."

Con digested that piece of information silently. Just more bad news he had to break to Robbie. It seemed as though that was all he ever did—bring her bad news. She'd been working like a madwoman for three days straight, and he knew it wasn't only because of him. She was missing the baby.

And so was he.

"I want to see him before then," he said. He was the boy's father. He had to have *some* rights.

"Certainly. Now that the DNA's back, you can have him every weekend if you like."

The tension in Con's gut slowly disintegrated. "I like. How soon can we pick him up?"

"Friday, anytime after four. Betty Williams will have him ready."

Robbie would be happy. Maybe even happy enough to forget what an ass he'd made of himself.

"Oh...Mr. Randolph? *If* you get placement, chances are good you'll get custody, too."

Con hung up the phone, suddenly energized. He'd heard Karen's *if* loud and clear, but he'd always taken things one step at a time. And in just two days he'd see his son again. Two days until he and Robbie could put their own troubles aside and be a team once more.

But sometime during those two days he had to tell Robbie about Cecily Barnhardt's reentry into their lives. How in hell did a man tell his wife she might lose her baby to a woman her husband had slept with, when he'd never even slept with *her?*

CON DIDN'T GET AROUND to telling Robbie about Cecily before Friday. She'd been working late both Wednesday and Thursday, and he'd been up and gone in the mornings before she appeared. He'd left her a note on the breakfast bar telling her they would pick up Joey for the weekend, so she'd be sure to come home early on Friday. It was true they'd been avoiding each other, but he was banking on the baby to bring them back together again—and to be the buffer that would help him keep his hands off her.

But once they had Joey that afternoon, although he told her about the placement hearing, he was loath to mention Cecily. Their time with the boy was too limited. The hours spent with him were the best hours Con had ever had, and he couldn't bring himself to tarnish them with the messy details of their future— or his past.

Stan and Susan drove down from Sedona on Saturday, bearing far too many gifts. With Joey on her lap, Robbie unwrapped each one, holding it up in front of the baby as if he really understood what it was or that it was for him. Joey obliged her by staring at each of the various brightly colored toys. He even reached for a couple. A mouse that squeaked. And a plastic hourglass that was filled with water and brightly colored confetti.

Susan marveled at every move the baby made. Even Stan got into the act, coaxing smile after smile out of the boy.

Con was content to watch, glad that Joey was getting the acceptance from this family he'd once craved so hopelessly for himself.

The weekend flew by. He and Robbie fell right back into parenting as if they'd been at it for years. They played with Joey; they shopped for more things they'd suddenly discovered they needed for him—a teething ring for one; they took turns feeding him and changing him.

Together they discovered new and amazing things about the little boy—the birthmark on his knee that was identical to Con's, the way he was starting to scoot himself around on his belly, the tooth they were sure was starting to come through. Together they pushed his stroller and answered proudly when people asked questions about him.

And together they drove him silently back to Gilbert on Sunday.

In one way this trip was made easier by the knowledge that they'd be getting Joey again in just five days. But for Con it was also more difficult. First, because as soon as the baby was gone, so would be the camaraderie he and Robbie had shared over the weekend.

And second, because he knew he had one more strike against him now, a strike Robbie knew nothing about. The boy's biological mother wanted him back.

THINGS WERE SHAPING UP. Now that he knew the woman was living with Randolph, he didn't have to watch the place so much. He still had to figure how he was going to get her out of there, but he had time. And ideas, too. He was having a real good time considering the ideas. He spent whole days just thinking about them. Yeah, maybe he'd take her at night. Maybe even when Randolph was home. Whatever way was going to make Randolph hurt the most.

He had the place to take her to. It was empty, but

he'd slept there last night. Not too many crickets, but hot. He'd had to sleep naked.

He'd thought about making Randolph watch him do it to her before he took her away. Except he wasn't keen on hurting the woman. Not until he had to. Or on giving Randolph a chance to stop him. The bastard was good, and a lot bigger than he was. He had to be smart about this, had to get it right. He'd only get one chance. And his black belt in karate probably wouldn't faze a guy like Randolph.

No, he'd probably grab her when Randolph wasn't home. His percentages would be better that way. He'd just have to make certain that Randolph suffered afterward. A lot.

ROBBIE LEFT the TV station in time to make it home for dinner Monday night. She'd missed Con last week. But she'd needed the time away from him, time to recover from his assault on her senses, her heart.

She pulled onto Con's street, *her* street now, too, waving at the teenager who was the neighborhood odd-job boy, out raking the gravel in the yard across the street.

Con had done her a favor, really. He'd been trying to shock her, make her not want him. But he'd also said something she'd needed to hear. It wasn't *her* his body was responding to, as she'd so desperately wanted to believe. It was his need for a woman. Any woman. He'd obviously been celibate for a while, and she had legs and breasts, both of which she'd shamelessly rubbed against him in the pool.

She pushed the button on the remote, and when the garage door opened, was disappointed to see that Con's car wasn't there. She pulled her truck into her side of the two-car garage, then lowered the door behind her.

She wasn't his type. She knew that. Had always known that. The women Con went for were her total opposite, helpless beauties every one of them. She'd seen enough of them come and go over the years. But she had something none of them had ever had, something far more precious than sex—Con's friendship.

She'd been content with that for twenty-five years. She couldn't let a little thing like this marriage change that.

Which was why she was glad he'd stopped when he had that night last week in the kitchen. As much as it had hurt, she knew it would have been a thousand times worse if they'd gotten as far as his bedroom or hers. By then it would have been too late to salvage anything. Not her heart. Not her marriage. And not their friendship.

She had spaghetti boiling in the pot when Con walked through the door half an hour later. She'd heard him pull in five minutes before and knew he'd been outside finishing his cigarette before he came in. She'd been very tempted to go out and join him. She hadn't had a cigarette in more than a week, and her nerves were jangling.

"I didn't expect you to be here," he said, throwing his keys on the breakfast bar next to one of Joey's pacifiers. There were clean bottles upside down on a towel on the counter, too.

Robbie shrugged, trying to remember how they used to act before they'd gotten married. "I was a little tired. Home sounded good."

He pulled a beer from the refrigerator, twisted off the cap and tossed it in the trash. "It's good to have you home," he said. She froze, her back to him, staring at the spaghetti as she blinked away a sudden rush of tears. He'd never said that to her before.

"Here—you want one?" he asked.

Robbie turned. He was holding out a beer.

Just like the old days. "Sure," she said, taking it from him, trying not to notice when his hand brushed hers. There was absolutely nothing seductive about the movement, but her body ignited, anyway. How in hell was she going to survive a lifetime of this?

"So what kind of blood and gore did you cover today?" he asked, getting out the tomato sauce for the spaghetti.

"I've been investigating a couple of nursing homes here in the valley," she said, ignoring her reactions to his nearness as best she could as they finished preparing the meal together.

He pulled a loaf of French bread from the freezer. "Why?"

"They're owned by a group of doctors, all internists who specialize in geriatrics," she explained, frowning. "We got this anonymous tip that the good doctors are convincing family members that patients need to be institutionalized before they really do."

"Are they?"

Robbie shook her head, her short hair bobbing against her ears. "That's just it, I don't know. I've visited the homes, Con, talked to many of the patients, and while some of them belong there without a doubt, there are others who seem perfectly capable of living at home. Yet the family members I've interviewed all insist they had no other choice."

"You could be going for the wrong story," Con said, slicing the frozen bread. "What you may have here are families who no longer want the burden of caring for their elderly."

Robbie rinsed the lettuce for a salad. "I don't think so, Con. One woman I spoke to was really broken up about having to institutionalize her husband. She spends every waking moment at the home with him. She'd do anything to have him back with her, but she's convinced he has to be there. So they're living the rest of their lives in a nursing home that's eating up all their savings."

Con frowned, quiet for so long that Robbie thought the discussion was over. She should have known better.

"I'd look for a younger family member," he finally said. "Maybe a son or daughter of the woman you just mentioned. Elderly people tend to be more dependent on their doctors, often taking a doctor's word as law. Possibly seeing symptoms they're told to see. They're also easier to convince. Someone younger might give you the insight you're missing."

Robbie nodded, knowing she should have come to

him before now. She always had before. The man was an expert when it came to human motivation. She supposed it came from years of trying to please disapproving caregivers, of always putting himself in others' shoes. Or maybe he'd developed a sixth sense during his years as an agent. Lord knew it had helped save his life a time or two.

"Thanks, friend, I will," she said, suddenly feeling better than she had in days.

"Anytime."

Anytime. This was what she had from him, an open-ended twenty-four-hour-a-day invitation into his life. She had to let it be enough.

"ROBBIE, CAN I SEE YOU?" Rick Hastings called out into the newsroom late Tuesday afternoon.

She dropped what she was working on and walked into the producer's office.

"What's up?"

"I've been going over the tape of your interview with Blackwell this morning. Great stuff."

"Thanks." She'd even dressed up for the occasion and was still wearing her new pair of black jeans and a white blouse.

"I'd like you to do the piece live on the air."

Robbie's gaze flew to Rick's. He had to be kidding. He'd always told her she was one hell of an investigative reporter, but she didn't have the right look to actually report the stories she uncovered. Which was why her pieces were always dubbed. Someone else narrated her stuff on air, paraphrasing the questions she'd asked to correspond with clips of the subject's answers.

"We're running it tomorrow night at six. Report to makeup by five."

"You got it," she said, grinning. She was going to be on the air!

"Better make that four-thirty and stop off at wardrobe on your way."

"I'm not wearing any of those low-cut show-your-cleavage things Megan wears on the air."

"She wears them off the air, too," Rick reminded her. "That's just Megan. We'll find you something. Don't worry."

She wasn't worried. She was ecstatic, thrilled, excited as hell. She had to call Con.

"Oh, and Robbie?"

She looked back at the producer. "Yeah?"

"Joan and I are having a cookout on August third. It's a Saturday. You think you and Con can make it?"

"I'll check with him and get back to you," she said, still grinning.

It felt great to be included again. Life was good. Life was really good.

SHE'D CALLED CON first thing, and when she got home he was waiting there with a bottle of champagne.

"Congratulations," he said, toasting her as they sat together in the living room, the open bottle on the coffee table. Still in her black jeans and white blouse, Robbie was sitting on the floor, leaning against the couch. Con had changed out of his suit to shorts and a cotton shirt and was lounging on the other end of the sofa. "Though I still say your reporting isn't grunt work. You have a real talent for getting to the truth."

"Thanks," she said, sipping her champagne. "You know, I really never thought this day would come."

"Why not? You wanted it."

She looked over at him. "What's that supposed to mean?"

"You always get what you want. Always have."

She burst out laughing. "I do not."

It was funny someone could know you for so long and still have an entirely different perception of you than you had of yourself. A false perception. She'd never had the one thing she'd always wanted most.

Him.

"What about that time you wanted to play football?"

"I was good enough to be on that team, Con. And I was a cop's kid. The team was for cop's kids. There was no reason I shouldn't have played."

His lips curved into the half grin she loved. "You were the only girl on the team, Rob."

So she'd caused a bit of ruckus, but she'd done the team and her father proud. "Yeah, well, you didn't seem to find anything wrong with it back then. If I remember correctly, you were the one who taught me to play in the first place."

They sipped silently for a couple of minutes. Her memories of those days had to be a whole lot happier than Con's.

"What about that Jeep you just had to have for your sixteenth birthday?" he asked.

"I worked hard for that Jeep, Con. I paid my dad back every cent, plus paid for insurance and gas."

He frowned. "I never said you didn't work hard. You've always worked hard. Which is why you always get what you want."

She smiled sadly into her champagne.

Not always.

CON MADE SURE he was home by six the next evening. He'd been looking forward to Robbie's debut all day. He was proud of her.

She'd called him that afternoon to tell him that her piece on Blackwell was being picked up by stations all over the country. He wasn't surprised. He'd always known she'd make it big. If not in news reporting, then doing something else. She was just one of those people.

After pulling a beer out of the fridge, he wandered into the bedroom and flipped on the television set while he stripped off his suit and tie. The temperature had been well over a hundred all week. He'd done nothing but sweat the whole time.

A swim sounded good. A nice cool swim. Right after the news.

He tossed his clothes on the end of his bed, which was huge and took up most of the room. He'd had to have the bed specially made so he could sleep without his feet hanging over the end.

He heard the news come on, listened to Megan

Brandt do the headlines. Padding in from the bathroom naked, he sat down on the end of the bed.

"We've all been reading his comics for years..." He heard Robbie's voice. He even made out the first few words she said. But the rest was lost on him as he sat and stared at his television set. Who was this woman? He hardly recognized her.

Her hair, normally flat against her head, was fluffed up like a fashion model's. She was wearing a dress, a navy thing that hugged her waist and ended several inches above her knees, exposing far more of her miles of legs than he was comfortable with. And she had makeup on, which widened her eyes and gave her lips a fuller "come kiss me" look.

How in hell was he supposed to convince himself she was still just his buddy when she looked like that?

He felt his body tighten as he continued to stare at the woman standing before him, who sounded every bit as confident as she looked.

Shit. He wanted her. Still.

"YOU WERE RIGHT," Robbie told Con later that evening. They were sitting in the kitchen, sharing a beer.

"Right about what?" He seemed awfully interested in his fingernails.

"Reporting isn't grunt work. It's what I love."

Con looked up. "Being on air wasn't all you thought it was?"

"Nope." She'd learned something about herself tonight. Something she'd thought she already knew, but apparently she'd needed the reminder. She was who she was. She couldn't change that.

She'd thought that if she looked like Megan Brandt she might be able to stir Con's blood. But she'd felt like an idiot. If Con didn't want her for herself, then so be it.

"I'm going to stick to reporting," she said, taking the beer from him. The bottle was still warm from his lips.

"Have you told Rick?"

"Uh-huh."

"And?"

She shrugged. "He said I was great at both. The choice is mine."

"Good."

She glanced up, surprised at the emphatic tone in his voice.

"You're too damn good at what you do to be a puppet, saying only what other people tell you to say."

Warmth flooded her. "Newscasters are more than that," she said, laughing to cover her sudden flare of desire for him.

Con grunted and finished off their beer.

"You still working on that nursing-home story?" he asked, and got up to throw away the empty bottle.

Robbie got to her feet, too. "Tomorrow I have an appointment with the daughter of the patient I told you about. She's having her father examined by another doctor."

Con nodded. He didn't seem surprised by her

about-face. Hell, he'd probably known all along it wouldn't take much for her to figure out where she belonged. He knew her that well.

"Rick's having a party on August third," she told him. "It's a Saturday. You wanna go?"

"Can Joey come along?"

She'd already asked that question herself. "Yep. It's for families."

"It's not a pool party, is it?" he asked, his back to her as he rinsed a couple of glasses in the sink.

She'd checked that out, too. Neither of them needed that kind of temptation again. "Nope."

"Sure, we can go."

Robbie moved to the door. "I'll tell Rick tomorrow," she said. "Good night."

"Night."

"Rob?" She was halfway down the hall when he called her back.

She stuck her head around the corner. "Yeah?"

"I was proud of you tonight."

As HE HEADED into work the next morning, Con realized he'd better tell Robbie about Cecily tonight, before they got Joey again for the weekend. He'd been putting off telling her because he hadn't wanted to spoil the truce they seemed to have reached last weekend. He'd also been preoccupied all week following the paper trail that would nail his local check counterfeiter.

Several hours later he was standing at the door of the apartment he'd traced his counterfeiter to, his backup in the apartment building next door. The folder beneath his arm was loaded with photocopies of enough evidence to put Tommy Boyer away for years.

Unless the guy wanted to help Con out by fingering his supplier. Because Con had discovered something interesting the day before. The paper Tommy Boyer was using to print his checks had the same pattern of red squares under ultraviolet light that several of the banks in the valley were using as a means of protection against check fraud. Which meant if a bank teller ran Boyer's checks under an ultraviolet light to see if the checks were valid, he or she would see the red squares and assume they were.

He'd only seen that paper fall into illegal hands once before. Nick Ramirez's. And Con had been certain he'd cleared out every contact in Ramirez's organization. He'd made it his personal project.

Holding his folder, which also contained an arrest warrant, in one hand, Con knocked on apartment number 2006. Boyer would be home. He liked to watch the cooking show that was on cable every day at noon.

"Just a minute," the young man called irritably through the door. Con heard some shuffling, as if something was being hurriedly put away, and then the door was cracked open.

"Yeah? Whaddaya want?" Tommy Boyer's pimply nose was about all Con could see.

"I have a deal. Martin sent me," Con said, playing a hunch and naming Ramirez's personal shopkeeper.

Whatever Ramirez needed, Martin had a contact who could supply it, whether it be Uzis or marked paper. Martin was doing twenty years in the federal penitentiary, compliments of Con, but apparently he still had someone on the outside Con didn't know about. Someone not as smart as Martin. Someone who'd made the mistake of doing business with a small-time crook like Tommy Boyer.

"You alone?" Boyer's voice had dropped to a near whisper.

"Yeah," Con said, lowering his voice, also. If clandestine was what Boyer expected, then clandestine was what Con would give him. He didn't want to alarm him by not playing the game the right way.

Boyer opened his door just enough to let Con inside, then shut the door quickly.

The young man's apartment looked like a computer nerd's dream. Con surveyed the living room, noticing the top-of-the-line equipment, desktop computer, color laser printer, even a scanner.

"Wow, man, ain't you hot in that suit?" Boyer said. "it's 120 degrees out there."

"No," Con said, staring at the young man, who was wearing glasses and a pair of boxer shorts. Period.

"You know Martin?" Boyer asked. The kid was still too cocky with his recent successes to be intimidated by Con's size. But that would come.

"You could say that."

"What kinda deal you got?"

Con stepped closer to him. The young man's glasses slid down his nose.

So he wasn't as cool as he wanted Con to think. Con relaxed. This was going to be a piece of cake. "It depends. How do you feel about prison?"

Boyer's hands started to shake. "Why?" He backed away. Behind him was an easy chair and an end table with a couple of drawers.

As Con started to reach into his inside jacket pocket for his FBI badge, Boyer sprung for the top drawer of the end table and came up with a pistol so fast he had to have practiced the maneuver. A lot.

Con had practice, too. He grabbed Boyer's arm. "Hold it right there," he said, his iron grip applying pressure in just the right spot to force Boyer to drop the gun. Then he picked it up, intending to empty it of bullets.

"You're a little jumpy there, aren't you, boy?" he asked, his voice calm, easy.

"It ain't even loaded," Boyer said, his hands still shaking. "What was you goin' for in your pocket just then?"

"Cigarettes." Con verified that the gun wasn't loaded, dropped it back on the table and pulled out his cigarettes. "You want one?"

"Lemme see 'em."

Con held the pack up. Anything to get the kid to cooperate. "See? Just cigarettes," Con said, pulling one from the pack with his lips and lighting it. "Got an ashtray?" he asked, looking around.

He knew exactly where Tommy's ashtray was.

Next to his desktop computer, with a half-smoked joint lying in it.

Tommy grabbed the ashtray. The joint was missing when he held it out to Con.

"You know, Martin gets nervous doing business with hotheads," Con said conversationally, leaning back against Boyer's dinette table. "I don't like it much, either."

"I didn't mean nothin'," Boyer said, then his tone turned pleading. "You ain't gonna tell him, are you?"

With his cigarette hanging from his mouth, Con reached into his jacket a second time.

"I'm with the FBI," he said, flipping out his badge.

He'd never seen the blood drain from someone's face so quickly. Tommy Boyer turned white and then a sickly green. "I didn't want to do it, man. They made me," he whined.

"Who are 'they'?" Con asked. This was going to be easier than easy.

Boyer's gaze darted around the room. "I don't know. They just have me collect information over the Internet."

He was lying. Con wasn't sure why.

"How do you contact them?"

"Someone comes here. I never know who or when." The words were coming too quickly, like they'd been practiced as many times as pulling the gun had been.

"Those old guys in prison, they've been locked up

so long they're really hungry for fresh young guys like you, you know that?'' Con asked. He wanted the truth. He wanted to know whether Martin and Ramirez were back in business. Or *still* in business.

Boyer started to tremble. ''Really, man, I don't do nothin' but surf the Net.''

Con had no idea what the kid was talking about. He had Boyer on check counterfeiting. Small-time sloppy check fraud. On professional paper. He stared silently at the young man.

''You said something about a deal. Was that just to get in here?'' Boyer blurted.

Con's eyes narrowed through his cigarette smoke. ''No.''

''Let's hear it.''

''I want Martin.''

Con saw relief flash across the kid's face at the same time as he heard a key in the door behind him. He wondered if maybe he should have brought someone inside with him, after all.

Feeling for the gun in his shoulder holster with the side of his arm, he gauged the distance between Boyer and the door.

''Hi, baby, I'm back,'' a woman called, coming inside. She didn't see Con right away. But the man right behind her did. He had his gun out and trained on a spot between Con's eyes as quickly as Con had drawn his own gun.

Con held his weapon steady, waiting for someone to move, swearing under his breath. The kid hadn't had a single visitor all week. Suddenly he had a damn

houseful. And Con had some quick thinking to do, a
new game to play.

Three against one.

WORD CAME OVER the police radio at the television
station that an FBI agent was trapped inside an apartment in Phoenix with three suspects, at least one of
them armed. The agent's partner was set up in an
apartment facing it, watching everything through an
unadorned window.

Rick Hastings heard the news first. And immediately sent George Nelson out to cover the unfolding
drama. "Take Darrin with you," he yelled, naming
the station's star photographer.

"I'm going along," Robbie said, her voice full of
steel.

"No." Rick didn't even look her way.

"Yes, Rick. I'm going," she insisted. Her heart
was pounding so hard she could hardly breathe, but
she had to go. She knew most of the local agents.

"No." Rick still didn't look up from the filing cabinet he was thumbing through.

"I'll see you tomorrow," she said, grabbing her
things, hoping to catch a ride with George and Darrin.

"It's Con, Robbie."

Rick's words stopped her in her tracks.

HE WAS GROCERY SHOPPING, figuring out which sug-
ared cereal was cheapest, when the music being piped
over the loudspeaker was suddenly interrupted. "FBI
Special Agent Connor Randolph is inside a west

Phoenix apartment believed to be occupied by at least one member of the Nick Ramirez organization. Ramirez's professional crime organization was broken up by Randolph's team almost two years ago. Randolph's partner on the investigation, FBI Agent Steve Corrinth, reports that two more individuals entered the apartment just moments ago. It is believed that at least one of the individuals is armed, though as of this report no shots have been fired. Agents have been called in and are surrounding the building...."

Damn! He let loose a string of expletives that would have made his mama cringe, left his half-full cart in the cereal aisle and walked out of the store. He had to get to a television. Find out what was happening.

They *couldn't* have him. They didn't deserve to have him. *He* was going to get Randolph. He was going to squeeze every last bit of anguish he could out of the bastard. The man didn't deserve a quick death. *He* was going to kill him slowly.

His plans were well under way. He was in the process of making the place real nice. He'd brought his mattress from home and bought some new sheets at the flea market. He was stocking up on food and soap and other stuff a woman might want or need. He'd bought some coffee, though he couldn't stand the stuff. She was going to be real comfortable. He'd even sprayed the place so the crickets wouldn't bug her. She wasn't going to suffer while he kept her. She'd never done anything to him. Randolph was the one who'd suffer, bit by excruciating bit. And at the end, of course, he'd have to kill her, too. To make it right.

But that was a long way off. First he was going to love telling Randolph he was balling his woman. He was making lists of all the things he was going to let Randolph think he was doing to the babe. Things he hadn't even known a guy *could* do till he started his research. He'd be ready by the end of the month. Ready to teach Randolph all he'd learned.

Provided, of course, they didn't kill Randolph first. Rage filled his soul as he thought about losing this chance. They couldn't kill him. Randolph was *his*.

CHAPTER ELEVEN

SITTING IN RICK'S OFFICE, a paper cup filled with brandy held between shaking hands, Robbie heard it all. Her boss was there, his wife, Joan, too, and everyone else not otherwise occupied at the station. She sipped the brandy slowly as she waited for news over the police radio, getting only a scrap of information at a time. She heard descriptions of the suspects, which agents were on the scene or close by. She heard Con's credentials.

She held herself together until reports came that a shot had been fired.

And then her whole body started to shake. All she could think about was Con lying in a pool of blood. The life seeping out of him.

She was hardly aware when Joan took her hand. If Con was dead, so was she. Con. Dead.

Stop it! she cried silently. Con was the best there was. He always got his man, even if there were three of them.

A second shot was reported and Robbie thought about Joey. He needed Con. He deserved to know him. To learn from him. To be loved by him. Huge tears rolled slowly down her cheeks.

Letting go of Joan's hand and putting down the cup of brandy, Robbie wrapped her arms around her middle, holding on for all she was worth. She just had to wait a little longer. Shots had been fired. The other agents would have moved in. Soon everyone would know what was happening. Soon they'd tell her Con was all right. She just had to hold on.

"NO! I'M NOT DOING TIME for murder!" Boyer yelled, interrupting the threats that had been passing back and forth between Con and Perez. Both men still had their guns trained on each other.

"Shut up, kid," Perez growled. The woman moved across the room, hovering by the easy chair and end table.

Con stood frozen, waiting for his moment. Then Boyer, eyes wild, lunged at Perez. "No, I didn't agree to any murder!"

He grabbed at the arm holding the gun, and Con made his move. He dived for Perez, grabbing the man's gun hand in a viselike grip above their heads as they started to fall. Con's gun dropped to the floor beneath them. Perez's gun went off.

Screaming, Boyer backed away. Con was vaguely aware of the kid sinking to the floor by the easy chair, mumbling incoherently. One down.

Con rolled with Perez, turning to take the knee intended for his groin in the thigh, instead, still holding Perez's gun hand above their heads, applying pressure for all he was worth. He'd lost track of the woman.

The gun went off a second time, the acrid smell filling the air.

Con landed a couple of good blows, one with his elbow, one with his fist. Perez wasn't as big as he was, but he was younger, and strong as an ox.

Rolling back on top, Con slammed the other man's arm to the floor. Perez still didn't lose the gun. Con pulled him up, then smashed him back to the floor. Perez doubled back with a fist to Con's nose and right eye.

"Hold it right there." Both men froze as the woman's voice came from right beside Con's head. She was holding a gun about a foot from Con's temple.

"Oh, God, no. He's FBI," he heard Boyer whimper. "You know what happens to you if you kill an FBI agent?"

"He's the scum who put your father behind bars," Perez said, relaxing his grip on his gun slightly as he saw the battle about to end in his favor. Con slammed Perez's hand against the floor one more time, knocking the gun loose—just as the gun in the woman's hand clicked quietly.

Boyer's gun.

Con flipped Perez over onto his stomach before the other man knew what was happening, then grabbed his own gun from the floor just as the door burst open to half a dozen FBI agents.

He got to his feet, wiped the blood from his nose, straightened his jacket and walked out of the apartment, leaving someone else to mop up—for now.

The world was full of Boyers and Perezes, Martins and Ramirezes. They just kept coming at him. And he just kept nailing them.

He found it one of life's cruel ironies that the only thing he was really good at was something he'd grown to hate.

ROBBIE WAS STILL trembling inside and out as she gripped the steering wheel, heading home after word had come that it was all over. Con was all right. Logically she knew that. He had a couple of bruises, that was all. He'd be on his way home soon.

But until she saw him, until she felt his warm body with her own two hands, her heart was afraid to believe. She'd almost lost Con today. Dear God, she'd almost lost him.

And once she'd assured herself that he was really all right, she was going to kill him for putting her through this hell.

CON WAS BEAT when he pulled into his driveway. His nose still throbbed and his muscles were going to be sore as hell in the morning.

But Ramirez was out of business again. Before Con had even known the guy was back up and running.

What had started out as a small-time arrest had turned into something with international ramifications. He'd gone after Tommy Boyer, curious about the small-time check counterfeiter's paper supplier, unaware that the kid was Martin's illegitimate son. Boyer had been working as Martin's Internet connection for the rebuilding of Ramirez's organization ever since Martin and Ramirez had gone to the slammer. Boyer had been passing information gleaned from hacking to Martin's girlfriend, who then passed it on to Martin during her weekly visits with him at the penitentiary.

But Martin had made a critical mistake when he'd trusted the son he'd run out on a decade before. A two-bit punk, Tommy Boyer had thought he was smarter than his father. He'd been running his own little check-counterfeiting business on the side with no one the wiser, using Martin's suppliers.

Which is how Con had become suspicious that Ramirez was back in business and made the decision to go after Boyer himself. Going in alone had proved more dangerous, but it had been the surest way to enlist Boyer's trust—to ultimately get Ramirez.

And no one had died, at least not yet. He didn't hold out much hope for Tommy Boyer. If the punk lived long enough to make it to prison, Ramirez would get him there. The stupid greedy kid had just handed the feds an entire organization.

Of course it hadn't all been Boyer's doing. Some of it had been pure luck. If Martin hadn't been on to his son, if he hadn't sent his hit man to take out Boyer at the exact moment Con was there, Con might not have put it all together so fast. But he'd recognized Perez. He'd just been a little surprised to see him alive, since the guy had been reportedly killed in a prison riot earlier in the summer.

Robbie's car was in the garage when he pulled in. Tired as he was, he was glad to see it there.

She was sitting at the breakfast bar when he entered the kitchen, an open pack of his cigarettes on the counter. Judging by the ashtray in front of her, she'd smoked at least half the pack.

His gaze went to her face.

Her cheeks were devoid of color. Her eyes were red-rimmed, as if she'd been crying. And they were wary.

"Hi," he said, still standing there staring at her. He didn't know what else to do.

"Hi."

"You have dinner yet?"

She shook her head. "I've been waiting for you."

His exhaustion lifted a little. It was still a novel experience coming home from a hard day to find someone waiting for him. Anyone waiting. But especially Robbie. "You heard?" he said.

He hadn't needed to ask. It was obvious she'd been worried as hell. It was written all over her face. "Yeah. I was at the station when it came in over the radio."

Con walked toward her, dropping his keys on the counter, then lighting himself a cigarette when she continued to watch him. What did she want from him?

"Boyer was Martin's illegitimate son," he said.

She nodded, but didn't seem to want to hear any more. "How's your eye?"

The intensity of her gaze had him on his guard.

Where was his hotshot reporter? The one who fired questions faster than he could answer them?

"Sore."

"You're gonna have quite a shiner by morning."

Con nodded, still watching her. She seemed so calm sitting there, but he sensed something roiling under the surface. He just couldn't fathom what it was.

She sat there for another moment and then ground out her cigarette and stood up. "Dammit, Con!" she yelled, all traces of calm gone. "Why in hell did you go in there alone? You have a family now! People who need you! How dare you do that to Joey?"

Her words took Con totally by surprise. His life, or death, had never mattered before. "It was going to be a piece of cake," he said.

"It doesn't matter what it was going to be! What matters is what was. When they said shots were fired, I thought you'd been killed, Con!"

There were tears in her voice.

"My job's dangerous. You've always known that."

"But you could have lessened the danger just by having someone else with you."

"We had a better shot of getting Boyer to talk if I went in alone."

"And your life was worth getting some rotten punk to talk? Damn you! Damn you to hell!"

In that second their whole relationship changed. Robbie had always cared about him, just as he'd cared about her—but without expectations, without investing more than they could afford to lose.

But Robbie was acting as if she'd almost lost something that would have mattered.

Reacting purely on instinct, he pulled her into his arms, holding her against his chest. "I'm sorry, Rob."

She shuddered, squeezing him tightly. "It was stupid, Con. Stupid to go in there alone. Joey needs you," she said, her words muffled against him.

"I'm sorry," he said again. He'd never had anyone who cared before, never had anyone to consider when he went to work. "I'll send someone else next time."

And he would, if he had any choice at all. Because it mattered. For the first time in his life *he* mattered to someone.

She looked up at him, her grin a little wobbly. "It's just a good thing you made it back okay. I didn't want to have to kill you for screwing up."

She was better.

He should let her go. He smiled at her, instead.

"He really got you good," she said, running her fingers softly along the tender skin beneath his right eye.

"I got him better."

"I'm sure you did."

They continued to gaze deeply into each other's eyes, assessing, wondering about things that hadn't been said. And slowly Robbie's eyes took on a light he'd never seen in them before. Determined, hungry and all woman.

"I'm sure you did," she said again softly. Then, hooking her hand around his neck, she pulled him gently down until his lips met hers.

There was passion in her kiss, kindling an answering passion in him, but there was something else, something Con craved even more. He followed her lead, opening his mouth to explore her sweetness.

The instant their tongues met, sweetness and whatever else he'd been seeking was forgotten. Everything was forgotten but the flames spreading through his body. He'd been living with her for weeks, listening to her shower and dress, undress and shower, climb into bed. He could no longer pretend he didn't want her with every fiber of his being.

His need drove him, deepening the kiss as his body hardened against hers.

His hands spread across her back, spanning her waist. His wife's waist.

She whimpered, but when he lifted his head she pulled it right back down, thrusting her tongue against his again. She wasn't letting him go.

His fingers slid lower, over the curves of her hips, down to cup her bottom. He was afraid he was going to explode. She was glorious. So much a woman. Firing him to the point of insanity.

So damn bold.

So Robbie.

Con jerked away from her, holding his hands up as if they didn't belong to him, as if he wasn't responsible for what they'd done. Where they'd been.

"Hell," he swore, turning away. He leaned one

hand on the breakfast bar, studying the pattern in the ceramic tiles.

He'd made a promise. And he'd made it for a damn good reason. Because as badly as he wanted her, he couldn't have her. He couldn't reduce what they'd spent most of their lives building to a few minutes of sex.

Because that was all it would be. All it could ever be with him. A few minutes of sex.

But it was equally obvious that they weren't going to be able to continue on as they were. For whatever reason, his damn libido had decided to notice Robbie after all these years. The simple truth was, he wanted her so badly he couldn't trust himself to stay away from her.

"We're going to have to end this marriage," he said, thinking out loud. It was the only solution. And he'd get used to the idea. He wouldn't hate it so much once he'd had some sleep. He was just worn-out.

Not saying a word, she stared at him, her eyes filled with pain. A raw naked pain he'd never seen there before. *Damn*. It might already be too late. He might already have lost her.

"I'll see to it in the morning," he said, brushing past her. He was in for one helluva long night.

"What about Joey?"

Her question stopped him. He turned around and stared at her, too tired to come up with any more answers, to make sense of anything. Could he continue to use Robbie to get his son? Was he really going to get his man, his boy, rather, at any cost?

"We can't lose him, Con. Not when we're this close."

"The marriage will have to end, Robbie," he said. There was no way he could last a lifetime of living with her and not touching her. And after he'd had her, he'd have killed the one good thing he'd ever had going for him.

She nodded, swallowing back tears. "But after we get Joey."

If they got Joey. He needed to tell her about Cecily, too, about the newest strike against him, but right now he was just too damned tired.

"The court date's in less than two weeks," she said when he remained silent.

Surely he could keep his fly done up for two more weeks. "Fine."

She bowed her head, and as much as he wanted to, Con couldn't just walk away from her.

"I'm sorry," he said.

"Don't be." Her head shot up. "I don't blame you, Con. You can't help the way you feel any more than I can help what I am."

He frowned at the strange tone in her voice.

"What you are?"

"Too aggressive, bossy. It's a turnoff. I understand."

"Is that what you think?"

"It's what I know," Robbie said. She'd blown it. And the only way she could see to salvage anything between them was just to get the problem out in the open. Maybe if they could talk about it, they could put it behind them. Maybe, someday, they could be friends again.

"You're nuts." Con was scowling at her, his face lined with fatigue.

"Let's just call it like it is and be done with it, Con. Twenty-five years of friendship allows that, at least, doesn't it?"

"I don't know," he said, suddenly wary.

"Look. This isn't the first time this has happened to me and it's probably not going to be the last. Why do you think I'm thirty-three years old and still not married?"

"You're married."

Robbie knew he was trying to spare her feelings, but he was only making things worse. She waved her hand dismissively. "I know all about it, Con. I've been told a number of times that if I'd only let a man be the man, I'd have a lot more luck getting one. My father warned me about my aggressive behavior the day I told him you and I were getting married. And I even overheard the guys at work talking about it."

"Talking about what?"

Robbie wanted to curl up and die, but she had to get through this. She'd never forgive herself if she couldn't at least salvage a friendship with Con.

"How going to bed with me would be nothing but a turnoff," she replied quickly, trying to sound as if she didn't care. "And the thing is, I understand. I really do. I'm aggressive. I take control. I'm bossy, even in bed. I like to be on top," she confessed, her voice breaking in spite of her attempts to control it.

"What?"

"It's okay, Con, really. I am who I am. I'm not willing to change that. So you see, the choice really is mine."

"There's nothing wrong with being on top," he said, hauling her against him.

Robbie fought him for all she was worth, pushing against his iron grasp. She didn't want him to touch her. Not now. Not like this. Not in pity.

"You got it wrong, babe, so damn wrong," he said, controlling her with very little effort.

"It's OK, Con. You don't have to lie to me," she said, going still in his arms. But she didn't look at him. She couldn't. She didn't trust herself not to settle for whatever crumbs he might throw her.

"I wish I *was* lying," he said harshly, grabbing her hand and putting it against his groin. "You feel that? That's what you do to me. And I don't know where you learned about sex, babe, but that isn't what I'd call a turnoff."

Robbie's hand cupped him. She shouldn't, she was making a huge mistake, but she couldn't stop herself. She had to feel him. Just once.

"It's been a while since you've had a woman," she said, reminding herself of the fact even while she ran her hand along the length of him. Oh, Lord, he was marvelous.

He didn't stop her. "It's you, Rob. All you."

She dropped her hand. "Maybe. I doubt it."

"Tell my body that," he said derisively.

Something in his tone, in the desperate look in his

eyes, got through to her. But still, she couldn't quite believe. "It's only until I do something that turns you off."

"I don't think there's anything you *could* do to turn me off," he said. "And God help me, I don't think there's any way I can resist, either. I gotta take you to bed, Rob. Now."

She wished he sounded happier about the prospect, but she was suddenly too needy to care. She could have lost him today. Her body, her heart, was starved for him. She couldn't pull away when he grabbed her hand and hauled her down the hall to his bedroom.

CON WASN'T a gentle lover. He wasn't a slow one, either. He fell with her to the bed immediately, his mouth covering hers even before she caught her breath. He rolled on top of her, his arms on either side of her head as he plundered her mouth, demanding everything she had.

His urgency fueled her, allowing her to be as wild with her passion as her nature demanded. Crazy with her unexpected freedom, she ran her hands all over him, touching him as she'd been dying to do for years. His body was rock solid. Everywhere. *He* was everywhere.

His huge hands spanned her body, making her feel fragile for the first time in her life. Fragile in a good way. A precious way.

He touched her face, her shoulders, her back, her buttocks again, pulling her against him, holding her right where she wanted to be. And then his hands were under her T-shirt, under her bra, cupping her breasts.

Robbie would gladly have died right then and there so perfect was the moment.

Except that Con had other plans.

He yanked her shorts down over her hips, pulled his slacks only as far as his thighs and positioned himself above her.

"You're a little hampered, there," Robbie said with a wobbly smile. She couldn't believe how nervous she was all of a sudden, or how glad that he wanted her this much. "Why not let me take it from here?"

She rolled over and straddled him, sitting above his rigid length. Con completed their union with one hard thrust.

And then brought her to an incredible climax. As she exploded around him, Robbie knew her life was never going to be the same again. There'd be no going back. No reclaiming what was hers. She'd just given herself utterly to him.

"God, you're good," Con said, his voice rough as he thrust again. His eyes were closed, his face a study of concentration.

"So good," he said, shuddering when he finally poured himself into her.

Robbie's heart soared as she watched him, as she went with him to paradise.

But the journey was far too short. When Con opened his eyes there was no love there, no warmth. Just the look of a satisfied male. The same impersonal look he might have given a stranger he'd happened to have sex with.

He rolled away almost immediately, then stood to yank his pants back up and fasten them. He still had his jacket on, his tie only slightly askew.

"I hope I convinced you," he said before he turned and left the room. A moment later she heard him leave the house.

CHAPTER TWELVE

THE PHONE WOKE Robbie from a troubled sleep early the next morning. She didn't even know Con was in the house until she heard him answer it. He hadn't yet returned home when she'd finally gone to bed sometime after three o'clock in the morning.

She hated herself for the relief she felt.

Con was nothing to her, she reminded herself. Twenty years of infatuation was over. Dead.

Though the night she had just spent had been the worst in her life, in a way she was grateful to Con. In less than half an hour, he'd cured her of a lifelong obsession. Because as good as her time in his arms had been, it wasn't anything she wanted to repeat. She'd rather live the rest of her life celibate than let Con touch her again under those terms.

She'd made love to him. She'd given him everything, her passion, her heart, her innermost being. She'd trusted him.

He'd had sex.

She'd showered twice after he'd gone, but she hadn't been able to erase the feel of him from her body.

"Robbie?" he called from just outside her door.

She pulled the covers up over her breasts, smoothing down the hair that she was sure was sticking up all over her head. "Yeah?"

She didn't want him to see her, didn't want to see *him.* She could hardly bear her memories of last night.

He opened the door, but she could have been a cleaner mopping the floor for all the notice he took of her.

"That was Karen Smith. The hearing's been moved up to this Monday at nine."

Monday at nine? She sat up. Something far more important than the last twenty-four hours was suddenly at stake. Joey. Did it have to be so soon? Were they ready? "Do we still get him today?" she asked.

He nodded. "I'm picking him up at four. Meet me here at three if you want to go along."

"Sure." Was this stranger the same man who'd swept her off to bed less than twelve hours before? Was he just going to pretend it had never happened?

"We still have to take him back on Sunday," he said. She watched him standing in her doorway and had a sudden vision of how he'd looked as she climbed astride him the night before.

Licking dry lips, she said, "I figured. But we get him back right away again Monday morning if the judge gives us placement, right?"

Con nodded. He hesitated as if there was more he wanted to say, and she held her breath. Could he somehow take away the terrible heartache he'd left when he'd walked out on her last night?

Could he explain why he'd treated her like a whore?

"See you at three," he said, and left.

Damn him to hell for not loving me.

Robbie damned the foolish tears that fell, too, as she rolled over and buried her face in the pillow.

SHE COULDN'T HATE HIM any more than he hated himself. But that didn't stop his gut from clenching, didn't stop him from hurting, when she avoided his touch as he opened the car door for her that afternoon. Nor did he hurt any less when she couldn't look at him.

He slammed the door after her, knowing he was getting what he deserved. He'd screwed her. And by doing so, he'd screwed them both. Right out of the best friendship, the only friendship, he'd ever had. Stan had been right—that simply by being with him Robbie was bound to be hurt sooner or later. And there wasn't a damn thing he could do about it.

Except be glad she hated him. She wasn't going to have any trouble getting on with her life once Joey's future had been decided. Con just wasn't so sure what he'd have left of his own.

THE BOY RECOGNIZED HIM. Standing just behind Robbie at the door of Joey's foster home, Con could hardly believe it when the kid smiled right at him and held out his arms. He scooped the boy up, holding him close to his heart. He didn't deserve this. He hadn't asked for this chance, had never intended to saddle a kid with a father like him or bring a kid into a world like his, but it had happened, anyway. And for once in his life he was going to make himself proud. He was going to be there for his kid, make Joey's life a good one.

God help the judge, the system, that tried to tell him he couldn't raise his son.

"How's our little boy?" Robbie crooned to the baby, tickling his toes, his chubby little legs where they peeked out of the one-piece outfit he was wearing.

Her eyes met Con's briefly, the first time they'd done so that day. They were wary, but they didn't scald him. The knot in Con's chest loosened just a little. He'd hurt her, but she was going to be OK.

"Let's go home," he said.

"You'll have him back by six on Sunday?" Betty Williams asked, reminding them that they weren't alone.

"Yeah," Con said, turning with his son in his arms to head back to the car.

"Have a good weekend," Con heard the woman call behind him. With Joey with them, they just might.

And maybe, if they got the boy again on Monday, he and Robbie could manage to have a good rest of their lives, too. Maybe they could live together, raise their son and never touch each other again.

Yeah, sure, Con thought derisively. Because getting Joey on Monday was a bigger "if" than he cared to contemplate at the moment, and keeping his hands off Robbie wasn't something he trusted himself to do, either. He'd never wanted a woman so much after he'd already had her. He wanted her again and again. On top. Underneath. And standing straight up.

But he wasn't going to lay a finger on her. He was going to keep his hands to himself until he could get her safely out of his life. Or at least out of his house. Because if he didn't, he'd keep using her until she was all used up. That was just the kind of guy he was.

THE WEEKEND was excruciating. Filled with the promise of dreams already lost. With the threat of broken futures. And at the same time, it was strangely happy. An interlude of right in a world of wrong.

Robbie suddenly understood how couples in unhappy marriages stayed together for years because of the children. Joey was a buffer. The need to lavish attention on him kept them from having to discuss anything personal. He was also the cement binding them together. In the battle of life it was the three of them against the world.

And with the responsibility of the baby drawing them closer, Robbie slowly started to heal. Not because she could ever forget the devastatingly impersonal way Con had had sex with her, but because all weekend long, in so many little ways, she could feel his caring, his respect.

He respected her opinion, even seeking it out on a number of occasions. He insisted on holding a fussy Joey so she could eat Friday night's meat loaf while it was still hot. He brought a cup of coffee in to her

Saturday morning when the baby woke her just after dawn for his bottle.

She could almost convince herself that they could still be a family just as they'd planned. Con hadn't said any more about ending the marriage. And in spite of everything, Robbie didn't want to end it, either. She loved Con. Had always loved him. And she loved his son. She wanted to raise Joey, be the one he ran to when he scraped his knee, the one he took for granted during adolescence. The one he thanked on national television when he grew up to be famous.

She even tried to convince herself that she'd be able to handle it when Con took other women to his bed in the coming years. After all, she now knew firsthand what they were getting. Or more importantly, what they weren't getting. She just had to not think about the incredible moments in Con's arms and concentrate on the seconds it took him to walk out on her afterward.

Or so she kept telling herself.

The low point of the weekend came during a visit from Susan and Stan on Sunday. Aware of the court date looming just a day away, Robbie's nerves were stretched to breaking point. And when Susan mentioned a photography special going on at the mall and suggested they take the baby there to have his picture taken, Robbie found herself frantic to have it done. Didn't all new parents have portraits of their babies? Wouldn't it make them seem like more of a real family, more solidly parents, if they took their son in to have his portrait taken?

At the very least, this way she'd have some pictures of her baby if the judge took Joey away from them tomorrow morning.

Con didn't see things that way.

"Let's wait till he's ours," he said when Robbie cornered him in the kitchen and mentioned Susan's idea.

She held Joey a little tighter. "He *is* ours."

Con turned back to the glasses he'd been filling with ice. "It's just one more day, Rob."

"One more day might be too late."

As she finally voiced what had been in the back of both their minds all weekend, his only reaction was a stiffening of his shoulders.

"Get him ready," he finally said.

Robbie left the room without another word.

They were in line for the pictures when Robbie discovered that Joey's security blanket was missing.

"It's in his crib," Con said, holding his son up above his head. He'd been entertaining the baby with such antics ever since they'd arrived at the mall.

Robbie had visions of the baby starting to cry just when it was his turn in front of the camera. Without his blanket, she'd never be able to calm him. "We need it," she said.

"He hasn't missed it, honey. He'll be fine," Susan said, smiling as she watched Con with the baby.

But Robbie dug in her heels. "We don't know how much longer it's going to be, and if he gets tired, he'll want it," she said, certain Joey could miss it any second. "I'm going to go get it."

"Wait." Con handed the baby to Robbie. "I left it. I'll go," he said, pulling his keys from his pocket.

Joey in her arms, Robbie nodded. "Thanks."

"Robbie!" Stan stepped up to his daughter. He'd been watching the exchange silently till now. "You can't really expect Con to drive all the way back to the house just for some little scrap of cloth."

"She can when she's right," Con told Stan. "The blanket's the one constant in Joey's life. He should have it."

"You don't have to let her run you in circles, boy!" Stan said, frowning as he looked between his daughter and Con. "We're not going to be here *that* long."

Robbie wanted to curl up and die.

"My relationship with my wife is my business," Con told Stan, rendering the older man speechless. He'd never spoken to her father that way.

"I'll be back as soon as I can," he said to Robbie before striding off across the mall.

In that moment, standing there with her parents, holding Con's son, Robbie felt married for the very first time.

ONE DAY AT A TIME. It was how he'd always lived his life. Sometimes one hour at a time. Monday morning he was taking it one minute at a time. And he was thankful that Robbie was spending the minutes with him.

He had no idea what the future would bring. Whether they'd get custody of Joey, whether they'd ever have sex with each other again. He couldn't even think about where their marriage might take them, or for how long. Not today. It was one minute at a time. With all the minutes leading directly to the judge's chamber and the verdict he would reach.

"We need to go," Robbie said softly, standing as she put out the cigarette he'd lit a moment before. She was wearing the same denim skirt and pink blouse she'd had on the day they'd first met Joey.

She picked up their coffee cups. "We don't want to be late."

Con looked around him at Joey's things, the high chair he was still too young to use, the bottles on the counter, and nodded.

"We'll have to find a cupboard for those," Robbie said, following his gaze.

"Yeah." He hoped to God she was right.

He needed—oh, how he needed!—to pull Robbie into his arms. He needed to hold her, to feel her warmth, her confidence. He needed to comfort her, to assure her that he'd take care of everything, that he'd find a way to make her happy again.

Except that he couldn't. He couldn't touch her. Not ever again. And he couldn't make her happy, either. He grabbed his suit coat off the chair and pulled it on.

"We have to take your car," Robbie said, following Con out to the garage.

"Right." But he knew that all the positive thinking in the world might not be enough today. Joey's car seat wouldn't be necessary if they were going to be coming home alone.

The drive to the courthouse was silent, as much of the morning had been, both of them drawing on the strength of the other, yet afraid to test that strength by voicing the fears, the doubts, the uncertainties that were forefront in their minds.

Con still hadn't told Robbie about Cecily; the moment had never seemed right. And there was no point telling her right now. Why add to her worries? If they didn't get Joey, she'd need never know, anyway. And if they did, the news of his biological mother's reentry into their lives wouldn't hurt so much if she heard it with Joey in her arms, already in her care. Besides, there was another six months of waiting ahead before they knew what kind of impact, if any, the woman would have on their lives.

They needed to worry about placement first.

One minute at a time.

ROBBIE'S STOMACH was cramped by the time they reached the courthouse. Her future had never been more insecure, and there wasn't a damn thing she could do but wait. Except...

"If we get him, we're staying married," she whispered to Con as they walked down the hall to the courtroom.

She'd had no idea how badly she'd needed to say those words until they were out.

"We'll talk about it later," Con said, looking straight ahead as they walked.

"We'll talk about it now, Randolph. I am not going in there to lose that baby or lose my place in both your lives when we come out."

He glanced down at her and then ahead again. They were almost there. "What place is that?" he asked, his frustration obvious.

"I don't know," she answered honestly, "but I'm not losing it." Before he could say another word, she sped up to enter the courtroom in front of him.

CON SAW a young blond woman turn to look at them as they walked in. She was sitting with a man he didn't know. He didn't recognize her, either, at first, only felt an instantaneous alarm, a sense that she was someone he never wanted to see again. She smiled at him.

And then he knew. Cecily Barnhardt.

He felt sick with dread. He didn't want to see her. Didn't want to have any connection with her. Ever. Didn't want Robbie to see her.

What was she doing there? He hadn't thought there was any reason to expect her to be present. She'd already signed away her rights. And even if she was unsigning them, if such a thing was really possible, she still had six months to go of proving herself.

Didn't she?

With his mind in turmoil, Con followed Robbie to the front of the room and took a seat beside her. How could his wife sit beside him when a woman he'd had sex with, made a baby with, was four feet away, smiling at him as if she'd like to do it again?

"Who is she?" Robbie whispered.

His throat thick, Con stared at Robbie.

He didn't know what to say, couldn't get even a name past his lips. He didn't want her to know that this was the woman he'd taken to bed and forgotten. Shame filled him. And bone-deep regret that he was bringing Robbie further and further into his world.

He was saved from answering when the judge chose that moment to enter the room. The hearing had begun.

ROBBIE'S HEART pumped in double time as the judge took his seat. The woman across the aisle was momentarily forgotten as Robbie studied the elderly judge's face. Was that disapproval in his eyes as he glanced their way? Or merely speculation? Had the man already made up his mind?

Con was the first to be called to the stand. Robbie grabbed his hand and squeezed it as he stood up. She'd sworn to herself she wouldn't ever reach out to him again, but she couldn't send him to the wolves alone. He'd proved many times over the weekend, over the years, what a good man he was, what a caring man.

The judge asked Con questions about his job, about his home, looking at the pictures Con's attorney produced of Joey's nursery, of the clothes hanging in his closet, the toys they'd purchased, the high chair in the kitchen. Con sat stiffly in the witness stand, answering all the judge's questions in monosyllables. Robbie stared at the judge, her stomach in knots, still unable to guess what the man was thinking.

"And what support can you offer this child?" the judge asked, frowning as he looked through his half glasses at the papers in front of him.

"You have my financial statement," Con said.

Robbie groaned silently at the faint look of annoyance on the judge's face. She ached for Con, for how hard this was for him, for how inadequate he felt. He'd been tried and found wanting all his life.

But he was going to have to do better than this if he hoped to win his son.

"Yes, I see, Mr. Randolph. Well, thank you. You may step—"

"The boy needs more than money can buy," Con interrupted the judge. The older man turned, peering at Con over his glasses. Robbie held her breath.

"He needs to know he's wanted. That he belongs simply by nature of the blood running through his veins."

Yes. Tears burned the backs of Robbie's eyes as she listened to Con tell the judge about the thing *he'd* missed out on as a child. The only thing he'd ever really wanted. Something he never spoke about, never even acknowledged, but the most important thing he had to offer his son.

"He needs unconditional acceptance, the kind a kid can take for granted and not ever have to earn. The kind he'll never have if he starts out life abandoned by the people who gave him life. An acceptance only a biological parent can offer him." Con swung his gaze to the people in the silent courtroom. Robbie couldn't stop the tears from trickling down her cheeks as she watched him. Her strong silent husband had spoken from his heart.

He turned back to the judge. "This is the support I offer my son," he said, then rose from the stand and took his seat next to Robbie.

Unable to say a word, Robbie reached for his hand and held it, even when his fingers didn't curl around her own. He'd retreated deep into that place in his soul where he hid when he felt vulnerable.

The judge cleared his throat, took off his glasses and put them back on again. "May I have Karen Smith to the stand, please?" he finally said.

The next half hour was filled with the case workers' reports, nothing particularly damning, but nothing encouraging, either. Until Sandra Muldoon reported that Con had abandoned his son at birth.

"That's not true," Robbie hissed in Con's ear. She hadn't had her chance on the stand yet, wasn't even sure she was going to get one at this rate, and she couldn't sit idly by and listen to these lies.

Con's muscles stiffened, his jaw so tight he couldn't possibly have said a word. He just shook his head at Robbie.

"That's her word against my client's, Your Honor." Con's attorney stood up. "My client had no knowledge of the child's existence until the state showed up on his doorstep last month."

"The child's mother told us she contacted the

boy's father and was refused support,'' Mrs. Muldoon insisted.

''I understand the boy's mother is here?'' the judge asked, looking over the courtroom.

Of course she isn't, Robbie thought.

Her gaze swung between the social worker and the judge. But even as she assured herself they were wrong, her heart froze, and she suddenly knew what was coming.

The woman who'd smiled at Con. That hadn't been the smile of a stranger.

''Yes, she's here, Your Honor.'' Robbie barely registered Mrs. Muldoon's words.

Ice filled her veins. If the judge had known the woman was going to be there, had Con known, too?

The judge called Ms. Cecily Barnhardt to the stand. Robbie couldn't look at the woman. She looked at her husband, instead. He didn't flinch, didn't show any reaction at all, other than resignation.

He'd known. He'd known and he hadn't told her.

There was no partnership between them. She was beginning to suspect there was nothing between them at all—except what her very fertile imagination produced. Had she simply conjured up what she wanted to see in order to justify forcing herself on him all these years?

And what chance in hell did they have of getting Joey if his biological mother was back in the picture? Or was she just there for testimony?

Why hadn't Con told her? Did she really matter so little? *And why should that come as any surprise?*

Con didn't look at Cecily Barnhardt as the judge started to question her, but Robbie couldn't look anywhere else. This was the woman Con had slept with, the woman who'd given birth to Joey.

"Tell us about your job, Ms. Barnhardt, your means of supporting the child."

Robbie tore her gaze away to glance at Con. Did that mean the mother *was* trying to get Joey back? Could she do such a thing?

Con, his face expressionless, continued to watch the judge.

"I'm not employed right now, but Joey'll be okay, anyway, with welfare and stuff," Cecily Barnhardt replied sweetly. "It's how I did it before."

She was everything Robbie had expected her to be. Con's type of woman exactly. Very beautiful and very feminine. And not very bright.

Robbie found it difficult to take much consolation from this last, however. For Cecily was truly gorgeous. Her curves were luscious where they needed to be, accented by the spaghetti-strap sundress she was wearing. Her legs were long and tanned, tapering to slim ankles and dainty feet encased in high-heeled sandals. Even her toenails were polished.

And suddenly, Robbie wanted to be as far away from Con as the seat would allow. He'd hurt her for the last time.

If it hadn't been for Joey, she'd have walked out of that courtroom and just kept going. But she couldn't walk out on Joey. Even with her heart burning up with jealousy, she couldn't walk away.

Ms. Barnhardt's state-appointed lawyer showed pictures of the trailer where she lived. The judge declared it clean and rather sweet, but apparently it had no provisions for the baby.

"I just don't have the money for those yet," Cecily explained, and then looked straight at Con.

"Please, Mr. Randolph, I know you're a really nice man, buying me that hamburger and all and letting me sit with you so's I didn't have to be all alone in my trailer, even with you being so upset about that poor woman who died. You'll take care of me and my baby, won't you? Tell them you will, Mr. Randolph." Cecily's big eyes filled with tears. "Please?"

Con looked away.

"Tell us, Ms. Barnhardt," the judge said, clearing his throat, "exactly what did Mr. Randolph say when you told him about the baby?"

Cecily blinked. "Oh, I never told Mr. Randolph about Joey."

"But we have it on record that you said the baby's father refused support," the judge said, reading from the file in front of him.

"But that wasn't Mr. Randolph," Cecily said innocently. "That was Joe. We were s'posed to get married. Ever since I was fifteen. He was s'posed to be little Joey's daddy."

Con sat up straighter, watching the woman intently. Robbie watched, too, listening, taut with tension, and caring far more than she wished she did.

"But you named Mr. Randolph as the father on the birth certificate."

Cecily shrugged one slender shoulder. "Well, I had to. You can't tell lies in writing, you know."

Robbie felt more than heard Con sigh. His hand slid over her knee, searching for and finding hers. She didn't want his touch, didn't want it to mean anything, but that didn't stop her fingers from curling around his.

He continued to hold her hand while Betty Williams gave her testimony, stating that Joey had obviously had excellent care each time Robbie and Con had kept him. She mentioned the new clothes and toys Joey had come home with, said that Robbie and Con had left their phone number in case an emergency arose. She even told the judge how Joey had reached for Con the last time he'd gone to collect him.

And then it was Robbie's turn to take the stand. She forgot Con. Forgot the mess they'd made of their lives as she fought for custody of the child who'd stolen her heart. Because whether Con wanted her or not was immaterial. In her heart of hearts, she truly believed that Joey would never have a better life than the one Con could give him.

Twenty minutes later, after listening to lawyers from all sides, the judge said he'd reached a decision. He asked them all to stand.

Con held tightly to Robbie's hand, telling her without the words he could never say how much the next moments meant to him. She squeezed his hand in return. Nothing mattered but the little boy whose entire future rested on the decision of one old man. Not her pain. Not Con's inability to love her.

"As Mr. Randolph so fluently pointed out, a child's biological parent can be an incredible asset to that child's emotional well-being. Which is why we hesitate to ever take a child from his mother's care if there's any hope that the child will find a loving home with her."

Robbie's heart sank as the judge paused. He looked at all three of them, his gaze serious.

"I feel that it is in Joey's best interests to give his mother, Cecily Barnhardt, six months to provide an acceptable home for her son."

No!

Con's grip crushed Robbie's fingers, but the tears that sprang to her eyes weren't from the physical pain.

"In the meantime," the judge continued, "I am placing the boy in the care of his father and stepmother with final custody to be determined six months from today."

Great sobs of relief racked Robbie's body as she threw herself into Con's waiting arms. He crushed her to him, lifting her right off the floor with the force of his embrace.

"Thank you," he said for her ears alone.

"You're welcome." And he was. Welcome in her life and in a secret part of her heart. Because in spite of the pain he'd caused her, the pain she feared he had yet to cause her, she was going to honor her wedding vows. She'd been standing by Con most of her life. She couldn't walk out on him now.

They had a son to raise.

CHAPTER THIRTEEN

BETTY WILLIAMS asked for a couple of hours for her family to say goodbye to Joey. The judge deferred her to Con.

He nodded his assent, partly because it felt so damn good to have the right to make the decision, but it still took everything he had to grant the request. He wanted his son at home. Now.

The future no longer seemed like a black hole. It suddenly had substance, a name. It had purpose.

And endless questions.

There were reams of papers to sign, details to go over. How soon could he have Joey added to his insurance? How often would they be bothered with visits from social services? Could they take him out of the state?

"He's really ours," Robbie whispered.

Warmth flooded Con, surprising him, almost scaring him for the brief second it took him to regain control. The same thing had happened to him in the courtroom moments ago, when the judge had told him he could have his son. But the feeling was just an aberration. A reaction to the changes that were taking place so rapidly in his life, which had been predictably the same for years. He wasn't falling back into that old trap again. He wouldn't start hoping. He couldn't. He was no longer capable.

Was he?

They still had an hour to kill after their business at the courthouse was finished. Con waited while Robbie went to a pay phone in the hall to give her parents a call and tell them the good news, and then walked with her out to his car.

She had something on her mind. He could tell by her sudden silence. He couldn't blame her if, now that it was over, she wanted out. Being a mother to Joey was hardly compensation enough for putting up with *him*. For withstanding a loveless marriage. He knew that.

Especially after he'd crossed that unforgivable line and used her body just for physical satisfaction. He'd known since he walked out of his bedroom the other night that it had only been a matter of time till she left him.

So why in hell did he still want to believe they could work something out?

"Where to?" he asked as they drove out of the parking lot. They didn't have time to make it home and all the way back to Gilbert in an hour.

"Someplace we can talk." Her softness was gone.

He glanced over at her, hoping to gauge where he stood, but she stared steadfastly out the windshield.

Without another word he pulled out into the traffic. A pack of cigarettes lay open on the console between them. Open, but untouched.

Con knew the city as well as he knew the lines on his face, and twenty minutes later they were parked out in the desert on a secluded dirt track, not ten minutes from the Williamses' home.

If Robbie wanted out of their marriage, he had to let her go. Somehow. Hell, he should probably make her leave even if by some miracle she didn't want to.

He left the engine running, allowing the air conditioner to continue cooling the interior of the car. The scenery was barren, just brown flat land as far as the eye could see, with an occasional cactus or sagebrush. He wondered if this view of the desert Robbie had always loved was a portent of their future. Barren.

He reached for the pack of cigarettes, then threw it down again, thrumming his fingers against the steering wheel, instead. He wasn't going to smell like smoke when he picked up his son. But would he be picking him up with Robbie at his side?

He waited as long as he could, until his chest grew tight with the dread of what was coming. "So talk." His words finally cut the silence.

"Why didn't you tell me about her?" Robbie's voice was filled with accusation. And hurt.

Disconcerted, Con looked away. He'd actually forgotten about Cecily. About what Robbie must be thinking of him now that she'd come face-to-face with the side of him she'd always refused to see. He'd been too busy thinking about Joey. And about sex with Robbie.

So how did he explain why he'd kept silent when he didn't even understand why himself? Robbie had always been the only thing good and pure in his life. Cecily was the embodiment of everything else. Somehow he'd understood that it would all be over when the two met.

"You knew about her, didn't you?" she asked, her voice resigned, but bitter, too.

He nodded. And then added, "Not that she was going to be there today, though." As if that made any difference. He'd disappointed Robbie, hurt her. She was disgusted with the man he was. The type of man who would bed a total stranger and not remember it in the morning. Seeing Cecily had finally opened Robbie's eyes.

"But you knew she wanted Joey back?"

He nodded again, still thrumming, still not looking at her.

"Out of curiosity, were you ever going to tell me?"

"Of course!" he said, surprised into looking at her. Didn't she know he discussed everything with her? That he always had? Eventually. "If it became necessary."

"Necessary? Today it wasn't necessary for me to know that I was going to be seeing the woman you impregnated? That I wouldn't care? That it wouldn't faze me a bit?"

If she was trying to make him hate himself even more, she'd succeeded. "I'm sorry," he said. He didn't know what else to say. He'd been telling her all her life what a jerk he was.

His gut clenched when he saw the tears in her eyes.

He could count on one hand the number of times he'd seen Robbie cry. And all of them because of him.

"You know, I believe you. You *are* sorry," she said softly, sadly. "But sorry isn't enough, Con. I had a right to know."

"Of course you did."

"So *why* didn't you tell me?" The anguish in her words confused him.

"Is that really what this is all about? Because I didn't *tell* you about her?" he asked.

"Yes!"

The relief he felt loosened his tongue. Maybe this time he could take away some of the pain he'd caused.

"I hoped she'd go away. That you'd never have to find out she'd appeared," he said, only just now realizing that that was what he'd been doing. Hoping. Even though he'd given up hoping years ago.

"You still should have told me, Con. I'm supposed to be your wife. Your partner in this thing. I should have been better prepared." Her tears continued to roll down her cheeks. There was so much pain. In her. In him.

Con pushed the console up and pulled her across the seat into his arms.

"I'm sorry, Rob." He wiped awkwardly at her tears with his thumb. "The time just never seemed right. The words wouldn't come."

She sat silently beside him, not pulling away, but not settling into his embrace, either. She needed more.

"I'm not proud of that night I spent with Cecily,"

Con said slowly. "Not eager for you to think less of me because of it," he finally admitted. To her. To himself.

She sank against him, turning to gaze up at him. "You sure you weren't just pushing me out of your life like you have everyone else you've ever known?"

"Hell, no!" He reeled back, shocked. "I can't imagine life without you in it, nagging me to death." He breathed a little easier when he saw a weak smile cross her lips. "And I don't push everyone else away, either," he felt compelled to add. "They leave of their own accord."

"Bullshit."

Feeling as though he'd just made it through a mine-field, he wasn't up for a battle. "Was that it? The talk you wanted?" he asked.

"No."

She sat up, surprising him again. There was more?

"I didn't mean to bring her up at all," she admitted sheepishly. "She just slipped out."

He frowned. "What, then?"

"I want your word that we're in this for the long haul—you, me and Joey. I love him already, Con. I don't want to lose him."

He was right back in the middle of the damn mine-field, after all. "As far as I'm concerned you'll always be his mother, no matter what happens between us," he said. Because it was only a matter of time before something did.

"I want your word, Randolph."

He turned away from her and looked out his side window. "I can't give it to you."

"Why?" The one word exploded into the car.

He looked back at her, his gaze impossible to mis-interpret. "I think you know why," he said, looking her body up and down. He'd used her. Every inch of her. The memory of it drove him crazy in the dark hours of night. He hated himself for it. And for want-ing to use her again.

"Because of the sex," she said bluntly. That was Robbie. Get the whole mess right out there on the table.

He nodded, still watching her.

"What about it?" she asked. He knew she was trying for nonchalance, but he heard the tiny catch in her throat.

"I still want it."

"Like it was last time?" Her gaze skittered away from him and then back.

"With me that's the only way there is." He couldn't lie to her. He'd never lied to her.

"It was horrible for me when you walked out of the room. You know that, don't you?"

His chest tightened as he saw the shadows in her eyes, but she had to know. When words wouldn't come, he nodded.

"Are you going to force me?" she asked, sounding belligerent now.

"No." Forcing a woman to have sex was one of the few things he'd never done. Besides, with Robbie he wasn't sure he'd have to. He wasn't the only one who'd responded that night.

"Then we've got nothing to worry about, because I didn't much like your performance, Randolph. At least not there at the end." Her eyes welled up with more tears. "I've felt like many things in my time, but I've never felt like a whore before. It's not an experience I care to repeat."

Her words were like a slap in the face, one he knew he deserved.

"Trust me," she said, her voice filled with disgust. "It won't be happening again."

CON TOOK A LEAVE of absence from work for the rest of the month, and since Robbie hadn't taken time off for a honeymoon, she also stayed home that first week. Neither wanted to leave Joey with a sitter; neither wanted to leave Joey at all. They were natural parents, welcoming the change in their lives, adjusting to the sudden absence of freedom with very little effort. Joey was a godsend. He provided a dimension both of them had needed in their lives.

Con offered to make a grocery run Tuesday afternoon while Joey was napping. They were going through diapers more rapidly than either of them had anticipated, and running low on formula, too. But Robbie was well aware of his ulterior motive. He needed a cigarette. During the hour he was away, she was envious of the smoking he must be doing.

She heard him pull into the garage and met him at the kitchen door, ready to tease him.

"I left one lit in the car ashtray. I'll deal with the groceries," he said before she could get in a shot.

Robbie was out in the garage and in the front seat of his car in a flash. He hadn't left one lit. He'd lit a fresh one. She had an entire cigarette to savor.

How was she ever going to fall out of love with Con when he was so damn nice to her?

He had everything put away by the time she was back in the house, except for a package on the counter. She picked it up.

"What's this?" she asked.

He turned from the cupboard where they now stored Joey's bottles. "Nicotine patches. I figured they couldn't hurt," he said a trifle sheepishly.

She set the box down. "No. You're right. They'll probably make quitting a little easier on you."

His mouth quirked in that endearing half grin. "There's some there for you, too."

IT SEEMED there was plenty of everything for everybody as long as Robbie didn't ask for Con's love. As unconventional as their lives were, she was almost able to convince herself they were going to be just fine, the three of them. A happy little family.

Almost.

On Thursday afternoon she followed Joey, who the day before had discovered he could actually go places when he scooted on his belly, into Con's bedroom. It was just as Con came walking out of his adjoining bathroom, a towel around his neck.

He stopped, stark naked, and stared at her.

Heart beating an erratic tempo, she automatically sought the part of him she had no business looking at. She swallowed. The man was male perfection.

He didn't cover himself immediately. Not when he caught her gazing at him. Not even when his body started to react.

"Why didn't you shut your door?" she snapped. *Damn.* With one look she was on fire for him, weak with need, filled with desire.

He still stood there, staring right back at her. Then Joey scooted into his line of vision and he strode over to his dresser to pull a pair of briefs from a drawer.

He had the best ass she'd ever seen.

"What the hell are you doing in here?" he said.

Dry-mouthed, Robbie couldn't move, feeling more like an awkward schoolgirl than a mature woman. "Joey was exploring," she mumbled.

"I'll close my door in the future." Con's words were weary as he disappeared back into his bathroom.

Robbie grabbed the baby and ran.

Much of the week was fraught with tension. The tension of unrequited love, of unfulfilled desire, of dying hopes and harsh realities. Robbie loved Con. He wanted her. But he was never going to love her back.

When Stan and Susan called, inviting them to Sedona on Saturday, Robbie jumped at the opportunity to get out of the house, to dispel some of the intimacy between her and Con. She was committed to her life with him, wanted it even. She was just going to need a little time to get over her love for him.

And he was going to need a night out now and then.

Nothing they couldn't handle.

The baby was asleep even before they hit the highway Saturday morning. He looked adorable in his baby-size blue-jean shorts and matching slugger shirt, his tiny face dimpled, even in sleep. He definitely had his daddy's chin. His new diaper bag, on the seat beside him, was stuffed with two more outfits and enough supplies to last them a week.

Con drove silently, his face a mask. Robbie wondered if he was happy—or at least *his* version of happy. Was he satisfied with the way things were working out?

"You getting anxious to get back to work?" she asked.

She hated not knowing what he was thinking, not knowing where she stood. Hated the lines she wasn't allowed to cross. Hated being dependent on him for any part of her emotional security.

He shrugged.

"There's not some case you're dying to crack? Some heathen to bring to justice?"

"There're always cases."

Her heart sank. Where was the man with a mission? The one who'd finally found a measure of peace with himself fifteen years before when he'd gone to work as a government agent?

The change in Con over the past couple of years really frightened her. She sometimes wondered if she was going to lose him completely to the purgatory that he'd forced himself to live in.

"Why don't you get out, Con?" she asked, unable to let it go. "No one said you had to be an agent forever."

"It's what I know."

She fiddled with the hem of her cutoffs. "But you hate it, don't you? Ever since that Ramirez deal last year."

"I'm good at it."

"You'd be good at anything you put your mind to."

He continued to drive, saying nothing, the cords in his neck tightening.

"It scares me to see what's happening to you," she said, daring to tread where she knew he didn't want her. But someone had to. "You used to take pride in your work. But now it's more like you hate yourself for doing it."

"I'm fine. Leave it." His voice had an edge of steel.

"Right."

They drove silently for miles. Robbie kept telling herself to let it go, to think about Joey, about their future. About being part of a family, instead of living alone.

"How are you going to love Joey if you can't love yourself?" she finally said into the stillness.

"I care for him just fine."

"Caring's not love, Con. Caring's lukewarm, detached. He needs total commitment."

"I'm committed."

She needed to holler at him, except that their baby was sleeping right behind them.

"We need your *love*, Con," she said, too upset to mind her words.

But he minded them. Plenty. "We?" he said, his voice hard, filled with ice. "You know my limits, Rob. You've always known them. I told you a long time ago that I'd never be that knight you were looking for."

What he'd told her was that he didn't believe in love. "You were just a kid then."

"I was never really a kid."

Anger swept through Robbie, anger at the life he'd had, the circumstances that had drained him of the things everyone needs—faith and hope and love. And anger at him, too.

"You want to be loved, Randolph. You've always wanted to be loved. Everybody does."

"Leave it, Rob," he said wearily.

"And what's more, you've got a little boy sitting back there who's going to idolize the ground you walk on," she continued, not even pausing for breath. "He's going to love you. And he's going to need your love in return. If you break his heart, you'll be no better than the people who broke yours."

He didn't say a word, just kept driving, jaw clenched so tight it was a wonder he didn't crack his teeth. She thought about what he'd said to the judge on Monday, about a kid deserving and needing to belong without having to earn the right. What he'd really been talking about was needing to be loved—unconditionally. He'd spent his entire childhood trying to earn that kind of love from anyone who might have some to spare. And he'd failed. Every time. Except with her. But that was the one place he'd never looked.

"It's time to quit running scared, Con," she said, her heart softening as she watched him. "It's time to allow the possibility that love is real. Because the only way you're going to get it or be able to give it is to believe it's there."

Con sent her a look that sparked real fear. Fear for him. For all of them. "You done?" he asked.

She wasn't reaching him. "Yeah."

So where did they go from there?

THE SKY CLOUDED OVER while Stan was cooking steaks on the grill. By the time they were eating dessert, winds were whipping across the land at well over seventy miles an hour, throwing debris across the yard and against the windows of the house.

"You can't drive home in this," Susan said, glancing worriedly out the dining-room window. She was holding Joey, sneaking him spoonfuls of her vanilla ice cream.

Robbie glanced at Con. There was no way they could stay. Her parents only had one spare bedroom. And Susan thought their marriage was normal.

But they'd be foolish to drive into the middle of a monsoon, to risk Joey's life. "If we had my truck—"

"We'll stay," he said, pushing his unfinished apple

pie à la mode away. He didn't look any happier about the prospect than she did.

THOUGH STAN WAS strangely reluctant, Susan was delighted to have her family stay over. She fussed over them, producing a couple of toothbrushes, putting fresh sheets on the queen-size bed in the guest room, even though Robbie was certain the ones she replaced were clean. And she gave Robbie a nightgown—silk, with spaghetti straps and lace.

The baby was asleep in the middle of the queen-size bed and Con was in the bathroom, giving her time, Robbie knew, to get herself safely under the covers. Her nerves already on edge, the feel of the nightgown as she moved almost sent her out of her skin. The silk skimmed sensuously across her breasts, her stomach, her thighs, leaving a pool of warmth in its wake.

Why couldn't it have been a flannel nightgown?

She was considering changing back into her overalls, sleeping in her clothes, when she heard the bathroom door open down the hall. Diving for the bed, she snuggled close to Joey, pulling the covers up to her chin. Her problem didn't really lie with the nightgown. She could be wearing galoshes and a winter coat, and she'd still be nervous about sleeping with Con. It just wasn't smart.

Her eyes were squeezed shut when he entered the room. She was incredibly aware of him—the sounds he made, the tangy smell of his aftershave. She couldn't risk looking at him, too. Not here. Not now.

"He still asleep?" Con asked softly, closing the door behind him.

"Uh-huh." She kept her voice low, as though she was almost asleep herself.

"You want me to sleep on the floor?"

And admit that she was the least bit tempted by him? After she'd assured him that she no longer had any interest in his kind of sex? "Of course not. The bed's big enough for three," she said.

The light went out and the covers rustled as he pulled them back and climbed in on Joey's other side. He was lying in the same bed with her. For the very first time.

Robbie was almost afraid to breathe, to attract his attention, holding herself stiffly so she wouldn't risk running into him somewhere on the mattress. She had no idea what he was wearing—or if he *was* wearing anything.

"Good night," he said, the words clipped.

"Night."

Ten minutes later her muscles were cramped from her frozen position, and Con was sound asleep. For once Robbie envied him his control. He issued an edict to sleep, and he slept. She had a feeling she was still going to be awake when the sun rose.

But eventually, lulled by the even breathing of her new son, of her recalcitrant husband, finding comfort in their nearness, she slept.

CHAPTER FOURTEEN

HER LEG WAS WARM and silky smooth against his foot. He traveled the length of it with his toes, inching under the silk that covered her at midthigh and then making a return journey. Only to begin again. His hand found her curved hip beneath the covers and cupped it, moving a little lower to squeeze her thigh. The warmth between her legs tempted him, lured him to delve further. She was more woman than any woman he'd ever had.

Her body shifted, angled so that her hips were just inches away from his straining groin. He knew he should stop. He just couldn't remember why. At the moment nothing seemed more important than his body finding solace inside Robbie's.

When her fingers found his penis, caressing his length, he knew they'd come too far to stop.

He pulled away and sat up.

"Con?" Her whispered word was an invitation—and a plea.

"Let me move him," he whispered back, sliding his arms carefully beneath the baby sleeping soundly between them. They had another hour before Joey would wake up for breakfast.

Con had Joey ensconced in the middle of the love

seat across the room, pillows packed firmly around him and on the floor beneath him, and was back in the bed in a flash.

"Are you sure this is what you want?" he asked, telling himself he was being noble even while his hands moved over her body, distracting her.

"Yes." Her soft acquiescence was filled with the same ache that was driving him. He needed her too much to care about right or wrong. To care whose house he was in or think about promises he'd made—and already broken. She was willing. He was going to take her.

He was only wearing briefs, and he quickly stripped them off, then did likewise with Robbie's nightgown. Her breasts seemed to beg for his touch and he was only too willing to comply. He sought the tiny scar that was all that was left of Robbie's run-in with Blackwell's dog, first with his finger and then with his lips, kissing it better before moving on. Her breasts were smooth and full, enticing him to taste. She was all woman. *His* woman.

And then, before he could reflect on that thought, on the fact that he'd even *had* that thought, he mounted her.

"I love you," she murmured, gazing up at him.

Con froze. This wasn't about love. It had nothing to do with love. It was sex. Plain and simple.

"I'm not asking you to love me back," she said. "But I can't do this the way you want to, Con. I can't hold back the most important part."

He rolled off her and off the bed in one movement, her words like a bucket of ice water thrown on his body. "I'll see you at breakfast," he said, grabbing the shorts and shirt he'd worn the day before and heading for the shower. She couldn't love him. He couldn't let her.

Because while he could give her his body, he couldn't give her his heart. He didn't have one.

ROBBIE HAD NO IDEA how she made it through breakfast with her parents, thankful only that it couldn't be a leisurely meal as Stan and Susan were on their way to church. And since she and Con only had the clothes they'd worn up the day before, they couldn't accompany them. They were back on the road to Phoenix by eight o'clock.

Con hadn't driven five miles before he turned off onto a secluded dirt road. Joey, who'd fallen asleep almost as soon as they'd put him in his car seat, didn't budge when the car came to a stop beside a couple of evergreen trees.

Robbie's heart sped up, afraid of what was coming.

With one arm along the back of the seat, Con turned to look at her, his eyes serious.

"I can give you my protection," he said. "You're welcome to whatever money and possessions I've accumulated, whatever comes in the future. I can give you my body, and my loyalty…"

Robbie's heart was breaking as she sat there and listened to him. Because she knew what was coming. Knew what he would not be including in that list. Knew that no matter what he offered her, it was never going to be enough.

"I need love, Con," she said softly, the words sticking in her throat. "*Your* love." There was no hiding from it any longer, no more pretending he wasn't aware of how she felt about him. She just wasn't strong enough for both of them.

"You're welcome to everything I have, Rob."

"Yes, you said—all your possessions, your body and your loyalty. Thanks, but it's not enough, Con. I need your love, your heart."

He stared at her silently for a moment, his lips moving without sound. "It's gone," he finally said.

And for the first time Robbie believed him. Not because she didn't still think that Con was capable of loving someone, but because he truly believed he wasn't.

"It withered away, little by little, Rob," he continued. "Until I woke up one day and just didn't feel it there anymore. And you know what?"

She shook her head.

"It was a relief."

Robbie had never heard anything sadder in her life. She was bone-deep sad, too sad even for tears.

"I can't live like that," she whispered. "I thought maybe I could, but I can't." The blue sky and sunshine outside the car was filled with promises, with brightness and hope. She looked out, trying desperately to find a thread of that hope, to keep believing, but nothing happened. Her heart was as dark as the night had been.

He didn't say a word. He just sat there, watching her. Waiting.

"I'll stay with you until the custody hearing, until we're sure Joey's yours, but that's it." She'd make it through the next six months. Somehow.

And then she'd find a way to leave him, find a way to care for Joey like any other divorced parent. Be-

cause if she didn't, she was going to end up just like
Con—a walking corpse.

"OK, LITTLE MAN, today we decide what we're going
to do with the rest of Daddy's life." Con lifted his
son off the changing table, talking to him as had become his habit in the past three days. Robbie had
returned to work the day after they'd come back from
Sedona, leaving Con alone with the baby.

"The month's up. I'm due back at the office tomorrow. And you, my boy, get to go to day care."

He wasn't overjoyed about Joey being in day care,
but there was little choice. The baby gave him a
happy toothless grin, cooing and gurgling. Con took
the response to mean that the boy understood every
word. He put Joey into the denim baby carrier he'd
bought on Monday, his first day alone with the child,
when it had seemed like he wasn't going to accomplish anything the entire day. Then, strapping the pack
to his back, he got the vacuum cleaner out of the
closet.

"The work I do in law enforcement is important.
I'm good at it," he said, plugging in the cord, then
turning on the switch. "It might give you something
to be proud of someday—before you find out what a
louse your old man really is." The hum of the cleaner
drowned out his words.

The telephone rang a few minutes later and Con
turned off the vacuum. The baby was pulling his hair.

"Randolph," he barked into the phone. Robbie
wouldn't be calling. She was avoiding him as much
as possible. And there wasn't anyone else he wanted
to talk to.

"Hello, Mr. Randolph. This is Karen Smith."

Especially not her.

"Yeah?"

"I just wanted to let you know we've heard from Joey's mother again, sir, and she says she doesn't need to set up visits with Joey."

"She's relinquishing her rights?"

"She didn't say that, sir, only that something else has come up and she wouldn't need to be setting up any visits."

Con didn't like the sound of that. "Is this common?" he asked, grateful for the weight of the boy on his back. Joey was with him. He was safe.

"To be honest, no, it isn't. But Cecily's a little...different. All I can tell you is she sounded happy. And if there's no more contact from her, I suspect the judge will waive the six-month waiting period to give you and your wife permanent custody."

"Good. Great," Con said, his mind racing. He'd move mountains to know that Joey's future was secure. And to be able to free Robbie to get on with her life, to learn whether he'd really destroyed her optimism as it seemed, or if, once she was away from him, she'd regain it. He'd give anything to make her happy again, and Karen's news was a big step in the right direction.

So why wasn't he overjoyed?

ROBBIE GOT the unenviable job of dropping Joey off at the day-care center the next morning. She and Con had chosen the place together, weeks before, and both were confident it was the best facility Scottsdale had to offer, but it was still a wrench to leave the baby with strangers again. She wished Con was with her. He'd have made the whole thing seem so common-place with his unemotional logic. But he'd been called in to the office at six that morning. Apparently some information had come in during the night, and Con's men had needed his expert assessment before formulating a game plan.

His job was the one thing they'd been able to talk about with any normalcy the night before. Con had finally figured out that he didn't do his job just be-cause he was good at it or because it was the one thing that had ever made him feel good about himself; he did it because he liked the work. Or most of it. But it was time for him to get out of the field. To take one of the many promotions they'd offered him over the years and do what he did best—plan. Strat-egize. And leave the fieldwork to guys who'd seen a little less, who still had some illusions, who hadn't had the heart sucked out of them.

"I'll be back for you lickety-split, little buddy," she said, kissing the baby as she unbuckled his seat from her truck, making certain that his security blan-ket was tucked beside him. "Mommy just has one story to write up and then we'll do lunch. How does that sound?" she asked. Joey grinned at her and shoved his fist in his mouth.

Anna Lewis, the woman who'd registered Joey all those weeks ago, was waiting for them, and she whisked Joey away long before Robbie was ready to say goodbye. Filled with panic for a second, she al-most ran after him. Joey had already spent too much of his life with strangers. Her only consolation was that she'd be back before lunch.

"It gets easier." Anna was back, a sympathetic smile on her face.

Robbie flushed. "I'm sorry, was I that obvious?"

Anna nodded. "But don't apologize. It's when the parents can't wait to get out of here that we worry."

"You'll make sure he has his blanket at all times?" Robbie asked, straining to see the room where Joey had been taken.

"Of course. Now, if you'll just sign him in?" Anna pushed a clipboard across the reception desk.

Robbie scrawled Joey's name, taking a little license and putting him down as Joey Randolph. He would be soon enough.

Sooner than they'd expected, according to what Con had told her about Cecily over dinner the night before. It hadn't seemed to faze him a bit that that meant she'd be leaving sooner. In fact, he'd seemed almost relieved. Not that she blamed him. The situation had been pretty unbearable between them since Sunday.

So why wasn't she relieved, too?

She pushed the clipboard across the desk. "I'll be back no later than eleven," she told Anna. And with one last longing look at the nursery door, she hurried out to her truck.

Joey was safe and that was all that mattered. She was going to have to get used to leaving him. It was soon going to be a way of life.

She cried all the way to the office.

CON WAS ENGROSSED in the contents of a file when the call came.

"Mr. Randolph? This is Anna Lewis at Rosemount Day Care."

Con stiffened, instantly alert. The woman sounded upset. "What's happened?"

"It's Joey, sir. He's gone!"

"What do you mean, gone?" he yelled.

"He's disappeared, Mr. Randolph." The woman gave a sob. "We can't find him anywhere!"

Con was out of his seat, reaching for his keys. "Have you called the police?"

"We thought maybe you'd want...since you're FBI and all..."

"I'm on my way," he said, slamming the phone down and running from his office.

He barked orders as he flew down the hall and out into the hot August sunshine, leaving a flurry of activity behind him. He wanted Cecily Barnhardt's ass found. Immediately. And an APB put out on his son. He wanted the airports and bus stations staked out. The highways blocked. He wanted Robbie.

The jacket of his suit caught on the door as he climbed into his car, and Con yanked it free, ripping the material. He shoved his key into the ignition and roared out of the parking lot and down the street, his heart racing, his thoughts tripping over themselves.

Would Cecily have done this? And if not her, who?

What was the possibility of a misunderstanding? Of the boy having simply been misplaced in the arms of one of the day-care workers, of him being there waiting for Con when he arrived? Slim to none.

He ran through his mind a list of all the people who had it in for him, but couldn't begin to calculate the possibilities. There were hundreds of people who'd threatened him over the years, who could have taken his son to get back at him. Hundreds of unsavory hate-filled people. Evil people who wouldn't think twice about...

It had to be Cecily. The woman was a little off, but she was as gentle as they came. Please, God, let it be Cecily.

Wherever Joey was, whoever he was with, there better not be one mark on him.

Did he have his blanket?

Panic seared him as he swung into the day-care parking lot. Panic and despair so unbearable he almost collapsed beneath its weight.

Except that his son needed him.

He climbed out of his car and raced to the building.

THIS ISN'T HAPPENING. It's all a mistake. It can't be happening. The words rolled through Robbie's mind over and over, a litany that preserved her sanity until she met Con outside the front door of the day care. One glance at his face and she couldn't breathe. He looked haggard, ten years older than he had that morning.

So it *was* true. Joey was missing.

"No!" The word tore from her throat just as Con's arms wrapped around her.

Robbie pressed against him, aware only of the steady beat of his heart beneath her cheek.

"We'll find him," she said then, afraid to let go of Con, afraid she'd fall to a heap at his feet, unable to help him. To help Joey.

She felt Con's nod, but more, she felt the desperation in his grasp as he held her. "If they hurt him,

I'll kill them." His voice was pure steel, and shaking with emotion.

Absurdly, the thought crossed Robbie's mind that a heartless man wouldn't shake with emotion.

"Let's go in," Con said, releasing her to open the door.

Anna was waiting for them inside. Her pretty face was blotchy, strained, streaked with tears. "I'm so sorry," she cried, wringing her hands. "This kind of thing doesn't happen here."

"Where was he last seen?" Con asked.

"In there," she pointed to the nursery door Robbie had watched her take Joey through earlier.

She followed as Con and Robbie hurried into the room.

"When?" Robbie asked.

"Nine-thirty or so. He'd just gone down for a nap."

It was ten-fifteen. He could be anywhere by now.

Three policeman were surrounding an empty crib on the far side of the room, questioning several day-care employees. Con joined them.

"Where are the other children?" Robbie asked, remaining in the doorway. She was loath to go near the crib. She couldn't bear to be close to it, to know that Joey had been there. To imagine someone reaching down, snatching him...

"Most of them have gone home," Anna said, pulling Robbie back from the darkness in her mind. "Those whose parents we couldn't reach are in the playroom with Maria and Joy." Anna's voice broke. "I'm so sorry, Mrs. Randolph," she said, starting to cry again.

Choking back her own sobs, Robbie turned from Anna and went to join Con. It was either that or rip the young woman to shreds. *Why in hell didn't she watch Joey better?*

"No one saw anyone unusual hanging around?" Con was asking the workers as Robbie walked up, wiping tears from her eyes.

Shrinking under Con's gaze, every one of the day-care employees shook their heads.

"The center's growing. We get new people almost every day," Anna said, coming over to them.

"Where was everyone?" Robbie asked. *Why weren't you watching him?*

"It was snack time," an older woman explained. "All the children were sitting at tables in the snack room, except the sleeping babies."

"One of you doesn't stay in the nursery?" A policemen asked.

The woman nodded, swallowing with obvious difficulty. "I do. I'd just gone down the hall to get another box of diapers. I'd used the last one," she said.

"How many babies were in here?" Robbie asked her.

"Three."

One of the policemen wrote on a pad he'd been holding.

"And the other two were untouched?" Con asked.

The woman nodded, her eyes flooding with tears.

Robbie exchanged a glance with Con, saw the confirmation of her fears in his eyes. Three babies asleep in a room. Only one taken. This wasn't a random kidnapping.

"Have you checked the windows and doors?" Con asked the policemen gathered around the crib.

"Yes, sir." All three nodded.

"And?"

"Nothing."

Just then a fourth policeman entered the room, and Robbie's heart sank, nausea overwhelming her when she saw the rag in his hand. "I just found this on the other side of the fence surrounding the playground. It was caught. Looks like someone tried to pull it loose," he said, bringing the material over to the crib.

Con stared.

"You recognize it?" the officer asked Con, holding up the bedraggled scrap.

Con's lips were pinched, his eyes bleak as he nodded.

Robbie fell against him, holding on to his arm as the world spun around her. A wave of blackness threatened, and then receded.

It was Joey's blanket.

CHAPTER FIFTEEN

LEAVING THE POLICE officers at the day care to continue the investigation, dust for fingerprints and comb the area behind the playground, Con followed Robbie home. He kept his eyes trained on his surroundings, looking for anyone he didn't recognize—or someone he did. But the neighborhood was quiet, as it usually was on a hot weekday morning. Even the boy who worked in the neighborhood had stayed in out of the heat.

He checked his mailbox as he drove up, but it was empty. At this point he didn't know whether to be relieved or not. If the kidnapper got in touch with him, he'd at least have something to go on.

Robbie had already gone in when he entered the kitchen, throwing his car keys down on the kitchen counter with such force they bounced off and onto the floor. He felt so helpless. So damn helpless.

"There's nothing at the front door or on the answering machine," Robbie said, rushing back into the kitchen.

Con found a pack of cigarettes in the back of his junk drawer and lit two. Robbie took one with shaking fingers.

"What do you think?" she asked.

"Let me make a phone call and then we'll talk."
He didn't know what to think. Except that if he didn't
stay busy, he'd go out of his mind.

He dialed the number by heart.

"Pete Mitchell."

Con breathed a little easier when his occasional and
usually reluctant partner answered. Pete was the best
there was at negotiating hostage releases.

"I may need your help," Con said, taking a long
drag on his cigarette.

"Where?" Pete asked without a moment's hesitation.

"This isn't official," Con said almost reluctantly.
He wasn't confident that Pete would still be willing
to help when he found out it was *Con* who needed
him, not the government.

"What's up? Is Robbie okay? And little Joey?"

"The boy's missing, taken from his crib at the day
care over an hour ago."

"You home?" Pete's voice was sharp.

"Yeah."

"Anything there?"

Con knew what Pete was asking. Had there been
any word from the kidnappers? "No."

"I'm on my way."

Pete hung up before Con even had a chance to
thank him. But he would never forget how quickly
Pete was willing to come to his aid. Con couldn't
remember a time he'd reached out to someone, asked
for something and not been rejected. Which was why
he usually didn't bother asking. He just gave orders.

"He's coming?" Robbie asked.

Con nodded, sat down and pulled her onto his lap.

Her face was lined with strain, with the effort it took to hold herself together.

"You got any ideas?" he asked her. He didn't tell her he was scared to death.

"Cecily."

Con nodded. He'd reached the same conclusion. "Why?"

"A man would've drawn attention. Someone would have remembered seeing him."

"And a man would've been strong enough to rip Joey's blanket free," Con added.

Robbie's short sandy hair was sticking up where she'd run her fingers through it. As he smoothed it down, a wave of helplessness washed over him again, paralyzing him. Every contact he had would be working on the case by now, but it wasn't enough. He needed the best.

And he was it.

"If Joey's with her, he's probably OK." Robbie spoke softly, like a child needing reassurance.

"Yeah. She's stupid, but she's not evil," Con agreed.

"At least when she abandoned him before, she took him to a hospital," Robbie said.

Con stubbed out his cigarette. "The state borders are all being patrolled. And chances are good she didn't think to change her appearance."

Robbie sat up, turning to look at him, fear in her eyes. "What about Mexico? She could take him to Mexico."

"We'll find him, Rob. We'll get him back," Con promised, hoping to God this was one promise he could keep.

Con tried for the millionth time to remember more about the night he'd spent at the Pink Lagoon Motel with Cecily Barnhardt. He had to figure out what was going on in her head to prepare for what might happen next.

"All she wants is to be taken care of," he said, repeating what Karen Smith had said. His own memories of the woman were so damn blurry! "She was afraid of something that night, I think. And happy as a clam as long as I let her sit there. Maybe that's why she ended up at the motel with me," he said, his head hurting with the effort it took to remember. "I can guarantee that I fully intended to be alone—falling-down drunk, but alone—when I rented that room earlier in the evening."

"Judging from the way she acted in court last week, I'd say you're definitely on the right track." Robbie's head was a welcome weight against his chest.

"Which probably means she won't go far. That if we just sit tight, she'll be contacting us."

Robbie stood up, crossing to the living-room window to stare out. "You think she'll be willing to trade Joey for monetary support?"

"Maybe. She wants to be supported—I know that for sure." Con joined Robbie at the window. The neighborhood looked like a picture in a travel brochure—beautifully landscaped yards, modern stucco homes with variegated tile roofs beneath gloriously blue skies. Not a hint that something could be so terribly wrong.

Robbie started to shake. "We have to give her

whatever she asks for," she said, her voice filled with the tears she'd been trying so hard to hold back.

"Pete's going to disagree with that," Con said, bracing himself against the tide of emotion that threatened his own control. "We'd just be reinforcing the danger of it happening again."

She turned to look at him, her eyes pools of sorrow, of fear. "We have to pay her, Con."

Swallowing the lump in his throat, Con pulled her into his arms. "We will. We'll do whatever's necessary."

THE MINUTES TICKED BY slowly, each one a lifetime, a hell on earth. Yet somehow the minutes became hours, and still the baby had not been found and still no one had contacted them. The longer the baby was gone without anyone contacting them, the greater the danger, Con knew. Pete had arrived, and it was past one o'clock when Con got a call from Martin Emerson, one of his agents.

"Cecily left town almost two hours ago," Con said, hanging up the phone. Pete and Robbie were sitting on stools at the breakfast bar, untouched cups of coffee in front of them. Con still couldn't believe that Pete had come rushing over the moment he'd called.

"Someone recognized her at the bus station. She's going by the name Cecily Armstrong."

"Does she have Joey?" Robbie asked, jumping up. Her arm knocked over the coffee in front of her, but she ignored the liquid as it spread across the counter.

Con grabbed a towel and wiped it up. "Emerson hasn't found anyone who could confirm that for sure, only that she was carrying a bundle that could have been a baby.''

He threw the wet towel into the empty washing machine, adding soap, then switched the appliance on. It took everything he had not to jump into his car and go after the woman.

''Where was she headed?'' Pete asked, frowning. Robbie was rinsing her coffee cup, her movements jerky.

''Flagstaff.''

''She's probably there already.''

''Or got off somewhere else. Emerson has men on that now.''

''You want to go after them, right?'' Pete said. Robbie turned around just in time to see Con nod.

''No!'' she said.

''You don't dare leave, Con,'' Pete said, calm but deadly serious. ''The woman's unstable. She's not going to like it if she can't reach you once she makes up her mind to ask for whatever it is she wants.''

It wasn't in Con's nature to sit back and let someone else conduct an investigation that was more important to him than all that had come before. But he realized the wisdom in Pete's words. He had a feeling that Cecily wouldn't talk to anybody but him.

The other two were watching him, waiting. He couldn't stand the pressure of their expectant gazes. He had to find something to do.

Without another word, he went out to the garage, gathered up a drill, a screwdriver and the child-safety latches he and Robbie had picked up weeks before. The way Joey was scooting around, he had no time to lose. He couldn't have the baby pulling all their pots and pans out onto the floor or finding something to hurt himself with.

PETE FOLLOWED ROBBIE into the living room. She'd heard Con wrestling with his tools out in the garage. And as soon as she'd known he wasn't going for his car, she'd decided to give him a little time to himself. Being alone was the only way Con knew how to deal with pain.

"Con's changed," the older man said.

"How do you mean, changed?" she asked, heading straight for the window, as though if she looked out long enough, the kidnapper would decide to bring Joey home.

God, please don't let him be hurt.

"I've wondered a time or two if the man ever felt anything at all," Pete said.

"Always," Robbie answered instantly. "More than anyone realizes."

Pete shook his head. "You could've fooled me. Don't get me wrong," he added when Robbie turned. "I've always respected him, admired his genuine self-lessness. I've just worried a time or two that he'd lost an important component in dealing with people. The *emotional* component."

Robbie nodded. She could understand that. She'd wondered a time or two herself. "I guess when all you see is ugliness, it's all you believe is there."

"Maybe." Pete shrugged. "But you and the baby have obviously convinced him differently. I've never seen him so broken up."

"I know." Robbie turned back to the window as a fresh bout of tears flooded her eyes. She just didn't know if the pain Con was feeling now would finally convince him he still had a heart or be the final nail in its coffin.

"He ran the washing machine for one little towel," Pete said, crossing to Robbie and putting an arm around her shoulders.

Robbie grinned through her tears, as she was sure Pete intended, and nodded.

They stood silently for a moment, until Con's curses started coming from the kitchen.

"Do you think it would be a good idea if I get something put on the news? Just in case someone recognizes Cecily or Joey?" she asked Pete suddenly. She had to do *something*.

"Can't see how it'd hurt," Pete said, considering. "She's got to know we're after her. And maybe someone will see them."

Pete stayed until after the film crew she called had come and gone. He even convinced Con to go on the air, to issue a plea to the kidnapper to return his son.

But the hours passed and still no word.

A CAR DROVE down the street. A black sedan Con recognized. His shoulders stiffened as his gaze followed the vehicle intently. It belonged to his neighbor across the street and disappeared into the man's garage. The knot in Con's stomach tightened. He couldn't stand much more of the waiting.

Jamming his hands into his pants pockets, he resumed pacing between the phone and the living-room window. Robbie was in the kitchen, where she'd been ever since Pete and the film crew had left, making a dinner neither one of them was going to eat.

His phone was wired, there were guards posted at each end of his street, and still nothing was happening. Had Joey been fed? Was someone changing his diaper?

Cursing, Con paused at the window yet again. The neighborhood was so quiet he couldn't stand it. Why did that damn kid who was always around have to take today off? At least he'd be someone to look at. At least there'd be something going on.

Images of what might be happening to his son invaded his mind. The world was filled with sickos, with evil people who wouldn't hesitate to hurt a tiny child to get back at the child's father. People who—

Suddenly Robbie was there, her arms creeping around his waist, holding him. She didn't say a word. There wasn't anything *to* say. But she was there, sharing her strength with him, chasing away the grotesque images that were haunting him more and more as the hours passed.

Cecily should have contacted them by now.

Con turned, sliding his arms around his friend. His wife. He needed her now in a way he never had before, needed her heart, her soul. Her gentle caring. Her eternal optimism.

He needed her if he was ever to find a way to hope again.

ROBBIE HELD CON, taking as much comfort from him as she gave. He was a rock, solid, sure. Capable of moving mountains. He always got his man. Always.

She wasn't sure exactly when his need changed, when she sensed a more immediate urgency, a physical urgency, within him. Without consciously knowing she was doing so, she floated from feeling a sense of comfort to feeling a desperate mind-numbing desire.

Desperate for the escape, she clutched him to her as he lowered his lips to hers. *Let him take me away, let him make me forget. Just for a minute. Let me forget.*

She kissed him hard, searching for something beyond the sex, some affirmation of a greater power, for the bond of strength born when two people become as one.

Stopping only long enough to close the living-room curtains, Con stripped her silently and lowered her to the floor. There was no foreplay. No patience for leisurely exploration, no time. Only the compulsion to connect to each other, to take everything, to give everything, to share the pain and fear that were eating them both alive.

Robbie didn't utter a word, either. She couldn't. There were no words for what they were seeking.

But they were seeking it together. Of that she was sure.

Con was powerful when he entered her, and she offered him sanctuary from the storm thrashing through him, finding her own sanctuary in the giving.

They could get through this. Together. They could do anything as long as they were together.

She flew with him to a place where only goodness and beauty existed. And she held on to him during the return to earth, to face again the pain of their missing son. But even in the midst of harsh reality, a miracle occurred. For Con didn't pull away from her. He didn't close his eyes or his heart. He stared straight into her eyes—and allowed her the first glimpse she'd ever seen of the man who'd been living alone inside him for more than thirty years.

"Thank you," he said, his eyes bright with the effort it was taking him to keep unfamiliar emotions from spilling over.

"I love you," Robbie whispered, suddenly knowing he was ready now to hear the words.

He nodded and crushed her to him. He might not ever be able to love her back, but at least he'd finally learned how to accept her love. To believe that someone could love him.

CHAPTER SIXTEEN

IT WAS MIDNIGHT and still no word. Con sat at his desk waiting for the phone to ring. Robbie was half reclining on the couch smoking a cigarette. She hadn't said a word in almost an hour.

He'd finally convinced her to call Stan and Susan before they had a chance to hear about the kidnapping on the news. They were on their way to Phoenix now. Con couldn't believe how anxiously he was awaiting their arrival. Not that their being here was going to make any difference to the kidnappers or to Joey's being found.

But they'd always been there for Robbie. They'd always kissed her hurts and made them better. Maybe Susan could at least talk her daughter into getting some sleep.

His heart slammed at the shrill ring of the telephone. Robbie jumped off the couch, rushing over to him as he picked up the receiver.

"Randolph."

He listened to the voice on the other end of the line with a sinking heart, avoiding Robbie's eyes as he hung up the phone. *Damn.*

"What? Who was it?" Robbie asked.

"Emerson. They found Cecily." He couldn't stand

the hope he saw in Robbie's eyes. Couldn't stand the pain he knew was going to follow. It was time to get to work.

"She didn't have him," he said bluntly.

"Didn't have him?" Robbie echoed in disbelief, leaning against the desk.

"She'd run off with some guy who's old enough to be her grandfather. He's rich as hell and promising to take care of her for the rest of her life."

"Why the false name? The secrecy?" Robbie asked, obviously not willing to give up hope yet.

"They're running from his grandchildren, who're trying to have him declared incompetent. Apparently they want his money, too." Con wasn't surprised, just damn tired of the rotten things people did, the lengths they were willing to go to when greed was in the driver's seat.

And sick at the thought of the implications the phone call had put on Joey's disappearance.

"What about the bundle she was carrying? Maybe she dumped Joey someplace."

Con shook his head. "She didn't have a suitcase. She'd rolled up the things she was taking with her in the blanket from her bed."

"Oh, God…" Robbie's words trailed off and a look of despair crossed her face.

Con wanted nothing more than to pull her into his arms, to wipe that look off her face. But they didn't have another minute to lose.

"We have to get to work, Rob. I need your help."

BY THE TIME an exhausted Susan called them to breakfast in the morning, Stan, Robbie and Con had

memorized every name left on the list Con had made
of possible suspects. The list had been several pages
long when Stan and Susan had arrived in the early
hours of the morning. It was now down to one sheet.

"I'll get the newspaper," Susan said as soon as
she'd filled coffee cups for all of them. "Robbie, Con,
eat."

Neither of them had eaten since breakfast the day
before.

Robbie didn't think she could choke down a bite
of the food Susan had prepared. The sight of the eggs
made her nauseous. The fluffy biscuits only made her
think of Joey and the time she'd given him half a
biscuit to gum. Most of it had landed on the floor, but
the baby had had the time of his life.

"Con! Stan! Come here!" Susan called from just
inside the front door.

Wiping tears from her eyes, Robbie ran into the
foyer after them.

"There's an envelope here," Susan said, holding
up the newspaper. A sheriff's wife for many years,
she knew better than to touch the envelope that was
nestled in the centerfold of the paper.

Grabbing a handkerchief from his pocket, Stan took
the envelope. It wasn't sealed. All four of them stared
at the single piece of paper that fell out and floated
to the floor.

Taking the handkerchief, Con picked it up. As his
eyes skimmed the page, the color drained from his
face.

Stan read the note over Con's shoulder and headed
for the bathroom. Susan grabbed a hold of Robbie
before she collapsed.

"Let me see it," Robbie said.

With an arm around both of them, Con held up the letter.

I have the kid. All I can say is he's alive—for now. And he cries good. Real good. If you're patient I might even let you hear him scream a time or two. Or maybe not. Have a good day.

Whoever had the baby had taken him out of malice. He wanted to make them suffer.

"I've got some calls to make," Con said, his voice dead.

Robbie started after him, but Susan pulled her back. "Let him go, honey."

"He's blaming himself," Robbie said. "I can't leave him alone like this. It isn't his fault the world is full of sick people. He can't blame himself for..." Her voice broke as more tears came.

"He has to work through it on his own, Robyn," Susan said in a tone of voice Robbie had never heard her use before. "You can talk to him until you're hoarse and he still won't believe. He has to learn to like himself on his own."

Feeling like a little girl again, Robbie buried her face against her mother's ample bosom, crying for all the wrongs there had been in one very good man's life. Crying, too, for the baby who was lying helplessly somewhere, crying, needing them.

By noon Con still had no idea who had taken his son. Throughout the morning most of the suspects on his list had been eliminated. A couple were even dead. And suddenly, despite his fear and exhaustion, the answer came to him. He remembered another threat he'd received. One he'd given no credence to whatsoever. A name that wasn't on his list.

"It's got to be the boy!" he exclaimed. Every pair of eyes around the table swung to him. Pete was there, Stan and Robbie, as well as Martin Emerson, who'd returned from Flagstaff midmorning.

"What boy?" Martin asked.

Just like that, things fell into place, the pieces of the puzzle fitting so perfectly Con knew he'd hit the mark.

"The woman who died last year in the Ramirez deal. She had a teenage son. He came after me at the funeral, refusing to let me in the church. Said he'd make me pay."

"A boy, Con?" Pete said doubtfully.

"He looked different then, had short hair, glasses."

Stan leaned forward. "You've seen him since?" he asked sharply.

"He's been working in the neighborhood. Doing odd jobs. Started a few months ago."

Robbie's mouth fell open in shock. "The boy who does the Waverlys' yard?"

Con nodded, his adrenaline pumping. "I just realized it's the same kid. It wouldn't have been all that difficult for him to get into the day care. Could've said he was an older sibling if someone stopped him." Con's instincts were telling him to move. He'd found his answer. He had to save his son.

"He wasn't around at all yesterday..." Robbie's voice trailed off.

Emerson grabbed the mobile phone from the middle of the table and ten seconds later was barking orders into the receiver. Every available man in the state would soon be searching for the boy.

"Pete, I need to know everything you can tell me about dealing with a hostage situation," Con said. He was going to do this one alone. No one else was going to die as a result of his orders.

"Stan, find out if he's purchased a gun in the past fifteen months, or ammunition to go with a gun his mother may have had."

"Robbie, how many of your snoops can you get to work on finding him?"

Robbie was on her feet. "All of them," she said on her way out the door. "Give me an hour."

She was exhausted, her face haggard, and still she was full of optimism. Of hope. And Con suddenly found himself buying into that hope.

If his hunch was right, the kid's main purpose was to make Con suffer a long slow living hell. Which meant Joey was still alive. And that was all Con cared about.

"I'VE FOUND HIM!" Robbie rushed into the living room two hours later. "He rented a migrant shack at the back of an orange grove twenty miles east of here."

Con was on his feet instantly, grabbing Robbie by the shoulders. "You're sure?" he asked.

She nodded. "Positive. The guy who rented him the shack was the same one who tipped me about that story I did about the dead greyhounds last year. Apparently the kid's been fixing up the place for weeks."

Which only reinforced Con's theory. The boy

planned to string Con on for a while, to squeeze every bit of suffering out of him. He wasn't going to settle for one nasty note. Which meant that in all likelihood Joey was still alive.

"I'm going after him," Con said.

"Wait a minute," Stan said, coming in on the tail end of the conversation. He and Pete had been in the kitchen coordinating a statewide search of gun shops by phone.

"He's armed. Bought himself a nice little automatic almost a year ago."

Robbie's eyes filled with fear as she looked from her father to Con. "Let Pete go in first, Con. He's trained to deal with this."

"No," Con said. Pete had a wife, a son and another child on the way. He might even have become his friend over the past twenty-four hours. Con wasn't going to let him risk his life. "This is between me and the kid. I'm going alone."

In spite of all the warnings to the contrary, in spite of a direct order from his boss, Con left the house alone ten minutes later. He wasn't waiting for a full-scale move. He wasn't waiting for assistance to be organized. What he was doing, Robbie knew in her heart, was giving up his life. He was going to offer himself to the kid in exchange for Joey.

An eye for an eye. A parent for a parent.

She'd heard him on the phone in his bedroom right before he left. He'd called his attorney and named Robbie as Joey's legal guardian in case anything happened to him.

He hadn't even kissed her goodbye. And she understood that, too. They'd become one spirit, one soul, the day before. If he got too close to her, he might not have the strength to separate from her again. To do what he had to do.

What she couldn't let him do.

"Pete, we have to go after Con. We can't let him do this alone," Robbie said, bursting into the kitchen after watching Con's car drive away.

Pete put down the phone and picked up his keys. "I've already called Emerson. They're going to meet us at the shack with backup," he said. "Let's go."

"Be careful," Susan said, hugging Robbie tight before pushing her out the door.

"Bring them both back alive," Stan said, and then picked up the phone. He was calling several of his former deputies to serve as additional backup. If the odds made any difference, they had a chance to pull this off.

But in law enforcement, the odds very rarely made a difference.

CON APPROACHED the shack on foot, his footsteps silent, like a panther on the hunt. The old one-room building wasn't air-conditioned, and the one window was wide open. Con heard the drone of a television, the steady hum of a high-voltage fan. Sweating in the hundred-plus temperature, he hoped to God the baby had survived the heat.

He was still wearing yesterday's slacks and shirt, with his holster strapped to his chest, and wondered if maybe he should have taken the time to change. The suit might intimidate the kid. It might make him do something crazy.

He could hear the television show quite distinctly

by the time he reached the window. It was an old "Happy Days" rerun. Two fans were humming. There was no sound of Joey.

Slowly, so slowly he barely felt himself move, Con peeked inside. He saw the kid immediately. He was sitting in the middle of a newish-looking couch, frowning at the television set. A baby bottle, half-full of what appeared to be juice, was standing on an old barrel being used as a coffee table. A box of diapers, a size too big, stood open on the floor beside the couch. There was no sign of Joey.

The kid glanced back to a corner by the refrigerator, the open refrigerator, Con noted. The kid glanced that way again several more times over the next minutes. A fan had been set up to one side.

Homemade air-conditioning. The baby was somewhere behind the refrigerator door. Con was sure of it.

As it turned out, it was almost too easy to take the kid. Con used a trick so old it never worked on experienced criminals. He threw a rock just outside the door of the shack, and as predicted, the kid came out to investigate. Con had him in a half nelson before the kid knew what had hit him. Before he could aim the gun he had cocked in his right hand.

The gun went off, a bullet ricocheting against the dirt to lodge in the outside wall of the shack.

"Easy, now, easy," Con said.

The boy was much stronger and better-trained than Con had anticipated, but he managed to wrestle him to the ground, disarming him at the same time.

"You!" the kid cried when he got his first look at his assailant.

"I came for my son," Con said, holding both the kid's arms with one hand while he took off his belt.

"I should've taken the woman," the kid grunted, using a decent karate maneuver that just missed Con's groin. "I'd at least have raped her by now."

Con twisted the kid's arms further, securing them with his belt. "You hurt either one of them, you're dead."

He meant it.

A FLASH OF MOVEMENT warned Con they were no longer alone. Dropping the end of the belt, he ripped open his shirt and grabbed his gun. His finger was on the trigger, ready to fire.

"Hold it, buddy," Pete said, coming out into the open as he assessed the situation. Robbie was right behind him, followed by a dozen agents and officers.

Just then Joey started to cry lustily from inside the cabin. Con handed his secured charge over to Pete and ran in. He grabbed his son up into his arms, holding him tightly against his chest. And suddenly he started to shake.

Joey was safe. His son was really safe. *Thank God.*

Weak with relief, he cuddled the boy, crooning softly to him.

"It's OK, son, Daddy's here," he said, his voice breaking as the baby's wails slowed to whimpers and then stopped altogether. Joey studied Con, a frown between his tiny brows.

"Daddy's got you now, Joey. Daddy's got you," he said, aware only of an intense need for Joey to know that he'd always be there for him.

The baby lifted his hand and began bopping Con's

cheek. Con reached up to take hold of the tiny fist and was startled to find his own face wet with tears.

In that moment he realized what he'd been feeling since the day Sandra Muldoon had knocked on his door.

"I love you, son," he said awkwardly, the words foreign to his tongue.

He was in love. With his own small son.

And with his wife.

He turned toward the door, looking for Robbie. He was going to do everything in his power, move the damn mountains she kept talking about if that was what it took, to make up to her for all the times he'd hurt her.

She was standing in the doorway, her face, too, streaked with tears. And she was, without a doubt, the most beautiful woman he'd ever seen.

"You said you love him," she murmured.

"Yes." Con felt vulnerable as he stood there, the baby his only protection.

"I'm glad." She smiled a radiant honest smile, asking for nothing at all. She was happy for him. Only him. And maybe a bit for the baby she adored, too.

The final dam in Con burst. He reached out a hand to her, daring to hope. She looked at his outstretched hand, and the seconds ticked slowly by while she glanced from his hand to his face, searching for something he hoped with all his being she'd find.

And then her fingers stole into his. He squeezed them, looking into her eyes, allowing her to see into his. And into his soul.

She wrapped her arms around him, buried her face between him and the baby and began to sob. Con held her and let her cry, knowing she was shedding tears for both of them, ridding them both of years of stored-up pain.

Joey grabbed a fistful of Robbie's hair and gave it a yank worthy of the offspring of Connor Randolph.

"Ow!" she cried, lifting her head to grin at her son through her tears. "I can see we'll have to teach you how to treat a lady, young man," she told him, freeing her hair from the baby's grip, and keeping his tiny hand captive within her own.

"I'll never be a knight in shining armor," Con said, needing to get things settled once and for all.

"I never said I wanted one. *You* said I did."

"You deserve one."

"But all I've ever wanted was you." The baby squirmed. "Let's take our son and go home, eh, Randolph?" Robbie took the baby from him.

That was it. Just like that, with nothing more from him, she was going to come home with him, make them the family he'd always wanted. She hugged Joey to her breast, pressing quick kisses to his neck. Laughing when Joey laughed.

Con couldn't let her do it. Couldn't let her settle for less than she deserved, less than she needed.

"Rob?" She was halfway to the door, but turned back when she heard him call her name.

"Yeah?"

"I love you."

"I know you do." Her voice broke, her chin trembling, as he finally admitted what had been there between them for a lifetime.

"I love you, too," she whispered. "I always have."

Tears poured down her cheeks again as Con scooped the woman of his dreams up into his arms, baby and all, holding her beneath his heart.

The heart she'd given back to him.

EPILOGUE

ROBBIE SAT with her father on the closed-in porch in Sedona, watching for Con to come back with their son. He'd taken Joey up the mountain to find a Christmas tree.

"The boy's only two. You think he knows what he's looking for?" Stan asked, puffing on his pipe.

"I don't think he cares as long as he's with his daddy."

"I always knew that husband of yours would make a fine family man if he ever lost that chip he carried on his shoulder."

"I'm not doing too badly in the wife department, either," Robbie said. She was still bothered sometimes by the conversation she'd had with her father on this very porch eighteen months before.

Stan cleared his throat and looked anywhere but at his daughter. "I was wrong, girl. I was looking at what I'd raised you to be, and seeing you all alone and lonely, I got to thinking I done you wrong. That it was my fault you were suffering so from loving a man who wasn't loving you back."

Robbie smiled, rubbing her hands over her extended belly. "He loves me," she said.

Stan glanced up the mountain, embarrassed. "'Course he does."

"Did I tell you the kid who took Joey is in counseling?" Robbie asked, deciding to let her father off the hook—for now.

Stan harrumphed. He'd made his opinion clear as far as that kid was concerned. Stan thought he should have been tried as an adult, locked away forever.

"He still has another year in detention until he's eighteen, but he wants to go to college, start over and put the past behind him."

Stan harrumphed again.

The baby kicked Robbie in the ribs and she gasped slightly. She tried to push the huge mound into a more comfortable position. Except that at thirty-five weeks, there wasn't one. She was loving every minute of this pregnancy. And with all the miracles that had taken place in her life, she could afford to be generous.

"The kid went a little crazy when he lost his mom, Pop, but he's basically a good kid. He went out of his way to make sure Joey was all right the whole time he had him."

"He was going to kill him," Stan said, his words sharp.

Robbie shook her head. "I don't think so. I don't think he'd have hurt Joey. Or me, either. He just wanted Con to suffer. And he knows now that Con was already suffering over the death of the kid's mother. Con wrote to him once, told the kid what really happened that day, how it happened."

He was also planning to pay for the kid's college education, but Robbie didn't think her father was ready to hear that yet.

"He's a better man than I—"

Stan broke off when Robbie gave a little cry. Con's younger son was a mighty determined little fellow. He'd never kicked her so hard.

"Susan!" Stan bellowed, his face white as he watched Robbie.

"What?" Susan came running from the kitchen, drying her hands on a dish towel.

"She's—"

"It's nothing, Mom," Robbie interrupted. It couldn't be. Not until Con got back. She was not going through this without him.

"Connor, Jr., just kicked a little harder than usual." Robbie rose from her chair, hoping to make more room for her unborn son, just as Con came walking across the desert field in front her. Joey was riding on his shoulders, an evergreen dragging behind them. Robbie couldn't tell whose grin was broader, Joey's or Con's.

Another fierce pain gripped Robbie, followed by a flood of warmth between her legs.

"Oh!" Susan said, grabbing Joey from Con's shoulders when they came through the door. Stan, meanwhile, tried to steer Robbie to the couch.

She stood her ground, her discomfort unimportant, as her gaze sought and found her husband's.

"What?" he asked, crossing to her immediately.

The look in his eyes told her everything she needed to hear. She returned the look and said simply, "It's time."

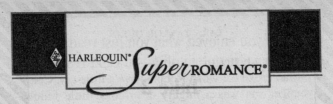
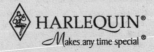

If you enjoyed what you just read,
then we've got an offer you can't resist!

Take 2
bestselling novels FREE!
Plus get a FREE surprise gift!

Clip this page and mail it to The Best of the Best™

IN U.S.A.	IN CANADA
3010 Walden Ave.	P.O. Box 609
P.O. Box 1867	Fort Erie, Ontario
Buffalo, N.Y. 14240-1867	L2A 5X3

YES! Please send me 2 free Best of the Best™ novels and my free surprise gift. Then send me 4 brand-new novels every month, which I will receive before they're available in stores. In the U.S.A., bill me at the bargain price of $4.24 plus 25¢ delivery per book and applicable sales tax, if any*. In Canada, bill me at the bargain price of $4.74 plus 25¢ delivery per book and applicable taxes**. That's the complete price and a savings of over 15% off the cover prices—what a great deal! I understand that accepting the 2 free books and gift places me under no obligation ever to buy any books. I can always return a shipment and cancel at any time. Even if I never buy another book from The Best of the Best™, the 2 free books and gift are mine to keep forever. So why not take us up on our invitation. You'll be glad you did!

185 MEN C229
385 MEN C23A

Name _____ (PLEASE PRINT)

Address _____ Apt.#

City _____ State/Prov. _____ Zip/Postal Code

* Terms and prices subject to change without notice. Sales tax applicable in N.Y.
** Canadian residents will be charged applicable provincial taxes and GST.
   All orders subject to approval. Offer limited to one per household.
   ® are registered trademarks of Harlequin Enterprises Limited.

BOB00   ©1998 Harlequin Enterprises Limited

USA *Today* bestselling author

S.TELLA CAMERON

and popular American Romance author

MURIEL JENSEN

come together in a special
Harlequin 2-in-1 collection.

Look for

Shadows and *Daddy in Demand*

On sale June 2001

HARLEQUIN®
Makes any time special ®